THE CHRONICLES OF
MALUS DARKBLADE
VOLUME TWO

WARHAMMER® CHRONICLES

- **THE LEGEND OF SIGMAR** -
Graham McNeill
BOOK ONE: *Heldenhammer*
BOOK TWO: *Empire*
BOOK THREE: *God King*

- **THE RISE OF NAGASH** -
Mike Lee
BOOK ONE: *Nagash the Sorcerer*
BOOK TWO: *Nagash the Unbroken*
BOOK THREE: *Nagash Immortal*

- **VAMPIRE WARS:
THE VON CARSTEIN TRILOGY** -
Steven Savile
BOOK ONE: *Inheritance*
BOOK TWO: *Dominion*
BOOK THREE: *Retribution*

- **THE SUNDERING** -
Gav Thorpe
BOOK ONE: *Malekith*
BOOK TWO: *Shadow King*
BOOK THREE: *Caledor*

- **CHAMPIONS OF CHAOS** -
Darius Hinks, S P Cawkwell & Ben Counter
BOOK ONE: *Sigvald*
BOOK TWO: *Valkia the Bloody*
BOOK THREE: *Van Horstmann*

- **THE WAR OF VENGEANCE** -
Nick Kyme, Chris Wraight & C L Werner
BOOK ONE: *The Great Betrayal*
BOOK TWO: *Master of Dragons*
BOOK THREE: *The Curse of the Phoenix Crown*

- **MATHIAS THULMANN:
WITCH HUNTER** -
C L Werner
BOOK ONE: *Witch Hunter*
BOOK TWO: *Witch Finder*
BOOK THREE: *Witch Killer*

- **ULRIKA THE VAMPIRE** -
Nathan Long
BOOK ONE: *Bloodborn*
BOOK TWO: *Bloodforged*
BOOK THREE: *Bloodsworn*

- **MASTERS OF STONE AND STEEL** -
Nick Kyme and Gav Thorpe
BOOK ONE: *The Doom of Dragonback*
BOOK TWO: *Grudge Bearer*
BOOK THREE: *Oathbreaker*
BOOK FOUR: *Honourkeeper*

- **THE TYRION & TECLIS OMNIBUS** -
William King
BOOK ONE: *Blood of Aenarion*
BOOK TWO: *Sword of Caldor*
BOOK THREE: *Bane of Malekith*

- **WARRIORS OF THE CHAOS WASTES** -
C L Werner
BOOK ONE: *Wulfrik*
BOOK TWO: *Palace of the Plague Lord*
BOOK THREE: *Blood for the Blood God*

- **KNIGHTS OF THE EMPIRE** -
Various Authors
BOOK ONE: *Hammers of Ulric*
BOOK TWO: *Reiksguard*
BOOK THREE: *Knight of the Blazing Sun*

- **WARLORDS OF KARAK
EIGHT PEAKS** -
Guy Haley & David Guymer
BOOK ONE: *Skarsnik*
BOOK TWO: *Headtaker*
BOOK THREE: *Thorgrim*

- **SKAVEN WARS:
THE BLACK PLAGUE TRILOGY** -
C L Werner
BOOK ONE: *Dead Winter*
BOOK TWO: *Blighted Empire*
BOOK THREE: *Wolf of Sigmar*

- **THE ORION TRILOGY** -
Darius Hinks
BOOK ONE: *The Vaults of Winter*
BOOK TWO: *Tears of Isha*
BOOK THREE: *The Council of Beasts*

- **BRUNNER THE BOUNTY HUNTER** -
C L Werner
BOOK ONE: *Blood Money*
BOOK TWO: *Blood and Steel*
BOOK THREE: *Blood of the Dragon*

- **THANQUOL AND BONERIPPER** -
C L Werner
BOOK ONE: *Grey Seer*
BOOK TWO: *Temple of the Serpent*
BOOK THREE: *Thanquol's Doom*

- **HEROES OF THE EMPIRE** -
Chris Wraight
BOOK ONE: *Sword of Justice*
BOOK TWO: *Sword of Vengeance*
BOOK THREE: *Luthor Huss*

WARHAMMER CHRONICLES

- **ELVES: THE OMNIBUS** •
Graham McNeill
BOOK ONE: *Defenders of Ulthuan*
BOOK TWO: *Sons of Ellyrion*
BOOK THREE: *Guardians of the Forest*

• **UNDEATH ASCENDANT:
A VAMPIRE COUNTS OMNIBUS** •
C L Werner, Robert Earl & Steven Savile
BOOK ONE: *The Red Duke*
BOOK TWO: *Ancient Blood*
BOOK THREE: *Curse of the Necrarch*

• **GOTREK & FELIX
THE FIRST OMNIBUS** •
William King
BOOK ONE: *Trollslayer*
BOOK TWO: *Skavenslayer*
BOOK THREE: *Daemonslayer*

• **GOTREK & FELIX
THE SECOND OMNIBUS** •
William King
BOOK ONE: *Dragonslayer*
BOOK TWO: *Beastslayer*
BOOK THREE: *Vampireslayer*

• **GOTREK & FELIX
THE THIRD OMNIBUS** •
William King & Nathan long
BOOK ONE: *Giantslayer*
BOOK TWO: *Orcslayer*
BOOK THREE: *Manslayer*

• **GOTREK & FELIX
THE FOURTH OMNIBUS** •
Nathan Long
BOOK ONE: *Elfslayer*
BOOK TWO: *Shamanslayer*
BOOK THREE: *Zombieslayer*

• **GOTREK & FELIX
THE FIFTH OMNIBUS** •
Josh Reynolds
BOOK ONE: *Road of Skulls*
BOOK TWO: *The Serpent Queen*
BOOK THREE: *Lost Tales*

• **GOTREK & FELIX
THE SIXTH OMNIBUS** •
David Guymer
BOOK ONE: *City of the Damned*
BOOK TWO: *Kinslayer*
BOOK THREE: *Slayer*

• **THE CHRONICLES OF MALUS
DARKBLADE: VOLUME ONE** •
Dan Abnett & Mike Lee
BOOK ONE: *The Daemon's Curse*
BOOK TWO: *Bloodstorm*
BOOK THREE: *Reaper of Souls*

• **GOTREK GURNISSON** •
Darius Hinks
Ghoulslayer
Gitslayer
Soulslayer

DOMINION
A novel by Darius Hinks

STORMVAULT
A novel by Andy Clark

THUNDERSTRIKE & OTHER STORIES
Various authors
An anthology of short stories

HARROWDEEP
Various authors
An anthology of novellas

A DYNASTY OF MONSTERS
A novel by David Annandale

CURSED CITY
A novel by C L Werner

THE END OF ENLIGHTENMENT
A novel by Richard Strachan

BEASTGRAVE
A novel by C L Werner

REALM-LORDS
A novel by Dale Lucas

HALLOWED GROUND
A novel by Richard Strachan

• **HALLOWED KNIGHTS** •
Josh Reynolds
BOOK ONE: *Plague Garden*
BOOK TWO: *Black Pyramid*

• **KHARADRON OVERLORDS** •
C L Werner
BOOK ONE: *Overlords of the Iron Dragon*
BOOK TWO: *Profit's Ruin*

WARHAMMER® CHRONICLES

THE CHRONICLES OF
MALUS DARKBLADE
VOLUME TWO

DAN ABNETT • MIKE LEE • C L WERNER

BLACK LIBRARY

A BLACK LIBRARY PUBLICATION

Warpsword and *Lord of Ruin* first published in 2007.
Deathblade first published in 2015.
'Bloodwalker' first published in *Black Library Weekender Anthology 2012: Volume Two* in 2012.
This edition published in Great Britain in 2022 by
Black Library, Games Workshop Ltd., Willow Road,
Nottingham, NG7 2WS, UK.

Represented by: Games Workshop Limited – Irish branch,
Unit 3, Lower Liffey Street, Dublin 1,
D01 K199, Ireland.

10 9 8 7 6 5 4 3 2 1

Produced by Games Workshop in Nottingham.
Cover illustration by Sebastian Szmyd.
Map by Nuala Kinrade.

The Chronicles of Malus Darkblade: Volume Two © Copyright Games Workshop Limited 2022. The Chronicles of Malus Darkblade: Volume Two, Warhammer Chronicles, GW, Games Workshop, Black Library, Warhammer, Warhammer Age of Sigmar, Stormcast Eternals, and all associated logos, illustrations, images, names, creatures, races, vehicles, locations, weapons, characters, and the distinctive likenesses thereof, are either ® or TM, and/or © Games Workshop Limited, variably registered around the world.
All Rights Reserved.

A CIP record for this book is available from the British Library.

ISBN 13: 978-1-80026-139-6

No part of this publication may be reproduced, stored in a retrieval system, or transmitted in any form or by any means, electronic, mechanical, photocopying, recording or otherwise, without the prior permission of the publishers.

This is a work of fiction. All the characters and events portrayed in this book are fictional, and any resemblance to real people or incidents is purely coincidental.

See Black Library on the internet at
blacklibrary.com

Find out more about Games Workshop
and the worlds of Warhammer at
games-workshop.com

Printed and bound by CPI Group (UK) Ltd, Croydon, CR0 4YY

This is a dark age, a bloody age, an age of daemons and of sorcery. It is an age of battle and death, and of the world's ending. Amidst all of the fire, flame and fury it is a time, too, of mighty heroes, of bold deeds and great courage.

At the heart of the Old World sprawls the Empire, the largest and most powerful of the human realms. Known for its engineers, sorcerers, traders and soldiers, it is a land of great mountains, mighty rivers, dark forests and vast cities. And from his throne in Altdorf reigns the Emperor Karl Franz, sacred descendant of the founder of these lands, Sigmar, and wielder of his magical warhammer.

But these are far from civilised times. Across the length and breadth of the Old World, from the knightly palaces of Bretonnia to ice-bound Kislev in the far north, come rumblings of war. In the towering World's Edge Mountains, the orc tribes are gathering for another assault. Bandits and renegades harry the wild southern lands of the Border Princes. There are rumours of rat-things, the skaven, emerging from the sewers and swamps across the land. And from the northern wildernesses there is the ever-present threat of Chaos, of daemons and beastmen corrupted by the foul powers of the Dark Gods. As the time of battle draws ever near, the Empire needs heroes like never before.

CONTENTS

Warpsword   13
Dan Abnett & Mike Lee

Lord of Ruin   229
Dan Abnett & Mike Lee

Deathblade   463
C L Werner

Bloodwalker   683
C L Werner

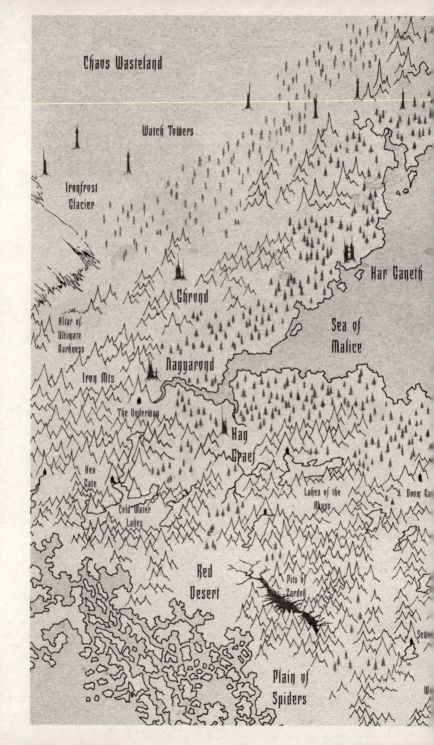

WARPSWORD

Dan Abnett & Mike Lee

CHAPTER ONE

BAG OF BONES

Two full moons hung low in the evening sky, gleaming like burnished pearls in a band of indigo just above the sharp mountain crags to the west. Their light cast a shimmer of faded gold across the restless surface of the Sea of Malice, and the wind blowing in from the water was cold and damp. Tendrils of mist coiled along the rocky shore, reaching tentatively northward through the rustling fields of yellow grass and touching lightly on the dark stones of the Slavers' Road. As the night wore on the mist would thicken, swallowing the road entirely and pressing hungrily into the dense forest of dark pine beyond.

The small group of druchii walking along the winding road eyed the swelling fog with a kind of weary dread. After many days of travel along the seacoast, they knew that the wind and the mist would sink through their light summer cloaks like an assassin's knife and settle deep in their bones. They were all young and strong – and had demonstrated so on more than one occasion since leaving their homes – but their muscles ached and their joints were stiff after weeks of sleeping on damp, cold earth. So when one of their number spied a small, cleared area with a fire pit at the edge of the tree line the band stopped in their tracks and spoke amongst themselves in low, hushed tones.

Their leader, a tall woman with finger bones plaited in her black hair, turned and looked along the road to the north, searching for a sign that their destination might only be a short way away. She wanted to press ahead a bit further, but when the man who'd first spied the clearing walked to the fire pit and pointed out a stack of ready firewood tucked beneath a nearby pine, that settled the debate. With a last, searching glance to the north the woman joined her compatriots by the fire pit, throwing back the folds of her cloak and shrugging her travel bags from her shoulders. Lengths of wood clunked and rattled as they were tossed into the pit and the druchii murmured easily amongst themselves, pleased at the thought of a warm fire to keep the fog at bay.

Preoccupied as they were with flint and tinder and unwrapping what remained of their meagre rations, none of them noticed the lean, haggard figure step quietly from the concealing mist close to the shore. Droplets of water glittered like shards of broken glass on the dark surface of Malus Darkblade's heavy, fur-mantled cloak and ran in thin streams across his worn and split-seamed boots. His long black hair hung loose in a thick, matted tangle, almost indistinguishable from the wolf-fur that weighed upon his narrow shoulders. Moonlight limned the hard lines of his weathered face, sharpening the bony angles of his cheekbones and the dagger-point of his pale chin.

Shadows pooled in the hollows of his cheeks and the sunken orbits of his eyes as he studied the four men and two women forming a circle around the fire pit just a few yards away. As he watched, one of the druchii stuffed a wad of tinder beneath the piled logs and took up his flint, scattering a stream of thin red sparks with a few deft strokes before bending low to blow gently on the smouldering wood shavings. Within moments a tongue of fire rose from the tinder and licked along the cured wood, and the druchii all leaned forwards expectantly, reaching out with slim, pale hands for the warmth that was soon to follow. Malus smiled coldly, scarcely noticing the offshore breeze caress his face with cold, damp fingers. A few moments more, he thought, nodding to himself. They'd taken the bait, but now he had to set the hook.

Within a few minutes the druchii had a roaring fire going, filling the clearing and painting the sides of the dark pines with flickering orange light. The druchii ate meals of hard biscuit, dried fish and cheese, and stretched their feet wearily towards the blaze. After a long, hard day of travel the men and women seemed to come unclenched at the heady sensation of warmth and food in their bellies. None of them noticed Malus's approach until he limped like one of the walking dead into the circle of the firelight.

Conversation stopped. Several of the druchii straightened, hands reaching for their swords. Their faces were carefully neutral, but Malus could see the calculating gleam in their eyes. They were sizing him up, deciding whether to treat him as predator or prey. Malus reached both hands from beneath the folds of his faded cloak and showed his empty palms. 'Well met, brothers and sisters,' Malus said carefully. The words came out in a low, hoarse voice – after two and a half months of living like an animal in the woods along the Slavers' Road he'd had little use for conversation. 'Might a fellow traveller share your fire for a while?'

Without waiting for a reply, he unclasped his cloak and pulled it from his shoulders. Beneath, Malus wore a ragged shirt of blackened mail and a battered kheitan of human hide, cut in a rustic style common to the north country. A broad, straight northern sword and a set of knives hung from his belt above a set of faded and torn woollen robes. His black boots were ragged as well, the soles pulling away from their pointed tips. But for a large ruby ring glinting brightly on his right hand and a plain silver band glinting on his left, he looked like a half-starved autarii or a crazed mountain hermit.

Malus spread the cloak carefully on the ground and shrugged a plain cloth bag from his shoulder. Sharp, measuring stares flicked from Malus's face to the stained brown canvas bag and back again. All of the travellers carried similar bags, kept close by their sides. Like Malus, the other druchii were dressed simply: plain robes and kheitans, light armour or none at all, and a single sword or broad knife to deal with encounters on the road. Had they horses and clinking bundles of slave irons they could have been traders on the way to Karond Kar in anticipation of the autumn flesh harvest.

After a moment the leader of the small band leaned forwards with a soft rustle of layered wool and studied Malus thoughtfully. Her hair was drawn back in a series of tight braids, accentuating her long face and severe features. The woman's brass-coloured eyes shone like polished coins in the firelight. 'Have you travelled far, brother?' she asked.

The highborn met the woman's gaze and struggled to conceal his surprise. The woman's eyes marked her as a high priestess of Khaine, the Bloody-Handed God. They set her apart even among other members of Khaine's temple as especially favoured by the Lord of Murder.

Malus nodded slowly. 'From Naggor,' he replied, thinking to describe his route down the Spear Road past Naggarond but holding back at the last moment. Say no more than you must, he cautioned himself. 'And you?'

'From the temple at Clar Karond,' the woman replied, and then nodded to two men to her right. 'And they from Hag Graef.'

Malus continued to nod, keeping his face carefully neutral and giving the two men only the briefest of glances. His mind raced and a fist tightened around his heart. A voice hissed inside his head, like a blade drawn across naked bone.

'I warned you of this, little druchii,' the daemon said, its voice dripping with contempt. 'They will recognise you any moment and your pathetic scheme will come undone.'

'After tonight you will not be able to return to Hag Graef,' his mother had told him, her voice cutting through the howling wind as the city burned around them. 'You must seek the Warpsword of Khaine in the city of Har Ganeth. Your brother Urial awaits you there, seeking to make the sword his own.'

And so he had travelled north and east, slipping from the corpse-choked Vale of Shadow with food taken from the ruins of the Naggorite camp. He moved at night and stayed off the roads whenever he could, knowing that his kin would be sniffing for his trail as soon as they were able. Once the fires had been put out and order restored in the city, his half-brother Isilvar would send his troops into the Vale to check every bloated and torn body to see if he lay among the fallen. When they realised he'd escaped, word would spread, and every druchii in the Land of Chill would be watching for him. For the man or woman who delivered Malus Darkblade – living or dead – into the clutches of the Witch King would reap a drachau's ransom in wealth and favour. Not because Malus had led an army against his former home, but for the crime of taking the life of his father Lurhan, the Vaulkhar of Hag Graef, and by extension a sworn vassal of Malekith himself. No one slew the Witch King's property without his leave, and for that Malus had lost everything – rank, property, wealth and ambition, all stricken from him with a single stroke of a sword.

He had thought himself clever, but in the end he'd played right into his enemies' hands. Now Isilvar was Hag Graef's vaulkhar and possessor of not only Lurhan's wealth, but Malus's as well. His half-sister Nagaira had conspired with Isilvar; together they'd known more about Malus and his secret quest on behalf of the daemon Tz'arkan than he'd realised. They knew of the five relics he needed to find in order to free the daemon from its prison and reclaim his stolen soul. They knew he would seek the Dagger of Torxus in the tomb of Eleuril the Damned, and so they'd arranged for Lurhan to get it first. And he, blind to everything except recovering the relics and ridding himself of the daemon, had done their bidding like a trained dog.

It had taken a week to reach the Slavers' Road, and two weeks more to reach Har Ganeth, City of Executioners. Malus had stopped there, hesitating warily before the city's open gates and sombre streets.

The gates of Har Ganeth never shut because the City of Executioners hungered for flesh and blood. It was Khaine's city, seat of the temple's worldly power, and no one came or went from it without the approval of the priests who ruled there.

Malus knew they would be watching for him. His half-brother Urial would have seen to that, if nothing else. Urial had every reason to hate and fear Malus, and desired the warpsword for reasons of his own. It figured into an ancient prophecy, one that the crippled highborn believed to be his birthright.

Malus had reason to believe otherwise. Prophecies were often slippery things, and had a tendency to turn in the hand of those who thought to wield them.

Nevertheless, he knew nothing of the city and hadn't a coin to his name to bribe anyone with, so he had no confidence that he could slip quietly into the city and remain hidden beneath Urial's very nose, much less go poking through the temple fortress in search of a sacred relic. More than once he found it bitterly amusing that before, when he had everything to lose he would have just charged headlong into the city, convinced he could think his way out of any mess he found himself in. Now, however, since he'd lost everything, he found himself much more circumspect.

He needed more information about the city and its inhabitants, he'd decided. So he retreated into the wooded foothills north of the city and waited for someone to leave.

The first thing he'd learned was that, unlike every other city in Naggaroth, few people came and went from Har Ganeth. It was almost a week before a lone traveller emerged from the city gates and headed west on horseback. Malus shadowed the solitary figure until nightfall, when the man left the road and built a fire at a campsite along the edge of the tree line. After watching the man for half an hour, Malus walked into the camp and offered to share some of his wine in exchange for a spot close to the fire. After sampling Malus's wine, the man grudgingly agreed.

He was a stranger to the city, as it happened – visiting a cousin in Har Ganeth who kept a chandler's shop close by the temple fortress. As Malus had feared, every stranger entering the city had to report to the temple straightaway and receive the blessing of the priestesses, or else he took his life in his hands. There were only three sorts of people in the City of Executioners: servants of the temple, guests of the temple and sacrifices to Khaine. A druchii caught on the street – by day or night – without the temple's blessing could be slain out of hand as an offering to the Lord of Murder, and the people of the city were zealous in their devotion to the Bloody-Handed God.

The man knew nothing about the temple fortress. Only members of the cult were permitted to enter, leaving the devout to worship at any one of a dozen smaller shrines located across the city. He had heard a recent bit of gossip, though. There were rumours throughout the city that a holy man had appeared before the temple elders bearing signs and portents that the culmination of a great prophecy was at hand. What that meant the man could not say, but there were acolytes in the streets exhorting the faithful to prepare themselves for a time of blood and fire, and bloodied skulls began to appear in piles on every street corner. Fearing that soon his head would be added to one of the piles, the man fled for his life.

The news filled Malus with dismay. They finished the wine in dreary silence, and then he stabbed the man in the heart and went through his belongings for anything useful. Spite feasted on man and horse that night, and Malus had bread and sausage for a week after.

As the days passed Malus settled into a grim routine, stalking travellers leaving the city and learning what he could from them. Sometimes the conversation ended at the point of a knife; other times he chose discretion and slipped away into the darkness once the wine was done. Once he nearly had the tables turned on him, and it was only the Dark Mother's own luck and his familiarity with the forest that allowed him to escape with a whole skin. Little by little, his knowledge of the city grew, but nothing he learned helped solve the most crucial riddles of all: how to avoid the notice of the temple without winding up an unwilling sacrifice, and how to find the Warpsword of Khaine.

It never once occurred to Malus to ask either Tz'arkan or his mother Eldire for help. The silver ring he wore had been a gift from his mother, one of the most potent sorceresses and seers in the Land of Chill. He could use it to speak with her on nights when the moon was bright. As for the daemon, it had never passed up a chance to tempt him with tastes of its supernatural powers – but after the night in the burning city, its behaviour had changed. It was warier now, questioning Malus's every move and offering nothing unless asked. The daemon feared Eldire's power for some reason, and that both pleased and troubled Malus.

As the summer wore on the pattern of travel changed. Druchii began heading for Har Ganeth – singly at first, and then in small groups of up to half a dozen, arriving at all hours of the day and night. They came down the Slavers' Road from the west or crossed the Sea of Malice in boats, and they all travelled surreptitiously, without fanfare or finery. They came from all walks of life, as near as Malus could tell: highborn and lowborn, princes, bakers and thieves and everything in between, and once they entered Har Ganeth, they didn't emerge again. Malus found himself thinking about Urial and his prophecy once more, and wondered whether there might be something to it after all.

Seeking answers, Malus headed down the road and looked for a solitary traveller to share a bottle of wine with.

The first man he found welcomed him like a long-lost brother and barely took a sip of wine before trying to cut Malus's throat. He'd laughed like a lunatic as they'd rolled across the damp ground, wrestling over the man's serrated knife. When Malus had finally gained the upper hand and searched the body afterwards he found a brown canvas bag filled with body parts: hands, ears, noses and genitals, many still sticky with gore.

Malus approached a second man a day later, and received another warm welcome. This time he was ready when the druchii leapt at him with a knife. He, too, had a bag full of freshly severed bits of flesh. In a fit of pique Malus tossed the druchii's head into the bag and took it with him.

After that he watched the people on the road much more closely. Man or woman, young or old, they all carried a sword or a broad-bladed knife and a stained bag hung from shoulder or belt.

Was there some holy ceremony in the offing, calling the faithful to the city to present their offerings to Khaine? He'd never heard of such a thing before. One thing was clear, however: the travellers seemed happy to kill any stranger they met except those carrying bags of their own. Malus had no idea why that mattered, but finally a glimmer of a plan began to take shape in his mind.

'Wine, brothers and sisters?' Malus pulled a clay bottle from a second carry-bag and offered it to the group. One of the men from Hag Graef leaned forwards and took the bottle eagerly. Malus caught the man's eye as he surrendered the wine, but saw no glint of recognition there.

'I hadn't realised there were any followers of the true faith living at the Black Ark,' the temple maiden said.

The true faith? What did that mean, Malus thought? 'I hadn't known of any in Karond Kar either,' he answered. 'I suppose that makes us even.' Eager to change the subject, he nodded his head eastward. 'We'll be in Har Ganeth by midday tomorrow.'

The other travellers from the Karond Kar murmured in approval. 'We should have listened to you after all, holy one,' the second woman said to the temple maiden. 'If we'd continued on we would have reached the holy city by midnight.'

'Let's go then,' one of the men declared. 'We have a sacred duty, do we not? The heretic and his minions could be battling with the faithful even now–'

The temple maiden cut the man off with a curt wave of her hand. Her gaze never left Malus. 'You look as if you've been wandering in the mountains for weeks,' she said to the highborn.

Malus affected a shrug, his mind churning. The heretic? That had to mean Urial. Who else had recently come to Har Ganeth shouting about the end of the world?

'I... well,' Malus stammered, looking away. 'I confess that I've tarried a while on the road, holy one.' He reached over and hefted the bloodstained sack. 'There are meagre pickings on the Spear Road this time of year, and I didn't want to reach Har Ganeth with a poor offering for the god.'

Several of the faithful nodded their heads approvingly. He'd taken a wild guess about the contents of the bag, and the gamble had paid off. The temple maiden considered him for a moment more, and then leaned back against a fallen log and resumed her meal.

The man from Clar Karond eyed Malus. 'Have you seen many other faithful on the road, brother?'

'Oh, yes,' Malus nodded. 'They've come from all over. I'd wager there are thousands in the holy city, ready to fight the heretic.'

At the news, the man's eyes glinted with a savage light. 'At last! The day of reckoning is at hand. We've suffered the heretic's lies long enough!'

'I couldn't agree more, brother,' Malus said with feeling. The man from Hag Graef passed the bottle back to him and he took a hearty swallow. This was going to work. If he kept his wits about him he could slip into the city with the rest of the faithful and no one – least of all Urial – would be the wiser.

Grinning broadly, the man from Clar Karond reached for the wine. 'With so many of the true faith returning to the city the streets must be busy indeed,' he said. 'We have a place prepared for us at the home of Sethra Veyl. Where will you be staying?'

'With my cousin,' Malus replied. 'He is a chandler, with a shop close to the temple fortress.'

The man from Clar Karond froze, his hand still reaching for the bottle. His grin faded. Suddenly Malus noticed that everyone else had fallen silent.

The temple maiden rose to her feet, a curved dagger in her hand.

'Seize the heretic,' she hissed.

CHAPTER TWO

EYES OF BRASS

Malus bit back a curse. So much for blending in with the herd, he thought bitterly. Thinking quickly, he grabbed his bag of offerings and rose slowly to his feet.

'Where I choose to stay inside the city is my business,' he said sharply, fixing the temple maiden with a steely glare. 'Just because I'm careful doesn't make me one of the enemy. Obviously you're as concerned about infiltrators in our ranks as I am, or you wouldn't be asking all these questions.'

Malus saw the two men from Hag Graef hesitate, their weapons half-drawn. They looked to the temple maiden for guidance.

She paused, the muscles in her jaw clenching as she wrestled with her bloodlust. The maiden opened her mouth to speak, but whatever she meant to say was lost as her female companion shrieked like a scalded slave and threw herself at Malus.

The woman's serrated dagger whistled through the air as she slashed at Malus's throat. He blocked the stroke with the stained bag of offerings, and the razor-edged blade split the damp cloth like wet paper. Withered, rotting body parts flew across the campsite, some landing in the fire with a sizzle and a flare of sparks. Malus planted his back foot and snapped the empty bag at the woman's eyes, checking her advance. Then he reversed his grip on the wine bottle and smashed it against the side of her head. She fell with a howl of rage and her companions took up the cry, rushing across the damp earth towards Malus with weapons held before them.

Malus back-pedalled, cursing fiercely as he dragged his broad sword from its scabbard. The zealots rushed at him from both sides, swinging wildly with swords and knives. The highborn blocked a knife stroke with his half-drawn sword and then twisted wildly to the left to dodge a downward slash of a sword that struck sparks from his shirt of blackened mail. With a roar he freed his blade and drove the zealots back a step with a fierce swipe at their eyes, but less than a second later they were back on the attack, hemming Malus in with a net of glinting steel.

What the zealots lacked in martial skill they made up for in utter fearlessness, apparently unafraid of losing their lives in the process of bringing Malus down. They kept up their relentless advance, forcing Malus to remain on the defensive against the flashing points of sword and knife. He could tell that the zealots were gauging his reflexes, and the attacks were falling into a deadly rhythm. The two men from Hag Graef pressed him from the right, while the temple maiden and the man from Clar Karond circled to his left. One of the men from Hag Graef reached in with a long thrust to Malus's neck. As he swept the blade aside with a quick shift of his sword, the temple maiden's dagger flickered in at the same moment and dug into his side. Mail rings popped and the dagger point carved a furrow through his leather kheitan, but the armour stopped the worst of the blow. Snarling, Malus aimed a savage blow at the maiden's neck, but she nimbly leapt back out of the highborn's long reach. As she did, the second man from Hag Graef stepped in and sank his dagger into Malus's right thigh.

The blow was overextended and weak and the point of the blade sank only a few inches into the muscle of Malus's leg, but the fiery explosion of pain made the highborn stumble. The man from Hag Graef showed his red-tinged blade to his fellows and cackled with glee, showing crudely filed teeth.

Malus met the man's frenzied stare and let out a furious bellow, swinging at the hand holding the bloodstained blade. The man leapt back, just as the temple maiden had done, but the move was wasted, because the highborn's attack was only a feint. Checking his blow at the last moment, Malus reversed his swing, just as the man from Clar Karond rushed in on his left. The man was at full extension, slashing low with his knife, and Malus's heavy sword buried itself in the side of his head. The druchii staggered beneath the blow, a choking, bloody rasp hissing past his shattered jaw. Then he let go of his knife and gripped Malus's sword in his bare hands, trapping it in a death grip.

The zealot fell, blood pouring from his ravaged face and hands, and pulled Malus along with him. Without thinking, Malus put his boot in the man's face and took hold of his sword hilt with both hands, but he was not fast enough to pull his weapon free. The dagger-man from Hag Graef tackled him around the waist, knocking the highborn off his feet.

Malus hit the ground with a roar, feeling the sword wrenched from his grip. The zealot's dagger was trapped beneath the highborn for the moment. Malus pounded and clawed at the druchii's head, but the zealot tucked in his chin and closed his eyes tight against the highborn's stabbing fingers.

The highborn changed tack, fumbling for his dagger, but the temple maiden and the remaining zealots swept down on him, weapons ready. 'Hold his arms,' she ordered. The maiden ran a pink tongue over gleaming white teeth. 'I want him to watch while I sip from his living heart.'

Malus thrashed and kicked, but the men from Hag Graef seized his wrists and pulled his arms back over his head. The maiden knelt and with one hand hiked up Malus's mail shirt until the leather kheitan was exposed. Her saw-edged blade would make quick work of the tough leather. She set the point of the knife just beneath Malus's ribs and flashed the highborn a lustful smile. 'Servant of the false Swordbearer,' she hissed, 'you were a fool to think you could face us alone. You placed your faith in a false prophet and now you will pay the price.'

The highborn tried to wrench free one last time, drawing muffled curses from the zealots, but their grip was like iron. Finally he subsided, shaking his head. 'Alone? I think not,' Malus said coldly. 'Let me show you where I place my faith, temple whore.' The highborn drew a lungful of air and bellowed. 'Spite!'

There was a shrieking hiss, like water poured on a hot forge, and a huge, dark shape burst from the deep shadows beneath the trees. The nauglir was small for its breed, no more than twenty-four feet long from blunt snout to tapered tail, but its gaping jaws held fangs as long as daggers and its taloned forepaws were as broad as a man's chest. It propelled itself forwards on two powerful hind legs, shaking the earth with its tread. Lean, cable-like muscle rolled fluidly beneath its armoured green hide as it charged like a lion at the stunned zealots. The woman from Clar Karond was rising to her feet, blood streaming from the side of her face as the cold one reached her. Her scream was cut off with a thick, wet crunch as Spite's jaws closed on her torso and bit her in half. The war beast never broke stride, throwing the lower half of the druchii's body high in the air with a sharp toss of his head and a thunderous roar.

The temple maiden met Spite's hunting bellow with a shriek of her own, but it was like a war scream in the face of a howling storm. She leapt to her feet, dagger ready, but the dagger-man from Hag Graef let out a terrified scream and ran for his life.

Spite was on them in moments, clawed feet crashing down to either side of Malus and the zealots holding him. Gobbets of flesh and poisonous slime dripped from the cold one's jaws as it snapped at the man still holding Malus's arm. The highborn cursed and screamed along with his foes, rolling on his side and pulling at his trapped arm for all he was worth. The cold one would just as easily bite off Malus's arm in the heat of the moment and never know the difference.

The man from Hag Graef refused to let go of Malus, yelling his own curses at the scaly war beast and the temple maiden alike. Spite lunged at the man, snapping his drooling jaws, but the zealot ducked at the last moment and narrowly avoided losing his head.

Still screaming in fury, the temple maiden tried to drive her knife into the cold one's neck, but she didn't reckon on the thickness of the nauglir's leathery hide. The serrated blade sank barely a couple of inches into the dark green scales and was caught fast. Spite snarled and rounded on the maiden, but the woman anticipated the move and leapt backwards, out of reach of the war beast's jaws. Or so she'd hoped.

Just as she made her move Malus caught her ankle with his free hand and checked her flight. The maiden stumbled, but Spite caught her before she hit the ground. Her scream of rage turned into a rising shriek of pain as the nauglir shook her like a rat in a terrier's jaws and then flung her at the man still holding Malus's arm. Both zealots went tumbling across the ground, the impact nearly wrenching the highborn's arm out of its socket before the druchii's grip was broken.

Spite leapt after his stunned prey, bloodstained jaws gaping, and Malus fumbled his dagger free as the man pinning his legs saw his chance to escape and tried to get clear. The zealot rolled to his feet, eyes bright with hate, and Malus threw his dagger left-handed, burying it in the man's throat.

By the time Malus staggered to his feet the only sound in the clearing was the crackle of the fire and the brittle crunch of bones. Spite stood over the remains of the temple maiden and the man from Hag Graef, devouring clothes, flesh and bone in quick, snapping bites. The highborn gave the cold one a wide berth while it fed, looking for the man who'd fled towards the Slavers' Road. After a moment he caught a glimpse of a pale face, several hundred yards along the road to the north-east. He could not see any details, but Malus could imagine the man running as hard as his legs would take him, casting terrified glances over his shoulder every few yards for fear that the terrible nauglir had given chase.

'Spite!' Malus called. The cold one looked up from its meal, steam rising from the hot blood coating its snout. It snapped its jaws once, scattering streams of gory slime, and then loped heavily towards the highborn like a faithful hound.

Malus pointed down the road. 'There, beast of the deep earth,' he said coldly. 'Smell his fear? Hunt, Spite. Hunt!'

The nauglir raised its snout, nostrils flaring, let out a rumbling growl and started off at a ground-eating trot. It wouldn't be long before the zealot cast a glance over his shoulder and saw nothing but red eyes and dagger-like teeth.

Malus turned back to the corpses of the faithful and bit back a snarl of dismay. 'Damnation,' he said wearily, reclaiming first his dagger and then his heavy sword. 'One day I'll have a plan that works to perfection. The shock of it will likely kill me.'

'You were a fool to think they would be deceived, little druchii,' Tz'arkan sneered. 'All cults are born of secrets and deception, the better to identify outsiders. One wrong word, one wrong look, and your skull will be sitting atop a pile on a Har Ganeth street corner.'

'And what would you have me do?' Malus shot back. 'March into Har Ganeth and ask them politely for the sword?'

The daemon's presence slithered against his ribs like silk. Malus had come to think of the sensation as Tz'arkan's version of a smile. 'Why not? It was meant for you, after all.'

Malus let out an involuntary snarl and began searching through the zealots' bags. One of them was bound to have a bottle of wine. 'I'm not interested in your riddles,' he growled. 'I am not bound by fate or prophecy – least of all yours.'

Back in ancient times, when the druchii still ruled lost Nagarythe, the cult of Khaine was outlawed for its violent excesses and refusal to acknowledge the authority of cursed Aenarion, king of the elves. In those days, the faithful who worshipped the Bloody-Handed God clung to a prophecy that one day the Lord of Murder would send his chosen servant to lead the druchii to eternal glory in a time of blood and fire.

Urial thought he was that man, chosen by Khaine for his purity and devotion in spite of his physical deformities. He certainly fit the criteria set forth in the prophecy. But then, so did Malus.

The Scourge was destined to take up the Warpsword of Khaine. If Urial was indeed the figure of prophecy, he was going to be very surprised indeed when Malus pried the blade out of his half-brother's cold, dead hands. He had to have that blade, and to the Outer Darkness with the rest.

'Your mother has filled your head with lies,' Tz'arkan hissed.

'You sound jealous,' Malus replied absently, tossing aside the last of the bags. No wonder the zealots were such miserable wretches. Not a drop of wine among them. It was unnatural.

'I have never lied to you,' the daemon said querulously. 'I have shared my power with you when you needed it, even when it caused me great pain to do so.'

'And you've destroyed me into the bargain,' Malus snapped. 'No wealth, no rank, no prospects – I've lost it all thanks to you.'

'Trinkets,' the daemon sneered. 'Cheap gewgaws unfit for one such as you.' Tz'arkan slithered gently beneath Malus's skin, setting the highborn's teeth on edge. 'Have you ever considered that perhaps this quest is but a test?'

'A test?' Malus spat. 'Of what?'

Again, came the silky, scaly rustle of the daemon's smile. 'Malus, dear Malus. Think for a moment. I am not born of flesh. I am Tz'arkan, Drinker of Worlds. I am eternal. Do you honestly think I suffer in my crystal prison to the north?'

The answer seemed evident. 'Of course.'

'Foolish druchii. To you, a millennium of entrapment is a horror beyond imagining, but to me? It is an eye blink. If I remain bound to that crystal until the sun goes dark in the heavens it would be about as onerous as wiling away a long afternoon.'

The highborn paused. 'So you do not truly care if you are freed?'

Tz'arkan laughed. 'I will be free, Malus. That is beyond doubt. The question is whether you will be able to free me.'

Malus frowned. 'Now you're speaking in riddles.'

'No, you're being obtuse. Must I spell it out for you? I care nothing for pitiful little worlds, or the nations of pale grubs that writhe upon them. I am like unto a god, Malus. You could be, too. If you are worthy.'

The highborn laughed, shaking his head in amazement. 'And you expect me to believe that? You'd make me a god, just like that?'

He expected the daemon to sneer at him. Instead, Tz'arkan's reply was strangely sombre. 'How else do you think gods are born?'

The thought brought Malus up short.

He's lying, the highborn thought. He must be. He's trying to get the upper hand again now that Eldire has allied herself with me. And yet... it all made a terrible kind of sense.

Malus thought it over. 'All right,' he said slowly. 'Give me my soul back.'

'What?'

'You heard me,' the highborn said. 'If this isn't about your freedom, there's no need to hold my soul to compel my cooperation. Give it back, and I'll get your relics for you.'

The daemon writhed within Malus's chest. 'Impertinent druchii! I offer you power undreamt of, and you insult me!'

'I'll take that as a no,' Malus said, pleased at the thought of discomfiting the daemon. Slowly but surely, he was learning how the game was played.

Tz'arkan roiled like a storm inside his chest, but Malus gritted his teeth and tried to focus on the matter at hand. He had thought that with a bag of bones and a quick wit he could pretend to be a pilgrim and bluff his way into the city, but he'd underestimated the tensions running within the cult. It sounded as if the temple was on the verge of civil war.

Still, now he knew more about the situation than he did previously. He knew that the faithful were flocking to Har Ganeth to stop the false Swordbearer, which was encouraging. He also knew that the zealots were gathering at the house of Sethra Veyl.

Deep in thought, Malus walked over to the remains of the temple maiden. Spite hadn't left much. Her head and part of one shoulder lay amid the pieces of the man she'd landed on. The maiden's face was frozen in a rictus of hate, defiant until the end.

The highborn knelt, studying the face. What he needed was an extra layer to his disguise, something that would make the zealots think twice about suspecting him.

'All right, daemon,' he said thoughtfully. 'Forget giving me the power of a god. Right now I'll settle for a pair of brass-coloured eyes.'

Tz'arkan had obliged without hesitation. That was a bad sign.

The pain had been immense, and it seemed to last for hours. There was a point when Malus thought that the daemon had decided to take him literally and turn his eyes to molten metal. After a while longer he wasn't thinking much of anything, hugging his arms tightly around his chest to keep from clawing his own eyes out.

The fog had reached the wood line and the fire had burned down to embers by the time the pain subsided. His face was flushed and each eye blink sent shivers of agony through his body.

Malus could hear Spite moving around the clearing, nibbling idly at the remains of the zealots. After some thought, the highborn rolled painfully onto his hands and knees and crawled towards the embers of the fire. Even the dull red light of the coals sent needles of pain into his eyes, but after some searching, he managed to find the maiden's offering bag. Malus called the cold one over and fumbled his way into the saddle. Then he pointed Spite up the road towards Har Ganeth and gave the nauglir its head.

They rode through the night. Malus swayed in the saddle, holding his eyes tightly shut. Well past midnight, his parched throat felt so tight he could barely breathe, and he groped behind his saddle for a water skin. The highborn drank deep of the brackish liquid, and then on impulse he poured a little into each eye. The pain was so sudden and sharp he cried out, but afterwards his eyes felt much better.

False dawn was colouring the mountains to the east when they reached the City of Executioners. The sea breeze shifted, carrying with it the burnt copper tang of blood, and Malus slowly opened his eyes.

The city shimmered like a ghost in the pearlescent light.

Har Ganeth, the Fortress of Ice. Before the druchii built Karond Kar at the mouth of the Slavers' Straits, Har Ganeth had been the northernmost city in the Land of Chill. Its walls and towers had been built from the purest white marble, quarried from the mountains near the Houses of the Dead. The Fortress of Ice was cold and cruel and everlasting, a symbol of the merciless druchii heart.

That had been before Malekith had given control of the city to the temple of Khaine, before the night of slaughter centuries past when the streets had turned to rivers of blood.

Walls of stone towered thirty feet above Malus, their sheer faces painted in layers of crimson from foot to crown. The bloodstained walls could be seen for miles, but up close, with the dawn light wakening the white marble beneath, Malus stared in wonder at hundreds upon hundreds of bloody hand prints, layered one on top of another to create subtle shades and murderous hues. The red sheen looked fresh. Malus was tempted despite himself to touch it, to add to it, deepening the mosaic of slaughter one thin layer more.

The city gate was unusually broad and low, wide enough for six mounted knights to ride comfortably abreast but not with their lances held high. An enormous gatehouse loomed overhead, its wide face pierced by arrow slits and murder holes. Oil gutters hung like arched tongues from the carved mouths of dragons and basilisks, ready to pour searing death on any invader. The gates of Har Ganeth were long gone, however, and its portcullis dismantled. The gateway yawned like the wide mouth of a leviathan, ever hungry for more prey.

There were no guards upon the battlements, no green light of witchfires burning behind the arrow slits. Beyond the gate Malus saw streets cloaked in eddies of pale fog.

Somewhere in the distance, a voice cried out in anger and pain. Malus put his heels to Spite's flanks and entered the City of Executioners, seeking the house of Sethra Veyl.

CHAPTER THREE

CITY OF RAVENS

Malus soon lost count of the dead.

They lay everywhere in Har Ganeth's streets and gutters, contorted by pain and violence and left to cool in drying pools of gore. Some were piled in narrow alleys like old rubbish; others lay slumped against the red-tinged marble walls, having painted the stone with bright swathes of their own blood. Most were druchii like him, although more than once Malus caught sight of the corpse of a slave, stripped naked but for his collar of service. Every victim had been hacked to death. Many bore the gruesome wounds of axe or draich, the great two-handed swords favoured by the temple Executioners. There were men and women, young druchii and old. Some died fighting, with swords and daggers in hand and mortal wounds to head and neck. Others simply ran and took their wounds in the back. The end result was the same.

Many of the victims had been beheaded. Their skulls had been added to pyramids of similar trophies, some stacked as high as a mounted man along the sides of the roadway or next to the door of a business or home. Nearly all of the piles of skulls rested in thick layers of dirty grey dust. The sight puzzled Malus at first, until he noticed that there was a gruesome stratum to the pyramids. The heads nearest the top were the freshest, of course, still cased in tattered flesh and skin. Closer to the bottom vermin and the elements had stripped them clean, leaving a layer of bleached bone at the very base. In time, even those sturdy bones crumbled, pressed down by the weight of the bones above and ground into pale dust.

The city stank like a battlefield. In the open squares it was bad enough, but climbing the narrow, winding streets towards the upper districts was like walking through a dimly lit abattoir. Spite grumbled and sniffed at the heavy odour of rotting blood and spilled organs, and Malus fought the urge to cover his face with a fold of his cloak. Even in the brutal battles on the road to Hag Graef he'd never seen the like.

The City of Executioners had been built on commanding ground on the shore of the Sea of Chill. At first just a collection of forbidding spires rising into the sky from atop a broad, granite hill, over the centuries the city had spread like a mantle of white stone down the hill slopes and along the flat ground around the hill's base. When Har Ganeth was given over to the temple by edict of the Witch King the temple in the lower city had been abandoned and the elders seized the districts surrounding the crown of the high hill. Many of the city's richest citizens had been turned out of their homes, and the buildings demolished to create the massive temple fortress that surrounded the drachau's stained white towers in a fist of dark stone. No matter where one stood in the lower city one felt the ominous shadow of the temple of Khaine.

Like all druchii cities, Har Ganeth was a warren of narrow, twisting streets and alleys, purposely designed to confound intruders. Tall, narrow buildings channelled would-be invaders into dead ends and cul-de-sacs where they would find themselves at the mercy of citizens waiting on wrought-iron balconies high overhead. But for a few main thoroughfares meant for commerce or war, no road was wide enough to admit more than two riders abreast, and in many cases the streets were narrower still. Sunlight rarely found its way into these claustrophobic lanes, and even in daylight every other house was lit by an intricately wrought, iron lamp hung outside the heavy oak door.

Upon entering Har Ganeth, Malus had found himself in the city's merchant district. Eddies of pale fog swirled around Spite's flanks as Malus led his mount past shuttered warehouses and through market commons littered with trash. Next came the slave quarter, with its broad squares and ironbound cages. The first of the city's many shrines lay just off the quarter, and it was here that the highborn saw the first signs of slaughter. Malus couldn't help but wonder how much flesh was bought at the markets and marched across the square just to bleed on the altar of the Lord of Murder.

The narrow streets of the artisans' quarters lay past Khaine's shrine, and further still were the flesh houses and blood pits of the entertainment district. Every lodging-house and tavern was tightly shut, their stoops empty of the indigent or the drunk. There were no signs of exhausted revelry, only piles of leering, tattered heads. For weeks he'd fantasised about a bath, bottles of wine and a soft bed in such a lodging-house, but the eerie stillness of the district drove all temptations from his mind.

Beyond the neighbourhood of lodging-houses and taverns the road began to climb the wide hill. The tall, shabby houses of the lowborn rose around him, and the way ahead became difficult. Malus's hair stood on end as he led Spite into the close-set streets. The narrow windows were shuttered and the overhanging balconies were empty, but he could not shake the sensation that he was being watched. The highborn drew his heavy sword and rested it in his lap, suddenly wishing he'd thought to put on the plate armour bound up in rolls of cloth and hung from the back of Spite's saddle.

The more scenes of carnage he passed, the more his wariness grew. Some of the bodies still steamed in the chilly morning air, suggesting that the killers were close by. The thought of a running battle with a mob of fanatics – on their home ground – set the highborn's teeth on edge.

He knew, from his conversations with travellers, that the highborn districts lay around the top of the hill, but he wasn't certain how to get there. How long could he wander down the maze-like streets before he stumbled across an armed band looking for more trophies to stack outside their door? Would his appearance give the attackers pause? Malus had no way of knowing. Nothing he'd seen so far made any sense to him. For the first time since the long, harrowing trip back from the Chaos Wastes, Malus felt vulnerable and exposed.

It wasn't as if he could go door-to-door and ask the way to the house of Sethra Veyl. Briefly he contemplated heading straight for the temple and simply presenting himself there – surely with a heresy simmering in the city the priestesses wouldn't scrutinise any offer of help too closely. The solution was simple and direct, but it gave Malus pause. There had to be a reason why the faithful were being lodged in houses in the city proper. Perhaps the temple ranks had been infiltrated? If so, how could he be certain that the priestess he spoke with wasn't a secret ally of Urial? With no other recourse open to him he nudged Spite onward, ears straining for the sounds of movement from the alleys or the balconies overhead.

As the dawn broke to the east Malus heard the first stirrings of life, high up in the shadows of the eaves along the street. Feathers rustled and bits of loose stone rattled down the stained facades of the houses. To Malus, far below, the shadowed ledges up near the slate roofs seemed to bob and writhe with invisible life. Then, with a querulous squawk and the beat of heavy wings, an enormous raven launched itself from the shadows and swooped low over Malus's head before alighting at the peak of a pyramid of fresh trophies. The carrion bird glared impetuously at the passing highborn before cocking its sleek head and contemplating its resplendent red feast.

Within minutes the air was black with gore-crows, flapping and calling to one another as they soared down the city streets. They passed so close to Malus that he felt the wind of their wings against his face, and they showed no fear at all of Spite. Once the cold one stepped right over a sprawled body covered in hungry ravens, and the birds paid no attention whatever to the lumbering nauglir.

The constant chatter of the birds made Malus uneasy. Some of the ravens even croaked at Malus in passable druhir. 'Sword and axe!' one bird called. 'Skulls! Skulls!' cried another. 'Blood and souls! Blood and souls!' croaked a third. Their eyes glittered cruelly as they jabbed at torn flesh with their dagger-like beaks.

He kicked Spite into a trot and rode on. Every house looked just like the next: stained walls and iron-banded doors of dark oak, without sign or symbol to identify who lived inside. At every turn Malus chose the uphill path, scattering ragged clouds of squawking birds before the nauglir's one-ton tread.

When Malus heard the ringing clash of steel and the screams of wounded men he turned Spite in the direction of the sounds without hesitation, his previous fears eclipsed by the morbid celebration of the birds.

He headed up a long, straight lane, certain the fight was dead ahead. Moments later Malus reached a dogleg and found himself abruptly heading downhill. Snarling, he pulled on the reins and turned Spite around in the cramped space to retrace his steps, and headed down another road that appeared to circle the hillside in the general direction of the battle.

That ended at a cul-de-sac piled with old bones and bare, white skulls. A lone, elderly druchii stood at the rail of an overhanging balcony, glaring down at Malus as he brought Spite about. The cold one knocked over piles of bones and crunched them underfoot, snapping irritably at the pall of fine dust kicked into the air. Snarling, the highborn kicked the nauglir into a canter, eager to be out from under the old man's silent stare.

He nearly missed the knife-slit of an alley as they careened back along the street. Malus caught the path out of the corner of his eye and reined Spite in roughly, causing the war beast to growl angrily and back-pedal along the cobblestones. The alley seemed to point in the direction of the fight, and was barely wide enough for the cold one to wriggle through. The fit was so tight that Malus had to draw up his feet and rest them on the saddle's cantle as the nauglir stalked down the narrow passage.

The alley intersected another street that seemed to climb the side of the hill at an angle. Malus reined in, cursing the damn labyrinth under his breath. Then he heard the unmistakeable ring of steel slicing flesh and a man's agonised shout just ahead. 'Slowly now, Spite,' Malus said quietly, prodding the cold one's flanks with his spurs.

They turned up the cross street and followed only a few dozen yards to the first bend. Predictably, the road came to a dead end just ten yards farther on. It was there that the killers had cornered their prey.

Five men had been backed up against the sheer wall at the end of the lane; only one of them was still standing, and he bled from a score of deep wounds. There were six druchii arrayed against him, locals, Malus guessed, by the similarity of the dark robes they wore. Their pale faces were streaked with patterns of dried blood – the five-fingered sigil of the Bloody-Handed God – and they wielded a mix of axes, clubs and knives. Their intended victim wore a highborn's kheitan and a breastplate of steel, and he fought with a knife in one hand and a long-hafted axe in the other. Despite his wounds, the man roared like a nauglir at his attackers, whirling his axe in a lethal pattern that drove the locals back. They had good reason to be wary of him; four others were already splayed out on the cobblestones, hacked open by the man's ferocious axe work.

As Malus watched, the locals gave ground before the man, staying just far enough back to avoid the reach of the axe, but close enough to threaten him if they got a chance. All they had to do was wait, the highborn thought. The axe wielder was already white as Har Ganeth marble, his robes dark and heavy with his own blood. Soon enough he would slow, and falter, and then the knives would strike home.

The highborn was just about to turn away when he saw the pile of cloth bags set neatly side by side along the sheer wall behind the beleaguered axe man. He was one of the faithful.

Malus slid quietly from the saddle and stepped close to Spite's head. He pointed to one of the locals. 'That one,' he told the cold one. 'Hunt!'

The cold one's jaws gaped wide as the war beast crept with surprising stealth towards the unsuspecting man. The highborn picked out a victim of his own and stole quietly up behind him, his broad sword raised.

At the last moment Spite's prey stiffened. Perhaps Khaine had sent him a premonition, or perhaps he'd simply caught a whiff of the nauglir's carrion breath. He whirled, weapon ready, and barely had time to scream before the cold one's jaws bit him in half. Blood and entrails splattered across the cobblestones as the nauglir latched onto the druchii's lower torso and began to feed.

Malus struck at the same moment, striking the man's head from his shoulders with a single, sweeping blow. The headless body collapsed, bright arterial blood pumping from the severed neck, and the highborn leapt at the next man in line with a savage scream.

The surviving attackers recovered with surprising speed and two men turned on Malus, deeming him the greater threat. One of the locals, teeth bared in a bloodthirsty snarl, rushed at the highborn with a sweeping diagonal cut aimed at the point of his right shoulder. At the same moment the second attacker swept in wide from the left and swung his bloodstained club at Malus's knee. Laughing hatefully, Malus gauged the speed of the axe and dodged backwards at the last second. Then he slapped the weapon aside with a hard stroke from his blade. It sent the man's axe into the path of his companion, snapping his shin with a brittle crack. The club wielder fell face first with an anguished shriek, and Malus finished off the axe wielder with a backhanded stroke that opened his throat to the spine. The highborn turned back to the fallen man and took a moment to kick him in the side of the head. Then he turned back to the wounded zealot, but his foe was already down, blood pumping from a half dozen brutal wounds.

Smiling in satisfaction, Malus went back and finished off the druchii with the broken leg. He gave the axe man a comradely grin. 'It's well for you that I came along when I did, brother.'

The zealot was still standing over the body of his fallen foe. His head hung low and his shoulders trembled. Rivulets of bright blood shone against the pallid skin of his face and hands. He took a single, racking breath. 'You... you saved me, holy one,' the man breathed.

Malus bent to wipe his sword clean on the dead druchii's hair. 'Well, I confess I had a question to ask you—'

Had the zealot not been half-dead from blood loss his first stroke would have split Malus from crown to navel. As it was, the highborn heard the faint scrape of the man's boot and battlefield instincts threw him to the side. The axe came whistling down and split the dead druchii in two, but the zealot scarcely skipped a beat. He pulled his weapon free and leapt after Malus, his expression a rictus of madness and hate.

There was no time for confusion or shouted commands; the axe was a crimson blur, reaching for Malus's head, neck and chest. The zealot's skill was incredible, and it was all Malus could do to parry the rain of razor-edged blows. The street rang from the clash of axe and sword, like the tolling of a madman's bell.

Malus gave ground, his anger rising with every step. The axe blade sang past the highborn's sword and sliced through the sleeve of his upper left arm. He felt warm blood soaking into the fabric of his robes. 'What kind of gratitude is this?' he snarled.

But the man only redoubled his attacks, howling in fury. The zealot leapt forwards, feinting at Malus's neck and then sweeping upwards to smash his skull. It was all the highborn could do to throw himself back out of the weapon's reach. He felt the edge of the blade nick his chin in passing.

'He can still answer questions without his arms,' the daemon suggested in its silky voice.

'True enough,' Malus gasped. Just then the man aimed a vicious backhanded cut at the highborn's head. Malus dropped to his knees and the swing of the heavy axe pulled the man off balance. Before he could recover the highborn hacked off the man's foot just above the ankle.

The zealot screamed and fell, still swinging at Malus. The axe scored a glancing blow to his right arm, popping mail rings in a long, ragged cut. Furious, the highborn rounded on the bleeding man and chopped off his right hand. Steel rang on the cobblestones as the axe cartwheeled across the street.

'Kill me!' the zealot moaned, trembling with shock and despair. 'Give me back my honour, holy one! I've done nothing to offend you.'

No, you just tried to turn me into sausage, Malus thought furiously. He leaned over the man. 'I care nothing for your honour, you fool,' he hissed. 'I just wanted to ask you a question. You brought this on yourself.'

'I did this? How? If you hadn't come along those men would have killed me. We'd been fighting for nearly an hour!'

The man was obviously delirious. Malus was frankly surprised the zealot had any blood left to lose. 'Just tell me: where is the house of Sethra Veyl?

That's all I want to know. Tell me...' Malus paused, trying to think of a suitable threat. 'Tell me... or I'll let you live.'

'No!' the man wailed, his eyes widening in horror.

'I can tie off your stumps; find a torch and cauterise the wounds. I could see to it you lived a long time.' He couldn't believe what he was saying.

The man looked at Malus as if he was a monster. 'All right, all right! His house is in the highborn quarter, near the city armoury. A house with a white door.'

'A white door, you say?' Malus snapped. 'That should be easy to spot in this blood-soaked place.' He rested the point of his sword against the man's neck. 'If you're lying...' The highborn paused. 'I'll... Oh, never mind.' He finished the man off. The zealot died with a grateful look in his eyes.

Shaking his head in wonder, Malus turned and called for Spite. 'In Har Ganeth you spare your foes and kill your friends,' he muttered. 'What do I do when I meet Sethra Veyl? Offer to burn his house down?'

By sheer luck – good or bad, Malus could no longer say – the next uphill street he found took him straight to the highborn quarter. The streets were starting to come to life; servants were emerging from the forbidding homes on errands for their masters, heading to the market or perhaps to restock the house's supply of slave flesh after a night's revelry. The servants moved with purpose, shoulders hunched and eyes downcast, never meeting another's eye or tarrying on the street for more than a moment. They wove gracefully among the piled skulls and the fresh bodies, and gave the fat, presumptuous ravens a respectful berth.

It took another hour of searching to find the city armoury, where the spears and armour of the city's militia were stored in anticipation of war. Using that as a point of reference Malus began exploring each nearby street, until at last he found a house with a spotless white door.

Malus dismounted, going over his story one last time in his head as he pounded his fist on the oak door.

Several minutes passed. Finally Malus heard the sound of a bolt being drawn back, and the door's spyhole opened. A dark eye regarded him dispassionately.

'Greetings brother,' Malus said. 'I've come a long way to answer the call of the faithful. I was told there would be a place for me here.'

The eye regarded him a moment more, and then the spyhole snapped shut. Larger bolts rattled in their housings and the door swung open. A young woman in startlingly white robes stood in the doorway. A long, fresh cut traced a red line down the side of her pale face, still seeping a thin line of blood. Her expression was eerily serene. 'Welcome, holy one,' she said in a measured voice.

Malus paused. Do I step inside or draw my sword, he thought?

He decided on the former. Stepping just inside the doorway, he found himself in a small, walled courtyard full of armed druchii. They all wore white robes, like the woman's, and little or no armour, but every one of the zealots had a bared blade in hand. They studied Malus with barely concealed belligerence.

Malus studiously avoided the stares of the assembled druchii, focusing on the wounded woman instead. 'I will need a place for my nauglir,' he said. It occurred to him that nearly every zealot he'd seen on the road had been travelling on foot.

'It will be seen to,' the woman said. 'There are nauglir pits in the quarter, with people we can trust.' She motioned to one of the armed men, who bowed and ran across the courtyard to a flight of steps that led into the house proper. 'Your arrival is propitious,' she told him. 'The heretics have learned how many of the faithful have slipped into the city over the last few weeks and they have decided to move against us.'

Malus nodded. 'I saw a bloody battle on the way here. The heretic's servants cornered five of our men and slew them not far from here. Where is Sethra Veyl?'

The woman's serene expression darkened. 'Dead, holy one. The heretics sent assassins in the night and slew Veyl while he slept. Tyran the Unscarred is the new elder, and he vows that the atrocity will not go unavenged.' A thought struck her. 'I should take you to him, holy one. You may be of great use to his plans.'

'Of course,' Malus said smoothly, considering the possibilities. Anything he could do to gain the zealots' confidence would make his position that much more secure. 'We will have to act quickly,' he said. 'Take me to the elder. If the heretics are on the move, then Urial must be close to claiming the sword.'

'Indeed,' the woman said with a fierce smile. 'The elders cannot deny him much longer. Soon he will take up the holy blade and we will sweep the heretics away on a tide of blood. If Tyran's plan succeeds, you will open the way for the Rite of the Sword to begin. Think of the rewards you will reap when the true faith is reborn and the Swordbearer takes his place at the head of the temple!'

CHAPTER FOUR

KEEPERS OF THE DEAD

The woman ushered him into a large, empty chamber on the top floor of the house, and left him to wait as she announced his arrival to Tyran the Unscarred. A variety of swords, axes and knives hung from three of the room's walls, and the floor had been dusted with talc. The room was clearly meant for practice and perhaps meditation, although it was strange to find it at the top floor with the master's quarters. There was no fireplace to warm the open space, and the woman had made no attempt to offer Malus food or drink. Cold, hungry and deeply confused, he walked to the tall windows that dominated the north wall of the room and glared down at the city streets below. Suddenly he was envious of all the damned ravens and their sleek, black wings. At that moment he wanted to fly from Har Ganeth as fast as he could.

'This place is a madhouse,' he muttered darkly. 'Urial is the hero of the faithful and the temple elders are the heretics? Is everything turned backwards in this cursed city?'

'Heresy is mostly a matter of perspective,' Tz'arkan replied, clearly amused. 'The true faith is the one ruthless enough to wipe out all its rivals.'

'Or the one that has the support of the State,' Malus said. 'The heretics in the temple fortress have the support of Malekith, and Urial has sided with the opposition. How interesting.' The highborn tapped his lower lip thoughtfully. 'I wonder how long this has been going on for.'

'How long has he believed himself to be the Swordbearer?'

Malus nodded. 'A good point. Urial survived Khaine's cauldron and was marked by the Lord of Murder, but perhaps the temple elders balked at the idea of a cripple emerging as the heir to their precious prophecy.'

'As well they might, for we know who the true Swordbearer is.'

The highborn grimaced. 'I'll take up that cursed sword because I must, and the prophecy be damned.'

Tz'arkan chuckled. 'A prophecy cares not what you think of it, Malus. It is like a map, showing the road ahead. You can curse it all you want, but the road remains unchanged.'

'Indeed?' Malus replied. 'Eldire thinks differently.'

'The witch knows nothing,' the daemon spat. 'She intends to shape you to her will, little druchii. You are her pawn, and she will cast you aside the moment you are no longer useful.'

Malus laughed scornfully. 'Next you will tell me that the sun is warm and the night is dark. You will have to do better than that, daemon,' the highborn sneered. 'At the moment she makes a far better ally than you. For one thing, she doesn't hold my soul in her clutches.'

'No,' Tz'arkan replied, 'but she sent you to me. Think on that.'

The highborn's smug grin faded. Before he could reply, the door to the practice room swung open. The druchii woman beckoned to him from the doorway. 'Tyran wishes to speak with you.'

Malus nodded curtly and joined her. She eyed him curiously. 'Are you troubled, holy one?' she asked.

'No more than usual,' he muttered. 'Life is never at a loss for ways to vex me, it seems.'

She led him to a tapestry a short way down the corridor and without preamble pulled it aside, revealing a narrow opening and another stairway climbing into darkness. The zealot bowed slightly, gesturing for him to precede her. Frowning warily, he stepped across the threshold and peered upwards. Pale light shone steadily from under another door at the top of a short flight of stairs.

Malus climbed the wooden steps carefully, feeling them creak beneath his boots. A breath of sorcerous power brushed across his face, setting his black hair on end and causing his cheeks to tingle. Tz'arkan tightened painfully around his heart, and cold threads of daemonic energy withdrew from Malus's extremities, receding like a tide back into his chest. The sudden absence made his entire body ache. When had he gotten to the point that he only felt Tz'arkan's power by virtue of its absence? *What will be left once I drive the daemon out,* he mused?

He paused at the top of the stair, his throbbing fingers brushing the door's cold, iron latch. Another wave of power brushed against him, invisible as the wind. He was reminded of his mother's sorcery at the top of the witch's convent at Hag Graef. *Tz'arkan isn't the only power in the world,* he reminded himself, *and where the soul is lacking there is always hate to sustain me. With hate, all things are possible.*

Malus thumbed the latch and pushed open the door, letting in a blaze of cold, biting sunlight.

The door opened onto the tower's flat roof, providing a panoramic view of the eastern highborn quarter and the white-capped sea off to the south. The dark bulwark of the temple fortress rose to the west, a permanent stain against the summer sky. A sea breeze whistled fretfully over the battlements and across the flat expanse of the roof, carrying to Malus hints of pungent incense and snatches of whispered chants from the ceremony unfolding only a few score paces away.

A block of polished black basalt sat at the exact centre of the roof, its head and foot oriented to face east and west respectively. The body of a man lay on the block, his pale face stained with dark blood and his hands wrapped around the hilt of a gleaming draich. His body was attired in the clothes in which he had died: simple white robes, similar to the other zealots, but his were soaked in red from a gaping wound that ran from his shoulder to his hip.

Three women danced slowly around the corpse, their thick, white hair billowing like banners in the wind. Each wore a witch's black headdress, and their naked bodies were sleek and voluptuous. Sweat glistened on their powerful arms and gleamed coldly from white throats and heavy breasts as the witches swayed to a rhythm only they could hear. Their eyes were like shadowed pools, depthless and dark, and their full lips moved, whispering words of power that he could feel pulsing against his skin. With a start, he saw that their slender fingers were tipped with long black talons, and their white teeth were sharp and fanged like a lion's. All at once Malus was reminded of the dreadful statues lining the road to the Houses of the Dead.

'Are they not magnificent? They are true blood-witches,' his guide whispered in his ear. Malus hadn't even heard her approach. 'Heshyr na Tuan, the Keepers of the Dead. No one, not even Sethra Veyl, knew any still existed.' The zealot's voice was tinged with awe. 'This rite hasn't been performed in thousands of years. It is a great honour just to witness it.'

And in full view of the temple fortress, Malus thought, looking up at the watchtowers looming at regular intervals from the black walls. Honour or not, he suspected that Tyran wanted to send the temple elders a message. More than a half-dozen zealots stood in a tight bunch just to the left of the doorway, dividing their attention between the fortress walls and the hypnotic movements of the ritual. They were taut and alert, as if expecting a flight of arrows to rise from the fortress battlements at any moment.

One man stood apart from the rest, about halfway between the ongoing rite and the doorway where Malus stood. His back was to Malus and he was bare to the waist, revealing broad, powerful shoulders and strong arms that could have been sculpted from pale marble. The man's black hair had been pulled back from his face and bound with a rough leather cord. A long, curved draich rested in one hand, its polished edge gleaming like ice in the sunlight. For all that he stood with the ready poise of a skilled and experienced swordsman, his bare skin bore not a single scar.

'That would be Tyran, I presume,' Malus said softly.

'Yes,' the guide replied. 'We will wait here for a few moments. The rite is almost complete.'

Malus wasn't certain how the woman could tell. The blood-witches continued their slow dance around the corpse of Sethra Veyl, staring at the body with their hooded eyes and whispering supplications to the Lord of Murder. As he watched, however, the trio suddenly stopped. One stood to either side of Veyl's body and the third stood just behind the man's head. The blood-witches reached towards the corpse, stretching their long, taloned fingers, and the woman at Veyl's head bent with a bestial grin and pressed her lips to his.

The corpse convulsed, arms and legs spasming as if in the throes of death. The blood-witches withdrew, throwing back their heads and letting out an ululating howl that set Malus's teeth on edge. Then with a furious roar Sethra Veyl sat bolt upright, his bloody face twisted in an expression of hatred.

Several of the druchii witnesses drew back with startled shouts. Tyran, however, spread his strong arms as if welcoming a lost brother, and let out a joyful laugh.

'Arise Sethra Veyl!' Tyran shouted. 'Shake off the black veil of death and heed your vow to Khaine!'

The risen corpse glared at Tyran. Veyl's face worked spasmodically, as if wishing to hurl curses at the laughing druchii but unable to make its mouth form the words. Nothing but a choked rattle escaped Veyl's bloodstained lips as he slid from the stone and raised his two-handed blade.

After a moment the corpse gave up trying to speak. Veyl's dark eyes glittered with bitter humour. Malus suddenly wondered if the dead elder wasn't trying to curse Tyran, but to impart some dark wisdom from Khaine's blood-soaked realm. The realisation barely had time to sink in before Veyl rushed soundlessly at Tyran, his sword flashing in a complex pattern of deadly blows.

The speed of the attack shocked Malus. Whatever else could be said of the zealots, their dedication to the arts of war was astonishing. Tyran was motionless, and the highborn wondered if he too was stunned by the ferocity of the corpse's assault. If so, there would soon be another corpse for the blood-witches to dance for.

But just as the corpse's long blade sliced for Tyran's throat the barechested zealot exploded into action. One moment his sword was hanging calmly from his hand, and the next he was past Veyl's onrushing form, his draich held high. Malus barely registered the ringing sound of steel against flesh.

Veyl staggered to a stop, still frozen in mid-swing as if confused. Then Malus heard a wet, slithering sound, and the upper quarter of the corpse's torso slid off at an angle and fell to the floor with a spray of clotted blood. Incredibly, the rest of Veyl's body remained upright for a moment more before toppling forwards and spilling steaming organs across the slate tiles.

With an ecstatic shriek the witches fell upon Veyl's bisected form, pulling away robes and tearing into the shorn flesh with fang and claw. Tyran turned gracefully on his heel, lowering his sword slowly to his side, and Malus was struck by the eerie, serene look on his handsome face.

Tyran approached the crouching witches, moving as if in a trance. The blood-witches eyed him over their carrion feast, their chins dark with blood. They studied Tyran with large, leonine eyes.

Tyran held out his left hand. 'Give me my due,' he said, 'in Khaine's holy name.'

One of the blood-witches smiled, showing bloodstained fangs. She reached into Veyl's ruptured chest and pulled forth his heart. Tyran took the organ respectfully, threw back his head and squeezed the heart's contents into his open mouth.

There was a subtle change in the air. Malus felt the sudden absence of an electric tension that he hadn't realised was there. A sigh went through the assembled zealots.

'Now Tyran possesses a part of Veyl's strength,' Malus's guide whispered, more for her own benefit than his. 'It was ever thus, when an elder died in ancient days. Truly our time of reckoning is nigh!'

When the last drop of blood was gone, Tyran turned to the looming walls of the distant fortress. Slowly and deliberately, he raised his blade and his grisly trophy high over his head. 'The call of blood is answered in sundered flesh!' he cried.

'Blood and souls for the Lord of Murder!' the faithful answered.

Tyran lowered his sword and returned the heart to the waiting blood-witches. His face, neck and upper chest were streaked with dark blood. At that moment he noticed Malus. Tyran favoured the highborn with a calculating smile. 'Ah, here is our new pilgrim,' the zealot said. 'How was your journey, holy one?'

Malus paused but a moment, uncertain how to respond. Tyran's eyes were dark, not brass-coloured like Urial's or like those belonging to the other favoured servants of the temple. How did one address such a man? Malus knew with icy certainty that if Tyran wished, the zealot could split him like a gourd before he even realised he was in danger. 'My travels were profitable,' he said carefully, 'although pickings between here and the Black Ark were poor.'

Tyran studied Malus thoughtfully. 'It looks as if you travelled through the mountains to get here,' he said. 'Did you take to hunting autarii for your offerings?'

The highborn shook his head. 'I have no skill at catching ghosts, elder.' He offered his stained bag to Tyran. 'I gathered what offerings I could along the road, but I confess that I spent more time out of doors than I'd intended.'

Tyran took the bag and emptied its contents onto the roof beside the hungry blood-witches. They eyed the collection of body parts with feline disdain. Tyran did not seem much impressed either. 'You say you came from the Black Ark of Naggor?'

The highborn took a slow breath. 'I did. The temple there is small, but there are still a few of us who honour the old ways.'

'I didn't know there were any.'

'Didn't Veyl tell you, elder?' Malus asked. 'He was expecting me.'

Tyran considered this. 'What of the rest? Surely you are not the only true believer at the ark?'

'The others are dead, elder,' Malus replied. 'Perhaps you have heard the news of the feud between the ark and Hag Graef? The Witch Lord lost his entire army against the forces of the Hag. It was a tragedy for the ark, but a glorious day for Khaine.'

Tyran's smile turned cold. 'It's a convenient story, holy one, but your manner is strange, and you could easily be a heretic spy.'

Malus forced himself to remain calm. 'You would not be the first man to mock my rustic manners,' he said, 'but why would the heretics bother with spying on you when you hold your rites in plain view of the fortress?'

The zealot's smile faltered, and Malus felt his guts clench. Then Tyran threw back his head and laughed.

'Well said, holy one,' he replied. 'Forgive my impertinence, a man's heart blood is heady stuff, and it's left me addled. Welcome to the house of Sethra Veyl. What is your name?'

'My name is–' he caught himself saying 'Malus' and paused. 'I am Hauclir. Tell me,' he said quickly, eager to change the subject, 'is it wise to provoke the temple with such displays?'

Tyran's expression darkened. 'Do you fear the heretics and their slaves?'

'Of course not,' Malus replied, 'but neither are we in a position to challenge them openly. Otherwise we would have destroyed the heretics long ago.' The highborn was making it all up as he went along, his pulse pounding in his chest.

The zealot shrugged. 'They already know we're here. The fact that they sent a handful of assassins last night instead of turning out the temple guard tells me that they don't wish to provoke a confrontation. If they did, they couldn't be certain of killing us all, and then they would have to explain to their worshippers why they tried to wipe out the Swordbearer's disciples.'

'And what news of Urial?'

Tyran chuckled. 'They remain cloistered in the Sanctum of the Holy Blade. When he and his sister came through the Vermillion Gate there were far too many witnesses for the temple elders to hush it up. Urial presented his sister as the Bride and declared himself Swordbearer in front of almost a hundred witnesses. So they've made a big show of honouring his claim and have spent the last three months using the scriptures to discredit him.'

'And?'

A gleam of triumph shone in the zealot's dark eyes. 'They have failed. Our sources in the temple say that the elders have already been forced to admit that Yasmir is indeed a living saint of the Bloody-Handed God. So now I expect they are panicking.'

Malus very much wanted to know why the temple elders would be panicked over such a thing, but he feared that the question might give him away. 'Which is why they killed Sethra Veyl.'

Tyran nodded. 'It was a clumsy, crude gesture, which speaks to me of the elders' desperation. They seek to thwart Khaine's will by silencing his true believers, as if that would spare them from his wrath.' The zealot stepped forwards and put his bloodstained hand on Malus's shoulder. 'That is why I wanted to speak with you.'

'Is there some rite you need me to perform?' Malus asked, praying fervently that there wasn't.

The zealot laughed. 'I like you, Hauclir. For a priest you've a fine sense of humour.' He took another step closer and lowered his voice. 'No, I need you to lead a band of true believers into the temple fortress and kill the bastards who were responsible for last night's attack.'

CHAPTER FIVE

THE ASSASSIN'S DOOR

The door lay at the end of a narrow street that only knew the touch of sunlight for about an hour each day. Tall houses, the homes of highborn lords, rose to either side of the close-set lane. Malus noted that the windows facing the street were tightly shuttered. Clearly the local nobles wanted little part in the temple's clandestine affairs.

He cursed himself for not anticipating Tyran's plan. In retrospect, the druchii's interest had been obvious. Veyl's death had to be avenged and the zealot leader needed expendable men for the job. Malus was new to the city, of uncertain provenance, and had no patrons to argue on his behalf. If he died in the depths of the temple fortress the zealots would scarcely feel the loss.

The highborn turned away from the mouth of the narrow alley and looked over at his two companions. The zealots were nearly invisible in the deep shadows of the rubbish-strewn passage, their faces concealed in dark woollen wrappings and shrouded by close-fitting hoods. They seemed utterly relaxed, poised and ready for action at a moment's notice. The prospect of certain death seemed to affect them not at all. For the first time, Malus found himself wondering what rewards the cult promised in return for their devotion. He'd never shown any interest in the temple as a child; many highborn families cultivated strong ties to the cult for political reasons, but the children of Lurhan the Vaulkhar had little need for such affiliations. What do you think awaits you beyond the veil of death, Malus thought? Splendid towers and vassals? A thousand virgins? Feasting halls and an eternity of battle? He could still vividly remember the night he walked in Urial's sanctum and trod on the threshold of Khaine's realm. The highborn wondered if the true believers would be quite so sanguine if they knew what awaited them.

Like the zealots, Malus had been forced to don the robes of a dead temple assassin. The black woollen robes had been carefully cleaned and patched during the day to conceal the fate of their previous owner, and Malus had been forced to scrub the dirt of the road from his face and clean his tangled nest of hair, which caused him no small amount of apprehension. The grime had served to conceal the grey cast of his skin and the thick, blue-black veins that climbed all the way up his right arm, across his shoulder and up the side of his neck. He'd been able to conceal the corrupting touch of the daemon's curse for a time by a simple act of will, but the more he'd opened himself to Tz'arkan's gifts, the more the taint had spread. Now gauntlets covered his hands and he kept his own scarves bunched tightly around his throat. Over his robes he wore the assassins' lightweight kheitan of human hide and a shirt of fine black mail. Two short, broad-bladed swords were buckled to a wide belt at his waist. Malus nodded to the pair and pulled his hood up over his head. 'The sun is setting,' he said quietly. 'It's time.'

Without waiting for a reply he turned and slipped out of the alley, the sound of his movements lost amid the noise of the bustling avenue at the other end of the shuttered street. Horses trod across the cobblestones, men shouted to one another or cursed their slaves, and servants chattered together as they hurried to complete their masters' business before the sun went down. By day, Malus found Har Ganeth was much like any other city in Naggaroth. It was during the hours of the night that it became a very different place indeed.

The Assassin's Door was made of bolted iron, with a small spyhole covered by a cage of steel bars. There was no latch or knob; the flat, tarnished surfaces of the metal plates were inscribed with ancient, rust-stained carvings of leering skulls and piled bones.

Malus raised his fist and pounded on the rusty iron, calling to mind the strange words Tyran had told him to say. Somehow the witches had got the password from the temple assassins. He wondered if they'd made the men talk before or after they'd died.

There was a sound of scraping metal immediately and the spyhole cover opened. A pair of dark eyes studied Malus and his companions warily.

The words tumbled from his lips, spilling out in a rush. The phrase was in an archaic form of druhir, the language of scholars and theologians. Perhaps it was a proverb of the temple, or an exhortation of the god – he simply concentrated on repeating the words as they'd been given to him. 'Khaine's will is done,' the highborn finished. He had no idea if it was the right thing to say, but it seemed appropriate. 'We have returned from the house of Sethra Veyl and must make our report.'

The spyhole shut so quickly that Malus feared he'd made a mistake. Then there was a rattle of heavy locks and the highborn relaxed slightly as the Assassin's Door creaked open. Without hesitation Malus stepped through the widening gap into the chill darkness beyond.

He found himself in a narrow tunnel lit by a pair of flickering tallow lamps. Long shadows flitted and danced along the curved, soot stained walls. A small, pale face peered around the edge of the iron door as Malus and the zealots stepped hurriedly inside. The druchii who pushed the door shut was no more than a boy, clad in stained white robes and wearing a brass hadrilkar fashioned in the shape of a ring of linked skulls. The young novice shot home the door's heavy locks and then sat back down on a wooden stool beneath one of the guttering lamps. The highborn noticed a second, empty stool and reasoned that someone had run ahead to warn the elders that their assassins had returned. With a nod to his companions, Malus set off down the tunnel at a swift pace.

The plan that Tyran and the other elders had devised was a sketchy one, but the zealot leader was very specific in his orders: only the temple's master of assassins and the elder or elders who ordered the death of Veyl were to be slain. Of course, no one knew which of the elders had sent the temple assassins to Veyl's house, nor did anyone know what the master of assassins looked like, or where he could be found. Finally, after lengthy debate, Tyran concluded that once Malus and his companions reached the temple their targets would invariably come to them. The elders and the master of assassins would want to hear their report of the attack, delivering them into the zealots' hands. There was a straightforward, audacious simplicity to the plan that Malus couldn't help but admire, although bitter experience left him appalled at the number of ways that the whole thing could go disastrously wrong.

Within a few dozen steps the zealots were swallowed in reeking darkness. Malus was forced to slow his pace and move more carefully, his senses straining to penetrate the cavernous blackness that surrounded him. His hands clutched the twin hilts of his stabbing swords, and not for the first time he wrestled with the notion of turning on the two men with him and cutting their throats. After more than two months he was finally within the walls of the sprawling temple fortress. He could leave the zealots' corpses rotting in the darkness and lose himself in the temple's maze of tunnels. Tyran and the true believers would simply think him dead, and if he went back and killed the boy at the assassin's door then there would be no one to describe him to the temple guards.

It was a tempting notion, but again, experience told him that things wouldn't be quite so simple. He had reason to believe that the blade he sought was kept within the Sanctum of the Sword, but he had no idea where that would be or how to get inside. Finding out would take time, which he suspected was in short supply. Urial was eager to claim the warpsword for himself, and it would be reasonable to assume that he and Tyran were plotting to force the temple's hand. Why the temple would be reluctant to accept Urial as Khaine's chosen one still intrigued Malus. What sort of agenda did the temple elders have, and how could it be turned to his advantage?

The highborn walked straight through the trailing edges of a dusty cobweb, the invisible tendrils clinging to his face and the rim of his hood. He snatched at the strands in irritation, slowing his steps even further.

I'm out of my element, he thought angrily. The intrigues of the temple were similar enough to politics in the Hag that he had a sense of what was happening, but the rules of the game were altogether stranger and more confusing than he was accustomed to. He needed more information before he could make his own play for the sword.

As preoccupied as he was, it was some moments before he was aware of a shifting orange glow outlining the far end of the passage up ahead. Malus resumed his brisk pace, quickly composing himself before stepping through the arch and finding himself in a vaulted, fire-lit gallery that stretched to either side of the highborn for as far as his eye could see. Pillars of white marble, stained and streaked with centuries of soot, rose more than thirty feet into the air, supporting thick stone arches worked in the shapes of fearsome, imperious blood-witches.

Don't gawk, he reminded himself fiercely, forcing himself to lower his eyes and study the gallery with feigned indifference. Red coals glowed and popped in the base of iron braziers set every dozen feet or so along the gallery, outlining narrow archways that opened off the gallery on either side. Many of these archways were dark, but in a few Malus saw rearing shadows and flickering candlelight glowing against the walls of narrow cells.

Acolytes of the temple shuffled quietly through the shadows, their heads bent in contemplation. They were pale-skinned, young and fit, and the highborn noticed that many of them moved with exceptional grace and speed. All at once Malus was reminded of his former retainer Arleth Vann, himself a former temple assassin who'd forsaken his oath and found his way into the highborn's service. The last he'd seen of Arleth Vann he was being dragged away into the darkness with two crossbow bolts in his back.

Such a waste, Malus thought bitterly. Like the rest of his retainers, Vann's honour had been ruined when Malus had slain his father at Vaelgor Keep. When the highborn had returned to the Hag at the head of the Naggorite army, the former assassin had done the only thing he could do to escape the stain of Malus's crime: he'd slipped into the Naggorite camp and tried to kill his former master. But for the timely arrival of a band of autarii scouts, Vann would have succeeded. Malus vividly remembered the touch of Vann's razor-edged sword at his throat. The man had most likely died in the forest outside Hag Graef, coughing up his life's blood and cursing Malus's name.

A figure in dark robes entered the gallery from a shadowy archway opposite Malus. For a moment the highborn was speechless, thinking he was looking at a ghost. The druchii's alabaster skin, pale hair and brass-coloured eyes resembled Arleth Vann's in eerie detail, as well as the paired swords that hung at the man's hip. Another young novice accompanied the assassin. He pointed at Malus and his companions and then backed away into the shadows, his head bowed.

The temple assassin stepped forwards, holding out his hands at waist height, palms up. 'The blessings of Khaine be upon you, brothers,' he said.

'This is a glorious day indeed. When you didn't return this morning we believed you had fallen to the blades of the heathens.'

Malus mirrored the assassin's gesture. 'Far from it,' he replied, speaking softly and counting on the hood to muffle his voice. 'The fools never saw us. We merely had to be patient in order to slip away while their leaders bemoaned Veyl's fate. In the process we heard much of the heathens' plans, and need to make our report.'

The assassin nodded. 'Master Suril has been summoned, as have the elders. Follow me.'

Malus relaxed slightly as he fell into step behind the temple assassin. As far as he was concerned, the hard part of the plan was over.

Their guide led the highborn and his companions back the way he'd come, up a narrow, spiral stairway that climbed past several more gallery levels until they emerged into a narrow room lit with pale witchlight. The transition from fire and shadow to the pale green light left Malus momentarily disorientated, a feeling that only deepened when the guide pushed open a tall door and led the men outside into the deep orange glow of the setting sun.

They exited through a portal built into the side of the fortress's thick wall, which emptied them out at street level at the end of a broad avenue lined on either side with some of the most palatial buildings Malus had ever seen.

Hidden behind the high walls of the temple fortress, the homes confiscated from the city's highborn by the order of the Witch King had not been transformed into dour vaults of worship. If anything, they had been made grander and more opulent than before. Long, roofed porches had been built along the fronts of most of the homes, with pillars of veined marble carved in the shapes of manticores, dragons and hydras. Windows had been broadened, and balconies built from soft stone instead of hard, ruthless iron. Malus saw door facings fashioned from gold and silver, wrought in intricate styles that could only have come from the hands of expensive dwarf slaves. The air was cool and smelled of incense. Priests and priestesses strolled casually along the street, wrapped in thick, red robes and kheitans of fine elf hide set with gold, rubies and pearls. The raw display of wealth and power nearly stopped Malus in his tracks. He'd known, like all druchii, that the temple of Khaine was universally feared. What he hadn't ever stopped to consider was that it was also very, very rich. Malekith's support had benefited the cult enormously.

The guide led them swiftly along the broad street, his eyes carefully downcast as he passed the high officials of the temple. He led them to the third house on the left, climbing a broad set of marble steps to a pair of gold-ornamented doors that slid open silently at his approach. Human slaves held open the doors and bowed from the waist as the druchii filed inside. Beyond was a spacious entry hall filled with expensive statues, some bearing the refined but effete style of the craftsmen of Ulthuan. They'd probably been tithed to the temple some time in the past by a noble seeking the elders' favour, Malus suspected.

They crossed the hall, the soles of their boots whispering across piled rugs, and climbed another flight of stairs. The druchii crossed another room lined with statues and hung with expensive tapestries, and were ushered into a small chamber set with a low table and half a dozen wooden chairs. A tray containing a plate of fruit and a bottle of wine sat on the table. The guide bowed to the men once more and left the room, closing the door behind him. Immediately the two zealots began a careful check of their weapons. Malus eyed the wine greedily, certain it would be a fine vintage and fighting the temptation to open it and find out.

He was still contemplating the bottle when the door swung open again and a small crowd of red-robed druchii bustled hurriedly into the room. The zealots immediately dropped to one knee, palms out, and Malus followed suit a moment later.

'Arch-Hierophant Rhulan will be along momentarily. In the meantime we shall hear your report,' a woman said in a harsh, businesslike voice. Malus looked up to see a tall, narrow-shouldered priestess striding purposefully towards him, walking with the aid of a slender, silver-chased staff. Her hair was white and bore the headdress of a witch elf, but she wore the heavy robes and ornamental kheitan of a temple dignitary. A short, broad man, also swathed in crimson robes came in behind her. A ring of gold glinted on each of his stubby fingers, and a pair of dark eyes glittered like chips of obsidian beneath a pair of jutting brows. A pair of temple novitiates bearing scrivener's easels, ink and quills and sheets of parchment attended him.

'It would not be proper to begin without Rhulan,' said the last man to enter the room. He was of middle height and whipcord-thin, with a long, pointed face that reminded Malus of a fox. His red robes were not as heavy as the others, and his kheitan was noticeably devoid of ornamentation. To Malus's surprise, the man carried no obvious weapons, but he had no doubt that he was looking at the temple's master of assassins.

'In the absence of the Arch-Hierophant I am the voice of the temple,' the woman snapped, 'and I will hear what these men have to say.' The two druchii exchanged heated stares, but after a tense moment the man deferred with a bow. 'Now then,' the woman said, turning back to the assassins, 'we watched the heathens dispose of Veyl this morning,' she said, 'so we know your mission was a success. What I want to hear is why you are only now returning to the temple?'

Malus quickly took stock of the situation. The two temple elders and the servants were closer, but less dangerous than the man by the door. He would have to kill the master of assassins at once, and that would leave him in a position to cut off the others' retreat. Then they could lie in wait for this Arch-Hierophant to arrive and deal with him at their leisure.

Suddenly an idea occurred to Malus. He considered his circumstances for a second time, and then smiled within the depths of his hood. Yes, there was an opportunity here.

The female elder leaned in close to Malus, near enough for him to feel her hot breath. 'Answer me, hound! You were told to return at once. Why did you tarry, when there is still more of Khaine's work to be done?'

Malus looked up, meeting the elder's glare. He smiled a killer's smile. 'Please accept our apologies,' he said. 'We would have been here sooner, but it took hours to get the blood out of these robes.'

The elder's face twisted into a bemused frown. She opened her mouth to speak, but the words were lost in a torrent of blood. The elder staggered, dropping her staff and fumbling at the gaping cut in the side of her throat with one hand while clawing at Malus with the other. But the highborn was already on his feet, blood dripping from his sword, and he charged across the room at the man by the door.

For a split second, the temple elders and their servants were frozen in shock, just as the highborn hoped. The zealots leapt into action a fraction of a second behind Malus. There was a whickering sound, and one of the stocky elder's novitiates let out a startled cry and collapsed with a thrown dagger jutting from his chest. Malus saw the remaining novitiate draw a pair of long daggers from his belt, but the highborn knew the man wouldn't have them ready in time. He would be on the master of assassins in another three steps.

To Malus's surprise, the fox-faced druchii still hadn't reacted to the sudden attack. This is their master of assassins, he thought?

Then came the blow against the side of Malus's neck, clipping him beneath the ear. His vision disappeared in a burst of white pain and the highborn fell face-first onto the piled rugs. Both swords tumbled from his nerveless fingers. He realised, too late, that he'd made a fatal mistake.

Malus rolled weakly onto his side as the stocky druchii stepped back from the highborn's stunned body and met the rush of one of the black-robed zealots with his bare hands. The zealot's daggers were a blur of motion, but the master of assassins slapped them aside with contemptuous ease and drove his stiffened fingertips into his attacker's throat. Bone crunched and the zealot fell to the floor, writhing and choking for breath.

The surviving novitiate leapt at Malus, intending to finish the highborn off, but was intercepted in mid-stride by the last zealot. As the two druchii began a whirling dance of razor-edged steel, Malus tried to drive the numbing paralysis from his body by sheer force of will. He fumbled for his blades with leaden fingers, knowing that he had scant moments to spare before the druchii by the door regained his senses and raised the alarm.

His fingertips brushed the pommel of one of his swords, and the physical contact seemed to focus Malus's energies. Groping, he drew the weapon quickly into his palm and rolled onto his knees. There was a grunt and a crack of bone and the surviving zealot tumbled across the rugs, his right arm twisted at an unnatural angle. Malus straightened and saw the fox-faced druchii with his hand on the door latch. The novitiate was sinking slowly to the floor, blood pouring from a wound over his heart, and the master of assassins was turning to face Malus once more, the rings on his fingers glittering coldly.

Malus's thin lips compressed into a grim line as he reversed his grip on his short blade and hurled it at the fox-faced elder just as a pair of fearsome blows hammered into his chest. The next thing he knew he was bouncing off the far wall, his ribs afire with pain. Expensive statues crashed to the ground, snapping off delicate arms and sweeping dragon wings.

Move, move, Malus thought desperately, biting back a groan of pain as he lurched to his feet. The master of assassins was advancing on him slowly and deliberately, reaching for Malus with his small, lethal hands. Desperate, the highborn glanced around for a weapon. He snatched up a stone arm and hurled it at the master's head, and then followed it with a piece of broken wing and a length of barbed tail. The master of assassins batted them easily out of the air, closing inexorably on the highborn.

Malus dodged the first blow at the last moment, ducking behind the statue of a rearing griffon. The second blow shattered the statue into pieces, lashing the highborn's face with chips of razor-edged stone. The highborn stumbled, landing hard on a scattering of stone limbs and wings.

The druchii master yanked back the highborn's hood and seized Malus by the hair the moment he hit the floor. 'Your technique is disgraceful,' the master of assassins hissed, his free hand poised to strike. 'Your every breath is an insult to the glory of Khaine.'

'I'm... flattered... you noticed,' Malus grunted, his face contorted in a grimace of pain. 'What I lack in... skill... I make up for... in... treachery.'

The highborn rolled to the side, lashing out with the stone limb he'd snagged during his fall. Bone snapped like kindling as he struck the master in the left ankle, bringing the master of assassins to his knees. Shouting in rage and pain Malus struck again, lashing out at the hand that held him and breaking the stunned druchii's wrist. He tore himself free of the master's grasp and swung a backhanded stroke that caught the druchii against the side of the head. There was a sickening crunch, and the master fell lifelessly to the floor.

Malus staggered to his feet, gasping for air. He struck the master twice more for good measure, and then tossed the bloodied stone arm aside. The man might have been a master at killing victims through stealth and guile, but he wouldn't have survived ten seconds on the battlefield.

Across the room the surviving zealot had struggled to his feet, his broken right arm clutched close to his side. Malus glared at the man. 'You might have helped,' he hissed through clenched teeth. It felt as if at least one of his ribs was cracked.

The zealot's eyes widened. 'And deprive you of the honour of the kill?' he said, aghast.

'Ah,' Malus said. 'That. Of course.'

The fox-faced elder still leaned against the door, pinned there by Malus's sword. The highborn limped over and pulled the weapon free with a grunt of pain. Just as the elder's body slid aside the door swung inward, and Malus found himself face to face with a druchii in rich, crimson robes, overlaid with a brass breastplate studded with rubies and pearls. Upon the elder's brow was a circlet of gold inlaid with garnets in the shape of tiny, glittering skulls. Like the female elder Malus had killed, the man held a short staff, this one chased with red gold.

The elder's face went pale with shock. There was a faint rustle of woollen robes behind Malus. He took a deep breath, switched his sword from his right hand to his left, and spun just as he heard the sound of the zealot's approach and drove his short blade through the man's chest. The zealot doubled over at the force of the blow, and his life left him in a single, gurgling gasp. The highborn pushed the corpse away and turned back to the stunned elder.

'Step inside, Arch-Hierophant,' Malus said, indicating the far table with a sweep of his blood-spattered hand. 'Take some wine. You and I have much to discuss.'

CHAPTER SIX

BALANCE OF TERROR

Arch-Hierophant Rhulan filled one of the brass goblets on the table to brim full with thick, plum-coloured wine and took a deep draught before turning back to face Malus. He had the face of an ascetic, with long, drawn features and a scrawny neck that bobbed furiously as he drank. The temple elder said nothing at first, surveying the room's grisly contents.

The highborn studied the man's reactions intently. Rhulan's eyes lit first on the female elder, lying close by in a spreading pool of dark blood. His thin lips pursed in a fleeting smile, and Malus could not mistake a smug gleam of satisfaction in Rhulan's brass-coloured eyes. The elder's gaze passed over the dead scribes and the contorted shape of the dead zealot, seeking out the slumped form of the fox-faced elder and grimacing in evident dissatisfaction. Malus could see the gears turning in the elder's mind as he took in the carnage, gauging new political equations within the temple. *Judging by your reaction it would appear that I've handed you quite an opportunity, Rhulan*, the highborn thought to himself.

It was only when the elder's searching gaze fell upon the battered form of the master of assassins that Rhulan was truly taken aback. Wine sloshed from the rim of his cup as he shot Malus a worried glance. 'You're not of the temple,' he said. 'Of that I'm certain. Who are you?'

'Who I am is not important,' Malus declared. 'My identity will not alter the situation you've found yourself in.' Unable to resist any longer, Malus walked stiffly to the table and helped himself to some wine. His ribs were aching madly, sending shooting waves of pain across his chest.

'And what situation would that be?' Rhulan snapped. The shock of what he'd seen was wearing off, and the elder was beginning to recover some of his composure.

'Save your bluster, holy man,' Malus shot back. 'The only reason you're still alive is because I'd rather bargain with you than kill you. Your city – nay, your very religion – is under siege by a small army of fanatics who believe you're denying Khaine's holy will, and they must be at least half-right, because you seem powerless to act against them directly.'

It was a feint, meant to upset Rhulan and get him talking, but Malus was inwardly shocked when the elder gritted his teeth and accepted the insult in silence. The highborn studied Rhulan intently. You truly are desperate, he thought. You suspect the zealots are right but you're trying to silence them. Why?

'How is it you bear the blessing of Khaine, but side with these heretics?'

Malus chuckled coldly. 'Rhulan, you shock me. How long have the zealots opposed the will of the temple? Did you honestly think that they could have survived as long as they have without the support of some among the priesthood? The temple fortress itself has been infiltrated, Arch-Hierophant. How else do you think I got in here?' It was another bluff, but judging by the look of terror that came over the elder's face, it was an allegation with bite to it.

'Who?' Rhulan stammered, his hand tightening on his cup.

This is almost too easy, Malus thought. He smiled. 'In due time, Arch-Hierophant. Let us first consider the crux of your problem. How are you dealing with Urial?'

The elder bristled. 'The man is deluded,' Rhulan snapped. 'We should have arranged for his death long ago. I knew that sooner or later he would try something like this.'

'Why then is he still within the Sanctum of the Sword if his claim is not legitimate?'

The knobbly muscles in the elder's jaw bunched tightly, like clenching fists. 'There is the matter of his sister,' Rhulan conceded, 'and his lineage. The situation is very complicated.'

Malus glanced at the thick liquid in his cup. He took a small taste and winced: too sweet by half. 'You accept that she is a living saint. The zealots know this.'

Rhulan shifted uncomfortably. 'Of that there can be no doubt,' he admitted. 'No one like her has been seen among the druchii since Nagarythe was lost,' the elder said, his voice tinged with wonder. 'There is much she could teach us once this... incident is resolved.'

'Is it your desire for Yasmir that keeps you from dismissing Urial's claims, or is he truly what he pretends to be? You must realise that the longer this draws out the more you play into the zealots' hands.'

Rhulan glared at Malus. It had been a long time since anyone had dared speak to him so brashly. 'His claim is compelling enough to demand exhaustive study before a decision can be made.'

Malus cut the man off with a sweep of his hand. 'The fact of the matter is that you think he might be right, but you don't want to hand him the sword, and I suspect your reasons have nothing to do with the will of Khaine.'

A tense silence filled the room. Rhulan had gone very still, his dark eyes narrowing warily as he studied Malus. The highborn took a sip of his wine contemplatively. I've hit a nerve, the highborn thought. What then was the temple's agenda?

'The temple keeps its own counsel in matters of the faith,' Rhulan said carefully. 'You said you had a bargain to make. I am listening.'

Malus fortified himself with a sip of the cloying wine and nodded curtly. 'Your position is untenable, Arch-Hierophant,' he said. 'Time is running out. You've been able to deny Urial so far, but his allies are preparing to take matters into their own hands.'

'How?'

The highborn shook his head. 'First things first. I can deliver the zealot leaders into your hands, but in return you will agree to grant me sanctuary in the temple fortress. Once we've dealt with the heretics inside the city, I can begin ferreting out their sympathisers within the temple fortress, leaving you to focus your efforts on Urial and his sister.'

Rhulan didn't reply immediately, contemplating the depths of his cup. 'I would need to discuss this with the council of elders,' he said.

Malus startled the man with a bark of laughter. 'Rhulan, ten minutes ago you were certain that the heretics couldn't possibly have agents within the temple fortress. Are you absolutely certain you can trust the elder council? The fewer people who know of this arrangement the more likely you are to turn the tables on the zealots.' Malus took a step towards the man. 'Choose, now.'

'All right!' Rhulan snapped. 'I accept your bargain. Woe betide you if you play me false.'

'I could say the same, Rhulan,' Malus replied, setting his cup aside. He searched for his second blade amid the bodies, and then held the weapon in his hand as he considered the two dead elders. 'Do not look at this as an adversarial arrangement, Arch-Hierophant. We both stand to benefit from this. When we're done the zealots will have been dealt a crippling blow, the temple will be cleansed of heretics and Urial will no longer be a problem.'

'And what of you? What do you stand to gain out of this?'

Malus smiled as he walked over to the body of the female elder. 'One thing at a time, Rhulan,' he said. 'Let's focus on you for the time being.' He grabbed the woman by the hair and pulled the head upright. The short blade flashed downward, biting into the corpse's neck, but it was too light for such butcher's work. Malus had to hack his way through the flesh and vertebrae, grimacing at the artlessness of the decapitation.

'What in the name of Khaine are you doing?' Rhulan gasped.

'I can't return to the zealots empty-handed,' Malus explained. Holding the grisly trophy by his side, he made for the fox-faced elder. 'For your part, I want you to stay here and help yourself to some more wine while I make my way back into the city. Wait half an hour before sounding the alarm, and then tell whomever you must that you arrived late to the meeting and found things as they are now.'

'Very well,' Rhulan said, uttering a sharp sigh as he reached for the wine bottle. 'How will we communicate? Will I find you skulking in my chambers tomorrow night?'

Malus chuckled. 'Nothing so dramatic. I still have some more enquiries to pursue among the zealots. When I have news worth sharing I will pass you a message through the shrine in the highborn quarter. Pick a trusted servant and have them check the offerings at the shrine each night.'

'And what will he look for?'

The highborn grunted in pain as he went to work again with his sword. 'Tell him to look for a head that's missing the tips of both ears,' he said, holding up the fox-faced elder's skull. 'I expect I'll have plenty of candidates to choose from in the coming days.'

Screams and the clash of steel lingered in the air over Har Ganeth, echoing like the cries of ghosts beneath the gleaming moons.

It was less than a mile from the Assassin's Door to the house of the late Sethra Veyl, but Malus spent more than three hours getting there. Armed bands were prowling the streets with swords and axes in hand, looking for offerings to the Blood God. Armed and armoured highborn with retinues of well-armed retainers passed gangs of commoners wielding meat cleavers and knotted cudgels, each gauging the strength of the other like packs of hungry wolves. The night was still young, but many of the roaming bands already sported one or two bloody trophies. From what Malus could tell, there seemed to be an unspoken rule to prey on solitary travellers rather than engage in big street battles. It was certainly safer for the killers that way.

He moved with care, using his dark robes to melt into the shadows whenever he heard a group of druchii approach. There was no way to be certain if the marauders would spare even a temple assassin once their blood was up. Once, the highborn stepped into a shadowed alley and found himself face-to-face with a white-robed zealot. The true believer was splattered with gore, and half a dozen trophies hung from his broad leather belt. The zealot had glided silently towards Malus, raising his stained blades, but at the last moment he recognised the highborn's face and bowed deeply, stepping past Malus and resuming his own hunt along the city streets.

Malus didn't begrudge the delay. It gave him time to think. Now that he had a way into the temple, he had to make good his part of the bargain and deliver the zealots into Rhulan's hands. Once that was done, he could bend his efforts to penetrating the confines of the Sanctum of the Sword and locating the damned warpsword. As he crept through the confines of the highborn quarter he considered his options. There was still much he did not know, but for the first time Malus saw a clear path to his goal. For the moment at least he had the upper hand, and he intended to make good use of it.

It was near to midnight by the time he turned onto the narrow street outside Veyl's white door. A pile of torn and headless bodies lay in a heap in the middle of the lane and a single bloodstained zealot stood guard outside the door, his dripping blades crossed over his chest. He bowed to Malus as the highborn approached, and stood aside as Malus pushed the door open and disappeared into the courtyard beyond.

The small square was all but empty; clearly the zealots had been turned out into the night to reap offerings in the name of Khaine. To Malus's surprise, he found Tyran standing near the steps of the house, speaking to a small group of new arrivals. When the zealot leader caught sight of the highborn his eyes lit up with interest. 'Well met, holy one,' he said gravely. 'You return alone.'

Malus nodded, pulling back his hood. 'My companions died in glorious battle,' he replied. It seemed like the proper thing to say.

'And you did not,' Tyran observed, the unspoken question clear in the tone of his voice.

The highborn pulled aside his cloak. Moonlight glimmered on pallid flesh and dark, dried blood as Malus pulled his trophies from his belt and held them up to Tyran. 'Someone had to return with the good news,' he said.

Tyran took a step forwards, peering closely at the three bloodstained faces. 'I see Aniya the Harrower,' he said, pointing at the head of the female elder, 'and this is Maghost,' he said, glancing at the fox-faced man. He frowned at the pulped mess of the third trophy. 'And this?'

'The master of assassins, as you commanded,' Malus replied. 'He wasn't as accommodating as the other two.'

A slow smile spread across Tyran's face, his suspicions forgotten as he considered the news. 'The temple Haru'ann is broken, while ours is nearly complete,' he said. 'This is a great victory for the faithful.' He beamed at Malus. 'Truly you are blessed, holy one! You have hastened the day when the Swordbearer shall walk among us.'

'Such is my fervent hope,' Malus said with convincing sincerity. 'What is our next move?'

Tyran took the heads from Malus, smiling proudly into their vacant eyes. 'Now we can contest with the temple for the hearts of the people,' he said. 'The surviving elders will be in disarray, and the assassins will be paralysed until they choose a new master.' The zealot leader indicated the new arrivals with his free hand. 'More and more true believers arrive each day,' he said. 'We are strong enough to make our case openly in the city streets.' The zealot leader beckoned for the waiting druchii to join them. 'We can even count another blessed soul such as yourself in our ranks.'

Malus was scarcely listening. 'Good news indeed,' he said absently, pondering what the Haru'ann might be, and how that figured into Tyran's scheme.

Tyran bowed to one of the hooded figures. 'Holy one, this is Hauclir, a true believer from Naggor,' he said, indicating Malus. 'Truly, it is a powerful omen that two blessed souls from feuding cities should be brought together in the common cause for the glory of Khaine.'

The zealot reached up with a pale hand, drawing back his hood. His long, white hair glowed like a ghostly shroud in the moonlight, and his brass eyes shone like hot coins as he fixed Malus with an enigmatic stare.

'Truly the ways of the Lord of Murder are mysterious indeed,' Arleth Vann said, staring into his former master's eyes.

'Prepare yourselves, oh servants of Khaine! The Time of Blood approaches!'

The zealot stood on a block of dirty white stone, his twin swords glittering in the sunlight as he held them up to the afternoon sky. Twin pyramids of stained skulls rose to either side of the true believer, offering a welcome meal to a murder of nodding ravens that listened with cursory interest to the zealot's fiery speech.

Barely a handful of druchii paused to listen to what the true believer had to say, thinking at first that he was a novitiate of the temple preaching to the citizens outside the marble-columned shrine of the highborn quarter. A steady stream of men and women were passing through the small square in front of the low building, bearing offerings to be deposited before the altar at the far end of the shrine. A pair of true novitiates stood at the entrance to the dimly-lit building, fingering the ceremonial sickles hanging from their belts and glaring at the zealot across the square with naked contempt.

Malus had positioned himself at the mouth of a narrow street leading into the square, allowing him a clear view of both the shrine and the zealot's energetic sermon. The man had been at it for an hour. Not long after he'd begun, Malus caught sight of a messenger dashing down the steps of the shrine and heading north, towards the temple fortress. The highborn figured they wouldn't have to wait much longer.

For the past three days the zealots had sent men and women into the city, declaiming their beliefs to the people of Har Ganeth. Prior to today, the zealots had stayed on the move, wandering the city streets and spreading the word but not providing the temple with a stationary target to vent their displeasure upon. Today, Tyran had decided to give them their wish, sending a man to preach the true faith outside every shrine in the city.

'The Bride of Ruin awaits in the Sanctum of the Sword!' the zealot declared to his sparse audience. 'She waits for her mate, but the temple elders deny her. They defy the will of the Bloody-Handed God, and soon they will suffer his wrath!'

Malus surveyed the square, trying to spot the other zealots lying in wait for the temple's response. Dressed in typical robes and unadorned kheitans, they were invisible among the steady stream of servants and retainers traversing the square on their masters' business.

Malus knew that Arleth Vann was out there somewhere, and the thought made his blood run cold.

He'd nearly given himself away when the assassin had shown himself that night. For a moment Malus had panicked, thinking he'd walked into a devilish trap. Surprisingly, it was the daemon that had stayed his hand, banishing the cold terror with a voice of iron and bone. 'Look in his eyes, Darkblade,' Tz'arkan had commanded. 'Look! He is as shocked as you are.'

And it was true. For a fleeting instant they had eyed each other warily, but then Tyran invited the new arrivals to join him inside, and Arleth Vann had simply turned away, falling into step with the zealot leader and not giving Malus a single backwards glance. His mind reeling, Malus had staggered to the spare, unfurnished cell set aside for him in Veyl's house and sat with his back against the stout wooden door, his straight northern sword naked in his lap. He'd sat in the darkness for hours, sleep dragging at his exhausted mind as he tried to decide what was going to happen. Were they waiting for more of the zealots to return before they confronted him? His instincts had told him to run while he could, slipping into the city before Arleth Vann could betray his identity to Tyran. Except that the zealots were his bargaining chip with Rhulan. If he broke his agreement with the Arch-Hierophant he doubted he could get anywhere near the Sanctum of the Sword. He was entangled thoroughly in a web of his own making. So, he'd waited in the darkness, wondering how and when Arleth Vann would try to take his revenge. The next thing he'd known he was blinking at the first rays of daybreak, his eyes gummy from sleep, his charade still intact.

He'd seen little of his former retainer since then. Tyran spent the next few days sending the zealots into the city, sniffing for news of the death of the elders. Malus caught glimpses of the former assassin at dawn and dusk, coming and going from the house like one of the city's ubiquitous ravens. The highborn did not know where Arleth Vann slept, or even if he slept at all, but it was clear that when he was at the house he spent much of his time in Tyran's company. It was a situation that troubled Malus no end, but he hadn't the slightest idea what to do about it, not when the former assassin could betray him whenever he chose. So the highborn had kept his distance, passing cursory messages to Rhulan that did little more than state the obvious: the zealots were agitating the people of the city to force a confrontation with the temple.

It took two days before Malus realised he wasn't in immediate danger. No one had moved against him, indeed, Tyran treated him no differently than before. Belatedly, Malus realised that Arleth Vann might be just as wary of him. After all, he was a renegade himself, an assassin who'd broken his oaths and abandoned the temple in years past. The cult's treatment of prodigals was legendary. They never forgave nor forgot those druchii who betrayed their trust. They would spare no effort to capture or kill Arleth Vann if they knew he was in the city. A few judicious words spoken in one of the city shrines would be enough. It was a tenuous stalemate.

But why was he here, Malus wondered? Had he been a zealot all along, nursing his heretical beliefs in secret, or did he track me here, seeking to finish the job he'd begun in the Valley of Shadow? The only thing he knew for certain was that he couldn't wait for Arleth Vann to show his hand. He had to find a way to kill the man without betraying himself into the bargain.

Movement at the edge of the square caught Malus's attention. A trio of black-robed men were making their way towards the ranting zealot, sunlight glinting on the edges of their long, curved draichs. Malus straightened, reaching for his sword. The temple had heard Tyran's message and here was the answer the zealots had expected.

The three warriors were not merely swordsmen: they were Draichnyr na Khaine, peerless slayers of men renowned for killing foes with a single, perfect stroke of their huge swords. He had seen men like them at work when Urial had led the warriors of the temple into battle against their sister Nagaira. Their reputation was richly deserved. The highborn set off after the men, sliding his long sword from its scabbard and concealing it beneath his cloak. He noticed two other cloaked figures on the move as well, stalking after the temple executioners like lean, hungry wolves.

'Even now the cowards in the temple fortress set their dogs upon me!' the zealot cried from his pedestal, pointing at the approaching swordsmen. 'Why? Because they do not wish their lies to be known! They have deceived you, brothers and sisters! They have tricked you, and stolen from you, and twisted the words of the Blood God to feed their own greed! The Bride of Ruin has come! The Time of Blood is nigh, sons and daughters of lost Nagarythe! Will you stand tall before the Scourge or be swept aside?'

'Heretic!' the lead executioner thundered, causing the zealot's small audience to scatter. 'You blaspheme in Khaine's holy city and impugn the honour of his devoted servants.' He raised his sword. 'Even the Lord of Blood repudiates you. Your skull is not fit to lie at Khaine's feet. After we've split you like a steer you'll be thrown into the sea for the fish to eat.'

Malus was less than ten steps from the rearmost of the executioners. He reached up to his cloak clasp, unfastening it and letting it fall to the cobblestones. Out of the corner of his eye he glimpsed his compatriots readying themselves as well. The highborn's hand tightened on the hilt of his blade as he drew in a deep breath and shouted in a voice fit for a battlefield.

'The Swordbearer has come! Blood and souls for the Swordbearer!'

To their credit, the executioners reacted to the surprise assault with speed and deadly skill. The man in front of Malus whirled at his shout, his draich making a fan of reflected light as it spun in a defensive circle around the swordsman. To his left, Malus heard the sharp ring of tempered steel and then the sound of a man's death rattle. A body hit the cobbles with a muted thud, but the highborn didn't dare look away from the warrior facing him. One wrong move and the executioner would strike his head from his shoulders.

Shrieking a terrible war scream, Malus rushed at the warrior. The executioner's curved blade paused in its circling movements, and for a split second Malus was reminded of Tyran, standing frozen in the face of Sethra Veyl's furious assault. He means to let me commit myself, and then strike the killing blow, Malus thought. He held his blow as he rushed ever closer, dropping the point of his sword as he went. If the executioner didn't react quickly he would be run through.

At the last possible moment, the executioner exploded into a blur of motion, sidestepping the highborn's thrust and aiming a blow at Malus's neck. But as the warrior committed himself to the motion Malus checked his advance, planting his leading foot and pivoting into a short, vicious cut across the warrior's midsection. The heavy sword bit into the executioner's thick kheitan and the hard muscle beneath, spinning the druchii half around with the force of the blow and throwing off his attack. Before the warrior could recover Malus pulled his blade free and drove its point into the side of the man's throat. Bright blood jetted from the wound and the executioner staggered, choking on his own fluids. Eyes bright with hate, the warrior swept his long blade around in an off-balance strike to Malus's head, but the highborn tore his sword free and blocked the blow easily, before lashing out with a backhanded stroke that decapitated the mortally wounded man.

Malus stepped out of the way as the headless body toppled over, quickly taking stock of the situation. A second executioner lay dead, his torso split by a terrible wound that ran from his collarbone down to his waist. The headless body of the zealot who attacked him lay several steps away. The leader of the executioners and another zealot circled one another warily, each searching for a weak spot in the other's guard. Malus took a step towards them, thinking to strike the man down while his back was turned, but then remembered the true believers' strange sensibilities. Far be it from me to deny the man an opportunity to die, Malus thought sourly, and left the zealot to his fate.

The highborn turned back to the man he'd slain, snatching up his blood-stained head. Moving swiftly, he sheathed his sword and pulled out a short knife as he walked over to one of the trophy pyramids by the preacher's stone block. With his back to the rest of the square, he reached up and sliced off the tips of the executioner's ears, before putting away the knife and pulling a folded strip of oilcloth from his belt. The cloth note went between the executioner's teeth in a single, deft move, and then Malus ostentatiously set the skull atop the pile.

Just then the highborn heard the sound of a blade striking home, and turned to see the executioner staggering away from his foe, clutching at a terrible wound in his chest. His long draich fell from nerveless fingers as he stumbled towards the shrine. The novitiates at the top of the stairs looked on in horror as the warrior fell onto his face and died.

'The Time of Blood is at hand!' Malus said again, repeating the words that Tyran had told him to say. He eyed the city dwellers still standing in the square, his face alight with righteous wrath. 'Shake the temple doors and command them to hearken to the Swordbearer! The Scourge is here, and he will strip the souls from the unworthy and fling them into the outer darkness!'

The people of Har Ganeth looked into Malus's eyes, and he saw that they believed him.

CHAPTER SEVEN

THE EXECUTIONER'S BLADE

They came for him that night.

It was well past midnight when the door to Malus's cell creaked open. His mind registered the noise, but it took precious seconds for him to force his exhausted body to awaken. By the time his eyes snapped open there was pale green light seeping into the room from the open doorway and he could see the shapes of men and women outlined in the corridor beyond. His hand closed on the hilt of his sword, but he knew instinctively that he was far, far too late. He was also so deeply exhausted that it was difficult to give much of a damn.

Malus lay there on his travel-worn bedroll, blinking stupidly in the witchlight for several long seconds. No one moved. 'If you've come to kill me, get on with it,' he growled. 'Otherwise let me sleep.'

Someone chuckled. 'Tyran sent us,' a woman's voice said. 'He wants to talk to you.'

Gods below, Malus thought, sitting stiffly upright. Did the bastard ever sleep? 'All right, all right,' he growled. 'Let me find my boots.'

He could feel them studying him as he collected his gear. Every inch of him ached, and his muscles refused to work as they should. He could sense their amusement as he fumbled clumsily with belt and sword. The zealots showed not the slightest sign of discomfort or fatigue.

For people who thought of themselves as the true worshippers of Khaine, the zealots had a strange notion of piety. Unlike the practices of the temple, with its devotionals and its catechisms, the only display of righteousness the zealots respected was the perfection of the killing arts. When they weren't out in the city ambushing temple warriors by day or collecting skulls on the blood-spattered streets each night the true believers were in the courtyard or the practice rooms of Veyl's house fighting with one another. Hour after hour, sparring with heavy wooden weapons or even live steel, the zealots devoted themselves body and soul to the craft of ending life as swiftly and irrevocably as possible. The temple's fearsome executioners were layabouts by comparison.

The more the zealots suffered the deprivations of hunger and exhaustion the more serene they became. They thrived on suffering, mortifying their flesh through exertion rather than by scourge or blade. Malus had thought himself a hard man before being thrust into the world of the zealots. Now he felt like an old, tired man trying to keep pace with a pack of lions. Give me the tender mercies of Slaanesh any night, he thought grimly. At least she expected her worshippers to sleep off their devotions.

Malus fell into line with the waiting zealots and followed them upstairs. The master's chambers were dark and silent. The highborn's tired mind registered fitful glimpses of dark hallways and turgid shadows cast by banked braziers. Before he knew it, he was climbing a familiar, narrow stairway and emerging onto the roof. A brisk wind off the sea blew salt mist into his face and banished the last vestiges of sleep. He took a deep breath of the briny air, looking out over the polished pewter surface of the Sea of Chill, and then to the west, where the moons peered bright and curious over the far mountains.

The zealots drew back their dark hoods and moved silently across the roof, settling down into a rough circle facing Tyran the Unscarred. The zealot leader's head was uncovered, his hair glistening with tiny drops of sea-spray. His draich lay across his folded knees, and he studied Malus thoughtfully. 'Come and join us holy one,' he said, 'we have much to discuss.'

Malus considered Tyran's words for signs of danger. It was possible the zealot leader was toying with him. If so, Malus thought, he would be made to regret it. 'A strange place for a meeting,' he mused, approaching the seated zealots.

Tyran shrugged. 'For a city dweller, perhaps. I've spent most of my life living under the open sky, moving from one city to the next or following armies on the march. This is as natural to me as a temple cell is to you,' he said. 'Besides, only a faithless heart hides itself behind walls of stone. We have nothing to fear from man nor beast, for the Lord of Murder is with us.'

The highborn bowed deeply. 'Well said.' He sat heavily on the slick roof tiles, wincing at the flare of pain from his stiff joints. Several of the zealots chuckled quietly, their faces hidden in shadow. Now fully awake, Malus surveyed his companions more carefully. There were six of them besides Tyran. He recognised nearly all of them, including the lone hunter he'd encountered on the streets on the way back from the temple fortress and the woman who'd first welcomed him into the house nearly a week ago. She returned his gaze with a frank, playful stare.

At the far end of the circle Malus found himself staring into a pair of brass-coloured eyes. Arleth Vann studied him with the expressionless interest of a rock adder. With an effort, Malus looked past the former assassin and focused on Tyran.

'Each day brings us closer to Khaine's triumph, brothers and sisters,' the zealot leader said with a fierce smile. 'Word of the Swordbearer and his bride spreads through the city, and the temple elders remain in disarray. Their assassins have gone into conclave, debating the choice of a new master, and the Haru'ann remains broken. The apostates have never suffered such setbacks before, and they are paralysed with fear: fear that the Time of Blood is indeed at hand and their lies are about to be exposed.'

Murmurs of approval rose from the assembled zealots. Tyran regained their attention with a raised hand. 'Their fear is so great that our allies within the temple fortress report that some of the apostates are considering recanting their decadent ways and joining with us for the greater glory of Khaine. One of them is a temple elder.'

The zealots glanced at one another, their eyes widening in surprise. One of the men snorted in disgust. 'They think to erase a lifetime of apostasy now that the hounds of Khaine are baying at their door? Let them offer their necks to the axe if they are so repentant.'

'Indeed,' Malus said. 'They knew all along what lies they were spreading. It's the fear of discovery that motivates them, not true faith.'

Several of the zealots nodded, muttering in agreement. In fact, it was fear of discovery that motivated Malus. Who was this elder? Was it Rhulan? What if the elder hoped to buy his survival by exposing the highborn's scheme?

'The ways of the Lord of Murder are mysterious and terrible,' Tyran replied, shaking his head. 'Like you, I have no mercy for those who turn aside from the holy path of slaughter, but there is a great opportunity here if we are bold enough to seize it.' The zealot leader folded his arms. 'So, after careful thought and prayer, I have decided to help this elder escape the clutches of the apostates.' He stared at each of the assembled druchii in turn, 'And I have chosen you to perform the rescue.'

Malus frowned. 'Entering the temple fortress so soon after our last effort will be very difficult,' he said. 'They will be watching for infiltrators at every door and gate.'

Tyran nodded. 'Of course. That is why the elder is going to come to us.' He met the zealots' confused expressions with a crafty smile. 'The confrontations across the city today have created an opportunity for us to exploit,' he said. 'Tomorrow, the temple elders will enter the city and appear at certain shrines to reassure the people and demonstrate their divine authority. The elder who wishes to join us has arranged to appear at the shrine here in the highborn district at noon.' Tyran smiled. 'Naturally, he will be under heavy guard, which itself provides us with another chance to demonstrate our righteous wrath. Your task is simple: slay the elder's bodyguards and escort him here, where we will test his devotion and plan our next move.'

Startled gasps rose from the zealots. Several prostrated themselves before their leader. 'This is a great honour,' the female druchii said, her eyes alight at the prospect of such a battle.

'If you succeed the rewards will be greater than you know,' Tyran said portentously. 'I believe Khaine has handed us this opportunity for a reason. If we prevail tomorrow, it will be a sign that our final victory is close at hand.' The zealot leader turned to Malus. 'Hauclir, I want you to lead this holy mission. Arleth Vann will be your lieutenant. You are both blessed by the Lord of Murder; together I know that you will prevail against the apostates.'

Malus felt his heart clench. He could feel Arleth Vann's reptilian gaze resting on him like the point of a knife. 'It... it's an honour to serve,' he managed to say.

The zealot leader nodded. 'After your exploits in the temple fortress, I have no doubt you will succeed,' he said, and then rose fluidly to his feet. 'You have ten hours, brothers and sisters. Prepare yourselves as your hearts dictate. Tomorrow the eyes of the Blood God will be upon you.'

As one, the zealots stood and took their leave of Tyran. Malus remained seated, lost in thought. Tyran was right in one sense; tomorrow would indeed present a golden opportunity, one that Malus could ill afford to ignore.

The question was, if he only had one chance to strike would it be better to kill Arleth Vann or the turncoat elder?

Rain blew in thin sheets across the small square outside the shrine, causing the passers-by to huddle inside their oiled cloaks and making life thoroughly miserable for the crowd waiting for the elder's arrival. Word had gone out just after dawn, when well-escorted town criers had walked the city streets, announcing that the elders of the temple would come before the people to denounce the words of the heretics that blasphemed against Khaine's holy cult. The announcement made things somewhat easier for Malus and the zealots, giving them much-needed concealment as they waited for the elder to arrive.

The highborn glanced up at the weeping grey sky and frowned. 'He's late,' the highborn muttered.

'He's probably offering sacrifices to Khaine to stop the rain,' the female zealot replied quietly. Her name, Malus had learned that morning, was Sariya. She was very young, the daughter of a highborn family in Karond Kar. 'The Lord of Murder forefend that his chosen servants get their feet wet walking down the street.'

Malus grinned at the girl's acid tongue. The zealots all stood together at the edge of the crowd, waiting for the highborn's instructions. He'd told them that he wouldn't know what they would do until nearly the last minute. There were simply too many unknowns: how large would the elder's escort be? Would he stop to speak to the crowd, or march straight into the temple? How closely would his guards hem him in? Until he saw firsthand what he was dealing with, he had no idea how to respond.

Malus fingered the hilts of a pair of heavy throwing knives beneath his sodden cloak. Shortly before dawn he'd finally decided on their target.

'More likely he's being hampered by his escort,' the highborn muttered darkly. 'A large contingent would have a hard time getting organised and moving quickly down these cramped streets.' He slowly scanned the assembled druchii, looking for anything untoward. 'That, or they are waiting to hear back from their informants to see if the square is safe to travel through.'

Sariya gave Malus a sidelong glance. 'My, holy one, you're a font of cheery news.'

'The true faith is not an easy one,' the highborn replied with a wry smile, 'but it is realistic.'

He turned to Arleth Vann and caught himself just before he asked if the former assassin had seen anything. The druchii was looking away at the time and didn't catch Malus's startled expression. Sariya's banter had almost caused him to forget himself. He's no retainer of mine, the highborn thought angrily, quickly looking away.

The tramp of armoured feet carried across the rain swept square from the east. Heads turned. Malus stood on his toes to peer above the throng and caught sight of a rank of four executioners, their lacquered armour gleaming wetly in the weak light. They marched with their draichs unsheathed and raised before them like a hedge of razor-edged steel. Their faces were grim and their dark eyes fixed on the crowd as if viewing them from across a battlefield. Malus paid no attention to the executioners, instead straining his ears to gauge the weight of the marching feet echoing across the cobblestones. He bit back a snarl. It sounded like a full company of swordsmen, possibly as much as two hundred men. The temple wanted to send a very clear message to the people of the city.

'Damnation,' Malus muttered, considering his options. There weren't many to choose from. From where he stood, it looked as if the swordsmen were marching directly at the assembled crowd, evidently intending to create a cordon for the elder between the audience and the shrine. After a moment he thought he understood what the temple contingent was planning.

'All right,' the highborn said, turning his back on the crowd and addressing the zealots in low, urgent tones. 'Here's what we're going to do.' Malus took a deep breath. 'Arleth Vann, take Sariya and get inside the shrine as quickly as you can. The rest of us will work to the front of the crowd and attack the executioners once the elder shows himself. When the fighting starts, he'll retreat inside the shrine, where you'll be waiting for him. Kill his escorts and take him straight to Tyran. We'll keep the executioners distracted until you get away.'

Malus looked first to Sariya, and then at Arleth Vann, making certain they understood their instructions. He met the former assassin's gaze and the druchii nodded curtly, acknowledging the order as he'd done countless times in the past. 'Go,' Malus said, and the two zealots headed swiftly away, circling around the edge of the crowd to get past the oncoming line of executioners.

The highborn turned back to his remaining men. 'Spread out and work your way up to the front of the crowd,' he said. 'No one acts until I give the order.' With that, he turned on his heel and started easing his way through the muttering throng.

Within moments Malus found himself fighting his way upstream against a press of people being pushed in the opposite direction. The executioners were using their blades to force the crowd to give ground, eliciting angry murmurs from the spectators. A long double line of armoured warriors was extending itself for twenty yards across the square in front of the shrine. A large block of troops was assembled near the mouth of the street the escort had emerged from, securing their line of retreat.

The tramp of feet fell silent, followed by the rattle of harnesses as the swordsmen adjusted their line. Malus stopped short behind the foremost line of spectators, first eyeing the warriors and their brandished blades and then trying to catch a glimpse of the steps to the shrine. He just caught sight of two hooded figures slipping inside the entrance to the building, and knew that Arleth Vann and Sariya were in position.

Movement near the mouth of the eastern lane caught the highborn's attention. All he could see over the line of troops was the tip of a gold-topped staff and a voluminous crimson hood. Was it Rhulan, he thought? There was no damned way to tell.

He watched the figure move along behind the line of executioners as he eased his sword from its scabbard beneath his cloak. Malus shifted slightly, taking up position almost directly behind a tall, scowling man who was glaring irritably at the temple soldiers.

Malus watched the elder begin to climb the temple steps, just as he'd anticipated – the man would need the extra height to address the crowd over the soldiers. The highborn took a deep breath and lowered his right shoulder. 'Blood and souls for the Swordbearer!' he roared, and shoved the unsuspecting man at the executioners as hard as he could. Taken by surprise, the spectator flew at the swordsmen with a startled shout, his arms flinging wide for balance, and the surprised executioner in front of him reacted out of instinct. A draich carved a flickering arc through the rain and the spectator screamed, blood rising in a fountain as the sword split him nearly in half.

The highborn struck at just that instant, while the executioner's blade was still deep in his victim's body. 'They mean to kill us all!' he shouted, stabbing his sword into the executioner's exposed throat. The swordsman reeled backwards, blood pouring down the front of his armour. More shouts and the clash of steel echoed up and down the line, adding to the pandemonium.

Malus leapt into the gap opened in the executioners' line, hacking left and right with his heavy blade. He struck the man to his left a heavy blow on the side of his helmet and then cut open the hamstring of the man on his right. The executioner collapsed with a scream, clutching at his leg, and the rest of the swordsmen lost their self-control and attacked the shouting crowd.

A draich swept down at Malus, but the swing had little real power and the highborn swept it aside with ease. The tight ranks of the executioners made for an imposing wall of men and steel, but it left the warriors with little room to use their long blades properly. He hacked at the man in front of him, feinting at his head and then altering the course of the blow to smash his heavy sword into the executioner's fingers. Two severed digits tumbled from the man's right gauntlet. Malus half-knocked the draich from the man's grip with a savage swipe and then smashed his sword into the executioner's face.

In the space of an instant the square had become a raging battlefield. The executioners lashed out at anything that moved, and spectators in the crowd were fighting back in an effort to save themselves. Screams and the stink of spilled blood filled the air. The executioner Malus had struck fell to his knees, his helmet crumpled by the highborn's savage blow. He stepped in and slit the man's throat with his sword, laughing like a madman in the ringing tumult. Malus felt the daemon respond to the terror and pain around it, writhing and squirming around the highborn's hammering heart. For a fleeting instant he was tempted to ask the daemon to share its power, just for the sheer joy of spilling blood. This was his element. He'd known it since the day he'd rescued the army of the black ark from the ambush at Blackwater Ford.

The line of swordsmen was disintegrating. Without orders, some men advanced into the crowd and others gave ground, splitting the force into isolated knots of struggling warriors. The cobblestones were black with pools of blood, men slipping and stumbling over fallen bodies or spilled entrails. As Malus watched, an executioner overbalanced and fell to the ground, only to be set upon by a trio of druchii who pounded his head and back with pieces of stone torn from the square itself.

A muffled shout drew his attention to the east where Malus caught sight of an executioner in ornate armour brandishing a rune-inscribed draich and shouting orders to the block of swordsmen covering the eastern road. Once they entered the fight the battle would be over in moments. The highborn spun in place, looking everywhere for signs of Arleth Vann and the temple elder.

There! Malus saw a pair of dark-cloaked figures herding another druchii with a crimson cloak towards the lane on the south side of the square. No one was paying any attention in the chaos of the battle. This was the only chance he was going to get.

Drawing one of his throwing knives, Malus cut back through the seething mob, staying low and skirting struggling opponents as he closed the distance with the fleeing trio. A bloodstained man grabbed at Malus's arm, bleeding from a head wound and babbling incoherently. Malus stabbed him in the leg with an angry snarl and shoved the man away.

They were nearly at the mouth of the street. Malus picked up his pace, running up to the edge of the mob. It would be a long shot, he realised with a grimace. The highborn took a deep breath, drew back his arm and hurled the knife as hard as he could at the elder's retreating form.

The knife was just a dark blur against the grey mist as it arced towards its target. It struck the red-cloaked figure just beneath the left shoulder blade. Malus watched as his victim staggered under the force of the blow, and then took two more stumbling steps before falling face-first onto the cobblestones. Malus watched Arleth Vann turn at the sound. The two cloaked figures paused only a moment, staring at the fallen body. Then they turned and made good their escape.

A tremendous shout echoed from the other side of the square as the reserve block of executioners charged into the fray. Malus couldn't see what had become of the remaining zealots. Perhaps they had already broken free, or maybe they lay among the dead littering the cobblestones. Either way, they were no longer his problem.

Malus headed south, pushing aside other fleeing city folk as he fled the oncoming executioners. As he approached his fallen victim, however, he was gripped by overpowering curiosity. Was it Rhulan? Had he made the right choice? On impulse, he skidded to a stop beside the body and pulled his knife free, before rolling the corpse over to peer inside the depths of the hood.

His heart clenched. 'Mother of Night,' he cursed, looking into Sariya's lifeless eyes.

CHAPTER EIGHT

REVELATIONS

Blood flowed in the streets of Har Ganeth, and the sounds of battle rang out all across the city as the warriors of the temple vented their fury on any druchii unlucky enough to be caught in their path. Men were chased down and hacked apart, their entrails spread for the ravens and their heads set aside as offerings to the Bloody-Handed God. Slaves were hunted and torn apart like wild animals. Market squares turned to charnel houses as the servants of the temple sought to drown their rage in rivers of blood.

An elder of the temple had been taken, so the rumours said, seized within the holy grounds of a city shrine while his bodyguards were slaughtered by a howling mob. Never in the history of the temple had such a crime been committed. It was an insult too great to be borne. Trumpets sounded from the temple walls all through the afternoon, and a flood of black-robed druchii streamed into the city streets with bared blades held in their hands, half-mad with anger and grief. The witch elves joined them late in the day, their muscular bodies painted with sweat and blood, and their eyes wild with murderous ecstasy. They sniffed the air and howled like wolves, their faces twisted in masks of bestial hunger, and when they could not find any more victims to kill on the city streets the brides of Khaine drove the temple servants to break down the doors of the lowborns' homes and flesh houses.

That was when the fighting began in earnest. For hundreds of years the people of the city had prospered under the terrible rule of the temple and bled for the Lord of Murder when necessary. The daylight was given over to the mundane needs of the city, but at night the streets were a place of holy communion, where sacrifices could be made to the Lord of Murder without fear of feud or reprisal. Highborn families would offer up clutches of slaves in hopes of a good flesh harvest or to call down a curse upon their enemies. Lowborn families, hungry for wealth and power, were forced to turn out their own kin in hopes of winning the Blood God's favour. One and all, they were prey to the armed bands that roamed the streets from dusk to dawn in search of victims to sate the eternal hunger of the temple.

The streets were given over to the Lord of Murder so that the houses of the citizens would remain inviolate by the unspoken rule that had allowed the city to survive for centuries. So when the servants of the temple tore down the doors of the lowborns' houses they did not find fearful victims waiting for the executioner's blade, but were welcomed with axes and spears like any other invader.

Malus Darkblade, the architect of the day's bloodshed, wandered the streets of Har Ganeth all through the afternoon, his face a mask of hate and his blade wet with blood. He staggered like a drunk and killed every living thing that crossed his path, furious with himself and with the city of madmen he found himself in.

Arleth Vann had anticipated him, forcing the elder to exchange his cloak with Sariya. Had it been a trap all along, designed to force his hand and show his true intentions to Tyran? Malus couldn't be sure, and wasn't certain it even mattered any more. The elder was doubtless safe at the house of Sethra Veyl, telling the zealot leader everything he knew. If Rhulan had told the elders of Malus's deal then he was certain to be exposed.

All this had gone through Malus's head as he'd crouched over Sariya's body. Then the fleeing mob surged around him, filling his ears with cries of anger and pain, and he let himself be caught up in it.

When he came back to his senses he was sitting in an alley surrounded by corpses. The sounds of battle raged in a small square just a few yards away. Malus listened to the clash of steel and the screams of the dying like another man would listen to the patter of rain or the whisper of wind in the trees. His robes were stiff with blood and his sword felt glued to his hand with layers of crusted filth. The stench of the battlefield filled his nostrils. His stomach rumbled and he recalled that he hadn't eaten all day.

A shadow passed over Malus's face, and he felt the beat of wings against his cheeks. The raven settled on the head of a man doubled over on the alley floor next to Malus. The bird studied him with one yellow eye and let out a croaking laugh. 'Blood and souls! Blood and souls!' the dreadful bird cried.

Malus took a half-hearted swipe at the damned raven, sending it squawking into the air. Exhausted, he slumped onto the bloodstained ground, rolling onto his back and staring up at a thin bar of cloudy sky between the alley's close-set buildings. He felt the daemon move within him, slithering against his ribs like a contented cat. The sensation repelled him.

His rage spent, the highborn wearily considered his options. There was a very real risk that his dealings with the temple had been exposed. Certainly Arleth Vann suspected him, but the former retainer might well have done that on nothing more than general principles.

The zealots were the key to the Sanctum of the Sword. He had to deliver Tyran and the other true believers into the hands of the temple, and that meant returning to the house of Sethra Veyl. Perhaps there were other ways to reach the warpsword, but they would take time to unearth, and time was one commodity he had in short supply.

I've got to go back, he thought grimly. I have to know what they're planning. Let Arleth Vann make his accusations. I've talked my way out of worse situations before.

Another shadow fell across Malus's vision. For a moment he thought the raven had returned, but then a bloodstained face and a pair of shoulders loomed into the highborn's view. A grimy hand reached for his hair, and a gore stained hatchet glinted in the fading light.

Malus rolled onto his side with a snarl and stabbed the man in the chest. The druchii, wearing the stained robes of a tradesman, groaned weakly and toppled onto his side. The man had a clutch of severed heads tied to his belt and a leather bag bulging with looted coin, gold earrings and silver bracelets. Malus had to admire the man's opportunism in the midst of chaos. The highborn helped himself to the bag and struck off the man's head for good measure.

A croaking laugh echoed down the alley. The raven looked up from its meal and eyed him knowingly. 'Gore-crow! Gore-crow!' the bird called mockingly.

Malus hit the bird squarely with the tradesman's head, sending it croaking angrily skyward in an explosion of greasy feathers. The damned skulls were good for something after all, he thought to himself.

The highborn district was relatively quiet after the bedlam of the lower quarters. Even in the depths of their anger the temple followers evidently knew better than to menace the city's well-armed nobility. Still, the tall houses were dark and tightly shuttered and the streets were largely deserted as Malus found his way to the house of Sethra Veyl.

There were no zealots standing guard outside the white door when the highborn arrived. Malus pounded on the door with the pommel of his blade, but got no reply. 'Open up, damn your eyes!' he roared over the wall, his previous anger returning. 'Since when do true believers cower behind stone walls?'

Within moments there was a rattle of bolts and the door opened. A white-robed zealot stood in the doorway, clutching his sword in a white-knuckled grip as he glared at Malus. 'No one enters tonight, holy one,' the man said, 'not even you. Tyran's orders.'

'If Tyran wishes to keep me out he can tell me himself!' Malus snarled, advancing on the man. The zealot raised his blade, but the highborn slapped it aside with his own and then shoved the man rudely in the chest. The true believer fell backwards onto the cobblestones and the men with him gave ground, stunned at Malus's bloody visage. To them he was the very image of the divine, anointed in the red wine of battle.

Malus raised his blade and levelled it at the astonished guards. 'Those of you who are ready to offer up your heads to Khaine need only stand in my path and I will give you gladly to the god.'

But the man Malus had struck wasn't so easily cowed. He sprang gracefully to his feet, a fierce expression on his face. 'Let us see who has the greater devotion, then,' he said, edging forwards with his sword held ready. 'I'll go to the Lord of Murder laughing with joy, knowing you'll soon be following me.'

'Enough!' cried a husky, female voice from across the small courtyard. 'Put aside your blades and let the man from Naggor pass. I can see the spirits of the dead that surround him. He has offered up a great bounty to our god this day, and punished the ranks of the blasphemers.'

The zealots reluctantly parted to allow Malus to pass. A woman waited on the steps leading up to the house, her pale face gleaming from the depths of a wide, black hood. The blood-witch studied Malus with a frank, predatory stare.

Malus made his way slowly across the courtyard, noticing for the first time that it was conspicuously empty. The zealots that had camped in the open space had all vanished, taking their meagre possessions with them. The highborn frowned up at the woman. 'Where is Tyran?' he asked.

'Elsewhere,' the blood-witch replied. 'When word of the elder's disappearance reached the temple the remaining leaders could not contain the fury of their servants. Once night has fallen and their bloodlust has been spent they will return to the fortress and the elders will send them against the houses of the true believers no matter where they lie.'

'And the elder who has joined us?'

The blood-witch smiled, showing her leonine fangs. 'He has proven worthy, holy one, and eager to witness the Time of Blood. Our Haru'ann is complete, while the temple remains in disarray.'

Malus paused, trying to puzzle out the full import of the blood-witch's words. If she knew so much and yet allowed him into the house then clearly the zealots still trusted him. Or perhaps they simply had no time to deal with him because something much more important was afoot. What was this damned Haru'ann everyone kept talking about?

'What would Tyran have of me?' he asked.

The blood-witch shrugged. 'When you did not return with the others it was assumed that you found a glorious death in the riots,' she said. 'Those of us who have no role in what is to come will take to the streets tonight and offer up tokens of devotion to the Bloody-Handed God.' She smiled again, her feline eyes glowing in the fading sunlight. 'I will dance with many men tonight, take many mates and bathe in their fluids. You may dance with me, if you wish.'

'That... that's quite an honour,' Malus managed to say, quite taken aback by the woman's feral gaze, 'but I am not worthy of your attentions. For one thing, I'm filthy.'

The blood-witch threw back her head and laughed. The sound both aroused and frightened Malus at the same time. 'Go then, as the Lord of Murder wishes,' she said. The blood-witch descended the steps, reaching up to gently trace a curved talon along the line of his jaw. 'Another night perhaps,' she said softly. 'Remember me, holy one. I might not recognise your freshly scrubbed face when we meet again.'

Malus strode swiftly down the deserted hall, his mind racing. Tyran was making his move tonight, of that he was certain, but what was his plan?

He reached the sparsely furnished cell that had been set aside for him and dashed inside, not bothering to shut the door behind him as he started gathering up his possessions. There was no way he was going to find the zealot leader before he set his plan in motion. The best he could do was to bluff his way into the temple and tell Rhulan what little he knew. Malus figured he could improvise the rest as the situation developed. It was not as if he had any other choice.

The highborn went to roll up his bedroll and realised that after everything that had happened he was still holding on to his sword. Malus stared at the long blade in irritation. Put the damned thing away, he thought. You wouldn't have made it this far if the zealots wanted to kill you.

Then a chill went down his spine as a dark shape moved through the light at his back. Malus whirled just as Arleth Vann struck.

The assassin was nearly invisible in the dimly lit room. The only warning Malus had was a glint of witchlight on metal as one of Arleth Vann's blades caught the light streaming in from the corridor beyond. The highborn raised his blade and narrowly parried a stroke that would have sliced open his throat. Pure, desperate instinct caused him to sweep his blade downwards and parry the assassin's second sword as it stabbed for his stomach.

Malus gave ground quickly, trying to circle around to the cell's doorway so he would be backlit by the corridor lights, but Arleth Vann anticipated this and darted swiftly to the side, aiming a flurry of blows at his former master's head and neck. The highborn parried stroke for stroke, but was forced inexorably backwards as he warded off the assassin's attacks. Malus fumbled for one of his throwing knives as the assassin shifted position again and melded back into the darkness.

The highborn pulled the dagger free as quietly as he could, reversing his grip on the blade with a flick of his wrist. He crouched low, sliding warily to the left. 'I continue to underestimate you, Arleth Vann,' he hissed. 'I never expected your little surprise in the Valley of Shadows, and here you nearly pulled the same trick on me again. Surely you realise that there's no honour left to reclaim by killing me. As far as the world knows, I died with the army outside Hag Graef.'

For a moment there was only silence. Malus waited, his ears straining for the slightest sound. Then there was a faint hint of movement and Arleth Vann spoke in a sepulchral whisper, like wind soughing through the cracks in a tomb. 'Would that I thought so as well,' he said, 'but in the absence of honour, the need for vengeance remains.'

Malus fixed on the source of the voice and hurled the dagger with all his strength, before bolting for the open doorway. He heard the discordant ring of steel behind him as Arleth Vann knocked the dagger aside and bit back a savage curse. He reached the shaft of light thrown by the hall lights and dashed for the relative safety of the corridor, only to be hauled roughly off his feet as Arleth Vann seized his bloodstained cloak.

The highborn crashed to the floor, swinging his sword wildly over his head. He felt the blade bite home, and Arleth Vann hissed a sibilant curse. Reaching up with his free hand, Malus undid the clasps of his cloak and rolled quickly to the side just as a curved sword thudded into the wooden floor where he'd been.

'What vengeance?' Malus spat, scrabbling backwards across the floor. 'I could understand such feelings from Silar or perhaps Dolthaic, even that rogue Hauclir, but you? I gave you a new life when you fled the temple. You owe me everything. It was you who was false. You swore fealty to me, when in secret your first loyalty was to these fanatics!'

There was a whirring in the air. A spinning shape passed through the weak light, and Malus caught sight of the hurled sword a moment too late. He moved to block the weapon but misjudged its trajectory. The back of the curved sword smashed into his right forearm. The highborn felt the bones break and cried out in pain. Then another blow knocked the broad sword from his nerveless fingers. Arleth Vann's hand closed around Malus's throat. His second sword hung poised above his head.

'My loyalty to you and to the temple was one and the same!' Arleth Vann snapped. 'I sought you out, across the length and breadth of Naggaroth. I served you for years, watching and waiting in secret because I was certain that you were the one. When the autarii foiled our attack in the Valley of Shadow I thought that it was Khaine's will, and I rejoiced.' The assassin bent lower, until Malus could see the anger and despair gleaming in his brass-coloured eyes. 'Then I returned to Har Ganeth to find your brother Urial in the Sanctum of the Sword, and I was forced to admit my mistake. I'd found the right house, but chosen the wrong son.'

Malus wrestled with Arleth Vann's choking grip, but the assassin's fingers were locked around his throat like a vice. Slowly, remorselessly, Malus's former retainer lowered his sword and placed its point above his master's racing heart. 'I do not know how you gained Khaine's blessing since I last saw you,' Arleth Vann said, 'but whatever piety you may have found here, I know you for the deceiver you truly are. You destroy everything you touch, Malus Darkblade. For the sake of the faith, and for the sake of blessed vengeance, your life ends here.'

Sparks swam in Malus's vision. Desperate, he switched his grip to Arleth Vann's sword wrist, but the blade sank inexorably lower, driven by a ruthless engine of hate. The assassin's words rebounded in the highborn's brain. *I served you for years, watching and waiting in secret because I was certain that you were the one.*

Arleth Vann's blade pierced his skin. Icy clarity focused the highborn's mind. *You know what to do. Act now or die!*

'Tz'arkan!' Malus growled under his breath. 'I have need of your strength!'

His body spasmed as his veins burned with a torrent of black ice, driving Malus deeper onto Arleth Vann's blade. A wave of crystalline agony tore a strangled scream from Malus's lips as the bones in his right arm re-knit. The darkness receded as the daemon's energies kindled his vision, and the highborn saw the look of fear and wonder spread across Arleth Vann's face.

Malus put his right hand on Arleth Vann's chest and with a single shove the druchii flew across the small room. The highborn flew upright as if weightless, his limbs burning with foul energies. It tasted like wine on his lips. How had he gone for so many months without the daemon's touch? The power was intoxicating. Malus heard laughter ringing in his ears, and thought it was his own.

He advanced on his former retainer, gliding like smoke across the floor. His eyes were molten, gleaming in the faint light. Malus channelled the daemon's seething power into his voice as he spoke.

'It is you who were deceived, Arleth Vann. Your faith deserted you in your time of trial and you doubted the Blood God's will. I am the Scourge, the anointed son of Khaine, and the Time of Blood is nigh.'

Arleth Vann looked up at Malus and cried out in awe. 'My lord!' he said, abasing himself at the highborn's feet. 'Truly I have failed you. My life is forfeit. Strike me down for my weakness and cast my soul into the Outer Darkness.' He drew a dagger from his belt with a trembling hand and offered it up to the highborn.

The gesture stunned Malus, rendering him speechless. What sort of madness was this religion that it drove men to offer up their lives like lambs? 'Put away your blade,' he snapped. 'I have no use for martyrs, Arleth Vann. If you would redeem yourself, then serve me as you once did, body and soul.'

Arleth Vann straightened, looking up at his master. Tears gleamed like gold in the reflected glow of Malus's blazing eyes. 'I swear it,' he said, 'body and soul, until death's release.' He bowed from the waist, pressing his forehead against the wooden floor.

Malus's eyes narrowed in triumph. Only then did he become aware of the laughter, still echoing within his mind.

'Now you accept your fate, Malus,' Tz'arkan said. 'I knew it was only a matter of time.'

'Tell me of the battle,' Malus said, peering out through the narrow window at the twin moons rising on the eastern horizon. 'What happened to you after the attack on my tent?'

Arleth Vann shrugged, the motion eliciting a grimace of pain as he dabbed at the cut oozing blood down the side of his left leg. 'There is not much to tell. The autarii nearly killed me. Had one of those bolts struck a finger's width more to the right it would have pierced my heart,' he said. 'I lost consciousness as I was being dragged from the camp. I awoke later, in a flesh house near the Slavers' Quarter. Silar had arranged for a chirurgeon to tend me, but it was many weeks before I was fully recovered.'

'What became of Silar and the rest?'

'Scattered like ravens, my lord,' Arleth Vann replied. 'They lost nearly everything when word came that you'd slain your father. All that treasure Silar had worked so hard to ferry from Karond Kar fell into Isilvar's hands when he seized your property. The new Vaulkhar was going to have us slain on the next Hanil Khar, but then he learned that you were heading for the city with an army from Naggor at your back. So we were given the chance to regain our honour if we returned to the Hag with your head.'

Malus nodded to himself, tasting bile in the back of his throat. 'I would have done the same, of course. It was by luck alone I survived.'

'We returned empty-handed, but Isilvar grudgingly credited us with causing enough of a diversion that the main attack was carried home successfully,' Arleth Vann said, wrapping a makeshift bandage around his leg. 'So we were given our freedom, such as it was. I think he wanted to seem magnanimous to the court, because he was still trying to win over many of the city's highborn. At any rate, Silar and Dolthaic left for Clar Karond, hoping to sign on with a corsair. Hauclir vanished. For all I know, he's still out there hunting for you.'

The highborn frowned. 'Did Isilvar not think me dead?'

'He said as much, but I doubt he truly believed it. We knew better. Scouts had turned up the body of Bale's only son, but you were nowhere to be found.'

'So how did you find my trail?'

Arleth Vann turned to face Malus, a bemused expression on his face. 'Your trail? I didn't come here looking for you, my lord. Word had spread among the true believers that Urial had appeared in Har Ganeth with the Bride of Ruin. The faithful were commanded to return to the Holy City and stand by his side as he petitioned the temple to perform the Swordbearer's Rite.'

Malus turned and approached the kneeling assassin, considering his words carefully. 'Arleth Vann, you have known me for many years.' He spread his hands and smiled sheepishly. 'You know I was never a worshipper at the temple. It was no accident that Khaine led you to me. I have need of a guide to illuminate the path I'm on.' He knelt beside his retainer. 'What is the Rite of the Swordbearer, and why would the temple be loath to perform it for Urial?'

'The Warpsword of Khaine is bound within ancient, powerful sorceries, wards that can only be undone by a special rite, and only in the presence of the prophesied one,' Arleth Vann said. 'Only the Haru'ann can perform the rite itself, which is why the temple–'

'Wait,' Malus said, raising his hand. 'What is the Haru'ann?'

Arleth Vann looked shocked. 'The Haru'ann is the council of elders that serves the Grand Carnifex,' he said. 'There are five members of the council, each bearing a sacred duty to the temple.'

Malus remembered the blood-witch's words outside the house. *Our Haru'ann is complete, while the temple remains in disarray.* Suddenly he knew what Tyran was planning.

While the temple turned out its warriors for an assault on the houses of the faithful, the zealots were going to sneak into the temple and perform the Swordbearer's Rite themselves, delivering the sword into Urial's hands.

CHAPTER NINE

CITADEL OF BONE

The pieces all fell into place. Malus realised that Tyran had manipulated the elders of the temple masterfully. The zealot leader would call on his agents in the temple fortress to admit him and his zealot council while the warriors of Khaine fought the bulk of the true believers in the city streets. There would be nothing to prevent them from reaching the Sanctum of the Sword and performing the Rite of the Swordbearer for Urial.

Malus rose and began to pace the room, considering his next move. 'Where are Tyran and the elders now?' he asked.

Arleth Vann shrugged. 'I don't know, my lord. I brought the elder here and found Tyran waiting for me in the courtyard with a cadre of warriors. They took charge of the elder and left immediately.'

The highborn bared his teeth. 'Likely he's gone to ground somewhere close to the temple, waiting for the right time to make his move, or he could be inside the temple even now, having slipped inside with the returning warriors.' Malus took a deep breath. There was only one viable course of action to take. 'I have to speak to Arch-Hierophant Rhulan,' he said. 'Can you get us inside the temple?'

Arleth Vann cinched the bandage tightly around his leg and eyed Malus with a frown. 'You wish to speak to the blasphemers? Why?'

Malus steeled himself, wondering if what he was about to say would spark off another fight. 'Because we must sound the alarm and stop Tyran and his men before they reach the sanctum.'

The retainer stared at Malus for a long time, his expression unreadable. 'Why would we want to do that?' he asked at last.

'Because Tyran has thrown his lot in with Urial,' Malus replied, 'and my half-brother will stop at nothing to get his hands on the warpsword.'

The assassin shook his head. 'He isn't the chosen one. The rite will not work for him.'

'Do you think that will sway him?' Malus asked. 'He thinks that he stands upon the brink of everlasting glory. He believes Yasmir is his for the taking. When the rite fails he won't fault himself, but Tyran and his council. He believes that he is the prophesied one, and he will stop at nothing to fulfil his ambitions, even if that means destroying the cult in the process.'

Tz'arkan wrapped tightly around his heart, his voice rasping softly in the highborn's ear. 'Speak for yourself,' the daemon hissed.

Arleth Vann considered the highborn's words at length, his expression troubled. Finally, he nodded. 'There is a way,' he said. 'It's known to few people even within the temple, so we should be able to reach Rhulan's chambers unobserved. The path is long, however, and it will take time.'

'Then let's go,' Malus said, eyeing his half-packed possessions and deciding to leave them behind. His truly valuable items – namely the Octagon of Praan, the Idol of Kolkuth and the Dagger of Torxus – were buried in a saddlebag strapped to Spite's back. He could get another bedroll and water bottle later, if need be. Right now, every minute counted.

If they moved quickly they could catch the zealots' leaders all in one place, far from any hope of assistance, and he could hand the temple elders a great victory. In the back of his mind, however, Malus harboured an even more ambitious plan. If he could reach the sanctum as the zealots were performing the rite, his presence would allow it to conclude successfully. Then he could make his own play for the relic, perhaps with the daemon's help.

The highborn smiled grimly as he worked. It would be worth it just to see the look on Urial's face.

Arleth Vann led Malus out into the darkened streets, heading south and east away from the fortress. Malus kept pace with his retainer, sword in hand and scanning the streets and alleys with care. The sounds of fighting still echoed in the lower parts of the city, and he could see the flickering glow of fires on the horizon near the warehouse district. Based on what he'd witnessed over the course of the afternoon, when the temple warriors were unleashed on the zealot strongholds around the city, things would spiral rapidly out of control.

The assassin led Malus out of the highborn district, following a zigzag course through twisting lanes that led inexorably down the long hillside. Along the way the pair slipped past armed bands of city dwellers, spattered with dried gore and drunk on bloodlust, in search of more heads to hang from their belts. Each time Arleth Vann slipped silently from one pool of shadow to the next, moving like a ghost past the exhausted druchii.

They moved quickly through the city's entertainment district. The flesh houses were tightly shuttered and many of the ale rooms had been looted over the course of the day. Many of the looted buildings sported piles of fresh, severed heads outside their broken doorways and windows. Malus imagined the proprietors letting the looters drink their fill and then descending on the drunken thieves with clubs and meat cleavers, determined to recoup their loss in flesh if not in coin.

After almost an hour Malus found himself in the lowborn district, near the city's great warehouses and tanneries. The acrid stink of the tanners mixed with the smoke of burning buildings, causing his eyes to water. Malus thought he heard the call of a single trumpet from high up the hill, and imagined the great gates of the temple fortress gaping like a dragon's maw, ready to unleash the temple's wrath upon the city.

He was so focused on the distant sound that he almost walked right into Arleth Vann. The assassin had stopped in a pool of deep shadow a few feet back from the mouth of a narrow alley and was studying a dark, shuttered house across the street. Malus crouched beside the retainer, eyeing the building. To his eyes, it looked very old and decrepit. The witchlamps over the door had long since expired, and at some point in the past one of the three iron balconies had given way, leaving only deep gouges in the stonework where the iron railings had once been. The door, Malus noted, was dark oak, and its iron hinges were thick and free of rust. 'What is this place?' he whispered.

Arleth Vann gave him a sidelong glance. 'This house is the reason why the temple chose Har Ganeth for their own.' He edged forwards and peered carefully up and down the street. 'I see no guards. Perhaps they were caught up in the fighting, or maybe the temple has grown lax over the years.' The assassin shrugged. 'Follow me.'

Moving quickly and quietly, the two druchii slipped across the moonlit street. At the door, Arleth Vann laid his hand on the dark wood and pushed. It slid open noiselessly, revealing abyssal darkness beyond.

Malus shot Arleth Vann a worried look. 'No guards and no locks?'

'No obvious ones,' the assassin replied, 'but the house is tightly warded, my lord. Be assured of that.'

The retainer stepped cautiously into the blackness. Malus followed, apprehension tickling his guts. As he crossed the threshold he felt a prickling sensation along his neck and scalp. Tz'arkan stirred. 'Old magic,' the daemon whispered. 'It tastes of rot and the grave. Be wary, Darkblade.'

Darkness, cold and dank, enveloped Malus. He stopped and waited for a moment, allowing his eyes to adjust. The entry hall of the old house was high ceilinged, like most druchii homes, and three narrow windows allowed only a trickle of moonlight past their grimy panes. Everything appeared to Malus in different shades of night. The ghostly arch of a stairway rose on his right, a fainter shade of black than the ebony surface of the floor. High overhead the perfect vault of shadow was smudged by a grey blob that Malus took to be an ancient witchlamp holder.

Arleth Vann turned back to Malus, his alabaster face hovering in the darkness like a disembodied spirit. 'There is a door at the base of the staircase. We'll follow it into the cellars,' he said, and disappeared into the gloom.

Malus lost sight of the assassin almost at once. Cursing to himself, he focused on the half-seen staircase, crossing the stone floor with care. After a few moments he reached the base of the stairs and worked his way along the wall until he almost bumped into Arleth Vann's nearly invisible form. Malus heard the creak of a door, and felt a gust of colder, wetter air against his cheek. He wrinkled his nose at the smell of damp earth and old rot. The doorway itself was a pool of darker shadow against the iron-grey of the wall. He sensed rather than saw Arleth Vann slip inside, and moved quickly in his wake.

Without warning, Malus's eyes were dazzled by an explosion of pale green light. He hissed a curse, trying to shield his eyes from the small globe of witchlight that burned in the palm of Arleth Vann's upraised hand.

'I never knew you were a sorcerer!' Malus exclaimed, blinking in surprise.

Arleth Vann shrugged. 'The temple teaches its assassins a few simple cantrips: how to make light, how to silence rusty hinges, things of that nature. Nothing like the knowledge possessed by someone such as Urial.'

They were in a narrow, enclosed stairway that led down to another iron-bound door. Arleth Vann descended slowly, testing each of the stone steps with a tentative boot before proceeding. 'One of these steps activates a poison trap,' he muttered, 'so follow my moves exactly.'

'You seem to know a great deal about this place,' Malus said, attempting to follow in the assassin's footsteps.

Arleth Vann shrugged. 'This was how I escaped the temple, many years ago.' He paused at the third step from the bottom, testing the riser carefully with the point of his boot. 'This is the one,' he said, stepping carefully over the trap and continuing to the door. There was a grating of metal as he turned the iron ring and pushed it open, letting in a blast of frigid air that sank right into Malus's bones.

The doorway opened onto a stone landing lit by a flickering green glow. The assassin doused his witchlight and stepped through the doorway. Malus followed close behind Arleth Vann, watching his breath turn to vapour in the chill air. His boots skidded on the dark stones, which were rimed with glittering frost. Arleth Vann caught his arm at once, helping his master steady himself. 'Careful, my lord,' he said quietly. 'You wouldn't want to take a fall right here.'

Malus steadied himself and looked around. The landing was barely three paces square and looked out over a cavernous space at least thirty feet deep. From where he stood he could see that the upper half of the space was square shaped and bounded with finished stone blocks. Another narrow staircase descended from the landing, following the rough wall towards the chamber floor. The source of the light came from below, radiating upwards in a flickering, ghostly nimbus.

Malus freed his arm from his retainer's grip and carefully approached the edge of the landing. Below, he saw a wide ribbon of dark, glossy stone, wide enough for four men to walk abreast, leading to a tall archway set into the side of the great hill. The archway was at least fifteen feet tall at its apex, and appeared to be formed from huge, polished bones the likes of which he'd never seen before. It looked as if arch and roadway had been excavated from the cold earth. The piles of rock and soil cleared from the path formed raised banks to either side of the road, packed down to rock-like hardness over the passage of centuries. Four iron spikes, each twelve feet long, had been driven into both banks alongside the road, making a rough octagon pattern with the roadway passing through its centre.

Corpses were impaled on each of the iron spikes, their dark, shrivelled bodies stacked one on top of the other so that Malus couldn't tell for certain where one body ended and the next began. They had all been bound hand and foot, their limbs twisted in the throes of long, agonising deaths. They had hung from the iron spikes for a very long time, and colonies of grave mould covered the corpses, emitting the pale light that filled the eerie space.

Malus glanced in wonder at Arleth Vann. 'What is this place?'

'Hundreds of years ago, when the city was first founded, a druchii named Cyrvan Thel built this house,' the assassin said in a hushed voice. 'Several years after the building was complete, Thel decided to add a lower level for a wine cellar, and the workers uncovered the roadway. The paving stones resisted every attempt to remove them, including sorcery, so Thel ordered the workmen to follow their course and see how far they went. That was how they came upon the archway. When the workers broke through into the tunnel beyond a breath of foul wind rushed out that killed them in an instant. Thel, being a devout man, took this as an omen. When the air had cleared enough for a slave to survive without ill effects, Thel and a handful of retainers entered the tunnel to see where it led.'

'And what did they find?'

'The Vermillion Gate,' the assassin replied. He pointed to the arch. 'The passage leads deep into the heart of the hill, to a circular chamber that might sink all the way to the heart of the world itself. A flat-topped spire rises in the centre of that chamber, spanned by a bridge of ancient bone, and on top of that spire sits the dreadful gate. No one knows who built it or why, but it is old beyond all reckoning.' He turned to Malus, a fearful look in his eyes. 'It leads to the very heart of the Lord of Murder's realm.'

The highborn was taken aback. 'Khaine is a druchii god. How can that be, if the gate was made in a time before Nagarythe was lost?'

Arleth Vann spread his hands. 'Thel looked upon the gate and thought it had been set here in anticipation of our coming, a gift from the Blood God to his chosen people. He took word of his discovery to the elders of the cult, and they came from across Naggaroth to look upon the gate. When they beheld it for the first time, they knew that from that moment forwards the hill and everything upon it must belong to the cult. Shortly after, the Witch King gave Har Ganeth to the temple of Khaine.'

Malus stared at the archway of bone and a feeling of dread turned his guts to ice. 'Urial spoke of the Vermillion Gate,' he said, 'on the way back from the Isle of Morhaut. He used it to reach Har Ganeth.'

The assassin nodded thoughtfully, as if the highborn had answered a worrying riddle. 'Some of the texts in the temple library claim that a true disciple of Khaine can call upon the power of the gate no matter where in the world he may be. He can reach the cavern beneath the hill in a single stride, if he makes the proper offerings. Spirits guard the gate from the unworthy, and if they are not provided for they will exact a terrible price from those who cross the threshold.'

'He rewarded them amply,' Malus growled, thinking of the slaughter on the main deck of the battered corsair, 'and from what little I saw he timed his crossing so that there was a crowd of worshippers waiting on the other side.'

The assassin shrugged. 'Every new moon the temple elders gather at the gate to perform sacred ceremonies of veneration. If Urial had emerged from the gate – with Yasmir in tow, no less – it would have seemed most portentous indeed.' He turned and headed for the narrow staircase leading to the cavern floor.

Malus followed warily, picking his way across the landing and then down the long flight of stairs. The risers glittered with frost. When he reached out a hand to steady himself along the wall he found that it was covered in a thin layer of ice.

Malus felt a prickling along his skin as they made their slow descent. The chamber was thick with sorcerous energies.

The highborn cleared his throat. 'About Urial–' he began.

Arleth Vann cut him off with an upraised hand. 'Quiet,' he said, his voice barely a whisper, 'we are about to pass the guardians.'

The stairway ended at the edge of the roadway. Up close, Malus saw that the stones of the dark path were like blocks of obsidian, polished to a mirror hue. It looked as if every stone had a flaw to it: a faint, pale smudge in each stone's centre. When he bent a little closer, however, he saw that it wasn't a blemish on the surface: there was something within each of the stones. The shapes were blurry, but there was just enough play of light and shadow for the objects to take on the quality of living faces.

Puzzled, Malus started to bend even closer, but the daemon's voice rasped in his ear. 'If you value your sanity, mortal, look no further,' Tz'arkan said coldly. 'There are some things no druchii – not even you – were meant to know.'

The highborn straightened with a start. Arleth Vann was already some distance away, approaching the first of the iron poles with his head bowed and his hands tucked into his robes.

Malus moved as quickly as he dared, hurriedly following suit just as the assassin reached the first set of poles. Suddenly a chorus of thin wails filled the air, rising piteously from the blackened mouths of the bound corpses.

A thrill of terror coursed down Malus's spine. He had heard that sound once before, in the depths of Urial's tower.

The highborn glanced fearfully at the pole to his right. Pale mist was leaking from the slack jaws and gaping eye sockets of the impaled figures. The tendrils danced and wove about in a spectral wind, taking the shape of pale, spindly figures with long fingers and emaciated faces. Their eyes were orbs of purest jet, soulless and cruel. 'The maelithii!' Malus breathed.

'Be not afraid,' Arleth Vann hissed. 'Avert your eyes and walk the ancient path. They are bound to do no harm to those who bear the blessings of Khaine.'

Malus averted his eyes, focusing on the black stones at his feet. They would not be fooled by his magically altered eyes. He imagined the maelithii swarming over him, sinking their black fangs into his flesh and feasting on his life force. When they were finished with him his skin would be the colour of a deep bruise, the blue-black of a corpse lost for months in the snow.

The vengeful spirits whistled and howled above Malus's head, drawing ever nearer. His legs began to tremble. There was no way to fight these spirits: swords passed straight through them and left the arm numb and frozen to boot. He fought the urge to turn and run for the staircase, wondering how much further he was from the archway.

One of the maelithii let out a shrill cry and swooped close enough to Malus for him to feel veins of frost spreading through his black hair. Other maeliths began a cacophony of wailing in reply. They've found me out, he thought!

Malus felt a needle of ice pierce his cheek, and just as swiftly he felt the daemon uncoil in his chest like a startled viper. Tz'arkan howled a challenge at the maelithii that set Malus's teeth on edge and the baleful spirits withdrew, wailing plaintively.

The highborn quickened his pace, not caring if he trampled Arleth Vann in the process. The sounds of the maelithii receded behind him with every step. Then without warning he was surrounded in a flare of witchlight. When Malus looked up he found himself standing beside his retainer, just past the tall arch of polished bone.

Arleth Vann was looking back the way they'd come, eyeing the eight maelithii circling above the centre of the octagon. 'They seemed interested in you for some reason,' he told Malus, 'and then they cried out in fear. I've never heard the like.'

Malus looked back at the tormented spirits. 'They tried to claim something that belongs to another,' he said grimly.

The assassin frowned. 'I don't understand.'

'Count yourself fortunate,' Malus replied. He gestured down the dark passage. 'Let's go.'

The passage seemed to go on forever. Arleth Vann's witchlight just barely reached the rounded walls to either side. To Malus's eyes they appeared to be made of dark, grainy stone, like granite, but worked in loops and strands as if the tunnel had been woven out of the stone rather than carved. He couldn't fathom how such a thing had been done, much less why. The strange patterns created many corners, niches and crevices among the coarse weave of the stonework, and over the centuries the worshippers of Khaine had filled those recesses with offerings to their god. Skulls by the thousand leered at the two druchii as they went deeper into the hill. Skeletal hands seemed to reach for them in the flickering aura of the witchlight. Malus saw leg bones and vertebrae, ribs and shoulder blades, all arranged to blend almost seamlessly with the fluid lines of the stonework. The dead pressed in on Malus from every side, setting his heart to race. He tried to focus on something else, and remembered the question he'd started to ask outside the archway.

'Why doesn't the temple want Urial to have the sword?'

Arleth Vann paused, turning to look back at his master with a rueful grin. 'Had you ever taken an interest in religion, my lord, you wouldn't have to ask such a question,' he replied. 'As far as the temple is concerned, they've already given the sword to another.'

'Another!' Malus exclaimed. 'Who?'

The assassin shook his head. 'Who else? Malekith, of course.'

'They think Malekith is the Scourge? How can this be?'

To Malus's surprise, Arleth Vann threw back his head and laughed. 'As clever a man as you are, my lord, I'm amazed you'd have to ask such a question. How do you think the temple of Khaine came to exist?'

Malus frowned. He didn't much care for the assassin's patronising tone. 'Malekith used the cult to consolidate his rule after Nagarythe was lost,' he snapped. 'They had every reason to hate most of the old houses, who worshipped Slaanesh and had persecuted them for hundreds of years. Malekith raised them up, made them the state religion, and in return they helped him break the power of the warlocks and assassinate any rivals to his throne.'

Arleth Vann nodded. 'Just so, my lord, but you must understand that the cult in those days was not like the temple as it is now. When you think of the temple, you envision people like your half-brother Urial, but back then they were true believers like Tyran. They were utterly devout, dedicated to the pure teachings of the Lord of Murder and the heirs of centuries of persecution.'

'They were fanatics,' Malus said, 'and I suppose they cared little for Malekith or his power plays.'

The retainer gave one of his rare smiles. 'Now you begin to see. The elders of the cult saw much to gain in Malekith's offer, however – power, legitimacy, wealth and influence – but they had to find a way to convince their followers that the alliance served the will of the Blood God.'

'So they claimed Malekith was Khaine's Scourge.'

'Indeed. For almost as long as the druchii have lingered in Naggaroth the temple has taught its followers that Malekith is their unquestioned master because he is the chosen Scourge of Khaine. When the time is right he will come to Har Ganeth and wed the Bride of Ruin. Then he will take up the Warpsword of Khaine and usher in the Time of Blood. Anything else is heresy.'

◄ CHAPTER TEN ►

FAITH AND MURDER

Malus stared dumbfounded at his retainer. 'You mean to tell me that all of this is built on a lie? The temple followers sold out their faith for the sake of political favour?'

Arleth Vann nodded. 'Does this trouble you?'

The highborn cocked his head thoughtfully. 'Actually, it's rather reassuring. These motives at least make sense to me, but clearly not all of the faithful believed the elders' pronouncement.'

'No,' the retainer said. 'The elders built a compelling case, of course, pointing to numerous obscure prophesies that seemed to support their claim. A devious mind can make the words of an oracle fit anything he wants if he tries hard enough, but it wasn't enough. Several cult leaders and their disciples saw through the elders' arguments and refused to take part in the alliance, regardless of the benefits. The debates raged for years, but the nascent temple continued to grow and gain legitimacy. Finally, the true believers saw that their power was waning fast. If they didn't act soon, the elders and their blasphemy would be too deeply rooted to eliminate.'

'So they fought.'

The assassin nodded. 'They fought. At the culmination of a weeklong holy festival – the Draich na Anlar – the schism leaders gathered their followers and attacked the elders in the midst of their consecrations. Somehow, the attempt failed. Some scholars suggest that the schism leaders were betrayed, while others point to divine intervention. At any rate, the five true believers that entered the temple to kill the blasphemous elders were never seen or heard from again. Other confrontations across the city degenerated into a chaotic riot that killed thousands. Fighting raged through the city streets all through the night, and by daybreak the White City was stained with rivers of blood. Afterwards the temple elders tore the city apart looking for the schism leaders and their allies, dragging those they found into the street and decapitating them on the spot. This is how Har Ganeth came to be known as the City of Executioners.'

'And the survivors?'

Arleth Vann shrugged. 'They fled the city, spreading out all across Naggaroth and beyond to keep the true faith alive. They knew that one day the true Scourge would appear, and there would be another day of reckoning with the blasphemers.'

'So the zealots returned to their roots, worshipping in secret as they'd been doing since time out of mind.'

The assassin nodded, resuming his course down the long tunnel. 'It was the proper way, regardless. Khaine is not meant to be worshipped in a temple, but on the battlefield or by the side of the road. We are exalted by testing our strength against others and taking their lives with skill and daring.'

Malus fell into step behind his retainer, thinking back to the constant training and superlative skill of the zealots. 'So Khaine is actually a god of combat?'

'No, he is a god of death,' Arleth Vann replied. 'What is the greatest power a man can have in this world?'

Malus shrugged. 'The power of a king.'

The assassin let out a snort. 'A king can die on the field of battle like anyone else. Think again.'

'Damned sorcery, then.'

The retainer shook his head. 'No, it is simpler than that. The greatest power in this world is the ability to end life. The one thing every man shares, whether he is a slave or the Witch King himself, is a beating heart. The power to stop that heartbeat in a single stroke is what brings us closer to Khaine. We become gods, holding the lives of those around us in the palms of our hands. Do you see?'

'I believe so,' Malus said. 'That is the purpose of the executioners, I suppose?'

The assassin nodded. 'In the days before the temple, every worshipper of Khaine was an executioner: a Sword of Khaine. The true believer killed his opponents with a single, perfect stroke, making it a gesture of worship and enhancing his power with every foe he slew in battle. It was only after the temple was founded and the elders required acolytes to devote themselves to sinful practices like tithe collection that the executioners became an isolated sect.'

'And the temple witches?'

Arleth Vann cast a sidelong glance over his shoulder at Malus. 'They suffered the worst degradations of all. Once, they were Khaine's bloody oracles and the enforcers of the Blood God's divine will. They had the power to summon back the souls of the fallen and partake of their powers. And now? Now they are degenerates, aping the glories of their forebears with drugs and pitiful necromancies. You have seen true blood-witches, my lord. Can the witches of the temple compare to their terrible majesty?'

'No,' Malus admitted, 'certainly not. So what happened?'

The assassin shrugged. 'The blood-witches tried to stay apart from the fray during the early years of the schism. The brides of Khaine did not concern themselves with such petty conflicts. After the true believers were driven from the city and the elders hemmed the rest of the cult into temples, their prestige gradually diminished. There hasn't been a true blood-witch serving the temple for at least two thousand years.'

As they walked, Malus began to notice narrow doorways cut into the ropy stonework of the tunnel walls. The doorframes were made of glossy white marble and carved with intricate runes in archaic druchast. Next to the strangely flowing weave of the walls the newer construction still seemed crude and awkward by comparison. 'What are these?' he asked.

'Those? They are tombs,' the retainer said. 'The temple has always interred the faithful, despite the Witch King's edict of cremation. Perhaps the elders venerate the spirits of the dead in the hope they will intercede on their behalf when Khaine returns in his wrath.' He gestured at the doorways with a sweep of his free hand. 'The entire hill is honeycombed with tomb complexes, and they reach far into the earth.'

The two druchii walked on in silence for a time, journeying down the dark road past the doorways of the dead. Some quality of the stone swallowed their footsteps, and for a while it felt as if they had left the physical world behind, trudging like ghosts through some forgotten underworld. Malus considered the implications of everything Arleth Vann had told him. *It did go a long way towards explaining the temple's odd behaviour... but his mind kept drifting back to his meeting with Rhulan, and the wary look on the elder's face. Urial's claim casts the entire history of the temple into doubt,* the highborn thought, *which was ample reason to keep him in seclusion and look for a way to silence him. However, that would be self-evident to anyone familiar with temple dictum. There's something more going on here,* he thought. *The elders have a secret that no one, not even the zealots, suspect.*

Arleth Vann stopped. Malus looked around and saw that they had reached a point where two curving stairways – one ascending, the other descending – were carved into the living rock to either side of the dark road. 'We'll go no further into the hill. The Vermillion Gate is close by, and it is always well-guarded by a cadre of witches and executioners.' He pointed to the climbing stairway. 'Here is where the journey becomes difficult.'

Malus eyed the staircase. 'More spirit wards?'

Arleth Vann shook his head. 'No. Just hundreds and hundreds of stairs.'

Malus lost all track of time as they trudged up the winding stairway. The journey passed as a blur of echoing steps and shadowy landings that opened onto ancient galleries and maze-like passageways leading to mouldy tombs. The temple hill was a labyrinth vaster and more convoluted than anything he had ever seen; even the tower of the mad sorcerer

Eradorius seemed smaller and less complicated by comparison. The highborn mused between gasps for breath that crossing paths with Arleth Vann had turned out to be a great boon. Alone he might have been fumbling about the hill and its passageways until the seas ran dry. He breathed the dry, dusty pall of bone dust at every turn, as centuries of temple servants rotted to dust in the niches and alcoves beneath the great temple. The dust made his nose itch and left the taste of the grave in the back of his throat.

At last, they emerged into a well-lit chamber glowing with the green fire of witchlamps. They were in a large space with low, vaulted ceilings, practically an underground plaza compared to the tight passageways and the narrow, enclosed staircase they'd travelled. Malus fought the urge to rub the ache from his trembling legs. 'Where are we?' he asked quietly.

'We're in the vaults beneath the temple proper,' Arleth Vann replied, eyeing the many passageways leading off from the chamber. 'From here we can reach almost every major building within the fortress, including the elders' private chambers.'

Malus nodded, gritting his teeth against the burning ache flaring from his knees. 'All right. Where are we likely to find Rhulan at this point?'

'When the elders are not conducting their rites, they typically retire to their chambers,' the assassin replied. 'No doubt to reflect on matters of the faith,' he said with a sneer.

'Yes, but this is no typical night. An elder has deserted the temple. The story on the street might be that the man was kidnapped, but I imagine the rest of the elders know the truth of the matter. Their warriors have taken to the streets to fight the true believers, and their sacred council remains broken. Where do the elders normally go when they meet in conclave?'

'The council chambers within the Citadel of Bone,' Arleth Vann replied, 'but if the elders are meeting there they will be well-guarded.'

'I thought the temple assassins were supposed to be invisible,' the highborn snapped.

'When the situation demands,' the retainer answered coolly. 'Can my lord say the same?'

Malus gave the man a hard stare. 'Just get us as close as you can. We'll improvise from there.'

'You mean we'll kill whoever gets in our way.'

'That is what I said, yes.'

Arleth Vann gave another of his ghostly smiles. 'It is good to know some things never change. Follow me, my lord.'

The assassin quickly led Malus out of the well-lit tunnels beneath the temple and into noisome passageways dripping with slime and tangled with dense layers of cobwebs. He made no effort to relight his sorcerous lamp, forcing Malus to crouch low and follow the almost undetectable sound of the retainer's footfalls. From time to time their path crossed better-travelled corridors, and once or twice the highborn caught snatches of whispered conversations as the servants of the temple went about their nightly tasks. Each time, Arleth Vann would pause at the junction and listen for several moments, gauging the servants' movements, before darting silently across the passageway into the darkened tunnel mouth opposite. Malus felt like a rat inside the walls of some vast city house, scuttling from shadow to shadow to avoid the master's house serpents.

After nearly half an hour, Arleth Vann stopped a few feet shy of the end of the passage and drew his twin blades. He turned to Malus. 'From here on out, I go ahead,' the assassin whispered. 'Wait three minutes and then follow after me.'

Malus frowned. 'Three minutes? How will I know where you've gone?'

The assassin looked at Malus over his shoulder. 'Look for the trail of bodies,' he said in a hard voice. Then he stepped out of the corridor and slipped off to the right.

Malus drew his own sword. His limbs felt leaden after the long climb through the heart of the hill, and the prospect of more fighting filled him with a weary kind of dread. I should drink of the daemon's power, he thought. Just a little, to lend me strength and take away this damned fatigue.

No sooner had the thought occurred to him than a wave of trembling wracked his body. His insides twisted with need as he thought about the glorious, icy vitality of the daemon's power. 'Mother of Night!' he breathed, dropping to one knee. The hunger felt bottomless, and his mind recoiled in terror from it.

It was several minutes before the trembling passed, leaving Malus feeling even weaker than before. His face and neck were bathed in cold sweat, and his guts felt tied in knots. The highborn clenched his sword tightly, focusing on the strain of his knuckles and the hard weight of the sword hilt digging into his palm. With an effort of will, he forced himself back onto his feet. A terrible sense of foreboding pressed down upon him. Had the daemon's recent silence been nothing more than the infinite patience of a predator, knowing its prey was but a single step away from ruin? Blessed mother, have I gone too far, Malus thought? Am I now beholden to the daemon, body and soul?

The daemon slithered across his ribs. 'Are you unwell, Malus?' Tz'arkan's voice slid into his ears like sweet poison. 'The temple elders await. Do you wish my aid?'

Yes, Malus thought. He bit his lips to keep the words from slipping past them. His mind roiled with horror and revulsion. Another wave of trembling passed through his taut frame.

'Come now, don't be proud,' the daemon whispered. 'I can feel your weakness, little druchii, your need. If you go before the elders like this they will see how weak you are. Let me make you strong again.'

Malus tasted blood on his tongue. He bit deeper into his torn lip, letting the pain kindle the fires of his hate. With hate all things are possible, he told himself. 'I... want nothing from you,' he gasped, sending a trickle of blood coursing down his chin. 'Nothing, you hear?'

The daemon chuckled, his manner smug and easy. 'That's an easy thing to say when you're alone and in the dark,' Tz'arkan said. 'You have no idea how pitiful you look. If the elders see you like this they will laugh in your face. Is that what you really want?'

Growling like a wounded beast, Malus forced his body to move; one step, and then another. Hate seethed in his heart, a weak fire compared to the icy torrent of the daemon's power, but it propelled him nonetheless. He bared red-stained teeth and spat onto the stone floor. 'They will see what I choose to show them,' the highborn said, feeling a little of his old strength return, 'nothing more or less.'

'Of course,' the daemon said in a patronising tone. 'I should have guessed you'd say such a thing. Perhaps you can manage a little longer without my help, but mark me: there will come a time very soon when you will find yourself in dire need of my power. Ask, and it will be yours.'

Malus staggered from the dark passageway, blinking owlishly in the light of the corridor beyond. Not ten feet to the right a temple servant lay on his face in a pool of spreading blood. The man had died without the slightest sound.

The highborn drew a shuddering breath, horrified that suddenly he felt unequal to the task before him. He'd thought he'd gained the upper hand over Tz'arkan, and the whole time the daemon had simply bided its time, like a spider sitting in the centre of its invisible web.

All is not lost just yet, the highborn thought. I still live. I still have my sword and my mother's ring; and my hate, always my hate. Dark Mother, let that be enough!

Licking bitter blood from his lips, Malus set off in the assassin's wake.

Arleth Vann was true to his word. The assassin left a trail of slaughter that a blind man could have followed. Malus passed more than a dozen temple servants in corridors and at junctions, each laid out on the floor as if slain in mid-stride. At one point he passed a trio of corpses propping one another upright, and Malus was struck with the image of the pale-faced assassin weaving his way through the close knit group and slaying them so quickly that they fell almost as one. The man's supernal skill filled Malus with admiration even as it reminded him of his own wretched state.

Finally Malus found himself at the end of a long corridor built from pale marble that glowed beneath globes of witchlight. An open doorway waited at the other end, beyond a pile of armoured guards. The highborn picked his way through the tangle of steel-clad bodies, his boots making tacky sounds as he crossed an enormous puddle of congealing blood.

Beyond lay a narrow chamber, dominated by a short ramp that led upwards to a large, echoing chamber. Arleth Vann waited at the base of the ramp, surrounded by half a dozen dead servants. The assassin was pausing to clean his twin blades with a cloth rag appropriated from one of the corpses. His pale face was spotted with blood and eerily serene. The roar of scores of angry voices rolled down the stone ramp from the chamber beyond, washing over Malus in seething waves.

'Where... where are we?' Malus stammered, raising his voice to be heard above the cacophony.

'Just beneath the council chamber,' Arleth Vann replied. 'This is the room where they remove claimants who fail to persuade their case before the council.'

At that moment a projectile hit the top of the ramp with a wet thud and bounced down the slope past the assassin. Malus caught the furious expression on the face of the severed head as it rolled across the floor.

The retainer looked up from his work. 'Are you well, my lord? You look–'

'I expect I look as if I'd crawled from a tomb, considering the route you took us through,' Malus snapped. 'It's a wonder I can see after all the webs I walked into.' He looked down at the grisly trophy and gave it a savage kick. The spiteful gesture heartened him a little. 'I'm fine,' he said, injecting a touch of steel into his voice, 'merely vexed at the foolishness of priests.' Without another word he moved past his retainer and climbed the ramp, his sword held at his side.

For a moment Malus was certain Arleth Vann had led him wrong. He found himself near the point of an oval chamber, ringed by a gallery that rose in tiers for at least twenty feet. Men and women crowded the tiers shouting and shaking their fists at the brawl that raged on the chamber's floor. The air stank of blood and shook with the inchoate thunder of an arena in the city's entertainment district. Not ten yards from where Malus stood more than a score of druchii pushed, pummelled and slashed at one another. At the centre of the fight two older men grappled with each other, their faces twisted with bestial hate. Broad bladed knives trembled in their white knuckled fists as they wrestled for the advantage. Each man wore rich, red robes and kheitans of fine leather studded with gold and precious stones. Their retainers were only slightly less bedecked themselves, their struggles having left a fortune in gilt and gems scattered across the marble floor. Wounded men stumbled or crawled away from the raging fight, clutching at their wounds and screaming encouragement to their respective sides. A handful of corpses lay forgotten underfoot.

Malus looked up at the gallery, realising that the shouting throng was made up of still more richly attired elders and their servants. Six large thrones were set around the perimeter of the chamber at the lowest gallery tier. Three of the seats were empty, although they were surrounded by elders and their retinues like hounds standing over a freshly killed deer. At the apex of the oval chamber, in a throne that surpassed all the rest in size and extravagance, sat an ancient druchii in vestments of hammered brass inlaid with diamonds and rubies. A mask of gold worked in the shape of a leering skull concealed his features, but his gnarled fists shook as he leaned forwards in his chair, shouting encouragements or curses upon the men fighting below. Malus caught sight of Rhulan sitting on the throne to the elder druchii's right. Of all the assembled elders, he seemed least interested in the fight. A gold mask lay in his hand as he leaned to one side and conferred with one of his followers.

The highborn looked over at Arleth Vann, who emerged from the ramp behind Malus. 'This is how the temple council conducts its affairs?' he shouted.

Arleth Vann shrugged. 'You must admit it's more entertaining than any drachau's court,' he shouted back.

The highborn shook his head irritably. 'To the Outer Darkness with this,' he snarled. He pointed at the reeling brawl. 'Make me a hole,' he said to the assassin.

Arleth Vann nodded grimly, raising his short blades. He glided swiftly towards the fight with Malus close behind and cut his way through the crowd like a thresher harvesting grain. Men fell away to either side, struck down by the assassin's flickering blades, and the rest recoiled in shock from the sudden assault. Within moments Malus reached the battling elders, each man lost in his own single-minded struggle. The assassin stepped aside with a bow. Malus walked up to the two men and swung his heavy blade, decapitating both elders in a single stroke.

Blood erupted in a bright fountain from the two slain men, their bodies falling against one another in a grisly embrace. The severed heads bounced audibly on the stone floor in the sudden, shocked silence.

Gore dripping from his blade, Malus turned, regarding the assembled elders with cold, brass eyes. 'Now that I have your attention,' he said, his voice echoing in the council chamber, 'I've come to bring a warning to the council. You must sound the call to arms and hurry to the Sanctum of the Sword. While you squabble here like dogs over a corpse, Urial and his supporters are closing their hands around the Warpsword of Khaine.'

Murmurs of shock and snarls of derision echoed from the assembly. At the far end of the chamber the Grand Carnifex of the temple rose portentously to his feet. To his right, the Arch-Hierophant turned pale, his dark eyes shifting from Malus to the leader of the temple and back again.

The Grand Carnifex's voice was a liquid rasp, bubbling up from old lungs thick with corruption. 'Who are you?' he said, his words carrying across the chamber in spite of the mask he wore.

'A servant of Khaine,' Malus answered. 'A man with a dire warning, and beyond that, what does it matter? Your enemies are on the verge of destroying you, Grand Carnifex: you and this house your predecessors have built. Will you act, or shall we sit here and waste precious time with introductions?'

The entire chamber resounded with a single intake of breath as the audience recoiled in shock at Malus's words. Steel rang as swords leapt from gilt scabbards, and a number of the temple elders barked at their retainers to make a way for them to reach the chamber floor. Then Rhulan leapt to his feet, calling out in a carrying voice. 'How do you know this?' he asked, looking meaningfully at Malus.

The highborn met the elder's gaze and nodded respectfully. 'Because I have spent the last four days at the feet of Tyran the Unscarred, the leader of the zealots who oppose you,' he answered. 'I have sat in their councils, and I know that they have agents within the temple itself.' He surveyed the outraged elders coldly. 'They have been in close contact with Urial since the moment they entered the city and everything they have done has been in preparation for this very night.' He raised his bloodstained sword and pointed at each of the empty thrones in turn. 'Do you think this was all some sort of accident? A stroke of cruel luck? No. They struck directly at the Haru'ann, sowing confusion and discord while they formed a learned council of their own. Now, with all your warriors pounding at the gates of empty houses across the city, they have slipped inside the temple and are performing the Rite of the Swordbearer even as we speak!'

'Let them!' A woman shouted. Her voice was an angry rasp, cutting jaggedly through the tense atmosphere. Malus saw a young priestess in the third tier of the gallery face the Grand Carnifex. 'We know Urial is not the Scourge. The ritual will fail, and we will have the opportunity we've been waiting for to denounce him!'

'If the rite fails the heretics will find fault in the men performing the rite, not in their would-be saviour,' Malus shot back. 'This can only end in death,' he snarled, looking to the Grand Carnifex. 'You know this.'

'I say this is the work of the heretics!' said an older druchii to Malus's left, leaning over the first tier railing and pointing a long finger at Malus. 'They've already sent assassins against us once. Perhaps they sent this loudmouth to draw us to the sanctum so they could slay us all!'

Malus gave the elder a cold stare. 'If you fear for your life, elder, then by all means run and cower beneath your overstuffed bed.' He met the Grand Carnifex's dark gaze. 'This is a matter for warriors.'

'This is nothing of the sort!' snapped the young priestess. 'If this is true, the zealots have handed us an opportunity! Let them try to complete their ritual. When it fails they will return to their followers and fall upon one another, looking for someone to blame. This crisis can solve itself in a single stroke.'

Malus watched the Grand Carnifex glance at the priestess, and for a brief moment he caught a flicker of uncertainty in the ancient druchii's eyes. He is afraid, Malus thought with a start.

'I have heard enough,' the Grand Carnifex declared. 'Summon the guards. We will march to the sanctum and offer prayers to the Lord of Murder for a bloody deliverance from the works of heretics.' He held out his hand and a retainer appeared from behind the tall throne to press a huge, rune carved axe into the Carnifex's palm. 'If there are trespassers within the sanctum we will offer them up as sacrifices to our lord.'

The Grand Carnifex rose to his feet. Ropy tendons stood out taut as steel wires beneath the skin of the elder's neck and arms as he levelled the axe at Malus. 'If not, I will strike off your head and pour your blood upon the sacred stone,' he declared. 'As you said, stranger, this can only end in death.'

CHAPTER ELEVEN

WARPSWORD

The sky over Har Ganeth was the colour of blood as the doors to the Citadel of Bone yawned open and Malus followed the elders of the temple into the battle torn night. More buildings were burning in the city below, sending towering plumes of cinders into the sky, and the air reverberated with the distant clash of arms. Malus knew that the streets would be choked with corpses come the dawn, but the madness and slaughter in the city was nothing more than a mummer's show. The true battle would be fought between a few score men and women within the towering structure barely thirty yards from the council chambers.

Witchlight globes swung from long, iron poles as a vanguard of temple executioners led the way, their bared blades glittering coldly as they fanned out into the deserted lane outside the gleaming citadel. Behind them came the temple elders, led by the Grand Carnifex in his grinning skull mask. The remaining officials and their retainers jockeyed for position behind their leader, brandishing broad knives and ornamented axes at the prospect of reaping fresh skulls for their hungry god.

All except for Rhulan. The narrow-faced elder had dutifully slipped on his skull mask, but let the mob sweep past him until he fell in among the guards escorting Malus and Arleth Vann. The executioner escort eyed Rhulan curiously as he paced along beside the highborn, but made no move to intervene.

'Why didn't you warn me?' the elder hissed. Unlike the Carnifex, his voice was muffled beneath the weight of his mask.

'There was no time,' Malus replied. 'The zealot leaders guarded their plans with care. No one was told until late this evening.'

Rhulan said nothing for a moment, staring into the night. Then the death's head turned back to Malus. 'If Tyran and his lieutenants die tonight, then their agents must be slain as well. We must sweep them all up in a single stroke. You understand?'

I understand that our arrangement is at an end, Malus thought grimly. 'I suspected as much,' he said coldly. It was unavoidable. Tyran had forced his hand, just as he'd forced the elders' hand.

If Tyran and Urial were stopped, Rhulan would force him to reveal what he knew about their network within the temple. Once they realised he was bluffing, he was finished.

Malus eyed the white stone of the temple rearing into the flame-shot sky like an upraised blade and thought he could sense the sorcery at work within. Somehow, in the midst of battle, he would have to make his move.

'Once you have the sword, what then?' the daemon whispered. 'Will you cut your way through the elders of the temple and into the city beyond?'

'First things first,' muttered Malus. Rhulan shook his head, thinking the words were meant for him.

'Fear not,' the elder said. 'However many agents this Tyran has, he could not have slipped into the temple undetected with more than a token force. There are nearly a hundred of us. We can bury the heretics in bodies if we have to. The zealot uprising ends tonight.'

'And Urial?' Malus asked. 'Surely you knew he would attempt this, sooner or later. The temple thought he was marked by Khaine from the moment he emerged from the sacrificial cauldron.'

'We knew nothing of the sort,' the elder snapped. 'Yes, clearly he was blessed by the Lord of Murder, but none of the witches could divine his destiny. Certainly no one believed that Khaine would anoint a cripple as his Scourge. His ambition has got the better of him.'

The highborn cocked his head at the quaver in Rhulan's voice. He studied the elder with narrowed eyes. 'You aren't so sure.'

'Do not presume,' Rhulan said archly. 'You heard me. He is a cripple. It's inconceivable that he could be Khaine's chosen one.'

'Then why do you sound so afraid?'

Just then a howl of challenge, fierce and joyous, rang out from the front of the great temple. 'Weep, unbelievers, for the great reckoning is at hand! The faithful stand in the presence of the sword and the Time of Blood draws nigh! Your wickedness will soon be revealed for all the people to witness, but see the gift of Khaine's mercy we bear in our hands. Come and redeem yourselves on our hungry blades!'

The procession of elders stumbled to a halt in a welter of angry shouts and bellowed curses. Seeing his chance, Malus nodded his head at Arleth Vann and quickened his pace, diving into the milling press of the elders and working his way towards the Grand Carnifex. Rhulan shouted something that Malus didn't catch. Then there was a rush of pounding feet as the highborn's escorts swept wide of the crowd and ran ahead to join the semicircle of warriors forming a cordon between the Carnifex and the five white-robed zealots that stood in his path.

They seemed like living shards of the shimmering, blade shaped tower that rose behind them. Moonlight shone on their unbound hair and glinted on the edges of their fearsome draichs. The zealots' dark eyes were alight with holy purpose. They were ready to shed their blood in holy sacrifice to the Lord of Murder. Malus thought he'd never seen five more dangerous warriors in all his life.

The Grand Carnifex however was not impressed. He raised his enchanted axe skyward and his voice trembled with rage. 'Be silent, unbeliever! Your every breath defiles this sacred place!' The elder spread his arms wide and commanded the executioners. 'Split their bodies asunder and cleanse this holy earth in libations of blood!'

With a shout the temple guards raised their long swords and charged at the waiting zealots, who met them with triumphant shouts and an intricate dance of death.

Malus watched in horrified wonder as the five zealots wove their way among four times their number of foes. Their swords were a gleaming blur as they rushed, ducked and spun, seeming to glide past a flurry of fearsome sword strokes and bypass their opponents' heavy armour with swift, precise blows. Executioners collapsed, clutching at the stumps of severed arms or hands, or doubled over from disembowelling strokes that slipped beneath the edge of their breastplates. Screams of anger and pain reverberated in the red tinged air, some cut short with a ringing note of steel.

The fight was over in moments. With a clatter of steel plates the last executioner stumbled away from the pile of fallen bodies, one hand outstretched towards the gleaming temple of Khaine. His draich tumbled from his fingers as he fell to his knees, and then toppled lifelessly to the ground.

One of the five zealots lay among a score of fallen temple guardsmen. The rest were streaked with splashes of gore, but their white robes made it plain that none of the blood belonged to them. Their leader raised his dripping blade to the Grand Carnifex and smiled.

'Your men are forgiven,' the zealot said with a smile. He'd just killed four men in as many seconds and wasn't even short of breath. 'Why do you hesitate, Grand Carnifex? Do you fear that the Bloody-Handed God has no cold mercy in his heart for one such as you? I assure you that he does.'

To Malus's surprise, the Grand Carnifex threw back his head and laughed. It was a terrible, bubbling sound, full of hatred and black fury. The Carnifex reached up and pulled away his ceremonial mask, revealing a ruin of broken bone and deep, twisted scars. The master of the temple was ancient, marked by hundreds of years of brutal war. The fearsome blow of a battle-axe had caved in the right side of his face, twisting his mouth into a feral, gap-toothed sneer. The tip of his nose was nothing more than a nub of ragged flesh, and his forehead was a patchwork of ancient scars, one on top of the other. The zealot leader met the Carnifex's baleful gaze, and Malus saw the briefest flicker of fear.

The Grand Carnifex hefted his enchanted axe. 'My god knows nothing of mercy, you moon-eyed fool,' he hissed. 'He does not forgive. He cares nothing for redemption. He simply hungers, and I live to see him fed.'

That was more like it, Malus thought. He drew his sword. 'Blood and souls for Khaine!' he roared, and the elders took up the shout just as the Grand Carnifex charged the zealot leader.

Malus glanced at Arleth Vann. 'Stick close,' he shouted, drawing one of his throwing knives.

The assassin shook his head. 'You can't possibly expect to fight these men, my lord. They are the best warriors Tyran has, and they have no fear of death. Their skill–'

'I'm not going to fight them, you fool. I'm going to kill them,' Malus snarled, and charged into the melee.

The zealots had resumed their deadly dance, reaping a red harvest among the elders and their retainers. They were constantly in motion, whirling and cutting with their long, curved swords as they wove among the howling mob. Their skill was transcendent and glorious in its purity and lethality. They were living works of the killer's art. Anyone who stepped within reach of their whirling blades was dead in seconds.

Malus watched the nearest zealot decapitate a howling acolyte and then spin gracefully on his heel to eviscerate a charging priestess. When he did the highborn struck the swordsman dead from fifteen paces away, burying his throwing knife in the back of the zealot's skull.

Shaking his head, the highborn peered through the melee for his next victim. Five yards away the Grand Carnifex fought the zealot leader in single combat. The master of the temple was already wounded in half a dozen places, but the speed and ferocity of his attacks was undiminished. Knowing better than to intercede, the highborn turned away and spotted a third zealot, hemmed in by a circle of wary elders. They pressed the swordsman from all sides, like wolves surrounding a mountain lion. When the zealot attacked they gave ground, providing him no opening to employ his deadly blade, but giving the druchii behind him a chance to strike at the swordsman's back.

Malus timed his move just as the zealot made another fierce rush. The elders fell back as before, but the highborn came up behind them and caught one of the men by the scruff of the neck. The elder let out a cry as Malus shoved him onto the zealot's blade. The razor edged sword sank deep into the man's chest and Malus continued to push the dying elder forwards, trapping the draich beneath the man's collapsing form. The zealot had just enough time to shout a bitter curse before the highborn split his skull like a melon.

A savage howl rang though the air. The highborn turned to see the priestess who had gainsayed him in the Citadel of Bone raise a bloody axe and a zealot's severed head to the burning sky. A deep wound scored her left shoulder, but her face was lit with a savage grin.

That left the zealot leader. If he knew his companions were dead the fanatic gave no sign. The swordsman held his draich before him, its point aimed at the Carnifex's throat. His body was taut, like a steel trap wound and ready to strike. The temple leader glared forbiddingly at the young warrior, flexing his two-handed grip on the haft of his great axe and shifting slightly from foot to foot. Blood flowed freely from deep wounds in his arms, chest and legs.

The two warriors faced each other for long moments, neither one presenting an opening to the other. No one moved. The temple elders observed the fight with reverent silence. Malus stole a glance at the temple and suppressed a snarl. His hand strayed to the other throwing dagger at his belt. 'Get it over with, for the Dark Mother's sake,' he muttered under his breath. 'I don't have time for this.'

It was the zealot who lost the test of wills. Thinking his foe was weak from blood loss and perhaps coveting the glory he'd gain from slaying the master of the temple, the swordsman exploded in a blur of motion, aiming a fearsome blow at the Carnifex's neck. The temple master was anything but weak, however, and as the long sword sang through the air he struck it with a backhanded blow from his axe. The enchanted steel broke the sword in three pieces. Then the Carnifex's return stroke sliced the man's head from his shoulders.

The temple master bent and plucked the zealot's skull from the ground. 'Take the heads of the others,' he ordered, tying the trophy to his belt. 'When this is done we will pile them high on the temple altar.'

Malus surveyed the grisly remains of the battle. Nearly two score of their number lay dead or dying, and he knew the worst was yet to come.

'Let us be swift,' the highborn said. 'We can catch Tyran and his heretic council as they attempt to perform the rite.'

'Blood and souls!' cried the axe wielding priestess, and the rest of the elders took up the shout. Their blood was up, and they rushed towards the temple in a ragged mob, eager to show their devotion to the Lord of Murder. The mob quickly left the Grand Carnifex behind as they swept up the white steps of the temple and through the tall, narrow doorway. Malus paced along behind them, checking to make sure that Arleth Vann was close by. He nodded to himself. This was going to work.

The temple was built from the same alabaster stone as the rest of the city, but there the similarities ended. The work of dwarf slaves – scores, perhaps even hundreds of them – was evident in the intricate design. The building centred on a single, narrow spire that rose like a sword into the burning sky, built from a broad, octagonal base supported by a cunning network of graceful buttresses that soared more than thirty feet into the air. The white marble was fitted with joins so precise that the whole structure looked more like a sculpture than a building, carved from the summit of the hill by the hands of a god. The temple was a symbol of wealth and power that could humble a drachau, much less a man such as Malus. He stared up at the great spire and could not help but feel a surge of black-hearted avarice.

The highborn raced up the temple steps, listening to the cries of the elders echoing angrily in the cavernous space beyond. Doors of dark oak plated in brass had been swung wide, providing a glimpse of the red shot blackness beyond.

Malus crossed the threshold and tasted blood in the air. Sorcerous energies pressed against his skin, pulsing in time to a rhythm he could not hear. Tz'arkan writhed in his chest, reacting hungrily to the power reverberating through the temple.

The space beyond was cavernous, lit by dozens of braziers that painted the walls and ceiling with leaping crimson shapes and menacing shadows. Pyramids of skulls, hundreds of them, were arranged in complex patterns across the black marble floor. Overhead, a red-tinged haze of smoke spread the bloody glow of the fires. The air reeked of rot and the sweet smell of cooking flesh. Malus's eyes burned and his throat ached, and for a moment it was as if he had been cast back in time, and was struggling through the red tinged realm of Urial's tower in the Hag.

At the far end of the chamber Malus saw another broad staircase, rising to another narrow doorway. He turned to Arleth Vann. 'Where do we go?' he asked.

The assassin nodded at the stairs. 'The temple has three sanctums. This chamber is reserved for acolytes and visitors. Up the steps yonder we will come to a smaller chapel where the temple priests and the elders make sacrifice and worship. Beyond that lies the Sanctum of the Sword.'

Malus nodded and started loping towards the stairs. 'When we reach the sanctum, I'll need a clear path to the sword. Do whatever you must.'

'I understand,' the assassin replied grimly. 'Khaine's will be done.'

The air grew thicker as Malus neared the steps to the second chapel. He felt a buzzing in his ears, like the distant shouts of a multitude. Again, he found himself reminded of Urial's tower, and steeled himself for what might lie ahead.

'You will need my power,' the daemon whispered. 'Take it, or you will die.'

The highborn paused, halfway up the broad stairway. 'No,' he hissed.

'Now is not the time for pride, Malus. You are weak. You know this. I can help. If you do not partake of my power you will be defeated. They are much too strong for you.'

A shudder wracked Malus's body. All at once he felt shrunken and starved, his muscles shrivelled and his bones aching from fatigue. Unbidden, he thought of Urial and his sorcery, and of Tyran's fearsome swordplay.

'I have my hate,' he whispered. 'I have my wits. They will suffice, daemon. They always have.'

'You know that isn't true. How many times would you have been lost had it not been for me?'

Malus bared his teeth, forcing doubt and fear from his mind by sheer, bloody-minded will. Then he heard the war screams and the shrieks of dying men coming from the chapel at the top of the stairs, and ran towards the sound.

The chapel was a smaller, oval-shaped chamber some eighty paces across, surrounded by roaring braziers that sent columns of scented smoke spiralling upwards to the peak of its arched ceiling. Between each brazier were deep, arched niches filled with stacks of gilded skulls, and a pile of similar, unadorned trophies lay in deep drifts around the raised dais at the far end of the room. A pall of shifting, reddish steam hung above the marble platform, rising from the brass mouth of an enormous cauldron sunk to knee height within the dais itself. Terrible power seethed from the vessel, its bubbling liquid hissing and spitting as if stirred to life by the desperate battle being fought nearby.

Another, narrower stairway rose beyond the dais, climbing towards a towering sculpture of the great god Khaine on his terrible brass throne. A doorway lit with crimson light gleamed at the base of the fearsome statue, and a fierce melee raged within feet of the glowing portal.

Another rearguard, Malus thought angrily. The crowd of temple elders and their retainers had swept up the short flight of stairs and swarmed around the fight just before the doorway. He couldn't see much of what was happening thanks to the haze of boiling blood rising from the cauldron, but he could clearly hear the clash of steel and the screams of the dying.

The air hummed with power. Malus felt pains shoot through his insides and a hot tear trace its way down his cheek. The drop broke over his lip and he tasted blood. Almost there, he thought. Just a little closer!

Malus pushed his way through stragglers on the near side of the dais and clambered onto it. He found himself looking down into the seething surface of the cauldron, where small skulls and delicate bones rolled in the dark, boiling liquid. He caught Arleth Vann climbing up beside him and shook his head. 'Go around the side,' he ordered in a rough voice. 'I'll draw the attention of the rearguard. You come in and attack them from the rear.'

The assassin nodded and dropped back off the dais. Malus turned back to the cauldron, took a deep breath, and leapt into the pall of steaming gore. Sword held ready, the highborn cleared the gaping maw of the sorcerous vessel and landed in a crouch on the other side.

He found himself looking over the heads of shouting elders as they tried to force their way up the narrow staircase and join in the fight. Figures pushed and stumbled over the bodies of the dead, and pale hands dragged bloody corpses away from the battle, leaving them to fetch up against the foot of the dais. Malus stood, peering intently at the swirling fight near the top of the stairway. A single figure spun and stabbed within a raging circle of temple elders. He caught sight of a long, tight braid of glossy black hair, and slim, alabaster arms moving in a swift, steady rhythm of slaughter.

Then the crowd recoiled under a fierce onslaught, and it seemed that the entire front rank of the elders simply collapsed like threshed wheat.

A pale, blood spattered face appeared, and Malus found himself staring into Yasmir's violet eyes.

She wore the ritual garb of a temple witch: a long crimson loincloth of silk held by a girdle of golden skulls that wrapped around her slender hips. Her torso was bare, decorated with streaks and loops of sticky blood, as were her long arms and her long, delicate fingers. A torc of golden skulls surrounded her slender throat and bands of gold and rubies gleamed at each wrist. Beneath the angular headdress of a temple witch her oval face was serene and achingly beautiful, like a flawless sculpture animated by the breath of the Blood God himself. Two long, needle-like daggers flickered in her dripping hands, licking through the air like adders' tongues to turn aside stabbing blades and pierce deep into yielding flesh.

When her eyes met his he felt a cold shock transfix him. It was like looking into the eyes of death itself, and at that moment he wanted nothing more than to sink into her embrace.

The crowd of elders surged back up the stairs, only to lose three more men to Yasmir's flickering blades. As they fell she extended a small foot and took a single step forwards. Her eyes never left his.

'She is coming for you, Malus,' Tz'arkan whispered. 'Accept my power, or she will kill you!'

If she reached him he would die. Her eyes told him that. He could feel her desire like a cold breath against his skin. Malus's hand tightened on his sword, but it felt no better than a bar of lead.

Three more elders leapt at Yasmir, striking at her almost simultaneously. They died before the blows were halfway to their target, stabbed through throat, eye and heart. She took another small step as the dead fell at her feet.

Malus couldn't take his eyes off her. Another few steps and she would be almost close enough to touch. Yet he could not move, transfixed by her violet gaze like a bird before the gliding serpent.

'Hear me, Darkblade, this is the moment of truth! The Bride of Ruin approaches, and without me you cannot prevail. Take what I offer you! Take it!'

A terrified cry went up from the elders, and they fell back before the onslaught of the living saint. One man realised he could not escape and simply sank to his knees before Yasmir, accepting a dagger point in his eye with a prayer upon his lips. Others at the base of the stairs turned and ran.

Less than ten feet separated them. Suddenly the very air resounded as if struck by the hammer of a god, and Malus sensed that the Rite of the Swordbearer had been completed. Somewhere beyond the red-lit doorway he knew that Urial was reaching for the Warpsword of Khaine, and the thought of being thwarted so close to his goal kindled a spark of bitter hate in his breast.

Death approached, bearing her dark knives, and damnation lay coiled in his breast. What could he do?

With a cry of despair three elders fell and poured out their blood on the marble steps, and Yasmir leapt like a deer onto the edge of the dais. Malus drew a shaky breath, gazing into her face. 'Hello sister,' he said.

That was when Arleth Vann appeared, crying out the name of the Blood God as he leapt at Yasmir's back. Quicker than lightning his short blades jabbed at her throat and arms, but she whirled with uncanny speed, flowing like water around his strokes and stabbing the assassin once, twice, thrice. Her long braid uncoiled like a whip, brushing Malus's cheek.

Without thinking he seized that thick rope of hair, and the spell was broken. His hate blazed like a furnace and he pulled with all his might, twisting into the motion and dropping to one knee. Yasmir was pulled from her feet, crashing into and over Malus and falling headfirst into the seething fluids of Khaine's cauldron.

Tz'arkan writhed and screamed in rage, raking along the inside of Malus's ribs, drawing an involuntary shout of pain from the highborn even as he bared his teeth in triumph. Arleth Vann sank against the side of the dais, one arm pressed tight against his chest. A trickle of blood leaked from the corner of his mouth. 'The will of Khaine be done,' the assassin gasped.

The way to the sanctum was clear, and Malus knew that speed meant everything now. Tyran and his ritual mates would be nearly spent from the exertions of the rite. He would deal with Urial now, and claim the warpsword for his own.

With a howl of bloodlust he leapt over Arleth Vann and charged up the stairs, his sword held ready.

A shadow loomed in the doorway just as he reached it. He felt an icy shock transfix him as his half-brother Urial stepped through the portal, clad in gleaming black armour. His brass-coloured eyes gleamed with triumph and his thin lips were drawn back in a savage smile.

Malus tried to raise his sword, but his body refused to obey. He staggered slightly, still off-balance, but something held him upright.

The highborn looked down at the length of dark, gleaming steel that pierced his chest. A thin line of blood ran down the surface of the warpsword, filling the runes etched along its surface.

'Looking for this?' Urial asked, and plunged the blade deeper into Malus's chest.

CHAPTER TWELVE

FROM THE CAULDRON BORN

Malus felt his heart clench in agony as the long blade slid between his ribs. His chest spasmed and he gasped, coughing up blood. Urial's sepulchral laugh rang in his ears.

'Glory to Khaine, greatest of gods!' Malus's half-brother shouted, his pale face alight with triumph. 'Truly it is a gift to find you here at the moment of my exaltation.' The former acolyte stepped closer, his twisted left foot dragging slightly across the polished marble. His withered right hand was tucked against his breastplate, its deformity hidden within a shell of dark steel armour. Urial's gaunt, hawk-like face was lit with a savage grin and his thick, white hair spilled unbound around his shoulders. He looked like a sorcerer prince out of the ancient legends, radiating icy cruelty and implacable power.

'It is fitting that you be the first to die,' Urial said, his voice almost a whisper. 'After all you and that whore Eldire have done to me, this will be sweet indeed.' He smiled, flexing his good hand on the warpsword's hilt. 'I'm going to split you from crotch to chin and let you bleed out on these steps. Then I'll command the blood-witches to call you back, and I'll look you in the eye as I feast upon your liver.' His grin hardened into a sneer. 'Once I've eaten of your spirit Darkblade you will be no more. I will take your strength – such as it is – and what is left will be lost to the Abyss forever.'

With a single, fluid motion, Urial jerked the warpsword free from Malus's torso. A wave of pain spread like ice through the highborn's body, so great it took his breath away. Blood leaked from his gaping mouth as he swayed on his feet. Then his knees buckled and Malus fell backwards, landing on his back and sliding limply down the marble steps. His sword, clutched in a death grip, rasped and rang as it was dragged along in his wake.

Malus fetched up at the base of the dais, his labouring heart sending cold waves of pain rippling through his chest. Tz'arkan stirred, and for a brief moment the agony subsided. 'I'm here, Malus,' the daemon whispered. 'Ask, and I shall heal you. The wound is deep, and you will die unless I intervene.'

It was hard to think and harder still to breathe. 'Not... possible,' Malus rasped, bloody froth collecting at the corners of his mouth. 'The prophecy...'

Urial looked out over the temple elders and raised the bloodstained sword, savouring their cries of dismay. Behind him came a slow procession of white-robed zealots, stiff and exhausted from their labours. Tyran led the way, his draich unsheathed by his side. He looked down at the crowd of elders and gave them the serene smile of an executioner. 'The Time of Blood is at hand!' the zealot leader proclaimed. 'Weep for the end of your world, you faithless curs! Khaine's truth gleams from the edge of the Scourge's blade. Prostrate yourselves at his feet and beg for his forgiveness!'

'Yes. Plead for a clean death to wash away your sins,' Urial hissed at the stricken throng. He brandished the warpsword at the crowd like a burning brand. 'When the cauldron spared me you knew that I was blessed by the Lord of Murder. You knew the prophecies of old, and yet you refused to believe the signs that were before your very eyes, because I was a cripple,' he spat, 'a bent and twisted man, unfit to wield a dagger, much less this sacred blade!' Urial took another slow step down the stairs. His face was taut with murderous rage and his eyes gleamed with savage glee.

'I say to you that these withered limbs were a warning, revealing your blindness and lack of faith! You chose the pleasing lie over the grim truth of Khaine's will, and you will reap the bitter fruit of your faithlessness!' The Swordbearer gave a bloodthirsty laugh. 'I have claimed the sword, and soon I shall take my magnificent bride. Then the world will burn – oh, how it will burn! – and we shall rise on a tide of blood as high as the stars themselves.' Urial levelled the warpsword at the temple elders. 'But these glories are not for the likes of you. The blood-witches will call you back and we will feed your guts to the ravens!'

'Be silent, heretic!' thundered the Grand Carnifex.

The crowd of elders fell away to either side from the fearsome master of the temple as he strode into the chapel and climbed onto the dais beside the bubbling cauldron. The Carnifex's face was a mask of fearsome, righteous rage, and fresh blood dripped from the long blade of his rune carved axe. The severed heads of the zealots slain outside the temple were clenched in his left fist, and his gold covered kheitan was smeared with dark splashes of gore. He was the image of an avenging hero, anointed in sacred blood, and the ferocious glare he laid upon Urial stopped the Swordbearer in his tracks.

'You are an abomination, Urial of Hag Graef,' the master of the temple proclaimed. 'You claim that the cauldron gave you back as a gift from Khaine, but I say the Lord of Murder spared you to test our beliefs, not fulfil them!' The Grand Carnifex surveyed the assembled elders, fixing each one with a stern glare. 'The will of the Bloody-Handed God is clear to the faithful: Malekith is his chosen Scourge, who will lead the faithful to glory!' He cast the severed heads into the cauldron and raised his axe to Urial. 'You are a deceiver and a false prophet,' he declared. 'You have defiled the holy sanctum and laid hands on the sacred blade of the Scourge.' The master of the temple stepped from the dais onto the steps, taking his axe in a two-handed grip. 'I condemn you and repudiate you, and it is my joyous duty to slay you in the Blood God's name!'

To Malus's surprise, Urial smiled and shook his head. 'The first man that dies by this blade is my half-brother. You aren't fit to bleed on my boots, you fraud.'

'Slay the blasphemer!' Tyran cried, and two zealots answered with a lusty roar, charging down the steps past Urial and brandishing their deadly blades. The Grand Carnifex met them with a howl of righteous fury, his axe whirling in deadly patterns as he advanced on Urial.

The charging zealots reached the Carnifex first, their blades flickering like lightning. The master of the temple gauged their advance, and with skill born of countless battles he shifted his stance and sidestepped to the left, meeting the left-most attacker blade to blade. The zealot's sword snapped as it met the temple master's ensorcelled axe, and the Carnifex responded with a lightning return stroke that split the man's torso crosswise, just beneath the ribs. His sudden dodge threw off the rightmost attacker's stroke just enough to spoil the man's killing blow, but not enough to fully escape the reach of the long blade. Malus felt the hot droplets of the old druchii's blood as the zealot's sword tore a deep cut through the Carnifex's side.

A torrent of blood and spilled organs tumbled down the steps around the temple master's feet as the two halves of the slain zealot emptied their contents onto the stairway. 'Blood and souls for Khaine!' the Grand Carnifex shouted, pivoting smoothly to meet the remaining zealot's charge. The old druchii parried a deft swing at his upper thigh and struck back with a reverse stroke at the zealot's head, but the robed warrior ducked nimbly beneath the blow. The zealot stepped into the temple master's guard with a blurring backspin, aiming an eviscerating cut at the Carnifex's midsection, but the old druchii gave ground and parried the blow against the long haft of his axe. The swordsman skidded slightly in the thick blood coating the stone steps, but with preternatural agility he checked his motion and leapt backwards, getting swinging room for his two-handed blade and chopping downwards into the Carnifex's right leg. The long sword bit deep into the meat of the temple master's thigh, but like an old, grizzled boar the Carnifex bellowed in rage and pressed the attack. Twisting slightly to trap the sword in the wound, the old druchii lashed out one-handed with his axe and hacked off the zealot's right arm just above the elbow.

The zealot let out a sharp hiss of pain, blood pumping from the severed limb, but his left hand tore the draich free from the temple master's leg and the swordsman got the long weapon into a defensive stance as the Carnifex lurched forwards. Drops of hot blood scattered like rain as the old druchii unleashed a barrage of blows against the zealot's faltering guard. On the third, ringing stroke the rune-carved axe snapped the draich just above the hilt and the curved blade buried itself in the zealot's face. Drunk on pain and slaughter the Grand Carnifex pulled the axe free and rounded on Urial. Laughing like a madman he ran his tongue along the edge of the gore-stained blade. 'The blood of slain warriors is sweet,' he proclaimed, 'but cowardice is bitter! I can smell your blood curdling to vinegar, Urial. The true Scourge of Khaine would not cower and leave others to fight on his behalf.'

The elders of the temple shouted their approval and the zealots responded with a maddened cry as the two sides threw themselves at one another. Robed figures poured around the dais like a black wave, surging up the stairs alongside their master as white-robed zealots rent the air with bloodthirsty howls and rushed to meet them. Blades flashed and rang and more blood poured down the black stairs as the battle was joined in earnest.

Amid the mayhem Malus felt strong hands grab his shoulders and try to pull him upright. Crying out in pain and coughing up more blood, the highborn tried to twist in the unseen grip and came round to find himself staring up into Arleth Vann's bloodstained face. 'Let go of me!' he croaked.
'Let go! You have to get to the Grand Carnifex. When Urial falls, you must claim the sword and bring it to me.'

The former assassin shook his head. 'It's hopeless,' he said in a dull voice. 'Urial has the warpsword. Not even the master of the temple can prevail against him.'

'But you can,' Tz'arkan whispered in Malus's head, 'with my help. Take it, Malus! Quickly, before it's too late!'

The highborn shook his head angrily. 'I don't need your damned help!' he gasped. His knees weakened and he slumped against Arleth Vann, who struggled to hold him upright. The ache in his guts belied his defiance. His lungs felt heavy, as if a great weight was pressing down on them, and a numbing coldness was spreading across his chest. Hissing in frustration, he tried to push himself back upright and catch a glimpse of Urial among the swirling melee raging on the stairway.

Urial and the Grand Carnifex raged at one another like demigods less than fifteen feet away, their sorcerous weapons striking showers of angry sparks as they clashed again and again in a flurry of artless, brutal blows. The master of the temple lashed at Urial relentlessly, but the former acolyte wielded the warpsword one-handed and blocked the Carnifex's two-handed blows with ease. Still, the Swordbearer was giving ground, falling back towards the sanctum one slow step at a time. Malus would have taken this as a good sign were it not for the vicious smile on Urial's gaunt face.

The master of the temple was weakening. Bleeding from deep wounds, any of which would have been enough to kill a lesser man, the old druchii was slowing a little with each murderous stroke. Whatever strength the Grand Carnifex had stolen from his foes was nearly spent, and Malus realised that with every step he took towards Urial he became more isolated from his fellow elders. He was already a solitary black figure in a surging sea of white.

With a bloodthirsty howl the old druchii feinted at Urial's waist, and then checked his swing and made a vicious, backhanded blow at the Swordbearer's knees. Again, Urial blocked the heavy blow with frightening speed, as if he was swinging nothing more than a willow-switch. The Grand Carnifex stumbled slightly, and Urial flicked his blade across the temple master's face, scattering a thin spray of blood. The old druchii barely flinched from the blow, redoubling his attack with a swipe at Urial's sword arm. Laughing, the former acolyte swayed back, letting the axe blade whistle through empty air. Then he straightened and slashed open the temple master's left arm from wrist to elbow.

Urial was toying with him, Malus realised, his heart sinking. He fumbled at his belt for his remaining throwing knife, but the hilt of the blade was slick with his own blood and slipped from his fingers. His bitter curse was lost amid the cacophony of screams and clashing blades echoing in the steamy air.

The Grand Carnifex reeled as Urial raked his blade across the old druchii's forehead. Another stroke sliced off the temple master's left ear. The wounded elder swayed on his feet, his chest heaving. Blood had soaked through his robes, making them gleam dully in the reddish light. Malus saw Urial say something to the Carnifex, but the words were lost in the tumult. The temple master responded with an angry shout and aimed a powerful stroke right at the centre of the Swordbearer's chest.

Urial blocked the blow easily, a smug expression on his face; one that turned to a look of horror as the canny old druchii hooked the blade of the sword with the beard of his axe and pulled the former acolyte off his feet. The Swordbearer crashed against the Grand Carnifex, his mouth gaping like a gaffed fish as the old druchii closed a powerful hand on Urial's narrow throat. The axe rose heavenward, trembling in the temple master's hand, and then plunged downwards into the former acolyte's left shoulder. Urial screamed in pain and fear as the sorcerous blade pierced his black armour and bit into flesh and bone.

For a moment, Malus thought Urial had dropped the sword. He saw the bloodstained blade dip, but then it flashed upwards, piercing the temple master's midsection and rising underneath the ribs until the point erupted from the elder's right collarbone. Both men froze for several long moments, and then the old druchii sagged, sinking to his knees.

A cry of horror went up from the temple elders as they saw their master fall, turning to wails of terror as Urial gritted his teeth and levered his blade upwards, splitting the old druchii's chest open like a slaughtered steer. The bloodstained axe fell from the temple master's lifeless hands, his ruptured body toppling onto its side.

'Blessed Mother of Night,' Malus hissed, as the zealots redoubled their attack and the temple elders recoiled in horror. He saw Urial searching the melee intently, and knew who his half-brother was looking for. The highborn looked to Arleth Vann. 'This is about to become a rout,' he snarled. 'We've got to get out of here!'

The former assassin nodded and without warning heaved Malus back onto the dais. Groaning in pain, the highborn pushed himself across the black marble, close enough to brush the lip of the brass cauldron in passing. He heard an exultant shout over the din: had Urial seen him? Fighting against waves of crushing pain he forced himself to crawl across the dais and into the crowd on the other side.

Shouts of panic and the frenzied cries of the zealots rang out behind Malus, and he felt the crowd around him surge backwards, like a black tide receding towards the far doorway. He let himself be borne along in the press, until he realised that the shouts of the dying were spreading around the sides of the dais like fire through tinder. Tyran and his men were closing in like a pack of wolves. Snarling angrily and spitting streams of dark blood, the highborn threw himself forwards, using the blade of his sword to batter his way through the panicked elders. He stumbled and kicked his way through piles of weathered skulls. 'Stand fast!' he managed to shout. 'Avenge your master and slay the unbelievers!'

If his words had any effect on the panicked elders and their men he could not say, but the men and women in front of him gave way rather than feel the bite of his sword. Arleth Vann appeared at his side, swords bared and facing back the way they'd come in case the zealots pressed too close.

They had forced their way through the far doorway within moments. Malus paused at the threshold and risked a backwards glance just as a great wail of despair went up from the servants of the temple. He saw that the zealots had swept past the dais and were wreaking a terrible slaughter among the panicked and demoralised elders. On top of the marble platform, shrouded in crimson steam, Urial the Forsaken stood before the great cauldron where he'd been sacrificed as a crippled babe, only to be reborn as one of Khaine's chosen. He held the Grand Carnifex's severed head over the mouth of the great vessel, letting streams of dark blood fall into its hissing brew. The Swordbearer's eyes were fever bright with divine madness, and his hateful gaze was fixed hungrily on Malus.

Then the contents of the cauldron erupted, showering Urial and the zealots with a rain of steaming fluids as Yasmir burst from the cauldron's depths. Heat shimmered from her naked form, and blood ran like quicksilver from her alabaster skin. Her raven hair had gone snowy white, and when her eyes opened Malus saw they were luminous and golden. They transfixed him, sinking like hooks into his labouring heart.

Yasmir smiled, revealing curved, leonine fangs. Long, black talons gleamed in the ruddy light as she gripped the edge of the cauldron and climbed gracefully onto the dais. The newborn blood-witch extended her sleek arm and beckoned to Malus, summoning him to her side.

Malus was already fleeing, stumbling like a child into the lesser sanctum with his own eyes screwed fearfully shut. He could still feel her stare upon him, like hot metal searing his skin.

He felt someone grab his arm as he stumbled on the broad stairway. After a dozen steps he dared open his eyes again and saw it was Arleth Vann at his side. Rhulan eyed him fearfully from the centre of the room. The Arch-Hierophant stood next to a slender female elder with a shaven head, her scalp tattooed in myriad intricate patterns that seemed to shift restlessly in the firelight. He had a fleeting memory of her in the Citadel of Bone, sitting in a throne almost directly across from the seat of the Grand Carnifex. She had to be the fifth member of the temple's Haru'ann. Malus suddenly realised that with the death of the Carnifex she and Rhulan were the only senior temple leaders still alive. They were surrounded by a thin cordon of temple retainers under the watchful eye of the young priestess that Malus had seen earlier.

'What has happened?' Rhulan asked, although from the look on his face it was clear that the elder already suspected the worst.

'We've failed,' Malus said bitterly. 'The Grand Carnifex is dead, and we're next if we don't get out of here.'

The tattooed woman gave Malus a look of contempt. 'You expect us to surrender the temple to a gang of heretics and thieves?' she snapped, her voice thick with a rustic northern accent.

'That's not a matter of debate,' the highborn shot back. 'You've already lost the temple. Your only choice is to stay here and throw your lives away or retreat and find another way to strike back.' He looked to Rhulan. 'We need real troops, and quickly. Are there any warriors left here at the fortress?'

Rhulan shook his head. 'We sent every swordsman and witch into the streets, hoping to overwhelm the zealots. If we sound the recall, the troops in the highborn district could be here within the hour.'

'By then it will be too late,' Malus snarled. He turned to ask something of Arleth Vann, but the question died on his lips. The highborn glanced back at Rhulan. 'What about the temple assassins?' he asked.

The Arch-Hierophant frowned. 'They have withdrawn into their tower to select a new master,' he said. 'After that they will swear vengeance upon the man who killed their former master and will not rest until he has been slain.'

Malus grinned. 'Is that so?' he asked. 'Well, then, I've got a proposition for them. If they want their vengeance they'll have to stop Urial from getting his first. Let's go.'

CHAPTER THIRTEEN

AMONG THE DEAD

At that moment a chorus of terrified wails erupted from the inner sanctum as the temple elders' courage finally gave out. The stream of wounded and demoralised temple servants pouring into the outer sanctum suddenly became a raging flood as scores of panicked druchii fled before Urial and his fearsome bride.

'Go!' Malus shouted at Rhulan. 'Gather your retainers and make for the temple doors.' Then he turned to face the tide of retreating temple servants and raised his bloodstained sword.

'Stand fast!' he roared, his face a mask of implacable rage. The shout was almost lost in the surf-like roar of the rout, but the leading rank of fleeing druchii saw the highborn's furious expression and pulled up short. He took a step towards the fearful elders. 'Turn and face the enemy! Defend your elders and the sanctity of the temple, for Khaine is watching!'

Each word was like a dagger, digging into Malus's chest. His lungs felt thick and swollen, and they couldn't seem to hold enough air. The daemon was right, Urial had wounded him badly. His chest heaved and he turned his head to spit a gobbet of blood onto the marble floor, but instead of fear, Malus felt only a black, boiling rage.

He stepped fearlessly into the press, forcing frightened men to either side. 'Skulls for the Blood God!' he cried, bloody foam flecking his thin lips. The front rank of temple servants turned with him, raising their weapons as Malus forced his way through the crowd towards the narrow door.

He knew that if he could reach the door they could hold it almost indefinitely. The battered temple retainers could form a tight ring around the portal and slay the zealots one at a time if they tried to fight their way through. The doorway was less than twenty feet away, but the path was crammed with thrashing, black-robed figures that contested each and every upward step. Malus snarled like a trapped wolf, laying about the men before him with the flat of his sword and eyeing the doorway with mounting dread. If the zealots could reach it before he did then all would be lost.

'Stand fast!' Malus shouted again, and succeeded in rallying the men closest to him. 'Drive for the door!' he ordered, and the men around him tried to force their way upwards, against the tide. The fleeing druchii pushed back, yelling and cursing. A temple retainer in front of Malus stabbed wildly at the highborn, and Malus split his skull without a moment's hesitation. He stepped into the gap the fallen man left behind and continued to press forwards. 'Hold them at the door!' he repeated. 'We'll stop them here!'

Had they been soldiers, accustomed to following orders amid the chaos of battle, the plan might have worked, but these were elders and temple acolytes, many of whom had not spilled another's blood except in temple rituals. The death of the Grand Carnifex and the slaughter visited upon them by the vengeful zealots had ground their courage to dust. Malus was halfway to the door when a chorus of thin cries rose to challenge his shouted commands.

'The Swordbearer is come! All hail Urial, the Scourge of Khaine!'

Men screamed as their fellow temple brethren turned on them, crying out Urial's name and stabbing their kin in hopes of saving themselves. The throng pressed with renewed vigour against Malus and his handful of rallied troops, but this time it was with knifepoints and axe-blades as well as elbows and fists.

The highborn heard the brittle snap of bones as the man in front of him was struck in the back by a retainer's axe. He fell with a gurgling scream, and his assailant pulled his weapon free with both hands and set upon Malus with a fevered gleam in his dark eyes. Malus blocked the frenzied axe-stroke with his upraised blade and then smashed the man in the face with the round pommel of his sword. The retainer staggered, fetching up against the men behind him, and Malus chopped his sword deep into the turncoat's neck.

A dagger lashed out from Malus's left, scoring a narrow track along his left bicep. He coughed and spat more blood, his breath coming in wet, rattling gasps. A short sword chopped at him from the right and Malus blocked the clumsy strokes without conscious thought. The crowd at the top of the stairs surged forwards. A man fell towards Malus, and he stabbed the druchii in the chest, unable to tell whether he was friend or foe. Then he saw it: a white sleeve spattered with red, holding up a bloodstained draich in front of the doorway to the inner sanctum. The zealots had seized the doorway to the sanctum, and there was no holding them back.

Another dagger reached for Malus. Unable to discern who held it in the tangle of bodies he took a swipe at the man's hand and severed a pair of fingers. Something sharp jabbed at his lower leg, causing him to shout in surprise. He stole quick glances left and right and saw the men beside him putting up a fight, but the weight of numbers had shifted against them. If they stayed where they were they would be overcome within minutes.

Malus gathered in as much breath as he could. 'Warriors of the temple!' he cried. 'One step back!'

The elders and their men eyed Malus with bewilderment, but their ragged line fell back a step. Several of the oncoming druchii overbalanced and fell at the feet of the retreating temple loyalists, and Malus was heartened to see his men despatch the turncoats with swift, merciless blows. The highborn risked a quick glance over his shoulder and saw Arleth Vann right behind him, his swords held low and to either side of his body. Malus noticed the rivulets of blood running from beneath both of the assassin's sleeves and dripping from his clenched fists, but the highborn had no doubt that his retainer could still fight and kill on command. 'We're retreating to the door!' he shouted. 'Watch our backs and keep the bastards from flanking us once we're off the stairs!'

Arleth Vann nodded grimly and turned his back on Malus, surveying the chapel floor.

'Warriors of the temple! One step back!' Malus commanded, and the retreat began in earnest.

The eighty paces back to the doorway were the longest steps of Malus's short life. Every loyal temple servant between Malus and the doorway was dead within moments and there was nothing in front of him but a bloodthirsty mob howling for his head. A man charged headlong at him, brandishing an axe, and the highborn dropped to one knee and stabbed the turncoat in the groin. Another rushed in and slashed for his face with a short sword. Malus pulled his sword from the axe man and blocked the sword stroke, forcing his assailant backwards with a jab to his face. He regained his feet and stepped backwards, taunting the men in front of him to try their luck against his blade.

And so it went: step, parry, kill and step again. As the temple loyalists came off the steps the mob spilled onto the chapel floor and lapped around the ends of the ragged line, slowly forcing the retreating fighters into a tight knot of weary men. The piled skulls on the chapel floor were a boon to the loyalists, breaking up the turncoat attacks so that they couldn't press the defenders from all sides. True to his word, Arleth Vann kept the line of retreat open, slaying every turncoat who crossed his path.

When they were slightly more than halfway to the doors, Malus was panting like a dog. Red spots swirled at the corners of his vision as he struggled for breath. He'd picked up a dagger from a fallen turncoat and fought on two-handed, blocking with the heavy northern sword and stabbing foes with the knife. He'd lost track of the number of men he'd killed. The rest paced in his wake like wolves, sensing that he was weakening and waiting for the right moment to strike. The highborn gasped like a landed fish, hardly daring to glance away from his opponents to see how well the rest of the loyalists were faring.

With each, halting breath he felt the daemon shift inside him, saying nothing but reminding him of its presence. Malus caught himself with the daemon's name on his lips, more than once, knowing that a single word could fill his lungs with fresh air and turn his blood to deadly ice. Each time he pushed temptation away with a snarl, although whether from fear or sheer, bloody-minded spite he could not say.

It was only when the turncoats redoubled their attacks that Malus knew they were nearly to the door. He heard the tempo of fighting increase to either side of him, and the three men who had been testing his defences for the last few minutes decided to rush him all at once. Two men held short, stabbing swords, while the druchii on the far right hefted a large, single bladed axe.

The axe man nearly got him, rushing forwards just as Malus tried to blink a swarm of bright spots from his eyes. He sensed more than saw the looming shape of his assailant and on instinct alone he leapt forwards and to the right, placing himself within the arc of the axe man's swing. Malus's attacker tried to adjust his aim by pivoting further to his right, but the move was a second too slow and his aim was poor, and the weapon struck one of the swordsmen in the back of the head instead. Before the axe man could recover Malus stabbed him twice in the chest and neck. Then he threw himself at the last swordsman, who was stepping over his fallen mate and thrusting his weapon at the highborn's throat. The turncoat's shorter blade meant he had to overextend himself in order to reach his target and the highborn made his foe pay dearly for it, sidestepping the thrust and chopping his sword deep into the side of the man's neck.

Malus risked a quick look backwards and saw the doorway only a few paces distant. Someone – probably one of Rhulan's men – had pulled the doors partly shut, so only one or two men could slip through at a time. Already there were only a bare handful of loyalists led by Arleth Vann remaining on the interior side of the door, barely keeping the escape route open. The highborn would have laughed out loud if he'd had the wind for it. Instead he turned back to the bloodthirsty turncoats, and found himself face to face with one of Tyran's zealots. The swordsman held his gore-crusted draich at the ready, a rapt smile on his face.

I can't beat him, damn it. I can barely breathe, he thought. Still, he leapt at the man with a rasping shout, holding his dagger close and feinting at the zealot's face to gauge his prowess. The swordsman was clearly spent from his exertions performing the Swordbearer's rite, because his killing stroke was just barely slow enough for Malus to block the blow with the flat of his dagger. Malus retreated from the swordsman, chest heaving, and the zealot glided after him, his expression hungry and intent.

Malus angled his course to head for the doorway, hoping his memory and blurred eyesight hadn't deceived him. He threw another short jab at the zealot's eyes, and pulled back just in time to avoid having his sword arm taken off at the elbow.

The zealot laughed. 'You disgrace yourself, blasphemer,' he said. 'I had hoped you would be a worthy foe, but you puff and stumble like a drunkard. Why don't you throw down your swords and accept Khaine's cold mercy?'

A ghostly grin came and went from Malus's bloody lips. 'Because I know something you don't.'

The zealot frowned. 'Such as?'

'Such as my retainer is about to stab you in the side of the neck.'

The swordsman whirled, raising his blade in a blurring defensive move. Malus leapt at the same time, catching the zealot's left arm at the crook of his elbow and shearing straight through it. The zealot staggered, but before he could regain his senses the highborn finished him off with a thrust to his neck.

Arleth Vann finished off the turncoat in front of him and took a step back, reaching Malus's side. He gave his master an accusatory look. 'I heard what you said,' he declared sternly, 'suggesting I would interfere in a sacred duel!'

'I'm a bit surprised he fell for it myself,' Malus replied. He grabbed the assassin by a blood soaked sleeve and pulled him back through the doorway. Wide-eyed druchii stood to either side of the threshold, their hands gripping the edges of the tall, oak doors.

'Shut them! Hurry!' Malus ordered. 'They're almost upon us!'

The retainers leapt to obey, pulling hard on the heavy panels. Frantic, bloodstained faces appeared in the narrowing gap and hands pounded fearfully on the closing doors. A pale hand shot through the gap, reaching desperately for Malus. With a curse the highborn stepped to the side and brought his sword down on the offending limb, severing it in a spray of blood. The loyalist's agonised shriek was lost in the heavy thud of the doors slamming shut.

Malus turned and sought out Rhulan, who stood ashen faced at the foot of the temple steps. 'Can you seal it?'

The temple elder started at Malus's voice, as if lost in a reverie. 'Seal?' he asked, blinking owlishly.

'The door, damn you!' the highborn snapped, his voice so sharp that Rhulan and his retainers flinched at the sound. 'Do you know some sorcery to lock the doors?'

'Oh, yes. Of course.' Rhulan strode forwards, raising his right hand. 'Step away from the doors,' he said.

Malus and Arleth Vann cleared the steps, and the rest of the temple servants scattered to either side. The heavy doors began to swing open almost immediately, giving vent to a chorus of fierce cries and pounding fists. A severed head rolled through the widening gap, bouncing wetly down the wide steps to stop at Malus's feet.

Then Rhulan straightened to his full height and spoke a single word of power that crackled in the air like the lash of a whip. He made a fist with his upraised hand and the twin doors slammed shut with a thunderous boom.

Malus nodded in weary satisfaction, revising his opinion of the frail-looking Rhulan somewhat. He quickly took stock of the motley band of loyalists who'd escaped the debacle within the temple. Rhulan had six men and women standing in a loose circle around him, and Malus saw the tattooed elder standing a short distance away, surrounded by her own coterie of retainers and hangers-on, including the axe-wielding priestess he'd seen fighting earlier. Four more loyalists stood near Malus at the foot of the steps. They were all that remained of the meagre force he'd led out of the building.

Out of the hundred druchii who'd followed the Grand Carnifex from the Citadel of Bone, less than twenty remained. Malus shook his head bitterly and tried to curse, but all he could manage was a wet, wracking cough that sent spasms of pain through his chest. He swayed on his feet, but Arleth Vann steadied him with a bloodstained grip.

'Are you well?' Rhulan asked, his face paling further.

With an effort, Malus bit back a sharp-tongued reply. He spat another mouthful of blood onto the ground and took a strangled breath. 'Well enough,' he managed to say.

'We haven't long,' the elder said, his voice hollow. 'What do we do?'

The daemon stirred. 'Listen to him,' Tz'arkan whispered. 'Time is running out for you, little druchii. You must choose.'

A sharp spike of pain lanced through Malus's chest, almost doubling him over with its intensity. Again, Arleth Vann's grip steadied him, but Malus jerked his arm away. With nothing but bitter rage to sustain him, he forced himself upright.

'We go talk to these assassins of yours,' he said through clenched teeth, 'and then we put an end to these fanatics once and for all.'

After the ivory eminence of the Citadel of Bone and the dwarf-wrought glory of the temple, Malus had no idea what to expect from the sanctum of the temple's holy assassins. A razor-edged keep wrought entirely of steel? A palace of ruby and garnet? Many fanciful visions passed through his mind as Arleth Vann shepherded him across the temple grounds.

It turned out to be a hole in the ground.

More accurately, it was accessed by a long, spiralling path, almost a hundred and twenty paces across, that wound its way deep into the earth. Large witchfire globes surrounded the perimeter of the wide spiral, throwing shifting patterns of light across the narrow pathways. The path was wide enough for only one traveller at a time, and it was formed of dark, crimson glass that glimmered like fresh blood in the sorcerous light.

Rhulan took the lead. The temple retainers – even the fearsome priestess with her bloodstained axe – looked to one another apprehensively as they fell into line behind their masters. Even Arleth Vann seemed hesitant to begin the descent, although Malus suspected that he had very practical reasons for avoiding his former comrades. He didn't expect that the silent knives of Khaine nurtured any compassion for those who broke their oaths and deserted the order.

The descent seemed to go on forever. It was fully five minutes of slow, methodical pacing before they'd completed the first circuit and began to sink below the earth. Malus gritted his teeth, one hand pressed against the wound in his chest, and expected to hear the sounds of pursuit at any moment. He couldn't imagine that Urial would be delayed overmuch by Rhulan's ward, nor would he waste a single moment in setting the hounds on his trail.

It was almost another five minutes before they were fully below ground. What in the Dark Mother's name was taking so long, he wondered? Were there traps for the unwary? Poison needles or voracious spirits? Everyone ahead of him seemed to be studying the path at their feet with intense interest. Concentrating on keeping his breathing even, Malus followed suit, watching the gleaming red stones for telltale pressure plates or tripwires.

On and on they went. The smell of damp earth filled his nostrils, and when they had passed beyond the light of the braziers their path was lit with the faint effulgence of grave mould, glowing from niches on the glistening stone walls.

He soon lost track of time. One step led to the next, their pace neither speeding up nor slowing down. A tight band of pain began to constrict around his chest, and from time to time a drop of blood would slip past his lips and fall heavily to the pathway. His breath bubbled in his throat, as if he was caught in the grip of a terrible ague. He heard the daemon whispering in his ears, but the sound was strangely faint, like the murmur of the tides, and he paid it little heed.

After a time Malus began to sense that their curving path was shrinking, drawing tighter and tighter with each revolution. He took heart, realising that they must be close to their destination, but he was careful not to get complacent and take his gaze from the perilous floor.

Not long afterwards he watched his steps glide across a narrow threshold, and looked up to see that they had reached a small, circular chamber carved from dark stone. Globes of witchlight gleamed from the walls, worked into carvings of dragons and leering daemons. Double doors stood on the opposite side of the circle. Rhulan gave the party a single backwards glance, his expression clearly indicating that they should wait here, and then went to stand before the doors. He spoke not a word, nor rapped upon the wooden panels, but nevertheless one door swung silently open, allowing him to slip inside.

After Rhulan was gone many of the loyalists sank wearily to the stone floor. Some checked their injuries, while others slumped into an exhausted stupor. The tattooed elder drew apart from the rest and sat with her back to one of the curving walls, closing her eyes as if to meditate or pray. The axe-wielding priestess sat, and then stood, and finally began to pace like a caged lion, her expression distant and vengeful.

Malus declined to sit as well, not so much out of nervousness, but because he wasn't certain he could get up again if he did. It was bad enough that Arleth Vann had to see him in such a weakened state; he would be damned if anyone had to carry him. The assassin leaned against the wall beside the entryway, resting his head against the carved stone. His gaunt features were scabbed with dried blood, and the front of his sleeves and kheitan were stiff and dark with gore.

The highborn glanced back the way they'd come. 'All that caution, and not a single trap or alarm,' he said. 'It appears that the assassins are less fearsome than their reputation suggests.'

Arleth Vann looked up at him, a bemused expression on his face. 'What are you talking about?'

Malus pointed back at the curving path. 'All that checking for traps,' he said, 'totally unnecessary.'

'Traps?' the retainer said. 'That was a labyrinth, my lord. A journey of meditation. Who lays traps in a labyrinth?'

The highborn blinked. 'Oh, well, no one, I suppose.' He frowned. 'What assassins' order forces you to walk a labyrinth to reach them?'

Arleth Vann studied his master for several moments, uncertain whether or not he was being mocked. 'We are not mere cutthroats, my lord,' he said at last. 'The Shayar Nuan are a holy order, much like the executioners or the temple witches.'

Malus raised an eyebrow at the name. 'The Blessed Dead? Is that what they call themselves?'

'That is the name we call ourselves,' the assassin said. He gave Malus one of his ghostly smiles. 'Now that you've heard it I have to kill you, of course.'

The highborn glowered at his servant. 'You speak as if you are still one of them.'

Arleth Vann shrugged. His brass-coloured eyes were haunted. 'We are Shayar Nuan when we emerge from the cauldron, my lord. Nothing can take that away.'

'I don't understand. I thought the cauldron was reserved only for sacrifices.'

The assassin sighed, trying to find a way to explain. 'Yes and no, my lord. The witches of the temple bathe in the cauldron. It is the source of their terrible allure and ageless vigour,' he said. 'That power is indeed born from sacrifice: prisoners, criminals, the weak and the crippled, as well as every neophyte assassin. It is the final rite of passage. We die, yet live on in service to Khaine.'

Malus peered closely at the assassin. 'You don't mean to say you're actually dead?'

'It's a metaphor, my lord. You're familiar with the term?'

'Don't get flippant with me,' Malus snarled weakly. 'In case you've forgotten, I was stabbed with a sword not too long ago, and I'm not in the mood.'

'Your pardon, my lord,' the retainer replied.

'Besides, with everything else I've seen in this damned city, I wouldn't be at all surprised.'

'No, I suppose not,' Arleth Vann replied. 'All right, consider this: how do you kill a man who is already dead?'

Malus considered the question. 'Cut off his head and limbs and burn the bits. It's the only way to be certain.'

The assassin's brow furrowed. 'I begin to see why your father never considered sending you to the temple,' he said. 'Let me be blunt: the greatest power a man can have is the ability to take the life of another. That is the central tenet of the executioners. If a man is already dead, however, not even the blessed swords of Khaine can touch him. He is a ghost, fearing nothing of this world or the next.'

Malus grunted, touching off a spasm of coughing. 'Interesting,' he said, wiping his mouth with the back of his hand. 'If I recall, you said that the order was a recent invention, not originally part of the Lord of Murder's cult.'

Arleth Vann eyed the other Khaineites warily. 'That is so,' he admitted softly. 'The Witch King needed a way to eliminate threats to the state without risking open war with the noble houses, and the temple needed a new reason to justify its authority after the last of the warlocks had been killed.' He shrugged. 'In the past, those who survived the depths of the cauldron were taken by the witches and trained in the ways of the cult. Many became priests, and others lived as exalted oracles or scholars. The temple elders gave them a new calling: the art of stealth and silent murder, a combination of the witch's magic and the executioner's skill.'

'And Urial was trained in these arts?'

The assassin shook his head. 'No, according to all reports, he was a voracious scholar and a potent sorcerer, but that was all. His deformities precluded him from mastering the arts of combat. As far as I know, he was never considered for inclusion into the order, nor could he truly be considered a priest, for even elders like Rhulan must be ready and able to march to war. Honestly, I don't think anyone quite knew what to do with your brother.'

'It's a pity they never asked me. I could have offered a number of pointed suggestions.' Malus studied the closed doors. 'Do you think they will help us, now that Urial has the sword?'

Arleth Vann shrugged. 'Truly, it's hard to say. Like the blood-witches of old, the order professes to take no interest in the affairs of the temple. Indeed, much of the witches' prestige and authority has been ceded to the assassins over the centuries. They may see Urial as usurping Malekith's role as the Scourge, or they may not care who wields the warpsword so long as Khaine's will is done.'

Another sharp jolt of pain stabbed through Malus. His breath was coming in shallow draughts, and shadows crowded at the edges of his vision. He knew that time was running out. Where was Rhulan? What was taking so long?

'It appears they need some persuading,' he said grimly, and lurched towards the doors.

Arleth Vann let out a startled shout, but Malus was at the doorway before anyone could react. He placed his hands against the cold, damp oak and pushed.

The doors opened easily, giving way to cave-like darkness. Without hesitation, Malus plunged through. He walked blindly forwards, expecting any moment to smash into a wall or plunge off the edge of a pit. He dimly heard Arleth Vann shouting his name, but he paid no mind.

After only a few moments he saw a dim light up ahead. A few steps later he could make out three figures, two standing and one kneeling before them. Malus guessed that the kneeling figure had to be Rhulan, and a dozen strides later, his suspicions were confirmed.

The Arch-Hierophant knelt in a circle of faint luminescence that seemed to emanate from the very air itself. Two robed figures stood before him, their faces hidden within deep hoods.

Rhulan glanced back fearfully at Malus's approach. His eyes widened as he recognised who it was. 'Blessed Murderer! What are you doing here? You were supposed to wait!'

'Time is more precious than gold at the moment,' Malus seethed, 'and we are growing poorer by the second.' He faced the hooded men. 'Are you among the elders of the order?'

One of the figures stepped forwards. 'The elders are in conclave,' a young man's voice replied. He reached up and drew back his hood, revealing the boyish features and dark eyes of an initiate.

Malus pointed at Rhulan. 'Do you not know who he is, boy?'

'Of course,' the initiate replied, 'but he has brought no blood tithe and nor have you. Not even the Grand Carnifex may speak to the elders without a suitable offering. The commandments of the order are clear-'

The highborn's hurled dagger struck the initiate in the forehead with a meaty thunk. The boy's body quivered for a moment, his mouth frozen in mid-sentence, and then the corpse collapsed to the floor.

Malus turned to the second hooded figure. 'All right,' he said coldly. 'There is my blood tithe. Take me to the elders.'

Rhulan let out a strangled gasp. The hooded figure considered the dead acolyte for a moment, and then faced Malus. 'Your tithe is... acceptable,' he said, 'but the elders are choosing a new master. They will speak to no one until their sacred duty is complete.'

'Do you not realise that a usurper has stolen the Warpsword of Khaine and killed the Grand Carnifex? If we do not move against him quickly he will seize the temple and then the city beyond!'

The figure said nothing.

Furious, Malus tried another tack. 'Are you not bound to avenge the death of your fallen master?'

'Yes,' the figure replied.

'Well it was I who slew him!' the highborn declared. 'I beat the fat oaf's brains out with a hunk of broken marble. If your damned elders don't get off their arses and do something about Urial, he'll kill me and rob them of their revenge.'

Someone shouted angrily. Malus couldn't be certain who it was. The room started to spin. A fierce jolt of pain shot through him, but with a shout of rage he fought to stay upright. The highborn groped for his sword, but powerful hands seized his arms and pulled him from his feet.

Malus never felt himself hit the ground.

He was floating through darkness. A hot wind hissed across his face and strange sounds echoed in his ears.

Visions came and went in brief, red flashes. He saw stone walls and robed men, twisting passages and narrow stairs. After a time he realised he was being carried, but he could not guess where or why.

Sometimes the sounds resolved themselves into voices, echoing in close, dark spaces. Sometimes they whispered, sometimes they shouted. He tried to answer them, but no words would come.

The next thing he knew, he was cold. No, he was laying on something cold. He tasted blood. There was another red flash, and Malus flinched, blinking in the sudden glare. Arleth Vann loomed over him, his pale face mere inches from Malus's own. Brass-coloured eyes peered deep into his.

Malus tried to speak. The sounds that came in response to his efforts were barely recognisable. 'Where... are... we?'

The assassin's face receded. The torchlight painted a wall of rock to Malus's right, revealing deep niches set at regular intervals from floor to ceiling. Skulls and piles of bones shone dully in the flickering light.

'Among the dead,' Arleth Vann replied. Then darkness closed in once more.

CHAPTER FOURTEEN

CONTEMPLATING THE ABYSS

A hot wind blew over Malus, tangling his unbound hair and blowing fine, rasping sand across his face. Flat plains stretched for miles, lifeless and inimical.

He lay on his chest, facing north, staring at the broken line of iron dark mountains that reared up from the edge of the burning world. Malus knew that one of the mountains had a cleft in it, as if it had been split by the axe-stroke of a god. At the foot of that mountain, in a dead and withered wood, there was a road of dark stones that led to an ancient temple.

He'd tried to do his part. He had tried to gather up all five of the lost relics, but in the end he'd failed. It was too much: too much for any one man to do.

Now the sands were running out. They were stolen from him by the desert wind, streaming away into the pale white sky.

He tried to rise to his knees, but his body refused to obey. A hot pain burned like a coal beneath his skin, stealing his breath away. He'd crawled for miles upon miles, trying to reach the temple and beg the daemon to release his tainted soul. Terror gripped him as the hour drew near, when Tz'arkan would claim his soul for all time.

A hand, cool and strong, gripped his shoulder. Sharp, writhing pain made him cry out as he was turned onto his back. Harsh, white light burned through his clenched eyelids. Then a shadow covered him, blotting out the merciless sun.

He felt a caress along the line of his blistered cheek. The skin was rough, calloused at fingertip and palm.

'Do you suffer, my lord?' her voice, throaty and deep, reminded him of the slave cruise, and the time before the daemon's curse.

'I have to get to the temple,' he croaked, his breath coming in bubbling gasps. His clumsy fingers pawed at the ragged tear in his robes. 'I'm hurt,' he said, bitter tears carving tracks through the grime caking his face. 'There is a daemon inside me–'

'Hush, my lord,' she said, 'the corruption has made you mad. I shall not let the daemon have you. Do not fear.'

Gentle fingertips probed at the tear. Malus opened his eyes and looked up into Lhunara's face. She smiled, causing the blood-filled orb that had been her right eye to bulge from its ruined socket. Blood and vile fluids seeped from the terrible wound in her skull and maggots writhed in the rotting brain matter, disturbed by the terrible heat.

Her fingers wriggled into the tear and then the open wound beneath. He felt the cold digits grasp the inside of his ribs and he screamed as she flexed her arms and pulled his ribcage apart. Flesh and bone parted with a rotten, tearing sound.

She lowered her face to the gaping hole and started to feed, tearing at his organs like a wolf, and it was all he could do to open his mouth and scream.

Hands shook him, gently at first, and then insistently. 'Wake up, my lord. For the Murderer's sake, wake up!'

Malus awoke, his rising scream silenced by a spasm of wracking coughs. His body was cold and damp, and his joints ached from lying on unyielding stone. He rolled onto his side, spitting clots of blood and phlegm from his mouth and struggling for a decent breath.

He lay on a mortuary slab in a small, rectangular cell. Its previous occupant, some withered temple elder from centuries past, had been dumped unceremoniously on the rough-hewn floor. Long niches lined the walls, filled with the tattered skeletons of favoured retainers and allies. A small oil lamp guttered from one of the higher niches, shedding a dim yellow light onto the ancient crypt. The air was dank and thick with dust, coating the back of his aching throat.

Strong hands gripped his shoulders, touching off a thrill of terror as he relived the last moments of his nightmare. He tried to fight back, but a fist of agony clenched around his left lung, leaving him near senseless with pain. Arleth Vann pulled his master back down onto the slab, studying him with concern.

'You had a nightmare, my lord,' he said quietly. 'It must have been a terrible one. I don't think I've ever heard you scream before.'

Malus wiped his face with a trembling hand. 'That's just because you haven't spent much time with me lately,' he replied, attempting a half-hearted smile. 'I've had occasion to hone my vocal skills over the last several months.' He pushed aside the retainer's hands and tried to sit up. 'Where in the Dark Mother's name are we?'

'Deep in the tombs,' the assassin replied. 'By the time we'd emerged from the assassin's sanctum Urial had already broken through the temple door and was well on his way to seizing the entire temple fortress. The great gates had been opened and a large force of zealots had slipped inside, reinforcing Urial's small band. They were killing every slave they could find and rounding up all the remaining acolytes. It was all we could do to sneak past their hunting parties and lose ourselves in the catacombs.'

Malus winced as another stabbing pain shot through his chest, but he refused to lie back down again. 'How long have I been out?'

'You've been in and out for most of a day,' the assassin said. He nodded to the narrow doorway over his shoulder. 'Rhulan and the rest are in the antechamber beyond. They haven't stopped bickering since we got here.'

The highborn muttered a curse. 'An entire day,' he said bitterly. 'Urial grows stronger with every minute. Do we know what is happening on the hill?'

Arleth Vann shrugged. 'I made a trip to the surface a few hours ago, hoping to get some food and water from the kitchens and maybe some hushalta,' he said. 'Urial is in complete control of the temple, and he's closed the fortress gates to the temple warriors still out in the city. Much of Har Ganeth continues to burn, and I could hear sounds of fighting in the highborn district.'

Malus nodded thoughtfully. 'A damned brilliant plan,' he admitted. 'Urial holds all the advantages.' He tried to slide his legs off the slab, grimacing in pain. 'If we don't do something very soon, all will be lost.'

Arleth Vann reached for the highborn. 'My lord, I'm not sure you should be moving,' he said. 'Your wound...' He paused, his face troubled.

Malus stopped. 'What about my wound?'

The retainer considered his words carefully. 'The warpsword pierced between your ribs and punctured your left lung,' he said. 'There was bloody froth on your lips, and you were gasping for air. Most men die from such a wound, even with the aid of a chirurgeon. Indeed, there were times during the morning when I was certain that you were about to take your last breath.'

'But?' the highborn enquired.

Arleth Vann started to reply, but words failed him. Helplessly, he pointed to the cut in Malus's robe.

Malus looked down, realising for the first time that his kheitan had been stripped off and his robe loosened. He felt a twinge of dread as he reached up with tentative fingers and pulled the dark cloth aside.

Arleth Vann had evidently used some of his plundered water to clean Malus's wound as best he could. The skin on the left side of his chest was mottled with dark, indigo-coloured bruises from his breastbone all the way to his navel. The puncture was a neat line almost as long as his finger, running between his fifth and sixth ribs. The ache in his back told him that a similar wound was present there as well.

The skin around the puncture was almost solid black. The injury itself was sealed shut, bound by a rope of thick, black tissue that wept a pale, foul smelling liquid.

Mother of Night, Malus thought, his blood running cold. What has Tz'arkan done to me?

Arleth Vann pointed hesitantly at the highborn's wound. 'I... I've never seen anything like that, my lord,' he said. 'What is it?'

Corruption, he thought, remembering Lhunara's words. The daemon's grip on his body was far worse than he'd imagined possible. Suddenly he remembered the stab wound he'd received in the battle on the Slavers' Road. He ran a hand over his thigh, finding not so much as a scab or scar. It was all he could do not to cry out in fear.

I'm teetering on the abyss, he thought. One more step, and I'm lost!

Belatedly, Malus realised that Arleth Vann was watching him, his expression growing more disturbed with each passing moment. He groped about for an explanation. 'It's... it's the blessing of Khaine,' he said. 'Am I not his Scourge?'

A cruel chuckle echoed in Malus's head. It was all he could do not to clench his fists and try to beat that sound out of his skull. 'What of you?' Malus asked, eager to think about something else. He studied his retainer's filthy, tattered robes and bloodstained skin. 'I saw what Yasmir did to you with her knives.'

The retainer averted his eyes, apparently willing to accept Malus's explanation, although his expression remained troubled. 'The wounds in my arms will heal,' he said simply. 'The witches teach us techniques to speed the healing process and knit torn flesh. As for the rest...' He reached up and pulled back a flap of his own robe. The faint light gleamed off polished rings of fine, close-set mail stitched to the inside of the assassin's clothes. 'They weren't as bad as they looked.'

Malus hazarded a weak chuckle. 'I thought you and your kin had no fear of death.'

The assassin shrugged. 'I don't fear death, my lord, but that's no reason to make things easy for my foes.'

Suddenly a heated exchange of words echoed from the antechamber beyond the tiny crypt. 'Speaking of making things easier on our foes,' Malus said. He drew as deep a breath as he could manage, and was both surprised and frightened to discover that he was breathing much easier than before. Then slowly, painfully, he pushed himself off the stone slab. His legs threatened to give way beneath him. Arleth Vann leaned forwards, reaching for him, but Malus waved him away. Another deep breath, and a measure of strength returned. The highborn adjusted his robes, cinching them tight, and then headed for the doorway.

Two more oil lamps threw fitful light on a rectangular chamber some thirty paces long. More crypt entrances, many still sealed by thin wooden doors, lined both of the long walls of the room, while larger entryways opened onto subterranean darkness at either of the short ends of the chamber. Alcoves had been carved into every free space on all of the room's walls and piled with skulls and cloth-wrapped bones. Ancient statuary lay in broken, moss-covered piles in each of the four corners, their original appearance long lost to the mists of time.

Rhulan stood in the centre of the room, glaring hotly at the young priestess who'd fought so well in the battle at the temple. Her hands were open in supplication, but Malus could see a steely glint in her eyes. There was a hint of anger and desperation in her voice. 'We deserve answers, Arch-Hierophant,' she said. 'If Urial is not the Swordbearer, how could this have happened?'

All eyes were on Rhulan. Every one of the temple loyalists sat on the bare stone floor, watching the exchange with hope and dread in equal measures. Even the tattooed elder had taken keen interest in the argument, sitting with her back to one of the piled sculptures, a pair of broad bladed knives lying naked in her lap.

'Does the writ of the temple not teach us that Malekith, lord and Witch King, is Khaine's chosen Scourge?' the priestess continued. 'Was the blade not bound by chains of sorcery, warding it so that only the Swordbearer could draw it forth?'

Malus saw a glimmer of fear in Rhulan's eyes. His lip trembled as he struggled for an answer. It looks as if he's living his worst nightmare, the highborn thought.

'No ward is perfect,' Malus interjected, causing everyone to jump. Startled faces turned to regard the highborn as if he'd risen from the dead.

'Urial is a potent sorcerer in his own right,' Malus continued, leaning against the doorframe for support, 'and has he not spent years studying the temple's lore? He's had plenty of time to uncover a means to circumvent the magic protecting the sword.'

'But the sword is meant for the Scourge alone.'

Malus studied Rhulan carefully. The elder was clearly very nervous. He knows that the sword has passed through many hands over the centuries, the highborn thought. Have they told the faithful it was passed directly from Khaine to the hands of the temple? 'The sword may be meant for the Scourge, but cannot others bear it? Wield it, even? After all, how long had the elders kept it before they came to Har Ganeth?'

The priestess glanced at Malus, her brow wrinkling in thought. 'Are we certain he is not the Scourge?'

'I am,' Malus said with utter conviction. He eyed Rhulan. *I'm not so certain about the Arch-Hierophant, though.*

'Malekith is the chosen one,' Rhulan said weakly, 'so it is written.'

'Then you had best get the blade out of Urial's hands before the Witch King learns of this,' Malus said.

'Why is that?' the tattooed elder asked, fixing Malus with a penetrating stare. 'This is a matter for the temple to resolve.'

Malus shook his head. 'Not if word of this coup makes it to the other cities,' he said. 'Malekith cannot see it as anything less than a challenge to his authority. He will have to take the sword from Urial, if only to prove that it is his by right. If other members of the temple decide that Urial is the true Scourge, the resulting feud could tear Naggaroth apart.'

'Blessed Murderer!' Rhulan said, placing a trembling hand over his mouth. 'What are we going to do?'

'We're going to fight them,' Malus said grimly. 'You should have been out in the city hours ago, rallying the faithful behind your banner. In a battle like this, the side that seizes the initiative will triumph, and I guarantee that Urial has already started moving against you.'

The priestess frowned. 'Urial can't possibly stop us,' she said. 'He has his zealots, but we have a small army at our command.'

'Urial has more than just his true believers,' Malus said. 'He has an entire city to call upon. Everything the zealots have done up to this point is to turn the citizens of Har Ganeth against the warriors of the temple. They goaded the temple into a campaign of fire and slaughter, and then they locked them out of their safe refuge, leaving them at the mercy of the people they savaged. Once Urial shows the people that he has taken up the sword and condemns the warriors of the church for their crimes, the streets will run red once more.' He pointed to the two elders. 'You must escape the fortress and rally the faithful. Denounce Urial and blame yesterday's bloodshed on the zealots, and then hunt down the heretics remaining in the city and turn your attention to retaking the fortress.'

The elder gave Malus a stricken look. 'We can't fight Urial,' he said.

'Why not?'

'The bearer of the warpsword cannot be defeated in battle,' the elder replied. 'So it is written.'

Malus started to argue, but then he understood. *You think Urial really is the chosen one*, he thought. *You know the truth about the prophecy, and you're trapped between the Witch King and the man you believe is the true Scourge.*

'Leave Urial to me,' the highborn said. 'I will remain behind with a handful of volunteers and strike the usurper directly while your forces hold his attention at the fortress gates.'

Rhulan said nothing for a moment, his dark eyes narrowing as he considered Malus's plan. Finally, he nodded. 'So be it.' He turned to the assembled loyalists. 'Mereia and I must join our brothers and sisters in the city. Who will remain behind and take the battle to the usurper?'

'I want no more than a dozen,' Malus said. 'We will have to strike hard and fast. Even then, there is little chance that many of us will survive.'

The priestess turned to the highborn, raising her chin haughtily. 'I will stay,' she said. Other druchii rose to their feet, singly or in small groups. Malus counted only ten, but he wasn't going to press the issue.

Rhulan surveyed the volunteers and nodded. 'The blessings of the Lord of Murder be upon you, brothers and sisters,' he proclaimed. 'Khaine's will be done.'

'Khaine's will be done,' the faithful answered.

Mereia, the tattooed elder, rose smoothly to her feet. 'How will we escape from the fortress?'

Malus looked to Arleth Vann.

'Take the winding staircase and follow the ancient road to Thel's house,' the assassin said. 'Even if there are guards watching the passage, you could still slip past them in the darkness. You could even call the maelithii down on them if you could fight your way to within sight of their iron anchors.'

Rhulan nodded. 'Then let us go. Every moment is precious.' As Mereia and their escorts gathered up their weapons, the Arch-Hierophant stepped close to the highborn.

'Are you certain you are capable of this?' he asked, studying Malus's face intently. 'Your wounds are grave.'

'I have suffered worse,' Malus said evenly. 'Never fear, Rhulan. I will fulfil my part of the plan. See that you do the same.'

'The fate of the temple – perhaps Naggaroth itself – rests in your hands. So far, Urial has yet to put the sword to the test, and if we can deal with him before he reveals the sword to the people then no one ever has to know this happened,' the elder said quietly. 'How will you separate Urial from the sword?'

Malus shrugged. 'I don't know for certain, but I expect it will involve a bit of bloodshed.'

'Remember what I said,' Rhulan whispered. 'Everyone knows the sword cannot be defeated in battle. You must find another way to best Urial and take the blade from him, and once in your possession it must never be used, by you or anyone else. Swear it!'

The highborn gave the elder a bemused look. 'As you wish, Arch-Hierophant.'

Rhulan nodded. 'Good. Very good. When you have the sword, bring it to me, and you will be well rewarded.'

Malus fought to keep his expression neutral. *What are you playing at now*, he wondered?

Before he could inquire further, a faint sound echoed from the dark passageway to Malus's left. Everyone in the antechamber froze upon hearing it.

'What is that?' the priestess whispered, clutching her axe.

The sound faded, but the echoes still lingered in Malus's mind. Setting his jaw, he slowly drew his sword.

'It sounded like a howl,' he said.

CHAPTER FIFTEEN

THE ABODE OF THE DEAD

The cry came again – a thin, almost despairing sound that wound faintly down the corridors of the crypt. The Khaineites shared apprehensive looks.

Malus looked to Arleth Vann. The assassin drew his twin blades, his expression tense. 'Whatever it is, it's coming this way,' the retainer said.

'Could it be a wight or a guardian spirit?' the highborn asked.

Rhulan answered, a quaver of fear in his voice. 'We built these tombs to contain the dead, not give them free rein.'

'Then I believe Urial has come looking for us,' Malus growled.

Mereia rose gracefully to her feet. 'What do we do?'

'You and Rhulan get out of here. Now.' Malus said. 'We'll buy you as much time as we can.'

The howl echoed down the eastern passage once again – then dissolved into a chorus of shrieking, gobbling cries that seemed to draw nearer by the moment. Galvanised by the horrific sounds, Rhulan, Mereia and their escorts dashed for the western corridor. The tattooed elder gave Malus a comradely nod as she passed. 'Kill one for me,' she said, drawing a vicious grin from the highborn.

Rhulan's parting look was far grimmer, as he paused at the mouth of the passageway and turned his gaze on the highborn. 'Remember what I said,' he said. 'The future of the temple depends on it.'

'I'll do what must be done,' Malus said gravely. 'Count upon it.' Providing I live through the next ten minutes, he thought.

He was in no shape to fight, of that alone he was certain. The wound in his chest ached when he moved, and his limbs felt clumsy and weak. Unbidden, he thought of the daemon. A taste, just the merest taste of Tz'arkan's power would make all the difference.

Could he take one more sip from the font of corruption without losing himself forever? He could bargain with the daemon. He could ask for just enough to get through the next battle, and no more. He could do that, couldn't he? If he died here, in the depths of this goddess-forsaken crypt, his soul would belong to the daemon anyway. Was it not better to live in corruption than to die and be enslaved forever?

The cries of the hunters drew nearer, and Malus felt all too keenly just how trapped he'd become.

More sounds emanated from the darkness: wet, slithering sounds, punctuated by the dry scrabbling of claws. One of the loyalists let out a frightened cry and shrank from the passageway. 'Blessed Murderer deliver us,' he said, his voice cracking with strain. 'We're all going to die!'

The words sent a tremor through the assembled Khaineites, but the axe-wielding priestess let out a derisive snort. 'Speak for yourself, wretch,' she said, spinning the haft of her weapon in her hands. 'I'm going to live long enough to make the bastards pay for what they've done.'

Arleth Vann chuckled. 'Never underestimate the power of sheer, bloody-minded spite,' the assassin said. 'Isn't that right, my lord?'

Malus thought it over. A wolfish smile spread across his face. 'Truer words were never spoken,' he said, hefting his sword. 'We'll meet them at the threshold,' he said, the words coming briskly as a plan of action took shape. 'Whatever's coming, I'd rather face them one at a time.'

The loyalists took heart from the highborn's fierce demeanour, readying their weapons and rushing to form a tight semicircle around the open doorway. The sounds of the approaching hunters stalking down the narrow passageway grew louder and more terrible: a cacophony of slithering, galloping, clawing madness that sent chills down the highborn's spine. Suddenly he was reminded of the twisted Chaos beasts that he fought in Urial's tower, many months past. As bad as those things were, this sounded a great deal worse.

The roiling tide of unnatural motion swept down on them in an avalanche of unsettling noise. Then it suddenly stopped. The druchii stared vainly into the cave-like darkness, more unsettled than ever.

An eerie stillness hung in the air, setting Malus's nerves on edge. He glanced at the man on his right. 'Fetch me one of those lamps,' he whispered, barely loud enough to be heard. The loyalist nodded and quickly snatched a lamp from the base of a broken statue. The brass vessel was hot to the touch as it was pressed into the highborn's hand.

'Let's see what we're dealing with,' Malus said, hurling the lamp down the passageway.

The palm sized lamp tumbled end over end, its tiny flame guttering until it struck the stone floor and broke apart. Orange fire whooshed into life as the wick ignited the spreading oil, revealing the hunters in all their horror.

There were three of them, their bulk so great that they could not stand side-by-side in the narrow, bone strewn corridor. Firelight shone on glistening, gelatinous flesh, shot through with thin, black veins and throbbing with unnatural strength. They had lean, powerful bodies similar to those of lions, their broad paws tipped with glossy, black claws, but their heads were like bloated octopi. The closest one to the fire reared back on its paws, its soft, bulbous skull pulsing with rage as it lashed the air with eight long, whip-like tentacles. Hundreds of suckers lined each tentacle, each one fitted with a barbed hook for trapping and shredding prey. At the centre of the mass of tentacles a cruel, glossy beak snapped furiously at the offending flame, unleashing a torrent of thin shrieks and gobbling cries.

The man beside Malus screamed like a child, and the Chaos beasts attacked.

The lead hunter bounded over the pool of flame and leapt for the screaming man, as if drawn by the sound. Its tentacles made a whirring sound in the air as they lashed at the terrified druchii. One slashed across the man's face, shredding the skin and muscle beneath as if they were rotted cloth. The stench of brine and rotted meat filled Malus's nostrils, making him gag. More tentacles wrapped around the hapless druchii, in the blink of an eye, enfolding him and pulling him from his feet. Wet, tearing sounds emanated from within the writhing web of fleshy ropes, and the druchii's frenzied screams of agony made Malus's blood run cold.

'Kill it!' Malus cried. 'In the Dark Mother's name, kill the thing!' He slashed at the beast's shoulder with his sword, but the creature's gelatinous flesh was deceptively strong, and his blade rebounded as if he'd struck solid oak. Arleth Vann darted at the thing, unleashing a flurry of stabbing blows. The blades sank barely an inch into the creature's flank, producing thin streams of clear, foul-smelling ichor.

Blows rained down on the creature from all sides. The priestess aimed a fearsome, two-handed blow at the creature's bulbous skull, but the axe blade left only a shallow cut in the heaving flesh. Undeterred, the Chaos beast continued to rip its victim apart. Blood poured from between the thrashing tentacles.

More tentacles whirred through the air, this time from the left side of the doorway. Malus heard a strangled scream and turned to see another man lifted from his feet by a second Chaos beast that clung to the wall of the passage like a spider. One broad paw had reached around the edge of the threshold and flattened itself against the wall of the chamber for support, and Malus saw that the base of the creature's feet were also lined with hooked suckers. The beast lifted its victim off the ground as if he was a child, wrapping one tentacle around the druchii's sword arm and ripping it off in a spray of hot blood.

'Mother of Night!' Malus cursed fearfully. They didn't stand a chance against these things. 'Run!' he shouted to his dwindling band. 'We can't stop them!'

The loyalists needed no convincing. They broke and ran for the western passage with barely a backward glance. Malus, Arleth Vann and the priestess were the last to break away, leaving the creatures to consume their prey. Though powerful, the beasts didn't seem to be much smarter than hunting hounds, easily distracted by the smell of blood, which suggested that their handlers were probably somewhere close by.

They were barely halfway across the antechamber when the third beast raced along the right wall of the passage and bounded heavily into the chamber, its tentacles waving sinuously as if it was tasting the air for prey.

The priestess let out a defiant scream and the beast oriented on her at once. Thinking quickly, Malus let out a war scream of his own and the beast turned to face him, spreading its tentacles wide and showing its clashing beak. The highborn raced for the nearest wall as the beast gathered itself and leapt with a keening wail.

It landed less than five paces from Malus, reaching for him with a blur of fleshy whips just as the highborn grabbed up the second of the three oil lamps and flung it at the creature's head. The lamp burst apart, covering its bulbous skull with blazing oil, and the beast recoiled with a tortured shriek as its wet flesh sizzled in the flame. The highborn took no time to savour the hurt he'd caused. The moment the beast was distracted he ran for the western passage as fast as his feet could carry him.

Malus plunged into near-total darkness without the faintest idea where he was going. He sensed he was in another narrow corridor, the twin of the passageway to the east. Somewhere up ahead he heard faint shouts, so he gritted his teeth and ran towards the sound. His feet struck a pile of spilled bones and he stumbled through the remains, cursing under his breath. Thin howls echoed behind him as the hounds began sniffing for new prey.

He reached a crossroads lit by patches of grave mould and paused, his heart hammering in his chest. The shouts seemed to be coming from everywhere at once, overlaid with the unsettling cries of the Chaos beasts. Thinking quickly, he glanced at the stone floor and saw hints of wet tracks following the passage to the left.

The highborn ran on, swallowed once again by suffocating darkness. The passage curved before he knew it and he bounced along the wall for several feet before it straightened out again. A piercing cry rang out behind him. It sounded as if one of the hounds had reached the crossroads, just a dozen yards or so away. Malus broke into a run, not caring if he ran headlong into another wall.

After another dozen yards the passageway opened into a larger, broader antechamber, bordered by half a dozen crypts and connecting three other passageways. Malus's heart leapt when he saw a small globe of green witchfire glowing at the mouth of the southern corridor. Arleth Vann beckoned to him urgently. 'Hurry, my lord! They're right behind you!'

An impertinent reply rose to his mind, but Malus elected to save his laboured breathing for more important work. Sharp daggers of pain shot through his chest as he struggled to breathe, and whenever he stood still it felt as if the chamber would start to spin. Focusing his will, he took the deepest breath he could and ran on.

The assassin took the lead, racing down the twisting passageway as fleet as a deer. Arleth Vann pulled steadily away from Malus, even as the sounds of the pursuing hounds drew closer. He could hear their wet, slithering strides and the click of their claws on the stone as they bounded steadily closer.

Malus could only utter a breathless curse as the retainer darted around a sharp corner up ahead, taking the faint light with him. The sounds of pursuit echoed all around him, and he found himself dreading the whip-like touch of the hounds' lashing tentacles against his back.

He was so focused on the sounds behind him that he missed the turn ahead, crashing against the wall hard enough to lose what meagre wind he had. He rebounded from the stone and reeled like a drunkard with the gobbling cries of the hunters punishing his ears.

He staggered a handful of steps around the corner, and found another long corridor glowing with patches of mould. A broad, jagged fissure ran across the passageway.

Arleth Vann was nowhere to be seen.

Grunting against the pain and loss of air, Malus lurched down the hall. He could hear the whirring of the tentacles. The hounds were just around the corner.

'My lord!'

Malus started at the sound. The assassin's voice was coming from the fissure. 'Down here!' The retainer said. 'Quickly!'

There was no time to argue. The first hunter rounded the corner with a wailing roar and Malus threw himself at the fissure. Fierce pain bloomed in his chest as he hit the stone floor and half-slid, half-rolled into the jagged opening. Clawed tentacles scraped the stone just a hand span behind him.

Malus felt a powerful sense of vertigo as he tumbled over the edge. The fissure was no mere cleft in the ground. It was a narrow crevasse, plunging deep into the earth. Arleth Vann let out a warning shout as Malus flailed desperately at the close-set, irregular walls. Pain bloomed in his knees and elbows as he managed to wedge himself tightly enough to stop his fall. His boots hung over empty space, leaving Malus giddy with fear.

'My lord!' the assassin cried from above. 'Are you all right?'

'Just fine,' Malus snarled. 'These jagged rocks managed to break my fall.'

A sharp howl echoed in the darkness and clawed tentacles lashed against the sides of the crevasse as one of the hunters tried to reach its prey. 'Keep going down!' the assassin shouted. 'The beasts won't be able to reach us.'

A tentacle slapped the wall of the crevasse less than a hand span from Malus's head. The highborn frantically groped about with the toes of his boots, trying to find some kind of foothold, but nothing gave him enough purchase.

Then Malus felt a sharp impact as one of the beast's tentacles struck him in the cheek. Another tentacle brushed against his neck. With a desperate shout the highborn relaxed his limbs and plummeted into blackness.

Strong hands pulled at Malus's shoulders, rolling him onto his back. His eyes fluttered open, and then snapped shut as a jagged pain lanced through his chest. The highborn bit back a tortured groan, hearing the sound echo in the space around him.

'My lord?' Arleth Vann said. The assassin bent close, examining Malus's chest. 'You're bleeding again. I think you tore your wound open in the fall.'

'Where in the Dark Mother's name are we?' he panted, forcing his eyes open again and peering around in the subterranean gloom. Faint witchlight played on smooth walls and square beams, hewn from living rock. The stone ceiling of the passage was split crosswise by a ragged cleft, its edges still spilling a faint spray of earth from his long, uncontrolled plunge.

'We're safe, for now,' the assassin said. 'The hunters can't fit into the cleft, and their handlers won't abandon the beasts to come after us alone. They might even think we're dead.'

Gritting his teeth, Malus tried to sit upright, but another flare of sharp-edged pain forced him to abandon the effort with a frustrated snarl. He pressed his hand to his left side and it came away sticky with fresh blood. 'They may not be all that far wrong,' he snarled, 'but that doesn't answer my question. Where in the Dark Mother's name are we?'

'We're outside the Lodge of the Delvers,' Arleth Vann said, reaching his hands under Malus's arms. Slowly, carefully, he pulled the highborn upright. 'There may be only a handful of people left in the temple who even know this place exists.'

Biting back waves of pain, Malus allowed himself to be pulled to his feet. The passageway was low-ceilinged, brushing the top of his head. The corridor itself ran as straight as an arrow, receding into blackness to the right. To the left, it ran for thirty paces and ended at a pair of stone doors hung on hinges of gleaming iron.

Arleth Vann helped Malus down the passage, towards the waiting portal. As they came closer, Malus could see that the surfaces of the doors were elaborately carved with underground scenes. Short, stout figures with braided beards came and went in fantastic scenes of subterranean splendour, bringing riches from the deeps and crafting them in works of cunning and art in a wondrous city chiselled from stone. It was like nothing the highborn had ever seen before.

He reached out and touched the surface of the doors, and the massive stone slabs swung inward on perfectly balanced hinges, revealing a broad, low-ceilinged room. A number of bare stone tables stood inside the chamber, each one short and broad. Four were arranged on each of the long sides of the room, their feet facing another, more ornately carved table in the room's centre. Another set of double doors stood at the chamber's opposite end.

Malus frowned. 'This is where the temple keeps its dwarf slaves?'

'In a manner of speaking,' the assassin replied. 'This is where the builders of the temple were entombed.'

The retainer helped Malus into the room, leading him to the central table and leaning the highborn against it. 'The elders entombed their dwarf slaves?' Malus asked, unsure at first if he'd heard the assassin correctly.

Arleth Vann nodded. 'It was a singular honour, a reward for their labours. Surely you noticed the craftsmanship of the building?'

'I had rather a lot on my mind at that point, but, yes, I noticed,' Malus replied irritably.

'That was just after the schism,' the assassin said, surveying the room appreciatively. 'With the dissenters driven out or slain, the first elders began work on the great temple in earnest. Over a hundred and twenty dwarf slaves laboured to build it, and construction took almost half a century. When the building was complete and the warpsword installed in its sanctum, the elders had the dwarfs build this splendid mausoleum for themselves. They told the delvers that their work had earned them a place of everlasting honour among the faithful, and that their spirits would be venerated for all time.'

'And then?'

Arleth Vann paused. 'Once they had completed the crypt the elders had them all killed and interred within.'

'Mother of Night,' Malus gasped. 'A hundred and twenty dwarfs, cut down in their prime?' The waste of so much valuable chattel staggered the imagination. A highborn could build and outfit a raiding ship for the cost of just one dwarf slave. Short of dragon eggs there was no more expensive commodity in all of Naggaroth.

The assassin shrugged. 'Bad for them, but good for us. The lodge was built deep below the hill – deeper even than the Vermillion Gate – and no one has come here for millennia. Only a few records of the place remain in existence, buried in the archives of the temple library.' He nodded to himself. 'It's a perfect base of operations, really: defensible and difficult to reach, but close enough for us to reach the passage leading to Thel's old house and communicate with the loyalists in the city if we need to.' He sighed. 'Now I've just got to get back up into the tunnels and lead the rest of our people down here past those damned beasts,' he said. 'This could take time. Will you be all right until I get back?'

Malus had nothing to say. When Arleth Vann looked over at his master he found the highborn had passed out once more.

CHAPTER SIXTEEN

DARKNESS AND DOUBT

'The wound is grave, my lord.'

Malus's eyes fluttered open. He was lying on the stone slab in the antechamber of the dwarf tombs. Someone had stripped away his kheitan and robes, and gooseflesh raced along his bare shoulders and back.

Firelight danced along the walls and limned a robed and hooded figure at work beside one of the long tables at the highborn's right. Malus heard the sound of metal ringing faintly on stone as the figure laid out a series of small tools. The voice he'd heard was familiar, but he couldn't place it.

He tried to rise, fearful that the figure would see the daemon's taint upon him, but ropes pulled tight at his wrists, shoulders and forehead. Memories of his days in his father's tower sent a cold thrill of panic racing up his spine. 'What is going on?'

'There is an infection,' the figure said. 'Your lung has collapsed, and the wound is... corrupted. Something must be done quickly, or you will die.'

A shiver of fear wracked his body. He knew what the figure was trying to say. 'You are going to have to cut the infection away,' Malus said, unable to keep a note of dread from his voice. 'Have you any hushalta?'

'No,' the figure said, holding a small, curved blade up to the light. 'You must brace yourself for what must be done, my lord. It is the only way.'

The figure turned towards him, reaching for his chest with a long-fingered hand. Orange light shone on the blade's razor edge. Malus could feel the wound in his side begin to throb and his heart quicken in fearful anticipation.

'I will work very quickly,' the figure said. Fingers played across Malus's ribs, fluttering like spider's legs over the raw, bleeding wound. 'You may scream if you wish. It will not trouble me.'

Malus opened his mouth to reply, but the words were lost in a terrible groan as the figure's bare fingers pressed into the cut and spread wide, enlarging the tear. Hot blood welled up in the wound, flowing down his side as the knife went to work. A spear of white-hot pain lanced again and again into his chest, stealing his breath away. Just when it seemed he could take no more he saw the figure straighten, holding up a lump of pink, glistening meat in its hand. The hooded face looked down at him.

'You see? Almost the size of a fist. As I said, very grave.'

A shudder passed through Malus. 'I feel... cold...'

'Of course,' the figure replied, tossing the flesh onto the floor. 'That is to be expected, but it is a small price to pay for your health, is it not?'

The figure raised the knife again, but this time its bloodstained hand pulled at the hem of its own robes. With a flick of its wrist it pulled its robe open and revealed bare, gleaming ribs stained black with corruption. Nearly all of the internal organs were missing, save for a wrinkled sac of flesh pulsing close to the breastbone.

'Nearly done,' the figure said. As it spoke, it reached up into its chest cavity and cut away the tattered, oozing remnant. 'The wound is painful, but it will heal, and then you and I will be stronger than ever.'

Malus tried to move, but the bonds held him fast. He screamed, shouting curses at the figure as it bent low and pushed the corrupted tissue into the highborn's gaping wound. At once, he felt the alien flesh wriggle and squirm inside him – and worse, he felt his organs heave and rise up to meet it.

The hooded head turned, close enough for Malus to see the face sheltered within. It was *his* face, pale and perfect, devoid of any daemonic taint. Only the eyes – black orbs like shards of the Outer Darkness itself – suggested the depths of the corruption that seethed within.

Tz'arkan smiled, showing jagged, obsidian fangs.

'You'll be a new man before you know it,' the daemon said with a gruesome chuckle.

'Careful! Careful! Hold him tight!'

Malus awoke with a shout, struggling against the grip of the four druchii who held him pinned to the stone slab. Arleth Vann loomed over him, pressing a hand to his clammy forehead and forcing a small vial between his lips. 'Drink,' he said, his voice hard and unyielding.

The taste of burnt copper flooded Malus's mouth. He gagged and tried to spit the hushalta out, but the assassin cursed fiercely and covered the highborn's mouth. Glaring at the retainer, he reluctantly swallowed the healing draught and forced himself to relax.

Arleth Vann studied Malus's eyes closely for a moment, and nodded in satisfaction. 'All right. You can let go,' he told the druchii, and the loyalists withdrew. They eyed Malus fearfully as they returned to sentry positions on either side of the dwarf lodge's entryway.

Malus raised a trembling hand and pressed it against his side. The wound ached fiercely. He pulled open his grimy robe and peered at his ribs, discovering the cut scabbed over and beginning to shrink. The black bruises remained, however, giving him the look of a week-old corpse. His mouth still tingled with the sharp taste of copper, and his joints creaked like dried leather. 'Water,' he said hoarsely.

The retainer lifted a leather water bottle to the highborn's lips, and Malus drank greedily. It was warm and brackish, but he savoured it like rare wine. When his fierce thirst abated somewhat, he glared at the grim faced assassin. 'You've been drugging me,' he croaked.

'You were going to die otherwise, Scourge or no,' Arleth Vann replied.

Malus drew a deep, slow breath, his eyes narrowing as he tested the extent of his injury. 'How long have you kept me out?'

'Three days.'

'Mother of Night!' Malus seethed, grabbing a handful of his retainer's robe. 'Have you any idea what you've done? Rhulan has been waiting outside the wall all this time! You may have damned us all!'

'Rhulan is not at the wall,' the assassin replied. 'In fact, I can't say for certain that he's even in the city any more.'

The highborn's anger faded. 'He hasn't rallied the warriors of the temple?'

Arleth Vann shrugged. 'If he tried, they evidently didn't listen,' he said gravely. 'I made my way out through the house of Cyrvan Thel the night after we reached the lodge, hoping to locate some food and other supplies,' he explained. 'The city had gone mad. Bloody riots were raging in the streets and much of the city was burning. From what I could discern, the temple warriors are holed up in scattered pockets all across Har Ganeth, cut off from one another by the raging mob. Certainly no one is directing their efforts to regroup and reach the temple.'

Malus took his hand away from Arleth Vann and slowly, painfully, he forced himself upright. The pain gave him something to focus on beside the rising tide of dismay that lapped at his brain. 'So Rhulan and Mereia ran afoul of the riots,' he said.

'It is possible. There are bodies everywhere,' the assassin replied. 'Or they might be trapped with one of the isolated warbands and can't find a way to communicate with the rest.'

The highborn gave his retainer an appraising stare. 'You don't think so,' he said.

Arleth Vann weighed his reply carefully. 'If he isn't dead, I think he's escaped the city,' he said with a sigh. 'Perhaps his courage failed him. Who knows? You heard him in the crypts. He thought Urial couldn't be beaten.'

'Damnation,' Malus spat. 'I thought at least Mereia would have been made of sterner stuff. We needed that diversion to help us reach Urial.'

The assassin straightened and set the water bottle on a nearby table. 'In a way, the temple warriors may be serving us better in the city than they would outside the temple gates,' he said. 'As long as the fighting continues, Urial must divide his forces between the temple fortress and the riots in the streets. He doesn't dare ease up on the pressure and allow the warbands to link together.'

Malus considered this. 'How easily can you move about the catacombs?'

'I can come and go as I wish, so long as I'm careful,' the assassin replied. 'The tunnel network is just too vast and interconnected to patrol effectively. I still hear Urial's hunters prowling through the crypts, but in truth they are poor trackers. So long as one is patient and quiet, they can be circumvented.'

'All right,' the highborn said with a sigh. He suddenly felt completely drained, as if the mere effort of sitting upright had consumed every ounce of his energy. 'How many of us are left?'

'Eight, counting you and me,' Arleth Vann replied. 'After the flight from the crypt I was able to find out where six of the volunteers were hiding and led them down here one at a time. Khaine alone knows what happened to the other two.'

The highborn nodded. His eyelids were getting heavy. He realised that it was because of the damned hushalta. 'No more mothers' milk,' he mumbled. 'No time to waste. Find where Urial is hiding... how he's being guarded...'

Arleth Vann said something in reply, but the assassin's voice seemed to fade into the distance as the healing drug pulled him under.

When he awoke again, Arleth Vann was gone.

Malus was ravenous. He took that as a good sign. The highborn lay on the stone slab in the centre of the dwarf lodge for several long minutes, gauging the stiffness of his limbs and the degree of pain in his chest. Finally, he summoned his resolve and swung his legs off the side of the table.

His knees nearly gave way beneath him when he slid to the stone floor. The sentries at the door stirred as Malus caught himself on the edge of the table. 'I'm all right,' he said, waving them back to their places. In point of fact, he felt anything but.

Malus looked around the chamber. Several small oil lamps flickered on three of the long side tables, and the assassin's water bottle still lay nearby. The door opposite the lodge's entrance stood open, and he thought he heard faint sounds echoing from beyond.

He reached for the water bottle and took several deep draughts, wincing at the vile taste. 'What time is it?' Malus asked the sentries.

The loyalists looked to one another and shrugged. 'Night time, I think,' one of them said. 'I no longer know what the hour is.'

Malus nodded thoughtfully. Then, gritting his teeth with effort, he walked towards the open doorway.

Beyond the low threshold he found himself in a long, irregular chamber that stretched off to his right. The features were a strange mixture of square-cut pillars and straight walls connecting small, rounded niches that had been carefully shaped to resemble natural caverns. In each niche the stone floor rose up to form a squat, rectangular tomb, inscribed with angular dwarf runes and overlaid with arcane magical sigils that glittered in the lamplight. There was no gilt-work or precious gems, no grave goods or mummified slaves, but the sheer scope and craftsmanship of the crypt was staggering. The caverns and their connecting passages had been hollowed out of solid rock, and the crypts constructed with surpassing skill.

Malus could see that the four tombs closest to him were open. He limped slowly to the nearest one, noticing a name inscribed at the foot of the stone coffin in druchast. *Thogrun Hammerhand*, it read, *Stonemaster*. A broad-shouldered dwarf clad in a slave's simple woollen robes lay in the coffin. His red beard was thick and stiff as wire, and his skin was the colour of granite. Only the faintest signs of decay could be seen around the stonemaster's seamed eyes and rounded nose. It was as if he'd been laid in the coffin only a few days before. The edges of the gaping cut that bisected the stonemaster's throat were only just beginning to shrivel. A veritable pall of sorcery hung over the figure, encasing it in a tight weave of magical energy.

More sounds echoed through the chamber from its far side: the scrape of stone, mutters, and faint, tired sounding curses. Frowning, the highborn sought out the source of the noise.

The room curved slightly to the right, following a logic that perhaps only a dwarf could appreciate. Malus walked past nine more crypts before the walls of the room narrowed to form a short, broad entryway into a connecting chamber. Two loyalists worked in front of the entryway, hauling heavy, rectangular stone panels into place to form a kind of defensive breastwork facing back the way Malus had come. They looked up at the highborn's approach and paused in their labour, wiping their faces with grimy rags.

Malus reviewed their work and nodded appreciatively, noticing that the stone panels were the thick lids used to seal the dwarf tombs.

'I see my retainer has been keeping everyone busy,' he said.

One of the men nodded. 'This is the last of them, my dread lord,' he said, a little breathlessly. 'There are more like this going all the way back to the prime chamber. We didn't have much to work with, since this place is practically built like a fortress already. A handful of people could hold off an army down here if they wanted to.'

Malus considered the crude fortifications and had to agree. With multiple, well-protected bastions to retreat to, they could take a fearsome toll of Urial's zealots if discovered. His half-brother's Chaos-spawned monsters were another matter, but he didn't think it wise to point that out. 'Where is our camp?' he asked.

The loyalist gestured over his shoulder. 'Five chambers further back, my lord,' he said, 'just outside the prime chamber. There's some food and water there if you're hungry. Your man brought in supplies a couple of days ago.'

Malus nodded again and carefully picked his way over the defensive barriers. 'With luck, we won't have to put these to the test,' he said, 'but carry on, all the same.' The men went back to work as the highborn disappeared into the chamber beyond.

The grave lodge wound back and forth through the rock beneath the hill like the track of a serpent. Each burial chamber was slightly curved, running away at an angle from the one before it. Possibly it was a technique to allow such a large number of tombs to fit within the stone confines of the region, but Malus suspected there was a ritual purpose to the layout, as if the curving lines of the chambers formed a sigil or sacred rune carved into the undying rock. At each entryway the druchii had built a defensive position using the lids of the tombs found nearby. One or two oil lamps sputtered in each chamber, providing just enough light to travel by.

By the time he'd passed through the second burial chamber the sounds of work behind him were swallowed by the stone walls, leaving Malus wrapped in funereal silence. For a brief time he felt truly alone, passing from shadow to shadow like a ghost amid the broken tombs, and it soothed him after a fashion.

'Did you have pleasant dreams?' whispered the daemon inside his head.

Malus paused at the entrance of the next burial chamber. Was it the fourth, or the fifth? He hadn't been keeping track. 'I dreamt of stuffing you into a chamber pot and throwing you into the deep sea,' he growled.

Tz'arkan chuckled. 'Dreams of vengeance and spite. I should have expected no less.' The daemon uncoiled itself within the highborn's breast. 'What of your wound? Are you healing well, little druchii?'

Malus's hands clenched into fists. 'You should know better than I, daemon. Soon I'll be no better than the wretches confined in these tombs, infused with so much sorcery that not even the worms will touch me.'

Obscene laughter raked along the inside of Malus's ribs. 'Such childishness! Such vanity! Your body has recovered from a mortal wound in less than a week. There are men who would think that an awesome gift, one worth almost any price.'

The highborn entered the next chamber, picking up his pace. 'The difference is that I see through your deceptions,' he replied. 'Every time I open myself to your power I let you increase your hold over me.'

'I have your soul, Darkblade.' The daemon sounded genuinely amused. 'What greater hold over you do I need?'

'Then why this?' Malus pulled open his robes, revealing the glossy, black scabs on his chest and the deep bruises in his flesh. 'Your gifts are making me into an abomination!'

Tz'arkan sighed. 'No, they are making you worthy of the fate that awaits you. Do not dissemble, Malus. I know your heart's deepest desires. You crave power. You dream of the day when all of Naggaroth bows before you.'

Malus continued on in silence, stalking angrily past the dwarf tombs.

'Did you think that mere treachery and cunning would be enough to supplant one such as the Witch King? You will need power beyond that of the greatest druchii heroes. That is what I offer you, yet you reject it at every turn.'

'I don't feel stronger, daemon. I feel... hollowed out.' Malus said. 'I feel twisted and diseased. You're corrupting me.'

'To what purpose?'

'To enslave me! What else?'

The daemon laughed. 'Stupid, stupid Darkblade! Why would I do such a thing? I know your fate. I laid its foundations millennia ago. In that sense, you were a slave to my wishes from the moment you were born. For the sake of argument, let's assume you are right. Let's say that I am subverting your will with each touch of my power. Tell me then: how is it you continue to resist me, even as your body weakens and your foes gain in strength? Have you lost one whit of your obstinate personality since you entered my temple in the north?'

Malus held his tongue. Part of him hungered for the daemon's power, like a drunkard ached for the taste of wine. If Tz'arkan didn't know it, he wasn't about to volunteer the information.

'Nothing to say? I thought not,' the daemon replied smugly.

The highborn crossed the dimly lit burial chamber and entered the next. Things were different here. More lamps burned along the curving chamber, outlining a meagre camp of bedrolls and cloth bags lying haphazardly in a dense cluster in the centre of the room. The priestess and a druchii novitiate lay wrapped in their cloaks, sleeping soundly on the stone floor. It struck Malus that after all this time he still didn't know the young priestess's name.

'So what will you do, Malus?' Tz'arkan asked. 'Will you continue to suffer needlessly, or will you allow me to renew your strength?'

Moving silently, the highborn picked his way among the snoring loyalists and sought out the far end of the room. Another set of defensive barricades had been placed there, but Malus also saw that a large stone door sealed this portal. Runes had been carved into the door's surface and inlaid with molten silver. Powerful charms and spirit wards radiated from the barrier, tingling across the highborn's skin.

Malus climbed over the barricades and carefully pushed the door open.

There were no oil lamps within. He pushed the stone door wide, letting the illumination at his back flow into the small room before him. It was similar to the burial niches he'd passed along the way, fashioned like an artificial cavern and containing a single tomb. Unlike the rest, the stone coffin was still sealed, and its surface was covered in a profusion of layered sigils and spells. *Gothar Grimmson*, the inscription read, *Ironmaster*.

Malus stepped inside the prime chamber and, after a moment, pushed the door closed. Darkness and silence swallowed him whole.

'How do I know you're telling me the truth?'

The daemon chuckled. 'Lies are for the weak and the stupid, Darkblade. I have little need of them. I have said this before, and I will say it again: I have never lied to you, ever.'

'You haven't told me the entire truth, either.'

'That, Malus, is a very different thing,' Tz'arkan replied archly. 'I've told you everything you needed to know at the time.'

'So what aren't you telling me now?'

The daemon paused. 'Nothing of import, I assure you.'

Malus smiled coldly. 'Then you'll understand if I look for answers elsewhere.'

'What does that mean?' the daemon hissed.

Wrapped in concealing darkness, Malus raised his hand and felt for the cold silver band that circled the finger of his left hand. The sentry had told him it was night outside, and as near as he could reckon the moon would be waxing bright.

Of course, Eldire hadn't bothered to explain to him how the damned ring actually worked. Lacking any other ideas, he clenched his fist and focused his will into a single word.

Mother.

Malus felt a ghostly breeze touch his face. He smelled the faint scent of ashes. Suddenly the daemon wrapped tightly around his heart, making him wince.

'Malus, what are you doing?' Tz'arkan asked sharply. 'What foolishness is this?'

The daemon's grip was relaxing and its voice fading. A strange, silvery glow, like faint moonlight, began to fill the small chamber. Malus felt his aches diminish, yet at the same time his body turned leaden and cold.

The light intensified, pushing back the shadows and drawing the sharp outline of a figure standing next to the ancient tomb. From one moment to the next the figure took on more and more solidity, swelling from little more than a silhouette to a tall, square-shouldered woman wearing the black robes of a seer. Long, white hair hung in a thick braid to below her waist, bound at the tip with a band of gold. She was statuesque and regal, with a face that was both beautiful and coldly forbidding. Wreathed in pearlescent light, she studied her surroundings with detached interest, entirely unfazed by his sorcerous summons.

'Eldire,' Malus said, inclining his head respectfully.

She turned at the sound of his voice. 'Hello, my son,' she replied. Her voice sounded clearly in the room, although it had a curious echo to it, as if she was speaking from the bottom of a well. Eldire's body remained somewhat ethereal, like a ghost's, and he could see the faint outline of the dwarf tomb through her vaporous form.

'It has been some time, Malus,' Eldire continued. 'I had begun to fear the worst.'

The thought made Malus chuckle. 'As if a seer of your power would have any need to worry.'

'Nothing is ever certain, child, especially where divination is concerned,' she said coolly. 'We deal in possibilities. Where you are concerned, the threads of fate are more tangled than most.'

The highborn frowned. 'That doesn't sound encouraging.'

'On the contrary, it means you are finally attempting to create your own fate instead of having one shaped for you,' she said. 'Of course, this necessarily means that things are less certain than they were before.'

'So you're saying I'm flirting with disaster.'

'More so than usual, yes,' Eldire said. Her lips quirked into the briefest of smiles.

'I'll try to take heart from that.'

'Good,' she said, turning to regard the tomb beside her. 'Now perhaps you can explain what you are doing in a dwarf crypt when you should be at Har Ganeth looking for the warpsword.'

And so he explained as best he could, describing how he'd finally gained entrance to the City of Executioners and then found himself caught up in the holy war waged between the temple loyalists and Tyran's zealots. He told her of the debacle in the sanctum and their retreat into the catacombs.

Then he spoke of the wound he'd been given, and the power of Tz'arkan's hold over him.

'He claims to be strengthening me,' Malus said bitterly. 'It makes some sense, come to think of it, but is it the truth? What other reason can there be, if not to enslave me completely?'

Eldire considered all that Malus had said. 'The daemon speaks the truth, as far as it goes,' she said carefully. 'It is true that Tz'arkan has stolen your soul, and that corrupting your body would not gain it any more influence over you than it already has, but I do not think it seeks to control you at this point. It intends to *become* you.'

A chill coursed down the highborn's spine. 'What do you mean?'

'Tz'arkan is transforming you, slowly and surely, to become a daemonhost,' the seer replied. 'Normally such a process takes a great deal of time, but your case is hardly normal, is it?'

'So the daemon seeks to... what? Wear me, like a glove?'

'In a manner of speaking, yes. Your soul will be destroyed, and Tz'arkan will take its place.'

Malus looked down at his chest. 'If the daemon's energies can heal me like this, how far gone am I?'

Eldire glided silently forwards and reached a ghostly hand towards the wound. Her expression darkened. 'You walk a knife's edge, my son,' she said. 'Chaos energies seethe within your flesh, but you have not yet been wholly consumed. Your will remains strong, and while it does you can keep the daemon at bay a little longer.'

Malus nodded, even though he felt anything but strong. Did he dare tell her how his limbs trembled at the thought of the daemon's power? He craved the icy rush of Tz'arkan's gifts, and he feared, deep in his bones, that he could not beat his half-brother without them.

'The battle ahead will be difficult,' he said. 'How will I be able to confront Urial alone and defeat him when he wields the warpsword?'

'How should I know?' Eldire asked irritably. 'I'm hundreds of leagues away. I've never set foot in Har Ganeth, much less examined the sword. You will simply have to find a way.'

Malus sighed, folding his arms tightly across his chest. 'Why couldn't you simply turn up and solve everything with a bit of arcane insight, like the sorcerers in all the legends?'

She leaned close. 'If we could truly do that, my son, we wouldn't have need of people like you,' the seer replied. 'Find a way. Your soul depends on it.'

'With hate, all things are possible,' he said, wishing the saying still had the power to reassure him.

Eldire smiled, brushing an insubstantial hand against his cheek, and then stepped away. She studied the tomb once more. 'Why so much effort for dwarfs?' she asked.

'It was a reward for building the temple,' Malus said sourly. 'A hundred and twenty prime dwarf slaves. Such a waste of very expensive flesh.'

The seer extended a long finger, tracing the sigils inscribed into the tomb. 'Dead, but their spirits remain,' she said. 'These are powerful wards of binding. A great deal of sorcery was invested in these tombs.'

'Who can fathom the wisdom of priests?' Malus asked with a shrug.

'Indeed,' Eldire admitted with a sigh.

'Has word reached the Hag about Urial?'

'No, not yet,' she said. 'If the priestesses at the temple know it, they are keeping the news to themselves. You are right of course, once Malekith learns that Urial has the sword, he will march on Har Ganeth. A fast rider could reach the Hateful Road from Har Ganeth in less than a week.'

Malus imagined Rhulan galloping down the Slavers' Road for all he was worth. 'And Isilvar?'

Eldire looked back at Malus. 'The Drachau has proclaimed him a hero for saving the city,' she said. 'His power grows by the day.'

'As powerful as Lurhan?'

'No, but powerful enough, in time,' she said. 'Forget him and Hag Graef, my son. Your future lies elsewhere.'

'My future is mine to decide, mother,' Malus said. 'You told me that. When the time is right, I will return to the Hag. I have unfinished business there.'

Eldire opened her mouth to respond, but thought better of it. She shrugged. 'As you wish, child. First, however, you must deal with Urial. That, I fear, will be challenge enough.'

With that, she was gone. There was no gesture of farewell – Eldire simply faded like a ghost, taking the penumbral light with her.

Malus was swallowed in darkness and doubt.

CHAPTER SEVENTEEN

SECRETS OF THE SWORD

When Arleth Vann returned to the lodge he found Malus sitting on the tomb of Gothar Grimmson, picking at a few scraps of stale bread and a piece of stringy meat spread out on a greasy cloth in his lap. An oil lamp sputtered on the top of the stone coffin, near the dwarf's feet.

The highborn glanced up as the assassin slipped quietly into the small crypt. 'Where did you find this awful stuff?' he asked, grimacing in distaste. He pulled a thread of the dark, stringy meat from the cloth and reluctantly put it in his mouth. 'If I didn't know better I'd say you robbed the temple kennels.'

'Nothing so fancy,' Arleth Vann replied.

Malus paused in mid-chew. 'Do I want to know?'

'Almost certainly not.'

The highborn eyed the rest of the food with dismay. 'Damnation,' he muttered wearily, and forced himself to continue eating.

'How are your injuries, my lord?'

'Better,' the highborn answered, hoping he sounded sincere. 'Or well enough for me to get out of this damned mausoleum, at any rate. What have you learned?'

The assassin glanced back into the chamber beyond, checking to see if anyone might be listening. Apparently satisfied, he sank to his haunches and steepled his fingers under his chin while he collected his thoughts.

'It's getting harder to move around the temple grounds,' he began. 'The zealots have killed most of the temple novitiates and slaves, and converted the rest. Those that remain have been given a brand in the centre of their foreheads in the shape of a sword. I think Tyran has done this to make infiltrators easier to spot.'

Malus considered the news. 'Are there still zealots in the fortress grounds?'

'Yes. I'm not certain how many, but most of them know one another on sight at this point.'

'I see,' the highborn replied. He pulled out his dagger and began sawing at the stale bread. 'Any news of the temple assassins?'

Arleth Vann shook his head. 'Incredibly, they remain in conclave. I suppose Urial's move has complicated their decision somewhat.'

'That doesn't sound good. If they were solidly for Rhulan and the loyalists they would have made up their minds by now.'

The retainer shrugged. He drew his own stained cloth parcel from the folds of his robe and unwrapped it across his knees. There was a piece of flatbread inside and a handful of small, dried fish. 'That's true, but at least they aren't actively opposed to us yet.'

'True enough,' Malus said. He stopped sawing at the bread and inspected his work, surprised that he'd barely made an impression on the stale lump. Frowning, he set the bread on the top of the tomb and hammered at it with the pommel of his knife. The blows made no mark at all. He held the lump up to the lamplight. 'If I could put a strap on this I'd use it as a shield,' he muttered darkly.

Arleth Vann pulled a small bottle of water from his belt and set it by his knee. Then he reached into the voluminous folds of his left sleeve and produced a small, clay jar. The assassin broke the wax seal around the lid of the jar and pulled off the lid, sniffing experimentally. Satisfied, he dipped one of the fish in the jar and popped it into his mouth, chewing contentedly.

'What have you learned about Urial and Yasmir?'

The assassin frowned, switching back to business. 'Nothing good, I'm afraid. It appears that your half-brother has taken his bride-to-be and retreated back into the Sanctum of the Sword. Only Tyran and a few other zealots are allowed inside to confer with him, and the temple is heavily guarded.'

Malus leaned back against the foot of the coffin. 'How heavily guarded?'

'I can only guess based on what I was able to overhear, but I would say at least a dozen zealots stand guard at the entrance to the sanctum, and twice that number on the stairs leading from the chapel on the ground floor.' The assassin shook his head. 'We can't fight our way through all that without raising an alarm.'

The highborn stared at the stone floor. He knew that there was a way. With the daemon's help he could carve through the true believers like a whirlwind, but Eldire's words dogged him. *You walk upon a knife's edge.*

'Surely there are secret passageways leading into the sanctum? Every other building on the hilltop seems riddled with them.'

Arleth Vann shook his head. 'The sanctum was created specifically to safeguard the sword and serve as the site for the temple's holiest rites. There is only one way in and out.'

Frustration gnawed at Malus, setting his teeth on edge. He leaned his head back and knocked it lightly against the tomb. 'There has to be another way in. Think, damn you!'

'Not unless you know a way to dig through dwarf-crafted stone,' the assassin replied grimly.

Malus froze. 'What did you say?'

The assassin frowned. 'I wasn't trying to be impertinent. I just said that unless you know a way to dig through dwarf-crafted stone–'

'That's it!' Malus said leaning forwards intently, 'Dwarf-crafted stone.' The highborn tapped his lower lip thoughtfully. Slowly, he turned and looked back at the tomb. 'Blessed Mother of Night,' he whispered in wonder.

Arleth Vann eyed his master warily. Surreptitiously, he picked up the jar of yellow sauce and sniffed it suspiciously, before setting it down again. 'Is everything all right, my lord?'

Malus stared thoughtfully at the foot of the coffin. 'Why is this room called the prime chamber?' he asked.

The assassin shrugged. 'That's not its real name. Dwarf burial rites are very secret affairs. Bodies are prepared in the antechamber yonder, away from the prying eyes of all but their kinsmen, and then laid to rest in their crypts.' He looked around the small room. 'I called this the prime chamber because there's just one tomb in here, unlike the others.'

'So this slave was someone important?'

'Most likely. A master of his craft, perhaps.'

Malus nodded, feeling his heart quicken. 'And the sanctum is made of stone? All of it?'

Arleth Vann could not help but give his master a condescending stare. 'Of course, my lord. Dwarfs don't build with wood. Every bit is cut stone, cunningly fitted together. What *are* you driving at?'

Once again, Eldire's words echoed in Malus's ears. *Why so much effort for dwarfs?*

The highborn reached up and touched the inscription on the tomb. 'Tell me,' he said, looking back at his retainer with a dawning smile, 'if the temple was built entirely of stone, what did the elders need with an ironmaster?'

Arleth Vann's eyes narrowed warily. 'I don't understand.'

'Gothar Grimmson here is an ironmaster, not a stone carver,' Malus said. His mind raced as he began putting the pieces together. He rose to his feet and began to pace the small room. 'What if the sword Urial took from the sanctum isn't the actual Warpsword of Khaine?'

The assassin was too stunned to speak for a moment. 'That's absurd,' he sputtered.

'Is it?' Malus asked. 'You said that the sanctum was built to safeguard the sword, but from what? The relic had been in the possession of the elders for centuries. Why the sudden need to enshrine it under layers of sorcerous wards?'

'I...' The retainer's voice faded as he wrestled with the notion. 'I don't know. Perhaps the elders feared the schism leaders would try to steal the sword at some point.'

'Or perhaps they already had!' the highborn exclaimed. 'You said that the five zealots who volunteered to kill the temple leaders were never heard from again. Doesn't that seem odd to you? If they had been caught or killed, wouldn't the elders have wanted to make a public spectacle of their deaths?'

'I suppose so.'

'Then it's reasonable to assume they weren't caught. So what happened to them?' Malus spun on his heel, his stride quickening along with his thoughts. 'What if they realised that their assassination attempt was doomed to fail, and decided on another course of action? Perhaps they couldn't kill the elders, but they could deprive them of the cult's most prized relic! So they took the sword and vanished.' The highborn nodded to himself. 'That's why the elders sent their warriors rampaging through the city afterwards. They weren't looking for the zealot leaders so much as they were looking for the warpsword itself!'

'But we know the assassins never returned from the fortress,' the retainer said. 'So where did they go?'

'Where else? Through the Vermillion Gate.'

Arleth Vann froze, a rebuttal dying on his lips. 'Blessed Murderer,' he swore softly. 'Of course.'

'One can imagine how frantic the elders were when they learned the sword had been taken,' Malus said. 'How could they claim to be the true servants of Khaine without the blade in their possession? What would become of their alliance with the Witch King? The elders may have survived the assassination attempt, but the zealots had dealt them a mortal blow all the same.

'Then a very strange thing happened. Days turned to weeks, and weeks into months, and nothing more was heard about the sword. If the zealots had it, they would have used it to discredit the temple publicly. So the elders realised they'd been given a sort of reprieve. For the moment, no one in Naggaroth knew of the warpsword's fate, so they hatched a desperate plan to save themselves.'

'They made a copy of the blade,' Arleth Vann said, his voice tinged with wonder.

'Exactly,' the highborn said. He patted the foot of the tomb. 'They had Gothar here make a perfect copy of the relic, and then made a grand show of installing it in the temple. The sanctum wasn't built to safeguard the sword at all, but to protect the temple's darkest secret.'

'That's why they killed the dwarf slaves,' the assassin said. 'They had to silence Gothar so he couldn't betray them, and murdered the rest to camouflage the act.'

'The elders even went so far as to bind their spirits into these tombs so that no sorcerer could question them later,' Malus said with admiration. 'That's why the elders kept Urial at arm's length all this time. Even if he had been the true Scourge, they couldn't give him what they didn't have.'

'So Rhulan and the other elders knew the truth?'

'Yes. That's why he told us we couldn't fight Urial directly – because the legend says the bearer of the warpsword can't be defeated in battle. If we put the lie to that claim, the rest of the deception would have begun to unravel.'

The assassin nodded thoughtfully. 'It all makes sense,' he said. Although from the sound of his voice he was loathe to believe it. Suddenly he straightened. 'Do you think Urial knows he doesn't have the real sword?'

'Honestly? I don't think so,' Malus said. 'Not yet, at least. Until the blade is put to the test he has no reason to think it is a replacement.'

'That's why Rhulan hasn't rallied the temple warriors. He doesn't dare spur a real confrontation with the zealots, despite the fact that he knows he has a good chance of defeating them.' The assassin shook his head ruefully. 'What madness!'

'Indeed,' Malus said. He continued to pace, tapping his chin furiously. 'Mother of Night,' he swore. 'The sword could be anywhere in the world. How are we going to find out where the assassins took it?' The rush of triumph he'd felt as all the pieces of the puzzle clicked into place turned to bitter frustration. For a moment he thought he'd found a way to cheat the daemon and claim the sword without having to confront Urial or Yasmir at all. He struggled with a flood of hopeless fury, so preoccupied that at first he didn't notice Arleth Vann had spoken. Malus caught the questioning look in the assassin's gaze and paused in mid-stride. 'What?' he asked.

'I said that I think I know a way,' Arleth Vann replied.

The assassin's right hand shot up and the small party froze in place. Malus and three of the surviving six loyalists settled onto their haunches, hands tightening on their weapons. Darkness flowed towards them as Arleth Vann closed his left hand, muffling the small globe of witchfire he'd conjured.

For several long moments Malus heard nothing but the sound of his own heart labouring in his ears. Then he heard a faint, keening wail, skirling out of the blackness somewhere up ahead of them. Two of the druchii behind Malus shifted nervously at the ominous howl. One let out a fearful moan.

'Hsst!' Malus whispered threateningly. 'Not a sound!'

No one moved. Malus caught himself holding his breath, straining to hear the telltale signs of discovery. A minute passed, and then another.

Finally Arleth Vann relaxed, opening his hand and filling the narrow tunnel with cold light. He turned his body slightly so he could glance back at Malus. 'The Chaos beasts are hunting somewhere up ahead, but they don't seem to be in our path,' he whispered to the highborn.

Malus nodded. He hadn't the faintest idea how the assassin could tell, but he knew better than to argue with the druchii's keen senses. 'How far to the citadel?' he asked.

'Another few minutes, if all goes well.'

'Let's go, then.'

The retainer rose silently to his feet. Malus followed suit. Behind him, the axe-wielding priestess – whose name he'd finally learned was Niryal – and two more loyalists made ready to move. They had been working their way through the tunnels beneath the hill for more than an hour, climbing from the deepest levels where the dwarf lodge was located and taking a circuitous route to the subterranean chambers of the Citadel of Bone. They had been forced to crouch in the darkness and hold their breath many times, while Urial's hunters prowled nearby, but so far the assassin had succeeded in leading them away from the horrific beasts. Arleth Vann's assessment had been correct; the monsters were fearsome killers but very poor trackers. Had the zealots turned a pack of nauglir loose in the tunnels the loyalists would have been in serious trouble.

Not for the first time, Malus wondered how Spite was faring in the wartorn city. Was he still being fed and boarded in the highborn district's nauglir pens, or had hunger or misadventure driven the cold one into the streets? He had no real fear for the nauglir's safety – the warbeast was more than a match for any but the most heavily armed warbands prowling Har Ganeth's streets. It was the safety of the relics in the cold one's saddlebags that gave the highborn cause for concern. He was haunted by visions of the cold one clawing its way through the doors of its pen and tearing its saddlebags off in the process, or having them ripped open in a fight and spilling their contents onto the street.

One thing he was coming to realise about sorcerous relics was that finding them was only half the challenge. *Keeping* them for any length of time was just as hard, if not harder.

If the zealots had stolen the sword and escaped through the Vermillion Gate hundreds of years ago, Malus hadn't the faintest idea how to track them, but Arleth Vann knew of a library in the Citadel of Bone that might contain some useful clues. All they had to do was slip past Urial's hunters and zealot patrols and infiltrate one of the most important buildings in the temple fortress undetected. As ever, the assassin volunteered to make the attempt alone, but Malus had insisted on sending a small party instead. There was simply too much at stake to risk sending a single man, even one as skilled as Arleth Vann. If anything went awry and Urial guessed their interest in the library, the would-be Scourge could place it under such heavy guard that they wouldn't be able to get anywhere near it – or worse, lay a sorcerous ambush to catch them unawares the next time they tried to reach it.

Holding the globe of witchlight over his head, Arleth Vann set off down the narrow, bone-strewn corridor. Many of the crypt passages had been thrown into disarray by the passage of the Chaos beasts. Skeletons had been scattered from their shelves and crushed to powder beneath the hunters' leonine paws. Some of the fresher ones even had the skulls and long bones split open in a vain search for meat. The assassin picked his way carefully among the drifts of bone and rotted cloth, leaving Malus and the loyalists to follow in his footsteps and watch every dark niche and side passage with a growing feeling of unease. No one spoke, but everyone shared the same sense of dread. The longer they spent in the tunnels, the greater the chance that the hunters would catch their scent. Sooner or later their luck would run out.

Arleth Vann moved unerringly through the maze of tunnels, pausing only occasionally to check his bearings at corridor junctions or antechambers. From what Malus could tell Niryal and the other temple servants were just as disorientated as he was. All he knew for certain was that they were close to the surface. The corridors showed signs of frequent traffic and were largely free of cobwebs and layers of dust. The highborn was surprised at how eager he was to get above ground, even for a short time. It had been almost six days since he'd been out in the open air, and the claustrophobic weight of the catacombs was beginning to tell on his nerves.

Long minutes passed, and Malus's impatience grew. One passageway led to another and every sound set the highborn's teeth on edge. They heard no more hunting howls echoing in the blackness. Did that mean the beasts had moved further away, or were they creeping stealthily closer, waiting until the very last moment before rushing at their prey in a cacophony of terrible, whistling shrieks?

Finally, Malus could take no more. He quickened his steps slightly, enough to catch up to Arleth Vann and pluck at a corner of his robe. The assassin stopped.

'You said just a few more minutes,' Malus whispered.

'We're nearly there,' the retainer replied. He pointed into the darkness ahead. 'There is a chamber just a few more yards that way. Beyond it will be a ramp leading up into the citadel's lower rooms.'

Malus took a deep breath, forcing himself to relax. 'All right,' he said, 'lead on.'

The assassin slipped quietly along the corridor, and within a few minutes more Malus saw the glow of the witchlight expand to fill a broad chamber just ahead. It was a rectangular room almost twenty paces across on its long sides, and its walls and corners were piled with skeletons and crumbling skulls. Passageways led off to the left and right, and a long, sloping ramp led upwards from the opposite side of the chamber. Arleth Vann stepped to one side as he entered the room, and Malus rushed past with the loyalists hot on his heels.

'Wait, my lord!' the assassin hissed in warning. 'Something's not right–'

Frowning, the highborn turned to ask what he was talking about, but his question went unasked as a chorus of high-pitched screams shattered the dank air.

CHAPTER EIGHTEEN

INTERROGATING THE DEAD

For the briefest instant, Malus froze in horror as the high-pitched shrieks reverberated across the dimly lit chamber. The attackers charged from the shadowy passageways, but instead of the rapacious Chaos beasts they expected, their foes were in the shape of men. They wore grey robes and kheitans beneath long shirts of blackened mail, and their skin and hair were smeared with a thick layer of soot or ash. Each man carried a short, cruelly hooked spear or a short, stabbing sword with a serrated edge, and their expressions were contorted in snarls of feral bloodlust.

Malus knew that these were not sorcerous monsters that shrugged off the touch of sharpened steel, and the knowledge filled him with murderous vigour. The highborn raised his sword and met the enemies' charge with a bloodthirsty laugh. 'Blood and souls for Khaine!' he cried, and rushed at the oncoming men.

The first man he reached lunged at Malus with his spear, his eyes widening in surprise at the highborn's reckless charge. Malus slapped the spearhead aside with the flat of his blade and then smashed the heavy sword into his attacker's face with a backhanded strike. Bone crunched as the keen edge struck the man just beneath his nose and split his skull in half. The corpse lurched on past the highborn for several more steps before collapsing to the floor.

The clangour of battle filled the air as the loyalists threw themselves at their foes. An ashen-faced attacker screamed as Niryal ducked beneath his spear thrust and hacked off his right leg just below the knee. Arleth Vann drew one of his blades and danced through the onrushing foes sweeping in from the left, toppling two men in a spray of bright crimson.

Two druchii rushed at Malus, holding their saw-bladed knives in an underhand grip. Still laughing furiously, he charged the first man, driving him back with a swipe at his face. The second man saw an opportunity and lunged in from the right, bringing up his blade in a disembowelling thrust, only to find he'd fallen into the highborn's trap. At the last moment Malus pivoted away from the thrust and severed the man's knife-hand with a short, powerful stroke. Hot blood sprayed across Malus's face as the maimed warrior reeled backwards, but the highborn had already turned his attention back to the second knife wielder. The druchii slashed at Malus's throat, but the highborn blocked the knife stroke easily, deflecting the smaller weapon away with his heavier blade. Before the druchii could recover Malus planted his left foot and lunged, driving his double-edged sword into the man's throat. The point of the blade grated against the druchii's spine and the mortally wounded man dropped lifelessly to the floor.

Suddenly Malus felt something curved and sharp circle his left ankle. He glanced left just in time to see one of the druchii leering triumphantly at him before hauling back on his spear. The weapon's curved billhook pulled Malus off his feet. Instinct and battle-hardened reflexes made him rotate in midair, letting him take the fall on his back instead of his sword arm, but the spearman was a quick and cunning fighter, stepping in swiftly and smashing his billhook against Malus's sword-hand. The highborn roared in pain and rage as his sword was sent spinning end over end across the room.

The spear swept around again, this time angling for Malus's neck, but the highborn caught the haft with both hands and pulled the druchii towards him. As the man stumbled forwards, Malus kicked the druchii hard in the groin and then smashed a heel against his attacker's left knee. The man fell hard, his face locked in a grimace of pain, and Malus pulled the spear from his hands. The highborn reversed his grip on the weapon and buried the spear's point in his foe's temple, and then crawled clear of the twitching body and scrambled for his lost blade.

Men were running past him. The ashen-faced attackers were in full retreat, demoralised by the ferocity of their foes' counterattack. There was a whirring of steel through the air and then a meaty *thunk*, and one of the fleeing druchii let out a strangled gasp and fell to the floor with Arleth Vann's sword buried in his back. Malus reached his sword and lurched to his feet, but by then the rest of the attackers had vanished, their footfalls receding swiftly into the darkness.

Arleth Vann dashed to his victim and pulled his sword free with a muttered curse. Malus took stock of his party and found that none of the loyalists had been injured in the brief fight. He turned to his retainer. 'Who in the name of the Outer Dark were they?'

'Beastmasters,' the assassin replied. 'The temple employs them to provide animals for festival games and to train its warriors.' He glanced down the left passageway, concern on his face. 'We must have surprised them as much as they did us, but they'll be calling the hunting beasts to them at any moment. We need to get inside the citadel, now!'

'Lead on,' Malus said, and Arleth Vann darted up the ramp without another word.

The ramp ran up through a series of large storerooms, switching back upon itself with each new level. They passed dusty crates and cracked clay urns that had once held expensive ink, bales of rotting cloth and sheaves of incense sticks that thickened the air with cloying, spicy scents. They saw no one as they raced for the upper levels of the tower, although in places Malus noticed a line of fresh boot prints running ahead of them through the layers of dust.

After several long minutes they reached the chamber and the top of the ramp, their noses clogged with dust and strange scents. A pair of broad, iron-banded doors stood at the other end of the room, and one of the heavy panels was slightly ajar. Arleth Vann rushed down an aisle of crates and pulled the door wider, as if he feared it might slam shut at any moment. Malus glimpsed a large, dimly lit room, beyond, piled high with more supplies. Stairs rose along the high, stone walls into the tower proper.

The assassin breathed a sigh of relief and doused his sorcerous light. 'We're in luck. The fools didn't think to bar the door. Quickly now!'

Malus and the loyalists filed through the doorway and Arleth Vann pulled the heavy door shut behind him. A broad, wooden wheel was mounted on a spindle set into the stone wall next to the doorway. The assassin grabbed the wheel's spokes and leaned against it, pushing with all his strength. Bemused, the highborn joined him on the wheel's opposite side and pulled, grimacing at the flare of pain in his chest. At first the wheel refused to budge. Then, inch-by-inch, it began to turn. There was a building screech of rusted iron, and then the doors trembled with a muted *thud*.

'That's it,' Arleth Vann said breathlessly, leaning against the wheel. 'The dwarfs built this to secure the citadel in times of war.' He pointed at the top of the threshold. 'Iron rods can be lowered into slots on the top of the doors, fixing them in place. The beasts can't get to us now.'

'How are we supposed to get back to the lodge?' Malus asked.

To his surprise, Arleth Vann gave him one of his ghostly smiles. 'Honestly, I have no idea. I'm more or less making this up as I go.'

Malus winced. 'Ah, well, that's comforting.'

'Would it help if I told you that it may not be a problem?'

'And why is that?'

'There's a good chance we'll all die once we reach the library.'

The highborn stared balefully at his retainer. 'I think you spent too much time with Hauclir back at the Hag. He's been a bad influence.'

Arleth Vann straightened. 'Really? That's interesting.'

'Why?'

'He said the same thing about you.'

Malus frowned. 'Impertinent wretch.'

'That's funny. He said the same thing–'

'Enough!' the highborn growled. 'Let's go see this damned library!'

Arleth Vann gave Malus a sketchy bow and dashed off, heading for a staircase on the far side of the room.

They climbed two more floors before they emerged into a corridor lit with globes of witchfire. The air smelled fresh, and Malus drank it in like wine. They were finally above ground.

Muted shouts echoed from one end of the corridor. Malus turned to Arleth Vann. 'What's that?'

'Urial must have men guarding the citadel,' the assassin said. 'The beastmen are raising the alarm.' He glanced down the opposite end of the passageway and seemed lost in thought for a moment. 'We'll take the servants' stairs,' he said after a moment. 'This way!'

Malus and the loyalists raced after the assassin, dashing through a maze of corridors before reaching a set of tightly curving stairs that led up into the higher levels of the tower. They climbed for a long while, their panting breaths echoing hollowly in the dark, cramped space. The highborn expected a wave of screaming zealots to sweep down on them from above at any moment, but many minutes later they left the staircase and emerged unchallenged into a brightly lit hallway. Arleth Vann raised his hand in warning, crept silently to the end of the passageway and peered into the space beyond. He motioned for the group to join him a moment later.

They crept from the passage into a large, open room not unlike a highborn's entry hall. A sweeping staircase rose to a gallery overlooking the room, and a circular platform sat in the centre of the chamber, piled high with severed skulls. Incense hung heavy in the air, attempting to mask the stench of rot rising from the putrefying trophies. A pair of heavy, gilded doors stood shut in a shadowed alcove beneath the gallery, opposite an open archway that led to an antechamber on the far side of the tower. The marble floor was covered in scraps of cheap brown paper. Malus frowned and stirred a pile of papers with his toe. Each sheet was covered in fine, archaic script. 'What's all this?' he asked quietly.

'Petitioners' writs,' Arleth Vann replied. 'Members of the temple may petition the Haru'ann for access to the libraries, and if their request is granted they are given a scrap of paper marked with the elder's signature and a verse or two from the *Parables of Sundered Flesh*. Then the petitioners are left here to wait and meditate upon the verses until the librarians call their names.' He gestured at the pile of grisly trophies. 'Many petitioners bring offerings in hope that the librarians will expedite their access, but the keepers of the sacred texts are rarely impressed.' The assassin pointed to the double doors. 'This level contains nothing more than histories and copies of sacred texts,' he said, indicating the gallery overhead. 'What we want is up there.'

Arleth Vann crossed the chamber and climbed the staircase two steps at a time. Malus went after him, noting that Niryal and the other loyalists followed with considerable reluctance. Priestesses and mere novitiates were not welcome in this place.

The gallery was furnished with thick rugs and plush, high-backed chairs arrayed in twin ranks before a single door of blooded oak. Side tables set off in the far corners were set with silver goblets and bottles of wine, clearly meant for the pleasure of the temple elders. Arleth Vann turned to Niryal and the loyalists. 'Wait here,' he said.

To Malus's surprise, Niryal glared at the assassin. 'We know our place,' she said. 'It is you who overstep your bounds. This is not proper!'

'You are welcome to complain to the Grand Carnifex,' the assassin said coolly. He pushed the door open and stepped into the room beyond as if he belonged there. Malus followed close behind.

The upper library was huge, its curving walls lined with bookshelves that stretched as much as three storeys high. Long ladders of blooded oak ran on tracks of polished brass that circled the towering shelves, allowing apprentice librarians to scurry up and retrieve volumes for their patrons. Thick rugs were piled on the stone floor around ranks of wooden carrels, their working surfaces brightly lit by a cluster of large witchlight globes suspended on a chain from the centre of the vaulted ceiling. The air was thick with the smell of dust, old leather and ancient paper. It reminded Malus of his half-sister Nagaira's former library back at the Hag. 'These places are nothing but trouble,' he muttered darkly.

Arleth Vann moved quickly to the far side of the room. There, beyond the furthest rank of work carrels, the rugs abruptly stopped at an expanse of polished black marble. A large circle of arcane sigils was carved into the stone, and beyond that stood a series of tall, wooden cabinets arrayed in a rough semicircle. The assassin studied each cabinet in turn before settling on the fourth in line and pulling its wooden doors open.

There were dozens of polished skulls inside, resting on shelves lined with black velvet. They all looked very old, and many were bound together with intricate nets of gold and silver wire.

'What is all this?' the highborn asked.

Arleth Vann looked over his shoulder at his master and smiled faintly. 'These are the real treasures of the library,' he said. 'Sacred texts are well and good, but the temple has always placed its greatest faith in the wisdom and insight of its elders. These cabinets contain the skulls of more than four hundred of the greatest men and women of the temple, stretching back for more than four thousand years. Their spirits remain tied to their skulls with powerful spells, so that they can continue to serve the faithful long after their deaths.'

The assassin reached into the cabinet and reverently lifted one of the skulls from its resting place. Malus noted that several spots on the shelves were empty, and thought of the skull that Urial had showed him in his quarters on the *Harrier*. A thought occurred to him. 'Why didn't Urial forsake the temple like the other zealots? He had to have known that the temple elders didn't dare acknowledge him even if he had been the true Scourge.'

Arleth Vann shrugged. 'I suppose it was greed. You've seen the wealth and luxury that the temple elders enjoy here. I suspect that Urial kept the zealots at arm's length for years, knowing he would need them when the time came to make his play for the sword, but looking to build his influence in the temple at the same time. Perhaps he seeks to reconcile the two in some fashion, letting him have the best of both worlds.'

Malus gave a cynical grunt. 'So much for the purity of faith,' he said. 'At least the Slaaneshi are honest about their appetites.'

The assassin shot the highborn a warning glare. 'Don't blaspheme,' he said, 'especially not in the presence of four hundred very pious, very savage ghosts.'

'Point taken,' Malus replied, watching his retainer carry the skull into the magic circle. 'For an assassin you seem to know a very great deal about the temple and its history,' he said.

Arleth Vann paused, staring down at the skull. 'I never wanted to be an assassin,' he said quietly. 'This is where I wanted to be, among the books and the old bones.'

'You wanted to be a librarian?' Malus said, not bothering to hide his disdain.

The retainer shrugged. 'I grew up here. My parents gave me to the temple when I was just a babe, like so many others. I grew up in the cells near the Assassin's Door, and when I was five I was given to the librarians to carry books and run errands. I took to letters well and could write by the time I was seven.' He looked up at the shelves. 'I was also good on the ladders, which the elderly librarians appreciated. I prided myself on getting up and down as quickly and quietly as possible.' His expression darkened, 'and that was my undoing, in a way. The librarians assigned me to a temple witch who was working on an important project, and she thought my skills were going to waste fetching books and picking up rubbish. So she spoke to the master librarian and at ten years old I began my tutelage with the temple assassins.'

Arleth Vann knelt and gently laid the skull in the centre of the circle. 'Once I entered the assassins' order, I was forbidden to enter the library, of course. So at night I would sneak into the crypts and slip back into the citadel, where I would spend hours poring through the old tomes. That's how I learned about the schism, and the deception the elders have practised for millennia. The truth is here, scattered in vague references and small details spread through scores of unrelated books.' He stood and pointed to one of the carrels near the back of the room. 'I was sitting right there the night I put all the pieces together. That was both the best and the worst night of my life. Nothing was the same after that.'

'So you threw in your lot with the zealots.'

The assassin gave Malus an indignant look. 'We're not talking about some petty highborn intrigue, where one's allegiance shifts with the wind. I was a servant of Khaine, and I had been practising heresy from the moment I entered the temple. So what other choice did I have but to leave Har Ganeth and seek the wisdom of the zealots?'

'That's why they sent you to Har Ganeth in search of the Scourge?'

'No,' the assassin replied, 'for all that you have seen of Tyran and his schemes here in the city, the true cult is not as dogmatic and rigid as the temple. Masters wander the land, practising their devotions and perfecting the killing arts, and aspirants to the cult must seek them out for instruction. When the master deems the student worthy, he or she is sent out into the world alone to worship the Bloody-Handed God and wait for the coming of the Scourge.' The assassin smiled faintly. 'Unlike most true believers, I wasn't content to simply wait for the Time of Blood to announce itself. I began searching for signs of the Scourge in every city I came to.'

'Why?'

The assassin shrugged. 'Redemption, I suppose, or revenge against the temple. At any rate,' he said with a sigh, 'that was how I found myself in a seer's hut outside Karond Kar several years ago, wagering my soul in a game of Dragon's Teeth in exchange for a divination. The woman was utterly mad, but her visions were true. She told me that the Scourge would be born of a witch in the City of Shadow, and would dwell in the house of chains.' He shook his head ruefully. 'The old wretch tried to serve me poisoned wine afterwards. The city folk had warned me she was a poor loser.'

Malus considered this and tried to hide his discomfort. He'd never inquired about Arleth Vann's beliefs when the assassin had served him at the Hag, and now he found all this talk about service and devotion more than a little disturbing. 'I hope you aren't expecting some kind of divine forgiveness from me,' he said, 'because I don't do that sort of thing.'

The assassin shook his head and chuckled softly. 'Khaine forfend!' he said. 'No, I simply serve, my lord. If the Lord of Murder wills it, I will find my own redemption. Speaking of which,' he said, drawing a deep breath, 'we're wasting time. Urial's men could be searching the citadel as we speak, and I don't know how long this summoning will take.'

'I thought you said that the assassins' order only taught you minor sorceries,' Malus said.

Arleth Vann nodded. 'That's right, but I've observed similar rituals many times in the past.'

'Meaning you've never done this before.'

The assassin hesitated. 'Strictly speaking, yes.'

'Mother of Night,' Malus cursed. 'What happens if the summoning goes wrong?'

'Well,' Arleth Vann said carefully, 'there is a very small possibility that I could lose control of the magical forces and cause a minor explosion.'

'Ah,' the highborn said, 'in that case, I'll wait in the gallery.'

'Very well, my lord.'

Malus turned on his heel and strode swiftly from the room, pulling the oak door shut behind him. Niryal and the two loyalists stood at the gallery's edge, peering over the rail at the space below. The priestess turned at his approach. 'Did you find what you were looking for?' she asked.

'My man is still searching,' the highborn replied. 'It shouldn't be long.' He joined her at the rail. The two temple servants stepped away, retreating to the top of the stairs.

Niryal resumed her watch, her expression troubled. She was tall and lean, with weathered skin stretched taut over hard, cable-like muscles. Faint scars marked the backs of her hands and the side of her thin face and neck, and her small mouth was set in a hard, determined line. 'How am I to address you?' she asked.

Malus gave her a sidelong look. 'What?'

Her dark eyes met his. 'You have a retainer – a man with the blessing of Khaine upon him and the swords of an assassin, no less – but for Rhulan, none of the other elders had any idea who you were. You know next to nothing about the temple, but you know things about the warpsword and about Urial that no one else does.' She looked him up and down. 'You dress like a beggar but shout commands like a highborn, and somehow you spent several days in the company of Tyran and his zealots, and then arrived unannounced in the council chambers to deliver an anonymous warning to the Grand Carnifex.' She cocked her head inquisitively. 'So, who... or what... are you?'

The highborn spread his hands and managed a smile to mask his concern. 'As I said to the council, I'm a servant of Khaine. What else matters?'

Niryal arched a whip thin eyebrow. 'I can think of a great many things, but let's start with this: how can you be so certain that Urial is not the Swordbearer after all? The more I think about it, the more trouble I have believing that he found a way to circumvent Khaine's will and claim the blade for himself.'

Malus hesitated. 'Malekith is the Scourge of Khaine, so it is written.'

'Yes, but written by whom? All I know is that the Witch King is in his tower at Naggarond, and Urial is here with the warpsword in his hands. I saw it with my own eyes, just as I saw him slay the Grand Carnifex in single combat. The Grand Carnifex! How can that be possible if Urial isn't Khaine's chosen one?'

The highborn's eyes narrowed warily. 'Because Urial is a sorcerer of fearsome power, and he has coveted the warpsword for many years. The Arch-Hierophant realised this. Why can't you?'

Niryal leaned close to Malus. 'The Arch-Hierophant has fled the city,' she whispered. 'I heard your retainer say so.'

Malus stiffened. 'Rhulan is a coward,' he hissed.

'Or he has no faith in you, and if he does not, then why should I?'

Out of the corner of his eye, Malus saw the loyalist sentries watching from the stairs drop into a crouch. He caught the warning movement a moment too late. Before he could react he heard shouts of alarm from the chamber below. The highborn gave a silent snarl as he saw a trio of temple beastmasters standing just inside the room. One of them locked eyes with Malus and levelled a short spear at his face.

'Damnation,' Malus cursed quietly, and the air shook with hoarse war screams as the beastmasters charged for the gallery stairs. Five of Tyran's zealots followed hot on their heels, their gleaming draichs held high.

'Stop them on the stairs!' the highborn shouted to the loyalists. The stairway was just wide enough for two men to walk abreast. If they could keep their foes off the gallery floor the zealots would be at a disadvantage with their long blades. As he raced past Niryal, Malus shot a nervous glance at the door to the upper library, but there was no hint as to what was happening on the other side. All he could do was hope Arleth Vann learned what he needed quickly. They couldn't hold out for long.

The beastmasters flung themselves at the loyalists, jabbing fiercely with their spears in an effort to drive them back. One of the men started to give ground, but Malus reached the top of the stairs and grabbed a fistful of the retreating man's robe, forcing him back. The highborn stood close, just above and behind the two loyalists, looking for an opportunity to strike.

One of the beastmasters blocked a spear thrust with his sword and then drew a ragged cut across his opponent's weapon arm. Seeing an opportunity, the second beastmaster feinted at the man in front of him and then threw a lightning quick thrust at the overextended swordsman, but Malus's sword flashed down like a thunderbolt, biting deep into the beastmaster's forearm. Bones snapped with a brittle crack and the beastmaster's howl of pain turned to a choked gurgle as his opponent recovered from the feint and stabbed him in the throat.

The dying beastmaster sagged to his left and tumbled off the stairs. His companion stepped forwards into the gap, aiming a low blow at his foe's legs. The loyalist tried to block the thrust, but the stroke was ill timed and the steel spearhead dug a deep gouge along his thigh. Screaming in pain, the temple servant slashed wildly at the beastmaster's head, but the warrior ducked beneath the blow and drove his spear deep into the loyalist's abdomen. Malus saw the sharp, steel point burst from the man's back and the loyalist died with a terrible groan.

Growling like a wolf, Malus kicked the dead loyalist in the back, sending the corpse crashing into his killer. The beastmaster shouted angrily and pushed the corpse off the stairs, but as he tried to pull his spear free of the falling body Malus swept down the stairs and split the man's skull. The beastmaster collapsed, blood spilling down his shattered face, and the highborn pivoted on the ball of his foot and drove his blade into the third beastmaster's chest.

The second blow nearly got him killed. Just as Malus pulled his sword free from the dying man he caught a flash of steel, and instinct caused him to fall backwards, away from the draich's blurring strike. The sword flashed through the space where his head had been, continuing downwards to slice across the highborn's forearm. He grimaced at the sudden flare of pain, but there was no time for concern – the zealot continued to press his attack, reversing his curved sword and slashing upwards at Malus's neck. The highborn rolled right, feeling the razor edged steel hiss through the air a finger's breadth from his jawbone. Then there was a meaty *crunch*, and hot blood sprayed across his face. He opened his eyes in time to see the zealot fall off the stairs, the top of his head shorn away by the stroke of Niryal's axe.

Legs pumping furiously, Malus scrambled backwards up the stairs. The zealots pressed forwards. On the highborn's left the surviving loyalist was also retreating, blood flowing from a deep wound in his shoulder. Niryal stood over Malus, her bloody axe swinging in vicious strokes to keep the enemy at bay. Then movement on the floor below caught the highborn's eye. Zealots and black robed temple converts were streaming into the room and adding their weight to the group pushing up the stairway.

'Fall back!' Malus shouted angrily. 'Back to the library!'

The wounded loyalist stole a glance at Malus upon hearing the order, and the mistake cost him his life. His opponent leapt forwards with a shout and brought his powerful blade down at the juncture of the man's neck and shoulder. The blow chopped through collarbone and ribs, splitting the breastbone and tearing through his vitals. Blood burst from the man's open mouth and he fell without a sound. Whether by luck or design the loyalist's body collapsed against the front rank of zealots, slowing their advance long enough for Malus to scramble to his feet and race for the library door.

The door latch was icy cold to the touch. Malus pulled the door open and a blast of freezing air lashed at his face. Frost glittered on the inside of the door, and the chamber was suffused with a shifting blue glow. At the far end of the room, Arleth Vann stood before the elder's skull, which floated in the air several feet above his head. Blue flames burned from the skull's eye sockets, and it was attached to a wispy body that twisted and writhed as it hung in the air.

Malus raced across the room, feeling the invisible tension of the sorcerous struggle seethe across his skin. Arleth Vann's back was arched and his head was thrown back, his mouth working silently as he waged a battle of wills against the elder's spirit. Niryal stumbled through the door behind Malus, her eyes going wide at the scene playing out before her.

'Into the circle!' Malus shouted to her as he stepped across the mystical lines. Power surged and crackled around him. He felt a wave of freezing cold against his face, and his hair stood on end. A seething crackle filled his ears. The highborn turned to find the priestess right on his heels. As she stepped into the circle they were buffeted by a cyclone of unstable energies. Arleth Vann's head snapped forwards, his face etched with strain and his eyes wide.

'Release the energy!' the highborn shouted into the building storm. 'Let it go!'

The door to the library burst open as the first of the zealots charged in. In half a dozen strides the swordsmen were halfway across the room. Malus started to shout at the assassin again when he heard Arleth Vann howl in agony and the world exploded in a blast of bluish flame.

CHAPTER NINETEEN

REVERSALS OF FORTUNE

A clap of thunder smote Malus's ears and he was yanked off his feet by the power of the blast, like a leaf caught up in the wake of a raging wind. He heard screams and the sound of splintering wood, and then he crashed into something hard and unyielding, knocking him senseless.

When his vision finally cleared, long moments later, he found himself sprawled beneath a pile of shredded, smouldering books at the base of one of the library's many bookshelves. The ringing in his ears began to fade, replaced by the groans of wounded men.

A hazy, bluish light hung in the air, seeming to emanate from the very stones of the floor, walls and ceiling. The witchlight globes had shattered in the blast, and drifts of shredded paper hung like fine ash in the unearthly glow. Everything caught in the blast had been destroyed. The study carrels had been smashed to pieces like a ship's rail hit by a catapult stone, and the hundreds of books lining the shelves around the room had been mulched by a storm of wooden shrapnel. The tall cabinets containing the skulls of former elders were likewise crushed, spilling a rain of bone fragments onto the floor.

Niryal lay against one of the bookshelves to Malus's left, covered in debris but apparently unhurt. As the highborn staggered to his feet he saw Arleth Vann rising in a daze on the opposite side of the room. The assassin's face was lined with pain and exhaustion, and his eyes were wide with horror at the devastation he'd wrought. The arcane circle laid in the floor was gone, its lines of silver obliterated by the release of magical energy. Malus reckoned that the only reason he and his companions were still alive was because the destructive force radiated outwards from the edge of the circle and dragged them along with it.

Their foes had not been so fortunate.

The zealots closest to the circle could not even be said to resemble men. Their swords had shattered and their clothes had burned away, but their bodies had simply melted like candle wax, leaving nothing but piles of steaming, red mush behind. The next rank of men had caught the full fury of the blast's shrapnel, riddling and slicing their bodies into tattered, dripping rags. Only those closest to the narrow doorway had escaped death, although the door itself had been torn to flinders and hurled into the gallery beyond. Bodies writhed on the floor, clutching seeping wounds or mangled limbs.

His breath turning to vapour in the unnaturally cold air, Malus cast about for his sword and found it embedded in a pair of thick, leather-bound tomes still resting on their shelf at roughly chest height. The highborn yanked the blade loose, spilling the torn contents of the books onto the glowing stone, and stumbled through the debris towards the wounded men with a grim look on his face.

'Blessed Murderer,' Niryal gasped, her face pale and furious as she surveyed the desolation. 'What have you done?'

'What was necessary,' Malus snapped, reaching the first pair of wounded men and despatching them with short, vicious strokes. Steaming sprays of blood arced heavily through the blue tinged air with each upswing of the double-edged blade. 'Would you rather have let these blasphemers kill us?'

'Of course!' the priestess cried. 'Our lives mean nothing compared to the knowledge within these walls–'

Malus rounded on her, levelling his dripping sword at her face. 'Don't start,' he warned. Nearby, a zealot rolled onto his stomach and began crawling towards a nearby blade. The highborn caught the movement and fell upon the wounded man, hacking remorselessly at his head and neck.

'None... of... this... is... yours!' Malus said, emphasising each word with a vicious sword stroke. The zealot collapsed, and the highborn searched for another victim. 'Every book, every damned skull, all of it belongs to Urial. Do you see?'

'What I see is another bloody disaster!' the priestess shot back. Somehow she'd managed to keep her grip on her axe during the explosion, and she pointed the curving tips of its twin blades at Malus. 'Everywhere you go, you leave death and ruin in your wake.'

Malus stepped over to an unmoving form and studied it. Quick as an adder he stabbed the man in the throat and was rewarded with a bright fountain of blood. The man began convulsing, and the highborn grunted in satisfaction. 'Didn't I say I was a servant of Khaine?' he replied, giving her a challenging stare.

'What servant of Khaine would leave his god's temple in ruins?' she said.

'One fighting a war,' the highborn replied. He pointed through the doorway with his sword. 'If you think that usurper in the sanctum is the true Scourge, then go to him and see how he rewards your misguided beliefs.'

The two druchii exchanged furious stares: Niryal trembling with anger, and Malus cold and still as stone.

A pile of debris shifted, revealing a badly wounded zealot. A bloody groan bubbled from the warrior's lips.

Niryal's face twisted in a bitter grimace. Hefting her axe, she took three swift strides and buried the heavy blade in the wounded man's chest. The priestess pulled her weapon free, spattering the surrounding books with spots of bright crimson, and then stalked from the room with a single, hateful glare. Moments later Malus heard the wet, butcher's sound of her axe cleaving into the survivors in the gallery.

Malus turned to Arleth Vann. The assassin's gaze still wandered through the ruins of his childhood, drifting from one devastated pile of books to another. The highborn joined him, picking his way carefully through the wreckage.

'Do not mourn,' the highborn said softly. 'You did what had to be done.'

Arleth Vann seemed to notice him for the first time, peering out of his bleak reverie. 'She was right,' he said, his voice hollow. 'You can't imagine what has been lost, my lord: so much knowledge... so much history!'

Malus took his retainer by the throat, pulling him close. 'Knowledge is illusory,' he growled. 'History is but prologue. Everything kept in this room was meant to shepherd the temple to this point in time. It served its purpose, Arleth Vann. The Time of Blood is nigh.'

The assassin stared at Malus, a stricken expression twisting his pale features. He nodded slowly. 'Yes, of course. You have the right of it, my lord.' Arleth Vann spoke intently, as if trying to convince himself. 'What's past is past.'

'Well said,' Malus replied. 'Did you learn anything from the elder?'

Arleth Vann glanced at the ruined circle. The elder's skull sat upright at its centre, miraculously unharmed by the blast. 'It was harder – much harder – than I expected,' he admitted, 'but, yes, the elder finally shared some of his knowledge.'

'And?'

The assassin breathed a misty sigh. 'There is no way to track the zealots through the gate,' he said. 'To do that would require a personal connection with one of them, like the blood of kinship or the power of a sorcerous oath.'

Malus growled deep in his throat. 'That is not helpful.'

Arleth Vann interrupted the highborn's protests with a raised hand. 'We have no tie to the zealots, but we do have a powerful connection to the sword itself.'

'What tie?'

'Why, you, of course,' the assassin replied. 'You're the Scourge. The blade is fated to be wielded by you during the Time of Blood. That destiny binds you to the warpsword, and with it you can navigate your passage through the Vermillion Gate.'

Damned fate! Malus thought bitterly. He imagined he felt the daemon swell with pleasure inside his chest. 'Then we shall leave at once,' he said brusquely, 'provided we can get back into the crypts.'

'We can't go back the way we came, obviously,' the assassin replied, his voice slowly regaining its strength as he shook off the strain of the ritual and its cataclysmic end, 'but if we move quickly we can slip out through the ground floor and find another entry point in one of the nearby buildings.'

'What about the guards?'

The assassin managed a faint chuckle. 'They're all up here and more will be coming any minute. Urial could not have helped but sense what happened here.'

'I shouldn't be surprised,' Malus said. 'Let's get out of here. Once we've reached the lodge, however, I've got another errand for you.'

'As you wish, my lord,' the retainer replied, stifling a weary sigh. 'May I ask a question?'

'Make it quick.'

Arleth Vann nodded in the direction of the gallery. 'Would you have let her go to Urial if she'd wished?'

Malus didn't dignify such foolishness with an answer.

The four remaining loyalists filed silently from the prime chamber, all of them casting troubled glances over their shoulder at Malus and the tomb of Gothar the Ironmaster. Niryal was the last. She hadn't said a single word since leaving the Citadel of Bone, but Malus could plainly see the anger and doubt warring behind her eyes. The conflict had only deepened when he'd told them his theory about the warpsword.

He could tell that they wanted to believe him, because it meant that there was still a chance to restore the rightful order in the temple and gain some vengeance in an otherwise hopeless situation. The fact that the temple elders had lied to the faithful about the sword for centuries hadn't made much of an impression yet, but that would come in time. Providing that any of them survived.

There was no telling what they would find on the other side of the gate. Malus had wracked his brain, trying to deduce where the zealots would have taken their prize, but he couldn't think of a single place that made any sense. He wanted some idea of what they would be up against when they emerged on the other side of the gate.

A shiver passed through Malus, making him cast a worried glance at the chamber door. Fortunately, the temple servants were gone, having been told to gather up their meagre camp and make ready to depart. The highborn wrapped his arms tightly around his chest and breathed deeply, trying to keep his knees from trembling.

Malus ached for a taste of the daemon's power. The need had come upon him as they slipped from the citadel and crept across the temple grounds. Maybe it had been the brush with sorcery in the library, or the after-effects of the battle, but as he'd walked he felt his muscles shrivel like old roots and his guts turn to ice. It was by sheer willpower alone that he forced himself to complete the long journey back to the lodge. He'd told the loyalists his plans while leaning against the tomb so they wouldn't see his body tremble.

Just a taste, he thought. Just a small taste. Eldire said all wasn't yet lost. My will is still strong.

Another wracking shudder passed through him. He felt his knees buckle and couldn't get his hand out in time to keep himself from landing hard on the stone floor. Malus bit back a stream of vicious curses, appalled at his own weakness.

'It will only get worse, little druchii,' the daemon whispered, sliding like oil across his brain. 'This is but a taste of the ordeals to come, unless you let me help you.'

'You're corrupting me,' the highborn growled wearily, 'chewing out my guts from the inside, like a rat. Do you think I can't see what you're doing?'

'Malus, you brought this on yourself,' the daemon replied, 'the ordeal in Lurhan's tower, and all those times afterward, when we returned to Naggaroth from the sea. You were too greedy, taking too much of my strength at once.'

'Don't put this on me!' the highborn shouted angrily. 'I did what I had to in order to survive! I took nothing but what I needed at the time.'

'If that's the way you insist upon looking at it, then I can't make you think otherwise,' Tz'arkan replied, 'but all that is in the past. You are what you are, and nothing can change that. Why make yourself miserable, and risk your continued existence into the bargain, by wallowing in this wretched state? Let me restore your strength. You're going to need it for what lies ahead.'

Malus clenched his fists. It all sounded like sweet reason. Why bother fighting it when he was already so far gone? What would be the point? If you're already damned, better to go out in a blaze of glory than shivering and whimpering in a corner. 'What does lie ahead?' he asked, desperate to change the subject. 'What do you know?'

'I know there will be struggle, of course, hard, desperate fighting and rivers of pain. It is your fate, little druchii.'

'Fate,' Malus spat, feeling a little of his old hatred flare to life. Mentally, he huddled around its wan flame. 'You mean the grand trap you built for me.' Suddenly, a thought occurred to him. 'How does Khaine fit into all this?'

'What are you talking about?'

'Your plan,' the highborn said. 'What does a daemon of Slaanesh have to do with the Scourge of Khaine? And how is it that one of the five relics used to bind you just happens to be the talisman of Khaine's chosen one?'

The daemon didn't respond at first. Malus took that to be a sign he was on to something.

'The sword has not always been called the Warpsword of Khaine,' Tz'arkan said. 'It is very, very old, and has had many names in its time.'

'What was it called when it was being wielded by the Chaos lord who bound you?'

'What's the point? You don't have the mouth parts to pronounce it properly anyway.'

The highborn put that unpleasant mental image aside. 'My point is that the relic wasn't handed down to the cultists by Khaine himself. It fell into their hands sometime after you were bound in the far north.' Malus's mind began to race as he considered the implications. 'They were meant to keep it until the day I would come and claim it. So, is the prophecy of the Scourge also part of your plan? Did you plant that seed as well as the sword?'

Tz'arkan chuckled gleefully. 'Who can understand the machinations of fate, Darkblade? Certainly not you. How could I possibly manipulate so much while trapped in my crystal prison hundreds of leagues distant?'

'I don't know. I was hoping you would tell me.'

'Then you are destined for disappointment, I fear.'

Malus relaxed a little. With his mind fully engaged, the aches in his body seemed to abate. 'All right. Let us suppose that Khaine handed down the prophecy of the Scourge, and you somehow inserted this relic into the legends, knowing that one day I – or some other misbegotten bastard like me – would come along to claim both. Aren't you courting Khaine's wrath in all this?'

The daemon sighed. 'Such a clever little beast you are sometimes. All right, as a token of pity for the sad state you are in, I will tell you this much: the Blood God does not care who spills blood in his name, or why, only that it flows.'

Malus considered this. 'Then, in truth, anyone can wield the blade.'

'Anyone? Hardly.'

'Obviously it isn't meant solely for the Scourge of Khaine, which means that I have no more a tie to the damned thing than anyone else.'

'No, but I do,' the daemon said. 'I have felt its bite, and it remembers the taste.'

The highborn's eyes widened. 'Then you knew that the sword in Urial's hand was a fake.'

'Of course. I knew it from the moment he stabbed you.'

'And it never occurred to you to tell me?'

'Certainly it did,' the daemon purred, 'but where would be the fun in that?'

Malus bared his teeth at the daemon's gleeful laughter, huddling against the stone tomb of the ironmaster as he felt another of the tremors begin.

He was dozing fitfully when Arleth Vann finally returned.

Malus awakened to a gentle tapping on his boot. The highborn opened his eyes to find the assassin crouching a polite distance away. Arleth Vann's pale face was smudged by soot and mottled with spots of dried blood.

'Where have you been?' the highborn asked, trying to rub the exhaustion from his face.

'In the city, of course,' the assassin replied wearily. 'Things have taken a turn for the worse.'

'Worse for us, or for them?' Malus winced. 'Never mind, the answer's obvious.' He tried to stand. 'Help me up.'

Arleth Vann pulled him upright, a worried frown creasing his face. 'Is it the old wound?'

'That and more, but I will survive,' the highborn said. 'Now tell me what's happened.'

The assassin nodded and headed for the doorway with Malus following close behind. 'Sometime this morning – most likely just after dawn – the temple warriors abandoned their holdouts and tried to fight their way out of the encirclements Urial threw around them.'

The highborn shook his head, bemused. 'Why now, of all times?'

Arleth Vann shrugged as they passed through the first of the burial chambers. The two temple loyalists resting there saw Malus on the move and rose to their feet, picking up cloth bags containing their supplies and falling into step behind the highborn.

'There are rumours on the street. Most people think that the holdouts ran out of food several days ago, so they had the choice of breaking out or starving to death. Others say that penny oracles in the merchants' district have had visions of a terrible army bearing down on Har Ganeth from the west.'

Malus hissed thoughtfully. Could the Witch King already be on the move, he wondered? 'Anything's possible,' he admitted. 'Were the breakouts successful?'

'Eventually,' Arleth Vann said. 'The fighting lasted all day, and there are rumours that hundreds of warriors and witches were slain. What little of the warehouse district hadn't burned before was put to the torch, it seems. Over the course of the day the isolated warbands managed to link up and fight their way to the city gate.'

The highborn stopped in his tracks. 'The *city* gate? Not the fortress gate?'

Arleth Vann nodded. 'They retreated about half a mile up the Slavers' Road to the west and they're building a camp by the shore.'

'Those fools,' Malus spat. 'Urial controls the entire damned city! It will be a hundred times harder to dislodge him now. Unless...'

'Unless perhaps those penny oracles were right and the temple witches have foreseen that Malekith is on the way.'

'Damnation,' Malus said. 'If it's true, then we're nearly out of time. If Urial is still in control of the city when the Witch King arrives, the die will be cast and there will be no stopping the war that will follow.' With a muted growl he leapt back into motion, speeding though the succession of chambers with long, impatient strides.

'Honestly, my lord, I'm surprised you care,' Arleth Vann said, moving swiftly to keep pace. 'Would a holy war not serve Khaine's purposes?'

The highborn gave his retainer a hard look. 'Under the circumstances, I believe that's for me to decide.'

'Of course, my lord.'

Malus continued on, rushing through the last of the crypts and coming to the open doorway of the lodge's antechamber. A familiar, acrid reek filled his nostrils, and he heard one of the accompanying loyalists let out a surprised curse at the smell. A sharp, drawn-out hiss sounded from within the antechamber, like steam whistling from a cracked kettle.

Though small for its breed, Spite took up nearly a third of the large, rectangular antechamber. Arleth Vann had left it resting on his haunches just inside the lodge's main doors, and even with its powerful tail tucked along his side, the nauglir was long enough to brush the ends of the long tables on either side of the room.

Malus raised a warning hand. 'Wait here,' he said to Arleth Vann and the loyalists. Spite, hearing his voice, rose onto its clawed feet and turned its huge, blocky snout in his direction. Nostrils flared wide as Spite tasted his master's scent.

The highborn slowly crossed the room, studying the cold one carefully for signs of danger. Before he'd sent Arleth Vann into the city to fetch Spite he'd applied a fresh coat of vrahsha to both his and his retainer's skin from a small vial tucked into his robes. The salve disguised a druchii's scent, but not the daemonic corruption that Malus knew was spreading through his body.

Spite's nostrils flared as it tasted Malus's scent. A low grumble rose from its chest.

'It's all right, you great, dumb beast,' Malus said lightly, 'it's me.'

The cold one lowered its head slightly. Venomous drool fell in long, ropy strands from its huge jaws. Spite growled threateningly as the highborn took another step forwards. Scales grated over stone as the nauglir uncurled its tail. The powerful, cable thick muscle brushed the room's centre table in passing and smashed one of the corners into powder with a sharp *crack*.

Malus stopped where he was, suddenly wary of getting within the cold one's reach. 'Where did you find him?' he asked.

'In the stables where Tyran's men left him,' the assassin replied. 'He'd broken out of the pen days ago and just seemed to be settling there.'

The highborn looked the nauglir over and noticed a number of recent wounds on the warbeast's armoured hide. None looked remotely life threatening. To his great relief, the saddle and bags on the cold one's back still looked intact. 'Has Spite been fed?'

'Oh, it's eaten well,' the retainer assured him. 'There were bits of flesh and pieces of broken bone all over the pen. It probably ate the attendants first, and then started hunting the locals over the last few days.'

Malus nodded. If Spite was well fed, this was as safe a time to approach the beast as any. Taking a deep breath, he took another step forwards.

The cold one settled slightly onto its haunches, assuming a defensive stance, another bad sign.

'What do you think you're doing?' Malus said to the warbeast. 'It's me, and I don't have time for your nonsense. There's hard riding to be done.'

He took another step forwards. Spite's jaws began to open, one slow inch at a time.

The highborn realised that Spite was getting ready to attack, and felt an overpowering rush of frustration. 'Now you listen here, you great lump of scales,' Malus snapped, levelling an angry finger at the one ton warbeast, 'I didn't come all this way to get made a meal of by my own mount. Now *stand*, and let me look at you!'

Malus's commanding shout rang from the chamber walls, startling the cold one. Spite jerked back, nostrils flaring, and snapped at the air with a bone-jarring crunch of dagger-length fangs. For an instant the highborn feared that the warbeast would turn and dart out of the antechamber into the tunnel beyond, but then it paused, blew steam from its nostrils and settled obediently onto its haunches.

Inwardly the highborn breathed a sigh of relief. 'That's better,' he said, and walked up to the nauglir. He circled the cold one and looked him over, checking talons, teeth, eyes, flanks and tail. Once he was convinced that the beast was essentially unhurt, he moved to check his possessions. 'Help me with this armour,' he called out to Arleth Vann.

Moving warily, the retainer joined Malus at Spite's side and helped remove the leather bags containing the highborn's plate harness. Arleth Vann worked quickly and efficiently, unwrapping the armour plates from their oiled cloths and then helping Malus into his old kheitan. Within minutes the highborn was buckling his sword belt over his mail fauld and almost feeling like his old self again.

'You said that fighting in the city lasted until around sunset,' Malus said, pulling on his armoured gauntlets, 'what time is it now?'

'About two hours past sunset, my lord,' the assassin replied.

Malus grimaced. The first light of false dawn had been paling the sky over the fortress when he, the assassin and Niryal had escaped the Citadel of Bone. 'We've lost a great deal of time,' he said. The highborn glanced at the lodge's main doors. 'Where's Niryal? She and one of the other loyalists were standing watch.'

Arleth Vann frowned. 'I didn't see anyone when I came in, my lord.'

Malus froze. A cold knot of dread tightened in his guts.

Suddenly, Spite turned, pointing his snout towards the tunnel outside and growling threateningly. At once, a chorus of gibbering howls answered.

CHAPTER TWENTY

BLOOD AND SOULS

'Bar the door!' Malus shouted, grabbing Spite's reins and leading the cold one deeper into the room. Arleth Vann and the loyalists leapt to obey, giving the hissing nauglir as wide a berth as possible. The three druchii reached the doors and pushed them shut. Then they picked up wedge-shaped pieces of stone they'd broken from the dwarf crypts and began jamming them as tightly as they could into the narrow space beneath the stone panels.

'What did you see?' the highborn asked his retainer as he guided Spite around the far end of the room's central table.

'I saw at least one of the hunting beasts,' the assassin replied, using a hammer looted from one of the tombs to drive the wedges home. Flecks of stone flew with every sharp blow. 'Worse, I saw witchlights.'

'How many?'

'At least a dozen,' Arleth Vann said grimly.

'Mother of Night,' Malus whispered. That many lights could mean fifty men or more. 'Any sign of Niryal or the other sentry?'

The retainer shook his head. 'If the assassins finally decided to join Urial they could have taken both of them and left no one the wiser. They probably let me through because I had Spite with me.'

'And they know we're trapped,' the highborn said grimly.

Something heavy smashed against the doors with a thunderous crash, causing even Spite to jump. Stone dust puffed through the doorjamb, and a gibbering howl echoed outside. Malus heard the scrape of thorny tentacles lashing against the stone.

'Get back,' Malus ordered, drawing his sword. Arleth Vann and the two loyalists retreated behind Spite. The nauglir was back in a defensive pose, growling ominously, its long tail extended. The highborn patted the cold one's neck as his companions drew their weapons and formed a small semicircle behind him.

They heard another fearsome crash, and a sharp crack of breaking stone.

'That won't hold for long,' Arleth Vann muttered.

'I don't suppose there's a secret passage out of here that you haven't told me about?' Malus asked.

'If there was, don't you think the dwarfs would have taken it?'

'Good point.'

Another blow struck the doors, and this time the druchii could see a pair of cracks spreading upwards and downwards from the centre of the leftmost panel.

Malus tried to think past the frantic sound of his pulse pounding in his ears. 'Perhaps we could hide in the tombs? Pretend we're dwarfs?'

Arleth Vann shook his head. 'It wouldn't work, my lord, Spite's too tall for a dwarf.'

'There is that,' Malus deadpanned. 'I suppose we'll just have to find a way to kill the bastards then.'

With a thunderous *crack*, the leftmost door exploded in a shower of dust and fragments, and the lean form of one of the Chaos beasts came tumbling into the chamber. Dust caked its damp, gelatinous hide, and its claws raked across the stone as it skidded to a halt. Tentacles lashed the air hungrily and one of the beast's fist sized eyes focused on the highborn, only a few yards away.

Spreading its fearsome, barbed whips and hissing through its glossy beak, the hunter gathered itself to leap. Malus slapped his hand against the nauglir's neck and shouted 'Hunt, Spite! *Hunt!*' just as the creature pounced.

The Chaos beast was swift as a hunting cat, but the nauglir let out a bellow that shook dust from the ceiling and met the fearsome creature mid-leap. The hunter was huge, but Spite's body was a third again larger and much more massive. The two creatures crashed together and the hunter was propelled backwards, its tentacles lashing furiously at Spite's armoured hide as the cold one dug its claws in and tore at the beast's throat. They landed with an earth-shaking crash, smashing two of the side-tables to pieces just as a wave of screaming druchii charged through the broken doorway.

They were a mismatched band, armed with an apparently random mix of weapons and armour. Black-robed temple servants brandished short swords and heavy axes next to knife wielding druchii in plain robes. One woman with the leather jerkin of a butcher hefted a gore-crusted cleaver beside a highborn wearing full armour and wielding paired swords. The only thing the mob had in common was the sign of the Blood God branded on their foreheads and the mindless look of bloodlust that burned in their dark eyes.

Their savage charge ran headlong into the path of the two wrestling beasts. Spite's lashing tail smashed three city folk off their feet, hurling their broken bodies back onto their companions. Lashing tentacles cut like saws through the enemy ranks, the barbed hooks ripping off hands, legs and faces with indiscriminate fury. Showers of blood and torn flesh burst among the charging druchii, but the survivors paid the carnage little heed. They saw Malus and his men across the room and scrambled past the thrashing creatures, their faces alight with the prospect of slaughter.

Malus bared his teeth at the oncoming mob. 'If they want a battle we'll give them one,' he said, raising his sword. 'Blood and souls!'

'Blood and souls!' the warriors of Khaine shouted, and the slaughter began in earnest.

The attackers were largely unskilled, making mistakes in their frenzy that no experienced soldier would have. Howling zealots raced around to either side of the large, central table that Malus had situated his men behind, thereby breaking the force of their charge, but some were so eager for bloodshed they scrambled atop the table itself. The highborn let them come, ducked low out of the reach of their shorter weapons, and hacked off their legs at the knees. Three city folk died that way, spilling huge gouts of blood onto the flat stone as they toppled off onto the heads of their compatriots.

To Malus's left, Arleth Vann slew every foe that came within reach, blocking with one sword and coolly despatching each opponent with a single thrust or cut from the other. To the highborn's right, the two surviving loyalists staggered against the frenzied assault of the zealots, but grimly held their ground, lashing at their foes with red stained swords.

With the tabletop clear Malus turned his attention to his right, using the corner of the table to keep the zealots at a distance where their knives and axes couldn't reach him. It was like slaying cattle. The frenzied city folk rushed at the loyalists, clashing blades, and Malus stabbed them in the throat or chest, dropping them to the ground. Whatever had robbed the attackers of their reason served to blind them to the murderous efficiency of the highborn's tactics.

The thrashing struggle of the huge beasts continued near the door. Spite's neck and flanks were criss-crossed with countless furrows from the hunter's barbed scales, but the nauglir had the Chaos beast by the throat, keeping its fearsome black beak at bay. The two creatures struggled to overbear one another, but Spite's greater bulk and long tail gave the cold one a powerful advantage. The nauglir found its feet and bore down with its jaws, forcing a strangled screech from the hunter. Its thick skin was more than enough to stave off sword and axe blows, but could not resist the fearsome might of the cold one's powerful bite. Runnels of clear ichor flowed off Spite's jaw as the warbeast lifted the hunter off the floor and shook it like a terrier shakes a rat. Tentacles flailed and bones snapped. Then Spite jerked his head and flung the creature across the room. It smashed into another of the long preparation tables, shattering it beneath its weight, and the hunter went limp.

Spite's bellow of victory shook the antechamber, drowning out even the zealots' frenzied screams. Barely a handful of attackers were left, out of the score or so who had charged into the room, and Malus felt his spirits lift.

If this was the best the zealots had available, then Malus and his followers could easily fight their way out to the gate.

The druchii woman with the two-handed cleaver charged at one of the loyalists with a piercing, bestial shriek, foam flying from her thin lips as she swung her filthy blade at the man's neck. The loyalist tried to parry the blow, but the heavier weapon knocked his blade aside and deflected into the man's shoulder. Before the butcher could pull her grisly weapon free Malus leaned in and took off the top of her head with his long sword. Bone and brain sprayed into the air, but the highborn looked on in shock as the frenzied druchii jerkily pulled her weapon free and tried to strike another blow before collapsing to the ground.

There were only two attackers left on Malus's right. On the left Arleth Vann duelled with the armoured highborn, blocking the noble's clumsy, frenzied attacks and darting in to strike at unprotected joints or exposed gaps in his plate harness. Leaving the assassin to finish the highborn, Malus edged in beside the wounded loyalist and took the battle to the zealots.

A man rushed at Malus with a bloody woodsman's axe held high. The highborn pivoted on his left foot as the blow fell, allowing the blade to pass harmlessly by, and stabbed the onrushing zealot through the heart. Sneering in disdain, Malus pulled his sword free and rounded on the second man, who was raining blows on the uninjured loyalist with a knotted club in one hand and a short sword in the other. The zealot was so intent on his victim that he never saw Malus step up beside him and split his skull from back to front, spraying the loyalist fighting him with bits of blood and bone.

On the other side of the table the armoured highborn slumped against the flat surface with a groan, succumbing to blood loss and a score of deep wounds. Arleth Vann stepped close, slicing his swords across the noble's neck in a scissoring motion, and the man's head went bouncing across the floor.

Malus himself leaned back against the other side of the table, panting like a hound and trying to ignore the dull pain throbbing in the side of his chest. Bodies were heaped everywhere, bleeding out onto the floor. The fight had lasted less than half a minute.

The loyalist who'd been struck by the cleaver was bleeding badly, the shoulder and sleeve of his robe already soaked and dripping. The other man appeared unhurt, as did Arleth Vann. All things considered, it could have gone much worse, the highborn thought.

Malus pushed himself away from the table and walked over to the body of the Chaos beast. The creature's neck was ripped open, revealing strange, yellowish muscles and a backbone that looked as if it belonged in a shark rather than a lion. Stepping carefully through the spreading pool of gluey ichor, the highborn raised his sword and began hacking at the flesh, working from the inside out. It was tough going, but within a few minutes the large, octopus-like head rolled free. He bent and picked the thing up by its tentacles, and walked to the shattered doorway. Grunting with effort, he took two quick steps and hurled the trophy through the doorway.

'We'll let them think on that for a bit,' the highborn said grimly. He turned to Arleth Vann. 'You check that one's arm. I'll look over Spite.'

They worked quickly, unsure what awaited them outside the lodge. A cursory check showed that Spite had dozens upon dozens of shallow cuts from the beast's tentacle hooks, but nothing that the nauglir's legendary constitution could not handle. Malus had moved on to check the state of his saddlebags when Arleth Vann joined him. 'The man's wound is deep,' he said quietly, 'and I've no means to close it. He'll die in a few minutes, maybe less.'

'Then we'd best get this over with quickly,' the highborn said. 'Let's take a look outside.'

The two druchii crept up to the doorway and peered into the tunnel beyond. Globes of witchlight filled the wide passage with ghostly luminescence, forcing Malus to squint into the cold glare. What he saw made his heart sink.

There were scores of white-robed zealots filling the tunnel, their robes and blades stained with smudges of soot and streaks of old blood. They stood in a packed group behind two more of the terrible Chaos beasts, which lashed at the air with their tentacles as if angered by the sight of their mate's severed head. A handful of beastmasters circled the creatures, holding their short spears and prods ready. They threw black looks at the broken doorway of the lodge, as if anticipating their own measure of revenge for their slain kin.

'Mother of Night,' Malus cursed softly, 'they must have pulled every zealot from the city back into the fortress.'

'With the temple warriors gone, why not?' the assassin replied, his face grim. 'They sent in those city folk just to take our measure and keep us occupied.'

'Well, what are they waiting for?'

As Malus said the words, a ripple of motion passed through the packed ranks of the zealots. Men stepped aside, bowing their heads as Urial moved through the crowd. A trio of blood-witches attended the usurper, and Urial carried the copy of the warpsword in his hand. The mere sight of the weapon seemed to leech the strength from Malus's limbs, reminding him of the wound he'd been dealt and of the daemon's poisonous touch.

The would-be Scourge of Khaine reached the front rank of the men and stopped. Urial eyed the head of the dead Chaos beast and laughed.

Malus fought a black tide of despair. He looked upon the assembled zealots, and the merciless arithmetic of the battlefield showed him the future as clearly as any seer could. There was no way they could prevail against such numbers, to say nothing of the sorcery of Urial and the blood-witches.

'We'll have to fall back,' he said. 'We can't possibly hold them here. We'll use the fortifications at each burial chamber to slow them down, bleed them–'

'No,' Arleth Vann said quietly.

'What?' Malus demanded, his expression incredulous.

'Don't be a fool, my lord,' the assassin said. 'You know better than that. We could fight them all the way back to the prime chamber, trade ten lives for each one of ours – twenty if you count Spite – and they would still have men left over. That's without counting your half-brother, much less the blood-witches.'

'Have you any better ideas?' Malus snarled.

The assassin nodded. 'When they attack, you mount Spite and ride straight through them. We'll cover your back as long as we can.'

'You can't be serious,' Malus said.

'Of course I am!' Arleth Vann said hotly. 'You have to escape and find the sword, for Khaine's sake! Otherwise the temple – even Naggaroth itself – could well tear itself apart.'

'Why would you do such a thing?' the highborn asked, torn between revulsion and awe. 'The temple owes you nothing.'

Arleth Vann turned away, eyeing the crowd of zealots and the leonine blood-witches. 'Do you remember what I said about seeking redemption, about a good death outweighing a bad life? What better chance than this to cleanse the taint from my honour?' He looked back at his lord. 'There's no glory in living as an outlaw, my lord, no matter what the bards say.'

Malus was surprised at how much the comment stung. 'You've been a highborn retainer for the last five years,' he growled.

'That didn't change who I was,' the assassin replied, 'but this will.'

The highborn bit back his anger. Fleeing the battle felt like cowardice, but the assassin's logic was unassailable. He could either stay and die – or worse, fall into Urial's clutches – or he could fight his way free and locate the sword. 'Damnation,' Malus snarled, and then turned and made his way to Spite.

Nearby, the two loyalists watched Malus intently. The wounded man was pale and shaky, using his left hand awkwardly to press a soaked bundle of cloth against his wounded shoulder. Their expressions were bleak.

'We're breaking out,' Malus told the men as he grabbed Spite's reins. 'I'm going to provoke the zealots into charging us, and then I'll counter charge with my nauglir and open a hole in their ranks. Stay close behind and keep our flanks clear, and we'll fight our way through. Understand?'

Both men nodded. The look in their eyes said they understood completely.

Malus nodded, and then headed Spite towards the doorway. The zealots hadn't moved. Urial appeared to be speaking to the assembled force, but Malus couldn't hear what his half-brother was saying. *He's probably ordering his men to take me alive,* he thought. *I expect he and the blood-witches have something special planned.*

The highborn turned to Arleth Vann. 'Are you ready?' he asked.

'I suppose I've been waiting for this for a long time,' the assassin said calmly. 'Farewell, my lord. When the Time of Blood comes, perhaps you and I will meet again.'

Malus didn't know what to say. He shook his head fiercely. 'If you see the Lord of Murder before I do, you march up to his throne and tell him I'm coming. Tell him that when I get there I'm going to kick his brass teeth straight down his throat.'

Before the assassin could reply, the highborn drew a deep breath and shouted into the tunnel. 'What are you waiting for, brother? More men, perhaps? I think these dead bakers and butchers had more courage between them than you and all your ilk!'

Malus heard Urial laugh. 'Is that you, brother?' the usurper asked. 'I was certain you'd died. The last time I saw you, that man of yours was dragging your limp body away from me as fast as he could.'

'What can I say, brother? He's a very pious man, and was afraid I'd hurt Khaine's Scourge.' Malus said, his voice dripping with contempt. 'Fear not, I set him straight. I told him all about the night on the *Harrier*, and what that damned skull of yours told me. Say, did the skull ever speak to you alone, or did you just forget to mention that to the temple elders? That was part of the prophecy, correct?'

'Shut your blasphemous mouth!' Urial snapped, the heat in his voice so strong that Tyran and the closest zealots gave the usurper questioning looks.

'How are things with your new bride? Is she still spurning you? I expect so,' Malus said, smiling despite himself. 'The Bride of Ruin is not meant for the likes of you, brother. She will never think of you as anything but a withered, pitiable man.'

The highborn's taunts were drowned by Urial's wordless shriek of rage.

Arleth Vann chuckled, readying his blades. 'You always did have a way with words, my lord.'

Malus swung into the saddle. 'Perhaps I'd have made a decent priest after all.'

The assassin smiled ruefully. 'I don't know if I'd go that far–'

A roar shook the tunnel as the zealots charged. Blades glinting, they flowed in a furious tide past the Chaos beasts, charging for the dwarf lodge at the command of their lord.

'Now?' Malus said, looking to Arleth Vann.

The assassin shook his head, peering into the tunnel. 'Not yet.'

Shouts of bloodlust echoed in the antechamber. The sounds of pounding feet filled Malus's ears.

'Now?'

'Not yet.'

Malus could make out individual voices in the thunder of the war shouts. He could hear the slap of boot heels on stone.

'We did decide to fight them in the tunnel, correct?' the highborn said pointedly.

The assassin looked at Malus and nodded solemnly. 'Go, my lord, and Khaine be with you.'

'Not if he knows what's good for him,' Malus growled. He put his boots to Spite's flanks. 'Charge!'

The warbeast leapt forwards with a bone jarring roar, its shoulder striking the edge of the right door and smashing the heavy panel from its hinges. Malus ducked at the last moment as they crossed the threshold, feeling the top of the doorframe scrape along his backplate.

When he looked up again he saw that they were rushing at the front rank of zealots, less than ten yards away. The charge of the white-robed druchii faltered as the nauglir bore down on them, its blunt jaws clashing together as it smelt the blood on the zealots' robes. Malus howled like a wolf as they plunged into the press, his blade falling left and right as he lashed out indiscriminately at the bodies flashing past.

Zealots screamed, flung like bloody dolls into the air by the nauglir's jaws or smashed aside by the beast's armoured shoulders. A blade struck Malus on the left thigh and glanced from the steel plate. On his right, the highborn slashed down at an upturned face, splitting the druchii's skull like a melon. He twisted his waist and cut to his left, knocking aside a blood-stained draich and slicing open another man's forehead.

The cold one plunged on, leaving torn and broken bodies in its wake. Zealots struck at the nauglir from all sides, opening deep wounds in the beast's muscular flanks, but the pain only enraged the cold one further. A zealot leapt for the nauglir's face, aiming a lightning thrust at Spite's left eye, but the cold one's training took over and the beast snapped at the flickering motion. The huge jaws bit off the swordsman's right arm at the elbow and spat his twisted sword onto the tunnel floor.

Malus looked over his shoulder to see how Arleth Vann and the others were keeping up. The wounded loyalist was already dead. His headless body lay only a few yards from the lodge's broken doors. The assassin and the last remaining warrior fought side-by-side close to the cold one's lashing tail.

Roars of rage turned to screams of anger, pain and fear. Men fell back to either side of the thundering cold one, stunned by the ferocity of the sudden attack. A tight semicircle of zealots formed between the nauglir and Urial. Malus smiled fiercely and aimed Spite directly for them.

The swordsmen held their ground, ready to die to protect their lord. Malus did everything in his power to give them their wish.

Spite let out a bloodthirsty roar and lunged at the man to his right, catching the swordsman's right arm and torso and biting them in half. The zealot to the cold one's left saw his opportunity and slashed with all his might at the nauglir's bent neck, but Malus anticipated the move and blocked the stroke with his sword. Hearing the sound, Spite jerked his huge head and smashed the zealot to the ground, where the beast crushed the screaming man beneath a clawed foot.

Malus caught a flicker of movement in the corner of his eye and instinctively dodged to his left. The movement saved his life, a draich glancing from his right pauldron as a zealot leapt onto Spite's flank and grabbed hold of Malus's saddle. Snarling, the highborn elbowed the man in the face, and then slashed open his throat as he reeled from the blow.

More zealots were closing in on both sides as the attackers recovered from the surprise charge. Urial stood just five yards away, surrounded by the fierce blood-witches. Letting out a battle scream, the highborn kicked Spite's flanks and charged.

Zealots were thrown left and right by the lunging warbeast, and Malus raised his sword for a decapitating stroke as he bore down on Urial. The blood-witches scattered, hissing curses, but the usurper stood his ground. With less than two yards between them, Malus saw his half-brother smile.

Suddenly Urial raised the sword in his left hand and shouted a word that smote Malus like a physical blow. Spite stopped dead in his tracks, roaring in pain and confusion. It took all of Malus's skill as a rider not to be thrown from the saddle by the force of the sudden stop.

'Forwards, Spite! Forwards!' the highborn roared, but the warbeast could only shake its head and bellow in pain, as if pressed against a wall of fire.

Urial laughed. 'He won't move, not if his life depends on it,' he said. 'Did you think me a fool, knowing you had your damned cold one with you?'

Malus shouted in impotent rage. Men were closing in from behind the nauglir and to either side, like wolves closing in for the kill.

Then there was a flash of movement and Urial ducked, catching Arleth Vann's hurled knife on the side of his head rather than in his throat. The knife scored a bloody line through the usurper's scalp, and in an eye blink, the spell was broken.

'Go, my lord!' Arleth Vann shouted, racing up beside Malus with the last surviving loyalist close behind. The assassin charged at Urial, blades reaching for the man's throat.

Zealots roared their bloodlust as they closed in on Spite. Malus gritted his teeth and once again spurred the nauglir forwards. 'Run, Spite, run!' he yelled, knowing that Urial could renew the spell at any moment.

Arleth Vann was determined not to give the usurper a chance. His short swords wove a pattern of death before him, stabbing at Urial's face and neck. Urial parried the attacks with unnatural agility, wielding his large sword as if it was a willow wand. Though no warpsword, it was clear that the dwarf ironsmith had imbued the weapon with considerable power.

Swallowing bitter bile, Malus spurred his mount past Urial. A lone voice cried 'Blood and souls!' as the last temple warrior charged at the witches. His sword sliced at one blood-witch's head, but she dodged the blow with unnatural speed, and her two compatriots fell upon the man from either side. His fierce shouts turned to a gurgling scream as their talons slashed open his throat. The witches bore the struggling man to the ground, and like lionesses, began to feed.

The last Malus saw of Arleth Vann, he was trading blows with his half-brother, circling and stabbing, leaping and slashing within a closing ring of zealots. Cursing venomously, he turned away and tried to guide his mount past the waiting Chaos beasts.

Unlike the zealots, the beastmasters knew very well how dangerous a charging cold one could be. They scattered like quail at the thundering nauglir's approach, shouting commands to the hunters in a strange, savage tongue. The air filled with the hunters' obscene, gibbering cries as they were unleashed upon Malus and Spite.

There was no point trying to fight. Malus knew all too well how useless his sword was against the monsters' hide. He bent low in the saddle and cried, 'Race like fire, beast of the deeps! Show these slugs how you can run!'

Rumbling like a cauldron, Spite obediently lowered his head and stretched his legs into a full, earthshaking gallop.

Malus angled their flight to pass the beasts on their right. The closest hunter flared its tentacles and screeched at the nauglir, but the cold one lunged at the Chaos beast and struck the creature a powerful blow with its shoulder. The hunter was knocked sideways, tentacles lashing, and the highborn was slapped on the side of his head by the back of one of the beast's fleshy whips. The blow nearly took his head off, throwing him hard to the left and almost pitching him from the saddle. Another tentacle brushed against his leg, the barbs scraping against his armour.

Suddenly, Spite lurched and bellowed in pain. The cold one's body slewed to the left, struck on its rear flank. Blinking tears of pain from his eyes, Malus glanced back and saw another of the hunters sinking its claws into Spite's powerful rear leg, much as a lion would pull down a gazelle. The highborn looked into the creature's right eye and heard the whirring of its tentacles as it reached up to pluck him from the saddle.

Malus hauled on the reins and planted his right heel in Spite's side, and the obedient warbeast slashed its tail to the left. The powerful motion flung the clutching Chaos beast over the nauglir's back, smashing it against the side of the tunnel. 'Go!' Malus shouted, spurring his mount forwards once more.

With the howls of the hunters echoing behind them, Malus and Spite raced down the broad passage. Darkness engulfed them, and the sounds of battle faded.

He gave Spite his head, trusting the cave-born nauglir's senses as they raced down the passageway. Arleth Vann had shown him where the tunnel ran, and he knew that after a hundred yards it ended in a large, empty chamber that once housed the dwarfs while they worked on their tomb. A spiral ramp at the west end of the chamber led up to the road of black stones that would take Malus to the Vermillion Gate.

When the echo of Spite's footfalls suddenly stopped, Malus knew he'd entered the housing chamber. He slowed the warbeast's pace and guided him to the left, allowing the nauglir to pick his way through the debris-strewn room. When he felt a breath of moving air against his cheek, he nudged the cold one's flanks. 'Climb the ramp,' Malus said, trusting it was there even though he couldn't see it. 'Up!'

With a grunt, the cold one padded forwards and sure enough, Malus felt them begin to climb. The ramp was just broad enough for the cold one to work its way up, and the highborn lay flat against the nauglir's back and tried to stay out of the way.

After several long minutes, Malus found he could see vague outlines of the ramp around him. They were almost at the top, where the road's glowing fungus shed a modicum of light. Two turns later Spite edged out into the main passageway, and the highborn breathed a sigh of relief.

He turned Spite's nose to the left, heading deeper into the hill, and let the warbeast lope down the tunnel. They rode on in silence for some minutes, until Malus began to feel the tingle of eldritch power against his skin. They were drawing close to the ancient gateway.

Moments later Malus found himself riding through a long, underground plaza, its ceiling lost in darkness high overhead. Stone statues flanked the long chamber, their features worn smooth over uncounted millennia. A heavy silence hung in the enormous chamber, and even Spite seemed to feel its weight.

The plaza led them to a large, semicircular gallery at the edge of a wide, natural pit. Here, statues of beautiful, fearsome blood-witches bore lamps of witchlight and robed executioners carried elegant swords of white marble. A slender bridge of stone ran from the gallery to a circular spire of rock that rose from the centre of the pit. The top of the spire was flat and capped with paving stones of glossy, black marble, and upon those stones rose an arch of seamless, reddish stone.

Taking a deep breath, Malus led Spite onto the bridge. He had no idea if the span would support the cold one's weight, and it was just barely wide enough to accommodate it. A cold void yawned beneath the bridge, leading perhaps to the heart of the world itself.

'Easy, Spite, easy,' he said. The nauglir seemed to understand, taking one slow step at a time as it edged its way across the abyss.

Nearly five minutes later they were just over halfway across the span, and Malus was starting to breathe easier. Then he heard the sounds of pounding feet behind him and turned just in time to see the Chaos beast leap at Spite with a chilling howl.

CHAPTER TWENTY-ONE

RED SKIES

The Chaos beast landed square on Spite's back, its talons sinking deep into the nauglir's hindquarters. The cold one roared in surprise and pain and instinctively turned to bite its attacker. The nauglir's right hind leg slipped from the bridge, and to Malus the world seemed to lurch vertiginously to the right. He threw himself to the left, away from the bottomless chasm, just as the hunter lashed at him with a pair of tentacles.

One of the barbed whips wrapped around his left arm and another wound around his waist. Screaming in fear and rage, Malus hacked at the tentacles with his sword, but the rubbery skin was barely marked. With no apparent effort the beast dragged him out of the saddle.

Malus looked down and saw nothing but emptiness and shadow. Then Spite's jaws snapped at the hunter and caught the tentacles in his fearsome maw.

The cold one's teeth parted the whips like thread, splashing Malus with sticky ichor. Still screaming, he fell like a stone, hitting the edge of the span and tumbling over it face-first.

By an equal mix of pure luck and desperation, Malus caught the raised edge of the span with his left hand and seized it like a drowning man. His legs swung past and he rocked like a pendulum over the pit as the two beasts raged above him. He heard the sounds of talons on stone as he fought for purchase, clawing at the other side of the bridge with his hind leg in an effort to force himself back onto the span. A stream of broken stone trickled into the blackness, and Malus heard an ominous crack.

His ichor covered hand and arm slid across the stone. With a thrill of terror, he realised he was slipping. The highborn threw his other hand over the edge of the bridge, hoping to stop his fall without losing his sword, but he hadn't reckoned on the slickness of the foul ooze coating his arms, and the sudden motion caused his left hand to slip.

Malus's stomach lurched as he dropped. Then he felt a heavy weight cover his arm and jerk him to a stop. He hung over the pit for an instant, his legs swinging uselessly. Then the mind numbing panic subsided and the highborn had the presence of mind to let go of his sword and try to find some kind of purchase with his right hand.

The weight on his left arm shifted slightly, and Malus distinctly felt the armoured shell of his vambrace bend beneath the pressure. Pain began to build at his forearm and wrist as they took the mounting strain. Gritting his teeth, Malus pulled himself upwards with his sword hand until he was able to get the crook of his arm over the bridge's rounded edge.

A clawed hand the size of his torso slashed past him, missing his head by inches. Spite had managed to regain his footing and was reaching back to claw and bite at his attacker. In doing so the one-ton warbeast had stepped on Malus's arm.

The Chaos beast still clung to Spite's hindquarters, tearing at one hip with its cruel beak and lashing at the warbeast's face with its remaining tentacles. The nauglir's clashing jaws had bitten off several more, and the stumps sprayed the cold one with gouts of clear, briny ichor. Spite roared and lashed his tail, hoping to dislodge the hunter from his back, but the Chaos beast only dug its claws in deeper and held on. The nauglir's foot ground down as it swung its tail, and the pain in Malus's arm intensified. He threw a leg over the edge of the bridge and pulled most of his body over. Then he grabbed up his sword and slapped at Spite's leg with the flat of the blade. 'Get *off*, you great lump of scales!'

Whether by accident or design, Spite lifted his leg and Malus yanked his arm free. The vambrace was crumpled, and a thin stream of blood leaked past the edges of the steel halves from where the armoured parts had bitten into his skin, but the highborn was not in any position to complain.

Spite shifted again, and Malus heard his jaws snap shut on empty air just above his head. A surge of terror shot through the highborn as he saw a shadow spread like a stain on the bridge around him, and out of pure instinct he rolled as far to the left as he could, just as a smothering weight of stinking flesh smashed against him.

He couldn't breathe for a moment, much less see, but then the Chaos beast drew back from its lunge and Malus saw how horrifyingly close he'd come to being impaled by the thing's beak. The shroud of flesh surrounding its mouth slid away from Malus, and without its weight to pin him he fell back over the edge of the span. Screaming, he flailed his hands and grabbed the first thing he could: a bleeding stump of wriggling tentacle. The highborn felt the clenching barbs of the thing's suckers scraping against his armoured glove as the creature screeched in his ear and tossed its head, flinging Malus high into the air.

The highborn held on for dear life as he was whipped about by the hunter's thrashings. More tentacles lashed around Malus, wrapping his legs and trying to pull him closer to the creature's rending maw. He groped at his belt, desperately trying to find some weapon he could use against the thing. The beast's strength was enormous, drawing him inexorably towards the great beak, and he had no illusions that his armoured breastplate would give the beast a second's pause before it tore him to pieces.

The monster's lunge had left it overextended, however, and Spite saw his chance. He darted forwards, closing his jaws around the hunter's neck. The Chaos beast shuddered and screamed, spraying Malus with spittle and gobs of sticky ichor.

He heard the creature's thin bones crunch as Spite bit deeper, and he knew what was soon to happen: the nauglir would break its neck with a savage shake and hurl the beast aside, just as it had down in the crypt. Frantically, he started to kick and thrash in the monster's grip, praying to the Dark Mother that it would start to weaken as its wounds began to tell.

With a fierce kick, Malus managed to pull his left leg free. He felt the beast begin to shift as Spite found his footing and started to lift. Acting on impulse, the highborn drew back his armoured leg and kicked the monster on the side of its beak. To his surprise, the monster howled and let go of his other leg.

Spite rumbled deep in his chest, lifted the hunter into the air, and started to shake. Malus heard bones crunch and felt the beast go limp. As the nauglir was wrenching the hunter back over the bridge the highborn took a deep breath and let go.

For a horrifying moment, Malus was certain he'd miscalculated. Rather than being thrown back onto the bridge, it seemed as if he was being hurled along its length, his arms flailing wildly as he began to plummet downward. At the last moment his left hand struck the edge of the bridge and he grabbed hold, his shoulder flaring in pain as it took the brunt of the impact. Without hesitating, Malus kicked up his feet and swung roughly over the edge of the span, just in time to see Spite hurl the broken body of the Chaos beast into the abyss.

Panting and giddy with terror, Malus rolled carefully onto his back and savoured the sensation of lying on something that wasn't writhing or clawing at him. Further back on the bridge, Spite lifted his snout and roared in triumph, and the highborn felt the curved bridge start to shift.

'Damn me,' Malus breathed, rolling onto his knees. He could see wide cracks spreading along the length of the bridge, racing towards him from the weakened section where the nauglir still stood. 'Spite!' Malus cried, waving his arms. 'Go! Move!'

The cold one looked curiously at his master. It blew a gobbet of ichor from its nostrils and shifted its weight, edging its way towards him.

'No! Not this way, you thick lizard! Back! Go back that way!' he yelled. He scrambled down the bridge, waving his hands wildly at the heavy cold one. Grumbling, the nauglir finally got the message and turned around, walking ponderously towards the Vermillion Gate.

The bridge groaned and crackled with each hair-raising step, but Malus managed to recover his sword and creep onto the spire without further incident. He fell to his knees beside the cold one, trembling with exertion.

'Well, I think it's safe to say we won't be going back that way,' he gasped.

The nauglir rumbled and turned to sniff at the red stone arch. After a moment, Malus managed to catch his breath and staggering back to his feet, he went to check on his cold one's injuries. He counted more than a dozen deep gouges torn by the hunter's beak, and applied a healing salve from his saddlebags to each before climbing back into the saddle.

No sooner had he taken up the reins than he heard a commotion at the gallery behind him. Malus turned in the saddle to see about a dozen zealots standing at the foot of the bridge, glaring angrily at him. Apparently they'd seen the damage to the middle of the span, and had no interest in testing its strength.

The highborn gave the zealots a mocking salute with his sword, and then nudged Spite towards the arch. Taking a deep breath, he addressed the daemon. 'I don't suppose you know anything about this gate?'

'I know a bit,' Tz'arkan admitted.

Malus bit back an angry curse. 'Well, why don't you tell me how it works?'

The daemon shifted within his chest. 'There's little to tell. Cross beneath the arch and fix your destination firmly in your mind.'

'I don't have a destination, as you damned well know,' Malus snapped.

'Don't be churlish, little druchii,' Tz'arkan sneered. 'I will guide us to where we need to go.'

They rode towards the archway. Malus studied it closely as they approached. There was not a single rune or sigil anywhere along its length. Whatever magic worked upon it was invisible to his uneducated eye. He could feel its power though, washing over him in pulsing waves that made his ears ring and set his teeth on edge.

As they passed beneath the arch, the highborn expected to see a portal of smoke or light, but nothing appeared. 'Are you sure you know how this works?' he said.

Then the world turned the colour of blood, and Malus felt himself twisted inside out.

Tz'arkan had neglected to mention the pain.

Malus was blind, plummeting through howling darkness, and it felt as if ravens were feeding on his organs. The highborn felt their sharp beaks tear at his heart and lungs, worrying out little pieces and pecking thoughtfully at his quivering flesh as if savouring a fine meal. He could not move, could not scream. All he could do was suffer the ravages of the carrion birds for what felt like an eternity.

Then there was a clap of thunder, a hot wind smote Malus in his face, and Spite was stumbling down a shallow hillside of loose stone and parched dirt.

The nauglir bellowed in confusion and pain. Malus reeled in the saddle, feeling sticky moisture on his face. His stomach heaved, and for a terrifying moment it felt like something was trying to force its way out.

Spite skidded to a stop at the base of the hill and Malus all but fell from the saddle. He landed hard on his knees and vomited a fountain of dark blood and glossy, black feathers onto the lifeless ground.

'Mother of Night,' he groaned, wiping his mouth with the back of his gauntlet. The armoured glove came away slick with blood. Gasping for breath, he straightened and tried to see where he was.

The hillside behind him emptied onto a dry and desolate plain under a swirling sky the colour of blood. Towering black mountains reared above the northern horizon, their iron flanks painted with chiaroscuros of jagged yellow lightning. The hot wind seemed to blow from every direction, shifting crazily around the compass at the whim of some lunatic god. It moaned and whispered in his ears with a susurrus of strange voices, hinting at things that he only dimly grasped, but the pieces he understood turned his guts to greasy ice.

A city of black iron and blasted stone sat on the plain like a vast, black spider. Tall, blade-like towers reared hungrily into the crimson sky behind ruined walls and craggy battlements. Pillars of inky smoke rose here and there across the cityscape, wreathing the ancient buildings in a pall of suffocating fumes and ash. Off to the east, huge, hulking shapes the size of citadels writhed and lumbered along the horizon, reaching skyward as if to grasp the fickle lightning, and bellowing in madness and rage.

The gate had sent him into the far north, into the Chaos Wastes. Nowhere else in the world could such a vision of torment exist.

Why had the zealots brought the warpsword here, he wondered? What had possessed them? Was it fear of discovery by the temple, or had the blade itself chosen its resting place?

'Where is the sword, daemon?' Malus croaked, his throat ravaged by his ordeal. 'Enough with your damned games. Just tell me where to find it so we can quit this accursed place!'

'It is yonder, I think,' Tz'arkan said. Malus knew the daemon meant the foul city on the plain.

'You *think*?'

'What am I, a hound that sniffs out swords?' Tz'arkan spat. 'The gate is not so precise as I imagined, or else my control was not quite as perfect as it might have been. We are in the proper area, and I feel a source of great power to the north. What else could it be?'

'Here? In the Wastes? It could be a great many things.' Before Malus could expound further, however, Spite looked back the way they'd come and sniffed the hot air warily.

The highborn looked back over his shoulder. Up the long, rocky hillside, perhaps two hundred yards away, a knot of horsemen regarded him from the hillcrest.

Malus glared sidelong at the nauglir. 'You and your damned bellowing,' he muttered, climbing to his feet. As he did so, the horsemen kneed their mounts forwards, walking them carefully down the treacherous slope.

'Time to be going,' the highborn said, reaching for his saddle. He swung himself onto Spite's back and kicked the nauglir into a trot. His mind racing, he led the warbeast out onto the plain.

The cold one's feet kicked up puffs of grey dust as the nauglir trotted across the wasteland towards the ruined city. The horsemen easily kept pace with the cold one, fanning out expertly into a semicircular formation once they came down off the hillside. Malus studied them intently as they rode, but he could make out few details except for the spears that rose above the riders' heads and the skill with which they rode. As near as the highborn could reckon there were at least a score of them. That either meant a large patrol or a small raiding force. Malus wasn't certain which possibility he preferred.

Spite made good time at first, but as the minutes wore on the highborn noticed that the great beast began to tire. His gait became uneven, and Malus let out a curse. The nauglir was going lame from the deep wounds in his hind legs. It was much harder to lame a nauglir than a horse, but with only two legs to drive it along, when it happened the effects were often much worse. The highborn snarled. He didn't dare stop to let the beast rest, but if he didn't slow down the cold one would eventually collapse. Having little choice, he reined in and slowed Spite to a walk.

The riders gained ground steadily, although they did not seem especially eager to get within spear distance of the lone druchii. The closer they got, however, the more they hemmed Malus in to left and right. Soon their intentions were clear: they were herding him closer to the city on the plain.

Malus considered his options as they rode on. As far as he knew, the sword was somewhere in the city, and it was entirely possible that whoever led those riders might know where it was. However, he doubted that anyone in this goddess-forsaken wasteland would have any interest in helping him. It was far more likely that they were herding him along like a prize cow for slaughter. That left fighting or running, and at the moment he couldn't manage either, unless he called upon the daemon.

With Tz'arkan's help he could wipe out the riders to the last man, with or without Spite, but at what cost?

Do I have a choice any more, Malus thought?

Behind him, the riders blew a strange, skirling horn. Malus's heart quickened, thinking the riders were about to charge, but when he looked back they were still keeping their distance a few hundred yards away.

They were only a few miles from the city. The highborn knew that he had to act soon. He had no intention of becoming a prisoner to these Chaos twisted savages. The more he thought about seeking the daemon's help the more he felt his body ache for the taste of Tz'arkan's power. How much more potent would it be here, with the energies of Chaos raging through the very skies? How like a god he could be!

Malus had the name of the daemon on his lips when they crested a gentle rise in the landscape and saw the riders waiting ahead of him.

There had been no warning of their approach, no horns or telltale dust clouds. They had mastered the terrain with devilish cunning, using its folds to manoeuvre directly into his path. Just like that, the trap closed shut around him. Horsemen from the trailing patrol had already reached the rise to either side of him, cutting him off from escape. The riders in front were less than a hundred yards away, waiting patiently.

He studied the men awaiting him as he guided Spite down the shallow slope. They were broad shouldered, powerful men, wearing animal furs and bits of ragged chainmail. Bracelets of silver or hammered brass adorned their arms, and steel helmets with mail skirts rested on their shaggy heads. Their skin was swarthy, almost like brown leather, and their bodies had been twisted by years of living beneath the boiling sky. Malus saw ram's horns sprouting from the forehead of one warrior, while another stared at the highborn with a single, catlike eye set in the centre of his forehead. Another man had two heads upon his neck, one broad and flat-nosed and the other shrivelled, scaly and bestial. Even their horses showed signs of terrible mutation, with cloven hooves and mangy bodies thick with cable-like muscles. Fangs protruded from their slack mouths, and their lolling tongues were long and forked like serpents'.

As he drew nearer, three of the riders kneed their mounts forwards upon some unspoken command. Each drew weapons that glinted in the bloody light. The man with one eye readied a long, curved sword and a steel buckler, while the two-headed man brandished a pair of long handled axes. A third man with piercing blue eyes and a ragged, drooling hole where his mouth should have been, uncoiled a long whip in his left hand and hefted a short, stubby mace in his right.

None of the other riders moved. Malus looked back at the men behind him, and saw them observing the scene from the rise many yards away. The highborn questioned whether this was some sort of challenge. He'd heard that some tribes of marauders favoured trials by combat, pitting their champions against those of their enemies. If that was their intent, he was happy to indulge them and see where it led. At worst, he could call the daemon's name and fight his way free if he had to.

The three riders spread out, edging their mounts forwards. Spite, smelling horseflesh, quickened his pace and let out a hungry roar, but the mutated animals were unfazed by the nauglir's hunting cry.

Malus realised that they were all going to attack him at once. He guessed that was supposed to be some sort of compliment. He drew his sword and decided to change the rules of the game.

Kicking his heels into Spite's flanks, Malus turned the nauglir hard right and charged at the two-headed man. The cold one closed the distance in an eye blink, but the horseman reacted with amazing speed, kicking his mount into a gallop and dodging nimbly out of the nauglir's path. Then he darted back at Malus, slashing at him with both deadly axes. Caught by surprise at the deft manoeuvre, it was all the highborn could do to get his sword up in time to block the flurry of strokes. Even so, the rider's last blow rang hard against Malus's pauldron, drawing a hiss of pain from his lips.

Malus reined Spite around, but already the two-headed man was darting away, his horse responding to his commands as if they were of one mind. The highborn started to lunge Spite after the horseman when a blur of motion to his right caught his eye. The one-eyed swordsman was charging at him from the flank, his sword gleaming redly. Malus cursed and twisted in the saddle, blocking the horseman's blow, but the attack had tremendous power behind it, nearly knocking his sword from his hand.

The one-eyed rider swept past, and Malus felt something wrap around his sword arm and haul backwards, wrenching the limb painfully in its socket. The blue-eyed man was behind Spite, hauling on his own reins and trying to pull the highborn from his saddle.

Gritting his teeth with pain, Malus wrenched his reins and applied his left boot, and Spite lashed out with his powerful tail. The blue eyed man had just enough time to comprehend his mistake before the muscular appendage slammed into his horse's side, splintering ribs and shattering the man's leg. The horse collapsed with a strangely human scream, but the wounded warrior held onto his whip with both hands, still drawing Malus with him towards the ground.

Hot pain lanced from the highborn's shoulder across his narrow chest as he heeled Spite around. He looked over his shoulder and saw the one-eyed swordsman sweeping in on his left flank, while the two-headed axe man was coming up fast just behind and to the right. He yanked at the whip wrapping his arm, but the braided rawhide bound him fast.

Facing the prone marauder, Malus kicked Spite into a trot. The blue-eyed warrior tried to roll aside, but the whip trapping the highborn worked against him as well. The marauder let out a terrible, gobbling cry as the nauglir crushed him underfoot.

Hooves thundered to Malus's left as the one-eyed swordsman swept in, aiming a mighty stroke for the back of the highborn's neck. Malus gauged the man's approach, and at the last moment he kneed Spite hard and threw up his left arm. The nauglir sidled towards the onrushing horse, closing the distance faster than the swordsman expected and throwing off his aim. The flashing sword smashed into the back of Malus's shoulder, hard enough for the highborn to hear the pauldron bending. Then Malus closed his hand around the marauder's wrist and dropped his arm, trapping the sword against his chest.

The one-eyed swordsman let out a savage curse and tried to ride past, but he was far too close to the cold one to escape. The nauglir's jaws closed on the horse's head and crushed it like an egg. The animal collapsed, throwing its rider forwards, and Malus let the man go. He rolled admirably with the fall, tumbling to a stop more than a dozen feet away. Spite leapt at the man like a cat upon a mouse. The swordsman barely had time to scream before the nauglir's bloody jaws clamped down and bit him in half.

Malus was just turning to look for the third rider when a pair of blows struck him from behind. One hit square between his shoulder blades, rocking him in the saddle, while the other struck a glancing blow against his head. Pain bloomed behind Malus's eyes and his body went slack. The next thing he felt was the jarring shock of hitting the dusty ground.

Vague noises came and went as he slowly regained his senses. He heard the sound of hooves and the roar of the cold one, both noises reverberating oddly in his head. He opened his eyes and saw the two-headed man swinging wide of the cold one and angling back towards him.

He tried to sit up, shouting as a spike of pain lanced through his skull. He felt hot blood running down his cheek and the back of his neck. Malus saw a glint of metal on the ground nearby and dimly recognised it as his sword. He rolled over and crawled towards it as the two-headed man kicked his horse into a gallop, bearing down on him. The ground shook as the horse drew closer, and Malus knew that there was no way he was going to reach the weapon in time.

As the thunder loomed over him Malus threw himself flat and rolled onto his back, looking up at the marauder leaning down out of his saddle to strike with his axe. The blade blurred through the air. Malus reached up and crossed his arms, forming an X, and the haft of the long blade crashed against them. The highborn grabbed the leather wrapped haft and held on for all he was worth. The marauder, already at the limit of his balance, came out of the saddle and hit the ground hard, close to Malus.

Malus yanked hard on the axe, pulling it from the marauder's hands, and then rolled drunkenly to his feet. His opponent was on his back, still clutching his second weapon. Without hesitation the highborn charged at the man, bringing his axe down on the marauder's head. The two-headed man brought up his axe and blocked the highborn's blow, but Malus twisted his weapon and hooked the beard of the axe around his opponent's haft, pulling it out of the way. He rushed in, hammered an armoured boot into the marauder's groin, and then broke several of his ribs. Grabbing his axe with both hands, he twisted the weapon out of his stunned opponent's grip and methodically cut away both of the warrior's heads.

The highborn straightened, his chest heaving, and looked for someone else to kill. The knot of riders at the base of the depression had not moved during the fight. Now one of their number slid gracefully from the saddle and approached Malus. He was a huge, broad shouldered warrior, with dark tattoos spiralling across his powerful chest. His skin was the colour of polished mahogany, and one of his eyes glowed a nacreous green, like trapped witchlight. Two large broadswords hung from a wide leather belt at his hips, but the man made no move to draw them.

A trickle of blood ran down Malus's cheek and touched his lips. He spat it into the dust. 'If you don't want to die empty-handed you'd best draw one of those blades,' he growled.

To his surprise, the warrior halted and addressed him in passable druhir. 'You were magnificent, holy one. Whom do I have the honour of addressing?'

The highborn frowned. This was just about the last thing he expected.

'I am Malus, of Hag Graef, a warrior of the druchii.'

The man bowed deeply. 'You bear the blessing of the Lord of Murder in your eyes.' He straightened and said gravely, 'You have come for the sword.'

The frankness of the question stunned Malus. 'Yes. Yes I have. How did you know?'

'It was foreseen,' the warrior said with a dreadful smile. His teeth were filed to jagged points. 'You are the Scourge. We have been waiting for you for a very long time.'

CHAPTER TWENTY-TWO

THE AGELESS KINGS

The dark-skinned warrior turned to his companions and shouted something in a foul, debased tongue. The warband erupted in cheers and savage howls that were echoed by the riders at the crest of the rise.

Malus frowned thoughtfully, considering what he'd heard. 'Who are you?' he asked.

The tattooed marauder bowed again, in a passable impersonation of a druchii retainer. 'I am Shebbolai, the chieftain of the Tribe of the Red Sword. We serve the Ageless Kings in the City of Khaine, yonder.'

At first Malus wasn't sure he'd heard the man correctly. The City of Khaine, he thought. 'Who are these Ageless Kings?'

'Servants of the Bloody-Handed God, who brought the great sword out of the hands of the blasphemers and kept it safe for many centuries, awaiting the day when Khaine's Scourge would walk out of the wasteland to claim his due.' The chieftain gave Malus another sharp-toothed smile and beckoned to him. 'Come, we must waste no time. The kings will want to see you at once.'

Malus was taken aback. Was it possible that the five assassins still lived after all this time, guarding the sword until the coming of the Time of Blood? It seemed incredible, but who knew what strange forces were at work here in the Wastes?

Slowly, painfully, the highborn recovered his sword. He looked at the bodies of the men he'd slain. 'Who were these warriors?'

'The champions of the tribe,' Shebbolai said proudly. 'Not even I could have defeated them all at once.'

Malus didn't think that spoke very highly of Shebbolai or the rest of his tribe, but the highborn judiciously held his tongue. On impulse he went to each of the men, struck off their heads, and carried the trophies over to Spite. The marauder chieftain watched, nodding in approval.

The highborn stuffed the heads into one of the empty sacks that had held his armour, and hung it from his belt like any zealot pilgrim. He took Spite by the reins and looked the cold one hard in the eye. 'Hunt, Spite,' he said.

'See what you can eat in this damned wasteland and wait for my call.' Then he slapped the nauglir on the neck and sent it loping off to the east. Whoever these Ageless Kings were, he wasn't about to trust them completely, not with his cache of Tz'arkan's relics at stake.

Malus turned back to Shebbolai. 'I'll take his mount,' he said, pointing to the two-headed man's horse.

The warrior nodded. 'He's yours,' the chieftain said. 'The horse and all three men's wives. It is your right.'

'Just the horse will do,' the highborn said, fighting to suppress a look of pure horror.

Shebbolai led the party through a ruined gate at the southern edge of Khaine's city, past towers of bleached skulls that rose more than thirty feet into the crimson sky. The city itself was huge, easily the size of Hag Graef, and looking at the sleek, black stone of its construction Malus couldn't help but see the hands of elves in its making. Certainly the Ageless Kings hadn't built it. The crumbling structures groaned under the weight of ages, perhaps going back as far as the Great War against Chaos or even earlier.

Malus and the marauders rode down deserted streets piled with broken stone. He found himself catching movement out of the corner of his eye more than once, but when he turned to look, he saw only a shadowy alley or an empty doorway. Piles of ancient skulls stood at every corner, reminding the highborn of Har Ganeth, hundreds of leagues distant.

'How did your tribe come to serve the Ageless Kings?' Malus asked.

Shebbolai chuckled, letting his horse find its own way along the avenue beside Malus. 'By conquest, of course. Long, long ago my tribe wandered these plains like the other tribes, but the Ageless Kings came from the cold lands and slew our chieftain and nearly all of his warriors with the power of the red sword. Then they took the wives and children of the tribe and brought them here, to the City of Khaine. We have served them ever since.' The marauder twisted in his saddle and pointed back to the plains from whence they had come. 'We rule all the land from east to west, and many tribes pay us tribute in flesh and treasure to cross our territory.' Shebbolai smiled proudly. 'Other tribes must journey for many leagues in search of wealth and glory to heap at the feet of the Old Gods, but we need only stretch out our hands and the tribes bury their faces in the dirt and give us all they have. There is no tribe more powerful or more favoured by the gods than ours.'

'A tribe's glory is wrought in battle, is it not?' Malus asked.

Shebbolai's smile faded. 'We fight from time to time, but few of the tribes dare to challenge the power of the sword. The Ageless Kings tell us to bide our time and wait for the coming of the Scourge, and then we will drown ourselves in hot blood!'

The highborn nodded thoughtfully. 'The Ageless Kings are wise,' he said. 'Tell me, how many of them are there?'

'The legends say there were five at first, but now only three remain,' the chieftain said. 'Once they rode alongside the tribe, bearing the red sword before them, but for many hundreds of years they have kept to the god's temple here in the city.' Shebbolai extended a hand. 'There it is, yonder.'

Malus saw a squat, square tower rising from a pile of ruins just ahead. Perhaps it had always been a temple or a citadel for one of the city lords. Now its sloped flanks were adorned with thousands upon thousands of skulls. The sheer scale of the offerings stunned the highborn. Not all of the temples in Naggaroth combined could equal it.

The closer they drew to the temple the more people Malus saw: hideous, twisted wretches, clothed in rags and bits of fur, who watched the passage of the chieftain and his retinue with hard, feral stares. Many of the buildings near the temple were inhabited, but few were in good repair. Whatever wealth the tribe had accumulated, it hadn't gone towards providing the marauders with luxury or comfort. As they rode through the more populated streets Malus could sense an undercurrent of tension rising out of the squalor, and wondered how he might turn that to his advantage.

Before they reached the temple the riders passed through a broad plaza. Princes and generals in ages past might have reviewed their armies in such an expanse. Now, however, it was a forest of iron poles bearing the rotting, headless corpses of thousands of sacrificial victims. The stench of decay was immense. Malus gritted his teeth and tried to keep his expression neutral as they worked their way through a miasma of death.

Malus studied the bodies closest to the narrow path. 'Many of these look quite fresh,' he observed. 'It seems you've been fighting recently.'

Shebbolai's expression darkened. 'Just the killing of dogs,' he said gruffly, and spoke no more.

Beyond the plaza of corpses the riders reached a broad flight of stone steps leading up to the tower. As they reined in, a pair of towering doors at the top of the steps groaned open, and a mob of cowering, naked human slaves spilled out. Their bodies were thin and sallow, covered with scars and weeping sores, and they raced to the bottom of the steps to take the marauders' horses and see to their needs. Malus slid gratefully from the saddle, happy to be rid of the mangy, stinking beast, and tossed its reins to one of the trembling humans before following Shebbolai up to the open doorway.

The chieftain ushered Malus across the threshold with a bow, and then returned to his fellows. A long, broad corridor stretched beyond, lit by globes of flickering witchlight. The highborn composed himself before striding swiftly down the long passageway. Tall figures in ornate, archaic brass armour stood sentinel along the corridor. The men were inhumanly strong, their bodies swollen to hideous proportions, and they held huge, double-headed axes in their broad, scarred hands. The highborn studied them as he walked past, feeling the weight of their gaze, but unable to see the expressions behind their helmets' ornate faceplates.

Malus stepped into a large, dimly lit space at the end of the passageway. A single shaft of light speared down into the centre of the chamber, falling upon a small stone altar carved of dark marble. Its square sides were anointed in fresh blood, and two grinning skulls rested upon it, their surfaces stained nearly brown by centuries of bloody libations.

Malus approached the ancient bones, noting that they were free from mutation and perfect in form. The cheekbones were sharp, the jaw lines angular. 'The two dead kings,' he murmured, reaching out to touch the remains of one of the five lost assassins.

'You are not worthy to touch the bones of the Ageless Kings!' hissed a voice from the darkness. The sound was eerie, like a keening wind whistling through bare branches and forming words Malus could understand. It echoed in the vast chamber, seeming to come from every direction at once. 'You defile this sacred place with your presence!'

Malus turned, seeking the source of the frail voice. 'Are you wraith or man?' he called out. 'Show yourself!'

Another voice spoke. Like the first, it was chillingly unnatural, like the groan of glacial ice. 'We are ageless,' it said, 'and we rule here, not you.'

The imperious tone in the groaning voice annoyed the highborn. 'You rule here? I thought you were waiting, serving the will of Khaine and guarding the warpsword until the arrival of the chosen one.'

A third voice answered, thin and creaking like old leather. 'Who are you to question us so?'

Malus took a deep breath. 'I am the Scourge,' he said. 'Your vigil is ended, for I have come for the sword. The Time of Blood is nigh.'

The echoes of his voice faded into the stillness. Malus waited, straining to locate the aged assassins in the depths of the room. After a moment he caught the faintest sound of movement to his left: a dry rustle of robes.

'Impossible,' the first voice said. 'You cannot be the chosen one.'

Malus turned to the source of movement. 'Can I not? Am I not druchii, like you? Do I not bear the blessing of Khaine upon my face? I have followed you here through the Vermillion Gate, drawn by the tie I have with the sword. How else could I have found you here in the Waste?' He held out his hand. 'Will you bring me my sword, or will you dishonour your long vigil here at its end?'

More faint hints of movement whispered in the darkness. The second voice spoke. 'You come from the temple,' it groaned.

'So did you, once upon a time,' Malus answered. 'The true believers count you among the dead. The heretics in the temple concealed the theft of the sword and have ruled unchallenged for centuries.'

'That is of no matter to us,' creaked the third voice. 'Let them rule atop their filthy hill. It will all be swept aside when the Time of Blood arrives.'

The voices were drawing closer. Malus was certain now. 'Why conceal your triumph from your fellows?' he asked. 'They might have swayed the people of the city to the true faith had they known.'

Faint shapes resolved themselves at the edges of the light. Malus saw the outlines of robed and hooded figures regarding him from the darkness. 'We are the true faith,' the first voice replied.

'Prove it,' Malus said. 'Give me the sword.'

'The sword is not here,' the second voice groaned, 'and you are not worthy.'

'You dare deny me?' the highborn snapped. 'I am Malus of Hag Graef, born in the city of shadow to the house of chains. My mother was a witch and I slew my father with my own hands. The skull of Aurun Var spoke to me through my sister, a living saint of the Lord of Murder. Have you forgotten your duty after so many centuries, or has your lust for power turned you into the very heretics you once rebelled against?'

All three voices shouted at once. 'Blasphemy!'

'A man blasphemes against the gods, not cowardly figures hiding in the shadows of a ruined temple,' Malus shouted. 'Did you steal the sword to keep it from the hands of the temple elders, or did you secretly covet its power? What are you but pathetic mockeries of the very heretics you once railed against?'

'Seize him!' the first voice shrieked. Malus reached for his sword, but huge figures loomed silently out of the shadows to either side of him. There had been more of the armoured guards standing a silent watch in the darkness of the room, and they grabbed Malus's arms and lifted him from the ground as if he was a child.

The robed figures crept slowly into the light, drawing back their hoods, and Malus looked upon them and cried out, horrified at what the assassins had become.

Their bodies were impossibly ancient, shrivelled and dried like mummies over thousands of years in the hot air of the Wastes. Two males and a woman – her paper thin lips framed a pair of yellow fangs that told Malus she had once been a blood-witch – little more than living skeletons with parchment skin stretched over sharp bones.

The man in the centre of the trio stepped close to Malus, studying him with cold, reptilian orbs that bore little resemblance to living eyes. 'You are young and strong,' the creature said, its voice whistling from the depths of dried lungs and past cracked lips. 'The people here are faithful, but their spirits are weak. We have lived on thin gruel for far too long,' the withered druchii said. 'You are blasphemous, but in a sense you are also a blessing from Khaine. Tonight we will kill you, so that tomorrow we may call back your spirit and consume it. Your energies will restore us and lend us strength for a very long time to come.'

'You would dare take the life of Khaine's chosen Scourge?' Malus raged.

The withered creature looked up at Malus and shook his head. 'The true Scourge would not have been taken so easily,' he said, and gestured to the guards.

'Take the heretic to the plaza and crucify him,' the Ageless King said.

CHAPTER TWENTY-THREE

THE BURNING BLADE

Malus roared like a trapped animal, thrashing and kicking in the guards' iron grip as they began to remove him from the altar room. Consumed with rage, he used their strength against them, twisting at the waist and kicking the man to his left in the side of the head. The highborn's armoured shin rang like a gong off the polished brass helmet and the guard staggered, allowing Malus to pull his arm free.

The guard on his right reacted quickly for a man of his immense size, reaching for Malus's throat with a wide, spade-like hand. Snarling, Malus ducked beneath the guard's lunge and tried to grab the bone handle of a dagger sheathed at the man's waist. The highborn's hand closed on the hilt and he drew the blade free, just as a clawed hand grasped the side of Malus's cheek and every nerve in his body exploded in icy pain.

Malus convulsed beneath the witch's agonising touch. His body arched, taut as a bow, and his face locked in a rictus of torment. Malus dimly heard a sharp, brittle *crack* near his waist and realised that the bone hilt had snapped in his clenched, quivering hand.

Armoured hands grabbed him roughly, tearing the dagger away and lifting him from the ground. His gaze was fixed. He could not move, could not breathe, could not even blink. The pain was so intense that he could barely think. Tz'arkan's name rose unbidden to his mind, but he had not the power to speak it.

The blood-witch recoiled from Malus with a frightened groan, her black eyes glittering with shock and horror as the guards dragged him away. The last thing he saw as darkness enfolded him was her white, withered face, its leathery features twisting into an expression of despair as the witch reeled from the glimpse she'd been given into Malus's soul.

In time, the pain began to recede, like a slow tide ebbing from his tortured frame. Visions of red slowly resolved into a crimson sky, painted with twisting shapes of black smoke and ashen clouds. Thunder rumbled in the distance.

Long shapes loomed at the edges of his vision. He lay on his back amid a forest of dying men, their ravaged bodies impaled upon iron stakes as tall as saplings. His body was contorted awkwardly on the wide paving stones, like a statue tumbled from its plinth. Figures moved slowly past the limits of his eyesight, their movements perceived as no more than shifting shadows playing across his contorted form.

He thought he heard a voice rise in anger, and moans of defeat and despair. Malus could not tell if they were real or part of a dream, and his mind wandered as he stared into the shifting, crimson sky.

Once he thought he saw the blood-witch standing over him, a curved knife trembling in her shrunken hand. Shrieks and groans echoed in the turgid air, and when he looked into her eyes she wailed like a ghost and shrank from his sight. He tried to laugh but managed only a low, tortured moan.

The sky darkened. Thunder rolled like war drums, and drops of blood mixed with gritty ash fell heavily against his face. Hands gripped him around his arms and lifted him. He rose into the air, wondering if he was being offered up to the storm.

Then he was falling again, being lowered onto a frame of rough wood in the shape of an X. The hands pulled at him, stretching his contorted limbs and laying them flat against the crossbars. His head sagged between the cross-posts, sending drops of dark red streaming down into his ears and hair.

He felt his gauntlets being pulled away. Something cold and sharp pressed against his right wrist. His mind drifted, unable to make sense of what was happening.

Then the first hammer blow struck, driving the spike deep into his wrist, and Malus began to scream.

Thunder crashed, vibrating his armour like a struck gong and startling him awake. His body jerked, and he cried out in the grip of raw, jagged pain as his broken wrists and ankles grated against the nails pinning him to beams. Agony caused his stomach to clench, and he vomited blood and bile onto the paving stones.

Darkness had fallen since the guards had nailed him to the wood and left him in the plaza to die. Lightning raged overhead, playing a nightmarish pantomime of shadows across the stones of the plaza. Blood and ashes had dried on his cheeks, forming a brittle death mask that lent a daemonic cast to his angular face.

Had it not been for his armour he would have been dead already, suffocated by his own ribcage as he hung from the upright wooden posts. As it was, the interlocking plates kept his body from sagging too far downwards, taking some of the weight off his mutilated wrists. He'd swum in and out of consciousness for hours, delirious from pain and loss of blood.

His mind was clearer now. Perhaps the last vestiges of the witch's touch had faded, or else his nerves no longer had the power to communicate the awful truth of his injuries. It was enough that he was able to notice the solitary figure outlined by the flash of lightning only a few yards away.

Grunting in pain, he managed to raise his head slightly and peer at the motionless figure. 'Sh... Shebbolai,' he whispered, his voice little more than a thready rasp.

The figure stirred. 'I thought you dead,' the chieftain replied. He stepped closer. Another flicker of lightning etched his dark skinned face in sharp relief, revealing an expression of anger and torment. 'How can this be?' he asked. 'You are the first warrior of Naggaroth to come here since the arrival of the Ageless Kings. You bested my finest warriors, and you bear the mark of Khaine in your eyes. You must be the Scourge!'

'The Ageless Kings have forgotten their duty to the Lord of Murder,' Malus rasped. 'They have been seduced by power and wealth. Long ago they ruled this land to safeguard Khaine's sword. Now they rule for their sakes alone.'

'Do not blaspheme!' Shebbolai snapped.

'You know it's true!' Malus said. He tried to look up at the bodies hanging nearby. 'On the way here you told me that your tribe rarely fought any more. Where, then, did all these men come from? They have the look of warriors, but were they foes taken in battle or members of your own tribe who rebelled against the Ageless Kings and their inglorious rule?'

'You're here now,' the chieftain said, 'and The Time of Blood is at hand! How can they deny you?'

'Because this is all they have,' Malus said. 'They've clung to life and power for so long that the struggle is all they know. They cannot return to Naggaroth, not as they are, and once I claim the sword, who will fear them? The centuries have made them mad, Shebbolai, and weak. Their time is at an end.' Malus met his eye. 'It's your time now. Of all the hundreds of chieftains who have led the red swords, it is you who will ride to battle beside Khaine's chosen Scourge.'

An expression of awe transformed Shebbolai's scarred face. 'What would you have me do?'

'Tell me where to find the warpsword.'

'It... it is not here,' the chieftain said. 'Long ago, when the kings first came here, the sword passed between them at the turning of each moon, so that all of them would share the burden of safeguarding it. One day the king who kept the sword refused to give it up, and they fought among themselves. The struggle lasted for centuries, or so the legends say.' Shebbolai turned and look back at the temple. 'Two of the kings died during the feud. You saw their skulls in the reliquary chamber.'

'And the sword?'

'They agreed to place it beyond their grasp except in the direst of circumstances, so that they would never feud amongst themselves again. They took the sword north, into the mountains, and hid it in a cave, so goes the legend,' Shebbolai said grimly, 'as it has been passed down through the line of chieftains. It is part of our pact with the Ageless Kings, to keep their secret from the rest of the world.'

'That's all very fascinating,' Malus wheezed impatiently, 'but how am I to find this cave?'

'Follow the skulls,' the chieftain said. 'They will lead you through the gullies to the cave and its guardian.'

'Guardian,' Malus spat, 'what sort of guardian?'

The chieftain shrugged. 'The legends do not say: something powerful enough to guard the warpsword for ages and not be tempted by it as the kings were.'

'Delightful,' the highborn snarled. The pain in his wrists was starting to build once more. Gritting his teeth, he tried to take some of the weight off of them, prompting a groan of torment as he bore down on the spikes penetrating his feet just below the ankles.

When the agony subsided and his vision cleared he focused his gaze on Shebbolai once more. 'You must pass the word to those of your tribe you can trust,' the highborn said. 'When I return with the sword the reign of the Ageless Kings will end. Do you understand?'

The chieftain nodded. 'I understand.'

'Good. Now get me down from this damned cross,' Malus groaned.

But Shebbolai was unmoved. He looked Malus in the eye. 'If all you say is true, and you are the Scourge of Khaine, you should be able to free yourself.' He backed away from the cross. 'I will await your return,' he said, and disappeared into the darkness.

Malus stifled a vicious curse. He had a plan for Shebbolai and his warriors, so for the moment he needed the chieftain on his side. Plus, he thought bitterly as he tried in vain to close his fists, there was not enough mothers' milk in the world to heal him from the guards' iron spikes.

Lightning flared overhead and arced among the iron poles of the plaza. Malus heard screams and smelled the sweet odour of burning flesh. He drew a deep breath.

This would not be any mere taste. He stood at the edge of an abyss. The next step he took would be into darkness.

Thunder crashed. 'Tz'arkan!' he screamed at the bleeding sky, and his veins burned with the daemon's icy touch.

Power coursed through him in an icy torrent, banishing fear, weakness and pain. The strength of a god flowed through him. Clenching his fists, he tore them free of the iron spikes and laughed like a madman as shattered bone and torn flesh re-knit. Reaching down, he pulled the lower spikes loose with his bare hands and fell to his knees upon the gore slick stones. Malus squeezed the spikes between his fingers as if they were half-melted wax, and threw them high into the air.

He felt the lightning coming before it flared overhead. He heard the heartbeats of the men slowly dying among the forest of iron poles. He could taste the scent of each and every living thing in the city, and see the peaks of the mountains to the north despite the roiling darkness overhead.

It was like nothing he had ever felt before. The daemon did not merely strengthen and heal him. He *was* the daemon, and the daemon was him.

He'd found the cold one a mile outside the city, tracking it through the darkness by its peculiar, acrid scent. It had growled threateningly at his approach, lowering its blocky head and snapping its fearsome jaws, but he had met its red eyes and bent his will upon the beast. The nauglir struggled against him but a moment, and then recoiled with a cry of pain. He advanced on the beast, lashing it again and again with his power, until it lay on its belly and allowed him to climb into the saddle.

Malus led Spite around the ruined city under the cover of darkness and up into the broken foothills to the north. His razor-keen senses banished the darkness and allowed him to traverse the narrow, labyrinthine gullies as if it was broad daylight.

Shebbolai had spoken true. He began to see the bones almost at once: smashed skeletons of men and horses, the long bones snapped and sucked clean of marrow and the skulls split open to get at the brains. Shorn armour and broken swords lay rusting in the dirt, enough to equip an army. For the first hour he'd amused himself by counting the skulls, trying to gauge how many souls had gone into the narrow defiles in search of Khaine's sword. Before the hour was up he'd counted a thousand, and didn't bother to continue from there.

Spite's broad feet were wading through drifts of old bones before long, crushing them and kicking them underfoot. They led unerringly upwards, many times branching off into twisting side paths, but Malus kept to the primary trail, knowing where it must eventually lead.

'Whoever lives here, daemon... has quite an appetite,' he said.

'Then let's hope he's sleeping, Malus,' Tz'arkan replied. The voice reverberated through his skull no differently than the highborn's own, as if he and the daemon were simply two spirits bound to the same body. 'Somewhere in these gullies lies the lost Warpsword of Khaine. We're not leaving until you've found it.'

The tone in the daemon's voice angered Malus, as if he was nothing more than a slave going about his master's business. For the moment, he chose to hold his tongue. Tz'arkan's power had subsided somewhat, but still flowed freely, infusing him with strength and power such as he hadn't known for months.

Up ahead the gully widened, forming a broad V that pointed to the mouth of a large cave. The gully floor outside the cave was literally carpeted with bones and the detritus of the dead. After many long months, he'd reached his goal at last.

Malus reined in Spite and slid carefully from the saddle. The nauglir shied away from him at once, retreating further down the length of the gully. He shot the beast a warning glance. 'I found you once, dragonlet. I can find you again,' he warned, and then turned his attention to the drifts of old bones that blanketed the rocky ground. It was a crude but effective alarm, providing the sword's guardian had sharp ears.

Choosing his course very carefully, Malus began to pick his way through the multitude of fallen treasure seekers. He tried not to think about the fact that many of them had probably attempted the very same thing.

'Quietly now, Darkblade,' Tz'arkan said, 'let's not wake anyone.'

'Your concern is touching,' the highborn murmured, slowly drawing his sword.

Lightning flickered silently overhead, making the landscape of bones appear to shift and slide. Disorientated, Malus tried to step over a yellowed skull directly in his path, and came down directly on it instead. The aged bone collapsed with a hollow *crunch* that seemed to echo like thunder between the gully walls.

Malus froze, not even daring to breathe. A moment passed, and then another. Still he waited, straining his ears for any signs of movement.

Two minutes passed. Only then did Malus relax, cursing his foul luck.

That was when the night air shook with an ear-splitting roar and an enormous figure emerged from the depths of the cave.

The guardian of the sword was huge. Its lower body alone was larger than a cold one, covered in scales of indigo and dusky red. Large legs, like those of a dragon, propelled it in a thunderous charge down the slope towards Malus, kicking up clouds of powdered bone with every ponderous step. Above the set of clawed forelegs where a dragon's neck and head would normally be there was instead a broad leather belt, decorated with scales of gold and a buckle shaped like a skull. Above the belt, towered the upper torso of a fearsome ogre, clad in crude armour that protected its midsection and capped its powerful shoulders. Tusks thick enough to disembowel a boar jutted from the shaggoth's thick lips, and its ice blue eyes gleamed beneath a craggy brow and a round steel helmet. In its platter sized hand, the guardian held a sword that was longer than Malus was tall, and the creature raised it angrily as it bore down on the stunned highborn.

'Mother of Night!' the highborn cursed.

'Malus, under the circumstances I think I'll let you run, now!'

The terrible sword whickered through the air. Galvanised by the daemon's shout, Malus hurled himself to the left, just out of the weapon's reach. The blade struck a pile of bones and sent shattered fragments spraying into the air. Still bellowing in rage, the dragon ogre charged past, quickly changing course to come around for another charge.

The creature was between Malus and his cold one. Frantically he cast around for other avenues of escape, but the walls of the gully were steep and sheer. 'There's nowhere to run!' he exclaimed.

The dragon ogre bore down on Malus again with a terrible crunching of bones. The highborn raised his sword warily. There was no way he could trade blows with something so massive. He would have to wear the monster down with lightning-fast strikes, much as he'd seen Arleth Vann kill the highborn in the crypt.

He crouched low as the beast charged into reach. Its sword swept down at an angle, aiming to cut the druchii in half from shoulder to hip. At the last second, Malus dodged to the left, cutting across the dragon ogre's path and fouling his swing. The creature let out a furious cry and the highborn answered with a druchii war scream as he put all his strength into a powerful cut aimed just below the shaggoth's belt.

The heavy northern sword, backed by the daemon's terrible strength, struck the monster dead on, and the steel blade shattered with a discordant clang. Malus barely had time to register his shock before the dragon ogre lashed out with a clawed forelimb and struck him a backhanded blow that sent him flying head over heels into the air.

Had the limb struck his chin it would have taken his head clean off. As it was, the shaggoth's paw had glanced off his chest and dented his thick breastplate. He felt as if he'd been kicked by a nauglir, and he gasped for breath as he hit a pile of old skulls near the side of the gully wall.

Malus rolled off the pile of bones, glaring helplessly at the monster. He tried to subdue it by force of will just as he'd done to the nauglir, but the dragon ogre was unfazed. Furious, he grabbed a skull and hurled it at the beast with all his strength. 'Curse you, creature!' he roared. 'Curse you back to hell!' The projectile struck the beast in the side of the head and shattered into pieces, leaving not a mark on the monster's thick skull.

Terror and despair raged through Malus. The daemon's gifts were useless. Had he surrendered the last vestiges of himself for nothing?

Bellowing like a bull, the dragon ogre came about, readying its massive sword.

Malus could feel Tz'arkan's strength pulsing through him. He could hear the blood rushing in his veins and feel the fury of the storm raging overhead, but not a bit of it mattered. In the next few moments the shaggoth would cut him apart.

As the dragon ogre trotted towards him, Malus's eyes turned to the dark mouth of the cave. I'll be damned if I'm going to die empty-handed, he thought.

The highborn pushed himself to his feet and sprinted up the gully. The dragon ogre bellowed angrily, surprised by the sudden move. Tz'arkan was surprised as well.

'Malus, where are you going? You're running towards the cave!'

'We still have a job to do, remember?' the highborn countered.

'You fool! It's right behind us!' the daemon said. 'You'll trap us in there!'

'I need a weapon,' Malus snarled. 'The warpsword is in there. That will do.'

Malus reached the entrance to the cave. A cacophony of pounding feet and crunching bone rose behind him as the shaggoth charged headlong up the gully.

'The Warpsword of Khaine is no pig stick to be used in brawling!' the daemon raged. 'It is a talisman of glorious power–'

'It's still a sword,' Malus said. 'Shut up, daemon!'

Malus rushed into the cave. He expected a long, carrion choked passageway, leading back into darkness. Instead he found himself in a broad, high-ceilinged cavern. The space was piled with bones and rotting bodies nevertheless, save for a cleared area near the centre of the chamber where the dragon ogre evidently slept. A plain stone altar stood on the other side of the cleared area, and upon that altar rested a sword.

The Warpsword of Khaine was a double-edged blade nearly as long as a draich, slightly wider at the point than at the hilt to give the weapon extra power to cut with. Its blade was sheathed in a scabbard of black lacquered bone, chased with gold and ornamented with fiery rubies. The weapon's hilt was long and slim, built for two hands and wrapped with dark leather. A large cabochon ruby, like a dragon's eye, gleamed at the point where hilt met blade. It glimmered with power, radiating from the entire blade in waves of invisible heat.

Malus looked upon the sword and saw the potential hidden within its depths. He saw red battlefields and toppled towers, looted cities and fallen kings. With such a blade a druchii could conquer the world.

'Malus, I forbid this!' the daemon snarled. Was there an edge of fear in Tz'arkan's voice?

The highborn dashed across the chamber. The shaggoth burst into the cavern just behind him, shaking the dank air with its furious cries.

'Then we die here,' Malus replied. 'The choice is yours.'

In truth it wasn't. Nothing the daemon could say or do would keep Malus from placing his hand upon the warpsword's hilt and drawing the weapon from its scabbard.

The hilt was hot to the touch, as if the ancient steel was still fresh from the forge. The warmth sank into his skin, suffusing his muscles with power. He drew the weapon in a single, smooth motion, marvelling at the blade's black finish. Its edge shone like fire in the gloom.

With a stentorian bellow the dragon ogre charged. Malus felt no fear. When he turned to face the onrushing beast he was smiling like a wolf.

Malus stepped into the shaggoth's charge, swinging the warpsword in a clean, perfect arc that was the virtual twin of the blow he'd struck before. The bright edges of the blade left an arc of ghostly light in the darkness as it sliced through the dragon ogre's midsection. The beast screamed, hurled backwards by the force of the blow. It landed in a broken heap close to the mouth of the cave, its armour half melted and smoke rising from the fearsome wound in its abdomen. The beast was dead, almost as if the blade had reached into its huge body and snuffed out its life like a candle.

The highborn stared at the sword in wonder. Its warmth coursed through him, banishing Tz'arkan's black ice. His heart hammered in his chest, and his mind was suffused with an emotion he hadn't felt in many months: hope.

'Good sword,' Malus said in an awed whisper. 'No wonder you wanted it for your collection.'

The daemon seemed to shrink inside Malus, dwindling in presence until it coiled like a serpent around the highborn's black heart. 'I despair of you Malus,' Tz'arkan said hatefully. 'When the final task is done there will be *such* a reckoning.'

Malus stared into the depths of the blade. A faint smile tugged at his lean face. 'I'm counting on it,' he said.

CHAPTER TWENTY-FOUR

THE SCOURGE OF KHAINE

Malus Darkblade rode into the city of the Ageless Kings with a gleaming sword in his hand and a Chaos storm raging at his back.

Lightning roiled the crimson skies, etching the broken walls and crumbled towers in stark relief. Thunder rolled, matched by the terrible growl of the nauglir as it stalked down the debris-choked lanes. Tribesmen rose from the furs they had been sleeping on, clutching axes or swords, and peered into the night, sensing something terrible was at hand.

Malus rode through the plaza of impaled men, passing the crossed timbers where he himself had hung mere hours before. The dark bulk of the temple reared before him, its skull adorned flanks silhouetted in flickering displays of brazen lightning. He reined in his cold one at the base of the towering steps and regarded the sealed doors coldly. Spite reared his head at the ancient building and roared, a raw sound of fury that echoed roughly from the temple's thick walls.

The double doors swung open within moments and a troop of temple guards swarmed out, brandishing long, heavy pole arms and axes. Malus slid from the saddle and took the warpsword in a two-handed grip, savouring the heat radiating from the unearthly blade. It pulsed in time with his beating heart, quickening hungrily at the prospect of battle.

The temple guards spread out at a run and charged down the steps shouting the name of Khaine, blessed Lord of Murder.

A wolfish smile spread across Malus's grim face. 'Blood and souls,' he whispered, and ran to meet them.

He saw the battle unfold with dreadful, icy clarity, as if it was a ritual dance unfolding in slow motion. A guard rushed in from the highborn's left, stabbing with his pole arm. Malus hacked off the spearhead with a desultory sweep of his blade and cut the man in half with a backhanded stroke. Without pause, Malus swept his sword to the right to block the sweep of another guardsman's axe, before reversing the blade and cutting off both of the warrior's legs just above the knee. Armour parted like rotted paper; flesh blackened and bone splintered at the sword's ravening touch. Men's screams wove a brutal threnody around Malus as he wove among his foes, scattering arcs of hot blood that sizzled and steamed in the air.

One guardsman swept low with his pole arm, aiming to knock Malus from his feet. Before the blow could land the highborn reached out and sank the point of the warpsword into the onrushing guard's neck, and then spun on his heel and severed both arms and the helmeted head of the guard charging at Malus from behind. The highborn laughed like a drunkard, spinning and cutting with the seething blade and climbing ever higher towards the temple doors.

A guard screamed in fury and leapt for him, heedless of the long fall to the plaza below. The move caught Malus off-guard for a fraction of a second, but with the battle fever on him his foe seemed to hang languorously in the air, his muscular arms outstretched like a child's. Fluid as a blade dancer, Malus half-spun and dropped to one knee, bringing the sword up in a glittering stroke that sliced the man open from groin to chin and propelled him in a bloody arc to the grey stones at the nauglir's feet.

There was a droning sound humming lazily towards Malus. He turned and swatted the thrown axe aside, and then dashed up the last few steps to the sole remaining guard. The warrior had barely enough time to unsheath his dagger before Malus reached him.

Both men regarded one another. The armoured giant towered over the lithe highborn, his masked face looking down at the druchii as if in startled bemusement. Then the guard let out a bubbling sigh and bright blood erupted from the air holes in his visor as the highborn pulled the warpsword free from the man's breastplate. Malus stepped gracefully to the side as the giant's body crashed face first onto the stone steps and slid towards the bottom on a dark trail of gore.

A pale figure regarded the highborn from just outside the temple doorway. The blood-witch sank slowly to her knees, her marble-like eyes glittering fearfully as Malus approached her. Thin, wrinkled lips pulled back from yellowed fangs in a frightful grimace of dread.

'I knew you would return,' she groaned. 'I tried to tell the others, but they would not believe what I had seen.' The ancient blood-witch spread her hands. 'You are death and ruin given form, oh son of the house of chains, and the blessings of the Dark Gods go with you. Our time is finished. Let the Time of Blood begin.'

She raised her chin, and the warpsword seemed to leap in Malus's hands. The black blade flickered through the air and the blood-witch stiffened in the wind of the sword's passing.

Malus studied the witch coldly for a moment. A trickle of dark blood welled in a thin line across her narrow throat. The highborn stepped up to her and reached out, taking a handful of her white hair in his fist and lifting her severed head from her neck.

The highborn hung the witch's head from his belt and stalked past her still upright body, heading into the darkness of the temple beyond.

When Malus emerged from the temple a short while later the tribe of the red sword was awaiting him.

They filled the plaza at the foot of the temple, standing like wraiths amid the forest of impaled men. Lightning picked out steel helms and glittering mail, sharpened swords and bared fangs. Warped faces turned upwards as the highborn's armoured figure strode to the top of the stairs, and every eye beheld the steaming sword and the trio of severed heads gripped in Malus's hands.

Shebbolai stood at the head of his tribe, waiting at the foot of the broad stairs with a look of grim joy on his face. Malus regarded him balefully, and then his gaze swept across the gathered warriors. Thunder rumbled from the north.

'The rule of the Ageless Kings is no more,' Malus said, his sharp voice ringing out across the plaza. 'They forgot their duty to the Lord of Murder, and Khaine has meted out his wrath, but their taint has spread to you, warriors of the red sword. The sons of Khaine do not hide in cities of stone and turn their faces from the battlefield! The glory of the Bloody-Handed God lies in death, not in slaves, nor gold, nor stone walls. The Ageless Kings chose to cling to life, and you joined in their depravity.'

A groan rose from the assembled warriors at the highborn's harsh words. Malus cut them off with a shout.

'When Khaine sent his chosen Scourge to claim his birthright from the kings, they were sunk so far in their iniquity that they did not know him.' Malus raised the terrible blade. 'Look upon the Warpsword of Khaine and know that his Scourge has arisen!'

The warriors replied with shouts of anger and despair. Men slashed their cheeks and their chests, offering up their bloodstained blades to the highborn. Warriors turned on the weaker men of the tribe and hacked their bodies apart, throwing glistening bits of flesh and bone upon the steps of the temple.

'We live to serve!' Shebbolai cried out, his face a mask of shame and despair. 'Forgive us, dreadful Scourge!'

'There is no forgiveness in the eyes of Khaine,' Malus snarled, 'only death. Blood alone can wash away your sins.'

'Then blood it will be!' Shebbolai roared. 'Show us the way, holy one. We live and die at your command!'

The highborn looked down upon the chieftain and smiled an executioner's smile. 'Follow me, sons of the red sword. Death and glory await.'

Malus led the tribe out into the wasteland, returning to the place where the Vermillion Gate had left him. He had no idea if it would make any difference, but it gave him some time to think and take stock of the forces at his command.

The Chaos warriors did not march as an army of Naggaroth, in ordered lines and divisions. They swept over the plain in a ragged mob, perhaps two hundred strong, riding swift, lean horses that moved as if they shared a single mind with their masters. Hoarse shouts and lusty war cries echoed in the darkness as the warriors followed the Scourge from the city. The prospect of battle had quickened their blood, banishing doubt and fear.

The same could not be said for Malus. He rode ahead of the unruly mob with the warpsword riding in its scabbard against his hip. With the weapon sheathed he felt cold again, the heat of Khaine's hunger leeching slowly from his muscles and leaving him wretched and weak. Every few moments his hand would stray to the weapon's hilt, as if he was warming himself by the side of a small fire.

Tz'arkan stirred within Malus. Where before the daemon's presence seemed to swell within the highborn's chest, now it caused his whole body to tremble. 'You grow overbold, little druchii,' the daemon sneered. 'You trifle with forces beyond your understanding, and you think to lead this pitiful mob to war with your brother?'

Malus looked back at Shebbolai, riding just a few yards behind the highborn, and beyond to the shifting crowd of riders spread out across the plain. 'I don't expect them to triumph,' he said coldly. 'I expect them to die, in as dramatic a fashion as possible. I will need a grand diversion if I'm to reach the Sanctum of the Sword and deal with Urial.'

It was a gamble, to be sure, and a desperate one. As fearsome as the warpsword was, Malus didn't care to pit himself against Tyran and his entire band of zealots. If he could distract them with a sudden attack inside the walls of the fortress, it might buy him enough time to reach the temple and confront Urial directly. He hoped that with his half-brother dead the zealots would accept him as the new Scourge or else lose heart and scatter into the night. Then he could deal with Rhulan or whoever was commanding the forces of the temple.

'You think that you can defeat Urial by yourself?' the daemon sneered.

Malus's hand strayed towards the hilt of the warpsword. 'With this I can.'

'You are a fool, Darkblade!'

'No, daemon. You put this sword into my hands. If you didn't think I'd take it up and use it to slay my enemies then you are the fool, not I.'

As he spoke, Malus caught sight of a trio of ragged shapes lying upon the lifeless ground and realised they'd reached the site of his battle with Shebbolai's champions. He prodded Spite into a canter and rode halfway up the shallow rise so he that could turn and regard the tribesmen. As the nauglir heeled about the riders brought their mounts to a halt and waited expectantly.

Malus drew the warpsword, shuddering slightly as the rush of heat flooded his body. 'Warriors of the red sword,' he cried, 'the hour of your redemption is at hand! Follow me and cleanse your souls in the blood of the foe! Kill every man who stands in your way!'

Shebbolai drew a fearsome, curved sword and waved it in the air. 'Blood for the Blood God!'

The night air erupted in a cacophony of bestial shouts to Khaine. Malus smiled, and focused his will upon the sword. *Open the gate,* he commanded. *Return us to the temple, you damned Lord of Murder, and we'll reap a red harvest in your name.*

An angry rumble shook the air. Whether it was thunder or the growl of a bloodthirsty god Malus could not say, for at that moment the warriors of the tribe cried out in terror and the world turned inside out.

They appeared under clear skies, with a bright pair of moons overhead. The transition was so jarring that for a moment Malus was completely disorientated.

Horses screamed and men shouted in wonder and fear. The night shook with the stern cry of trumpets and Malus heard shouts of alarm echoing down the lanes of the temple fortress. Then the world snapped back into focus.

Malus and the warriors found themselves in the broad avenue between the Citadel of Bone and the dwarf-built temple. White-robed zealots were charging from every building and pathway, and the alarm trumpets continued to sound. It was as if their arrival had been expected somehow, the highborn thought. If so, his gambit had already failed.

The sounds of battle revivified the Chaos warriors, however, and already screams and clashes of steel echoed across the avenue. Malus stood in his saddle. 'Warriors of Khaine, redeem yourselves in the blood of your foes!'

With a bloodthirsty roar the marauders spurred their horses and threw themselves headlong at the zealots, and in moments a fierce, swirling melee raged along the length of the avenue. More zealots were streaming in from every direction, but for the moment the horsemen had an edge in both numbers and mobility. The highborn knew the tide would turn soon enough.

Malus put his heels to Spite's flanks and dashed for the temple.

White-robed warriors raced across his path from left and right, trying to cut him off. The highborn pulled on his reins and headed directly at the zealot on his right. To his credit, the zealot held his ground, readying his weapon to strike at Spite's head, but at the last moment Malus changed direction again, veering left and swiping his sword at the warrior as he went past. The zealot's draich bit into Spite's shoulder just as Malus took off the top of the warrior's skull.

Steel rang on Malus's left side. He glanced over his shoulder in time to see the second zealot's headless body collapsing to the ground. Shebbolai and half a dozen marauders had fallen in behind Malus, using spears and swords to kill anyone who came too close. The marauder chieftain raised his sword to the heavens, laughing like a fiend. Malus grinned cruelly and put his boots to Spite's flanks.

The doors to the temple were open as Malus reined in before the building's broad steps. Fearing an ambush, he dismounted quickly and let Shebbolai and the marauders take the lead. The Chaos warriors raced across the threshold, and almost immediately Malus heard screams and the sounds of battle. As he charged through the doorway, he found the marauders slaughtering a group of temple servants who had been stacking a new set of trophies near the doors.

'This way!' Malus shouted as he dashed across the large chamber. Shebbolai and the men followed the highborn as he raced up the stairs to the chapel. He burst into the chamber expecting at least a handful of zealot guards, but the smaller chamber was empty.

Something's wrong, Malus thought, feeling the first twinges of dread tickle at his heart. The Cauldron of Khaine seethed and bubbled on the ceremonial dais with no one to attend it. It felt like an ambush, but how could Urial have possibly expected this?

Gritting his teeth, Malus decided that it didn't matter. He was committed, one way or the other, and would have to see things through to the bitter end. Taking a deep breath, he made his way to the sanctum stairs.

Shebbolai and the marauders gasped at the towering statue of Khaine as they worked their way around the dais and climbed to the red-lit doorway. Malus gripped the warpsword tightly, drawing strength from its heat as he approached the door. He remembered all too well what had happened the last time he'd stood at that narrow threshold.

Raw power seethed from the doorway, washing over Malus's skin and making the warpsword vibrate in his hands. 'Be ready for anything,' the highborn warned the marauders, and stepped inside.

Malus was not prepared for what he found.

The very air howled and shimmered with pain.

Malus stood at the foot of a broad bridge fashioned from skulls that crossed a sea of seething red. Heat and light rose from its surface like the glow of a furnace, searing his skin and filling his ears with the cries of the damned.

At the far end of the bridge stood another doorway leading into the sanctum, and at the bridge's midpoint, naked and gleaming in the ruddy light, stood Yasmir.

Malus looked upon her and felt smaller and weaker than he'd ever known before. She was unearthly, radiant in her lethal beauty. Her dark eyes met his and she smiled, revealing her leonine fangs. Behind Malus, one of the marauders moaned like a frightened child.

'Who is she?' asked Shebbolai, his voice full of dread.

Malus didn't know what to say. Finally he shrugged. 'She is my bride,' he said grimly, and went to meet her.

She waited for his approach, spreading her arms slightly. Had it not been for the slim, needle-like knives in her hands she might have been offering herself to her lover.

The highborn clenched the warpsword tightly. One did not fight Yasmir; one offered oneself up to die. For an instant he thought of the daemon, but he pushed the idea away. The warpsword would have to be enough.

Her gaze was inscrutable. It was as if she stared through him, seeing some vista beyond the ken of mortals. When she was within reach of his longer sword he came to a halt. His fingers flexed on the sword's leather wrapped hilt.

Yasmir made no move. She continued to stare through him as if he wasn't even there. Malus frowned. 'Hello, sister,' he said.

At the sound of his voice her expression changed. Her eyes shifted slightly, as if she was seeing him for the first time, and then she was flying at him, her daggers reaching for his throat.

Malus brought the warpsword up in the nick of time, barely deflecting the lethal strikes, but there was no time to recover, as the living saint switched targets and began a series of deadly thrusts at his face, chest and groin. She never stopped moving, flowing towards him like a dancer and making a lethal move with each and every step.

He had no time to be afraid. The warpsword seemed to move of its own accord, matching Yasmir blow for blow. Once again, he saw the fight unfold with a detached clarity, as if he was a spectator rather than a combatant. Her speed and grace were devastating. Even though he could read Yasmir's next attack his body was hard-pressed to counter it.

She drove him back steadily, keeping him constantly on the defensive. A dagger thrust sank a quarter of an inch into his throat, but he scarcely felt it. Another blow stung him like an adder just below his eye.

The next one was going to hit his hip, right where the breastplate met his fauld. Malus waited until the last possible moment, and then pivoted on his left foot and let her thrust slide past. He continued the spin, turning it into a lightning quick backhanded cut aimed for her neck. The warpsword hissed through the air, but Yasmir was already gone, rolling forwards out of the sword's path.

Malus rushed at her, but Yasmir recovered from the roll at once and whirled, knocking aside his stop thrust, and making a blurring stab for his neck. The highborn sensed the strike and faded back, deflecting the thrust with the flat of his blade.

Two marauders charged at Yasmir, their weapons aiming for her slender back. She reversed her daggers with a flourish and stabbed both warriors through the heart, before pushing their corpses off and tucking into a tight roll towards the highborn. When she came up out of the roll her blades were reaching for his throat and a terrible smile of joy lit her unearthly face.

Malus had anticipated her attack and ducked beneath the thrust. His sword swept up at her torso and her knives fell into a cross block, trapping his sword. Malus yanked his sword clear, feinted low and then thrust at her neck, just as she twisted her body, deflecting the attack with her right hand dagger and stabbing at Malus with her left.

The point of her dagger scratched the hollow of his throat and stopped. She could reach no further with her right hand blocking Malus's sword. They were at a deadlock.

Yasmir looked into Malus's eyes. She seemed to truly recognise him for the first time. 'I cannot kill him,' she said breathily.

Malus gave her a bemused frown, and then realised that she wasn't speaking to him.

From behind the highborn, back towards the doorway at the far end of the bridge, he heard Urial's angry voice. 'What is this foolishness?'

Malus thought quickly. 'She cannot kill me because we are too evenly matched,' he said. Slowly, carefully, he stepped away from Yasmir and lowered his sword. She mirrored his moves exactly. 'As befits a bride and a groom, don't you think?'

Angry shouts from the other end of the bridge caught his attention. The marauders were retreating from a group of bloodstained zealots, and two fearsome grey figures that crawled like spiders down the stone walls above the doorway to the chapel. The Chaos beasts lashed their tentacles hungrily as they sank closer to their prey.

There was a meaty *thump* near Malus's feet and something bounced heavily off his calf. He looked down and saw Arleth Vann's bloodstained head roll to a stop at his feet.

'He told me everything,' Urial hissed. 'An assassin's body can resist torture, but his spirits are powerless to one such as I.'

Malus turned to face his half-brother, pure murder dancing in his eyes. 'If he told you where I went,' he said raising the warpsword, 'then you know what *this* is.'

Urial stood at the far end of the bridge, the copy of the warpsword clutched in his left hand. His face twisted with rage. 'It is not yours, you misbegotten cur! It is meant for *me*! I was reborn in the cauldron while you were whelped by that Naggorite whore. If you are here it is because Khaine willed it so. You are here so that I may take the sword from your broken and bleeding body.'

Malus smiled. 'Do you want it, brother? Come then, and take it.'

Urial screamed like one of the damned and charged at Malus, his sword held ready. Behind the highborn Shebbolai roared a challenge at the zealots, and suddenly the air rang with the clash of steel and the screams of the dying.

Malus charged at his half-brother, a war scream bursting from his throat. He read Urial's every move, knowing his blade would come slashing down for his shoulder half a second before the blow fell. The warpsword swept up, knocking the blow aside. Then Malus reversed the stroke and sliced at Urial's chest. Before the blow could connect, however, Urial's form blurred, and the sword passed through the space where he had been.

Damned sorcery! Malus whirled just as Urial's blade whipped at his face from an unexpected angle. Caught by surprise, the sword sliced neatly across his cheek. Hot blood poured down his face, and Urial laughed.

Malus stabbed at his half-brother, but again, the sorcerer's form blurred and seemed to coalesce three feet to the left. Urial's sword stabbed out, glancing from Malus's armour, and the highborn spun and slashed down at the extended arm, but once again, it was like cutting at air. Urial blurred and then reformed again to Malus's right. This time the highborn was expecting an attack and was ready when Urial lashed out at his neck. Malus parried the blow and stepped in for a thrust, but again, his half-brother turned to smoke and reappeared three feet to the highborn's right. His half-brother's sword flashed, and Malus felt a spike of pain lance through his right thigh.

The highborn roared in anger, and rushed at his half-brother just as a heavy weight landed on the bridge behind him. He heard the tentacles hissing through the air a fraction too late as the Chaos beast entwined his sword arm and waist and lifted him into the air.

Hissing, gobbling howls rang in Malus's ears as the beast reared onto its hind legs and lashed at Malus with the rest of its tentacles. Barbed hooks grated across Malus's armour as he was spun through the air. He could hear Urial cursing the beast, but the hunter paid the sorcerer no mind, intent on drawing Malus towards its clashing beak.

Snarling, Malus shifted the warpsword to his free hand and slashed at the tentacles holding him. The warpsword parted the flesh whips in a spray of steaming ichor and he plunged face first to the bridge. He hit hard on his left shoulder and rolled away down the beast's right flank. Malus rolled to his feet as the Chaos beast rounded on him, and he buried his sword in the creature's neck just as two of its tentacles smashed against the side of his head. The blows knocked the highborn to the ground and he rolled clear, dragging his sword with him.

When his vision cleared Malus found himself facing back towards the chapel end of the bridge. The second Chaos beast had leapt from the wall and clung to the side of the stone span, snatching men in the midst of the melee and lifting them clear. As Malus watched, the hunter snatched one of the marauders from the battle and lifted the wriggling body high overhead, whereupon it began to pull the man limb from limb.

Tyran and Shebbolai faced one another, trading blows with their curved swords in a blur of razor edged motion. All around them zealots and marauders tore at one another with single-minded ferocity, although it was clear that with the Chaos beast on their side the zealots would soon gain the upper hand. Yasmir stood apart from the battle, watching the slaughter with dispassionate interest.

A shadow loomed over Malus. Urial's sword whirred through the air and struck the bridge where the highborn had been, but Malus had rolled away and was clambering unsteadily to his feet.

Roaring with hate, Urial charged at his half-brother, launching a series of powerful blows that Malus blocked with steady, deft strokes. Malus didn't attempt to strike back, knowing that it would only give Urial a chance to discorporate and strike him from an unexpected angle. Instead he gave ground, defending himself easily and trying to think of a way to turn the tables.

With every step Malus drew closer to the melee at the end of the bridge. On impulse he blocked Urial's next attack, and turned and ran towards the battle. Behind him, Urial laughed in disdain and lurched after him, dragging his twisted foot across the smooth stone.

A zealot struck down one of the Chaos warriors and stepped in Malus's path. The highborn cut the man in half and dashed past before the bloody halves hit the ground. He raced right for the last Chaos beast, which saw him coming and reached for him with eight thrashing tentacles. He seemed to race directly into the creature's embrace, but at the last moment he threw himself to the ground and rolled beneath the creature's head.

As he'd hoped, Urial ran headlong into the monster's clutches. The Chaos beast, not able to tell the difference between friend and foe, reached for Urial as eagerly as it had tried to grab Malus, but again the sorcerer's form blurred and he appeared three feet to the left of where he'd stood. Half mad with fury, Urial stabbed the beast in the eye, and it plunged from the edge of the bridge with a shriek. One of the last marauders leapt at Urial from behind, but the usurper twisted at the waist and sliced the man in half with a savage swipe of his blade.

There was a scream to Malus's left as the last zealot leapt at the two remaining marauders. Both Chaos warriors buried their blades in the druchii's chest, but the zealot crashed heavily into the two men, bearing all three over the edge of the bridge and into the red sea beneath. Their screams ended as they sank beneath the heaving liquid and did not rise again.

Only Tyran and Shebbolai were left. Both men circled one another warily, bleeding from scores of deep wounds on their chests and arms. Shebbolai raised his sword and charged Tyran with a fierce roar, as Malus looked on. The zealot leader watched the man come and ducked the chieftain's swing at the last second, thrusting with his draich and taking Shebbolai squarely in the chest. The onrushing warrior impaled himself on Tyran's blade, the draich bursting from Shebbolai's back. Before Tyran could pull his blade free, the chieftain grabbed the zealot leader's wrist. Smiling madly, the chieftain pulled Tyran towards him, driving the man's sword deeper into his chest. Tyran tried to pull away, but the Chaos warrior's grip was like iron. Shebbolai's sword flashed, and Tyran's sword arm was hacked away at the shoulder. The zealot staggered back with a hideous scream and fell backwards off the bridge. Still smiling, Shebbolai sank to the ground and toppled over dead.

Urial charged Malus with a roar, thrusting at the highborn's neck. Malus blocked the thrust and swung at Urial's head, but again the sorcerer's body blurred and reappeared three feet away. The usurper's sudden counter-attack nearly took Malus's head off, but he saw the blow just in time and ducked out of the way.

Malus's half-brother laughed. 'You're done for, Darkblade,' he taunted. 'I can do this all night long if I must.'

'I know,' Malus snapped, swinging at Urial's chest. The sorcerer's form blurred – but the highborn continued the swing, aiming for a point three feet to the left.

Urial screamed, staring down at the black sword jutting from between his ribs. Blood poured down the length of the warpsword, turning to steam against its hot edge.

'It makes you predictable,' Malus said, and pulled his sword free.

Urial staggered backwards, his sword falling from his hands. Blood poured in a rush down the front of his armour. He fell back, and found himself enfolded in Yasmir's slender arms.

She laid him gently on the ground, cradling his head in her hands. Urial stared up at her, a look of longing in his eyes. His mouth worked breathlessly.

Yasmir rose and walked around him, kneeling at his side. Smiling lovingly, she placed her hands at the join of his breastplate and pulled. Rivets popped and straps broke as she tore the armour away, revealing Urial's misshapen chest. Then the living saint ran a delicate finger down the usurper's uneven sternum until she found the spot she wanted, and dug in with both hands. Cartilage popped wetly as Yasmir ripped her brother's chest open.

The last thing Urial saw was his beloved sister feeding on his still-beating heart.

As it happened, the warriors of the red sword acquitted themselves far better than Malus had ever expected. After slaying all the zealots and temple servants they could find, they opened the gates of the fortress and rampaged out into the ravaged city. Several of their bodies were found as far away as the warehouse district when the warriors of the temple made their way back into Har Ganeth.

Malus sat back in the throne of the Grand Carnifex as Arch-Hierophant Rhulan entered the council arena, attended by a handful of priests and priestesses. When the elder saw Malus, his relieved expression turned to a look of abject horror.

'You!' he exclaimed. 'What happened? Where's Urial?'

The highborn eyed the elder contemptuously. 'Why, Arch-Hierophant, don't you remember the plan? I said I would find a way to strike at the usurper directly, and so I did. He will trouble the temple no more.' He leaned back in the throne, his right hand resting on the pommel of the unsheathed warpsword. 'I would have resolved this more quickly, but the diversion I'd been led to expect never materialised.'

Rhulan gaped at Malus, his eyes widening in fear. 'It... that is, we tried, but the citizens had gone mad. We couldn't reach the temple–'

'Where is that other elder?' Malus interjected, 'the striking one with the tattoos?'

'Mereia?' Rhulan stammered. 'She... she died trying to reach one of the more isolated warbands.'

'Meaning she tried to fulfil your part of the plan and died fighting while you cowered in a basement somewhere,' Malus snarled.

'Do not presume to judge me,' Rhulan cried. 'I did what I thought best.' He looked back at his attendants, and then fixed Malus with a conspiratorial stare. 'You couldn't have beaten Urial. He had the warpsword. He couldn't be defeated in battle.'

Malus smiled coldly. 'Ah, yes, the scriptures, so, let me understand this correctly: in the interests of doctrinal veracity, you betrayed me and left me to die. Is that right?'

Rhulan began to tremble. 'No, no, it wasn't like that. We had to wait for Malekith to arrive. He could have found a way to stop the usurper.'

'Fortunately for our people, he won't have to.' Malus rose from the throne, holding the fake warpsword in his left hand. Stepping to the edge of the railing, he jumped off and landed on the arena floor. A flare of pain in his wounded leg made him wince, but he pushed the feeling aside. Actually, the discomfort was a good sign. It meant that the daemon's power wasn't healing him as well as it had been. The power of the sword was somehow counterbalancing it. He didn't know how, but he wasn't going to question it for the time being.

Malus straightened and stalked over to Rhulan. 'This, I believe, belongs to the temple,' he said, dropping the fake blade with a clang at the Arch-Hierophant's feet. 'The Grand Carnifex can return it to the sanctum, and as far as the rest of Naggaroth is concerned, it never left its home.'

Rhulan frowned. 'I don't understand–'

'I know,' Malus said, and beheaded Rhulan with the warpsword.

Men and women screamed in horror as the Arch-Hierophant's body collapsed to the floor. Malus silenced them with a cold glare. Then he levelled his sword at one of the priestesses. 'You, come here.'

Niryal stepped from the crowd. She'd put aside her axe at some point, and changed into better clothes. Unlike Rhulan, she mastered her fear, keeping her chin up as she stepped closer to the bloodstained sword.

Malus gave the priestess a murderous look. 'You weren't taken by assassins. You slew the other sentry and then betrayed us to Urial.'

The priestess never flinched. 'I was certain you were deceiving us, and, as it happened, you were.'

'Then, as soon as Urial was dead you switched sides again.'

'I serve the temple,' Niryal said.

Malus smiled. 'I thought you would say as much. That's why I'm making you the new Grand Carnifex. Of all the people in this damned fortress you're the only one whose motives I can understand.'

The other attendants gasped. Even Niryal was stunned. 'You can't do that,' she said.

Malus raised the warpsword. 'I am Khaine's chosen, Niryal, I most certainly can.' He surveyed the other loyalists. 'And they shall be your new Haru'ann. They seem a dim sort, but since they know the truth about the sword, we can either kill them or make use of them.'

Niryal struggled with her sudden change in fortunes for a moment more, and then managed to recover her composure. 'What would you have us do, holy one?' she asked.

The highborn smiled. 'That's better. You will return the counterfeit sword to the sanctum. At this point, no one who saw Urial with the blade is still alive except for us.'

'What about the Witch King? He is probably marching up the Slavers' Road even now.'

'When he arrives you'll receive him with luxurious hospitality and inform him of Urial's usurpation,' Malus said. 'Tell him that Urial and a cabal of zealots used Chaos magic to sow discord among the citizens and slay the temple elders. There was fighting in the streets for almost a week, but in the end you sent a group of volunteers through the tunnels and they managed to assassinate the usurper and the ringleaders. The Witch King will probably want to publicly execute some citizens to vent his pique, but other than that he should be satisfied with the outcome.' He raised the sword in warning. 'You will not tell him anything about me, or Yasmir. She is to remain in the sanctum until such time as the Witch King departs. After that, she may do as she will.'

Niryal thought everything over and finally nodded in satisfaction. 'It shall be as you say, holy one, but what about you?'

'I am leaving,' Malus said. 'Summer is almost done, and I have pressing business elsewhere.'

Malus reluctantly slid the warpsword into its scabbard. Spite waited in the fortress's beast pen, packed and ready to ride. Somewhere out there was the Amulet of Vaurog, the final relic the daemon required. Time was growing short.

He pushed his way through the crowd of stunned attendants, walking briskly to the door, when Niryal called out. 'I don't understand. You're the

Scourge. The Warpsword of Khaine is yours. What about the Time of Blood? Are you not here to lead us into an age of death and fire?'

Malus paused. He looked back through the crowd at Niryal, his hand straying to the hilt of the burning blade.

'Perhaps,' he said with a ghostly smile, 'but not today. The apocalypse will have to wait.'

LORD OF RUIN

Dan Abnett & Mike Lee

CHAPTER ONE

THE MOUNTAIN IN THE NORTH

The Chaos Wastes, first week of winter

The cold wind shifted, blowing gusts of snow from the south-east and whispering in torment through the topmost branches of the trees. Urghal froze in place, settling on his haunches amid the snow-covered undergrowth. The beastman's nostrils flared, scenting prey, and his thin lips pulled back in a rictus of feral hunger.

Urghal swung his horned head left and right, catching glimpses of his two fellow hunters, Aghar and Shuk, as they split up and slid into concealment as well. The dense mountain forest had gone deathly silent save for the keening wind, and the beastman's long, tufted ears twitched restlessly as he strained to hear signs of movement from farther down the long slope. Heavy muscles bunched and relaxed along the beastman's broad shoulders, causing the dark, spiral tattoos etched into his thick hide to roll and shift in unnerving patterns. He breathed slowly and deeply, his clawed fingers flexing around the knotty grip of the rough-hewn club resting in his broad hands. The hunting had been poor since the herd had crept back to the cleft mountain and reclaimed their former territory. Soon the new master of the herd would begin culling out the weak and the slow and butchering them for the cook fires. Urghal had no intention of being one of them.

Silence stretched across the dark wood, broken only by the shrill buzzing of flies circling the open sores on the beastman's bony snout. Then without warning came the rustle and crash of bramble and fern, and Urghal heard the drumming sound of hooves racing over the loamy earth.

The beastman listened intently as the herd of deer stampeded up the slope directly at him. Ferns and thick shrubs were trampled and torn as the panicked animals forced their way through the dense undergrowth. Urghal could smell them now, perhaps as many as a dozen, the scent of their fear burning in his nostrils. He ran a thick, black tongue over his jagged teeth, lusting for the taste of hot, salty blood.

Twenty yards. Ten. Urghal caught glimpses of swaying branches now as the herd drew near. He heard the slight sounds of his fellow hunters readying themselves to strike. The beastman's muscles tensed like coiled springs just as the herd crashed over him like a wave.

A doe burst from the undergrowth to Urghal's left, dodging nimbly around the bole of a dark oak tree in a blur of frenzied motion. The beastman caught a glimpse of wide, terrified eyes as he sprang from his crouch and lashed out with his heavy club. The length of hardened oak smashed into the doe's side, splintering ribs and snapping the animal's spine with a brittle *crack*. The deer squealed in agony and plunged headfirst onto the ground.

Howls and hungry roars shook the air as Aghar and Shuk joined in the bloodletting, slashing at the plunging, leaping bodies with dagger and claw. Urghal smelled bitter blood in the air and bellowed cruel laughter as a huge stag burst from the foliage to the beastman's right. The stag saw the beastman at the very same moment; consumed with terror the deer tossed its antlered head and tried to spring away, but Urghal swept his blood-stained cudgel in a whistling arc, shattering the stag's gleaming antlers and smashing its skull. The deer hit the snowy earth with a heavy thud, its legs thrashing in the throes of death, and Urghal dropped his club and fell upon it, tearing at its warm throat with his teeth. The beastman ate greedily of its flesh as it trembled and died, tearing away ragged bites and choking them down whole in an effort to sate his frenzied hunger.

It was several long moments before Urghal realised how quiet the forest still was, and as the all-consuming hunger began to ebb he wondered what could have panicked the woods-wise deer in the first place.

The beastman raised his gore-smeared snout, licking his nostrils clean and tasting the frigid air once more. The wind rose and fell; over the rich scent of blood and spilt entrails he caught the faint whiff of something strange and bitter that sent a thrill down his knobby spine. His companions ate on, oblivious to everything except the steaming feast laid before them.

A premonition of fear tightened Urghal's throat. Baring his blood-slicked teeth, the beastman looked about frantically for his club and saw it lying on the bloody snow a dozen paces away. He lunged for the weapon, barking out a warning to his herd-mates just as the air shook with a thunderous roar and a huge shape leapt from the shadows beneath the trees.

The beast was massive, shaking the earth as it landed on two taloned feet among the surprised beastmen. Nearly thirty feet long from snout to tail, it filled the small clearing where the hunters had ambushed their prey. Its hide was dark green and scaled like a dragon's, and its muscular haunches were covered in scars from hundreds of deadly battles. Long, skinny forelimbs were tucked in tight against the beast's narrow chest; the creature's muscular, cable-like tail balanced its lunging motion as it snapped up a pair of deer carcasses in its huge, lizard-like jaws and swallowed them in a few crunching bites. Rivulets of blood mingled with tendrils of ropy spittle that drooled from between the creature's dagger-like teeth. Eyes the colour of spilled blood rolled wildly within deep, bony oculars as the beast searched about for more prey. Quick as a snake it lunged again, tossing the body of a deer into the air and eating it in a single gulp.

Shouts and bellows of fright echoed across the clearing as the hunters reeled from the beast's sudden assault. Urghal snatched up his club, snarling in rage. Hunger warred with fear as he watched the monster feed upon their kills. As the creature lunged for another deer, Urghal realised that it was oblivious to the three beastmen surrounding it. Its long, powerful tail now drooped, partly dragging the ground, and the flesh covering its bony head was shrunken, stretched across the skull like thick parchment. As it ate, Urghal saw its ribs standing out sharply from its flanks. It was starving, the beastman saw. He understood that madness all too well.

The beastman noticed the empty, weathered saddle strapped around the monster's back, just behind the sloping shoulders. Ragged saddlebags were strapped down behind it, their sides tattered and frayed by hard use and indifferent care. Silver rings glinted in the beast's leathery cheeks where reins had once been fitted. Then he saw the long, black-hilted sword buckled to the side of the saddle and knew that its rider had to be long dead.

Urghal bared his blackened teeth and barked commands to his fellow hunters. The creature was weak and stupid with hunger, he said. They could leap upon its back and kill it while it fed and feast off its acrid flesh for many days. Aghar and Shuk listened, and their shrunken bellies lent them courage they might not otherwise have possessed. Gripping their weapons tightly, the beastmen circled around the creature's flanks. Aghar sidled up along the creature's right side, raising his dagger for a deep thrust into the monster's neck. Shuk crept near the base of the creature's tail, ready to throw his massive bulk onto the appendage and weight it down, hampering its movement. Urghal crept up along the left side, drawing closer to the saddle. He would leap up and draw the black blade, then plunge it into the back of the monster's neck. The beast would be dead before it realised it was in danger.

Grinning viciously, Urghal turned to Shuk – and, too late, saw a dark shape leap from the depths of the forest and land upon the beastman's back with a terrifying shriek. Urghal heard the clatter of metal as the attacker pounced upon Shuk's bare torso, then saw pallid hands reach around the beastman's broad chest and plunge claw-like fingers through scarred hide and slab-like muscle. Shuk bellowed in terror and pain, throwing back his horned head and reaching over his shoulder to try and pry free his assailant, but the pale-skinned attacker clung to his victim like a cave spider, pressing close to the beastman's back.

Urghal caught a glimpse of a pale, angular face framed by loose, matted black hair as the armoured attacker lunged for Shuk's throat. Eyes as dark as the Abyss burned into Urghal's own. Bluish lips skinned back over perfect white teeth, and the figure tore open the beastman's muscular throat.

Blood burst from Shuk's lips as he tried to staunch the fountain of crimson jetting from the ragged wound in his neck. Urghal watched the black-eyed monster bury its face into the gaping wound, tearing away mouthfuls of flesh like a frenzied rat.

The dying beastman fell to his knees, choking on his own blood. Urghal gripped his cudgel and bellowed a challenge – just as the scaled beast beside him turned and lunged for Aghar. The creature's whip-like tail slashed in the opposite direction, crashing into Urghal's chest. Ribs snapped like twigs beneath the powerful blow; Urghal was flung backwards across the clearing and dashed against the bole of a towering oak tree. Stunned by the double impact the beastman toppled onto his side, feeling broken bones grate together in his chest.

As his breath rattled wetly in his throat, Urghal saw Aghar charge at the black-armoured attacker. The hunter bellowed in berserk fury, and the lithe figure responded with a bestial growl of his own. Bloody mouth agape, the armoured warrior leapt to his feet with disquieting speed and met the beastman's rush head-on.

Aghar was head and shoulders taller than his foe and half again as wide. Urghal expected the armoured attacker to be smashed to the ground by the hunter's furious charge, but instead the two crashed together in a clatter of flesh and steel. A pale hand reached up and took hold of the beastman's throat, and the pair grappled for the space of several heartbeats. Savage snarls and guttural growls rose from the desperate struggle; Urghal could not say for sure from which throat the terrible sounds came. Then, with a sudden, convulsive wrench Aghar pulled his dagger-arm free and stabbed at the armoured figure again and again, the blows ringing against the smaller assailant's steel breastplate and pauldrons.

There was a muffled heavy thud and a crunch of broken bones. Aghar shuddered at the blow, his cloven feet lifting off the ground from the impact. The beastman doubled over, choking in agony from a shattered breastbone, and the black-eyed attacker grabbed Aghar's ridged horns and wrenched them around in a neck-snapping twist.

Urghal felt the cold gaze of the killer settle on him. Growling in pain, the beastman struggled to rise onto his knees. Without warning an armoured boot crashed into his shoulder, flipping him back onto the ground. The pale-skinned warrior had crossed the dozen yards between them in the blink of an eye. The beastman growled defiantly, hefting his club one-handed – but as he met the warrior's face the weapon tumbled from his stunned grasp.

Depthless black eyes, without iris or pupil, regarded Urghal with the soulless hunger of the Abyss. The warrior's mouth and pointed chin dripped with clotted gore, spattering the ornate gilt-work of his plate armour. Trickles of red flowed into the crevices and corners of three golden skulls affixed to the foe's breastplate, and a thick torc of red-gold enclosed his wiry neck.

Just above the burnished gold curve of the torc jutted the rusty hilt of Aghar's dagger. The long blade had been driven clean through the warrior's throat, its broad point emerging at an angle just below the warrior's right ear.

As Urghal watched, the warrior reached up with a red-stained hand and slowly pulled the dagger free. A trickle of thick, black ichor leaked from the gruesome wound. Ropy black veins pulsed and writhed like worms beneath the skin of the warrior's throat and along the back of his hands.

The warrior let the dagger tumble slowly from his dripping fingers. It landed right beside Urghal's head, but the beastman made no move to pick it up. With a ghastly red grin, the black-eyed warrior opened his mouth and uttered a sound no living throat could possibly make, and the beastman's fevered mind shattered at the sound of it.

Urghal's cry of terror shook the black-limbed trees as the killer reached for him with claw-like hands.

Little by little, as the beastman's raw flesh filled his wasted belly, a measure of sanity returned to Malus Darkblade. His body, withered like a shrunken root by the nightmarish ordeals of his journey, began to shudder and ache as the daemon relaxed its remorseless grip. The shock of consciousness was so intense that for an agonising moment the highborn was certain that he was going to die. He fell onto his back, still clutching tattered scraps of flesh in his hands, and howled his wretched hate to the roiling northern sky.

Part of him was certain he was already dead. His mind recoiled from the few memories he had of the past few weeks, driven ever northwards by the daemon's merciless will. No sleep, no food, no rest for weeks on end, driven to lengths no living body ought to endure. Even Spite's near limitless stamina had been driven to the breaking point and beyond.

But they had reached the broken mountain. Nearby lay the pale road and the dreadful temple. Many times in the last few weeks he hadn't thought such a thing possible, but now, so close to his goal he wanted nothing more than to die. He wept bitterly at the thought, feeling icy tears course down his hollow cheeks.

'Rise, Darkblade,' the daemon said, and his body responded to the implacable command. Ravaged muscles tautened painfully, propelling Malus upright with a groan of helpless rage. 'Your final hour approaches.'

Malus's body lurched across the clearing towards Spite. His mouth worked silently, trying to utter dark curses from his ruined throat. From somewhere farther up the wooded slope came a chorus of howls and the rolling, mournful notes of horns. The clamour of the battle had reached as far as the beastman camp, and now the herd was on the move.

As he approached the saddle the cold one groaned and cowered, snapping at him fearfully. The daemon lashed the nauglir with its black will, and the cold one whined in submission, allowing the highborn to clamber jerkily onto its back. Still groaning, the nauglir rose wearily onto its feet and was mentally lashed into motion, beginning the last leg of its long, hellish odyssey.

The horn calls faded but the howls of the beastmen drew nearer as the daemon led Spite around the flank of the mountainside. Darkness fell as they rode. Malus swayed in the saddle, his gaze drifting to the black-hilted sword resting by his left knee. With all his might he tried to force his hand to reach for the sorcerous blade, but Tz'arkan's will held him fast.

All for nothing, he thought, as the daemon drove him onward to the temple like a sacrificial lamb. He thought of Hauclir, and the fields of the dead. He thought of the daemon-haunted shade and the soul-shattering screams of his sister. All for nothing.

Hatred and loathing burned like a seething coal in his ravaged chest – and the little finger on his left hand twitched.

Malus scarcely dared to breathe. He couldn't bring himself to hope, but even in the depths of privation and despair there was always room enough for hate. With hate all things are possible, he thought. His bloodied lips trembled in a palsied smile.

Half-formed memories dogged in the highborn's wake as they plunged on through thicket and fern. The echoes of the hunting beastmen called to mind a desperate flight through these same woods exactly one year before. Every now and then they passed a stand of trees or a wooded hollow that seemed familiar to him, though part of him knew that it was only a trick of the mind.

The shouts of the beastman herd were close now – perhaps a half-mile further upslope, hidden by the depths of the forest. Without warning the ground suddenly levelled out, and Malus found himself on a road of pale, snow-covered stones untouched by the passage of millennia. It was a road built for the tread of conquerors, with each stone carved in the shape of a skull and standing stones set at intervals along its length, praising the Ruinous Powers and exalting the deeds of the Chaos champions who ruled there. A year before, the blasphemous runes of the standing stones held no meaning for Malus; now he looked at them through daemon-tainted eyes, and the names carved on the menhirs burned themselves into his brain. Malus could feel his sanity crumbling with each passing moment as they drew nearer to the temple; desperately he turned to his hate, stoking it with all the bitterness and rage his year of servitude had wrought in him. The highborn focused on the hilt of the sword and prayed to every cursed god he could name for the strength to tear the unholy blade from its scabbard.

The air hummed and crackled with unseen energies as the daemon within Malus drew closer to the temple. Unearthly power crackled over his tortured skin, and the black-limbed trees lining the road rattled and shook in an invisible wind. Spite's pace quickened steadily, as though the nauglir was being drawn forward like iron to a lodestone. A strange, buzzing hum began to build in the back of Malus's skull.

By the time they swept around the final bend of the winding road Spite was nearly at a gallop. His drumming feet echoed off the close-set trees, and for a dizzying moment Malus felt as though he'd been cast back in time, riding with a troop of armoured retainers at his back. He thought of Dalvar, the dagger-wielding rogue, and Vanhir, the haughty, hateful knight.

He thought of Lhunara, riding quietly at his side, her fierce smile gleaming in the darkness. Choking back bitter bile, the highborn pushed the memory away.

And then the air trembled with the shout of a hundred furious voices as the beastmen raised their weapons and challenged the lone rider bearing down the road towards them. The herd had guessed where he was headed and had cut him off just short of his goal, exactly as they'd done just twelve months past.

But there were no armoured retainers to open the way for him this time. The beastmen stood in a roaring, bellowing mob that filled the tree-lined avenue before him. Axes, cudgels and rusty two-handed swords were brandished by the light of guttering torches. Spite stumbled to a halt, hissing and screeching in agitation as the mob surged forward.

Malus sensed his chance. The daemon would have to let him draw the warpsword before they were overwhelmed. With all his hate-fuelled will he tried to force his hand to reach for the blade.

But just a few yards short of the cold one the howling mob fell to their knees and pressed their horned heads to the skull-faced stones. In the midst of the mob a shaman with a single red eye gleaming from the middle of his narrow skull bleated: 'The prophecy is fulfilled! The Drinker of Worlds is come! Bow before the blessed Prince of Slaanesh, and let the dirge of Eternal Night be sung!'

Once again the daemon lashed at the nauglir's beleaguered mind, and the warbeast lurched forward, trotting down a path that opened through the centre of the prostrate mob. Malus trembled with impotent rage as they passed unchallenged through the herd and rode on a short way until the trees parted before them. Beyond rose a square, tiered structure of sheer, black stone, windowless and devoid of ornamentation, as cold and soulless as the Abyss itself. Surrounding the temple was a wall formed of similar stone, and a square-arched gateway. A desperate battle had been fought there a year before; skeletons of beastmen and misshapen Chaos beasts still littered the ground where they had fallen to druchii crossbows and swords. They crunched beneath Spite's heavy tread as the cold one walked beneath the gateway and came to a halt within the courtyard beyond.

There were more bones here, speaking of another scene of slaughter. Huge skulls and piles of dark bones that once had been nauglir, and druchii skeletons in rusting armour. They lay in the white snow where he'd slain them almost twelve months before.

He'd killed his own retainers out of shame, unable to bear having them see how the daemon had enslaved him. Now he met their black, empty stares and wished he could grind their grey bones into dust.

Malus's body lurched into motion, sliding awkwardly from the saddle. His face contorted into a rictus of thwarted rage, the highborn could only watch helplessly as his hands unbuckled the warpsword from the saddle and then collected the frayed bag containing the rest of the daemon's relics. As he pulled the sack free, Spite collapsed onto its side, as though unburdened at last of a terrible weight. Its flanks shuddered and heaved, and its breath came in ragged gasps.

'It is time,' the daemon said, its cruel voice reverberating in Malus's skull. 'Quickly now! Carry the relics to the crystal chamber, and soon your curse will be at an end.'

Filled with dread, Malus turned his back on the dying nauglir and marched like a condemned man into the shadow of the daemon's temple.

CHAPTER TWO

THE DOUBLE-EDGED SWORD

The city of Har Ganeth, eight weeks before

Smoke hung like a pall over the City of Executioners, wreathing the broad hill in streamers of grey that tasted of cinders and the grease of cooked flesh. High in the blade-like towers of the temple fortress the sacrificial bells were ringing, calling to the faithful to bare their blades and give thanks for Har Ganeth's deliverance. Tortured screams and the howl of hungry mobs rose like a paean into the cloudy summer sky.

The fighting had raged for more than a week, and the lower quarters of Har Ganeth had suffered the worst. Two days after the riots had ended the narrow, maze-like streets were still choked with corpses and the charred remains of burnt-out buildings. Fresh splashes of vivid red painted the rust-coloured walls of the White City, and the shadowy avenues reeked of the charnel stench of the battlefield. Shopkeepers and tradesmen picked their way carefully amongst the piled debris, looking for useful bits of salvage. Groups of young children ran along the cobblestone streets, brandishing tiny, stained knives and rawhide cords strung with severed fingers decorated with rings of silver and gold. Axes and meat cleavers flashed and *thunked* into dead flesh, separating vertebrae with a wet crackle as the druchii collected severed heads to stack outside their bloodstained doors. Only a few days before, many of those same folk had taken up torch and blade and risen against the priests of Khaine's temple, believing that the apocalypse was at hand. But the would-be Swordbearer of Khaine was revealed to be an impostor, and the leaders of the uprising either driven off or slain, so the people of the city bent their heads and piled skulls outside their shops and homes, praying that the vengeful shadow of the temple executioners would pass them by. At the sound of tramping feet they hunched their shoulders and lowered their gaze to the bloody stones, fearful of attracting the attention of the temple executioners, or worse, the hungry gaze of Khaine's bloodthirsty brides.

Thus, when the heavy tread of a nauglir and the dull clatter of armour echoed down the narrow streets the people of Har Ganeth hid their eyes and paid no heed to the highborn rider – or the black-hilted blade buckled at his side. Only the city's ravens took notice of his passage, raising gore-stained beaks from their bloated meals and flapping great, glossy wings. 'Blood and souls!' they croaked exultantly, regarding Malus Darkblade with lantern-yellow eyes. 'Scourge! Scourge!'

Damned nuisances, Malus thought, his scowl deepening the hollows of his sunken cheeks and drawing dark lines around his thin lips. Spite, sensing its master's irritation, tossed its blocky head and snapped at the capering ravens, scattering venomous drool from its toothy maw. The highborn settled the cold one with an expert tug on the reins and guided the warbeast around the burnt wreckage of an overturned wagon. More black shapes circled overhead, floating like shadows in his wake. The ravens were sacred to Khaine, he'd learned. Is it the sword that stirs them so, he thought, or is it me?

Something cold and hard slithered serpentine around Malus's heart. A voice hissed like molten lead along his bones, setting his teeth on edge. 'A meaningless distinction,' Tz'arkan sneered. 'You and the burning blade are now one and the same.'

The highborn jerked upright in his saddle, armoured fists clenching the thick reins hard enough to make the leather creak as a wave of freezing pressure swelled behind his eyes. He bit back a savage curse, blinking at the black spots that drifted like ashes across his vision. His pulse throbbed turgidly in his temples, veins thick with oily, black ice.

Tz'arkan's hold over him was nearly complete.

It was the daemon's damnable curse that had brought him to Har Ganeth in the first place, seeking one of the five arcane relics that would free Tz'arkan from his crystal prison in the Chaos Wastes – and allow Malus to reclaim his stolen soul. The Warpsword of Khaine was one such relic, but in the millennia since the daemon's imprisonment the weapon had found its way into the possession of the Temple of Khaine, where it was kept in anticipation of the day when the Lord of Murder's chosen one would claim it and usher in the cataclysmic Time of Blood. According to the elders of the temple, that chosen one was none other than Malekith himself, the merciless Witch King of Naggaroth, but Malus knew that to be a convenient fiction, a lie told in the pursuit of temporal wealth and power.

The truth, as it often happened in the Land of Chill, was rather murkier than that.

Malus managed a bitter chuckle. 'Could it be that the great daemon has wound himself up in his own webs of deceit?' he growled. 'Are you sorry now for making me your catspaw? It was your own machinations that put the blade into my hands, after all. My *fate*, as you so gleefully put it.'

He'd learned a lot about fate in the ten months since he'd entered Tz'arkan's chamber in the far north. Fate was the word that puppets used to describe the tugging of invisible strings. It hadn't been fate that had drawn Malus to the north in search of power and wealth; he had been pointed at Tz'arkan's temple and loosed like an arrow, manipulated into undertaking the expedition by his half-sister Nagaira. Yet she herself was being manipulated in turn by Malus's own mother, the sorceress Eldire. Eldire had known of the daemon and its ages-old schemes somehow. She had learned of the prophecy and the Time of Blood, and had spent untold years shaping people and events to bring about their fruition. Not to serve Tz'arkan, but to usurp the daemon's machinations for her own secret purposes. It was an act of towering ambition and ruthlessness that culminated in the birth of her son, Malus. She had shaped him to be the lever that would set the daemon's inscrutable designs into motion.

But prophecies, by their very nature, were slippery, treacherous things. Others had tried to bend him to their will, or claim the mantle of prophecy for their own. Nagaira had tried to bend him through deception and sorcery, seeking to turn the daemon to her own purposes. Worse still, his twisted half-brother Urial, poisoned in the womb by Eldire herself and given to the temple as a sacrifice, had survived the Cauldron of Blood and been initiated into the mysteries of Khaine's cult. Dissident members of the cult who refused to accept Malekith as Khaine's Swordbearer believed that Urial was the chosen one, and the circumstances of the prophecy fit well enough. He was secretly groomed to claim the sword when the time was right, and after his beloved half-sister Yasmir was revealed as a living saint of the Bloody-Handed God he betrayed Malus and fled to Har Ganeth, where he summoned the temple zealots to cast down the heretical elders of the cult.

For a week the City of Executioners tore itself apart as the zealots led its citizens in a bloody uprising. Urial had come very close indeed to achieving his aims. Too close for comfort, Malus admitted to himself, absently raising a hand to his breastplate where Urial's sword had slipped between his ribs. But for the daemon's power, he would have died.

Tz'arkan had sunk its talons deep into his body, spreading its corruption a little more each time Malus had drawn upon its infernal strength. Even now, his skin felt like ice, his muscles shrivelled and weak, aching for another taste of daemonic power. He had only a few months left to claim the last of the daemon's five artefacts and return them to the temple in the north or his soul would be forever lost, but Malus couldn't help but wonder if he wasn't already too late. Had he fought for the last ten months to reclaim his soul only to become a daemonhost once Tz'arkan was free?

Malus had good reason to believe that had been the daemon's plan all along.

'Foolish druchii,' the daemon spat, 'The warpsword was not meant to be wielded by the likes of you. You see it as nothing more than a sharp blade, but it is a talisman of supernal power. As ever, you trifle with forces beyond your ability to contemplate.'

The highborn caught Spite sniffing at the bloated corpse of a dead horse, still trapped in the overturned wagon's traces. Malus put his spurs to the warbeast's flanks and startled the nauglir back into a heavy-footed trot. 'Oh, but you are mistaken,' he replied. 'I see it as a fine weapon *and* a talisman of great power – one I have every intention of using as I see fit. What do you care, so long as I am doing your damned bidding?'

In truth, Malus suspected he knew the source of the daemon's concern. The warpsword radiated power like a burning brand – even now he could feel its heat, seeping from its scabbard and sinking into his bones. Power enough to supplant the daemon's icy gifts and resist Tz'arkan's will, or so he hoped.

'You imagine that you carry a mere blade on your hip? No. That is Khaine's own hunger given form,' the daemon hissed.

'Then I will see that it is kept well-fed,' Malus replied.

'Of course you will,' Tz'arkan said mockingly. 'You have no choice. The sword has claimed you, and like all those who wielded it before you it will one day turn in your hand when you fail to give its due.'

Something in the daemon's voice gave Malus pause. He glanced down at the warpsword's black hilt and felt a sudden chill.

It's just another lie, he told himself. Malus laid a hand on the sword's black pommel and savoured its warmth. It's the only chance you have against Tz'arkan, and the daemon knows it. 'Best for you then if we part ways before the blade gets the better of me,' the highborn said.

The daemon's laughter etched itself like acid into Malus's bones. 'No, best for *you*, Darkblade. Bad enough that your allotted time is running out – now you trifle with an eldritch artefact that hungers for your life's blood. Don't you understand? Your doom is sealed! The best you can hope for now is to find the Amulet of Vaurog and return to my temple in the north before you are undone. Otherwise your soul will belong to me until the end of time.'

With the daemon's mirth echoing jaggedly in his head Malus kicked Spite into a canter, no longer caring what the cold one caught between its snapping jaws or crushed to paste underfoot. His thoughts roiled like the murderous brew in Khaine's own cauldron as he contemplated his next move.

The farther down the wide hill Malus went the worse the devastation became. The highborn districts around the temple fortress near the summit had been largely untouched; each home was like a small citadel unto itself, ideally designed to fend off all but the most determined assaults. The lowborn districts further down the slope had suffered far more, first at the hands of the temple warriors and then the successive riots that had raged across Har Ganeth for days on end. Many of the stone structures had been blackened by fire and several had collapsed completely, spilling their charred contents onto the streets.

But it was the merchants' quarter and the warehouse districts at the base of the hill that had suffered worst of all. Many shopkeepers had shut their doors and hoped to weather the storm, but as the riots gave way to open warfare between the zealots and the temple loyalists the quarter became a no-man's-land caught between the warring factions. Shops were pillaged or burned in the riots, then had their bones picked clean by scavengers as the fighting wore on.

Beyond the merchants' quarter the slave market and the warehouse district were in ruins. It was here that the fighting raged hottest, once Urial and his zealots seized the temple and trapped the loyalists out on the streets. Large warbands of blood-witches and executioners had been isolated by mobs of frenzied citizens and forced to take refuge in slavekeepers' stables or shipping houses. Fires touched off by the vicious street fighting had raged unchecked for days, and the air around the wreckage was thick with tendrils of turgid, stinking smoke. When the wind shifted Malus could catch glimpses of the city walls, rising untouched above the devastation. If anything the walls had only served to hem in the carnage, turning Har Ganeth's rage back upon itself as the city tore itself apart.

He was still within the warehouse district, less than half a mile from the city gate when he heard the first stirrings of the mob. Their bloodthirsty roar shook him from his bitter reverie, their cries of 'Blood for the Blood God!' echoing weirdly along the ruined streets. The sounds seemed to be coming from just up ahead, though he couldn't be certain of anything in the shifting smoke. For a fleeting moment he contemplated altering his course, but with a flash of irritation he pushed the thought aside. He could guess what the mob was after, and it didn't include the likes of him. The highborn spurred his mount on through the smoke, the nauglir's broad feet crunching cinders and scorched bones with every step.

The sounds of the mob ebbed and flowed, muffled by the wreckage and the shifting wind as he continued down the rubble-strewn avenue, until Malus began to believe that the druchii were heading away from him, moving off to the west. The cries tapered off, and after he'd ridden on in relative silence for a few minutes he finally allowed himself to relax. Just at that moment, as though stirred by the laugh of a capricious god, a gust of wind banished the concealing smoke that surrounded the highborn and the mob erupted in a bloodthirsty cheer less than a dozen yards to Malus's left.

There were thirty or forty of them, filling a broad side street next to the wreckage of a long, single-storey warehouse. Most of them were lowborn citizens in soot-stained robes, clutching swords or axes in their grimy hands, but the ringleaders of the band were a pair of young blood-witches and a handful of temple executioners. The servants of the temple were standing on a broad pile of fallen stones to give the crowd a better view of their efforts. The white stones beneath them were stained in patterns of red: striations of vivid crimson bled into a dull brick red, then to a dark reddish-brown where the congealing gore had settled into crevices and cracks among the stones. Headless bodies sprawled down the rockslides, spilling their contents onto the gritty cobblestones.

Several druchii squirmed and hissed in the grip of the mob, awaiting their turn before the drachms of the executioners. They had made the mistake of siding with the zealots during the revolt and had lacked the wit to switch sides again once the uprising had failed. Or perhaps they had simply been caught in the wrong place at the wrong time; one of them, Malus noted, looked more like a trader from Karond Kar, with his indigo-hued kheitan and a set of slaver's chains hanging from his hip.

For the moment, the hapless prisoners had been granted a short reprieve. The servants of the temple had far sweeter offerings to occupy their attentions.

Two druchii swayed atop the stone pile, held upright in the iron grips of the executioners. They had been stripped to the waist, but Malus noted the filthy white robes and torn sleeves that were bunched around their hips. Their muscular chests and arms were severely bruised and blackened; looking at them the highborn could well believe they'd been hauled from the rubble of one of the buildings nearby. Tellingly, neither man bore the mark of sword nor axe on their bodies, despite the days of hard fighting that had raged across the city.

They were zealots, members of the renegade splinter cult that worshipped Khaine's true faith. Killers without peer, they wore no armour in battle and clothed themselves in white to better show the red favours of their god. Hundreds of them had flocked to Har Ganeth at Urial's call and had taken a fearful toll of the temple warriors during the uprising. Once it had become clear that the uprising had failed, most of the survivors had scattered back into the countryside – which made zealot prisoners all the more enticing to the vengeful blood-witches. These two would suffer for weeks under the witches' expert hands before their remains were given to the Cauldron of Blood. It was the worst fate possible for the true believers, who prayed to Khaine daily for a glorious death in battle.

Malus eyed the doomed men coldly and thanked the Dark Mother for the distraction. Better you than me, he thought, then frowned irritably as Spite slowed to a near stop as it caught the scent of fresh blood. The highborn glared at his scaly mount and made to spur the beast back into a canter when suddenly an anguished cry rang out from the rock pile.

'Deliver us, holy one!' the zealot cried to Malus. 'Draw your sword and slay us, in the Blessed Murderer's name!'

Heads turned. Malus felt the predatory stares of the blood-witches against his skin and felt his hair stand on end. All at once the air seemed charged with pent-up tension, crackling with furious energies like the moments before a summer storm. Spite sensed the change, too, and rumbled threateningly at the crowd.

Of all the damnable luck, the highborn cursed. He didn't recognise either of the zealots' pleading faces. Malus had fallen in with the true believers by accident when he'd first made his way into the city, looking for his own secret path into the temple fortress. He had even taken a hand in stirring up the early riots, hoping to distract the temple elders further, and had wound up with far more trouble than he'd bargained for.

The mob eyed Malus like a pack of feral dogs. In his worn robes and scarred plate armour, he had the look of a landless knight or an exiled noble rather than a wild-eyed heretic. The highborn's face was gaunt, emphasising his sharp cheekbones and pointed chin. Eyes the colour of brass shone from sunken eye sockets, marking him as one of Khaine's chosen. More forbidding still was the grey pallor of his face, like a druchii in the grip of a terrible sickness.

'No one is going to save you from your sins, heretic,' Malus spat, wrenching at Spite's reins. 'Khaine has no cold mercies for the likes of you.'

The nauglir shook its massive head and sidestepped, unwilling to turn away from the mob. It clashed its massive jaws and growled menacingly, and the mob hissed in reply.

One of the temple witches levelled her sword at Malus. Lines and loops of fresh blood glistened on her muscular arms and her long, bare legs. 'You are not a temple priest,' she said in a throaty voice, like cold air rising up from a tomb.

'I have never claimed to be,' Malus said tightly, trying to get the cold one under control. Spite circled and stamped, pacing away and then angling back towards the crowd like iron drawn to a lodestone. The tension in the air continued to build, setting the highborn's teeth on edge. What in the name of the Dark Mother was going on?

'Coward! Apostate!' the zealot screamed, surging against the grip of the executioners.

'Seize him,' the witch said coldly.

The mob erupted into lusty shouts, brandishing their weapons as they rushed at the highborn, and Spite lunged at them with an answering roar, nearly jerking Malus out of the saddle.

He could feel the pent-up tension burst in a rush that crackled through the air and sizzled across his bare skin. It was like the seething flare of an open flame or a lash of summer lightning. Malus cried out in bewilderment and anger, struggling to stay upright as Spite tore into the mob. Bones crunched and blood sprayed in the air as the cold one caught a man by the shoulder and bit off his right arm. The druchii's anguished scream set Malus's nerves on fire.

Spite roared and lunged at another man running past the cold one's flank, catching the druchii by the hip and flinging him into the air. Malus cursed and pounded the beast's flanks with his spurs, but the nauglir had gone berserk, tearing at its foes with reckless abandon.

The mob surged hungrily around the snapping beast. A sword blade rang off Malus's breastplate. Pale, blood-streaked faces glared up at him, their dark eyes burning with battle-lust. Bare hands seized his mail fauld and his right leg, trying to pull him out of the saddle. Snarling like a wolf, Malus pulled his leg free and planted his heel in a man's upturned face, but more hands closed about his ankle and dragged him downwards.

He felt himself sliding inexorably from his seat. Rage and desperation seethed through his veins. Without thinking, Malus reached for the warpsword. Its hilt was hot to the touch, and the long, eldritch blade seemed to leap from its scabbard with an ominous hiss.

Roaring blasphemies, Malus raised the ebon blade to the stormy sky. Above the cacophonous shouts of the mob, the highborn heard a horrified shriek from one of the temple witches, then he swept the sword in a vicious arc through the arms and heads of the grasping crowd. Flesh blackened and withered as the sword drank deep of hot blood and mortal pain.

Roars of bloodlust turned to screams of terror and despair. The mob reeled back from the smoking corpses of their brethren, crying out Khaine's name. Malus leapt after them, his face set in a mask of berserk rage.

Overhead, the croaking laughter of ravens echoed across the stormy sky.

The blood-witch's face was oddly serene. Malus admired the alabaster perfection of her high cheekbones and the subtle curve of her elegant jaw. Her brass-coloured eyes were calm, her round lips slightly parted and vivid with the blush of youth. In another time she could have been a violet-eyed princess of lost Nagarythe, about to whisper her secrets into the ear of a lover.

Close enough to kiss those perfect lips, Malus drew a shuddering breath and pulled the warpsword free. The ancient blade scraped against stone as it slid from the pile of rubble at the witch's back, leaving her body to slip from the long blade and slump lifelessly to the ground.

For a moment the highborn blinked drunkenly at the witch's body, as though seeing it for the first time. His skin was hot, as though flushed with fever, and his nerves still sang with fading notes of bloodlust. His gaze drifted to the drooping tip of the warpsword. A faint curl of crimson vapour rose from its razor edge.

With an effort of will Malus raised his head and beheld the trail of slaughter that stretched the length of the long, broad street.

Ruptured bodies and severed limbs lay in a tangled carpet across the cobblestones. Many bore their wounds upon their back, cut down as they tried to escape. Broken weapons glinted in the weak sunlight, showing where others had tried to fight the hunger of a god. Every face Malus could see was twisted in a rictus of terror and pain – all but the two zealot prisoners. Their headless bodies still knelt upright on the cobblestones, their arms outstretched in a gesture of religious ecstasy.

'Blessed Mother of Night,' Malus whispered in horrified awe. 'What have I done?'

'You have slaked the thirst of the burning blade,' Tz'arkan hissed. 'For now.'

Dozens of people, the highborn thought, unable to tear his eyes away from the carnage. *Dozens* of damned people. The last thing he remembered clearly was drawing the sword. After that... only laughter and terrible screams. The thought of such a loss of control terrified him.

Shouts echoed in the distance, back in the direction of the merchant's quarter. The highborn looked for the temple executioners and found their bodies at the base of the rock pile just a few yards away, surrounding the corpse of the second blood-witch. He tried to count the bodies of the lowborn, but gave up in disgust. There was no telling how many there were for certain, or if any might have escaped the slaughter and run for help.

Malus forced his body to work, weaving his way quickly among the fallen bodies. He noted absently how little blood there was – just blackened flesh and shrivelled organs.

Spite was not far from where Malus had dismounted, feeding warily on one of the dead men. The nauglir shied away at the highborn's approach. Malus snarled irritably at the warbeast. '*Stand*, damn you!' he shouted – and caught his hand tightening slowly around the hilt of the warpsword.

Malus froze. Eyeing the black blade warily, he slowly and deliberately slipped the sword back into its scabbard. Twice it seemed to get caught in the scabbard's mouth, forcing him to draw it out slightly and try to sheathe it again. When the weapon finally slid home the highborn breathed a sigh of relief.

Within moments the heat suffusing his muscles began to fade, like an iron plucked from the fire, leaving him feeling wretched and cold once more.

Caught between the dragon and the deep sea, Malus thought, fighting a wave of black despair. Which was the worse fate?

⊰ CHAPTER THREE ⊱

PORTENTS OF DARKNESS

Moonlight gleamed along the gold fittings of the warpsword's scabbard and kindled a dusky fire in the depths of the oblong ruby set at the juncture of hilt and blade. Malus admired the relic fearfully for a moment, holding the sheathed weapon carefully in both hands. He fancied he could feel its heat, pulsing softly like a sleeping heart. He licked his cold lips nervously, then with a deep breath he laid the weapon on the fabric spread across his knees and wrapped it tightly from end-to-end in layers of frayed and dirty sailcloth. With each turn of the cloth he felt a bit colder, a bit smaller and more withered than before. When he was done, Malus tied off the bundle with loops of rough twine and then carried the wrapped weapon over to Spite. The cold one was crouched beneath the trees on the opposite side of the small forest clearing, watching its master warily with its red-ember eyes.

His face set in a mask of grim determination, Malus stowed the warpsword with his saddlebags, securing it tightly to his saddle beside the bag where the rest of the daemon's relics were kept. Reluctantly, he took his hands from the blade and patted the nauglir's flanks. 'No hunting tonight,' he said quietly, eyeing the dark depths of the surrounding wood. 'There's no telling what you might run into.'

It was only a few hours past sundown, and they were almost ten miles from Har Ganeth, deep in the wooded hills north and west of the city. The clearing was one he'd used often in the two months he'd prowled the Slaver's Road outside the City of Executioners. There was even a small lean-to built from pine boughs to provide some shelter from the elements and a store of firewood laid by. Lighting a fire was out of the question, however. The last thing he wanted to do was to advertise his presence, and he doubted the flame would warm his cursed bones anyway.

He'd escaped the city without further incident, though by the time he'd reached the wide city gate he could hear the first cries of alarm from the scene of the massacre. Malus trusted that the citizens would blame the attack on a band of zealots but he had no intention of putting his theory to the test. The highborn had all but galloped through the open gateway, relieved to find the Slaver's Road nearly empty of traffic. For the next few hours he'd worked his way westward along the road, keeping a wary eye out for plumes of dust rising on the horizon.

Malus had a very good reason for wanting to get out of Har Ganeth as quickly as he could: there was every chance that Malekith was on the way to the city with an army at his back, alerted by news of the temple uprising. Though he'd personally ended Urial's coup, the highborn doubted that the Witch King would show him any gratitude. Malus had been a fugitive since early summer after murdering his father at Vaelgor Keep, scarcely twenty miles to the north-east. He'd done it to gain possession of the Dagger of Torxus, another of the daemon's damned relics, not that the motive made any difference according to the laws of the land. Malus's father had been the Vaulkhar of Hag Graef, one of the Witch King's lieutenants, and no one slew one of Malekith's vassals without his leave. He hoped that the Witch King thought him dead, slain along with thousands of druchii in a confused night battle outside Hag Graef several months before, though it wasn't something he was willing to bet his life on. His half-brother Isilvar, now Lurhan's only heir and Hag Graef's Vaulkhar, almost certainly knew the truth. The question was what would he do with the knowledge? Isilvar had very good reasons to want him dead, the least of which was a nasty scar across his throat that Malus had given him in a battle beneath their sister Nagaira's tower a few months ago.

Frowning in thought, Malus combed through his saddlebags and pulled out an oil-stained cloth bag and a small bottle of wine. Then he drew the heavy battle-axe from a loop on the nauglir's saddle and sank wearily to the ground beside the cold one's armoured flank. As he leaned back against the nauglir's side the great beast shifted, its blocky head swinging around to fix him with a beady glare. Malus gave the beast a haughty glare. 'Settle down,' he warned, and tried to get comfortable once more. Again, the nauglir recoiled from his touch, rising to its feet and giving its master a warning hiss.

'All right, all right!' Malus snapped, snatching up his axe and his store of food and stalking to the other side of the encampment. He sat down heavily with his back to a rotting log and fixed the warbeast with a murderous look. 'See if I let you eat the next dead horse we come to.'

After a few moments Spite lowered carefully back onto its haunches and rested its snout on the ground so that it could keep a wary eye on Malus. The nauglir had been acting very strangely ever since they'd returned from the City of the Ageless Kings, far north in the Chaos Wastes. He'd gone there in search of the real warpsword, only to fall into the clutches of the power-mad druchii zealots who'd stolen it. They had intended to kill him and feed upon his life essence, and so they'd crucified him in the broad plaza outside their temple.

He'd had no choice but to call upon Tz'arkan's power to escape. Events after that were somewhat hazy. The next thing he recalled clearly was standing on the bridge of stone outside the Sanctum of the Sword in the temple fortress in Har Ganeth and watching his half-sister Yasmir eating their brother Urial's still-beating heart.

The prophecy of the Scourge maintained that he was destined to marry Yasmir, now considered a living saint of the Bloody-Handed God. After witnessing what she'd done to Urial the very idea of wedding her made his blood run cold. *Perhaps if I'm lucky the warpsword will kill me before that becomes an issue,* Malus thought bleakly.

It was getting colder in the clearing as the moons climbed into the cloudy sky. Even in late summer the Land of Chill was true to its name. Malus unwrapped his meagre bundle of salted fish and yellow sauce and began to eat, chewing doggedly at the tough flesh and washing it down with swigs of vinegary wine. He took his time with the meal; as wretched as it tasted, it was still better than the hardtack that he would be eating come the morrow.

By the time he was done the moons were shining almost directly overhead and his breath made a faint mist in the cold air. Malus doggedly finished off the terrible wine and summoned up his nerve. The other reason he'd chosen such an isolated campsite was because he was in sore need of information, and some conversations were best kept private.

He also had a dreadful feeling that he wasn't going to like what he was about to learn.

Malus wiped his face and put away the cloth and empty flask, then sat cross-legged with his back to the fallen log and his stolen axe within easy reach. The highborn pulled off the armoured gauntlet covering his left hand. A plain silver ring glinted on his finger like a band of purest ice. He held it up to the moonlight, noting with a grimace that the veins on the back of his hand were black with the daemon's corruption.

The highborn made a fist, focusing his remorseless will on a single thought. *Eldire.*

A faint, familiar breeze ghosted across Malus's face – and the daemon inside him writhed in anger. His muscles seized and his guts curdled; Malus toppled onto his side with a groan, doubling over with the sudden wave of nausea and pain. Pressure built within his head, as though the daemon had his brain in a vice, causing sparks to dance before his eyes. Malus rolled onto his stomach and vomited his meal onto the cold, hard ground, his breath coming in shallow gasps timed to the pounding in his skull.

The highborn rolled back onto his side, fetching up against the side of the log. He caught the scent of ashes, and then suddenly the pain and sickness was receding like a black, oily tide. The pounding in his skull eased, and Malus thought that he heard the daemon's angry voice receding into an infinite distance. When it was gone he was left trembling with a leaden cold that seemed to radiate from his very bones.

'What have you done?' spoke a woman's voice, hard and cold as carved marble. The words had a peculiar echo to them, as though spoken from deep within a well. 'You fool! Malus, what have you done?'

The highborn's eyes flickered open. Above him loomed a glowing apparition wreathed in pale silver light. 'Hello, mother,' he said, managing a bitter laugh. 'How I've missed your loving voice.'

She was statuesque and regal, clothed in the heavy, dark robes of the witches' convent. Her pale hands were clasped before her and her braided white hair seemed wrought from moonlight, haloing the cruel angles of her face. Her form was insubstantial – the highborn could see through her as though she were made of fog, picking out Spite's sloping form and red-ember eyes on the other side of the clearing. For all that, Malus felt the weight of Eldire's stare like a dagger-point against his skin.

'Impertinent wretch!' Eldire snapped. 'Your body belongs wholly to the daemon now. Your veins pulse with foul energies. I can even see the daemon itself, sliding like a leviathan beneath your pallid skin!'

'Does it coil about my heart like a nest of serpents?' Malus sneered, wiping his mouth with the back of his hand. 'Does it clutch my shrivelled brain in its dripping jaws? Your gifts are wasted in this case, mother. I've known this every minute of every day for nearly a year.'

Eldire's ghostly face blazed with fury. 'This is far worse than mere possession, child! You have taken the final step. I warned you of this, back in the dwarf tombs!'

'Do you imagine I did this by choice?' the highborn shot back. Grimacing against the pain in his guts, he pushed himself wearily upright and rested the back of his head against the moss-covered log. 'The damned warpsword wasn't in the temple after all. I had to go into the Chaos Wastes to claim it.' His gaze fell upon the back of his black-veined hand and his anger faded in a wave of disgust. 'It was either this or death; there were no other choices open to me. For now, I live, and while I live, I can fight.' He met the seer's forbidding gaze. 'And now I have the sword.'

Eldire's dark eyes widened a fraction of an inch. The fury ebbed from her alabaster face. 'You drew the burning blade,' she said, her voice slightly more hollow than before.

'There were very compelling reasons at the time. I won't bore you with the details,' Malus said darkly. 'Tz'arkan was even less pleased than you. It makes me wonder if perhaps the warpsword's power is strong enough to counteract the daemon's influence.'

Eldire frowned at her son. 'Perhaps,' she allowed, with a sigh like a wind seeping from a tomb. 'Khaine's hunger cares little for the schemes of other beings, even daemons as potent as Tz'arkan. In fact,' she said, her expression turning angry again, 'the warpsword is likely the only reason you have any consciousness left. Looking at you, it's a wonder that the daemon isn't able to make you dance like a puppet.'

The idea sent a chill down Malus's spine. His gaze drifted to the wrapped bundle of the warpsword. Could he afford to keep feeding its hunger? Could he afford not to? 'The daemon may possess my body, but I assure you, my will remains intact,' he said. 'I dance for no one, least of all that damnable fiend.' He paused, watching the black veins throb beneath his skin. 'What I want to know is what will happen once the daemon is freed.'

The seer's lips pursed in thought. 'That is an interesting question,' she said. 'By rights, your soul would be snuffed out like a candle flame as Tz'arkan claims your body as its host. Now, however...' After a moment Eldire made a faint shrug. 'I cannot say. It is possible that the sword might counteract the daemon's claim over you, but you may be certain that until the moment arrives Tz'arkan will take whatever steps it can to help decide the matter in its favour.'

Malus gave his mother a hard look. 'So you're saying all is not lost.'

'I'm saying that if you are very clever and very lucky you might manage to trade one doom for another,' the seer replied archly. 'The warpsword will kill you sooner or later, Malus. Now that you've drawn it you can't turn it loose.'

The highborn let out a weary sigh. 'All of us die, mother,' he said, staring into the darkness. 'So it's not much of a price to pay, now is it?'

'Bold words for someone who has never spoken with the dead,' Eldire replied. 'Nevertheless,' she said, raising a hand to pre-empt a retort from her son, 'what's done is done. You have the sword, and that is what is important. That leaves just one relic to reclaim.'

'The Amulet of Vaurog,' Malus said ruefully. 'I've no idea where it is and precious little time to look for it. As near as I can tell I have two months left to return to the temple and set the daemon free, and the trip alone takes almost a month and a half.' He shot Eldire a sidelong glance. 'So unless you've got the power to make me fly, I've only got two weeks left to find the last relic.'

Eldire hitched up the ghostly hem of her robe and bent close to Malus, so that mother and son were almost nose-to-nose. 'Would you like a pair of wings, Malus?' she asked, her voice dangerously sweet.

Malus's sarcastic reply turned to ice at the tone in his mother's voice. 'That's... generous...' he said carefully. 'But perhaps I should worry about finding the relic first and making the trip afterward.'

Eldire smiled a wolf's smile. 'A very wise decision,' she said, straightening once again. 'My time grows short,' she announced. 'Speaking to you in this way is very taxing, especially now that the daemon has grown so strong. Is there aught that you wish of me?'

'I was hoping you knew something about the amulet,' Malus said quickly, forcing himself to sit up straight. 'That was why I called you in the first place.'

'The amulet?' Eldire said. Already her form was losing its nebulous consistency, melting like morning fog. 'It is a potent talisman, wrought from meteoric iron in ages past. No weapon can harm the warrior who wears it.'

'Never mind what it does!' Malus cried. 'Do you know where it is?'

Eldire's image began to blur, dissolving into formless mist. Her answer was little more than a sigh.

'The path to the fifth amulet leads to Naggarond,' the seer replied. 'Seek the amulet in the lightless halls of the Fortress of Iron.'

By the time Malus had recovered his wits, Eldire was gone. He looked to Spite. The nauglir raised its massive head and let out an irritated snort.

'I couldn't have said it better myself,' the highborn said darkly, folding his arms tightly across his chest. 'The Witch King's own fortress. I should have known.'

One doom for another, he thought bitterly to himself, feeling the daemon's corruption rise like a black tide from his bones and spread beneath his skin.

Malus awoke to aches and pains from head to toe. The clearing was bathed in the pearly light of false dawn, and wisps of fog curled along the ground. He was laying on his side, wrapped tightly in a heavy cloak sodden with morning dew. A few feet away Spite slept with its head tucked behind its long, whip-like tail, hissing like a boiling kettle.

Long fingers teased gently at his scalp, the tips warm against his clammy skin. His sleep-fogged mind savoured the sensation as the fingers brushed against his right ear, sending a trickle of warmth flowing along its curved outer edge.

Another rivulet of heat flowed across his cheek and over the top of his lips. It tasted of salt and iron.

The highborn's eyes went wide. He opened his mouth to speak, but the words were blotted out by a crushing wave of agony that radiated from his skull. Malus writhed within the tight confines of his cloak, but try as he might he could not pull himself free.

Blood ran in a freshet across his face and down his neck. It flowed into his right eye and he gasped at another, fiercer wave of pain.

Helpless, blinking away the drops of blood catching in his eyelashes, Malus turned his head and looked up to find an armoured figure crouching at his shoulder. More blood poured down the back of his head as though his skull were a broken jug of wine.

Bright blood painted Lhunara's pale grey hands, pooling beneath torn black fingernails and running in jagged courses along her wrists. Her blue lips parted in a lunatic smile, and her one good eye shone with a fevered gleam. The other eye, swollen and black with rotting blood, rolled aimlessly in its socket.

'We are of one mind, my lord,' she said, her voice bubbling from liquefying lungs as she raised her hands to the awful wound on the right side of her skull. With a wet, slithering sound she pressed the grey matter in her palms deep into the maggot-infested cavity.

'One mind,' she said, then reached for his face. 'One heart. One eye...'

* * *

Malus awoke screaming, thrashing about in slick, dewy loam.

His heart lurched in terror as he found that his arms and legs were wrapped tight. Still half-blind and witless, he writhed and kicked, sputtering and howling like the damned. Then with a convulsive heave he tore one leg free and realised that he was tangled in his heavy cloak.

Panting furiously, Malus forced himself to close his eyes and rest his head against the damp earth. When the hammering in his heart had eased, he slowly and purposefully untangled his limbs and spread the cloak open, heedless of the early morning chill.

Finally, when his breathing had slowed, the highborn opened his eyes. It was well past dawn, and weak sunlight was streaming through the close-set branches of the tree over his head. A thick root bulged up from the ground under his back, pressing hard against his spine.

Frowning, Malus raised his head. He was lying on an animal path between stands of tall oaks. Green, dripping ferns brushed against his cheeks, making him shudder.

He was nowhere near the clearing he'd camped in.

Cursing blearily, he clambered to his feet. The forest stretched away in every direction. Bits of foliage were caught between the plates of his armour, and the palms of his hands were caked with dirt. Blessed Mother of Night, he thought. How did I get here? Memories of the night before were fuzzy at best. He remembered sitting in the darkness, trying to envision a way into Naggarond of all places... and then things became vague. Did I get drunk on that damned vinegary wine, he thought?

He did a slow turn about, casting his gaze frantically about in an attempt to get his bearings. The game trail looked familiar and at least headed south towards the edge of the forest. Rubbing his face with a grimy palm he started walking down the trail, suddenly conscious of the fact that his battle-axe was nowhere to be seen.

Malus followed the trail for nearly a mile through the dense foliage, growing more confused and apprehensive by the moment. As he went he began to notice signs that he might have followed the path previously. From the shallow footprints and broken branches it looked as though he'd been reeling along like a drunkard in the darkness. It was a wonder he hadn't impaled himself on a low branch or cracked open his skull against the side of a tree.

After walking a mile and a half he found himself fighting back a rising tide of panic. Then, off to the south-west, he heard a familiar steam-kettle hiss. With a sigh of relief the highborn left the path and made for the sound, thrashing impatiently through the undergrowth. After about a dozen yards the trees began to thin out, until finally he stumbled onto the edge of his campsite. Spite rose to its feet at his sudden appearance, wide nostrils flaring as it tasted his scent.

Malus stopped dead at the edge of the clearing, scanning the small space warily. His axe was still where he left it. Even the folded parcel of cloth that had contained his evening meal was still where he'd left it. Moving carefully, he crossed the campsite and approached the nauglir. 'Easy, Spite,' he said, reaching for his saddlebags. The cold one snorted at him, one red eye regarding him balefully as the highborn searched through his gear.

The three remaining wine bottles hadn't been touched. He checked each wax seal and found them perfectly intact.

Spite shifted on its broad, taloned feet and grumbled irritably. 'All right, all right,' Malus said, securing the saddlebags and slapping the cold one on the flank. 'Go. Hunt. I need to think.'

The highborn stepped away as the huge warbeast slipped with surprising stealth into the thick undergrowth. Then he turned and once more scanned the ground near where he'd sat. There was no sign of a disturbance. It was as though he'd simply stood up and walked off into the darkness.

Malus settled wearily against the log and tried to clean some of the dirt from his hands. Try as he might, he couldn't remember much of the night after he'd spoken with Eldire. Could she have done something to him? If so, why? He shook his head irritably. The idea made no sense.

Then there was the nightmare. He'd heard of druchii who cried out, even got up and moved about in the grips of a powerful nightmare. Had there been more to the dream that he didn't remember? Had the ghastly vision of Lhunara sent him fleeing into the depths of the forest? 'I may have to start drinking myself to sleep again,' he muttered sourly. 'Or hobbling myself at night like a horse.'

From off to the north came a sudden eruption of frenzied movement – something huge thrashed through the forest, snapping branches and slapping heavily against tree trunks. Malus grunted softly. Spite had already found a morning meal.

Then, as if in answer, came sounds of movement to the south, back in the direction of the road.

Without thinking, Malus snatched up his axe and rolled quietly into a crouch, peering warily over the top of the fallen log. Scarcely daring to breathe, he held perfectly still and strained his senses to the utmost. Moments later he heard a much fainter rustle in the undergrowth, perhaps twenty yards to the south-east. The highborn closed his eyes and tried to picture the surrounding terrain in his mind. Whatever it was, it sounded like it was working its way up the game trail he'd recently been following.

Then came another crackle of broken branches – this time directly to the south. The highborn bared his teeth.

It sounded like a hunting party. And it was coming his way.

CHAPTER FOUR

THE ENDLESS

After everything he'd been through in the last ten months, Malus no longer believed in luck. Whoever the hunters were, they hadn't simply stumbled onto him by accident. He doubted they were city folk from Har Ganeth – the camp was too far away and too deep in the woods to catch the attention of a band of refugees. An autarii hunting party was a possibility. The Shades claimed the entire mountain range and hill country north of the Slaver's Road, and it wasn't unheard of for small raiding bands to find their way to the southern foothills to steal from westbound slave caravans. But no autarii worth his salt would be so clumsy as to give away his position, particularly in the deep woods.

That left only one possibility: they were men from Malekith's army.

Malus's hands tightened on the haft of his battle-axe and peered over the top of the log into the shadows beneath the thick trees. It was possible they were just a foraging party, hunting for deer or pheasant to feed the Witch King's warband. It was also possible that they were hunters of a different kind, combing the woods in search of him. But how could they have found me, Malus thought? He reckoned he knew these woods better than any soldier from Naggarond, and he'd been careful to cover his trail the evening before.

Undergrowth rustled off to the highborn's right, still some fifteen yards away. The hunters were moving cautiously and swinging a little further to the west. He turned his gaze to the east, hoping to catch some sign of movement from the second hunting party, but the dense foliage stymied him. Still, he thought, if I can't yet see them, they can't see me.

Then came the sharp sound of a branch snapping near the game trail. Ten yards away, he reckoned, and also a bit farther east. The two groups were swinging around the edge of the campsite. What was more, he suddenly realised that he'd heard no indications of movement from directly south. They know where the campsite is, he thought, feeling the hairs bristle on the back of his neck. They are trying to surround it, cutting me off from fleeing further northward.

He had to move now, before the noose closed around him. Fortunately Spite was somewhere north of him now, feeding on his morning meal. If he could reach the nauglir he was sure that he could outpace whoever was stalking him, fleeing northward into the foothills. Of course, that meant he'd be trespassing on autarii land, but first he had to survive to get there.

Still crouching low to the ground, Malus turned and scuttled across the campsite. As he did, the sounds of movement erupted from east and west. The hunters were making their move.

Malus ducked his head and followed the path that Spite had taken upon leaving camp. At least, he tried – not two feet beyond the edge of the clearing he crashed headlong into a briar thicket that the iron-skinned cold one had simply muscled its way through. Thorny branches lashed at the highborn's face and neck, eliciting a strangled hiss of pain. Malus lashed at the hedge with his axe, hoping that a few good strokes would be enough to hew his way past, but the thin, green branches rebounded from the weapon and lashed back at him like whipcords. Worse, the attempt made considerable noise, causing him to feel dangerously exposed. Malus gave up after a handful of noisy strokes and rushed to the west, looking for a clearer path through the undergrowth.

He heard someone burst from cover and dash into the clearing only a half-dozen yards behind him. Not waiting to see who it was, Malus ducked and dodged past thin saplings and drooping ferns, reaching the end of the thicket and cutting back northward again. His tense gaze scanned left and right, hoping to catch some sign of the nauglir's trail, but the cold one's path was almost invisible to his unskilled eyes. *The damn thing is almost thirty feet long and weighs a ton*, he thought irritably, *yet it can move like an autarii in the woods when it wants to.* For a moment he contemplated whistling for Spite – easier to bring the cold one to him than the other way around – but he was certain the hunters would hear him as well. He had no idea what would happen then, and didn't want to find out.

Malus strained his ears for the sound of pursuit and kept to the parts of the wood that offered the least amount of resistance, trading concealment for speed. The ground began to slope gently upward, starting the slow climb to the low foothills that were still more than a mile distant. Within a few minutes he came upon a small wooded hollow and on impulse he headed inside rather than skirt it.

The shadows beneath the close-set trees were deep, but at least it meant that there was less undergrowth to fight through. Almost immediately Malus found a narrow game trail winding through the centre of the hollow and followed it without hesitation. Seconds later he came upon a large pool of fresh blood splashed across the trail and found a pair of large, familiar footprints nearby.

Malus settled into a crouch, breathing heavily. He'd found the spot where Spite had ambushed his prey but the damned cold one was nowhere to be seen. Nauglir, like many predators, preferred to drag their food somewhere more secure before they felt safe enough to eat. Which meant that the warbeast could have gone off in nearly any direction.

A flicker of movement in the shadows to Malus's left brought him around, weapon at the ready. No one was there. The highborn turned in a slow circle, looking for any signs of danger. As near as he could tell, however, he was alone.

Branches crackled perhaps a dozen yards behind him. The hunters had reached the south end of the hollow.

Malus sank into a crouch, quickly sizing up the surrounding terrain. Did he dare make a stand here, or keep running? Now he regretted leaving the warpsword bound to Spite's saddle!

Moving as quietly as he could, Malus swung around the bloodstain so as not to leave a trail his enemies could follow, and sidled into the dense woods to the west of the path. Vines and brambles tugged at his hair and scraped against his steel armour, but he resisted the temptation to swipe them away with his axe. Instead he burrowed deeper, hoping to draw the vegetation behind him like a cloak.

A few yards further on the highborn came to the burnt and blasted trunk of an old oak tree. Clearly felled by lightning years ago, the shell of the old tree rose less than ten feet and terminated in a jagged, moss-covered stump. A cleft in the wide trunk ran from root level up to about waist height. Thinking quickly, Malus hurried to the cleft and carefully wormed his way inside.

Rotten, pulpy wood and squirming insects rained down on him as the edges of his armour plates scraped the inside of the tree. Malus closed his eyes and clamped his mouth tightly shut against the dank-smelling debris and braced his back against the far side of the tree. Then, moving carefully, he raised a foot and felt about for a toehold a few feet off the ground. Within moments his boot found a ridge that would support his weight. Gritting his teeth, the highborn pressed his back against the trunk and heaved upward. As his other foot came off the ground he fumbled quickly for another foothold and found one just above the cleft.

Working quickly, Malus forced his way three more feet up into the hollow trunk and hung there, scarcely daring to breathe.

No sooner had he stopped moving than he heard faint sounds of movement in the woods outside. The highborn stifled a bitter curse. He heard the swish of branches and the crackle of dead wood, and for the first time he heard hushed voices speaking in what sounded like druhir. From what he could tell there were at least three of them, but he couldn't quite make out what they were saying.

The voices drew nearer. The highborn heard the muted rattle of plate harness and the faint clatter of sword scabbards. Malus looked down at the narrow shaft of pale light shining through the cleft. As he watched, a shadow passed across the opening. He held his breath, expecting to see a head peer into the opening at any moment.

For several long moments the conversation continued. The words were strangely muffled; again, Malus couldn't quite divine their meaning, but he could guess from their cadence and tone that they were discussing where to look for him next. At length, one of the hunters seemed to arrive at a decision. With a grunt, the hunters moved off, apparently continuing to head farther west. The highborn let out a slow breath. Once he could no longer hear any sounds of movement he counted slowly to one hundred, then carefully eased himself back to earth.

Getting out of the cleft proved much more difficult than getting in. In the end he was forced to turn about and sink to his knees, then crawl backwards out of the hole. At any moment he expected blades or crossbow bolts to bite into his back, but within a few moments he was free. Brushing rotted wood and insects out of his hair, Malus regained his bearings and headed off east as fast as he could manage.

He hadn't gone more than a few yards when he heard a familiar growl some ways to the north. Now at least he knew which direction the cold one had gone in. The question was whether or not the hunters had heard the same thing, and what they would make of it.

Malus continued west, heading back to the game trail. He could follow the faint trail as far north as he could, hopefully making better time than his pursuers, but if they were now heading in Spite's direction as well he was sure to cross their path. Unless he continued west, crossing the game trail and then doubling back in a wide circle to come at Spite from the east. But doing so would take time. Which risk was more worthwhile?

Caught up in his internal debate, Malus almost missed the flicker of movement to his right. Certain that this time it wasn't his imagination, he fetched up against the bole of a tree and dropped to a crouch, scanning the deep shadows all around him.

Nothing moved. There were no sounds save for the restless wind. Malus waited for ten seconds, seeing nothing, then took a deep breath and started off once more. He went for ten yards and then abruptly stopped, whirling to the right.

There! He saw a shadow flit from the darkness beneath one tree to the next. It was the size of a raven, and darted through the air at shoulder height. The hair on the highborn's neck stood on end. He was being hounded by a shade, no doubt reporting his location back to its master. Even now, Malus imagined the huntsmen he'd encountered were doubling back, following the call of their unearthly hound.

The time for stealth was past. Malus turned and ran for the game trail as fast as he could. With the weight of his armour his footfalls echoed through the dense wood, but all that counted now was speed. Such was his haste that he ran full-tilt into the same thicket he'd encountered earlier.

Needle-like thorns raked his face and hands, but with a savage snarl he hacked wildly at the branches with his axe and bulled his way through.

Panting like a dog Malus stumbled onto the game trail – and saw at once that he was not alone.

Three figures stood in a tight group a few yards down the trail to Malus's right. They wore black, woollen robes over breeches and boots, and their torsos were protected by silver steel breastplates engraved with elaborate designs and sorcerous runes. Their bodies were wrapped in heavy, hooded cloaks, and their faces were hidden behind masks of polished silver. Three female faces worked in cold metal regarded him curiously, their polished features seeming to float within the black depths of their hoods. One of the figures raised a black-gloved hand, and Malus turned and ran northward as fast as his feet would carry him.

'Spite!' Malus called, throwing all caution to the wind. Fortunately for him, the game trail twisted and turned, quickly carrying him out of sight of the three shade-casters. Had he run afoul of the autarii after all? The three women he'd seen were witches, of that he had no doubt, but no witches he'd ever seen wore masks and archaic armour over their robes.

Shouts and sounds of movement rang out from Malus's left; the hunters he'd met by the tree were closing in. Off to the north he thought he heard another low growl from Spite. He tried to gauge how far off the sound was when he turned another corner and an armoured figure stepped onto the path directly in front of him.

For a fleeting second Malus thought one of the witches had somehow flown ahead to cut him off. The figure wore black robes and silver steel armour, but the ornate, archaic plates covered the hunter from neck to toe like a proper knight. Two swords hung from the hunter's belt and his face was hidden behind a mask worked in the shape of a leering daemon. A hadrilkar of polished gold glinted from the depths of the man's hood.

The hunter raised a gauntleted hand. Malus was too close to swing the axe, so instead he held the haft out before him and crashed directly into the man. With a crash of wood against steel the masked figure fell backwards and Malus leapt over him without breaking stride.

More shouts sounded behind him, and then he heard a whickering sound slice through the air behind him. Something heavy struck him between the shoulder blades and then a steel web wrapped his chest and arms in a fearsome embrace. Barbed hooks scraped across his armour and locked inside its crevices, and suddenly Malus was off-balance and stumbling forward. With a furious effort he tried to regain his balance, but then his foot struck a protruding root and he crashed headlong to the ground.

The highborn thrashed and rolled, wrestling with the implacable grip of the net. Footfalls sounded behind him as he struggled, and three masked figures loomed into view over him. One grabbed his ankles, flipping him expertly onto his back, while another grabbed the folds of the net that laid across his chest. The third warrior stood a few feet away and slowly drew his sword.

With a snarl Malus pulled one foot free as the man holding the net began to straighten. On impulse the highborn kicked the warrior in the side of the head, and he fell sideways with a muffled curse. As he did he inadvertently pulled part of the net with him, freeing Malus's right arm. The warrior who had been holding his feet let go and lunged for the highborn, but Malus rolled quickly to his left and unrolled himself from the barbed trap. Driving the second warrior back with a savage sweep of his axe, Malus struggled to his feet – just as the masked swordsman lunged in from the highborn's left.

The warrior's blade was just a silver flicker in the forest gloom. Battlefield instincts alone spared Malus; without thinking he pivoted on his right foot and blocked the sword stroke with the haft of his axe. As it was, the force of the blow nearly drove Malus back to his knees, and before he could recover the swordsman pressed his attack, landing two more solid blows that nearly knocked the highborn off his feet.

Whoever the warriors were, they were tough and skilled opponents. Without a word shared between them the masked men fanned out in a loose semicircle, clearly working to hem him in. The other men kept their swords in their scabbards, however, leaving the lone swordsman to batter Malus's failing guard. The highborn gave ground quickly, retreating further north up the path, but within moments one of the hunters was going to cut behind him and seal off his retreat.

Malus suffered another ringing blow to the haft of his axe and risked a hurried feint at the swordsman's face. The short swing checked the warrior's advance for half a second, but it was enough for the highborn to spin on the ball of his left foot and then lunge at the masked hunter who had circled around behind him. Caught off guard, the warrior tried to retreat, but the highborn charged him with a bestial roar and caught him with a vicious blow that struck sparks from his ornate breastplate. The force of the blow knocked the man from his feet, and the highborn charged past him and continued along the path.

'Spite!' Malus called again, and immediately was answered with a sharp hiss just ten yards off the path to his right. Without hesitation the highborn plunged into the undergrowth, hacking bushes and saplings out of his path with wild sweeps of his axe. If he could just get to the nauglir's side he could turn the tide of the battle in his favour.

Malus caught the sharp smell of spilled blood. Up ahead he caught sight of the nauglir's scaled back and grinned fiercely. The cold one had dragged his kill to another clearing almost a hundred yards farther up the hollow.

'Up, Spite, up!' he cried to the crouching warbeast. Malus could hear the sounds of the masked warriors in close pursuit a scant few yards behind him. As he plunged into the clearing his looked for the wrapped bundle of the warpsword on the cold one's back.

Instead he saw a black-robed figure standing close to the nauglir's saddle. One gloved hand rested on the side of Spite's neck, and the nauglir's eyes were downcast in submission. The witch regarded him impassively from the depths of her silver mask as Malus ground to a sudden halt.

Two more witches glided silently from the shadows to Malus's left and right, attended by two warriors each who advanced with swords in hand. The highborn's three pursuers charged into the clearing directly behind him, completing the encirclement.

Malus turned slowly in place, regarding each of the hunters in turn. His gaze passed from masked face to masked face, dismayed and bewildered by their strange appearance. These were no autarii, he realised. No group of shades would be so regimented.

The highborn stopped in his tracks. Each of the warriors wore the same golden collar. *Gold*, not silver or even silver steel. Peering closely at one of the hadrilkars, Malus saw that it was worked in the shape of a pair of twining dragons.

His breath caught in his throat. These were no mere hunters, Malus realised. He knew who they were, though few had ever seen them face-to-face.

They were the personal bodyguards and agents of the Witch King. They were the Endless.

⚔ CHAPTER FIVE ⚔

FORTRESS OF IRON

Black ice poured from Malus's veins as the seven warriors closed in around him.

The rush of daemonic power shocked him, drawing a horrified cry from the highborn's throat. Time stretched like a bowstring; the movements of the Endless slowed to a turgid crawl, even as Malus's own body seethed with merciless vigour. Inwardly the highborn recoiled in terror and disgust from his unexpected salvation.

'I did not ask for this, daemon,' he hissed. 'You cannot force your damned gifts upon me!'

'Things have changed, Darkblade,' Tz'arkan said. His laughter trembled along Malus's skin. 'I am now free to protect you as I see fit. I would think you would be grateful. Do you imagine that Malekith despatched his chosen with orders to kill you? Had he wanted you dead he could have sent ten thousand spearmen into the woods to root you out like a boar. No, they are here to drag you back to Naggarond in chains, where you will suffer torments that no sane druchii can imagine.'

'Take it back!' Malus snarled. 'Take your cursed ice from my veins. I neither want nor need it!'

'You cannot turn back the seasons,' Tz'arkan replied coldly. 'You had your spring and your summer, little druchii. Soon it will be autumn. Winter cannot be far behind. The ice will come whether you wish it or not.'

Malus clenched his fists around the battered haft of his axe and roared like a wounded beast. The masked warriors were still gliding towards him, poised between one step and the next. Were he able to see their faces he imagined that they would be stretching like melted wax, surprise registering by degrees as the highborn seemed to blur before them. Then, like a butcher, he settled on his first victim and prepared to drown his misery in a tide of hot blood. Yet before he could take a single step a cold, melodious voice spoke in his ear.

'Your sorcery is impressive, Malus of Hag Graef, but in the end it changes nothing.'

The highborn whirled, fear tightening his throat. His axe sang through the air, angling for the witch's neck, but she moved as though he were standing still. She reached forward without apparent effort and touched her fingertips to his armoured chest.

Blue fire exploded behind his eyes. He felt himself falling, the silver face of the witch receding into darkness. Her voice tolled after him like a bell.

'You belong to the Witch King now.'

Night had fallen by the time he woke again. Malus opened his eyes to the shifting hues of the northern lights in an unsettlingly clear late-summer sky. The stars were cold and pitiless as diamonds, and the twin moons cast strange shadows across the foggy landscape. Black-robed figures moved silently at the corners of his vision, and he heard people speaking in terse, hushed tones.

He was stretched out like a corpse on the hard ground, still cased in his battered armour. He wasn't bound in any way, but his body felt like lead. With a grunt, he tried to sit upright. It was all he could do just to prop himself up on his elbows.

Malus saw at once that he was in the middle of a small camp, somewhere along the Slaver's Road west of Har Ganeth. There were no fires, only small globes of witchlight resting on low, iron tripods, and perhaps a dozen tents set in orderly clusters around the spot where he lay. Masked warriors were busy dismantling and stowing the tents as the highborn watched, while another group saddled a score of coal-black horses hitched to a picket line a dozen yards away. Grey sea fog curled around the steeds' glossy black hooves, and their eyes glowed green in the reflected witchlight.

The Endless went about their tasks all around Malus, paying him as much attention as they might give to a bedroll. A quick check showed that his axe was nowhere to be seen, and they'd plucked his two daggers from his belt. There were no irons to bind his wrists or ankles, which implied a great deal about his captors' capabilities. If he tried to run, the Endless and their witches were certain he would not get far.

'You are awake,' spoke an unearthly, musical voice. It was cold and sweet as a trumpet or a silver bell, and sent shivers down the highborn's spine. He tried to turn his head to glance at the witch, but the effort left him exhausted. Malus sank back to the ground as the masked druchii circled around him and knelt gracefully at his side. She held a narrow decanter of cut red glass in one hand and a polished silver cup in the other. 'That is good. We will be leaving soon.'

She poured a small measure of a black liquid into the cup and held it out to Malus. The highborn studied her eyes warily. They were wide and dark within the gleaming oculars of the mask, and reminded him of nothing so much as the frank, earnest stare of a child. Setting his jaw, he lifted himself up on one elbow and slowly reached for the cup. 'Where is the army?' he asked wearily.

The witch cocked her head to one side. 'Army? There is no army.'

Malus frowned, his dark brows furrowing in consternation. He studied the black liquid at the bottom of his cup and took a small sip. The potent liquor seared his tongue and flowed like molten iron down his throat. Tears sprang to his eyes. 'Then where is Malekith?' he gasped, fighting the urge to cough.

'The Witch King is in Naggarond,' she said, as though it explained everything. 'We have been commanded to bring you to him.'

The liquor seethed inside Malus's guts, but it also returned a small measure of strength to his limbs. Steeling himself, he finished off the cup. 'Reminds me of the time I drank some lamp oil as a child,' he said hoarsely. 'Honestly, the oil had more flavour.'

'It is a dwarf liquor called barvalk,' the witch said, taking the cup from him. 'Dark riders carry it on cold winter nights. It keeps the blood hot and the mind sharp.'

'Probably takes the tarnish off silver as well,' he muttered, but silently admitted that his limbs had begun to loosen and his mind was alert and awake. With a rueful grin he levered himself fully upright and stretched his arms and shoulders.

The witch was well within reach. Her stare was guileless and her manner relaxed. It would take no effort at all to seize her and close his hands around her neck. But what then, Malus thought? Was she the witch that had felled him in the wood with but a single touch? He could not tell. And even if he did slay her, what then? He was surrounded by more than a dozen warriors, and even if he could somehow fight his way free, the Endless had already demonstrated they could track him easily with their magic.

Malus's shoulders slumped within the confines of his armour. Putting him in irons was redundant. There was nowhere he could go, and they knew it.

Then he remembered what Eldire had told him: *the path to the fifth relic leads to Naggarond.*

It was just possible that falling into the clutches of the Endless was a blessing in disguise.

'All right,' Malus said, trying to sound resigned to his fate. 'What next?'

The witch rose to her feet. 'There is food prepared in the tent yonder,' she said, pointing over Malus's shoulder. 'If you are hungry, eat. We will be riding through the night and will not pause again until midday tomorrow.'

Malus nodded. In truth, food was the last thing on his mind at that point, but better to fuel mind and body while he could. 'Where is my mount?'

The witch turned and inclined her gleaming mask towards the line of trees to the north. 'Your cold one is being tended to there, beyond the camp,' she said. 'Go to it after you have broken your fast, and wait for the order to depart.'

Without so much as a farewell the witch began to walk away. 'Wait!' Malus called. 'What is your name?'

The druchii paused. Her head turned slightly, moonlight glinting on one rounded cheek. 'I have no name,' she said, childlike amusement in her voice. 'I am Endless.' Without waiting for a reply she joined a group of figures packing saddlebags nearby. Soon Malus couldn't tell for sure which of the identical figures was her.

The highborn shook his head wearily and clambered to his feet. Malekith's bodyguards continued breaking camp swiftly and efficiently, hardly sparing their prisoner a sideways glance. Not twenty yards to the south a caravan of flesh merchants were driving their wheeled cages northward up the Slaver's Road, heading for Karond Kar. He listened to the drovers curse the stolid oxen as they went, harangued in turn by the slave master and his sons. One of the young druchii slavers looked up at that moment and stared curiously at the small encampment. He saw Malus watching him and raised his coiled scourge in salute.

Malus raised his hand in return, and the young slaver spurred his horse and cantered to the head of the caravan. Still shaking his head, the highborn headed for the tent that the witch had indicated, hoping that the bodyguards had brought some meat and cheese, and perhaps a bit of decent wine.

Once camp was broken and the baggage packed the Endless set a gruelling pace as they bore their prisoner back to Naggarond. Mounted on their preternatural steeds the masked druchii rode all through the night and half of the following day before finally calling a halt in the middle of a cold and desultory rain.

Horses snorted and stamped, their breath pluming in the chilly air as they were led off the road into the tall grass. The animals paid no heed at all to the cold one in their midst; sired from thoroughbred stock brought from drowned Nagarythe, the dark steeds were foaled in the sorcerous stables of Naggarond itself, and feared neither man nor beast. Cousins to the dark steeds that the kingdom's messengers rode, they were fleet as storm winds when given their head, and could run for days without tiring.

For Spite's part, the nauglir paid little heed to anything, including Malus himself. Since the encounter with the Endless near their camp in the woods, the cold one had been strangely subdued and passive, following commands as meekly as a whipped slave. On the road the cold one loped along at the same pace as the rest of the party, ignoring the highborn's subtle commands.

The nauglir followed the horses off the road and settled onto its haunches, its head perking up a bit at the welcome caress of the rain. Malus slid from the saddle and tried to stretch the kinks out of his hips and shoulders. Though no stranger to hard riding, more than fourteen hours in the saddle left him feeling as though he'd been beaten with a club.

Masked druchii slid effortlessly from their saddles and silently inspected their mounts, checking hooves, muscles and tendons with expert hands. Malus did the same for Spite, although the highborn was checking for telltales of a very different kind.

He found the cluster of magical runes within moments, painted with some kind of indigo dye onto the nauglir's bony skull. The rain had no effect on them, nor did they blur when he rubbed them with his thumb. Malus patted Spite's neck resignedly. The Endless had usurped his control over his own mount and effectively turned Spite into a jailer of sorts. He couldn't spur the cold one to turn on the riders even if he wanted to.

With nothing else to do, Malus leaned against Spite's flank and waited. After a few minutes one of the warriors made his way down the line, holding a bottle of barvalk and half a sausage. Malus steeled himself and took the proffered cup when his turn came, then wolfed down a thick slice of sausage. As soon as the warrior had finished making his rounds he jogged back to the head of the line and without a word the Endless climbed back into the saddle. Their midday break had lasted little more than fifteen minutes.

They rode through the rest of the day and well into the night. Ahead of them went the dragon banner of the Witch King of Naggaroth, and slave caravans travelling in either direction pulled aside and waited with heads bowed as the black riders thundered past. It was nearly four hours past sunset when the Endless finally called a halt, leading their mounts off the road and preparing a cold meal by witchlight. Cold, wet and aching from head to toe, Malus pulled his bedroll from the saddle and fell wearily to the ground beside Spite.

No sooner had he closed his eyes than one of the witches was kneeling beside him with a handful of salted fish and a hunk of bread wrapped in a greasy square of cloth. He took the food without thinking, his exhausted brain only dimly aware that it was close to midnight and the warriors were climbing back in their saddles again. Groaning, the highborn stowed his bedroll and climbed back onto his mount. He ate his meagre rations as they rode.

By the end of the second evening the black riders had reached the western end of the Sea of Malice, and were within a day's ride of the great crossroads where the Slaver's Road met the Spear Road as it headed north to the Wastes. The ration of barvalk at each rest stop had grown more generous, and Malus found himself growing accustomed to the taste. It didn't relieve the aches and pains of the endless ride but it made them slightly more tolerable. As the riders ate and rested, Malus resisted his body's demand for sleep and spent the time carefully arranging his bags. He dug into the pack where three of the daemon's relics were hid and fished out the wrapped bundle that contained the Idol of Kolkuth. He could feel the coldness of the brass figure through the layers of frayed cloth as he set it atop the rest of the bag's contents. During the day's travel he'd worked out a plan of escape. Once the Endless had got him inside the Iron Fortress he would wait until the last moment before seizing the idol and using its power to transport himself away from his captors. He felt certain that once he was inside the fortress he could find ample hiding places from which to begin his hunt for the Amulet of Vaurog.

Providing, of course, that the witches couldn't simply use their shades to locate him once more – and that their sorcerous hold on Spite didn't force the nauglir to turn on his own master.

The Endless rotated their riders through different points in their formation as they travelled; Malus wasn't sure of the reason why, unless perhaps it was to limit their exposure to him as much as possible. After the second day he thought to start a conversation with one of the witches riding beside him, and was surprised when she answered every question he put to her. She told him how the Endless were given to the Iron Fortress as babes, taken as a sort of tithe from each of the highborn families in Naggarond. The witches received training by Morathi herself, while the warriors were taught by a highborn named Lord Nuarc, the finest warlord in the Witch King's warband. They served Malekith until death, at which point their mask and gear were given to a waiting neophyte. There were always a thousand of the Endless, guarding the precincts of the Iron Fortress and marching with the Witch King when the druchii went to war.

From what Malus could determine, the bodyguards wanted for nothing and possessed not a shred of independent thought or ambition. They were essentially incorruptible, a realisation that both frustrated and horrified him at the same time.

Tempted by the witch's loquacity and her apparent lack of guile, Malus asked her how they'd managed to find him. 'It must have been sorcery,' he said offhandedly. 'How else would you have known to look in a nameless clearing in the middle of a vast forest?'

'We are all trained in shade-casting,' the witch replied. Her childlike voice was tinged with surprise, as though it were the most obvious question in the world. 'It is nothing to summon a fetch and have it search for you, providing you have the subject's name.'

'A fetch?' Malus asked.

The witch giggled behind her silver mask. 'The weakest of shades; little more than a fragment of spirit essence, intelligent enough to command but utterly devoid of will or initiative. They can be set to simple tasks, but their reach isn't very long.' She regarded Malus with a condescending shake of her head. 'I'm surprised you know so little, given your demonstration in the forest.'

'My knowledge is... specialised,' Malus replied. 'You say their reach is short?'

She nodded. 'Yes. They have little strength of their own, and must depend upon the energies of the summoner to remain active in the physical realm. A shade-caster can command a fetch over a few dozen miles, perhaps, but no more.'

The highborn looked away, pretending to study the faint line of Dachlan Keep in order to mask his frown of dismay. A dozen miles, he thought? Not much distance for a sorcerer, perhaps, but that would mean he would have to use the idol to leave Naggarond completely in order to escape their reach. Perhaps if he could find a place to hide somewhere in the nearby hills and then use the idol to come and go from the fortress...

Suddenly he straightened in the saddle. Malus turned to the witch. 'You said that a fetch couldn't reach for more than a few dozen miles?'

'Of course,' she replied.

'Then how did you know where to look for me? I could have been in Har Ganeth, or on the road to Karond Kar – I could have been at sea aboard a corsair, for the Dark Mother's sake.'

The witch shrugged. 'We were told to look for you along the Slaver's Road,' she said.

And how did Malekith know that, Malus thought? He was certain that he wasn't going to like the answer.

They came upon the crossroads at well past midnight of the fourth day. The air was cool and clear, and the highborn shivered in the saddle from exhaustion as much as dread as the riders slowed their mounts to a walk and passed among the forest of burning souls.

The last time Malus had been this way was at the head of a small army, marching south to conquer Hag Graef in the name of Balneth Bale. The withered figures, wired to tall iron poles all around the crossroads and set alight with sorcerous fire, had held little terror for him then. Now he found himself listening to their faint, maddened cries and dreading the sight of the empty stake that the Witch King had set aside for him. Only those highborn who'd broken Malekith's laws were sentenced to burn at the crossroads, some lingering in agony for years as the elements wore away their bodies inch by inch. As Malus rode among the guttering lamps that used to be powerful men he could not help but tremble at the fate that awaited him. He reached back and checked the bag where the idol was kept, making certain he could reach it quickly when the time came.

On the other side of the crossroads lay a narrow ribbon of road that gleamed ghostly white under the moonlight. The Hateful Road led to Naggarond alone, and was paved with the skulls of a hundred thousand elves. The hooves of the dark steeds clattered hollowly on the magically treated bones and the riders sat straighter in the saddle as they drew closer to home.

The road wound among dark, lifeless hills and through echoing hollows dense with oak and ash, while in the distance the high walls and pointed towers of Naggarond rose ever higher into the indigo sky. Glimmering witchlight shone like a thousand eyes from the buildings of the fortress city, lending it a kind of cold, brooding life. This was not a place built upon ruthless power like Hag Graef, or stained with bloodlust like Har

Ganeth – Naggarond was black, eternal hate quarried from cold marble and unyielding iron. It was the implacable heart of the druchii given form.

They travelled the Hateful Road for another hour, until finally they crested a rocky ridge and came upon a flat, featureless plain that stretched between the curving arms of a bleak mountainside. Naggarond curled upon itself like an enormous dragon upon the plain, surrounded by a gleaming wall nearly sixty feet high. Tall towers bristling with iron spikes rose from the wall every mile or so along its length, sited to rain clouds of arrows and heavy stones upon any invader. Ahead, Malus could see a massive gatehouse that was a small fortress unto itself, looming over a double portal wrought from slabs of polished iron nearly twenty feet high. The highborn shook his head in wonder. He'd once thought that Hag Graef's fortifications were fearsome, but nothing compared to Naggarond's forbidding bulk.

The dark riders led their steeds directly across the plain and approached the iron gates. No challenge issued from the gatehouse's jagged battlements; evidently the mere sight of the gleaming silver masks of the Endless was sufficient. With a terrible, echoing groan one of the massive gates swung open and the column trotted down a long, wide tunnel that ran beneath the gatehouse. Darkness pressed in from all sides, and the highborn fought to keep from hunching his shoulders at the thought of the murder holes and oil flues that doubtless pierced the stone overhead.

Malus expected to emerge from the tunnel into a large, open square, much as in the style of other druchii cities. Instead he found himself in a narrow lane overlooked by tall, stone buildings with deep-set oaken doors. Witchlights glowed from sconces hanging over many of the doorways, creating pools of flickering light amid a twisting path of abyssal shadow. The hooves of the dark steeds struck sparks from the grey cobblestones and sent up a thunderous clatter that reverberated from the close-set walls.

All druchii cities were treacherous, labyrinthine places, full of blind alleys and confusing turns designed to entrap and kill the unwary, but Naggarond was unlike any living city Malus had ever seen. Once inside the walls there were no landmarks to navigate by; nearly every street ended at a crossroads that connected to three other narrow lanes, all leading off in unpredictable directions. None of the buildings he saw bore signs or sigils that told what they were, and if there were market squares anywhere he never saw them. Within minutes he was utterly lost, and he knew full well they had only just entered the outer wards of the city.

They rode for more than an hour through the labyrinth, alone but for the echoes of their passage. Malus saw not a single living thing along the way: no citizens or city guards, no drunkards or thieves, penny oracles or cutthroats. It reminded him of nothing more than the houses of the dead, that city of crypts in the east where the ancient dead of Nagarythe were bound fearfully in vaults of stone.

There were three more defensive walls that subdivided the city, closed by three more heavy gates of iron. Tall, silent houses pressed hard against either side of these inner walls; as the first of the six cities, Malus had the sense that it had grown in fits and starts as the kingdom prospered, expanding beyond its own walls again and again until it was ringed like an old, gnarled tree.

Thus, when they paused before a fourth wall of gleaming stone it took several long moments before Malus's exhausted mind registered the narrow, arched gate and the gatehouse formed of blades of forged iron. Witchlights shone from the oculars of iron dragons that rose to either side of the formidable gate, their spread wings formed of hammered iron plates as sharp-edged as swords. Beyond the gatehouse rose a profusion of close-set towers like a thicket of polished spear-blades, pierced by slitted windows that glowed with sorcerous fire. Tendrils of vapour rose from behind the walls of the iron fortress, rising among the towers and reaching for the twin moons with claw-like fingers.

They had come at last to the Fortress of Iron, citadel of the undying Witch King.

CHAPTER SIX

THE WITCH KING

A rattling boom reverberated from the iron gatehouse, startling Malus from his exhausted stupor, and the arched gate swung inward on ancient, dwarf-wrought hinges. The highborn felt a chill race down his spine as the black gate swung open and he stared into the blackness beyond. He feared to tread any deeper into the Witch King's domain, but he knew that he had to get at least a glimpse at the fortress grounds to allow the Idol of Kolkuth to get him inside. As the first of the riders nudged their dark steeds forward Malus reached back and loosened the flap on the bag where the idol was kept.

The passage through the gate was shorter than he expected, barely twelve feet from one end of the tunnel to the other. Beyond lay a small courtyard paved with flagstones of polished slate and bounded by statues of imposing druchii knights and rearing dragons. Above them loomed the sharp-edged towers of Malekith's citadel and the vassal lords of his warband, casting a deep shadow over the weary travellers. As Malus led Spite into the courtyard he felt the weight of a terrible gaze fall upon him; for a moment he felt like a rabbit caught in the shadow of a swooping hawk, and cold, unreasoning terror seized his heart and turned his muscles to ice. Even Spite felt it, causing the massive warbeast to sink onto its haunches and snap its jaws at the empty air. Just as quickly as it struck, the terrible pressure eased, and Malus caught the hint of a sinuous shifting amid the thick shadows that lay across the paving stones. He stole a glance upwards and caught a faint hint of motion, as though a great serpent were coiling about one of the citadel's tallest towers. Then he glimpsed the outline of a long, narrow head silhouetted against the moonlight, and a pair of glowing red eyes that brooded over the dark city with lordly disdain. A black dragon, Malus realised with a shudder. His jaw gaped at the terrible sight.

Malus was so caught up with the sight of the fearsome beast that he paid no heed whatsoever to the highborn that awaited them in the middle of the courtyard until he spoke. 'Are you certain you have the right man?' the highborn rasped in a powerful, commanding voice. 'He looks like a corpse.'

The highborn's tone snapped Malus out of his reverie. He saw the Endless sliding from their saddles and watched the masked warriors bow their heads respectfully to the druchii lord, who returned the gesture with a disapproving scowl. Exhaustion and spite emboldened Malus's tongue. 'Lord Nuarc, I presume?'

'Did I give you leave to open your damned mouth, boy?' Lord Nuarc snarled. He was a tall and powerfully built druchii, clad in enamelled plate armour ornamented with gilt etchings and potent runes of protection over a skirt of shining ithilmar mail. His paired swords were masterworks, their pommels set with rubies the size of sparrow's eggs and resting in scabbards decorated with ruddy gold, and a cloak of glossy black dragonscale hung about his broad shoulders. Even without the thick gold hadrilkar circling his neck it was clear that he was a powerful noble and a member of the Witch King's personal retinue. His sharp nose was scarred in two places by sword-strokes, and a star-shaped dimple of scar tissue on the side of his neck spoke of the spear thrust that had ravaged his voice. The druchii's black eyes shone with keen wit and hinted at a will stronger than steel. His black hair, streaked with grey, was pulled back from his lean face and bound with a band of gold.

'He can be no other, my lord,' said one of the warriors, speaking in a voice eerily identical to the witch Malus had spoken with in their time on the road. 'We found him in the forest near Har Ganeth as you said. By his name the shades knew him.'

Malus leaned back and reached his hand beneath the flap of his saddlebag. The idol's icy surface burned against his fingertips. He tried to visualise a spot back along the road, someplace near woods and hills where he could lie low and plan his next move.

Nuarc looked Malus over again and shook his head. 'I wouldn't have believed it.' He looked the highborn in the eye. 'How did a shrivelled wretch like yourself kill Lurhan of Hag Graef?'

'With a sword. How else?' Malus sneered, his ire getting the better of him. If Nuarc was expecting excuses or snivelling pleas for mercy he was going to be disappointed. 'People have a habit of underestimating me, Lord Nuarc. I tend to make them regret it.'

Nuarc studied Malus for a moment, then nodded appraisingly. 'Brave but stupid,' he declared. 'I suspected as much.' He frowned at the highborn. 'Take your hand out of your bag, boy,' he snapped. 'We didn't bring you all this way to steal your trinkets.'

'No, you brought me here to hang me at the crossroads,' Malus shot back. 'Am I supposed to feel grateful that you won't steal my possessions until after I'm dead?'

'Dead?' Nuarc exclaimed. 'If the Witch King wanted you dead you and I would be having a very different kind of conversation right now.' His lip curled in disdain. 'For the moment, Malekith simply wishes to speak to you.'

Malus had to stop and replay Nuarc's words in his head. 'He wants to speak to me?' he echoed. His exhausted mind couldn't make sense of what he'd been told.

'I'm not in the habit of repeating myself, boy,' Nuarc growled. 'Now get out of that damned saddle. The Witch King knows you've arrived, but I won't send you to the Dragon Court looking like some flea-bitten autarii.'

Nuarc's iron-tinged rasp galvanised Malus's near-senseless body into motion. Before he was fully aware of it he was climbing down from Spite and standing uneasily on the slate paving stones. As if on cue, a pair of beastmasters with ornate kheitans and beast prods appeared from the shadows, ready to take charge of the sullen nauglir.

'Follow me,' the warlord commanded, and turned on his heel. Malus, his mind reeling from the sudden change in circumstances, quickly cinched up the saddlebag containing the relics and stumbled after Nuarc.

What was going on, he thought as he followed the warlord through an ironbound door into the citadel proper. Again, the words of his mother echoed in his mind. *Seek the amulet in the lightless halls of the Fortress of Iron.*

What did she know that he didn't?

Nuarc led him to a cold, austere apartment in one of the citadel's towers – it might have been the warlord's own keep, as far as Malus knew – where a trio of silent, efficient servants waited to make him presentable for an audience with the Witch King. They stripped away his battered armour and kheitan, as well as his stained and tattered robes, and laid out food and wine while they drew a steaming bath to wash away the dust of the road. He ate like a wolf while he waited for the hot water to be poured, eyeing the wine wistfully but leaving the bottle untouched. His wits were addled enough as it was.

While he waited a pair of masked warriors slipped silently into the apartment with his bags piled in their arms. Malus masked his fear with a curt nod and quickly checked them after they'd gone. For a wonder, nothing had been disturbed.

Perhaps I've fallen asleep in the saddle and this is all a bizarre dream, he thought. Nothing else makes much sense.

The servants scrubbed him industriously and said nothing about the fresh scars on either side of his torso where Urial's sword had run him through, nor did they show concern for the web work of black veins that ran from his right hand all the way across his shoulder and up the side of his neck. No doubt the servants were spying on behalf of someone – or several someones – but there was little Malus could do about that. Let them make their report. He doubted it could make his situation any more precarious than it already was.

The food and the hot water preyed upon him, making his eyelids droop.

Malus splashed a bit of water on his face and tried to concentrate on the facts at hand. In retrospect, his treatment at the hands of the Endless now made a bit more sense. He hadn't been their prisoner at all, just a highborn who had been summoned to the Witch King's court with all dispatch.

And now this, Malus thought, his weary gaze sweeping around the apartment. He wasn't being treated like a guest, necessarily, but certainly as something more than an outlaw. So what could possibly account for that, the highborn thought?

The obvious answer was that Malekith wanted something from him. Something that couldn't be got using the end of a red-hot iron or a torturer's knives.

He waved the servants away and leaned back in the tub. He eyed his bags piled near the door. Was it the warpsword? He tugged thoughtfully at his lip. From all indications it appeared that Malekith had never received word of the uprising at Har Ganeth, so as far as he knew the blade still rested in the Sanctum of the Sword back at the temple. And even if he did know the truth, it wasn't as though the Witch King needed his permission to take it.

Or did he? Since he'd drawn the sword, did that mean no one else could claim until so long as he lived? Malus grinned ruefully. It wasn't as though that would be much of a problem for Malekith either.

What then did he possess that Malekith couldn't simply take from him? He went over everything Nuarc had said in the courtyard outside the citadel, looking for clues as to why he'd been summoned. All Nuarc had seemed to care about was Lurhan's death. The highborn's brows knitted in thought. Could that be it?

Other than his half-brother Isilvar, who now held their father's rank and properties, Malus was Lurhan's only male descendant. And while he was now an outlaw and stripped of any claim to Lurhan's legacy, Isilvar had secretly broken the Witch King's laws as well. Both Isilvar and their sister Nagaira had been members of the cult of Slaanesh; indeed, Malus strongly suspected that Isilvar had been the cult's Heirophant inside the city. After the cult had been exposed and most of its members killed, Malus suspected that Lurhan had discovered his son's involvement and covered it up.

Had Malekith found out? If so, there was no one left who could offer proof... except for him. Malus steepled his fingers beneath his chin. That was an intriguing possibility indeed.

The door to the apartment banged open and Nuarc swept inside like a storm wind, scattering cowed servants like leaves. 'This isn't some damned flesh house, boy,' the warlord growled disdainfully. 'Get dressed. The Witch King is waiting.'

Gritting his teeth, Malus rose from the tub and did as he was told. He heard Nuarc let out a surprised hiss as the warlord got a look at the daemon's handiwork, but the druchii lord asked no awkward questions.

The servants had laid out a fine set of black robes and a court kheitan of soft human hide. Hands plucked at his head; he rounded on the servants with a snarl, belatedly realising the servants were trying to comb his long, tangled hair. Frowning irritably, he let them finish their work and bind the hair back with leather and gold wire.

There was no armour to replace his old harness, and certainly no paired swords to wear at his hip. It was clear that Malekith's interest was entirely conditional. The new outfit he wore would look just as fitting hanging from an iron pole as it would at court. 'All right,' he said grimly, pulling on a pair of new boots. 'Lead on.'

On the way out the door, Malus spared one last look at his piled baggage. He tried to reassure himself that if Malekith wanted him dead the Witch King wouldn't have bothered to give him the opportunity to unpack.

Malus followed Nuarc through a maze of dark, empty corridors, each one as silent as a tomb. Witchlamps set in iron sconces cast solitary pools of light along the way, making the darkness seem even deeper and more oppressive. Before long the silence began to prey upon Malus, setting his nerves on edge. There was none of the hectic bustle he was accustomed to at the citadel of Uthlan Tyr, drachau of Hag Graef. Though it was the centre of power for the entire kingdom, the Iron Fortress was cold and still, filled only with echoes.

At first he'd tried to memorise their route, but after a quarter of an hour's worth of twists and turns he gave it up as a lost cause. Like the city outside the fortress, there were no landmarks by which to navigate; only those who belonged there had any hope of finding their way. Malus couldn't imagine how long one had to wander these funereal halls before they gave up their secrets.

Lord Nuarc found his way effortlessly. Within half an hour they passed through an archway into a long, empty chamber lit by massive witchlamps suspended by chains along the arched ceiling. Here Malus began to notice the furtive movements of other druchii: masked Endless, nobles going about the business of state, temple bureaucrats and scarred, nervous servants, all gliding quietly through the shadows to and from the Witch King's court. All made way for the brisk, commanding stride of Lord Nuarc, who swept past them without so much as a nod.

One long chamber led to another. In most druchii cities a drachau's audience chamber was divided into two spaces: the throne room proper and the lower room, where lesser highborn and common folk waited in hopes of a brief audience with their overlord. Here Malus counted no less than four lower chambers, each one large enough to hold a thousand druchii or more. Each room was slightly more ornate than the first; bare walls of polished black marble gave way to statues of druchii princes clad in the raiment of lost Nagarythe, which in turn gave way to titanic columns of red-veined basalt and bas-reliefs of mighty battles between the druchii and their foes. The final lower room was dominated by a tremendous flame that rose in a hissing, seething pillar in the centre of the chamber. The shifting light picked out threads of silver and gold in ancient, enormous tapestries that told of Malekith's suffering in the fires of Asuryan and the Seven Treacheries of Aenarion.

At the far end of the fiery vault stood a pair of iron doors twenty feet high, engraved with the sinuous forms of rearing dragons. The twin drakes seemed to glare down at Nuarc and Malus as they approached the Witch King's throne room. Four of the Endless stood watch at the doors with bared blades in their hands. They bowed as Nuarc approached and gave way before their master. With a single backwards glance at Malus, the warlord placed his hands on the great doors and pushed. The massive iron panels swung open on perfectly balanced hinges, throwing a rectangle of shifting blue light across a floor of gleaming black marble.

Nuarc stepped into the chamber, head held high. As Malus crossed the threshold he felt Tz'arkan contract fiercely around his heart, his power drawing back from his limbs like a swiftly receding tide.

'Step carefully here, little druchii,' the daemon hissed. 'And remember that there are worse things than death.'

Beyond the doorway the Court of Dragons was all but devoid of light. The change brought Malus up short, leaving him near blind and intensely vulnerable in the space of a single step – an effect that of course could only be deliberate. As his vision adjusted to the gloom he saw that he was standing at one end of a surprisingly small octagonal room, barely thirty paces across. Again, after the lofty space of the previous chambers Malus couldn't help but feel the weight of the dressed stone walls pressing in on him. All around the perimeter of the room stood huge dragons carved cunningly from onyx, their wings spread like cloaks as they bowed in obeisance before the tall dais at the far end of the room. There, in shadows as deep as the eternal Abyss, glowed a pair of red-orange eyes that shone with the banked fire of a furnace.

The huge iron doors swung silently shut behind Malus, plunging the chamber into darkness. Malus felt the burning gaze of the Witch King upon him and bowed his head in genuine fear and dread.

Nuarc's voice rang out in the blackness. 'As your dread majesty commands, I have come with Malus the outlaw, formerly of the house of Lurhan the Vaulkhar, late of Hag Graef.'

The voice that replied sounded like nothing formed from a living throat – it was as hard and unyielding as hammered iron, the words rumbling out like the hot wind from a forge. '*I see you, kinslayer,*' the Witch King said. Malekith shifted slightly in the darkness, causing red light to seep from between the seams of his enchanted armour. '*Did you think to escape my wrath, Malus Darkblade? Your father was sworn to my service, and lived and died by my command alone. There can be no forgiveness for such a crime.*'

Silence fell. Malus blinked owlishly as he considered the Witch King's words. Was this some kind of test? He shrugged, wondering if Malekith could see the gesture. 'As you wish,' he replied.

There was the sound of steel rasping against steel, and more ruddy light outlined the segments of the Witch King's form. *'Will you not beg for mercy, kinslayer? Will you not bow down before my throne and treat with me, offering all that you possess if only I would stay my wrath?'*

The suggestion took Malus aback. 'Am I to believe that you would be moved by such a pathetic display? Do I seem so foolish as that?' he said, his tone indignant. 'I think not. You are the Witch King. Who am I to persuade you of anything? If you mean to exact your vengeance upon me, then so be it.'

'Kneel, then, and show your fealty to me.'

Malus gave the Witch King a bitter smile. Part of his mind gibbered in terror at his effrontery, but he'd suffered enough humiliation at the hands of Tz'arkan to last a dozen lifetimes. 'Only a vassal bows his knee,' the highborn said. 'But I am a vassal no longer. I am an outlaw now, by your own decree.' He squared his shoulders, drunk on suicidal defiance. 'So I believe I would rather stand.'

The red eyes narrowed, and Malus knew he'd gone a step too far. He drew a deep breath, believing it to be his last – when suddenly a woman's laughter, rich and cruel, rang from the darkness beside the throne.

Pale green light flickered to life across the throne room, kindled in the depths of witchlamps set in iron stands arrayed around the chamber. Again, Malus was momentarily disoriented, his defiance forgotten. Through slitted eyes he dimly perceived a tall, black throne at the top of the dais, and upon that seat of barbed iron he glimpsed the terrible visage of Malekith himself.

But it was the laughter that drew the highborn's eye. A woman was gracefully descending from the dais, clad in black robes as befitted a druchii witch or seer. She was tall and regal, with features that seemed cruel even in the depths of her mirth. White hair fell past her waist, wound with gold wire and delicate finger bones. Her dark eyes flashed with a cold, draconic intellect, her stare cutting through him as cleanly as an obsidian knife.

'Tell me,' she said, her voice belling out in the same cold tones as the witches of the Endless, 'do you come by such reckless courage naturally, or does it come from the daemon curled around your heart?'

CHAPTER SEVEN

THE EMISSARY

The Witch King leaned forward upon his barbed throne. Visible heat radiated from the seams of his armour, blurring the air around him. '*Daemon?*' Malekith hissed, his burning eyes narrowing further. Behind Malus, just a few steps from his left shoulder, he heard the cold rasp of steel sliding from its scabbard.

Malus felt sharp talons sink into his heart. It might have been a warning from the daemon or it might have been a sudden rush of fear. Regardless, he took a few moments to master his composure before he answered the seer's question.

'My recklessness is the very reason there is a daemon inside me, Lady Morathi,' he said. He kept his gaze focused straight ahead, fearful of what else the seer might unearth from the depths of his eyes.

Morathi glided past him, circling him slowly. He could feel her icy gaze sweep over him, reminding him of the passing stare of the dragon in the courtyard outside. 'You are no sorcerer,' she declared, 'despite your parentage and the rumours of forbidden practices performed by your siblings.'

'It is a curse, dread lady,' Malus said quickly. 'The daemon entrapped me while I was on an expedition into the Chaos Wastes.'

'Entrapped? To what purpose?' the seer asked, as lightly as if she were inquiring of the weather. Her cold, unnatural voice was sweet, but like any polished tone it was brittle. If it broke, Malus dreaded to hear what lay beneath.

'It is entrapped in turn, dread lady, inside a crystal far to the north. I have been given a year to perform certain tasks to gain its freedom, or else my soul is forfeit.'

'Did one of those tasks involve killing your father?' Nuarc growled.

Malus glanced over his shoulder at the warlord, glad for any excuse to look away from the throne. 'Not directly, no,' the highborn said. 'Lurhan simply got in my way.'

'*The daemon forced you to do this?*' Malekith inquired.

Malus couldn't help but frown. Where was all this leading? 'Forced?

Certainly not, dread majesty. I am master of my own fate. But the circumstances were... complicated.' The highborn tried to think of a way to explain things, but gave up with a shrug. 'Let us just say it wasn't my choice. I did what I had to do.'

Lady Morathi appeared on Malus's left side, still studying him intently. They were close enough to touch and the force of her presence was tangible, like a cold razor being drawn delicately across his skin. She radiated power in a way that not even his mother Eldire did. Her face was youthful, her features regal and severe; she was handsome rather than classically beautiful, with a broad face and a rounded chin that was almost square rather than pointed. Her eyes were like windows onto the Abyss, drinking in everything around her. 'Does this daemon have a name?' she asked, her lips quirking in wry amusement.

She knows more than she's letting on, Malus thought. She's testing me, seeing how much I know. Again, he affected a shrug. 'If it does, it hasn't shared it with me,' he said. 'Why would it? Wouldn't that give me power to control it?'

'Daemons go by many names,' Morathi said. 'But only one true name, which they hide as best they can.' She stepped forward, pinning him with her gaze. 'What does this daemon call itself when it speaks to you?'

'Itself? Why, nothing,' Malus replied sourly, 'although it has more than a few choice names for *me*.'

Malus heard a harsh bark of laughter from Lord Nuarc. Morathi stared at him for a moment more, a faint smile quirking the corners of her mouth. 'I have little trouble believing that,' she said, then turned back to the dais. 'It explains much,' she said to the Witch King as she climbed the stairs to take her place beside the iron throne.

The highborn shook his head in consternation. 'From my perspective it explains nothing, dread majesty. Why have I been brought here, if not to answer for my crimes?'

A rumbling hiss escaped from Malekith's horned helmet. '*Oh, you shall answer for what you have done, Darkblade,*' the Witch King said. '*But the payment shall be of mine own choosing.*' Malekith stretched an upturned hand to the ceiling. '*Observe.*'

There was a ponderous groan of machinery overhead. Malus glanced upwards and saw a dark, circular opening in the centre of the domed ceiling. With a thunderous rattle of heavy iron links a spherical shape descended from the opening. First the witchlight picked out curved bars of polished iron, formed into a cage or basket large enough to hold a grown druchii. At first Malus thought the cage was meant for him, but as it sank closer he saw the greenish light reflecting on a huge, uncut crystal held within the iron frame. Suddenly the highborn realised what it was. 'The Ainur Tel,' he hissed.

Malekith nodded slowly. '*The Eye of Fate,*' he said. '*One of the few relics of power brought with us out of Nagarythe millennia ago, carved from the root of the world in aeons past.'*

The great crystal was lowered on four massive chains, sinking into the room until it hung directly before Malus's eyes. With a clash of gears the chains locked in place, and a mote of faint, white light began to glow within the crystal's depths. Slowly the light began to pulse, like the beat of a tremendous heart. The glow intensified with each beat, growing in strength until the huge crystal shone like a pale sun. Malus could feel its energies washing over his skin in turgid waves, setting his nerves on fire. It was all he could do not to recoil from the legendary relic. Only by a supreme effort of will did he manage to still his shaking limbs and look unflinchingly into the light.

Morathi's voice called out to him from the dais. 'Stare into the eye, son of Lurhan,' she said. 'Cast your gaze a hundred leagues to the north.'

Frowning, Malus stared fixedly into the white glare. At first he saw nothing. His eyes grew weak and his lids fluttered – then all at once the harsh light faded and Malus saw blurry images take shape within the crystal. He saw a single, blackened watchtower rising above a bleak and desolate plain. The walls of the keep were blasted and broken and the single gate had been smashed aside, buried beneath a mound of twisted, misshapen bodies. Moonlight shone on the armoured bodies of druchii warriors in the tower's courtyard, and Malus imagined many more in the burnt-out shell of the citadel itself. Hundreds of horned beastmen and savage, tattooed marauders lay among the fallen defenders, struck down by crossbow bolts or pierced by axe or sword. It was clear to him that the watchtower had been taken by storm, its warriors overwhelmed in a single, savage assault.

Within moments the vision blurred and reformed again. The image showed another watchtower, this one standing atop a rocky hill above a swift-flowing river. Again, the walls of the keep were blackened by fire, and the fortifications were gouged and torn as though clawed by monstrous hands. Armoured corpses were splayed across the battlements, and Malus could see a knot of charred corpses where the last of the citadel's defenders made their final stand at the foot of their burning tower.

The image shifted again. Malus was shown another ruined watchtower. His bemused frown deepened into a look of genuine alarm. He glanced worriedly at Morathi – and by the time he looked back at the glowing crystal it was showing yet another border keep that had been put to the torch. This one had been attacked within only a couple of days; tendrils of smoke still rose from the fires smouldering in the wreckage of the tower. Malus's eyes widened as he saw the rubble of the watchtower gate, crushed beneath the weight of a giant whose naked body had been riddled by the tower's powerful bolt throwers.

'What is the meaning of this?' Malus exclaimed. Raiding parties of Chaos-tainted savages riding out of the Wastes was an ever-present threat, which was why there was a line of watchtower keeps along the northern frontier. But raiders went out of their way to avoid the towers as much as possible rather than spend their strength against them. 'I've never heard of a border keep being overrun, much less *four* of them,' he said. A sudden thought sent a thrill down his spine. 'Is this an invasion?'

The Witch King pointed at the relic. '*Behold.*'

This time when the vision cleared Malus saw a sky full of fire. A dark tower stood against the backdrop of a burning forest, and beneath that roiling, flame-shot sky raged a horde of howling monstrosities that crashed in a frenzied wave against the watchtower's battered walls. Spear tips glinted atop the battlements and axes flashed as the beleaguered defenders hacked at scaling-ropes or fended off ladders thrown up by maddened beastmen and furious, blood-soaked barbarians. Crossbow bolts flickered in a black rain from the tall watchtower, wreaking havoc among the ranks of the enemy, but for every attacker that fell it seemed that three more rushed to take its place.

Huge shapes waded through the raging horde: hunched, misshapen trolls and terrible giants dragging clubs made from gnarled tree trunks. As Malus watched, twin streaks of light sped from the top of the watchtower and struck one of the giants squarely in its muscular chest. In an instant the huge creature was wreathed in unnatural green flame – the terrible, liquid dragon's fire both prized and feared by druchii alchemists and corsairs alike. The giant reeled in agony, beating clumsily at the hungry flames consuming its body and throwing off gobbets of sizzling, burning flesh that fell upon the Chaos marauders swirling about its huge feet. Malus imagined the furious cheer that no doubt rose from the battlements as the giant staggered, its face melting and its mouth open in a roar of mortal agony as it toppled onto a herd of onrushing beastmen with an earth-shaking crash.

But the assault did not falter. Other giants lumbered to the watchtower gate and began to batter it with their clubs, seemingly heedless of the stinging bolts that prickled their thick hides. Sorcerous lightning rent the burning sky and flocks of hideous, winged daemons swooped over the battlements, plucking spearmen from the ramparts and dropping them to the stones fifty feet below. Packs of snarling trolls reached the base of the walls and began to climb atop one another to reach the defenders, their beady black eyes glinting hungrily.

Another bolt of dragon's fire arced from the watchtower, striking one of the giants at the gate and setting it alight. The monster dropped its club and stampeded back through the oncoming horde, sowing carnage with every step, but the damage had already been done. Pulverised stone and shattered fittings spun through the air as the remaining giant smote the gate with its club and smashed it to the ground in a cloud of dust and debris. Into the breach swept the tide of savage marauders, and Malus snarled with impotent rage as he saw that the keep was doomed.

'Bhelgaur Keep has fallen,' Morathi declared, and the vision within the crystal faded to darkness.

Malus's mind raced as he tried to make sense of what he'd seen. 'I'm not familiar with Bhelgaur or any of the other keeps you showed me, but if they neighbour one another then that horde has torn a hole in our frontier defences more than *sixty leagues* across,' he said darkly. 'There must be tens of thousands of them.' He shook his head in terrible wonder. 'Such a thing isn't unheard of in the so-called Old World of the humans, but here? It's unimaginable.' The highborn turned to the Witch King, his former defiance and suspicion momentarily overcome by the glamour of war. 'What more do we know of these invaders, dread majesty?'

But it was not the Witch King who replied. 'Their scouts crossed the frontier almost a month ago,' Nuarc said tersely. 'Then came a flood of raiding parties, perhaps twelve or eighteen in number. Four of the watchtowers were struck within days of one another and their defenders put to the sword. Then the raiding parties came together into a single warband and marched on Bhelgaur Keep, the western anchor of our border defences.'

'That puts them within a few days' march of the Tower of Ghrond,' Malus exclaimed. If they made it past the Black Tower then the Chaos host would be at the northern end of the Spear Road and less than two weeks' march from the walls of Naggarond itself.

It was a full-scale invasion the likes of which Naggaroth had never seen before, the highborn realised at once. And it had struck the Land of Chill at the worst possible time, with the campaign season still underway and at least two-thirds of the nobility at sea or away from home. Now Malus understood why the Witch King hadn't marched on Har Ganeth when he'd learned of the uprising. What was more, he knew all too well how badly weakened the armies of the druchii were after the fighting in the City of Executioners and the brief but savage feud between the Black Ark and Hag Graef.

'But why now?' Malus said. 'Other than small raids the tribes of the Wastes have never warred against us. Who is leading this horde, and what does he want?'

Morathi eyed the highborn coldly. 'What, indeed?' she said.

At some unspoken command the doors to the throne room swung open, and Malus heard limping, shuffling footsteps slide across the polished floor. He turned – and his pale face twisted into a grimace of revulsion at the horrid figure lurching towards him.

The highborn's pallid skin was greenish-grey in the witchlight, darkening to a purple-black around the deep wounds in his forehead and neck. His armour had been savaged by blows from axe, sword and talon, scoring deep lines across his breastplate and tearing his right pauldron completely away. The noble's mail skirt was rent in a half-dozen places, and the robes beneath were stiff with rotting blood. Half of his left hand had been shorn away by a heavy blade, and his right arm ended in a chewed stump just above the elbow. Malus reckoned by the stench that the highborn had been dead for almost a fortnight.

Every inch of the noble's battered armour was covered with intricate runes, apparently inscribed with the druchii's own blood. His eyes were a ghostly white – no pupil or iris could be seen, and they glowed with sorcerous life under the gleam of the witchlights. The corpse, escorted by a pair of masked warriors, shambled towards Malus, apparently heedless of his presence. Hissing in disgust, the highborn backed away – and the revenant stopped, his head turning at the sound. Blind white eyes searched for Malus. The corpse's slack lips twitched as it tried to form words.

Malus's hand went to his hip, reaching instinctively for a blade that was no longer there. He glanced over his shoulder at Nuarc, who glared balefully at the animated corpse. 'What in the name of the Dark Mother is this?' he cried.

'This,' Nuarc growled, 'is Lord Suharc. His watchtower, near as we can tell, was one of the first to fall. Eight days ago a patrol found him stumbling along the Spear Road, and they followed him all the way to the gates of Naggarond itself.' The warlord's hand tightened on the hilt of his drawn sword. 'He came bearing a message from the master of the Chaos horde.'

Before Nuarc could speak further Morathi's voice rang across the hall. 'We have done as you wished, revenant,' she said. 'Malus of Hag Graef has been found and stands before you. Now deliver your message.'

The seer's command left Malus dumbstruck. But the revenant was galvanised by the news. With a sudden burst of energy the corpse stumbled towards him, reaching for the highborn's face with what remained of his ruined hand. Malus recoiled from the creature with a startled cry – only to fetch up against Nuarc, who grabbed the highborn by the back of the neck and shoved him rudely at the oncoming creature.

Cold, stinking flesh closed about Malus's face. He felt the splintered bones of the highborn's hand dig into his cheek as the revenant clumsily studied the shape of his features. With a savage cry the highborn wrenched free of Nuarc's grip and shoved the corpse away. It staggered backwards a few steps but did not fall, turning instead to face the iron throne. Air whistled through the pulped gristle of the revenant's throat as it filled its shrivelled lungs. When the corpse spoke its voice was a bubbling, croaking hiss, and Malus reeled in terror at the hideous sound. Bad enough that the words issued from the throat of a man long dead – worse still was the awful realisation that the voice was one he knew all too well.

'You hold your salvation in your hands, Witch King,' Nagaira said, speaking through the revenant's ruined throat. 'Even now your watchtowers lie in ruins, and my army marches on the Black Tower of Ghrond. The power of the Black Ark is broken, and Hag Graef has been dealt a crippling blow. Your kingdom lies upon the brink of ruin – unless you give this outlaw to me.'

The revenant raised its mangled hand and pointed to Malus. 'Deliver my brother, and the war ends in a single stroke. Otherwise the Tower of Ghrond will burn, and Naggarond will follow. Make your choice, Witch King. Naggaroth will burn until you do.'

A rumbling hiss echoed from Malekith's sealed helm. '*I have heard enough.*'

There was a rustle of movement and a flash of steel. The Endless drew and struck the emissary at the same moment, their swords slicing the revenant apart. As the head and the severed limbs struck the floor they burst into hissing flame, filling the chamber with a searing stench.

Malus swayed on his feet, still thunderstruck at all that had transpired. His half-sister had worshipped Slaanesh in secret for many years, but after he'd betrayed her to the Temple of Khaine months before she had escaped and sworn revenge on him. She had made obscene pacts with the Ruinous Powers that had granted her daemonic powers, but now this...

'Now the matter is clear,' Morathi said, fixing Malus with an appraising stare. 'It is not you she wants, son of Lurhan. She is after the daemon inside you. No doubt she believes that she can bend it to her will.'

With supreme effort the highborn got hold of himself. 'No doubt you are right, dread lady,' he said shakily. And who knows, he thought fearfully. Perhaps Nagaira can.

But that mattered little to Malus just then. His eyes darted about the throne room, taking in the position of the Endless and trying to gauge where Nuarc was standing. He had to escape, and quickly. Could he reach the warlord and take the druchii's sword? Could he call upon the daemon's strength to fight his way free? If he could somehow reach Spite he might have a chance...

Malus heard footsteps close behind him, crossing slowly from right to left. 'The Endless can be ready to ride within the hour,' Nuarc said, sounding near enough to be speaking in the highborn's ear. 'Now that we know where the Chaos horde is, we can give this witch what she wants and see them on their way.'

The highborn whirled, reaching for the warlord – only to find Nuarc's sword point less than a finger's width from his throat. Nuarc chuckled cruelly, shaking his head. 'Not so fast, boy,' he said. 'The witch didn't say anything about you getting to her in one piece, so if you want to keep your hands and feet you'll hold as still as a statue.'

Malus glared hatefully at Nuarc, but his reply was directed at Malekith instead. 'You cannot give her what she wants,' he snapped. 'It won't turn aside the horde. Nagaira will simply use me and the daemon to further her own plans of conquest.' He turned slowly to face the throne. 'She means to supplant you, dread majesty. Why else would she have raised so large an army?' How she'd managed to raise such a horde was another question altogether, the highborn thought.

The seer pursed her thin lips thoughtfully. 'Unless we could master the daemon ourselves,' she murmured. 'We could command it to slay the witch, then give Malus to her.'

'You can't control the daemon without its name,' Malus said quickly, trying to keep the desperation from his voice.

Nuarc stepped forward and seized a handful of Malus's hair. 'Then I say we send the witch his head and show her that the daemon will forever be out of her reach!'

'*Enough!*' Malekith roared, his armour flaring like an open furnace. '*No one makes demands of the druchii,*' he rumbled, leaning forward on his barbed throne. His red gaze burned against Malus's skin. '*She will get nothing from us but wrack and ruin.*' He stretched out an armoured hand and pointed imperiously at the highborn. '*You will see to this. When you slew the great Lurhan you deprived me of my rightful property. Now you belong to me instead.*'

Malus tried to tug his hair free, but Nuarc held him fast. 'I live to serve, dread majesty,' he growled through clenched teeth. 'What is your command?'

'*Go to the Black Tower of Ghrond,*' the Witch King said. '*Lord Kuall is the Vaulkhar there. It is he who failed to turn aside the Chaos horde, and you will express to him my displeasure.*' Malekith's armoured gauntlet clenched into a fist. '*Your exploits against Hag Graef are well known, son of Lurhan. Take command of the forces at Ghrond and lead them against the invaders until I arrive with the army of Naggaroth. You will hold them at the Black Tower until I arrive. Do you understand?*'

The highborn took a deep breath. He understood all too well. 'Your will be done, dread majesty,' he said without hesitation. 'I will serve you with all the vigour I possess.' As he considered the situation, his predatory mind saw a possible opportunity. 'There is one matter to consider, however,' he said carefully. 'The people of Naggaroth still consider me an outcast and a criminal. That will make it difficult to speak with any authority.'

Malekith glared implacably at the highborn. '*You are a member of my retinue now, Darkblade,*' he hissed. '*You will ride to Ghrond with the Endless and bear a writ signed with my name.*'

For the first time, Malus essayed a smile. 'Then I may reclaim my rights and status as a highborn?'

The Witch King paused, considering Malus carefully. '*In time, perhaps. Serve me well and you will be rewarded in kind.*'

'Yes. Of course, dread majesty,' Malus said, bowing deeply. 'Then, with your permission, I will return to my chambers and prepare to depart.' The sooner he got away from the iron fortress the better, he thought.

The Witch King dismissed Malus with a wave of his gauntleted hand. The highborn turned on his heel and strode swiftly for the chamber doors, giving Nuarc a defiant glare as he swept past. Already his mind was racing, contemplating all that he had to do when he reached the Black Tower.

For a short while at least, he would command an army again. He never dreamed such a day would come again. *And I have you to thank, dear sister,* the highborn thought with a feral grin.

As he reached the iron doors Morathi called after him. 'The daemon has sunk its roots deep into your flesh,' she said. 'What do you think is going to happen once you set it free?'

The highborn laid his hand on the iron panel. 'If I serve the daemon well it promises to reward me in kind,' he said, and then was gone.

CHAPTER EIGHT

THE BLACK TOWER

The pain built steadily as Malus stalked down the echoing corridors of the Witch King's palace, pressing against the backs of his eyes like steam swelling in a kettle. Blood pounded in his temples like a funeral drum, reverberating across his narrow skull until he swore he could feel it in his teeth. The highborn's thin lips pulled back in a feral grimace of pain, drawing uneasy glances from the nobles and state servants who stepped hurriedly out of his path as he swept by.

His limbs worked mechanically as his exhausted mind struggled to come to grips with his latest change of fortune. How had Nagaira managed to take command of an army? It had only been three months since he'd faced her in the tunnels beneath Hag Graef, when she'd attempted to destroy the city in an act of bloodthirsty vengeance. He had given her a terrible wound with the Dagger of Torxus, a magical weapon that severed the tie between body and spirit and pinned the soul to the spot where it was slain, to suffer as a tormented spirit for all time. Yet his half-sister had not died; like Malus, she had no soul for the dagger to steal. She had entered into a blasphemous pact with the Chaos Gods, receiving unimaginable powers in exchange for her service. Perhaps she had used her new-found might to subjugate some of the northern tribes, or perhaps they had been given to her as part of her arcane pact. The Ruinous Powers were free with their gifts, he'd learned bitterly, so long as their own interests were fulfilled as well.

And yet the sheer scope of Nagaira's actions staggered Malus. What were her true motives? It had to be more than mere revenge, surely. Was it Tz'arkan she was after, as Morathi believed? Could the daemon alone be worth so much effort? Malus felt a chill course down his spine as he considered the possibility. No less than five Chaos champions, mighty warlords and sorcerers all, had combined their fearsome powers to summoning and entrapping the daemon in the temple far in the north. As potent as they were, the champions knew that the daemon would make them more powerful still, and as far as the highborn had been able to determine,

Tz'arkan had done just that. For a time the champions had bestrode the earth like gods themselves, causing the world to tremble beneath their feet.

Nagaira would know the tales far better than he, Malus knew. His cold hands clenched into fists as he stalked the twisting corridors. She would understand the awesome potential of the being lurking beneath his skin, and would know how to bend it to her will.

Once I'm in her clutches she'll bargain with the daemon through me, Malus realised. His expression turned bleak. She might even let the daemon take my soul as a token of good will, then use the five relics to bargain with Tz'arkan for even more power. She would have her revenge upon him and grow vastly more potent in the bargain – the very sweetest sort of revenge, as far as he was concerned. And then? Who knew? Perhaps she would march on Naggarond anyway, coming to grips with Malekith himself. With Tz'arkan bound to her, Nagaira might just overthrow the Witch King and claim the Land of Chill as her own.

The pain continued to worsen as he left the Court of Dragons behind. The pressure behind his eyes sharpened into needle-like points that pricked out white pinholes of light at the corners of his eyes. After ten minutes it hurt just to breathe. The air seemed to rasp like a file over his lips and teeth. He staggered, throwing out a hand to steady himself against the bare stone walls as he forced his legs to carry him onward.

He reached the door to his chambers without realising it, fetching up against the oaken panels and fumbling for the iron ring in a blind haze of pain. How he'd found his way back from the court through the maze-like passageways of the fortress was a mystery that he hadn't the wherewithal to consider. The door banged open and he staggered into the brightly lit room, startling a trio of slaves who were busy laying out new clothes and arranging a set of polished plate armour on an arming stand at the foot of the bed. His stolen axe had been cleaned and sharpened, and lay gleaming on a tabletop nearby.

'Out, all of you,' Malus snarled, waving angrily at the blurry shapes that bowed uncertainly on the other side of the room. He staggered to the table and closed his hands on the hilt of the axe. 'I said *out!*' he roared, brandishing the terrible weapon, and the slaves fled from the room in a silent rush, their hands thrown protectively over their heads. As the door thudded shut he let the axe tumble from his hands and lurched to the bed, burying his face in the sheets with a bestial groan.

And then he heard the voice, hissing in his ears like a serpent. *You disappoint me little druchii,* the daemon whispered hatefully, and then he felt the nest of vipers coiled about his heart suddenly contract.

The pain was like nothing he had ever felt before. All the air went out of him; Malus gasped like a landed fish, his eyes wide and his hands clawing futilely at his armoured chest. The highborn slumped to the floor, rolling onto his side in a clatter of steel as he struggled for breath.

'What foolishness is this, bending the knee to that parody of a king and playing at war when you and I have unfinished business,' Tz'arkan continued. 'Have you grown too accustomed to my presence these last few months? Did you forget the bargain you and I made? I assure you, Darkblade, that I have not.'

There was a roaring in his ears, and his vision was turning red, like a tide of blood rising from the edges of his vision. Trembling with effort, Malus drew in a thin gulp of air. 'The relic...' he gasped. 'My... mother...'

The grip on his heart drew sharply tighter; for half an instant Malus was certain that it would burst. All he could see was red; with a faint groan the highborn squeezed his eyes shut.

'What does that witch have to do with this?' the daemon growled. Malus could feel the cold touch of Tz'arkan's anger in his bones. 'Is this another of her pathetic schemes?'

'She said... she said the path to the relic lies here,' the highborn moaned. 'Perhaps... it's... in the Black Tower...'

'Perhaps?' The daemon seethed. 'You would hang your very soul from so slim a thread?'

'For now it's... all I have,' Malus gasped. There was a roaring in his ears, growing stronger by the moment. Darkness beckoned, and he sensed he lay closer to death than he'd ever been before. 'Whatever she plans... I'm a part of it,' he whispered. 'So... she would not lead me... astray. Not yet at least.'

The daemon didn't reply. For a single, agonising instant, Malus felt Tz'arkan's grip continue to tighten – and then without warning it was simply gone. He sucked in air like a drowning man, rolling onto his stomach and biting his lip to keep from crying out. The daemon coiled and slithered within his chest, sliding black tendrils up the back of his neck and across his skull.

'Pray that you are right, little druchii,' Tz'arkan said. 'Whatever her motives, she is not the one you should be wary of. I grow stronger with every beat of your miserable heart. Soon I'll be able to hurt you in ways you can't even imagine. And I will be watching every move you make, Darkblade. Step carefully.'

He could feel the daemon's presence dwindle. The pressure in his head began to fade. It was several minutes before he could push himself upright and blink owlishly in the glow of the pale witchlights. Every muscle in his body ached. With a groan he slowly rose onto his knees. Heavy drops spattered on the stone beneath his head, and he realised that his upper lip was damp. Malus touched it with trembling fingertips, and they came away stained with a cold, black ichor.

There was a looking glass over by the now-empty bathtub. Malus staggered over to it, peering intently into the silvered pane. The face looking back at him was one he only barely recognised. His face was even more drawn and haggard than he remembered, the grey skin pulled tight over corded muscle and fine, white scars to create a fevered mask of cruelty and hate. Streams of ichor ran from his sharp nose, his pointed ears and the corners of his eyes.

His eyes! Malus realised with a start that they were no longer the colour of heated brass – instead the irises were orbs of polished jet, so large that almost no whites were visible. When had Tz'arkan's disguise faded? The thought that the daemon could now alter or change his body at its whim frightened Malus to the core.

Behind him, he heard the chamber door creak open. Hurriedly, Malus snatched up a damp cloth hanging from the edge of the bathtub and pressed it to his face. 'Take another step and I'll split your skull,' he snarled at the intruder.

'You're welcome to try,' came Nuarc's familiar rasp. 'But daemon or no, I think you'd regret it.'

The highborn masked his surprise by scrubbing fiercely at his cheeks. 'Your pardon, my lord,' he said. 'I thought you were one of those damned servants.' After checking to make sure he'd cleaned away the last of the ichor he quickly wadded up the stained cloth and tossed it into the tub. He turned to face the general, gesturing tiredly at the clothes and armour laid at the bed. 'Give me a moment to change and I can leave the fortress at once.'

Nuarc gave Malus a penetrating stare, his expression doubtful. 'You don't look fit to pull off your boots, let alone manage another forced march,' he growled, but then grudgingly nodded. 'Not that I expect you'd let such a thing stop you. You're a hard-hearted, spiteful bastard, right enough.' The warlord pulled a metal plaque from his belt and walked over to the highborn. 'Here is the Witch King's writ,' he said, offering it to Malus as casually as though he were sharing a bottle of wine. 'I'd caution you to use it wisely, but what's the point? With that piece of paper in your hand you can do damn well whatever you please and no one will look sideways at you.'

Malus took the plaque from Nuarc's hand. It was very like the Writ of Iron he'd once been granted by the drachau of Hag Graef. This one was a bit longer, perhaps eighteen inches long, and the protective metal was unpolished silver instead of steel. He opened the hinged plaque and studied the parchment within.

He had expected a lengthy statement detailing his rights and privileges in exacting detail. Instead there were just two simple sentences. *The bearer of this writ, Malus of Hag Graef, belongs to me and acts solely in my name. Do as he bids, or risk my wrath.*

Below the archaic line of druchast was pressed the dragon seal of Malekith, Witch King of Naggaroth.

Malus closed the plaque carefully, savouring the feel of the cool metal on his fingertips. This is what absolute power feels like, he thought. With that writ in hand there was very little he could not do within the borders of the kingdom. Only the highest nobles in the land were immune from his authority, and he answered to no one but the Witch King himself. A slow, hungry smile spread across his face.

'It's a trap of course,' the warlord said, reading the look in Malus's black eyes. 'You realise that I'm sure.'

The highborn paused, his smile fading. 'A trap?' he replied, setting the plaque carefully upon the bed.

Now it was Nuarc's turn to smile. 'Of course it is. Consider the situation,' he said, pacing slowly around the room. 'This sister of yours has attacked the kingdom at a time when we are at our most vulnerable. She knows this – her remarks about Hag Graef and the Black Ark tells us that she is well aware of how weakened we are. The only way to stop her is to keep her occupied long enough for Malekith to scour the cities for every warrior he can lay hands on and form a large enough army to match her.' The general pointed a long finger at Malus. 'And you are the one thing guaranteed to hold Nagaira's attention.'

Malus thought it over. 'If so, why not simply send me to the Black Tower in chains? Nagaira would still tear the city apart trying to get at me, writ or no writ.'

Nuarc gave Malus a sidelong glance. 'Put a druchii in chains and he'll look for the first chance to escape. Put a druchii in power and he'll fight like a daemon to stay there, regardless of the risk.' He crossed the chamber and picked up the writ. 'This piece of parchment is stronger than any chain ever forged,' he rasped. 'You may think yourself clever, but Malekith can see right through you. You are just another pawn to him. He'll use you as a stalking horse to draw Nagaira to the Black Tower, then once she has been beaten back you'll be nothing but an outlaw once more.'

Malus reached up and took the plaque from Nuarc's hand. 'Then why tell me all this? Aren't you betraying your master's secret designs?'

The warlord let out a harsh, rasping laugh. 'Better for the Witch King that you understand the position you are in, and to know that there is nothing you can do to change it! I've heard reports about your generalship in the latest fighting between the Black Ark and Hag Graef; you did passably well against Isilvar's forces. You're young and headstrong, but you've got a sharp mind underneath all that foolishness. What's more, you can be damned unpredictable, and that's the reason I'm here,' he said. 'I want you to understand how tightly Malekith has boxed you in. Don't try anything stupid; it won't work, and it will likely leave us in an even less tenable position than we're in now. The best chance you have of keeping your head on your neck is to follow orders and enjoy the power you've got while you've got it.'

'Until the danger is past,' Malus said coldly. 'And then you'll tie me to a pole at the crossroads.'

Nuarc met the highborn's gaze unflinchingly. 'Would you rather face your sister's tender mercies instead?'

Malus sighed. 'You've made your point, my lord,' he said, tossing the plaque back onto the mattress. He began working at the lacings of his armour. 'I should be ready to ride within the hour.'

'Very good,' the general said with a curt nod, then turned to leave the room. 'I'll send the servants back in to help you change and bring in a good meal. It'll likely be the only one you'll get for the next few days.'

Nuarc stepped into the corridor outside Malus's chamber, barking orders for the servants. Malus jerked the lacings of his breastplate free with sharp, angry movements, glaring balefully at the Witch King's writ as he worked.

The dark steeds of the Endless swept over the wooded ridge and thundered down the reverse slope, their lathered flanks heaving and their glossy hooves beating upon the packed cinders of the Spear Road as they came at last to the Plain of Ghrond. A light snow was falling, stirred into stinging gusts by a cold north wind that whispered among the dark pines.

At the top of the ridgeline Malus reined in Spite and surveyed the broad plain, baring his teeth at the biting wind. His cheeks and nose were already chapped from the cold, but the pain kept him awake and alert better than any dose of barvalk could. His exhausted, aching body reeled in the saddle; Nuarc had commanded the Endless to bear him to the Black Tower with all dispatch, and their pace had made the trip down the Slaver's Road seem leisurely by comparison. They stopped only once every few days for a cold meal and a ration of the dwarf liquor, and what little sleep the highborn got was on the move. Malus could no longer say for certain what day it was, but to the best of his reckoning they'd covered the week and a half ride to the Black Tower in just four days. Even the dark steeds seemed to be at the limits of their endurance, something the highborn hadn't thought possible.

Below him the lead riders of the Endless stirred up a cloud of pale grey dust as they galloped along the black ribbon of road that crossed the desolate plain. The ashen expanse stretched to east and west as far as the eye could see, while the horizon to the north was edged with a broken, iron-grey line of mountains that marked the edge of the Chaos Wastes. Perhaps a league to the north, rising out of the pale ash like a sentinel's black spear, rose the Tower of Ghrond.

Each of Naggaroth's six great cities served a purpose for the druchii as a whole: Karond Kar built the sleek black ships that corsair captains used on their slave raids, while Klar Karond was the clearing-house for the flesh trade that the corsairs supplied. Similarly, Har Ganeth forged the weapons and armour that armed the warriors of the state, while the Black Tower could be said to be the forge that made the warriors themselves. Every unit of troops raised across the Land of Chill was sent to the Black Tower to be trained in the arts of war. Units of spearmen and cavalry took their turn manning the watchtowers along the northern frontier and blooded themselves on cross-border raids into the Wastes, led by sons of prominent highborn families who were there to learn the rudiments of command.

The Black Tower was the lynchpin of the northern marches, built during a time when the druchii feared that an invasion from the Wastes was an ever-present threat.

The nauglir reached the base of the steep slope in a few loping strides, grumbling querulously as the highborn spurred the cold one into a ground-eating trot. What little he knew of the Black Tower had come from books in his father's library; Lurhan hadn't thought it necessary to give his bastard son the customary training that his elder sons had received.

Ghrond was a city only in the sense of its population and density of structures; in reality it was a permanent military camp, its buildings devoted solely to martial pursuits. The fortress city had a hexagonal-shaped outer wall more than forty feet high that was wide enough at the top for a troop of knights to ride their nauglir two abreast along its length. Each corner of the hexagon was further fortified into a triangular-shaped redoubt that was a citadel unto itself, with its own barracks, armoury and storerooms. The redoubts extended some ways out from the walls, so that archers and bolt throwers could fire down their length and catch attackers in a withering crossfire. Like the redoubts, the city's two gates were likewise fortified with imposing gatehouses that could rain death upon any attempt to break through their iron-banded doors.

From the southern gatehouse the sentries could see the entire length of the Spear Road, all the way back to the far ridge. As the Endless drew closer the forbidding wail of a horn rose above the battlements and the massive portal slowly swung open. One look at the silver faces of the riders and their black steeds was enough to convince the sentries of their identity.

Within minutes Malus was riding beneath the arch of the southern gate and into a narrow tunnel lit only by a handful of witchlamps. Heavy stone blocks seemed to press in from every side, and the highborn made out narrow murder-holes and arrow slits along both the walls and ceiling of the space. After about ten yards, the highborn was surprised to find the tunnel angle sharply to the right, then dogleg back to the left again. It made a difficult turn for wagons and an impossible one for a battering ram, he noted with approval. An attacker who managed to penetrate the first gate would find himself stuck in the dark confines of the tunnel and ruthlessly slaughtered by the gatehouse's defenders.

After another ten yards the highborn emerged from the inner gate into a small marshalling square lined with low, stone barracks. Foot soldiers were drilling in formation in the square, and the air rang with the clash of hammers from nearby forges as armourers readied the garrison for battle. The commander of the footmen raised his sword in salute as the riders passed, then resumed bellowing orders to his men.

The space between the outer wall and inner wall of the city was close-packed with barracks, stables, storehouses, forges and kitchens, organised into fortified districts that could operate as independent strongpoints in the event the outer wall was breached. An invader would have to spend precious time and thousands of lives clearing these buildings and fighting along the narrow streets before he even reached the inner wall itself. Malus had read somewhere that each building had been further built so that the people inside could collapse it when all hope was lost, further denying its fortifications to their conquerors.

Unlike other druchii cities, the streets of Ghrond were laid out in neat, orderly lines to facilitate the rapid movement of troops. Malus and the Endless made good time riding down the bustling avenues. Ahead of them loomed the black bulk of the fortress's inner wall, its spiked battlements rising sixty feet above the city's fortified districts.

Like the outer wall, the inner wall was built in a hexagonal shape with six small redoubts of its own and a single, solidly built gatehouse. Beyond rose the black tower itself, supported by lesser towers like any drachau's citadel and bristling with spiked turrets fitted with an array of heavy bolt throwers. As the highborn and the Endless were admitted through the inner gatehouse he could not help but shake his head in admiration. All of the power of the watchtowers combined could not equal the strength built into this fortress. A few thousand druchii could hold the Black Tower against a force more than ten times their number. It was an expertly designed death trap, built solely to ruin an invading army. And he, Malus noted bitterly, was meant to be the bait.

Beyond the inner wall Malus found himself in a small, shadowy courtyard at the feet of the great tower. A troop of Black Guard stood watch at the courtyard's far end, their white faces impassive and their wicked-looking halberds held ready. Attendants in light armour and the livery of the tower's drachau raced from an adjoining stable as the Endless slipped heavily from their saddles. Malus did likewise, pausing only to check the pack containing the daemon's relics and to run a possessive hand over the wrapped hilt of the warpsword. He felt its banked heat through the layers of cloth and was sorely tempted to draw it free and buckle it to his harness. Who here would recognise it, after all? But the memory of the slaughter at Har Ganeth forced him to push the temptation aside. He couldn't afford another mindless slaughter here. With a deep breath the highborn pulled his hand away, removing instead the axe from its loop on the nauglir's saddle and then checking to make certain that the writ was securely tucked into his belt. As he did so there was a clatter of steel as a young highborn dashed from the tower into the courtyard.

The young druchii clearly came from a wealthy family. The hilts of his twin swords were chased with gold and set with small rubies, and his lacquered armour was embossed with silver runes of warding and decorated with gold scrollwork. A hadrilkar of silver encircled his slender neck, worked in the shape of twining serpents. His narrow, pointed face was flushed from his quick sprint, and tendrils of black hair had come loose from the band of gold at the base of his neck. He surveyed the assembled riders quickly and sized up Malus as their obvious leader. The young highborn advanced to a proper hithuan and bowed deeply. 'Welcome to the Black Tower, my lord,' he said. 'I am Shevael, a knight in service to the drachau, Lord Myrchas. How may I assist you?'

Malus could well imagine the thoughts going through the young highborn's mind. His new armour was filigreed with gold and wrought with its own powerful spells of protection, and the heavy gold hadrilkar of the Witch King hung about his neck. Yet he bore no swords to mark his station; instead he clutched the worn hilt of a battle-axe in his had. *The boy probably thinks I'm Malekith's own executioner, come to pay a call on his lord the drachau*, the highborn thought. *And, as it happens, he's not far wrong.*

'Where is Lord Myrchas and his vaulkhar?' Malus said, his voice hoarse from exhaustion.

Shevael's eyes widened. 'I... he... that is, they are in council at present–'

'Excellent,' Malus replied. 'Take me there.'

The young highborn went pale. 'But... that is, perhaps you would care for some refreshment after your long ride?'

'Did I ask for refreshment?' Malus snapped. He let the axe hang loosely from his hands. 'Take me to your master, boy, or would you rather hear the Witch King's decree yourself?'

Shevael took a step back. 'No, of course not, my lord! That is – I mean – please follow me!'

The young druchii turned on his heel and strode swiftly to the tower. Malus followed, grinning wolfishly, and the Endless fell silently into step around him.

⚔ CHAPTER NINE ⚔

THE WITCH KING'S VOICE

The drachau's council chambers lay near the very top of the tower, which did nothing to improve Malus's mood. The climb, up narrow, twisting stairways and down dimly-lit, bustling corridors, seemed to last for hours. By the time the young knight led him and his Endless bodyguards into the council chamber's anteroom he was entirely out of patience. Pulling the writ from his belt he pushed past the startled Shevael and strode purposefully up to the chamber door. The two Black Guard halberdiers assigned to watch the door glanced from Malus to his silver-masked attendants and stepped carefully aside.

Smiling grimly, Malus put his boot against the door and kicked for all he was worth.

The oaken door swung open, rebounding from the stone wall with a thunderous bang. Nobles and retainers in the room beyond leapt to their feet with startled shouts and wrathful curses. Malus rushed within, catching the recoiling door with the flat of his axe and stopping it with a hollow clang.

Across the large, square chamber lay a broad table, covered with maps, parchment notes, wine goblets and pewter plates littered with half-eaten meals. A dozen armoured highborn and their retainers glared fiercely at Malus's intrusion, many with their hands on the hilt of their blades. Four more Black Guardsmen dashed from the shadows, two on either side of the axe-wielding highborn, the spearheads of their halberds aimed for Malus's throat.

Opposite the chamber door, at the far end of the table, sat an older highborn clad in ornate, enchanted armour. Sigils of coiled serpents were worked in gold across his lacquered breastplate, and his right hand was encased in a taloned gauntlet of a type that Malus knew all too well. It was the literal Fist of Night, the magical symbol of a drachau's authority. Lord Myrchas, the drachau of the Black Tower, studied Malus with small, bright black eyes. His long face, accentuated by a narrow, drooping moustache, was marked by dozens of minor scars from the bite of sword and claw. He reminded Malus somewhat of his late father Lurhan, which blackened the highborn's mood even further.

At the drachau's right hand stood a towering, lanky figure in ornate armour, marked with the sigil of a tower engraved upon his breastplate. He was older than Malus, but not so old as the drachau, and his skin was darkened by years of exposure from campaigning in the field. His sword belt and scabbards were studded with gems, doubtless looted on dozens of raids into the Wastes. The lord was bald as a nauglir's egg, and his face and scalp bore the marks of a great many battles. He might have been handsome once, but that changed the day his nose was broken for the fourth time and his right ear was shorn almost completely away by some foeman's blade. His left cheek was scarred and crumpled, lending his angry scowl a horrid, unbalanced cast. 'What is your name, fool?' the scarred druchii roared. 'I want to know whose head I'll be hanging from the spikes atop the inner gate.'

'I am Malus of Hag Graef,' the highborn replied coldly.

Lord Myrchas straightened. 'Malus the kinslayer?' he exclaimed. 'The outlaw?'

Malus smiled. 'No longer.' He raised the writ for the assembled lords to see. 'His dread majesty the Witch King has seen fit to put my notorious talents to good use.'

The drachau held out his taloned hand. 'Let me be the judge of that,' he declared. 'I've heard of your deeds, wretch. For all I know there's nothing in between those metal plates but a fish-wife's tally sheet.'

Malus bowed his head, genuinely amused by the drachau's accusation, and passed the plaque to the nearest lord, who in turn handed it around the table to Lord Myrchas. As the drachau opened the plaque and studied the parchment within, Malus waved a hand at the Endless. 'I suppose these would be the fish-wife's daughters in disguise?'

Lord Myrchas read the parchment, then scrutinised the seal closely. His face turned pale. 'Blessed Mother of Night,' he said softly, raising his eyes to Malus. 'The world has turned upside down.'

'As it is wont to do from time to time,' Malus said darkly. 'Which is why the Witch King requires the services of people like myself.'

The drachau blanched even further, and Malus couldn't help but feel a rush of cruel glee. This was a role he could come to enjoy, he thought. He turned to the tall lord next to Myrchas. 'Now you have me at a disadvantage, my lord. Who might you be?'

The glint of rage in the druchii lord's eye faltered slightly at the sudden change of events. 'I am Lord Kuall Blackhand, Vaulkhar of the Black Tower.'

Malus's smile widened. 'Ah, yes, Lord Kuall. I've come a long way in a very short time to bring you a message from the Witch King himself.'

A stir went through the assembled nobles. Even the drachau leaned back in his chair and stole a bleak look at the vaulkhar. Lord Kuall straightened at the news, the muscles bunching at the sides of his scarred jaws. Whatever his failings, the vaulkhar of the tower was no coward. 'Very well,' he said, his voice tight. 'Let's hear it then.'

Malus nodded formally. 'As you wish. My lord and master has watched your efforts here in the north since the coming of the Chaos horde, Lord Kuall, and he is displeased with what he has seen. *Very* displeased.'

Worried murmurs passed through the assembled lords, and the drachau's eyes narrowed warily. Lord Kuall, however, went white with rage. 'And what would Malekith have me do?' he cried. 'Meet that damned multitude in the field?' He snatched up a pile of parchments and threw them across the table at Malus. 'Has the Witch King read my scouts' reports? The Chaos horde is immense! When it moves it raises so much dust that you can see it from the sentry posts at the top of the tower. You expect me to form lines of battle and try to defeat such a force? We would be completely overrun!' He banged his armoured gauntlet on the heavy table, causing the goblets to jump. 'I've commanded the army of the tower for two hundred years, and I've lead countless raids into the Wastes. In all that time I've never seen a horde such as this. This fortress – ' Kuall pointed a finger at the ceiling – 'was built to break a Chaos horde against its walls. If you had an ounce of sense you could have seen that just riding through the gates. The only sensible course of action is to conserve our forces and prepare for the coming onslaught, where we can bleed the enemy dry against our fortifications.'

The assembled lords listened and nodded, casting uneasy glances between Lord Kuall and Malus. But the highborn was unimpressed.

'So while you cowered in your hole like a rabbit the enemy has systematically destroyed nearly a third of our frontier watchtowers,' he replied coldly, 'not to mention slaughtered hundreds of isolated troops who stood their ground expecting reinforcements that never arrived. Instead you cowered behind these walls to preserve your own skin, and now the kingdom will be vulnerable to Chaos raids for years to come.'

'The Chaos horde must overcome the Black Tower if they hope to press further into Naggaroth!' Kuall shot back. 'They have no choice but to attack us, and here we are in a position of strength.'

'Are you?' Malus said. 'If I recall correctly, slightly more than half your garrison is made up of cavalry. How useful will they be to you in a protracted siege, unless you plan on putting the cavalrymen on the walls and sending their mounts to the kitchens?' He glared hotly at the vaulkhar. 'You have a powerful, and above all, a mobile force at your command, Lord Kuall, and yet you feared to put it to the test against a mass of ignorant savages. Out of timidity you hoped to fight the enemy with half an army while you sat here in your chair and waited for Malekith to come to your rescue. That is not how our people fight, Lord Kuall. That is not how the state responds to animals that trespass on our domain.'

'You dare call me a coward!' Kuall shouted, tearing his sword from its scabbard. The gathered nobles backed hurriedly away from the enraged lord, knocking over chairs and upending cups in their escape.

'I call you nothing,' Malus sneered. 'When I speak it is with the Witch

King's own voice, and he calls you nothing less than a failure.' Malus gestured to the Endless. 'Take this wretch and impale him upon the spikes above the inner gate. With luck he'll live long enough to witness the defeat of the horde.'

The masked bodyguards swept forward in a silent rush, swords suddenly appearing in their hands. With a cry of rage, Kuall gave ground, threatening the implacable Endless with the point of his blade. But the warriors scarcely broke stride, advancing fearlessly into reach of the lord's long sword and trapping it with their own. Two more warriors seized Kuall by the arms, and within moments they were dragging the thrashing druchii across the chamber and out the door.

Malus savoured the shocked silence that fell upon Lord Kuall's sudden exit. His black eyes sought out the drachau and he waited for Lord Myrchas to make the next move.

The drachau met the highborn's stare, and Malus could see that Myrchas was weighing his options. For the moment the drachau was untouchable; as one of the Witch King's personal vassals he was beyond Malus's reach, but the reverse was true as well. Finally his expression softened slightly and the highborn knew he'd won.

'What is our dread majesty's command?' the drachau asked.

'The Witch King is assembling the army of Naggaroth and preparing to march here at once,' the highborn replied, feeling a thrill of triumph. 'Until such time as he arrives I will command the forces of the Black Tower.'

Myrchas bristled at the news. 'Malekith cannot name you vaulkhar without the approval of the tower lords!'

The highborn cut off the drachau's protest with a raised hand. 'I did not claim to be the vaulkhar, Lord Myrchas. I said that I will command the army. It is a fine distinction, but an important one, as I'm sure you'll agree.'

'Very well,' the drachau said darkly, realising that he'd been outmanoeuvred.

'Excellent,' Malus said, then raised his axe and embedded it in the tabletop with a thunderous crash. All of the assembled highborn leapt back with startled oaths, and Malus leaned forward and picked up an empty wine goblet with a fierce grin. 'Now as my first official command I want a bottle of good wine brought out, then you can tell me who you are and report as to the disposition of our forces.'

The reports lasted for almost three hours. Malus listened closely to each and every one, forcing himself to stay awake and drinking in every detail he could. His brief time as the lieutenant of Fuerlan's small force had in no way prepared him for the magnitude of commanding the army of the Black Tower.

Malus struggled with the names of the many highborn who came forward to report on one of the many facets of the garrison and the tower's defensive preparations. Lists were presented, detailing the numbers of troops in each regiment, the status of their equipment and their overall readiness, the quantity and quality of their food and the amount of time left in their training period before they were to be sent to their home city. Detailed tallies were given of arrows, crossbow bolts, heavy bolts, spare armour, spare shields, swords, spearheads, arrowheads, catapult stones, gallons of oil, bundles of torches –

'All right, all right!' Malus interjected, waving his goblet at the pair of highborn who were currently reporting on the status of the kitchens. 'I've heard enough.' The two druchii bowed quickly and returned to their seats, grateful to have escaped Malus's notice with their skins intact. Wincing painfully, the highborn shifted in the uncomfortable council chair and drained the dregs of the goblet in a single gulp.

The highborn did his best to collect his scattered impressions as he held out his goblet to be refilled by a waiting attendant. The Endless had taken up positions by the door, watching the council members from behind their implacable masks.

'It is clear to me that the Black Tower has not squandered its time since the appearance of the horde. Your preparations were misguided, but your dedication and effort are to be commended,' he said. The assembled highborn nodded their heads respectfully. Beside Malus, the drachau's high-backed chair stood empty. Lord Myrchas had taken his leave a couple of hours before.

The highborn focused on a druchii noble across the table who had introduced himself as the commander of the cavalry. He was a whipcord-lean figure in dark armour, swathed in a heavy cloak of glossy bearskin. Malus couldn't remember the druchii's name to save himself. 'Let us get back to basics. How many light cavalry did you say we had, lord...'

'Irhaut, dread lord,' the highborn replied smoothly. Lord Irhaut had a long, hooked nose and three gold earrings that glinted roguishly in his left ear, hinting at a successful former career as a corsair. 'We currently muster six thousand light horse, arrayed in six banners.'

Malus nodded. 'Very good.' He turned to the broad-shouldered highborn sitting beside Irhaut. 'And our infantry, Lord Murmon?'

'Meiron, my lord,' the highborn corrected with a pained expression. He had blunt, craggy features and unusually shaggy brows for a druchii. Malus wondered idly if Lord Meiron's mother hadn't mated with a bear to produce such a child. Lord Meiron consulted his reports and drew himself straight. 'We currently muster fifteen thousand spearmen and a thousand Black Guard in sixteen banners, although four of those banners are scheduled to return home–'

'No one is going home until the horde has been destroyed,' Malus said sternly. Lord Meiron blinked beneath his shaggy brows and nodded hesitantly. The highborn scowled. They've been training troops and leading raids for so long that they can't seem to comprehend anything else, he thought. Well, they'd have a chance to revise their thinking soon enough.

Malus realised his goblet was full and took a deep, appreciative draught. He made a mental note to get a tally of the fortress's wine stores when he had a moment. 'Lord Suheir,' he said, turning to the armoured giant on his right. 'How fare the household knights?'

Lord Suheir turned slightly in his chair to face Malus, appearing a bit surprised that his new commander actually remembered his name. Suheir was head and shoulders taller than any other druchii in the room, and looked strong enough to crack walnuts with his hands. If Lord Meiron's mother had mated with a bear, then Suheir's ill-fated dam had lain with a nauglir. He had a wide face and an almost square chin, an unfortunate combination for a druchii lord. 'The household knights are fifteen hundred strong,' he replied in a booming voice. 'As well as five hundred chariots that haven't been used in a single battle as far as I know.'

Malus rolled the numbers over in his mind as he swirled the wine in his cup. Twenty-four thousand troops! It was easily twice the size of any other garrison in Naggaroth, with the possible exception of Naggarond itself. The notion was far more intoxicating than any vintage he'd ever drunk. The amount of power at his disposal was immense. As he contemplated this his eyes fell to the burnished silver plaque resting on the table before him.

Now he understood Nuarc's words all too well.

The highborn took a deep breath. 'All right. What have we learned about the enemy?'

Heads turned. At the end of the table the oldest druchii present sat up straight in his chair and leaned forward, resting his elbows on the edge of the table. Lord Rasthlan's hair had more grey in it than black, and was pulled back and plaited with plain finger bones and silver wire. Unlike the other highborn he wore only a shirt of close-fitting mail over a kheitan cut in a rustic, almost autarii style. His right cheek was decorated with a swirling tattoo of a snarling hound – a mark of considerable honour among the shades, if Malus's memory served him correctly. Rasthlan certainly looked more at home among the cushions and rugs of an autarii lodge than sitting at a table with civilised folk.

'Our scouts have been tracking the horde since it came together after sacking the majority of the hill forts almost a month ago,' Rasthlan said in a gravelly voice. 'Kuall spoke truly: the army is the largest I have ever seen. Tens of thousands of beastmen, and human tribes besides.'

'Any heavily armoured troops?' Malus asked.

'None that my scouts saw, dread lord,' the scout commander replied. 'But there were giants, and great hill-trolls, and possibly even more terrible things marching along with them in the centre of the host. It appears the horde is led by a very powerful sorcerer or shaman, for the air reeked of dark magic.'

'You may be assured of that,' the highborn replied. 'So, what is your most honest estimate? How large a force are we facing?'

Rasthlan paused, swallowing hard. He looked to the men beside him. 'I could not say for certain, dread lord.'

Malus's dark eyes bored into the older lord. 'Give me your best guess, then. Thirty thousand? Fifty thousand?'

The druchii's gaze fell to the table. 'I wouldn't want to guess...'

'I understand,' Malus said, a hint of steel creeping into his voice. 'So you may take this as an order: tell me, in your best estimate, how large you think the Chaos horde is.'

Lord Rasthlan took a deep breath, then met the highborn's gaze. 'A hundred and twenty thousand, give or take,' he said levelly. 'I've seen them myself. They darken the plains with their numbers. It's like nothing I've ever seen before.'

The rest of the highborn looked uneasily at one another, shock evident in their expressions. Lord Suheir looked at his wide hands. 'Kuall had the right of it,' he said slowly. 'There's no way we can challenge such an army in the field. It would be a massacre.'

Even Malus himself was shocked at such a number, but he kept his face carefully neutral. He studied Rasthlan closely. 'Are you certain of this?' he asked.

The scout commander nodded at once. 'I didn't want to believe it myself, which is why I went and counted their numbers myself.'

Malus nodded slowly, his gaze dropping to the map spread across the table. 'And where are they now?'

Rasthlan rose from his chair and came around the table. 'The horde moves slowly,' he said, 'Less than a dozen miles or so a day. After razing Bhelgaur Keep they turned towards the Black Tower, which means they would be about here.' He pointed to an area of foothills north and west of the Plain of Ghrond, perhaps fifteen leagues distant.

Malus considered the distances and studied the terrain. For the last four days he'd been thinking over all that Nuarc had told him, trying to find a way out of the many snares that had been laid for him. One plan after another had been discarded, until an idea struck him in the early hours of the morning that suggested a possibility of success. Now, looking at the map, he made up his mind. 'Very well. My thanks to you gentlemen. You've given me everything I need to develop a plan of action.' He threw back his head and finished off the contents of the goblet, then set the wine cup carefully on the tabletop. 'It's been a very long day for all of us, I expect. I'm going to find a bed and get a few hours' sleep. We will meet again on the morrow, when I will provide detailed orders for each of the divisions.' Bracing his hands carefully on the arms of his chair, the highborn pushed himself to his feet. 'Until then, you are dismissed. I suggest you all get as much rest as you can. There will be little of it to go around in the next few days.'

The army staff rose to their feet, exchanging bewildered glances as Malus strode purposely towards the door. Finally it was Lord Suheir who summoned up enough courage to speak. 'Dread lord?'

Malus paused, his head swimming with wine and fatigue. 'Yes?'

'Is there something you know that we don't?' he rumbled. 'Lord Rasthlan says that the horde is moving only a dozen miles a day. That means they won't reach the Black Tower for almost a week.'

Malus looked at the captain of knights and gave him a wolfish smile. 'I know. That gives us just enough time to launch our attack.' Then he disappeared from the room, bounded by the swift shadows of the Endless.

CHAPTER TEN

WARRIOR OF NAGGAROTH

Malus dreamt he was back in the forest near the City of Executioners, racing through the close-set trees beneath the light of the twin moons. Something was following him; he could hear its ponderous footfalls and the brittle crack of the tree boughs as it forced its way through the woods in his wake. And he knew somehow that if whatever it was managed to catch him it would consume his very soul.

His armour and axe were gone, and the brambles tore at his face and clothes. Like razor-edged claws they shredded his thick kheitan and the robes beneath, and peeled away the skin across his cheeks and forehead. Hot blood coursed down his skin, but he felt no pain. He felt nothing but pure, mortal terror that the thing was going to catch him no matter how hard he ran.

And, sure enough, the heavy footfalls sounded closer, as though his pursuer were a giant, covering leagues with every step. Choking back a cry of fear he ran all the harder, the branches and the briars cutting ever deeper into his skin. He longed to find Spite, but the nauglir was nowhere to be seen. Malus strained to hear the familiar howl of the cold one, thinking it had to be hunting somewhere deep in the wood, but he could hear nothing over the pounding of his heart and the steady *thump* of his pursuer's tread. It sounded as though it was just a few scant yards behind him now; the skin on the back of his neck prickled, but he didn't dare look back, fearful of what might be reaching for him with outstretched talons.

Then without warning he burst into a thickly wooded hollow, finding himself on his knees on a narrow game trail running along its length. With a shudder of relief he realised where he was.

The tree. He had to find the tree. If he could climb back inside his pursuer couldn't find him.

Frantically he leapt to his feet and ran north along the path until he found the bloodstain he remembered on the trail. His heart hammering in his throat he risked a quick glance behind him, and saw that for the moment his pursuer was still just out of sight. Quickly he circled the broad stain and dived deep into the woods on the western side of the path. Thorny vines and brambles cut deep into already bleeding wounds, but he pushed on nonetheless, praying to the Dark Mother that the darkness and the vegetation would conceal him.

Within moments he found himself beside the blasted tree. The old trunk shone softly in the moonlight, like a gift from the goddess. Stifling a cry of relief he forced himself into the dark cleft. Showers of insects and rotten wood rained down on him as he straightened in the darkness, and he took it as a blessing from the goddess.

In his dream the tree was larger inside than without. He turned as the footsteps drew nearer, backing away from the thin slice of moonlight coming through the cleft from outside.

The footfalls were so close now that he could feel the earth tremble with each step. *Thud. Thud. Thud.* He held his breath, his eyes fixed on the thin slant of moonlight before him.

A shadow passed across the cleft. Malus saw a pair of booted feet through the slanted opening, barely a yard away from his hiding place. He took another involuntary step back, deeper into shadow.

The boots shifted left, then right. A voice called out. 'I know you're here little druchii,' Tz'arkan said, his voice slick and deadly as oiled steel. 'It's no use hiding. I can smell you. You're almost close enough to *taste*.'

A shudder passed through Malus at the sound of the daemon's voice. The boots shifted back to the right – then paused. One foot stepped towards the tree.

'Are you in there?' the daemon said. 'Yes, I think you are.'

A scream bubbled up in Malus's throat. He took another step back and fetched up against the uneven bole of the tree. He smelled rot and the wet stink of earthworms. The substance behind him gave slightly beneath his weight, like soft flesh.

Then a hand reached around him and pressed tightly over his mouth and another snaked tight around his waist. Malus smelled the stink of the grave and tasted putrefied flesh on his lips. Worms wriggled from the dead thing's wrist and landed, squirming, on his throat.

'Do not fear, my lord,' a familiar voice breathed in his ear. A cold breath, foul with the stench of rotting meat, lay damply along his cheek. 'The daemon cannot have you. I claimed you first.'

Malus writhed and squirmed in Lhunara's embrace, but her dead limbs held him in an iron embrace. He could smell nothing now but fleshy rot and the bitter smell of grave-dirt. His frantic gaze turned to the shaft of light and he saw the daemon pause outside, suddenly unsure. He tried to scream, to call out the daemon's name. Better to offer up his soul to the daemon's hunger than linger one moment more in Lhunara's foul embrace! But her gelid hand clamped his mouth tightly shut, and he could not get enough air through the reeking miasma that seeped from her decaying skin.

Outside, the boots turned slowly away. 'You can't hide forever, Darkblade,' the daemon called. 'It's only a matter of time before I find you.' Then, to Malus's horror, Tz'arkan walked away. The heavy footsteps receded quickly into the distance.

A cold, slimy tongue traced lightly along the side of Malus's neck. 'You see, I told you I would keep you safe,' Lhunara said, her breath close against his throat. 'No one is going to hurt you but me.'

Then her perfect teeth bit deep into his skin, and for the first time he found the breath to scream.

'My lord! My lord, wake up!'

Malus awoke staring upwards at a starry sky framed by an arch of stone. He lay upon his back, dressed only in a sleeping robe that had somehow tangled around his legs. A cold wind blew against his cheek, tasting of snow. His heart laboured painfully in his chest, hammering like the drumming feet of a charging nauglir.

A dark silhouette hovered over him, backlit by the moonlight. He thrashed violently, still partially in the grip of the nightmare and the figure gripped his arm tightly. 'Be still, my lord! You could throw yourself over the rail!'

The sharp warning penetrated his dulled senses. He blinked away the last vestiges of the dream and realised that he lay on the floor of a narrow balcony, high up on the flank of the Black Tower. Moving slowly and cautiously, he sat upright, helped along by the strong hands of the shadowy attendant. Malus looked out across the white plain, which shimmered faintly in the moonlight. He saw the dark mountains off to the north, limned with the shifting light of the northern aurora. Off to the north-west he could just make out a faint white line of foothills. Beyond them, many leagues north and west, lay Nagaira and the Chaos horde.

'A dream. A terrible dream,' he said to himself, rubbing dazedly at his chin. His body ached and his mouth tasted like a chamber pot. 'I drank too much,' he said absently. 'Never again. Do you hear that Hauclir? Never again, you damned rogue. No matter how much I beg.'

'Hauclir, my lord?' the figure said worriedly. 'It's me, Shevael. The drachau assigned me to serve as your retainer. Don't you remember?'

Malus turned away from the balcony rail and stared closely at the man beside him. 'Ah. Yes. Shevael,' he said in a hollow voice. 'Shevael. Never mind my rambling, lad. It's just wine and memories.'

'Yes, my lord, of course,' the young highborn said, sounding anything but reassured. 'How did you come to be on the balcony in the first place? When I last checked you were sound asleep in your bed.'

Malus rose unsteadily to his feet. The double doors leading from the bedroom to the balcony were wide open; within he could see the banked glow of a pair of braziers, weakly illuminating the wide bed and the tangle of bed sheets that pointed like a trail to where he lay.

'I must have got up in the night,' he said weakly. But he recalled the time in the forest when he'd awoke far from where he'd bedded down. What in the Dark Mother's name is happening to me, he thought? For the first time he found himself missing the constant presence of the Endless. After escorting him safely to the Black Tower and seeing him installed as the commander of the army their duty was done, and they left him to begin the task of preparing a set of chambers for the Witch King's imminent arrival.

The highborn let Shevael lead him back to the bed and pile the sheets and blankets over him. Malus stared at the ceiling. 'What is the hour?'

'It is the hour of the wolf, my lord,' the young highborn answered. 'Dawn will break in another hour and a half. Light comes early this far north.'

'I know, lad, I know,' Malus answered. 'Let me rest here until daybreak, then turn me out. We'll be on the march by midday.'

'Very good, my lord,' the young highborn answered, and retreated from the room. At the door he paused to glance fearfully at the highborn, then slipped out of sight.

Malus paid no heed. He was lost in thought, staring though the open balcony doors at the shifting lights to the north.

The thunder of three thousand marching feet reverberated down the length of the marshalling square and vibrated against Malus's ribcage. He felt the measured tramp of boots through the heavy stone of the outer gatehouse, and it brought a feral smile of joy to his pallid face.

He had issued his orders scarcely an hour past dawn, and the forces he'd chosen had assembled in good order barely three hours after that. To their credit, his highborn staff hadn't blinked an eye when he'd laid out his plan. Possibly they'd drunk their fears into submission the night before, much as he had.

The scouts, as always, were the first to depart. They'd left almost immediately after meeting with his lieutenants. Lord Rasthlan had left with them, garbed in dark robes and mail just like the autarii themselves. Glancing up at the midday sun, Malus reckoned that the shades were leagues away by now.

Just an hour before a fanfare of horns sounded from the outer gatehouse, and the first three banners of cavalry left as the army's vanguard. The last few squadrons of those horsemen were just departing through the massive gate, and the regiment of Black Guard were crossing the square next. Their captain raised his sword in salute to Malus as they passed beneath the high arch, and he returned the gesture proudly with his upraised axe.

Beyond the Black Guard waited two more regiments of spearmen, then the household knights and the cold one chariots, destined for the battlefield at last. Farther still waited the remaining three banners of the light cavalry to act as the rearguard. The garrison's entire cavalry force and almost a quarter of its infantry – almost half of the entire army, on balance – were being wagered on a single, desperate gamble. The thought chilled him to the marrow, but anything less would have doomed the expedition to certain failure.

Suddenly a loud commotion arose at the far end of the battlements. Malus heard angry shouts over the heavy tramp of feet and glanced along the walkway to see what was happening. The soldiers of the gate watch who were watching the army alongside him suddenly shifted and dodged about as a single figure stormed down the battlements in Malus's direction. The highborn couldn't see who it was, but he had a fairly good idea.

He straightened and made certain his gleaming armour was presentable as the drachau of the Black Tower burst into view. Lord Myrchas was livid, his entire body trembling with rage.

'What do you think you are doing?' the drachau said in a strangled voice. 'Stop this madness at once and return these troops back to their barracks!'

Malus bowed his head regretfully. 'I cannot,' he replied. 'And you have no authority to command me, even if I were your vaulkhar.'

For a moment it looked as though Myrchas would reach for his sword. His hands trembled with fury… and no small amount of fear, the highborn imagined. 'You cannot defeat the horde in pitched battle!' the drachau cried. 'You're sending these men to certain death and leaving the Black Tower defenceless!'

'Defenceless?' the highborn arched an eyebrow. 'Hardly. I've left you with thirteen thousand well-trained spearmen to defend the fortress walls. That should be more than sufficient to hold the Black Tower against ten times their number. And if my plan succeeds, they will not be needed at all.'

The drachau would not be mollified. 'But the horde–'

'My lord, I have no intention of fighting the Chaos army in a pitched battle,' Malus snapped, fixing Myrchas with a fiery stare. 'A horde like that is not held together by training or discipline. It is a clumsy weapon wielded rather tenuously by its war leader. If the leader dies, the army will turn upon itself like a pack of maddened dogs.' Malus pointed a gauntleted finger northward. 'I am taking the most mobile force I can manage and I plan to launch a night attack aimed right at the horde's beating heart. We're going to cut our way to the war leader's tent and I plan on splitting her skull myself.'

'Her?' the drachau said, momentarily confused.

'Never mind, my lord,' Malus said. 'The point of the matter is that a quick, decisive strike could stop this invasion in its tracks. I need the cavalry's mobility and hitting power, and the spearmen will provide a solid rearguard for the squadrons to rally behind.' He leaned close to the drachau. 'Think of the glory when Malekith arrives with his army to find the war leader's head hanging from a gatehouse spike. They'll sing of your heroism the length and breadth of Naggaroth.'

Myrchas thought it over. A faint gleam of avarice shone in his eyes. 'The rewards for such a victory would be great,' he allowed, then frowned worriedly. 'Are you absolutely certain this will work?'

The highborn shook his head. 'Nothing in war is certain, my lord. But believe me when I tell you that while the Chaos war leader is a mighty sorceress, she has no experience whatsoever as a general. She will not expect an attack like this, which gives us a great advantage. At worst we will be able to inflict tremendous losses and sow terrible confusion on the enemy, which will allow us to retire back to the fortress in good order.'

Malus put every ounce of sincerity he possessed into his argument. He believed in the plan; it was the only one he could conceive that would give him a chance of escaping Malekith's clutches, locating the relic and fleeing northward in time. If he could kill Nagaira before the Witch King arrived with his army then he would be able to use his temporary authority to search for the relic in the Black Tower – and the ruins of the Chaos encampment if necessary – without interference. Then he could slip out of the fortress and disappear into the Wastes with no one the wiser.

The highborn struggled to remain patient while the drachau thought it over. Finally, Myrchas nodded. 'I can find no fault with your plan,' he said at last. 'Go with the Dark Mother's blessing and sow fear and loathing among our foes.' He smiled. 'Naturally I regret not being able to accompany you–'

'Say no more, my lord,' Malus assured him. 'Someone must remain behind to command the garrison and await the Witch King's arrival. With luck I should return with the army in about five days.'

The drachau smiled. 'We will be awaiting your return,' he said. 'And now that you mention it, there are a great many matters that I must see to before the Witch King arrives, so I will take my leave.'

'Of course, my lord,' Malus said, bowing deeply. He held the bow as the drachau hurried away, hiding the grim smile of satisfaction on his lips.

The army marched for the rest of the day and well past nightfall. Malus kept the pace brisk but measured; he'd had enough forced marches in the last two weeks to last a lifetime. Spite seemed to have recovered completely from his exertions on the road with little more than a day's rest and half a ton of horseflesh to renew his strength.

On the following day they marched at a cautious pace through the foothills, awaiting the first reports from the far-ranging scouts. Malus kept the army moving at a walk, both to minimise the amount of telltale dust and to avoid running headlong into the oncoming Chaos army. Timing their approach to the horde would be the trickiest part of the attack.

At midday Lord Rasthlan appeared before the vanguard with a pair of autarii in tow. Malus called a halt and met the scouts beneath the shadow of a copse of fir trees on the reverse slope of a low hill.

'Where are they?' the highborn asked as Shevael passed bread, cheese and wine to the tired-looking scouts.

'About five leagues to the north,' Rasthlan said, drinking deeply from his cup. The shades crouched beneath the trees and ate in silence, gazing inscrutably at Malus. Lord Rasthlan tore off a hunk of bread and stuffed it quickly in his mouth, nearly swallowing it whole. 'They've picked up their pace somewhat, but they shouldn't cover more than two or three leagues before nightfall,' he continued.

Malus nodded thoughtfully. The distance would be just about perfect. 'Do you know for certain where the war leader's tent can be found?'

Rasthlan grimaced and shook his head. 'The Chaos savages are thick as flies along the ground,' he said. 'From the edge of their encampment it is nearly three miles to the centre. Too risky to penetrate, even for these ghosts,' he said, indicating the autarii. 'The war leader's tents will lie in the middle of the camp. They should be easy to find, even in the dark.'

The highborn nodded. 'Will your men be ready by nightfall?'

One of the autarii snorted disdainfully. Rasthlan grinned. 'They are ready now, my lord,' he said. 'We will uphold our end of the plan, never fear.'

'Very well,' Malus replied, feeling the first twinges of anticipation. 'Then we wait here until nightfall.' He turned to Shevael. 'Summon the division commanders to attend a war council in three hours to go over final preparations,' he ordered. As the young highborn rushed off, Malus turned back to the scouts. 'And as for you, I suggest you get some rest. It will likely be a very long night.'

The larger of the two moons was still low on the horizon when the army rose from their temporary camp and began their march to the enemy encampment. During the day they had wrapped their arms, armour and tack in layers of cloth to muffle any telltale noises while they moved. Each regiment and banner marched with a pair of autarii in the lead, holding small, shuttered witchlamps to signal their fellows and act as pathfinders, guiding the army to its objective.

Solitary flakes of snow drifted from a seemingly clear sky, and Malus's breath sent frosty plumes into the air as he rode alongside the household knights. They travelled in remarkable silence for so huge a force, and the highborn could not help but admire the mettle of the troops under his command. A general with sufficient daring could do much with such an army at his back, he mused, and smiled up at the starry sky.

It took more than two hours to travel two leagues across the foothills, then the pathfinders raised their lanterns and called a halt. As the army slowly ground to a stop, Rasthlan suddenly appeared at Malus's side. 'You may form your lines here, my lord,' he whispered, as though the Chaos troops were just on the other side of the hill instead of nearly a mile away. 'We will go ahead from here and deal with their sentries,' he said. 'Wait for the signal.'

Malus nodded. 'The Dark Mother's fortune be with you, Rasthlan,' he said, and the old druchii vanished like a spectre.

Lantern signals were passed all along the column, and slowly, carefully, the army formed line of battle behind the slope of a long, wooded ridge. Once again, the shades and their shuttered lanterns were invaluable, guiding each regiment and banner into the proper position with a minimum of confusion. Still, it was nearly two hours before the army was properly arrayed. After that there was nothing to do but watch the moons creep across the sky and try not to focus too much on the battle ahead.

The wait seemed to last forever. Each moment Malus strained his senses to detect the slightest sign of alarm, even though he knew intellectually that he was too far away from the enemy camp to hear anything short of war horns. Knights shifted uneasily in their saddles, the creak of leather seemingly sharp as a thunderclap to the highborn's strained nerves. Nauglir grunted and stamped. Tiny bits of harness jingled despite every precaution. After almost an hour Malus discovered that his fingertips had gone numb from holding the reins in a nervous, white-knuckled grip. With a deep breath the forced himself to relax and slowly unclenched his aching hands.

Then came the sign they were waiting for. A hunched figure appeared at the top of the hill and flashed open the cover of his shuttered witchlamp: once, twice, thrice. Other pathfinders were sending the same signal all along the druchii line; the shades had done their deadly work and slain the enemy sentries along a one-mile front. There would be no one to give warning to the beastmen and marauders slumbering in their tents until it was far too late.

Malus looked to the left, just spying the edge of the banners of horse that stretched away to his flank; a similar formation waited at the right end of the knight's battle line, their loose formations stretching for more than a mile to either side. To his immediate right, the bristling line of the household knights checked their reins and stirrups and quietly drew their blades. Behind the knights waited the long line of scythe-armed chariots. A torch burned low in the back of each war machine, ready to light the arrows of the archers who waited alongside the charioteers. Still farther back, the highborn could see the three regiments of spearmen, dressing their lines in long ranks of two. Their spearheads glinted cruelly in the moonlight, though if all went well the footmen would never enter the battle at all. They were a veritable wall of silver and steel that disorganised cavalry units could retreat to and shake off any pursuers so they could rally and return to the fight.

Slowly and deliberately the highborn reached down and unhooked the axe from his saddle. He'd been sorely tempted to carry the warpsword into battle instead, but once again the episode at Har Ganeth gave him pause. What if he succumbed to the killing madness again at a time when he needed to be clear-headed and issue orders to the army? There were no guarantees, he finally admitted, and so he'd left the blade – and the bag with the relics – back at the Black Tower. As much as it worried him to leave the artefacts untended, worse still was the thought of them falling into the hands of his half-sister by some awful mischance. She'd already taken the items from him once before; Malus doubted he'd be so lucky as to retrieve them again.

He turned to the household knights, arrayed in a gleaming line two ranks deep that stretched off into the darkness for more than half a mile, well beyond his line of sight. Closest to the highborn were Lord Suheir, the knight-captain and Malus's retainer Shevael. Both eyed him with a mixture of excitement and wary unease. Every man in the small army knew what they were up against; he'd made certain of it before the troops left the Black Tower. If they won, the Chaos threat would be over. If they lost, few if any of them would return home again. They had to win or die.

Malus leaned over in his saddle and spoke quietly to Suheir and Shevael, certain that his words would be repeated on down the line. 'Remember, we are the spear tip,' he said, his expression fierce. 'Leave the chariots and the light cavalry to do most of the butcher's work. Our only task is to cut our way to the Chaos war leader's tent at the centre of the camp, regardless of the cost. Once we're there, I'll put an end to this invasion once and for all. Clear?'

Both men nodded solemnly. Already he could hear the next men in line whispering his words to the comrade beside him.

Lord Suheir raised his curved sword in salute. 'We are with you, my lord,' he rumbled.

Malus nodded and sat up straight. At that moment he realised that twelve thousand men hung on his next word, awaiting the command to unleash a grim slaughter upon their foes. He smiled to himself, savouring the sensation of power. Suddenly the risks inherent in his plan became meaningless. Could any risk in the wide world be great enough to sour the terrible joy he felt?

The highborn turned his gaze to the summit of the wide hill before him and raised his axe high into the air. 'The household knights will advance,' he said in a low voice, then brought the weapon down in a shining arc. 'Forward!'

Spite lurched forward at a steady walk, head lowering as it sensed that a battle was close to hand. The cold ones of the front rank followed suit, rippling forward like the flick of a long, steel whip. Malus spurred the cold one up the hill slope, eager to crest the summit and see what he could of the vast movement occurring around him.

When he reached the top of the hill he looked immediately ahead and found only more rolling terrain stretching off to the horizon, but to left and right the light horse were surging in a black tide over their own series of foothills, moonlight burning coldly on the tops of their long spears. Behind him came the faint rattle and groan of chariot wheels, growing steadily quieter as the war machines picked up speed.

The druchii army swept across the hills like storm clouds, low thunder murmuring in the fall of thousands of shining hooves. Malus raised his axe once more at the top of the next hill and swept it downwards. As one, eight thousand knights and cavalrymen spurred their mounts to a trot.

Now the earth shook with the heavy tread of the cavalry, and the iron wheels of the chariots added their own deep-throated rumble as they picked up speed. The barren hills were flashing past now. The nauglir of the household knights were gliding over the rolling terrain like hunting hounds, venomous drool trailing from their dagger-like fangs. As they rode the wind shifted, and in the distance a herd of northern ponies shrieked in terror as they caught the cold ones' scent. Malus could just catch glimpses of dark tent roofs a half-mile ahead, just beyond a trio of low, broken hills. The highborn swung his axe over his head and put the spurs to Spite's flanks, urging him into a canter.

Spite plunged down the steep slope and bounded swiftly up the opposite hillside, long legs at full extension and a growl rumbling from the cold one's snout as it scented prey just ahead. This time when they streaked over the summit Malus saw that the rolling slopes beyond were carpeted in low, round tents made from crudely sewn hides. The tents of the horde covered everything from horizon to horizon, darkening the hillsides and hollows like a vile disease. The stench of spilled blood and corrupted flesh rolled over him like a cloud, thick enough to hang like a faint haze over the squalid tents of the camp.

The sheer size of the horde struck Malus like an invisible blow. It was one thing to comprehend what a hundred thousand troops represented, but another thing entirely to see it with one's own eyes. We're like a bucket of water being thrown into a furnace, he finally realised. How can we possibly defeat such a foe?

Despair began to seep like poison into his heart – but just then a tent flap opened almost a dozen yards away and a bewildered beastman staggered out into the night air. Its heavy, horned head swung left and right, taking in the oncoming druchii riders and struggling to make sense of what it saw. Then, in a single moment its expression changed from aggravation to stark panic, and the highborn grinned like a daemon from the Abyss.

One foe at a time, he realised. We beat them one foe at a time.

I'm coming for you, dear sister, the highborn thought with savage joy. Now, after so many months, so many schemes and betrayals, there will finally be a reckoning.

Fixing the terrified beastman with a predatory glare Malus raised his axe and screamed to the heavens.

'Warriors of Naggaroth! CHARGE!'

CHAPTER ELEVEN

NIGHT AND FIRE

Shevael raised a long, curving horn to his lips at Malus's command and blew a wild, howling note that was answered up and down the druchii line. The household knights roared their bloodlust to the heavens and broke into the Chaos camp in a storm of steel and red ruin.

Malus screamed like a tormented shade, his face alight with daemonic wrath as he drove Spite down a narrow, filth-strewn lane between leaning rawhide tents. Tent ropes parted like threads and poles crackled like kindling as the heavy cold ones smashed headlong through the closely-packed tents. Shouts and screams echoed from within as the nauglir crushed trapped beastmen underfoot or snapped at flailing shapes struggling to escape their collapsed shelters. Geysers of red sparks shot skyward as fires were scattered or stomped by rushing, scaly feet, and orange flames flared brightly where coals landed on brittle hides or oily bedding.

A dark, hulking shape burst from a tent just ahead and to Malus's right. He dropped his reins and raised his axe in a two-handed grip, striking the beastman in the side of the head in a vicious, underhanded swing that shattered the monster's skull. Another beastman erupted from the shadows of his tent ahead and to the left, brandishing a long, rusty sword. The horned fiend swung at Spite's toothy snout, but the nauglir ducked its bony head and bit off the attacker's left leg just above the knee. The beastman's wail of agony swept over the onrushing highborn and was quickly lost behind him as Malus drove ever deeper into the enemy encampment.

Sounds of battle and the thunder of hooves mingled into an echoing roar like the grinding fury of an avalanche. Pandemonium reigned inside the Chaos camp; some beastmen ran for their lives while others lashed out at anything that moved. Swarms of fiery motes traced glowing arcs overhead as the druchii charioteers shot flaming arrows deeper into the camp. Horns blew, horses screamed and marauders shouted hoarse, blasphemous curses to the sky.

Ahead, the reeking path abruptly jogged to the right around a tent festooned with skulls and bloody scraps of freshly skinned druchii hides.

Snarling, Malus put his spurs to Spite's flanks and ran right over the rawhide shelter. Something wailed and gibbered within, its cries cut short by one of the nauglir's stamping feet. On the opposite side of the tent a dark shape stumbled out into the open, clutching a curling staff of grey wood. Malus caught a brief glimpse of the bray shaman whirling on its cloven hooves and raising a clawed hand to cast some terrible spell before Spite lunged at the beastman and bit its head off.

The highborn leaned back in the saddle as his mount leapt clear of the collapsed tent. Malus looked frantically to the right, trying to keep track of his knights, but saw only the reeling sides of half-collapsed tents and glimpses of helmeted heads and hacking, red-stained swords rising above the low shelters. Where had his trumpeter gone? 'Shevael!' he shouted, his voice instantly swept away in the maelstrom of battle.

'Here, my lord!' came a faint reply, just on the other side of the tents to Malus's right. One of the shelters burst apart in a cloud of tattered hides and flailing ropes as the young highborn rode his nauglir through it. The knight's pale face was streaked with blood and his eyes shone with battle-lust. 'We have them on the run!' he said, shouting to be heard even though he and Malus were only a few yards apart. 'I've never seen such a slaughter!'

'Stick close to me, lad!' Malus shouted back. 'Sound the signal for the knights to rally! We're getting scattered by these damned tents!' The highborn knew that time was not on their side. For now they had the advantage of surprise, but once the shock wore off the Chaos horde could overwhelm the druchii attackers by sheer force of numbers.

Shevael, wrestling with the reins of his agitated cold one, stared quizzically at Malus. 'What was that about the tents?' he shouted. Then suddenly his eyes went wide. 'Look out, my lord!'

Malus whirled, but Spite had seen the onrushing beastmen first. The cold one spun to the left, nearly throwing Malus out of the saddle, and the axe blow aimed for Malus's neck glanced off his left pauldron instead. The highborn cursed, fighting for balance, and threw a wild swing at the beastman's upturned snout that hacked off part of the misshapen beast's left horn.

Four of the goat-headed monstrosities had rushed out of the darkness at Malus, and now they swarmed around the flank of the cold one, aiming blows at both Spite and Malus alike. One of the beastmen thrust a spear at the cold one's snout, gouging a deep furrow just above the warbeast's upper fangs, while another slashed at Spite's neck with a heavy, broad bladed cleaver. The axe-wielder brayed a blasphemous oath and swung again at Malus's chest. Malus anticipated the blow and tried to lean back out of the weapon's reach – but the fourth beastman leapt up and grabbed the highborn's left arm, trying to drag him from the saddle.

Whether by accident or design, Malus was pulled full into the axe's path and the weapon struck him in the chest, just over his heart. A mundane steel breastplate would have crumpled under the savage blow, but the sigils of protection woven into the armour held fast and turned the blade aside with a discordant clang and a shower of blue sparks. Before the beastman could recover and strike another blow Malus shouted a curse and brought down his axe on the warrior's head, striking the beastman right between the eyes. The warrior fell, spilling blood and brains from the cleft in his skull, and the highborn planted a heel in Spite's right side before the creature holding his arm could pull him to the ground. On command the warbeast pivoted right, slashing its powerful tail in an arc to the left. It struck the unwary beastman full in the back with bone-crushing force, tearing the warrior free from Malus and sending its broken body hurtling through the air.

Foam dripping from its fanged snout, the beastman with the cleaver switched targets and charged at Malus, but Spite lunged forward and caught the running warrior in its teeth, shaking the creature like a dog shakes a rabbit. Bones cracked and snapped, and the cleaver spun out of the beastman's lifeless hands. The nauglir took a quick, convulsive bite and the warrior fell in two bloody pieces. That left the lone spearman who turned and ran for its life, bleating in terror as it headed deeper into the camp.

Malus settled himself back in the saddle and grabbed the reins in his left fist. 'Sound the call for the knights to rally and follow me!' he shouted at Shevael, and kicked Spite into a run.

The sky above the Chaos camp glowed a dull orange from the fires of burning tents. Sounds of battle echoed from every side; he wondered how the cavalry was faring to either side of his knights but there was no way to tell from where he was sitting. He cut the straightest path through the camp he could manage, driving Spite over and through any tent in his path. Behind him he heard Shevael sound his war-horn and then distant shouts and thudding feet as the household knights responded.

Trusting that the knights were right behind him, Malus plunged ahead, searching desperately for any signs he was nearing Nagaira's tent. How far into the camp was he? A mile, a mile and a half? There was no way to be sure. The scouts said three miles to the centre of camp, he thought grimly, watching hunched-over beastmen scramble out of the path of the charging cold one. One of the creatures stumbled on a rope, and before it could recover he hacked off its head as he swept by, splashing dark blood against the side of a nearby tent.

Without warning Spite burst into a large, cleared area surrounded by tents. Malus quickly stole a look behind him to see if Shevael and the knights were back there, and the lapse of attention very nearly cost him his life.

Suddenly the air rang with the shrill scream of horses and the bitter oaths of men. Two small objects struck Malus in quick succession, one bouncing off his breastplate and the other ricocheting from his pauldron and scoring a bloody line across his cheek. Startled, the highborn brought his head around just as another hand axe spun by, missing his nose by inches.

He'd ridden right into an improvised picket line where a band of marauders had tied up their horses for the night. The small, grassy space was packed with a dozen screaming, rearing horses and their men, who now turned on the highborn and attacked him with whatever weapons were to hand.

Spite, smelling horseflesh, bellowed hungrily and leapt for the nearest animal. The horse shrieked and reared, slashing at the air with its hooves as its rider shouted vile oaths and struggled to keep his seat. Malus was in a similar predicament, shouting and cursing at the warbeast as it clamped its jaws around the horse's neck and pushed forward on its powerful hind legs, trying to bear the animal to the ground.

Another axe hissed past Malus's head. Shouting, tattooed warriors rushed at him from left and right, brandishing swords and short spears. The highborn jerked at the reins, trying to get Spite to release the squealing horse, but the nauglir refused to give up its prey. The nauglir surged forward, driving the animal over onto its side. Its rider leapt clear, but Malus, caught unawares by the sudden movement was catapulted from the saddle. He flew over Spite's bloodied head and landed just on the other side of the thrashing, dying horse – a few scant feet from its enraged owner.

The marauder was on him in an instant, bellowing a war cry in his barbarian tongue. A rough hand seized the highborn's dark hair and pulled his head up, exposing his throat to the marauder's upraised blade. Malus caught the downward-sweeping sword against the side of his axe, and then drove the end of its haft into the marauder's leg just above the knee. The blunt haft rebounded from the human's thick muscles, but the painful blow staggered him for a moment. Malus jabbed him again, this time in the groin, and the marauder's grip on his hair loosened. The highborn tore himself free and rolled quickly away, scrambling to his feet beside the dying horse to receive the barbarian's charge – and a hurled axe flew out of the darkness and hit Malus in the side of the head.

The axe had been poorly thrown, and struck Malus with the top edge instead of the blade. But the world dissolved in a flash of searing pain, and he dimly felt the impact as his body hit the ground once more. Sounds came and went, and though he could still see, his mind couldn't quite make sense of what was happening. He felt, distinctly, a rivulet of ichor make its way slowly down the side of his head and begin to pool in the hollow of his throat.

He felt the ground shake beneath him, and an awful, low moaning reverberate through the air. The world seemed to grow dark, and for a moment an icy rage galvanised him at the thought that he was about to die.

At that moment, everything snapped back into place – and he saw that the darkness was the shadow of the howling marauder, looming over him with sword upraised.

With a shout Malus tried to roll further away but fetched up against the twitching corpse of the marauder's horse. The sword swept down in a blurring arc and the highborn caught the blow on the haft of his axe. More blows rained down amid a stream of burning curses, several slipping past his guard and ringing off his enchanted armour. Gritting his teeth, Malus threw up his left arm and caught the next blow on his vambrace, then chopped one-handed at the human's right knee. He felt the keen blade split the kneecap and the man fell onto the highborn's lower body, bellowing in rage and pain.

Quick to follow up on his success, Malus sat up and swung hard for the marauder's shaggy head – but the man caught the haft of the axe in his left hand and stopped it cold. Glaring balefully from beneath craggy brows, the marauder let out a lunatic chuckle and flexed his powerful shoulders and arms, forcing the weapon back. Malus cursed and spat, the axe quivering in his hands, but the human's fearsome strength was far greater than his own. Slowly but surely the highborn was pushed backwards and the Chaos warrior dragged himself up the highborn's body, drawing a long, serrated dagger from a sheath at his belt.

Malus's axe was forced past his head and the curved blade driven into the blood-soaked ground. The marauder loomed over him, his scarred lips pulling back to reveal crudely filed teeth. Hot, foetid breath blew in the highborn's face. The marauder whispered something in his bestial tongue and raised his dagger to strike.

Suddenly the highborn's body spasmed and searing ice flowed through his veins. He cried out in shock as needles of pain wracked his eyes. The marauder, seeing what was etched in them, recoiled from Malus with a shriek of wordless terror that ended in a bone-jarring crunch as Spite lunged over the horse's ravaged body and bit the man cleanly in half. Malus was deluged in a shower of blood and spilled entrails as the marauder's lower torso emptied itself onto his chest.

'Mother of Night!' Malus cursed furiously, shoving the steaming remains away and climbing to his feet. Spite had returned to feasting on the horse's innards, and the highborn swatted the nauglir across its bloody snout with the flat of his axe. 'Stop thinking with your damned stomach, you great lump of scales!' he shouted hoarsely. The nauglir flinched from the blow, shaking its gore-stained snout like a large dog, and lowered obediently onto its haunches.

Druchii knights swarmed through the cleared area, and the mangled bodies of horses and marauders lay in bloody heaps all around. Malus staggered over to the nauglir and rested his pounding head against the saddle for a moment before putting his foot in the stirrup and levering himself back into his seat.

'My lord!' Shevael cried from the other side of the cleared area. He hauled on his reins and trotted quickly to his master's side, his bloodstained sword resting against his shoulder. 'I saw you go down, and then the marauders came at me, and – Blessed Murderer! You're wounded!'

The highborn rubbed at the sticky mess covering his face and neck. 'Most of this isn't mine,' he growled, scanning the area quickly. He counted close to fifty knights milling about the picket area, their armour splashed with streaks of gore. Overhead the sky glowed a fierce orange, and the stink of burning hair hung like a pall over the battlefield. There were faint shouts off to the north and the east, but the sounds of fighting had all but tapered away. 'Where are the chariots?' he demanded, spitting bits of human flesh out of his mouth.

Shevael gave Malus a blank look. 'I... don't know,' he said sheepishly. 'We lost sight of them right after I sounded the call to rally. We must have got separated in the confusion.'

Malus cursed under his breath. He had been depending on the chariots to support their withdrawal after they killed Nagaira. The highborn stood as straight in the saddle as he could and tried to see over the leaning tops of wrecked tents, but with the darkness and the columns of smoke rising from nearly every direction it was impossible to see where his troops were. The sea of rough tents was acting against the druchii now, channelling the riders into a dark, twisting maze that worked to separate the banners from one another. 'It's too quiet,' he said uneasily.

'It's been like that for several minutes,' Shevael said. 'The Chaos horde is in full flight. The attack has filled them with panic!' he said excitedly.

But the highborn shook his head worriedly. 'Something's not right,' he said. 'We've got to get moving, Shevael. Where is Lord Suheir?'

Shevael pointed to the north. 'He continued on with most of the knights a few moments ago,' the young highborn replied. 'He said that he caught sight of a cluster of tents on a nearby hill that might be the war leader's pavilion.'

Malus gathered up Spite's reins. 'That's where we need to be,' he snapped. 'Household knights!' he cried, raising his gory axe. 'With me!'

Lord Suheir's knights had blazed broad trails through the jumble of tents, trampling everything in their path as they drove relentlessly north. Malus picked the centre path and led the knights along at a brisk trot, searching the twisting side lanes for enemy activity as they rode. Could the enemy have panicked so completely? If so, would Nagaira still be in her tents? He tried to guess how long it had been since the attack began: five minutes, perhaps? Ten? It was hard to be sure. Time became elastic in the heat of battle, seeming to rush by in some moments and slow to a crawl in others.

They rushed forward into darkness, hearing the roaring of the flames swell around and ahead of them. Fires had leapt out of control among the filthy tents, and the night sky was thickening with stinking smoke. His eyes strained to make out the nearby hill that Shevael spoke of, but he could see nothing in the shifting murk. Worry started to eat at his nerves; his army was no longer under his control, which meant that he had almost no way of pulling them back if something went disastrously wrong. In case they were separated, all of the banner and regimental officers knew a series of locations to retreat to along the route back to the Black Tower, but would they turn back in time? A moment's indecision could cost thousands of lives. For a moment he was tempted to order Shevael to sound a general retreat, then lead the household knights himself on to find Nagaira's tent. But the Chaos horde would hear the horn as well, and once they saw the druchii forces breaking away they would rush in pursuit, leaving Malus and his men advancing right into their teeth. He beat his armoured gauntlet on the cantle of his saddle in frustration. There were no good options that he could determine.

Suddenly a wild shout and the clash of arms echoed through the murk in the near distance. As if on cue, the wind shifted, drawing back the veil of smoke and revealing a roughly circular cluster of low, indigo-hued tents covering a broad hill less than a quarter mile ahead. A fierce melee had erupted at the base of the hill; Malus could see Lord Suheir's knights hacking away at a large force of beastmen, who fought with ferocious zeal against their better-armed foes. Suheir's larger force was moving quickly to surround the base of the hill completely, cutting it off from the rest of the camp. Clearly the knight-captain believed that he'd found their objective, and looking up at the cluster of tents, Malus agreed.

'This is it!' he cried to the knights following in his wake. 'Forward up the hill – kill everything that gets in your way!' With a shout, the knights of the Black Tower spurred their mounts forward, forming into a wedge formation as compact and powerful as a spearhead. 'Shevael, sound the charge!'

The young highborn let out a long, howling note from his horn and like a bolt shot from a crossbow the wedge of knights hurtled towards the hill. Lord Suheir's knights heard the horn and saw Malus's approach, and riders scrambled to open a gap in their lines for the wedge to pass through. Howling, roaring beastmen swarmed into the gap, oblivious to the doom bearing down on them.

At the point of the wedge, Malus raised his axe above his head and gave his foes a savage, red-toothed grin. Horned heads turned at the thunder of the knights' approach. Braying calls rang out from the knot of beastmen, and the huge creatures hefted clubs, mattocks and axes to receive the highborn's charge.

The highborn gauged the distance carefully, glaring balefully at the snarling mob of beastmen. At the last moment, just before Spite crashed into their ranks, he planted his heels in the nauglir's flanks and hauled back on the reins. 'Up, Spite!' he cried. 'Up!'

With a thunderous roar the cold one bent low – and leapt into the mass of enemy troops. The one-ton warbeast smashed into the enemy like a hammer, scattering and trampling the beastmen with bone-crushing force. Malus chopped at upturned snouts and chests, alternating blows to his left and his right, inflicting horrific wounds on his stunned foes. Thick, bitter blood burst from ruptured arteries and shattered skulls.

But the rear ranks of the beastmen refused to give way – if anything they redoubled their attack in the face of Malus's charge. A howling beast rushed at the highborn from the right, smashing his club into Malus's hip. His armour turned aside much of the blow, but he roared out in pain and buried his axe deep in the beastman's shoulder. Spite lunged forward and bit off another beastman's head, its skull and horns crunching between the nauglir's jaws like brittle wood. An axe blow glanced from the highborn's left leg. Malus yanked his weapon free from his victim's shoulder and brought it down on the head of his foe to the left. Brains spattered against the highborn's face. Then a surge of armoured figures swept up on Malus's flanks as the rest of the knights cut their way to his side.

'Again, Spite! Up!' he shouted, kicking his heels. The nauglir obeyed, gathering itself and leaping up and through the thin line of beastmen blocking their way. As they landed, Malus pivoted the nauglir hard to the right, using its powerful tail to smash aside a pair of beastmen that had escaped the cold one's rush. Their numbers scattered by the brute force of Malus's manoeuvre, the beastmen became easy prey to the knights following in his wake, and the remaining warriors fighting against Lord Suheir's troops began a fighting withdrawal up the hill. Malus turned to his men and pointed at the beastmen with his axe. 'At them! Into their flanks!' He put his spurs to Spite's flanks and led the knights up the hill at a shallow angle, intercepting the retreating beastmen. Pressed hard from behind and now attacked from the flank, the beastman rearguard collapsed.

Malus kept Spite moving steadily uphill, riding down a fleeing beastman and burying his axe into the warrior's back. Spite lunged forward and caught another in its jaws, biting through its abdomen and letting legs and torso roll bloodily downhill. The nauglir's lashing tail accounted for another foe, breaking its legs with a vicious sweep and leaving the beastman to be trampled by the oncoming knights.

Ahead, a single surviving beastman disappeared inside the shadowy opening of the first tent. Malus reined in Spite outside the enclosure and leapt to the ground, axe at the ready. Within moments he was surrounded by a half-dozen more knights, including Shevael and Lord Suheir. 'Well done, Suheir,' Malus said, saluting the knight-captain, then he addressed the assembled druchii. 'Remember, we're after a potent sorceress. She's no doubt defended by all manner of magical traps and summoned beasts. When we reach her, hold our line of retreat open and let me deal with her.'

Suheir and the knights nodded their helmeted heads, saving their breath for the hard fighting ahead. Malus adjusted his grip on the blood-slick axe haft. *You'll not escape me this time sister,* the highborn thought grimly. *You should have fled while you had the chance.*

'All right,' he said. 'Let's go.'

Weapons ready, the druchii entered the gloomy confines of the first tent. The enclosure was dimly lit by a few guttering oil lamps, and the air was thick with a musky incense. Within lay piles of metal that glittered dully in the weak light: fine swords and battered armour, many still marked with dried blood and bits of flesh, as well as silver plates, goblets and other bits of valuable plunder looted from the razed watchtowers. Lord Suheir eyed the piles with some bemusement. 'A funny place for a treasure trove,' he murmured.

'They are offerings to the sorceress,' Malus replied. 'The beastmen and the marauders give her their best plunder as a sign of subservience. It's a statement of power, not greed.'

'It sounds as though you know this sorceress well,' Suheir mused.

'More than I'd like,' the highborn replied, edging across the enclosure.

At the far end of the wide tent lay a heavy hanging of red-dyed canvas. Malus paused before the hanging, uncertain of what lay beyond. Suheir shouldered his way through the group, hefting his shield. 'I'll go first,' he said quietly, stepping carefully up to the covered opening. He studied the cloth and its borders carefully, and finding no strange markings, he slashed his sword across the hanging, revealing the beastman waiting in ambush on the other side.

With a braying roar the horned warrior lunged at Suheir, chopping at the knight's helmeted head. Suheir absorbed the blow against the face of his shield and stabbed low with his sword, catching the beastman in the belly. The warrior staggered, bellowing in rage and pain, and the knight-captain slashed his sword across the creature's abdomen, spilling its guts onto the grassy floor. The beastman collapsed with a groan and Suheir knocked it aside with his shield, then advanced warily into the space beyond with Malus close behind.

The second enclosure was even darker and smokier than the previous one. Huddled shapes knelt in groups of eight in each corner of the space, their heads bowed in supplication as they faced four pathways through the square space. Each pathway led to another cloth hanging, including the one the druchii entered through. Suheir started upon seeing the silhouetted figures, then bent close and prodded one with the point of his sword. 'Dead,' he grunted. 'Looks like mummified beastmen. The incense covers the stink, I suppose.'

Malus nodded silently, gooseflesh racing down his spine as he remembered a similar chamber in the daemon's temple far to the north. 'We're in the right place,' he whispered. 'Head through the opening on the other side of the tent.'

Suheir stepped warily among the mummified corpses and cut down the hanging on the opposite end of the tent. Beyond lay a long, rectangular tent, lit at the far end with two small witchlamps. Along the length of the tent treble rows of kneeling figures lined both sides of a narrow aisle. 'Blessed Murderer,' Suheir cursed softly, studying the mummified attendants.

They were not beastmen this time, but druchii highborn, clad in battered armour and ragged, bloodstained kheitans. Some had limbs and heads crudely stitched back into place. Their helmets had been removed, revealing gaping head wounds here and there, and showing the looks of fear and agony frozen on their pallid features.

'More tribute for the war leader,' Malus growled. 'We're close now. Press on.'

Suheir took a deep breath and nodded gravely, then edged his way down the long aisle. At the far end lay a pair of hangings this time, their indigo panels stitched with arcane sigils in gold and silver thread. An invisible nimbus of magic hung about the portal, setting Malus's hair on end.

The highborn turned to the men behind him. 'Wait here,' he said. 'Suheir and Shevael, come with me.'

Steeling himself, he shouldered past the knight-captain and pushed his way past the heavy cloth panels. Everything about this felt wrong. Where were the attendants? The guards? He feared that the pavilion had been abandoned when the attack began, and their bold assault had been for nothing.

Malus stepped past the hangings into a spacious tent set with tables, small bookshelves and chairs, all of which were piled with books, papers and yellowed scrolls. Candles burned on several tables, and a pair of braziers near the centre filled the space with reddish light.

At the far end of the enclosure, on a small dais set with a low-backed chair, sat a solitary figure in a dark, hooded robe.

For a moment Malus was too stunned to react. He could feel the intensity of the figure's gaze smouldering hatefully from the shadows of the wide hood.

'It's a trap,' he declared, and knew with an awful certainty that his intuition was true. He couldn't imagine how Nagaira could have anticipated his attack, but she'd waited here in her tent, knowing that he would come for her.

Grabbing his axe tightly, Malus charged across the room. 'Hear me, Tz'arkan!' he hissed. 'Grant me your gifts!' It was the one and only advantage he possessed, and he'd planned to use it when he came face-to-face with his sister. Now he prayed that if he struck swiftly enough he could forestall whatever ambuscade she'd devised.

Black corruption seethed in Malus's veins, spreading like a cold fire beneath his skin. He crossed the room in an eye blink propelled by a daemonic wind. With a savage curse burning on his lips he struck at the hooded figure with all his strength.

The axe blurred through the air, straight for the figure's head. Quicker than the eye could follow, a pair of long blades swept up from beneath the robes and blocked the highborn's downward stroke with a flare of sparks and a ringing clash of steel. The loose robe fell away and the figure rose, effortlessly pushing Malus backward off the dais.

Instead of Nagaira, Malus found himself face-to-face with an armoured Chaos knight, clad in armour similar to a druchii knight but covered in patterns of blasphemous runes painted in blood. Red light seeped sullenly from gaps in the sorcerous armour, and shone from the oculars of the champion's ornate, horned helmet. Twin druchii longswords held Malus's axe at bay with fearsome strength. Around the champion's neck rested a heavy, red-gold torc.

'The Amulet of Vaurog!' Tz'arkan hissed, roiling inside Malus's chest.

And with that, the trap was sprung.

CHAPTER TWELVE

SHIELDS AND SPEARS

A second champion, Malus realised with a sense of ominous dread. Suddenly the tremendous size of the Chaos horde made terrible sense. Nagaira hadn't raised the horde alone, but had allied herself with a powerful warlord and won him to her cause.

There was a tremor in the air of Nagaira's tent, like the movement of unseen spirits, and suddenly a chorus of screams and the clash of steel rang out in the antechamber behind the druchii. Then in the far distance Malus heard a roaring, skirling sound that cried out from all along the invisible horizon – it was the wailing of hundreds of war horns, loosing the Chaos horde at last.

With a shriek of rage Malus drew back his axe and hammered the Chaos champion with a storm of vicious strokes at head, neck, chest and arms. Sparks flew and tempered steel sang, but the champion blocked the furious blows with superhuman speed. A return stroke slipped easily past Malus's guard and rang off his pauldron; another struck like an adder and glanced off his right wrist. The champion's twin swords clashed and whirled in a graceful, deadly dance, driving the highborn inexorably backwards in spite of Tz'arkan's potent gifts.

Malus blocked a lightning thrust to his stomach with the haft of his axe and thrust upwards, hoping to catch the champion beneath the chin with the weapon's curved upper edge, but the armoured warrior checked his advance at the last moment and let the axe slide harmlessly by. Without stopping the highborn pivoted smoothly on his heel and swung around and down, aiming for the warrior's right knee, but the champion anticipated the blow and his right-hand sword parried the stroke with ease. At the same time his left-hand blade blurred at Malus's head, and only the daemon's inhuman reflexes drew him back in time. Even so, the sword drew a shallow cut across the highborn's forehead, sending thick streams of ichor down the side of his face.

He'd heard tales of the phenomenal power and skill of warriors chosen by the Chaos gods, but the reality was far more terrifying than he'd imagined.

Even the zealots of the cult of Khaine, who worshipped the art of killing, could not compare with the champion's implacable skill. Thinking quickly, Malus retreated from the armoured warrior, desperately looking for some way to turn the battle to his advantage.

The momentary distraction was nearly enough to seal his fate. A sword leapt like lighting at the highborn's face; Malus twisted at the last moment, dodging the blow with a hiss of surprise, but realised, too late, that the attack was a feint. The champion's second sword swung down in a vicious arc and caught his left leg, just above the side of the knee. Fiery pain shot up Malus's leg and it gave way beneath him, toppling him to the matted earth. He fetched up next to an oak table plundered from one of the fallen watchtowers as the champion pressed his advantage and loomed over the highborn like a swooping hawk.

Malus threw a frantic swing at the warrior's midsection, hoping to spoil his attack, but the swing was off-balance and only served to leave him more exposed than before. The champion's right-hand blade rose above his helmeted head and chopped down in a backhanded blow that struck the haft of Malus's axe above his right hand and sheared through it like a sapling. The warrior's left-hand sword plummeted like a thunderbolt, and the highborn raised the severed length of axe-haft and caught the fearsome blow on the seasoned oak between his white-knuckled fists. The keen blade split the haft once again and the sword struck the highborn's breastplate hard enough to drive the air from his lungs.

Then Malus heard a roar like an angry bull and an onrushing shadow swept over him from behind. There was a crash of steel against iron and a shower of fiery orange coals seemed to drift lazily through the air as Lord Suheir smashed aside one of the braziers in a headlong charge at the Chaos champion. The powerfully built knight-captain swung a fearsome stroke at the champion's helm, but the warrior swayed backwards with serpentine grace and let the blade pass harmlessly by, then lashed out with his right-hand sword in a backhanded stroke that struck Suheir's vambrace a glancing blow. Malus saw a spray of blood burst from the point of impact, then watched as the champion thrust with his left-hand sword and stab its reinforced point into the knight-captain's side. The sword punched cleanly through Suheir's breastplate and sank an inch deep, just above the waist. Suheir staggered for just a moment, then lashed out with a backhanded stroke of his own that knocked the champion's stabbing blade aside before rushing the armoured warrior with his steel-rimmed shield held before him. For the first time the champion seemed taken by surprise, and back-pedalled furiously in the face of Suheir's bull-like charge.

Hands grabbed at Malus's shoulders, trying to pull him upright. The highborn looked up to see Shevael's pale, terrified face. The young knight's movements seemed clumsy and slow to the highborn's daemonic reflexes. 'How do we kill him?' Shevael moaned.

The Chaos champion's retreat was swift, but not swift enough. With a roar, Suheir struck the warrior's breastplate with the edge of his shield and set the champion crashing backwards through a small bookcase. Malus grabbed Shevael's arm and staggered upright, biting back a savage curse at the pain in his damaged leg.

Just a few feet away Suheir pressed his attack, hammering at the champion with one fearsome blow after another that tried to batter aside the warrior's defences. The champion blocked each stroke with nimble movements of his left-hand sword. Then, just as Suheir drew back for another punishing stroke, the champion lashed out at the knight-captain's shield arm, knocking it wide so that he could lunge forward with his right-hand sword and strike the side of Suheir's left knee. The knight-captain's armour didn't carry the same enchantments as Malus's did; steel pins snapped, lames and poleyn shattered and the champion's sword carved deep into the knee-joint. The druchii fell onto his good knee with a bellow of pain, covering his wounded leg with his shield as the Chaos warrior sprang to his feet like a hill-cat and levelled his weapons at Suheir's head.

The Chaos warrior was so intent on finishing the knight-captain that he didn't see the table Malus hurled at him until it was far too late. With no time to duck or dodge the solid oaken tabletop the champion could only raise his swords and smash the hurtling furniture to bits with his twin swords.

Above the splintering crash of the thick wood rose a furious roar and the ringing clash of steel on steel. The Chaos champion staggered back half a step – and slowly lowered his head to the length of druchii steel jutting from his midsection. Suheir's fearsome strength had driven his blade clean through the champion's torso, emerging more than a foot from the warrior's steel backplate.

And yet the champion did not fall. For an appalling instant the two warriors were transfixed, each staring at the wound Suheir's sword had made. A line of thick, black ichor flowed heavily down the back of the silver steel blade. Then with a guttural growl the champion's swords flashed and Suheir's head bounced across the matted earth. The knight-captain's body toppled onto its side, pouring a freshet of blood onto the ground, while the champion drove his right-hand sword into the dirt and used his free hand to reach for Suheir's sword, still jutting from his abdomen.

Shevael let out a panicked wail and Malus pushed him away, gritting his teeth at the pain as he limped quickly across the chamber. Flames were climbing the back wall of the tent and licking at several of the bookshelves, kindled by the scattered coals from the upended brazier.

The young highborn staggered, his face a pale mask of terror and rage. With a trembling hand he drew his second sword, and with a deep breath a sense of eerie calm stole across his features. 'Make your escape, my lord,' the young highborn shouted. 'I'll cover your retreat.'

Shevael's grim tone brought Malus up short. 'No, you young fool!' he cried. 'You don't stand a chance–'

But the young highborn wasn't listening. With a furious shout he charged at the struggling champion, his twin swords describing a deadly figure-eight pattern. The Chaos champion lurched backwards in the wake of the sudden attack, stumbling on a pile of spilled books, and Shevael's swords struck the warrior multiple times in the head, chest and leg. But the young highborn's blows were hasty and poorly aimed, and could not penetrate the champion's heavy armour. The Chaos warrior righted himself and with a convulsive motion wrenched Suheir's ichor-stained sword from his body. Still shouting curses at the champion, Shevael pressed his attack, but he underestimated the Chaos warrior's skill. As the young highborn rushed in the champion backhanded Shevael across the face with the pommel of Suheir's dripping blade and in the same motion extended his left arm and stabbed the young knight in the throat. Bright, red blood burst from the awful wound and Shevael collapsed to the ground, gasping and choking for air.

Cursing bitterly, Malus reached his objective. His armoured fingers closed about the iron grillwork of the second brazier, the drying blood on his armoured fingers hissing on contact. Using his daemonically-infused strength he lifted the red-hot container and hurled it at the champion, catching the Chaos warrior full in the chest. The warrior fell with a resounding clang and a hiss of scorched flesh, his body covered in searing coals and ash. More embers scattered across the enclosure, burning holes in the tent wall and starting more fires among the shredded papers.

Malus leapt to Shevael's side, but already the blood flow from this torn throat was ebbing and his eyes were glassy and unfocused. The highborn shook the young druchii roughly. 'Don't die on me, you damned fool!' the highborn snarled, but it was already far too late. Shevael's eyes rolled back in his head and his body went limp.

Cursing bitterly, the highborn pulled the horn from around Shevael's neck and with a grim look in his eye he pulled off the young highborn's sword belt and buckled it about his waist. The tent by this point was blazing on every side, and waves of heat and choking smoke surrounded him. Coughing furiously, he snatched up the young highborn's swords just as the Chaos champion regained his senses and kicked his way clear of the burning brazier.

Malus fought a tide of black rage as the champion struggled to his feet. He wanted nothing more than to avenge himself upon the foul warrior, but this was not the time. The Chaos fiends had sprung their ambush, and if he didn't get his troops out of the camp they were going to be slaughtered. He'd sooner see his soul lost to Tz'arkan for all time than suffer such a black stain to his honour. With a last, hateful look at the Chaos champion, Malus turned and raced back the way he'd come.

As he pulled back the double hangings however, he was brought up short by a nightmarish scene of carnage. The long, rectangular tent swarmed with the pale figures of the living dead. The druchii corpses that had knelt in supplication along the narrow aisle had sprung to grisly life at some invisible command and attacked the knights Malus had left behind as a rearguard. Many of the stitched-together revenants had been hacked apart, but the rest now hunched over the ruptured bodies of the tower knights, their chalk-white hands slick with blood and torn meat. Several slack-jawed faces turned in Malus's direction as he stood upon the threshold, and the highborn recoiled from the charnel scene with a blasphemous curse.

Behind him the champion lurched to his feet and gathered up his swords. Malus looked quickly about, seeing nothing but flames to left and right, and came to a decision. Taking a deep breath, he raised Shevael's blades and dived headlong through the blazing canvas to his left.

Heat and smoke washed over him for a searing instant, and then he was stumbling through the darkened confines of an adjoining tent, piled high with cushions and sleeping furs. Malus staggered headlong across the tent and slashed at the far wall with both swords. A draught of cool air washed over the highborn's face and he leapt through the shredded cloth, emerging into the night air. Screams and wild howls echoed through the flame-shot darkness all around the hill as the Chaos horde charged out of their hidden positions outside the camp and rushed at the druchii raiders. Knowing that every second counted for the isolated bands of cavalry and footmen, the highborn put Shevael's horn to his lips and blew the general retreat as loudly as he could. He sounded the call three more times, pointing the horn to the east, north and west, then let the instrument fall to his side and headed back to the waiting knights as quickly as he could. As Nagaira's pavilion burned, Malus cut his way through two more tents that lay between him and the mounted warriors, kicking aside piles of skulls and golden plunder as he went.

At last he emerged, bloodied and smoke-stained, before the nervous household knights. They were facing outwards in a large circle, listening to the echoing cries of the enemy and waiting for the onslaught to begin. Even the nauglir sensed the peril approaching, pawing the earth and lowering their heads threateningly.

'Here, Spite!' Malus called as he staggered up to the circle. The knights started at the ghastly apparition of the highborn. 'My lord!' one of the druchii cried out. 'We feared the worst–'

'And you were right to do so,' the highborn said grimly, sheathing his left-hand sword. 'I've led us straight into an ambush.' Without waiting for Spite to sink to his haunches the highborn took a deep breath and hauled himself into the saddle. For good measure he drew the war-horn and sounded the retreat one last time, eliciting a chorus of savage howls from the darkness close by. 'That's it,' he shouted. 'Close order formation!

We're falling back to the spearmen and we're not stopping for anyone or anything.' He raised the sword in his right hand.

'Household knights! Forward!' Malus said, and kicked Spite into a run just as the first mobs of beastmen came howling out of the burning night.

Malus and the knights came thundering down out of the charred outskirts of the Chaos encampment with a screaming horde at their heels. True to his word, they'd smashed through or trampled over everything that stood in their path. The highborn's sword streamed thick ropes of blood into the ashen wind, and the nauglirs' snouts glistened with the vital fluids of beastmen and marauders who had been caught before the avalanche of steel and scale.

More than a dozen riderless cold ones loped in the formation's wake, following along with the rest of the pack now that no rider lived to guide them. Knights had been pulled from the saddle by leaping horrors, or felled by flung axes or spears. Each loss was a blow to Malus's pride, a mark of failure that burned worse than any blade and added its weight to the disaster unfolding around him.

As they burst from the smoking confines of the camp Malus looked to the brim of the low hill ahead and his spirits rose as he saw the long lines of spearmen, their shields and spear tips gleaming against the firelight. If they could hold long enough...

Malus pointed his sword to the left and the household knights responded, pivoting smartly and thundering past the spear wall's right flank. The highborn saw the wide-eyed faces of the front ranks as they galloped by, and sensed the fear gripping the young spearmen. No one had told them what was going on, but they knew something wasn't right.

The highborn led the knights down the reverse slope of the hill and called a halt. Off to the right, some fifty yards away, stood a knot of some two hundred cavalrymen. One banner of horse out of six; Malus glanced quickly about and bit back a curse when he could find no more. He turned back to the knights. 'Who is the senior knight now that Lord Suheir is dead?'

Searching glances passed between the assembled warriors. Finally a gruff-looking older knight raised his hand. 'I am, my lord. Dachvar of Klar Karond.'

'Very well, Dachvar. You're in command now,' Malus said. 'Rest your men and see to your mounts. I expect to have need of you again shortly.' Without waiting for a reply he turned Spite about and headed up behind the spear regiments at a run.

The three units stood in close formation, nearly shield-to-shield about a quarter of the way down the hill-slope. Each spearman carried not only his spear, shield and short sword, but also a heavy repeating crossbow and a quiver of black bolts. These were now being loaded by the rear two ranks of each company as the highborn reached the crest of the hill and found Lord Meiron and Lord Rasthlan studying the howling, roaring mob of Chaos troops massing on the far hillside some two hundred yards distant. A short distance down the reverse slope he saw Rasthlan's autarii scouts crouched together in a small group, smoking pipes and speaking to one another in low tones.

Malus reined in beside the two commanders and hastily returned their salutes.

'My compliments on your deployment, Lord Meiron,' the highborn said, using the advantage of height to study the disposition of the spear regiments. 'I'd hoped we wouldn't have need of your spears, but now it appears you'll anchor our rearguard. Has there been any sign of our chariots or the rest of our cavalry?'

'None, my lord,' Meiron replied gravely. 'It's possible the chariots were caught in the fires that swept through the enemy camp – we haven't heard the rumble of their wheels for some time.' He gave the highborn a shrug. 'As to the cavalry, they may be half a dozen leagues away by now. Most of those young bravos are like wolf cubs – they'll chase anything that moves.'

'Lord Irhaut thinks like a hill bandit, my lord,' Rasthlan interjected. 'He has trained his banner leaders to retreat in the face of a superior foe and lead pursuers away from the rest of the army. What Lord Meiron means is that the light horse could be miles away to east and west, drawing off as many of the Chaos forces as possible.'

From the look on Meiron's face it was clear he meant to say no such thing – he was a dyed-in-the-wool infantry commander with nothing but disdain for cavalrymen – but Malus accepted Rasthlan's explanation with a knowing nod. 'Then let us pray to the Dark Mother that he and his men are successful,' the highborn said, his expression grim. 'Because it looks like we have all we can handle right here.'

A cacophonous roar filled the air at the edge of the Chaos encampment. Beastmen threw back their heads and brayed to the smoke-shrouded moon and tattooed humans beat their swords against their shields and howled the names of their blasphemous gods. They swelled in number with every passing moment, spilling like a black tide down the slopes of the far hill. Malus couldn't guess at the size of the mob, but it was certain that the druchii were heavily outnumbered. The noise washed over the spear formations and murmurs of fear could be heard from among the state regiments. The Black Guard, holding the centre of the line, were silent and still as statues, waiting simply for the battle to begin.

Lord Meiron turned to the spearmen and bellowed in a leathery voice that sawed through the raucous din. 'Stand fast, you whoresons!' he snarled. 'Shields up and eyes front! Those degenerate bastards are working up the courage to charge up this hill and throw away their lives! If I were a holy man I would fall to the ground and thank Khaine almighty for foes as stupid as these!'

Cheers and hisses of laughter went up from the ranks, and the spearmen shook their weapons at the swelling horde. Lord Meiron turned back to Malus and smiled proudly. 'Fear not, my lord,' he said. 'We'll see to these animals.'

'I'll hold you to that, Lord Meiron,' Malus said with a nod, then wheeled Spite about and rode downhill to the group of cavalrymen. The light horsemen were stragglers from a number of different banners and were clearly exhausted, their faces and armour stained with layers of smoke and blood. As the highborn approached, the riders sat straighter in the saddle and chivvied their mounts into something resembling a formation. Malus pulled quickly into shouting distance and cried, 'Secure the spears' left flank! The household knights will take the right.' The banner leader acknowledged the order with a salute and began shouting orders to his men, and the highborn turned Spite about and raced back to the waiting knights.

By the time he reached Dachvar the Chaos warriors were on the move. They seethed down the long slope in a ragged, bloodthirsty mass, running, shambling and loping with twisted and slithering strides. They waved crude weapons above their misshapen heads and screamed for the blood of their foes. To Malus's eyes there looked to be more than ten thousand of them, a sight that filled even his black heart with dread. It never should have come to this, he thought bitterly. How had Nagaira anticipated him?

The ground shook to the thunder of thousands of pounding feet. Horned heads and upraised swords stood out blackly against the hellish backdrop of the burning Chaos encampment.

When the first of the enemy warriors were a third of the way from the bottom of the far hill, Malus heard the rough voice of Lord Meiron cry out, 'Sa'an'ishar!' Instantly a rustle ran through the spear regiments as warriors readied their shields and levelled their long spear. Then: 'Rear ranks! Ready crossbows!'

A ripple of armoured forms ran the length of the battle line as druchii warriors raised their repeating crossbows to their shoulders and angled the weapons skyward. Lord Meiron raised his sword. 'Ready... ready... fire!'

Fifteen hundred crossbows thrummed, and a rain of black bolts hissed through the air. Not a one could fail to find a mark as they plunged into the mass of enemy troops, and howls of rage turned to agonised shrieks as the bolts tore through the poorly armoured warriors. Hundreds of humans and beastmen fell, their bodies trampled by their fellows as the rest of the mob ran on.

The charging Chaos troops had reached the bottom of the hill. An oiled rattle echoed up and down the line as the druchii quickly reloaded their weapons. 'Ready!' Lord Meiron cried. 'Fire!'

Another hissing storm of bolts plunged into the Chaos ranks. Hundreds more were wounded or slain, their bodies piling up at the base of the slope. Savage beastmen clambered over riddled corpses or knocked their injured mates aside, some crawling on all fours as they tried to reach the druchii line.

Once again the repeater crossbows rattled, readying another volley. The front ranks of the foemen were less than fifty yards away. 'First two ranks kneel!' Lord Meiron cried, and the spearmen dropped obediently to one knee. 'Rear ranks, fire!'

Black death scythed through the attackers, the powerful bolts punching completely through the closest enemy troops. The first three ranks of the Chaos warriors toppled like threshed wheat, and even Malus shook his head in awe at the scale of the slaughter. In less than a minute the hill slopes had become a killing field, carpeted with the bodies of the dead.

Yet still the Chaos horde came on.

They struck the line of spearmen with a great, rending crash of steel on wood that echoed from the hillsides. Axes, clubs, swords and claws battered against shield and helm, and the druchii line staggered beneath the weight of the enemy assault. It bent backwards a slow step at a time... then stopped. Malus could hear the rough voice of Lord Meiron spitting savage oaths at the troops, and the Black Guard responded with a collective roar. Spears flickered and stabbed into the press of foes, and howls of rage turned to screams of agony as the druchii warriors put their training and discipline to lethal effect.

But would it be enough? Beastmen and marauders were dying by the score, but from Malus's vantage point he could see spearmen pulled from the ranks and torn apart, or dashed to the ground by terrible blows. The flanking regiments were taking the worst of the punishment, their rear ranks rippling like wheat as wounded men were pulled from the line and new men rotated to take their place. The Chaos attack showed no signs of faltering, and more troops were streaming from the camp every minute to add their weight to the battle. If just one of the regiments broke and ran, the other two would be overwhelmed in moments.

They couldn't remain on the defensive for long, Malus saw. Their only option was to attack.

He drew his bloodstained sword and turned to Dachvar. 'We've got to take the pressure off the spearmen,' he said. 'The household knights will form line and we'll charge the Chaos bastards in the flank.'

'Aye, my lord,' Dachvar replied with a nod, then wheeled his nauglir about and trotted the length of the formation. 'Form line and prepare to charge!' he cried, and the knights readied themselves for battle.

Taking the lead, Malus angled Spite to the east and led the formation of knights around the side of the hill, where they could sweep around the slope and strike the Chaos warriors from the left flank. Long minutes passed while the large formation repositioned itself. Malus listened intently to the battle raging on the hilltop, knowing that every passing minute pushed the spearmen closer to the breaking point. Finally, Dachvar signalled at the far end of the line that all was in readiness, and Malus raised his sword. 'Sa'an'ishar! The household knights will advance at the charge!' Then he lowered his blade and the knights let out an exultant roar, kicking their mounts into a run.

There was neither the time nor the distance to work the formation up into a proper charge; the knights swept around the slope like a huge pack of wolves, plunging into the flank of the enemy with a bone-crushing impact of claws, teeth and steel. Spite trampled two beastmen beneath his broad feet and bit the head off another; Malus stabbed a stunned beastman in the back and slashed his sword across a leaping marauder's neck. The mob recoiled at the sudden shock, and the knights forced their way deeper into the mass, their red swords rising and falling and their cold ones flinging mangled bodies high into the air. Meiron's spearmen cheered and redoubled their efforts, reclaiming the few yards of ground they'd lost and pushing the enemy back down the slope.

Axes and clubs battered at Malus's armoured legs. A beastman tried to climb onto Spite's neck, swinging a cleaver-like sword at the highborn's chest. Malus caught the creature's sword-arm with a blow to the wrist that severed its hand, then stabbed the howling fiend in the chest. Its body left a gleaming trail of blood as it slid from the cold one back into the seething mob below, but another beastman literally leapt to take its place. Malus cursed, trading blows with the creature even as he felt another pair of hands to his left trying to pull him from the saddle. The charge had inflicted considerable damage but the mob continued to hold its ground, bolstered by its reinforcements and motivated by fear of its terrible leaders. Now that the knights were stuck in they'd lost their most crucial asset: mobility. Soon the greater numbers of the enemy would tell against them.

Malus feinted a cut at the beastman in front of him, inviting a response. When the creature lunged at him with its sword he was ready, stabbing it in the throat. The beast fell to the ground, coughing blood, and the highborn turned his attention to the braying monster pulling at his left leg. Distantly, he heard an ominous rumble of thunder roll from the depths of the Chaos encampment. What new threat was Nagaira sending his way?

A quick look uphill showed that the spear regiments had ceased their advance, fighting from their original positions at the brow of the hill. To his immediate left, one of the spear units had no foes to contend with at all thanks to the arrival of the knights. Still the enemy mob fought on, surrounding the hard-pressed knights and tearing at them in a frenzy of hate. No sooner had Malus despatched the beastman on his left than a heavy blow smashed into his hip on the right. Desperation began to take hold, and he considered calling a retreat.

Then suddenly the roll of thunder swelled in volume and Malus heard a titanic crash off to his right. Screams and howls of fear rent the air, and it seemed as though the entire enemy mob recoiled like a living thing. Malus heard the spearmen to his left start to cheer, and then he saw that the Chaos warriors were *retreating*, scattering into the darkness to the north-west. The household knights spurred their cold ones in pursuit, cutting down the fleeing foes, until shouted commands from Dachvar brought them to a halt.

A rattling rumble echoed up the slope behind Malus; he turned and saw it was one of the war chariots that had accompanied them from the Black Tower. Standing up in his stirrups, he could see more of the chariots milling about at the base of the hill, their wheels and fearsome scythe blades dripping with blood.

The charioteer behind the highborn reined in his paired cold ones, and the knight standing beside him dismounted and hurried over to Malus. 'My apologies for losing you during the advance, my lord,' the knight said gravely. 'We were forced to stick to those damned, twisting paths, and once we diverged it seemed that we never could head back in the right direction again.'

Malus leaned back in his saddle, breathing heavily and watching the last of the beastmen disappear into the smoke. 'The loss was sorely felt,' the highborn said. 'But your return more than made up for it. Gather your chariots, commander. You are now the rearguard. The spears must fall back to the next rally point with all haste, while we still have a little breathing room.'

The commander of the chariots saluted and headed quickly back to his mount. Malus reached behind him for his war horn, trying to remember how to sound a proper recall and withdrawal. By the grace of the goddess he'd won a momentary reprieve, but he still had to get the remainder of his army back to the tower before they were overrun.

CHAPTER THIRTEEN

THE LONG, BLOODY ROAD

'Here they come again!' one of the spearmen cried, his voice cracking with exhaustion and strain.

The marauder horsemen were pouring back over the ashen ridge, the hooves of their lean-limbed horses kicking up plumes of chalky dust that clung to the bare arms and faces of their riders. Ululating howls rose from the horsemen as they picked up speed down the shallow slope and thundered directly towards the ragged lines of the retreating druchii force.

Spears and shields rattled awkwardly as the exhausted soldiers readied themselves for yet another attack. Lord Meiron took a quick swig of watered wine from a leather flask at his hip and barked out hoarsely. 'No one shoots this time! Conserve your bolts until ordered to fire. Front ranks keep your damned shields up this time!'

Malus leaned back against his saddle and tried to rub the grit and exhaustion from his eyes. The band of horsemen was larger this time – yet another knot of marauders had caught up with the limping druchii raiders. The hit-and-run attacks were getting larger and more frequent. For the thousandth time since dawn he turned in the saddle and looked to the south. They had reached the Plain of Ghrond just at first light, and the sight of the distant tower had renewed their spirits somewhat, but for the last four hours they had only managed half a dozen miles. Chaos horsemen had been harassing them constantly, nipping at their heels like packs of wolves. The attacks had grown so numerous that the spearmen were forced to march in battle formation, limping along in a ragged line six hundred yards across.

They had marched all through the night, probed constantly by hunting parties of Chaos horsemen who struck at the rear columns of the retreating army and faded back into the darkness. For most of the night the surviving banner of light horse had fought hard to keep the enemy cavalry at bay, but now the horses were exhausted. Malus had realised belatedly that this was part of the marauders' strategy, but now it was too late. As the marauders swept down on the waiting spearmen the druchii cavalry could only watch helplessly from their staggering mounts, well behind the lines.

Lord Irhaut and the bulk of the light horse had never reappeared over the course of the night. Malus had kept the retreating force as long as he could at each of the rendezvous points, but there had been no sign of the lost horsemen. Finally, at the last rendezvous, the highborn had been forced to make a difficult decision. He'd summoned Lord Rasthlan and ordered him and his autarii scouts to break off and try to locate the scattered cavalry and link them up with the main body of the force. Rasthlan had accepted the order stoically, though it was clear from his manner that he didn't expect to find anyone still alive. That was the last Malus saw of him and his scouts.

Now he was out of ideas. For the last five hours the only horsemen who'd come riding over the ashen ridges had been painted in crude tattoos and crying for druchii blood.

The marauder horsemen fanned out into a thundering line as they charged at the druchii spearmen. Wild, tattooed faces screamed the names of blasphemous northern gods, and sunlight flashed on the tips of their short spears. The druchii had learned from experience that the marauders would play at pressing home a charge, then launch their spears at nearly point-blank range and wheel away, retreating back up the ridge to prepare for another attack. For the first few attacks the druchii had punished the marauders severely, meeting them with volleys of crossbow bolts that cut down riders and mounts alike. But now their store of bolts was running low. They'd emptied the chariots of all their remaining ammunition, but even so they only had enough for a few volleys left.

The chariots had long since been given over to carrying the wounded. As for the nauglir, they were fearsome shock weapons, but Malus knew better than to pit them in a pursuit against the nimble marauder horses. Like the light cavalry, the knights and the surviving chariots could only sit and watch as the Chaos attack thundered home.

The marauders thundered closer, screaming like tormented shades and wreathed in clouds of ashen dust. At twenty yards the line of druchii spearmen crouched as one, raising their battered shields to cover their exposed faces.

With a furious shout the marauders let fly, hurling a cloud of black spears in a long arc onto the druchii soldiers. They struck the upraised shields with a staccato rattle; some glanced from curved helms or caught on mailed shoulders. Here and there a warrior screamed and fell, clutching at the spear driven deep into his body.

As the last of the spears struck home Malus felt himself relaxing. He could see the spearmen do the same, straightening slightly and lowering their shields a bit as they waited for the horsemen to turn and head back for the ridge.

This time, however, they didn't. In half a second the marauders were past the point where they always turned about, and Malus saw that something was wrong. By the time his exhausted mind realised what was happening it was already too late.

The marauders let out another roaring shout, plucking swords and axes from their belts and crashed full-tilt into the druchii line. By luck or by design the marauders struck one of the battered state regiments, and the spearmen reeled from the impact. Unprepared for the sudden charge, the front ranks of the regiment fell screaming beneath the blows of the howling Chaos warriors. The rear ranks, overcome with shock, began to break away and flee for the illusory safety of the nearby chariots.

'Goddess curse them!' Malus snarled. He turned to his knights. 'Dachvar! We're going in!'

Dachvar wearily drew his sword. 'The household knights are ready, my lord,' he said gravely. The side of his face and neck were black with dried blood from a spear attack during the night. Already, shouted cries were spreading among the surviving knights as they readied themselves for battle. After a night of running they were eager to spill more of the enemy's blood.

The broken spearmen were in full flight now, dropping their weapons and running in terror from the raging marauders. Malus welcomed the black rage that swelled up from his heart and filled his limbs with hateful strength. 'Sa'an'ishar!' he snarled. 'Charge!'

Spite leapt forward with a growl, eager at the prospect of horseflesh. The marauders had possessed enough sense to attack the far end of the battle-line, away from the weary knights, but the charging cold ones covered the few hundred yards in less than ten seconds. The marauders were heedless of their doom, lost in their orgy of slaughter until it was far too late.

Malus gave Spite its head, drawing both of his long blades as the nauglir leapt upon the lead marauder horse. The mangy equine was borne over with a hideous scream, its spine severed by the cold one's snapping jaws. Its rider leapt clear with a savage curse, only to have his skull split as Dachvar thundered past.

'On, Spite! On!' the highborn cried, driving the cold one forward with spurs and knees. Roaring hungrily, the cold one lunged for another nimble horse, catching one out-flung foreleg and biting it off in a spray of bitter blood. The animal fell end-for-end, shrieking and writhing, and the nauglir landed right on top of it, biting and snapping at its back and hindquarters.

The beat of rushing hooves brought Malus's head around – a marauder was racing at him from behind and to the left. The highborn seized the reins with the fingers of his left hand and hauled for all he was worth, pulling the nauglir free of its prey and turning the beast to face the oncoming threat. He only managed it halfway, turning the cold one perpendicular to the charging horseman. The marauder had to choose between swinging wide of the cold one's jaws and passing out of range of Malus, or turning in the opposite direction and risking the cold one's deadly tail for a chance of exchanging blows with its rider. Grinning like a fiend, the marauder chose the latter.

Malus met the oncoming rider with a furious scream, slashing left-handed at the horse's reins and following up with a furious right-handed thrust for the barbarian's eyes. The reins parted like a snapped thread, but the horsemen turned aside the highborn's second blade with the steel rim of his round shield. Laughing, the horseman lashed out with his axe, and Malus felt the blade strike home just above his collarbone. The iron axe head rebounded from his enchanted armour; another six inches higher and the weapon would have slashed his throat open to the spine.

Spite roared and turned in place, snapping at the horse's hindquarters, but the marauder forced his mount tight against the cold one's flank and kept hammering away at Malus's guard. The axe arced down again, aiming for Malus's head, but this time the highborn caught the curving beard of the weapon against the back of his left-hand sword and tried to pull it towards him. But his exhausted limbs were weaker than he imagined, and the marauder seemed to have arms of spring steel. Still laughing, the barbarian snarled something in his bestial tongue and pulled his axe back, neatly dragging Malus from his saddle. The next thing the highborn saw was the scratched iron boss of the horseman's shield as he smashed it into Malus's face. He screamed in rage and pain, blinded by the blow, and swung his right-hand sword in a wild stroke that connected with the horse's ribs and the marauder's leg. Both beasts let out a pained yell, but the marauder continued to pull on the highborn's sword with his axe.

Malus couldn't breathe, his mouth filling with ichor from his broken nose. Blinking away tears of pain, he looked up to see the horseman raising his ichor-stained shield and taking aim at the highborn's outstretched neck. With a shout Malus twisted painfully at the waist and stabbed upwards with his free blade. The point of the sword sank into the marauder's side, just beneath the edge of his broad leather belt. The horseman stiffened, his laughter stilled at last. Red blood ran thickly down the side of the druchii's dark blade; Malus clenched his fist and twisted the sword in the wound. With a convulsive wrench he tore the blade free and the horseman slid lifelessly from the saddle.

As the riderless horse bolted away, Malus levered himself back into his seat and rubbed the back of his left gauntlet over his stinging face. The battle was already over; a bare handful of marauders were racing back to the safety of the ridgeline and the household knights were sitting on their mounts amid a field thick with the bodies of humans and savaged horses. A weary cheer went up from the ranks of the Black Guard, but the sound was lost in the roll and rumble of thunder to the north.

Frowning, Malus looked to the ridgeline and saw that the sky overhead was a roiling mass of black and purple clouds. Streaks of pale lightning crackled in their midst, and a cold wind tasting of old blood stirred the dust and brushed at the faces of the battered druchii host.

Now the purpose of the steady attacks became clear. The marauders had slowed the retreating army to a crawl so that the rest of the horde could press on and catch them.

Lord Meiron was shouting savage curses at the survivors of the broken regiment, chivvying them back into ranks. The household knights turned their mounts back towards the rear of the battle line, casting uneasy glances at the ridge to the north. Malus sat in place for a moment, weighing the odds. He looked to the south, at the distant image of the tower. So close. So damned close.

Lost in his bleak reverie, Malus was startled by the sound of Lord Meiron's voice. 'My apologies, my lord,' he said gruffly. 'The captain of the regiment was one of the first men slain in the charge. I've taken command of the unit personally, and I assure you they won't turn their backs on the enemy again.'

The highborn turned his gaze to the ridgeline. 'There's a storm about to break, Lord Meiron.'

'So I see, my lord,' Meiron answered calmly.

'We don't have much time,' Malus said. 'I reckon we're still a good five miles from the tower. How fast can your men run?'

'Run, my lord?' the infantry commander said. 'We've done all the running we're going to. No, this is where we'll make our stand.'

Malus met Lord Meiron's eyes. 'We can't,' he said. 'We'll be cut to bits. That's the main body of the horde over there.'

'I know, my lord. That's why there's no point running. They've got us. If we run their horsemen will just ride us down.' Lord Meiron drew himself up to his full height. 'And I have never run from a foe in all my life, least of all these animals. I'll not start now.'

Malus narrowed his black eyes. 'I could order you.'

Meiron stiffened. 'Then you'd make me a mutineer, my lord,' he said. 'You'd best get the nauglir and those dandy horsemen moving. I don't expect we have much time now.'

A look of understanding passed between the two druchii. Malus nodded. 'Very well, Lord Meiron,' he said darkly. 'I will not forget this, and I swear to you, neither will the enemy.'

The druchii lord nodded solemnly. 'I'll hold you to that, Malus of Hag Graef. In this life and the next.' Without another word the infantry commander turned on his heel and marched back to his men.

Malus watched him go, his heart bitter. 'In this life and the next,' he said to himself, and drew upon the reins. He kicked Spite to a trot and headed for the waiting knights. With enough of a head start the mounted troops could reach the tower safely, and it shamed him to think that a part of him was glad to be escaping Nagaira's trap.

You will pay for this, sister, he thought. By the Dark Mother I swear it. You will suffer a hundredfold for every man of mine you slay.

He reached Dachvar and the knights and spoke a few, quiet orders, then turned about and rode to the light horse. The cavalry he ordered to move at once, then as they started for the tower he went to the chariots and got them moving as well. The last to go were the knights, and behind them all rode Malus himself.

The black clouds were past the ridgeline now, heading inexorably south towards the tower. Lighting lashed across the sky and smote the backs of the mounted men with blows of thunder.

The last sight Malus had of the battered ranks of spearmen was a line of straight backs and a thicket of spears, aimed towards the storm rolling from the north. He caught sight of Meiron's square-shouldered form standing in the front rank of his regiment, eyes forward, awaiting the coming of the foe.

Along the rear ranks of the spear regiments, young druchii stole quick glances over their shoulder at the retreating cavalry and knights, their faces pale and uncomprehending.

The storm clouds paced the dispirited riders all the way back to the tower, dogging their heels with flashes of pale lighting and imprecations of thunder. It took them nearly an hour to reach the high, black walls, and the entire time Malus would catch himself looking back over his shoulder, wondering if Meiron and his men still fought on.

Sombre faces lined the outer walls as the riders made their way to the tower gate. As they came near the gatehouse Malus saw four banners flying from the battlements, their heavy fabrics shifting listlessly in the faint wind. He saw a black crag on a white field surmounted by a silver circlet, and a blue banner with three black masts. Between them was a grey banner with a rearing, dark green nauglir, and above all rose the cloth-of-gold banner of lost Nagarythe, bearing the sign of the dragon and the crown.

Malekith had arrived with his army, and the armies of Clar Karond, Hag Graef and the Black Ark of Naggor rode with him.

On the long ride northward he'd imagined returning to the tower at the head of a victorious army, listening to a fanfare of trumpets from the walls as he bore the head of his sister before him. Now he returned in defeat, with but a broken remnant of the warriors he once led. He felt the weight of each soldier's stare as he led Spite aside and watched the survivors of his army make their way inside the fortress. As the last of his knights disappeared inside the walls, a mournful chorus of horns rose from the gatehouse. The highborn turned in the saddle to see the white plain behind him awash with a black tide of marching troops. Nagaira's horde had reached the Black Tower at last.

With a creak of great hinges the gates of the fortress began to grind shut. Malus took a last look northward before spurring his nauglir inside.

The remainder of his troops waited in the marshalling square beyond the gate, arrayed in parade ranks to either side of the centre path. A single druchii waited in the centre of the square, sitting astride a huge black destrier. Malus approached the old general wearily. Even Spite was too tired to more than sniff in the horse's direction.

Nuarc crossed his hands over the cantle of his saddle and gave the highborn an appraising stare. 'You look like someone dragged you through a butcher's shop,' he said without preamble.

'A *burning* butcher's shop,' Malus corrected, glaring back at the general.

To the highborn's surprise, Nuarc nodded sombrely. 'I know the place,' he said quietly. His expression turned businesslike. 'Malekith wishes to hear your report.'

'Yes, I expect he does,' Malus answered with a sigh. A bitter smile played across his bloodstained face.

Nuarc frowned. 'Something amuses you?'

'I was thinking that a thousand brave druchii just gave their lives so I could safely make it to my execution,' he said. 'Lead on, Nuarc. Let's not keep the Witch King waiting.'

Nuarc offered to give Malus time to clean up, but he declined with a mirthless smile. Better that the Witch King and the assembled lords see what the future held for them, he thought.

The general led the weary highborn through the inner gate and into the high tower. Malus's gait was as unsteady as a babe's. Belatedly he realised that he'd been in the saddle for two days straight. It was a wonder his legs worked at all.

He did notice that he felt no pain from his wounds. Some experimental prodding along his scalp and his knee hinted that the injuries were healing very quickly indeed, thanks to the daemon's black corruption. The highborn wondered perversely how many strokes a headsman would need to take off his head. Would his body keep wriggling for hours afterward, like a snake?

Nuarc cast a curious look over his shoulder at the highborn. Had he laughed aloud? He couldn't recall.

The general led him to a pair of tall doors etched with the tower sigil of Ghrond. A score of black-robed Endless watched Malus impassively as the doors swung open and he was admitted inside.

Malekith studied him with burning eyes from an iron throne no less impressive than the one he presided from at Naggarond. The throne room was larger than the Court of Dragons, built to admit several hundred nobles and their retinues. At the foot of the dais were four ornate chairs, arranged in a semicircle. Four druchii nobles, clad in martial finery, bolted to their feet as Malus and Nuarc made the long walk across the echoing chamber. Malus felt their hot glares like irons against his skin, but the heat made little impression upon him after all the fire he'd recently endured.

He recognised Lord Myrchas at once. The Drachau of the Black Tower was pale with rage, but a glitter of fear shone in his black eyes as Malus was brought before the assembled lords. No doubt he remembers our conversation at the tower, the highborn thought, and he fears that I shall pull him down with me. A not unreasonable assumption.

Then Malus recognised the druchii standing beside Myrchas and felt his heart skip a beat. For a moment he fancied that the vengeful shade of his father Lurhan had risen from the Abyss to torment him. He recognised his father's ornate armour and the great sword Slachyr, the ancient blade of Hag Graef's vaulkhar, but the face of the man wearing the armour looked strange to him. The last time he'd seen his half-brother Isilvar's face it was a pallid green, soft and paunchy from decades of fleshy decadence. Now all that soft skin had melted away, leaving sharp bones and deeply sunken eyes that glittered with almost feral hate. His black hair, still bound in wires with hidden barbs and hooks, was held back with a golden circlet, and his ropy neck was bound by the thick gold hadrilkar of the Witch King's retinue. Malus noted that Isilvar wore his collar of service on the outside of a high collar of supple suede. No doubt to keep the heavy gold from chafing his delicate skin, the highborn thought sarcastically.

Next to Isilvar stood a lanky druchii clad in vivid blue robes and polished silver armour, and of all the nobles in the room only he looked at Malus with something other than anger or hate. Malus supposed he was the drachau of Clar Karond, the one ruler of the six cities he hadn't managed to mortally offend in the last year. The drachau regarded the highborn bemusedly, as if uncertain what all the fuss was about. It took him a moment to realise that the ruler of Clar Karond was somewhat drunk.

On the opposite side of Lord Myrchas stood a tall, narrow-shouldered figure in ornate armour chased with silver and gold. He had a long face and a small, square chin – a handsome man that reminded Malus at once of his mother Eldire. But there was nothing welcoming in Balneth Bale's eyes, only a black gulf of endless hate.

If the assembled lords expected him to quail before their withering stares they were disappointed. He spared them only the briefest of glances, focusing the majority of his attention on the armoured figure upon the throne. When he reached the foot of the dais – surrounded by the circle of hateful lords – he sank slowly to one knee. 'I come at your command, dread majesty,' he said simply.

'*Have you done my bidding, Malus of Hag Graef?*' Malekith asked, his voice seething from his ornate helm like air from a banked forge.

'I live to serve, dread majesty.'

'*Then tell me of all you have done.*'

And so he did, relating his arrival at the Black Tower and his failed attack on Nagaira's camp. He left out no particular – even, to his surprise relating the heroism and self-sacrifice of Lord Meiron and his spearmen. 'It was because of their courage that I stand here to relate these facts, dread majesty,' Malus said. 'I am ashamed that I led so many of your finest warriors to their deaths.'

'There, you see, he freely damns himself!' Lord Myrchas declared, levelling an accusing finger at the highborn. Once it became clear that Malus wasn't going to scapegoat him for the loss of the battle, the drachau's demeanour had reverted to type. 'He deserves the same fate that Lord Kuall suffered! At least Kuall didn't throw away ten thousand of our best men!'

'For all we know, he led those men to their deaths as part of a plan he's worked out with Nagaira herself,' said the new Vaulkhar of Hag Graef. Isilvar's voice, once silken and refined, was now a guttural ruin, worse even than the hoarse growl of Nuarc. The sound brought a smile to Malus's face, though he was careful to keep his face turned to the floor. 'He and my sister have engaged in conspiracies for years, dread majesty. It was she who wrought such ruin in my home city last spring, and it was he who so disfigured our drachau that he remains convalescing to this day. It is clear to me that they were working together to destroy Hag Graef, and I believe they now conspire to destroy the Black Tower and perhaps supplant you as well. He should be slain at once!'

'If he is to die, dread majesty, let it be by my hand!' swore Balneth Bale. The self-styled Witch Lord of the Black Ark stepped beside Malus, his hands clenched into fists. 'He led my son and his army to ruin before the walls of Hag Graef. This is a matter of blood feud!'

'Let Balneth Bale strike him down, dread majesty!' Isilvar declared. 'Let him avenge his son and the feud between our cities will end as well!'

But Malekith seemed not to hear the pleas of his own vassals. '*What of this second Chaos champion?*' he asked.

Malus shrugged. 'I do not know, dread majesty. His appearance in Nagaira's tent was a surprise to me. But he is mighty; he bears tokens of favour from the Ruinous Powers, and his body cannot be harmed by mundane weapons. I suspect that he is the real power behind the horde. The warriors serve him, while he in turn serves Nagaira.'

'*And how large is the host that is arrayed against us?*'

Malus paused. Now he knew how Rasthlan had felt when he'd put the man to the question days earlier. 'I would say that the enemy still numbers around a hundred thousand warriors, dread majesty.'

The number shocked even Isilvar into silence. Malus could clearly hear the scrape of steel against steel as the Witch King turned his head to regard Nuarc. '*How does our own army fare?*'

'We were able to muster forty-four thousand troops, dread majesty: eighteen thousand from Naggarond, two thousand from the Black Ark, and ten thousand each from Hag Graef and Clar Karond, plus two thousand mercenaries scraped from the harbour leavings at the City of Ships. Taking Malus's losses into account that puts the garrison here at around fourteen thousand. So we can muster fifty-eight thousand effectives against Nagaira's host – more than enough to bleed her army dry against these walls. When our additional forces from Karond Kar and Har Ganeth arrive we will be in position to pin the enemy against the walls of the fortress and destroy them.'

'Providing Nagaira employs none of her sorcery,' Isilvar said darkly. 'Or we face no treachery from within.'

Malus could take no more. He was battered and torn, physically exhausted and now his knees were beginning to ache. With painful effort he struggled to his feet. 'If it please your dread majesty to slay me then let us be done with it,' he said. 'I acknowledge my failure in the field. What is your decision?'

For a moment no one spoke. Even Malekith seemed taken aback by the highborn's weary frankness. *'I see no failure here,'* the Witch King said at length. *'You drew Nagaira to the Black Tower as I commanded.'*

'But, dread majesty,' Myrchas exclaimed. 'He lost half the army—'

'Lost?' the Witch King said. *'No. He spent them as a warlord must to achieve his aims, fighting an enemy that has invaded our kingdom. Something none of you have done.'*

'But... you can't intend to install him as Ghrond's vaulkhar!' Myrchas cried. 'I won't have it, not with all the offences he has perpetrated against my fellow lords.'

'No. He will not be Vaulkhar of the Black Tower,' Malekith said. *'He will no longer command armies in the field.'* The Witch King leaned forward on his throne and stretched out a claw-like hand to Malus. *'Instead, I name him my champion, to confront the enemies of the state and slay them on my behalf.'*

'You can't mean that,' Malus heard someone say. It took a moment to realise it was him.

'It is my decree, Malus of Hag Graef, that you will be named my champion, and will bear the three golden skulls of Tyran upon your armour so that both friend and foe know that you fight in my name. The honour of the kingdom rests upon your shoulders. Do not forsake it, or the wrath of the Dark Mother shall be upon you.'

'I... I hear and obey, dread majesty,' Malus replied, bowing before the throne. This wasn't a true reward, he knew, but another facet of Malekith's game. He was just too tired to see what the Witch King's stratagem was. Regardless, it wasn't as though he could refuse.

'How can this be?' said Isilvar, his ruined voice charged with genuine outrage. 'He has committed grave crimes against the kingdom, and against you personally, dread majesty. How is it he not only continues to live, but is deemed worthy of such an honour.'

'He lives because it serves the Witch King's purposes that he do so,' said an iron voice from across the hall. Morathi slid silently out of the shadows, her eyes glittering with cold menace and authority. 'It is a lesson that all of you would do well to learn.'

'What of my brides, Morathi?' Malekith asked, referring to the witches cloistered in the Black Tower's convent.

'They are foolish, weak-willed girls,' Morathi replied disdainfully. 'But we may yet get some decent work out of them before the siege is finished. There are gaps in their training I must take steps to rectify.'

'*Make it so,*' the Witch King said, then regarded his vassal lords once more. '*Go now, and prepare for the coming assault. Nagaira's warriors encircle the city even as we speak. Serve me well, and your rewards will be great.*'

None of the assembled lords had any question what the alternative would be.

CHAPTER FOURTEEN

THE TEMPLE OF TZ'ARKAN

The Chaos Wastes, first week of winter

Beyond the shadowy portal of the great temple an inky darkness awaited, pulsing with blasphemous power. It swirled and eddied about Malus as he staggered along the narrow processional, recoiling from the possessed druchii as if in supplication to the daemon that rode within him.

The temple was much changed since he'd last been inside. No, it was *changing* – potent energies coursed through the ponderous stones and prickled invisibly across his icy skin. Tz'arkan swelled painfully within the highborn's tortured frame, and the forces at work within the great building responded, ordering themselves according to the daemon's will.

Malus's body moved of its own volition, driving him forward like one of the risen dead. At the far end of the processional he reached the temple antechamber. More than a hundred figures dressed in ceremonial robes lined the narrow aisle that ran through the large hall. The ancient forms had knelt in obeisance for so long that the bodies within had long since crumbled to dust, leaving behind only petrified shells of leather garments and rune-carved bone. He remembered the first time he'd seen these wretched figures, and how he'd wondered what sort of awful terror could have inspired the temple slaves to press their foreheads to the stone floor until they finally died.

Now he knew all too well.

His boot heels echoed forlornly along the dusty marble floor as he walked among the ranks of the damned. Suddenly he heard a rustling sound, like the crumbling of ancient parchment and the crackle of ruined leather, and his heart went cold as he saw the ranks of the temple servants slowly, jerkily straighten. Dust swirled within the depths of their drooping hoods, coalescing in the ghostly shapes of skeletal faces. Green globes of bale-light shone eerily from their shadowy eye sockets and their spectral mouths moved in silent adoration of their returning overlord. Ethereal hands brushed against his boots and the hem of his robes, and Tz'arkan's cruel will measured his every step, basking in the horrid worship of those agonised souls. At the far end of the chamber corroded steel creaked wearily as the armoured shells standing guard over the chamber raised their rusting blades in salute. Green fires burned within the oculars of the guards' helmets, and the runes worked into their Chaos armour crawled with sorcerous energies.

'Do you see, Darkblade? This is but a glimpse of the glories to come. The dead will rise to do my bidding even as the living give their souls to sate my glorious appetites. These are but the smallest tastes of the wonders that could have been yours had you simply chosen to serve me.'

On he went, past the tormented ghosts and into another large hall containing the altars of the four gods of the north. Behind each altar rose a horrific idol dedicated to one of the Ruinous Powers; Tz'arkan led Malus to the idol of Slaanesh and forced the highborn to his knees before the abominable figure. His hands made twisting signs in the air and his lips formed debased words that no mortal was even meant to speak. Ichor bubbled from his throat and trickled down his pallid cheeks as the daemon forced him to participate in the horrid worship of the Great Devourer. On and on the ritual went, until he feared his teeth would splinter and his lips run like tallow, and his tortured mind screamed for release.

The next sound he recognised was the daemon's laughter, cruel and cold, echoing in his brain. 'You are weak, Darkblade. So weak. This is the so-called hero of Ghrond? Your mind could not even fathom a simple acolyte's benediction. And to think I once saw such potential in you.'

Tz'arkan dragged Malus to his feet and forced him onward, into the great, cavernous space where the bridge of fire waited.

Blistering heat smote the highborn's pallid face; the reek of sulphur stung his nose and caked his aching throat. The earth itself roared angrily in the vast open space, stirred to wrath by the unnatural being trapped in the chamber above. At the far end of the long plaza, some fifty yards away, stood the statue of a winged daemon, crouching on its talons and limned by the sullen, red glow of the lake of fire at its back. The sight of the muscular, human-shaped daemon with its snarling animal face seemed almost comical now after the horrors he had witnessed during the siege of the Black Tower.

With each step the heat beating against his skin increased, and with each step the fearful energies of the daemon seemed to grow as well. Tz'arkan's power radiated from his body; he could feel it seeping from his pores like venom, soaking into the dark, stone walls and tainting them from within.

There was an angry crash, and a plume of molten stone burst from the great chasm that lay beyond the waiting daemon. Malus dimly recalled the last time he'd travelled the floating stair the river of burning stone had lain hundreds of feet below the level of the plaza. Now, it surged and roiled just a few dozen feet from the edge of the square. The heat was unbearable.

Malus could feel his skin baking and his lungs ached fiercely with each shallow breath. He tried to close his eyes against the burning air, but the daemon held him in a merciless grip, forcing him onward towards the fire.

Before long he couldn't breathe. Wisps of smoke rose from his tattered robes, and he feared his eyes would burst. He fought against the daemon's control, his efforts growing more and more frantic as he was pressed ever closer to the inferno.

Tz'arkan hissed with delight. 'Your fear is sweet. There is nothing so delicious as a mortal's death throes! But I will not permit you to die Malus, not yet.'

There was a furious hiss and an eruption of steam from the edge of the precipice. Huge boulders rose in serried ranks from the boiling rock, their faceted surfaces glowing with incandescent heat and dripping streams of liquid fire onto the roiling sea below. They formed a floating stairway to a spur of rock that hung from the ceiling of the great cavern. Beyond, Malus knew, lay the chambers of the temple sorcerers and then, the tribute chamber and prison of the daemon itself.

His skin was burning. He could smell his hair singeing in the heat. His lungs clenched, aching for a taste of cool air, and his eyes felt as dry as leather. Yet he was helpless to resist the daemon's iron control.

He seeks to break you, Malus thought. Here, at the very last, he wants to ensure his control over you. Even now he fears you may be able to circumvent his plans. Malus focused on that notion, taking hope from it even as his body was wracked with burning pain and forced to do the bidding of an inhuman will.

The highborn mounted the steps concealed in the daemon statue's flanks, noting the molten glow of heat along the trailing edges of its stone wings. His mind reeled for lack of air, but his body worked like a wood puppet, leaping heavily from one floating stone to the next.

Beyond the rocks curved a stone staircase, intricately carved with dozens of naked figures writhing in eternal torment. He vaguely remembered a body that lay sprawled along the stairs, its forearms slit from wrist to elbow. How he wished he'd taken heed of the corpse's silent warning!

Slowly and painfully the daemon drove him onward, up the stairs and into the charnel house of the sorcerers' sanctums. Here the five Chaos champions had built chambers for themselves and their servants. Those same servants had turned upon one another in the end, their minds broken by the daemon's manipulations as they waited in vain for the return of their masters until they slew one another in an orgy of cannibalism and murder. Looking back, it amazed him how blind he'd been to the dire portents laid right before his eyes. He'd been such a fool – and what ruin had been borne from it!

The daemon drove him past the lifeless, blood-streaked apartments, strewn with crumbling debris from the brutal fights that had raged there.

After a few minutes he frowned, his gaze sweeping the floors of the rooms he passed and peering along the dimly lit corridors. Where had all the bodies gone? Had they finally crumbled to dust once the daemon invoked its hideous curse?

Finally he came to the great ramp, worked with hundreds of runes and leering alabaster skulls, and the tall double doors made from solid gold. A nameless dread seized Malus's throat at the sight of them, like a condemned man catching sight of the impaling stake. Beyond those doors lay the entrance to the daemon's chamber and the end of his terrible quest.

And so it comes down to this, he thought bleakly. I've walked alone out of the Chaos Wastes, fought daemon cultists and Chaos-tainted pirates, commanded armies and fleets and fought grim battles for the fate of entire cities. Not long ago a whole kingdom rested in my hands. But this is how it ends, walking like a lamb to slaughter. It was enough to make the fiercest druchii weep tears of rage.

He had nothing left now. Desperately he wracked his brain for some trick, some stratagem to turn the tables on the daemon before it was too late. But how could he fight a creature when he couldn't even master his own wretched body?

Up the ramp the daemon drove him. The golden doors, balanced on perfect hinges, swung open at the touch of invisible hands.

Beyond, Malus heard the skeletal rustle of ancient fabrics and the creak of dried skin. It was the bodies, he realised. The bodies of the dead scholars and servants.

'See? The dead rise and serve the worthy.'

Tz'arkan forced him across the threshold before a bowing assembly of mutilated corpses, worn and withered by time. Heads rose to behold their immortal master, their dried lips smeared against their faces in unctuous, lunatic grins. Skeletal fingers clenched into claws and hollow eye sockets gaped at infernal wonders beyond the ken of mortals.

'Here are your servants, Darkblade,' the daemon declared mockingly. 'They will aid you in what must be done, for there is little time left.'

The undead servants scraped and rustled as the highborn moved stiffly among them. They shambled ahead on the stumps of ruined feet, driven by the same implacable will as he, across the gleaming marble floor and the curving lines of the sorcerous wards that had kept the daemon imprisoned for thousands of years. Their frail robes fluttered in the waves of invisible power that reverberated through the air. They paused before the great, basalt doors, flanked by massive statues of winged daemons, and waited for his approach. In the shadows to either side of the waiting slaves swirled figures of brown dust. They cringed and genuflected to Malus, and he remembered the hideous mummies who'd lain in a torturous half-life before those self-same doors, unable to find release in death thanks to the powers of the binding spells laid like a trap beneath them.

As Malus crossed the first of the arcing silver lines he felt a tremor pass through him. As cold as he'd been before, now he felt as though he were frozen in ice, his spirit wreathed in powers he could barely comprehend. He wondered if he would linger here, trapped within these terrible wards once the daemon feasted upon his soul.

Deep within the bleak despair gripping his brain, the tiny spark of an idea flickered to life. He scarcely dared consider it, half-afraid the daemon would read his thoughts. Malus frowned. Could it be possible? Did he dare?

Did he have any choice?

The undying servants pushed the black doors aside and ushered Malus into the cold radiance of the tribute chamber. The vast hall contained the wealth of dozens of plundered kingdoms now lost to time: coin and gems, plate and graven statues – more wealth than any man could spend in a thousand lifetimes. Even now, despite his dire straits, the sight of the treasure chamber kindled his avaricious heart.

But of all the wonders piled high in the tribute chamber, none could match the enormous crystal that dominated the centre of the room. It was roughly faceted and larger than a man, set in a low tripod of iron. The enormous stone glowed with a softly pulsing blue light, a strangely alluring colour considering the black evil that lay within.

His gaze drifted to the small, unassuming pedestal just a few yards inside the room. It had lain empty for a year now, he thought grimly. Hands trembling, he pulled off his gauntlets and gazed bleakly at the red stone planted on his finger. If he'd had any real courage he would have tried sawing it off rather than leave this place wearing it!

The servants shuffled amid the gleaming splendour, searching for the tools that the daemon desired. Malus's body spasmed as the daemon reasserted its fearsome control. 'The relics, little druchii,' Tz'arkan commanded. 'Lay them out and prepare yourself for the ritual.'

His heart sinking, Malus could only watch as his body obeyed the daemon's commands like a dog. He laid his saddlebag carefully on the stone floor and drew out four of the relics, each one wrapped in dirty cloth. First the Octagon of Praan, then the Idol of Kolkuth and the Dagger of Torxus. Finally he pulled free the Amulet of Vaurog, and his heart went cold at the ordeal he'd gone through to get it. Of all he'd endured to gain Tz'arkan his relics, the price he'd paid for the damned amulet would haunt him for all time. Last of all, he reached for the warpsword at his belt.

'No,' the daemon commanded, forcefully enough to send ichor running from the highborn's eyes and ears. 'The servants will see to the blade.'

Two of the shambling corpses knelt beside Malus and slid the long, black sword from its scabbard. Wisps of smoke rose from their withered hands as they handled the burning blade.

Malus watched the servants lay the blade beside the other relics, while another pair of servants approached from deeper within the chamber.

One carried an urn made from gold and etched with spirals of sorcerous runes. The other held a tablet of ancient, weathered stone, carved with dense lines of blasphemous script.

'Take the urn,' the daemon said. 'Remove the cover, and I will show you what must be done.'

He tried to fight it, like the condemned man fights against the grip of his executioners. But for the first time his indomitable will failed him. Malus watched helplessly as his hands took the heavy urn from the corpse's hands and pulled free the lid. Inside was a grey powder that reeked of the crypt.

The highborn could feel the daemon's joy as the urn was opened. 'The bones of my tormentors,' it said. 'Gathered from the far corners of the world. All five of the champions who trapped me were ground up to fill that bowl. All but that scheming fool Ehrenlish – in the end I got all but his skull, but that will be enough.'

Tz'arkan turned Malus bodily and marched him to the crystal. 'Use the dust to lay out the sigil precisely as I command, the daemon said. You must do this alone, Darkblade. I cannot force you. Follow my instructions in every particular. Your soul depends on it.'

All at once he felt the grip of the daemon loosen – the change was so sudden Malus swayed on his feet, stopping his fall only by effort of will. His gaze drifted to the black blade, lying on the stone just a few feet away.

'Do not attempt it,' the daemon said. 'I will stop you before you take a single step, then I will make you suffer in ways you never dreamt possible. Remember the chamber of the altars? That was a gentle kiss compared to what I could do if I were truly displeased. And in the end you would have even less time to save your eternal spirit. Now, begin.'

The instructions flowed like icy filth into the highborn's brain. He gasped at the hideous images flowing through his mind and reached into the urn for a handful of dust.

CHAPTER FIFTEEN

THE CORPSE-HANDLERS

The Black Tower of Ghrond, four weeks before

The crash of thunder smote the walls of the fortress like a hammer blow, causing many of the defenders on the wall to duck their heads and cry out in fear. The earth-shaking roar all but drowned out the high, skirling wail of the horns, crying their shrill warnings from the redoubts. Malus rose to his feet from the base of the battlements and peered out at the lightning-shot blackness. A savage, reeking wind roared in his face and tangled the loose strands of his sweat-streaked hair.

All was darkness upon the ashen plain. He counted the seconds, waiting for a flash of pale lightning. There! A bolt of fire burnt across the heavens, revealing a rushing tide of monstrosities charging for the walls.

'Sa'an'ishar!' he shouted to the spearmen crouching against the battlements beside him. 'On your feet! Here they come!'

Now the roaring of the advancing army could be heard above the raging tempest, and the strobe and flicker of the lightning increased overhead, pushing back the clinging shadows and revealing the oncoming attackers less than twenty yards from the base of the wall. Already the ground there was carpeted with the bodies of marauders and beastmen, and as Malus watched, a black rain of crossbow bolts began to fall upon the screaming horde from the sloping redoubts to the left and right. Horned, half-naked beastmen screamed and stumbled, pierced through by the deadly bolts. Some ran on, while others fell to the blood-soaked earth and died. Still the seething mob charged forward, undaunted by the deadly hail. Long ladders bobbed above lines of grim-faced barbarians; when one of the ladder-men was struck down another marauder ran to take his place. Some men kept going with two or three bolts jutting from their bodies, driven forward by unholy battle-lust and the blessings of their fearful northern gods.

Malus drew his swords and set his jaw in a grim line as the attackers drew closer. Already his armour was splashed with dried blood and stinking ichor, and his arms felt leaden from all the killing he'd done. He couldn't recall if this was the third assault or the fourth. At this point he didn't even know if it was day or night. The clouds that had rolled in before the advancing horde had tightened about the Black Tower like a shroud, blocking out the pale northern sunlight. Once the fighting began, time lost all meaning.

With groans and bitter curses the druchii company assigned to hold this stretch of wall clambered slowly to their feet. They were state troops from Clar Karond, evidenced by their blue robes and the short, lightweight kheitans favoured by druchii corsairs. When the first attack had begun the troops were in high spirits, but now their faces were tired and grim, stained with grime and other men's blood. They looped their arms through battered shields and took up their weapons – one warrior in three hefted a repeater crossbow, while the rest drew their short, stabbing swords. They tested their footing amid the pools of drying blood that stained the paving stones and watched the oncoming mob to see where the ladders would likely land. A young druchii ran down the line, scattering sawdust from a wooden bucket. It would soak up some of the blood once the fighting started in earnest, but there was never quite enough.

Malus leaned back and peered down the length of the wall, checking to make sure all the troops were standing to. He saw a pair of legs still stretched out across the paving stones and jogged down to take a look. 'On your feet, spearman,' the highborn growled, kneeling before the warrior. The warrior was a young woman, called up to fight with the regiment in the wake of Malekith's proclamation of war. There wasn't a mark on her that Malus could see, but her face was white as chalk and her lips were blue. Most likely the blow of a hammer or club had ruptured something beneath the skin and she'd bled to death in her sleep. Taking hold of her mail shirt, Malus dragged her over to the inner side of the wall and rolled her over the edge. Already there were deep drifts of corpses piled on the flagstones forty feet below. Men were stripping the bodies of armour and weapons and dragging the corpses to the furnaces. Even in these cold climes, the dead could carry pestilence that could decimate the fortress city's defenders.

The rest of the line looked ready, as far as he could see. Each of the eight sections of wall was held by a single regiment, stretching for more than two and a half miles between the hulking redoubts. The regimental commander anchored the far end, while Malus's end had been anchored by the second-in-command. That fellow's brains had been splashed against the side of the embrasure just a few yards to Malus's right. He'd happened to be nearby when the officer died, and without thinking had stepped in to take his place. That had been during the second assault, and he'd remained ever since.

Malekith had given him no orders after declaring him champion. With no troops to command – not even a retinue to call his own – it was as though he'd been swept aside in the haste and confusion of the impending attack.

He'd found his way to his chambers, found servants to fill a bath and bring him food, and watched as a pair of smiths from the fortress armoury affixed a set of three golden skulls to the breastplate of his armour. The skulls marked him as the Witch King's champion: Athlan na Dyr, the Taker of Heads. As far as Malus was concerned, they made him a tempting target for every bull-head and barbarian that came over the walls.

Nevertheless, when the horns began to wail he had buckled on his harness and headed for the wall.

He'd hoped that when the attack began it would be led by Nagaira's champion. The warrior, aided by the Amulet of Vaurog, would be a literal engine of destruction atop the city walls, but Malus hoped that with enough spearmen behind him the champion could be pulled down long enough for him to pull the artefact from around his thin neck. After that they could hack the bastard to pieces and hang his helmeted head from the battlements, and Malus would find a way to slip out of the fortress and make his way into the Wastes.

But nothing had gone according to plan so far. The champion had yet to show himself among the screaming throngs, and most of the warriors on the wall regarded Malus with open resentment and hostility. The spearmen of the Black Tower had heard the stories of his disastrous expedition to the north, and blamed him for the loss of their mates and of their commander, Lord Meiron. But they were far from the worst – as Malus walked the battlements he came upon warriors from Hag Graef and the Black Ark, both of whom saw him as the blackest of villains after the ill-fated events of the previous spring. They were just as likely to stab him in the back or throw him from the walls in the middle of an attack, Witch King's champion or no. He'd stayed so long with the regiment from Clar Karond simply because he was just another officer to them.

The crossbows along the battlements were firing now, and Malus could hear the screams of the dying, forty feet below. 'Ladders coming up!' one of the warriors shouted, and the highborn rushed up to the battlements to see how many had landed nearby.

There were only two: one was very close to the redoubt at his right, while the other was almost ten yards to his left. Others going up farther down the line were someone else's problem. Swift-footed barbarians were already scrambling up the long ladders, many with a throwing-axe gripped in their teeth. More barbarians at the base of the wall were flinging axes up at the defenders, but the druchii paid them little heed.

'Crossbows cover the ladders!' the highborn yelled, although there was little need. The men on this part of the wall knew the routine well by now. Bolts from their crossbows and from the firing slits of the nearby redoubt raked along the line of men climbing hard for the wall. The marauders advanced fearlessly into the storm of black-fletched bolts, pressing on even after being shot multiple times. When they could climb no more they hurled themselves clear of the ladder, screaming or laughing like madmen the whole way to the ground, and those below would redouble their efforts to reach the top.

And reach the top they would. They always did, despite the appalling losses they suffered. The crossbows could only fire so fast, and the Chaos warriors had no fear of death. Slowly but surely the line of warriors inched closer to the battlements.

'Four men on each ladder!' Malus roared, rushing forward to welcome the first foe who came over the battlements. Obediently the troops crowded close around the end of each ladder, ready to strike the attackers from multiple directions at once. This wasn't duelling or elegant swordplay – this was pure butchery, killing men as quickly and efficiently as possible. So long as they kept the enemy warriors from gaining a foothold on the battlements they could almost slaughter the oncoming attackers at will.

Suddenly the air hummed with half a dozen thrown axes, burning through the air in short, glittering arcs as the warriors closest to the top let fly. There was a clash of steel and a warrior beside Malus toppled without a sound; a hurled axe had cleft the spearman's helmet and buried itself in his forehead. 'Shields up, damn you!' the highborn shouted. 'Mind their axes!' He himself reached up and checked the strap on his new helmet. Malus hated wearing the thing, but it was far better than the alternative.

A face appeared at the top of the ladder, grinning like a daemon. Malus leapt at him with a shout, and just missed having a hurled axe embedded in his face. His sudden move threw the man's aim off, sending the spinning projectile blurring past his ear, and before the warrior could drag out his sword Malus stabbed him through the throat. Blood poured in a flood down the barbarian's tattooed chest, but the warrior kept coming, forcing his way up the ladder and onto the battlements. Spearmen dashed in from both sides, stabbing and hacking at the man, and Malus tucked his shoulder in and crashed into the reeling man's bloody midsection, sending him flying out into space.

But the warrior's last seconds bought more time for the man behind him. A sword thrust slid off Malus's armoured belly, and then the screaming beastman lowered his horned head and butted the highborn in the chest. The force of the impact hurled him back a few feet, and the bellowing warrior leapt quickly onto the battlements. Druchii warriors pressed in on either side of the foe, stabbing and slashing with their short blades. Roaring in fury, Malus leapt back into the fray as well, catching the warrior in the middle of a turn and hacking through the side of his neck. Hot blood sprayed across the spearman as the horned warrior staggered beneath the blow. One of the spearmen rushed at the warrior, intent on finishing the creature off, but the beastman was far from finished. With a braying shout it lowered its broad sword and caught the onrushing spearman with a thrust to his right thigh that tore clean through the muscle and cut a major artery.

The druchii fell with a scream, clutching at the mortal wound, while his companions plunged their blades into the beastman's back.

A barbarian reached the battlements next and leapt over the dying beastman straight at Malus, his face twisted with madness and his arms outstretched in a deadly embrace. Snarling in disdain the highborn ducked clear of the warrior's foolhardy attack, then rushed after the madman's tumbling body and kicked it off the edge of the inner wall. The dying druchii was trying to drag his way clear of the melee, leaving a thick trail of blood through the newly lain sawdust.

Another druchii fell to the paving stones, grappling with a dagger-wielding barbarian. Malus rushed over, planted a foot between the marauder's shoulders and split his skull with a downward sweep of his sword. Two more Chaos warriors had made their way onto the battlements, and a third waited at the top of the ladder, looking for a space to clamber across. Cursing lustily, the highborn dived back into the fray, using his longer swords to telling effect.

One beastman went down, his neck carved to the spine while he traded blows with a nearby spearman, while the marauder to the beastman's left collapsed with the point of the highborn's left-hand sword buried in his kidney. The warrior on the ladder leapt to take their place, but Malus was ready for him. He rushed in as the barbarian jumped, effectively moving in beneath the hulking warrior and stabbing upwards into the man's unprotected belly. The barbarian screamed, bringing his axe down on the highborn's back, but his enchanted plates turned aside the powerful blow. Gritting his teeth, Malus staggered beneath the weight of the dying warrior, but he summoned up his hate and pushed forwards with all his might, unloading the limp form onto the next man scrambling up the ladder. Taken by surprise, both marauders plummeted, screaming, to the ground.

The next warrior up the ladder never reached the top before a crossbow bolt buried itself in the side of his head. For the space of a few seconds the defenders had some precious breathing room. 'Close up ranks!' Malus shouted. He pointed to the limp form of the mortally wounded druchii. 'Someone drag him out of the way. Quickly now!'

A quick check of the other ladder showed that the druchii there had things well in hand; so far none of the attackers had even reached the battlements before dying underneath the defenders' blades.

More spearmen rushed over to surround the ladder next to Malus. Breathing heavily, the highborn stepped back to let the fresh warriors take their turn. He rubbed a gauntleted hand across his mouth, inadvertently smearing his lips with a foeman's blood. Mother of Night, I could use a drink, he thought.

Just then he heard a shrill note sounding from the redoubt to his right. He frowned, trying to puzzle out his meaning – then he heard the guttural roars and agonised screams coming from the next wall over. Spitting a blasphemous curse, Malus turned and ran for the redoubt's iron door, just a few yards to his right. He pounded on the portal with the hilt of his sword shouting imprecations to the druchii on the other side. Within moments the bolts were drawn back and the heavy door opened to admit him.

The highborn brushed past the sentry at the door and ran down the long, narrow passageway that connected to the next wall over. Shouts and commands echoed up and down the corridor from the crossbow and bolt thrower teams firing from inside the fortification, calling out targets and shouting for more ammunition. He passed barrels of water that held long, heavy bolts tipped with glass orbs that glowed a baleful green: they were dangerous and volatile dragonsfire bolts, held in reserve in case the enemy horde sent giants or other huge creatures against the walls.

The passage ran on for almost fifty yards, then angled sharply right. Another fifty yards later and the highborn reached another iron door, watched over by a pair of nervous sentries. Hands and sword hilts were pounding frantically on the other side of the door. The sentries saw Malus coming and snapped to attention. 'The enemy has reached the wall,' one of the warriors began.

'I heard the horn,' Malus snapped. 'Open the door and let me through.'

The two men hesitated – then saw the fearsome look on the highborn's face. As one, the warriors turned to the door and drew back the heavy bolts.

Almost at once there were panicked warriors pushing the door open from the outside. Snarling with rage, Malus drew the iron portal open and roared at the men on the other side. 'Stand to, you worthless dogs!' he said, blocking the doorway with his bloodstained form.

The white-faced spearmen recoiled at the wrathful figure standing before them, and Malus quickly stepped into the space they vacated. Behind him the iron door slammed shut again and the bolts shot home. 'Where do you bastards think you're going?' the highborn raged. 'You're here to defend this wall or die in the attempt. Those were the orders the Witch King gave you!'

But Malus saw at once that the situation was very grave indeed. The battlements near the redoubt were littered with dead and dying spearmen, and marauders were pouring over the battlements. There were fifty spearmen between Malus and the raging battle, all crammed tightly against the side of the redoubt. As far as he could tell the enemy was also pushing hard in the other direction, trying to reach one of the ramps that led down into the city proper. If that happened there might well be no stopping them.

There was a ramp just to Malus's right, and the marauders were fighting hard to reach it. Only the sheer press of the panicked spearmen were holding them momentarily at bay. 'Move forward, damn your eyes!' the highborn commanded. 'There's no safety back here! If the foemen don't kill you I surely will!'

The men wavered, weighing their options. One look at Malus showed that the highborn was deadly serious and perfectly capable of carrying out his threat. One of the spearmen, a senior warrior, exclaimed 'Our commander is dead, highborn, and we don't have enough soldiers to drive the enemy back!'

Malus considered calling for reinforcements from the redoubt, but quickly cast the notion aside. Jostling a pair of spearmen aside, he checked the avenue at the base of the ramp and saw no less than two hundred druchii poring through the piled bodies at the base of the wall. 'Who are they?' he demanded, pointing at the corpse-handlers with his sword.

The exasperated trooper glanced down at the druchii band. Despite his panic, his lip curled in distaste. 'Mercenaries,' he replied. 'Harbour scum hired by the drachau of Clar Karond. Captain Thurlayr refused to have them on the wall. Said gulls like them were only fit for picking over the dead.'

Malus shook his head in disbelief. 'That kind of thinking is what got Thurlayr killed, soldier,' he snapped. He grabbed the front of the trooper's mail shirt and pulled him close. 'What's your name?'

The warrior looked into the highborn's black eyes and went pale. 'Euthen, my lord.'

'Well, now you're *Captain* Euthen,' Malus hissed. 'Take charge of these fools and get them back in the battle by the time I return or I'm throwing you off the wall myself. Do you understand?'

'Y... yes sir. Clear sir.'

'Then get to it, Captain,' Malus shouted, pushing the man away. Without waiting for a reply he shoved past another spearman and raced down the long ramp towards the mercenaries.

The harbour rats had the look of corsairs, from what Malus could see at a distance. Tattered robes of different hues, lightweight kheitans and blackened mail were common, and the warriors carried a wild assortment of weapons, including a profusion of daggers and looted throwing axes. Approximately half the mercenaries were poring over the bodies at the base of the wall, stripping them not only of weapons and armour but valuables as well. As he watched, one of the druchii took a dagger to the ring finger of a druchii officer, popping the digit loose with a practiced motion – and then losing it among the pile of corpses beneath him. The rest of the mercenaries sat on the paving stones of the avenue and played at dice or dragon's teeth, seemingly oblivious to the desperate battle being waged on the battlements above.

'Form up!' Malus shouted at the cutthroats. 'The enemy is on the battlements, and it's time you earned your keep!'

The corsairs looked up at the distant figure of the highborn as though he were speaking in a foreign tongue. The looter who'd been groping among the corpses for the officer's severed finger frowned up at Malus. 'We're not allowed,' he shouted back in a bemused voice. 'This one here – ' he pointed at the officer's corpse – 'said we weren't fit to stand 'mongst real soldiers.'

'Besides,' chuckled a female, scooping up her dice, 'it's a good deal safer down here.'

'It won't be for long once the enemy reaches the ramps!' Malus snapped. 'And you can't spend your ill-gotten coin if you're hanging from some beastman's banner-pole! Now get off your arses and get up here!'

The cutthroats looked to one another, considering their options. Malus didn't wait for them to reply – arguing with them would only weaken his already shaky authority, so it was better to act as though he expected them to obey. He turned and ran back up the ramp, and within moments was gratified to hear someone down below start barking orders in a surprisingly professional tone. At least someone down there knows what he's doing, Malus thought.

On the battlements, things looked grim indeed. The Chaos foothold was already more than fifteen yards wide and expanding steadily. Euthen had managed to bully the panicked spearmen back into the fight, but their numbers were too few to accomplish much more than keeping the enemy away from the near ramp.

Malus shoved his way into the crowd. 'Form a wedge!' he shouted, elbowing cursing spearmen into a rough semblance of the formation. 'Wider! All the way to the edges of the parapet!'

Trusting that the soldiers would follow his command, the highborn worked his way to where the tip of the wedge would begin. He found Euthen there, fighting valiantly against a leering Chaos marauder wielding twin axes in his knotty hands. As Malus approached, he watched the marauder carefully, looking for a sign that he was about to strike. Euthen lunged in, attempting a half-hearted swipe at the marauder's leg, and the barbarian tore into the spearman with a terrible howl, hacking into the druchii's left shoulder with one axe while the other sent the captain's short sword spinning off the edge of the parapet. But while the warrior was savaging the hapless Euthen, Malus rushed in and stabbed the barbarian cleanly through the heart.

The warrior sank to the stones with a curse on his lips. Meanwhile, Malus took the injured Euthen by the collar and gave him a gentle shove in the direction of the ramp. 'Warriors of Clar Karond!' he cried, raising his sword. 'Form wedge on me!'

No sooner had he said this than a red-haired barbarian rushed at Malus with a savage yell, his greatsword swinging in a wide arc for the highborn's head. Malus saw the move and hissed disdainfully, ducking and stepping into the stroke so that the wild blow passed harmlessly overhead, then stabbing the warrior in the groin with both of his blades. The man fell with a terrible scream, and Malus quickly stepped past him, deeper into the press of foes. 'Advance!' he ordered.

Miraculously, the spearmen did. Now Malus had foes on three sides, but the men to the left and right aimed their blows at the soldiers in front of them. The warrior before Malus snarled and chopped at him with his axe; the highborn blocked the blow with his left-hand sword and then slashed open the thigh of the warrior to his right. The injured marauder faltered and the spearman in front of him finished the man with a thrust to the neck. When the axe-wielding barbarian attacked again, Malus blocked with his right-hand sword and stabbed his other blade into the marauder on the left. Then he devoted his sole attention to the warrior in front of him, trapping the warrior's axe with a sweep of his left sword and stabbing the marauder in the eye with the blade in his right.

And so the slaughter began. Coldly, methodically, the druchii began to reduce the Chaos foothold. Malus knew that if they could at least fight their way to the enemy ladders then they could cut off their foes' reinforcements, then eventually sheer numbers would eliminate the rest of the marauders that had made it to the walls.

Working together the spearmen made steady progress. Soldiers were struck down to either side of the highborn, only to be replaced by the next spearmen in line. After almost ten yards there were no spearmen left, but Malus saw that the corpse-pickers had taken their place. The mercenaries were clearly in their element in this style of fighting, accustomed as they were to the tight quarters and close sword-work of boarding actions aboard ship. They struck down barbarians with underhanded cuts to their legs, or knives flung into their throats. Sometimes Malus would strike at a man to his flank and then look back to see the foe in front of him collapsing with a throwing axe buried in his skull.

Finally they'd cut off all of the enemy ladders and had cut the marauders down to less than a dozen warriors – and that was when things became truly dangerous. The surviving marauders realised they were trapped, and as one they decided to take as many of their hated foes with them as they could.

A warrior came screaming at Malus with a bloodstained sword in his right hand and a battered shield in his left. Eyes wild and foam flying from the corners of his mouth, he unleashed a flurry of blows that the highborn had to devote all his energy to deflect. He tried to knock the man off his stride with a lightning stroke to his eyes, but the marauder simply caught the blow on the edge of his shield and barrelled on, hammering away at Malus's guard.

So intent was the highborn on this frenzied warrior that he failed to notice when the man on his left slipped in a pool of blood and went to one knee. His opponent crowed in triumph and brought down his heavy warhammer – against the side of Malus's head.

The shock was all-powerful. One moment Malus was locked in a deadly battle with the man in front of him and the next he was hurtling to the ground. He bounced off the paving stones face-first, his brain unable to grasp how he'd got there.

There was a roaring in his ears, like a raging surf that ebbed and flowed just above his head. Everything blurred; the only thing he felt with perfect clarity was a thin trickle of ichor leaking down his cheek.

I'm bleeding, he thought stupidly, and realised that he was likely about to die.

But instead of seeing a sword or hammer descend on his skull, he saw a druchii boot heel come down just inches from his face. The roaring continued, and the boot moved on, to be replaced by another.

He lay there watching boots stamp and slide past him for what seemed like a very long time, and it wasn't until the roaring in his ears tapered away that he realised he hadn't been killed after all.

The next thing he knew there were rough hands pulling at him, trying to roll him over. 'That was the damnedest thing I've ever seen, if you don't mind me saying so, captain,' said a voice. 'Reminds me of this damn-fool highborn I used to know–'

The hands rolled him over, and Malus found himself looking up into a dark-eyed, grinning face. He recognised the scarred features at once, and let out a bemused grunt.

'There you are, Hauclir, you damned rogue,' he said. 'Where is that wine I asked for?' And with that the world went utterly dark.

CHAPTER SIXTEEN

DAEMONS AND CUTTHROATS

Cold water splashed Malus in the face. He came to, sputtering and coughing, propped up against the hard stone of the battlements. Pools of blood and body parts littered the paving stones around him.

A figure knelt in front of the highborn, holding an upended water bottle. 'Sorry to wake you, my lord,' Hauclir said calmly, 'but it looks like we're about to be attacked again, so I don't have the luxury of allowing you to sleep off that little knock you got on the head. You and I have a bit of talking to do while we're both still able to do it.'

Malus tried to rub the water out of his rheumy eyes. When his vision returned, he found Hauclir to be studying him intently, paying especial attention to his face and neck. The former guard captain was dressed much like the rest of the mercenaries, though the cut of his robes were finer and better kept, and his kheitan was thick, sturdy dwarf-hide. He wore his customary mail hauberk, and his short sword sat in its oiled scabbard. A long, knotted oak cudgel dangled loosely from his right hand.

The highborn shook his head bemusedly. 'I thought I was dreaming,' he muttered thickly. With tentative fingers he reached up and prodded at the side of his head.

'I had much the same reaction,' Hauclir said dryly. His lips twisted in a sarcastic grin, but his dark eyes were cold and hard. 'Now, I'm not going to ask how you somehow went from a closely-hunted outlaw to the Witch King's personal champion; I've seen the way your damned mind works, and nothing you do surprises me any more. Instead, I want you to tell me, in very compelling detail, why you saw fit to betray each and every man in your service after we left you at Karond Kar.'

Malus's own expression hardened. His former retainer's impertinent tone caused the highborn to bristle. 'You were my damned vassal!' he snapped. 'Your life was mine to use as I pleased! I owe you no explanation.'

But Hauclir was far from cowed by the highborn's imperious tone. A slow, dangerous smile spread across his scarred, angular face. 'Look around you, my lord. Do you fancy you're reclining in your high tower back at the

Hag? No. You're sitting on a battlefield, surrounded by blood and spilled guts, and the nearest nobleman for two miles is lying at the bottom of the wall with the rest of the rubbish. Right at the moment I own this part of the fortress wall, so you're going to play things by my rules. So let's hear your story, my lord, and it better be a good one, or else I'll chuck you over this damned wall myself.'

The former retainer's tone was light, even cheerful, but Malus looked in his eyes and saw the anger burning there. He had absolutely no doubt that Hauclir meant every word he said. So he shrugged, and told the former guardsman everything.

Or at least he tried to. He hadn't got much past receiving Tz'arkan's curse when the next wave of attackers came howling at the walls. Malus was forced to wait while Hauclir and his men drove off the assault. His weapons had been taken from him, and he wasn't sure he could stand up yet, anyway.

They were interrupted twice more by enemy assaults before Malus finally got Hauclir to the moment their paths crossed once again. The former retainer sat wearily against the battlements beside Malus, picking dried bits of blood from his haggard face. For a long time he didn't speak at all. 'So. A daemon, you say?'

Malus nodded. 'A daemon.'

Hauclir grunted. 'Well, that explains your eyes. And the fact that your head wasn't splattered across the flagstones by that damned hammer.'

The highborn sighed. 'I don't deny there are certain advantages to the situation.'

'And you had no idea it was your father who was at Vaelgor Keep?' the former guardsman asked. 'Who else did you think it could be?'

'It could have been anyone, Hauclir. Lurhan wasn't flying his banner outside the keep, after all. At the time it made more sense that it was Isilvar, working in conjunction with my sister.'

Hauclir grudgingly nodded. 'Yes. I suppose you're right.' He looked sidelong at his former master. 'But you realise that now I have an even more compelling reason to throw you over the wall.'

Malus spread his hands. 'You wanted the truth, Hauclir. Can I have my swords back now?'

'Certainly not. You're a damned daemonhost!'

'For the Dark Mother's sake, Hauclir!' Malus snapped. 'I had a daemon inside me from the moment I returned from the north. Did I ever once try to kill you? No. In fact, I made you a very rich man.'

'Before you broke one of the cardinal laws of the land and I had it all stripped away from me.'

The highborn folded his arms tightly about his chest. 'Shall I beg your pardon, then? What do you want from me, Hauclir? I did what I had to do. Do you think you could have done any better in my place?'

'Gods Below, my lord. I have no idea,' the former guardsman said. He sighed. 'To be honest, it didn't hit me as hard as some of the others. Your man Silar took it the worst, him and Arleth Vann. Dolthaic, he was just angry about losing all the gold.'

Malus nodded thoughtfully. 'Arleth Vann thought that all of you had gone to sea after the battle outside Hag Graef.'

The former retainer shrugged. 'That was Silar and Dolthaic's idea. I just followed along. Couldn't stay in Hag Graef any more, so why not? The two of them put to sea a day after we got there. Looked up the master of the *Shadowblade*; Dolthaic said he knew the captain from a raiding cruise the summer before. They asked if I wanted to go, but I've seen all the ocean I ever want to see. So, I stayed on around the dockyards, picking up the odd work here and there. And then I fell in with these rats,' he said, indicating the mercenaries sitting a discreet distance away. 'We were shaking down bridge travellers for tolls when Malekith's call to arms reached the city. The drachau scooped a lot of the gangs up after that. I'm sure he hopes none of us survive to go back and dirty up his precious city.'

Malus nodded. He reached down and picked up his dented helmet. 'So, it appears I owe you my life.'

'Again.'

The highborn grinned. 'Yes. Again.'

'You don't expect me to serve you again, do you?' Hauclir asked. 'I'm not your man any more, my lord. Not after all that's happened.'

Malus shook his head. 'I'm still technically an outlaw, despite all the finery. I couldn't hold you to your oath if I wanted to.'

'But you still need my help,' Hauclir said.

'Do I?'

'Oh, yes, my lord, you do. And you damned well know it.'

The highborn spread his hands. 'Nothing escapes you, it seems. All right. Name your price.'

Hauclir made a show of thinking things over. 'That Chaos champion has the amulet you need, correct?'

'Correct.'

'And your sister's tent was chock full of loot, correct?'

'Before I burnt it to the ground, yes.'

The former guardsman nodded. 'Well, I expect your path is going to take you back into her vicinity before all is said and done,' he said thoughtfully. 'Me and mine get all the loot we can carry, and we're yours for the asking.'

The highborn looked at Hauclir bemusedly. 'You're a fool. You realise that, I trust?'

'So my mother told me,' he answered. 'Do we have a deal, or not?'

Malus nodded. 'Done.'

'All right then,' Hauclir said, rising to his feet. 'I'll go and explain things to the troops.'

The highborn watched his former retainer go, shaking his head in amazement. For the life of him, he couldn't be certain who was getting the better end of the deal, but all of a sudden he felt much better about his chances of getting the amulet and getting out of the Black Tower alive.

Sometime later Hauclir remembered to return Malus his swords. The rubies in both pommels had been carefully pried away.

It was not long after the twelfth assault that the roiling darkness suddenly receded, leaving the fortress's defenders blinking wearily in the pale light of early morning. Cheers went up from within the city, as the soldiers took the sunlight as a sign the siege had been lifted, but the exhausted warriors holding the battlements saw the enemy encampment for the first time and knew that their ordeal was perhaps only just beginning.

The Chaos horde was camped in a broad band that completely surrounded the fortress city. Cook fires by the hundreds sent thin tendrils of smoke into the sky, and herds of northern horses mingled in great corrals around the camp's circular perimeter. The dusty ground seethed with motion, the dark figures moving about on their errands like a multitude of ravening ants. Malus looked out over the part of the encampment opposite his part of the wall and shook his head in awe. Was there no end to the damned beasts?

If he stood at the far left end of the wall and leaned out far enough to see past the rightward redoubt he could glimpse a pavilion of indigo-dyed tents, just like the ones he'd burned a few days ago. There was a strange distortion in the air above and around the tent, similar to the haze of hot air over a forge. That was where Nagaira and her champion would be found.

His eyes ached and his stomach rumbled, and he hadn't been clean since the Dark Mother alone knew when. Most of the mercenaries were sound asleep, stretched out on the filthy paving stones with their weapons across their chests. Over the last two days he'd got to know many of the sell-swords in the company. None of them had names; only nicknames, to make it harder for the city watch or anyone else to track them down using sorcery. He met a professional killer named Cutter, an unlucky cutpurse named Ten-thumbs, a gambler named Pockets and too many others to count. The highborn learned at length that Hauclir's nickname was Knock-knock, which privately amused Malus.

There were nearly a hundred of the cutthroats to begin with, but after throwing back no less than seven attacks their numbers had dwindled to sixty-five. Almost half that number was wounded to a greater or lesser degree; supposedly there were aid stations and orderlies to patrol the walls and remove injured soldiers, but they'd seen nothing like that since taking charge of their stretch of wall. They had long since run out of bolts for their crossbows as well. Malus had tried to use his authority to get more from the closest redoubt, but the captain in charge had flatly refused, claiming that only Lord Myrchas could authorise such a transfer. The highborn hadn't pursued the matter further. The less he had to deal with that den of snakes in the citadel the better.

He did send some of his more talented foragers into the city in search of food and drink, once it became clear that no one was going to send them anything to eat. In this, the mercenaries were singularly successful, returning to the wall with roast fowl, boiled eggs, fresh bread and cheese and several bottles of decent wine. Malus didn't ask any questions, and the foragers were happy to not give any answers.

Three hours into the morning, Malus was sipping from one such bottle when the iron door of the far redoubt swung open and a ramrod-straight figure in gleaming armour strode into the sunlight. Nuarc made his way slowly but purposefully down the length of the wall, eyeing the snoring mercenaries with a look that was somewhere between outrage and bemusement. The few cutthroats still awake returned the general's gaze with the flat stare of hungry wolves.

When the general reached Malus's reclining form his expression of shock only deepened. 'By the Dark Mother!' he exclaimed. 'We were starting to think you'd been killed. No one's seen you at your apartments for days.' Nuarc jerked his head in the direction of the mercenaries. 'What in the Blessed Murderer's name are you doing with this rabble?' he asked. Then his face turned deadly serious and he leaned close to the highborn. 'They aren't holding you for some sort of ransom, are they?'

The notion gave Malus the first real laugh he'd had in a very long time. 'No, my lord. They know very well that I'm not worth the trouble.' He cocked his head at the general. 'Out for a stroll in the sunshine, general?'

Nuarc glowered at the grinning highborn. 'Out to see what the enemy is up to, and to check on things along the wall,' he said darkly. 'And to get away from those caterwauling fools back at the citadel, truth be told.'

Malus held up the pilfered bottle. 'Can I interest you in some wine, general?' Much to the highborn's surprise, Nuarc accepted the offer and took a deep draught before handing it back. The gesture sobered Malus at once.

'How bad is our situation, my lord?'

On reflex, the general glanced at the mercenaries some feet away to make certain they were out of likely earshot. 'Things could be better,' he admitted. 'We've held the walls for almost three days now, but the regiments have taken a bad beating. The hardest hit units have been rotated off the walls, but our reserves are being stretched thin.'

'Rotated?' Malus exclaimed. 'We've been up here for two days! No one's brought us food or ammunition, and no one's sent orderlies for our wounded.'

'That's because no one knows you're here,' the general answered grimly. 'None of the mercenary companies are part of the army's muster list, and no one back at the citadel is capable of thinking past their own damned agendas.'

The thought shocked Malus. 'You mean to tell me no one is in command?'

Nuarc shook his head. 'Each drachau thinks of nothing but his own honour and prestige. They intrigue against one another constantly, and no one will cooperate towards the city's defence. They've staked out which walls belong to each drachau, and they spare no thought for the others.'

'But... but that's absurd!' Malus cried. 'What does the Witch King say about this?'

The general shrugged. 'He watches and waits to see which lord will assert himself. It's his way. But Myrchas is too timid, Isilvar is too inexperienced, Balneth Bale is too weak and Jhedir of Clar Karond is too drunk. About the only consensus Myrchas, Isilvar and Bale have reached is that you have to be put to death at the first available opportunity. Fortunately for you, they can't decide what manner of execution to use.'

Malus shook his head in stupefied wonder. 'What about our reinforcements, then?'

Nuarc took a deep breath. 'Any forces from Karond Kar would have a long way to travel, even if they commandeered every available boat and sailed them to the western shore of the Sea of Malice,' he said. 'They aren't expected for a week or more. Troops from Har Ganeth, on the other hand, should have been here by now. No one knows what could have caused their delay.'

Malus could venture a guess, but thought it wiser not to say. He took a long draught from the bottle and rolled it around his tongue. 'I regret that I cost the army a further ten thousand troops,' he said bitterly.

'Nonsense,' the old general barked. 'I might have done the same thing. It was a good plan, but you assumed too much.'

The highborn considered this, and nodded. 'All right. What do you think we should do now?'

'Me?' Nuarc replied, a bit surprised at the question. He looked out at the enemy encampment for a moment before replying. 'I would pull the army back to the inner wall.'

Malus blinked. 'But then we'd be trapped.'

'We're trapped *now*, boy,' the general shot back. 'The inner wall is higher, and there's less ground to have to defend. We could rotate units more often and still make the enemy pay a steep price every time they tested us. We're very well supplied, so Nagaira can't starve us out, and ultimately time is not on her side. Our warriors at sea are returning home even now, and within a month she would be facing a powerful army of highborn marching up from the south.' The general shrugged. 'But no one has asked my thoughts on the matter.'

The highborn took another drink and turned his face to the sky. 'Well, at least the sun is shining.'

'I know. That's what worries me the most,' the general said.

'And how is that, my lord?' Malus asked.

'Because up until now your sister has put a great deal of effort into keeping the city locked in darkness. According to Morathi, the cost of such effort is considerable, especially in the face of opposition from her and the city's convent.'

'Morathi has been fighting against Nagaira? I hadn't noticed.'

'Did you imagine all that lightning was your sister's doing?' Nuarc asked. 'It doesn't make much sense when one is spending all that energy to keep things dark, now does it?'

'No, I suppose not,' Malus replied peevishly.

'So there you are. She pits her strength against Morathi and the witches for three days – and now this.' Nuarc raised his head slightly, almost as though he were sniffing the air. 'Something's up, boy. She's changing tactics.'

That was when they heard the sound. Malus had no words for it; it was a horrible, wailing, tearing noise that seemed to reverberate through the air and yet not be a part of it. One thing Malus was certain of – it came from the direction of Nagaira's tent.

Tz'arkan reacted immediately, its daemonic energies rippling along Malus's skin. 'Your sister's gifts are potent indeed,' it hissed. 'She has opened a great doorway between the worlds.'

'Between the worlds?' Malus muttered. Then he understood. 'Chaos,' he said to Nuarc. 'Nagaira is calling upon the storms of Chaos. She's summoning monsters to send against the walls!'

At that same moment the alarm horns howled from the redoubts. The mercenaries were awake at once, scrambling warily to their feet. 'We need crossbow bolts,' the highborn said. 'Quickly!'

The old general nodded. 'I'll see to it,' he said, and hurried back to the nearby redoubt.

Malus drew his swords. 'Stand to, you wolves!' he called to the cutthroats. 'The bastards are going to try their luck again!'

Hauclir came striding swiftly down the line, barking commands to his men. 'What's going on now?' he asked, his sword and cudgel ready.

The highborn gave him a bleak look. 'Remember the Isle of Morhaut?'

'Oh, damnation,' Hauclir said, his face turning pale.

At the far end of the line the redoubt door opened and a pair of soldiers were all but hurled out onto the parapet by Nuarc, each one carrying a barrel full of crossbow bolts. 'Load the crossbows! Quickly now!' Malus yelled. 'We haven't much time.'

And indeed, he was right. No sooner had he spoken than he heard the heavy *bang* of the redoubt's bolt throwers, and something not of the mortal world screamed and gibbered just out of sight around the redoubt's sloping flank. Everyone on the parapet turned in the direction of the sound, their faces full of dread.

CHAPTER SEVENTEEN

MOVE AND COUNTERMOVE

The slithering thing that lurched into view from around the corner of the redoubt was a hideous knot of roiling muscle and misshapen bone as large as a nauglir. Mouths that were little more than muscular tubes lined with dagger-like teeth writhed and gaped like serpents above the fleshy mass, and great, scythe-bladed arms lashed and stabbed at the air, reaching madly for prey. The abomination had been pierced by a bolt from one of the redoubt's bolt throwers, and its body was wreathed in seething green sorcerous flame. It lurched a few more steps towards the wall, shrieking an agonising, lunatic wail, then collapsed into a shrivelling, burning mass.

The cutthroats' cheer of relief was short-lived however, as it became clear the otherworldly creature was far from alone.

A huge pack of smaller creatures came racing around the end of the redoubt, loping, slithering, bounding and scuttling with hideous, predatory grace. They flowed past the burning Chaos creature and charged straight for the fortress wall, throwing back their bald heads and screeching hungrily at the defenders above. Behind them lurched three more of the larger, more powerful monstrosities, bellowing angrily as they dragged their bulk across the ashen ground.

Hard-bitten cutthroats screamed like frightened children as the seething pack of Chaos beasts reached the wall and began to scuttle up its sheer height like spiders. 'Stand to, you dogs!' Malus roared. 'Crossbows! Don't just stand there! Open fire!'

Galvanised by the steely tone in Malus's voice the handful of crossbowmen stepped to the battlements and leaned over the edge and fired at the monsters rushing up the fortress wall. Two bolts struck home, dislodging a pair of the screeching fiends and sending them plummeting to the ground, where they struck hard and curled in upon themselves like dead insects. Reassured by the knowledge that the monsters could die like any other living thing, the mercenaries regained some of their lost courage and readied their weapons as the beasts drew nearer.

The heavy bolt throwers in the redoubt banged once more, and twin streaks of green fire plunged down at the shambling behemoths still crawling towards the wall. One of the dragons-fire bolts missed, splashing a pool of searing fire along the ground, but the other struck home. The blazing monster continued to shamble forwards even as it died, its wails adding to the cacophony of noise assaulting the defenders' senses.

More war horns blared, and cries of battle echoed all across the northern quadrant of the fortress. Cursing under his breath, Malus dashed to the inner edge of the parapet and leaned out as far as he dared, peering at the section of wall on the other side of the redoubt to his right. The next wall over was the scene of a desperate battle as the spearmen there grappled with a furious pack of Chaos beasts. On the other side of these spearmen lay the north gatehouse. Malus had no doubt that was where the monsters would go. If the gatehouse fell then the whole outer wall was lost.

Screeching and roaring, the first of the Chaos beasts came scrambling over the battlements and threw themselves at the waiting mercenaries. A druchii went down with a multi-legged monster wrapped around his torso, his sword driven clean through the beast's midsection. Another creature crouched on the battlements and lashed at two of the cutthroats with whip-like tentacles lined with tiny, fanged mouths. Malus saw Hauclir block a lunging beast's charge with his heavy cudgel and hack the thing open with his short sword. Ten-thumbs levelled his crossbow and shot another point-blank, the heavy bolt punching clean through the monster's body. Another mercenary shrieked in agony as a monster drove its blade-like forelegs into his eyes.

More and more of the creatures were swarming over the wall every moment. Blood and ichor stained the parapet in equal measure. Malus saw Nuarc standing by the redoubt's open door, slicing a charging monster neatly in half with his rune-marked sword. 'We need reinforcements!' the highborn yelled over the din. 'We can't keep this up for long!'

But Nuarc shook his head. 'They'll never get here in time,' he cried, rushing forward and stabbing another beast that had fastened onto a mercenary's throat. 'We hold the wall with what we have or not at all!'

Damn those fools in the citadel, Malus thought! Their petty intrigues were doing Nagaira's work for her.

Just then a fierce wind rushed over the top of the redoubt and buffeted Malus's face. He smelled brimstone and old blood, and heard a vast rushing of wings. Instinct spurred Malus into motion even before the wave of flapping figures burst overhead. 'Get down!' he yelled at Nuarc, crashing into the older druchii and driving him back against the redoubt wall just as a swarm of winged monsters came roaring down the length of the parapet. The creatures lashed at the struggling druchii with their long, saw-bladed tails; a few snatched up unsuspecting mercenaries in their talons and flung them screaming from the wall. Under assault now from two sides, the defenders' courage began to waver, and they started to give ground to the snarling beasts.

Malus pushed away from Nuarc with an angry snarl. 'Not another step back!' he roared at his men. 'You can stand and fight or run and die! Kill these bastards before they kill you!' To the terrified crossbowmen he yelled, 'Shoot those damned flying beasts out of the air!'

Once again the defenders redoubled their efforts under the lash of Darkblade's tongue, but Malus knew that he couldn't keep things going for long. Another major reversal and the battle could turn into a rout.

A long, lean shape with six legs and a gaping, tooth-lined orifice in place of a head clawed its way up the body of the mercenary nearest Malus and then launched itself at the highborn. Roaring an oath, he caught the monstrosity on the point of his blade and threw it screaming over the battlements. The winged creatures came rushing in again, but this time several tumbled from the sky with crossbow bolts buried in their pale bodies. Malus sliced off another's wing as it shot past, sending it careening full-tilt into the side of the redoubt. Another of the mercenaries was plucked from the parapet, but this time both druchii and monster went tumbling to the ground with the cutthroat's dagger buried in the creature's chest.

Malus sensed that the tide of battle was starting to turn in the defenders' favour. No more of the swift creatures were appearing over the battlements, at least, and the mercenaries were rallying themselves and ganging up on the monsters that remained.

Then he heard the wailing cry from the other side of the wall and his heart lurched in his chest. He'd forgotten about the two behemoths.

Malus dashed to the battlements and peered over – then ducked his head back just as quickly. One of the monsters was almost within arm's reach, trailing a slick of yellow slime as it slithered its way up the wall. The second creature had flattened against the wall of the redoubt to avoid the punishing fire of the bolt throwers and was nearly to the top of the wall as well. Malus pounded on the edge of the battlements in frustration. He couldn't imagine anything less than a dragonsfire bolt being able to destroy the huge creatures.

His gaze drifted to the open redoubt door. Maybe he didn't need the bolt throwers at all.

Malus dashed inside the redoubt. The two sentries who normally stood watch at the door had evidently fled, or perhaps been killed out on the parapet when the Chaos beasts first attacked. He ran down the long corridor for another few yards, until he came to a water barrel holding a pair of the long, glass-tipped dragon's breath bolts. He pulled the long, spear-like bolts from the water, taking great care not to knock them together, then turned and hurried back the way he came.

Nuarc was waiting for him just as he emerged from the doorway. The general recoiled from the highborn with a startled hiss. 'What in the name of the Murderer are you doing with those!' he exclaimed.

'Taking care of some pests,' Malus replied, just as the first of the behemoths appeared at the edge of the battlements with a wailing roar.

'Get back!' Malus yelled at the mercenaries nearby – who were already falling over one another trying to escape the monster's thrashing limbs. Then he hefted one of the long bolts like a javelin, took two quick steps and hurled it at the monster's side.

The bolt wobbled in the air as it flew the short distance to the target. Faster than Malus thought possible, the beast saw the projectile coming and smashed it out of the air with the sweep of a scythe-like arm, breaking the glass globe at the bolt's tip and showering itself with liquid flame. Shrieking and flailing in agony, the monster sizzled like fat dropped in a fire, then fell away from the battlements and tumbled like a comet to the ground.

Even as the first monster was plummeting to earth Malus took up his second bolt and peered cautiously over the battlements. Instantly a pair of scythe-arms lashed at him, missing his face by scant inches. The behemoth was only perhaps a dozen feet below, clashing its multiple jaws and undulating inexorably upwards. With a cruel grin the highborn held his ground and took deliberate aim. All he really had to do was drop the bolt onto the creature, and within moments it too was burning in a greasy heap at the base of the wall.

The last of the smaller Chaos beasts took another of the mercenaries with it when it died – farther down the wall one of the druchii fell from the battlements with a scream, still stabbing at the beast that was burrowing its way into his chest. Malus watched beast and victim fall to their deaths and said a silent thanks to the Dark Mother that it was the last of them.

Leaning against the battlements, Malus took in the scene of carnage that stretched the entire length of the long wall before him. Bodies and pieces of bodies lay strewn everywhere, amid puddles of congealing blood and stinking ichor. The mercenaries were pulling their wounded comrades to their feet, but there were too few of them. Not three minutes ago there had been sixty-five mercenaries fighting alongside him, and now he was hard-pressed to count more than thirty that were still breathing. He scanned the battered cutthroats for a glimpse of Hauclir, and found the former guard captain at the far end of the line, working hard to get the mercenaries ready in case of another attack.

Nuarc stood just a few feet away with his back to the redoubt wall, wiping dark fluid from the length of his blade with a coarse piece of cloth. 'A near run thing,' the general said, 'That was an inspired piece of lunacy, fetching those dragon's breath bolts. Never seen that done before.'

Malus grinned tiredly and was about to reply when a warhorn wailed a shrill, insistent note from the gatehouse. Nuarc stiffened, and Malus saw the briefest flicker of fear in his dark eyes. 'What is it?' he asked.

Cursing under his breath, Nuarc dropped his cleaning cloth and dashed a few yards down the wall. Malus joined him, following the warlord's gaze to the scene of slaughter unfolding along the neighbouring wall.

Chaos beasts were swarming over the battlements in a glistening flood, racing over the torn corpses of the defenders and pouring down the long ramps into the city beyond. At the far end of the wall where it met the gatehouse, two of the huge Chaos monsters were hammering and prying at the iron door leading into the gatehouse proper.

Behind the monsters, bloodstained swords in hand, stood Nagaira's Chaos champion.

The armoured figure was surrounded by lesser Chaos beasts, which circled his heels like hunting hounds. Worse still, more than a dozen armoured Chaos warriors stood ready on the battlements behind the champion, waiting for the door to come down. As Malus watched, a half-dozen of the winged nightmares flapped heavily up from the base of the wall, each one clutching another armoured warrior in its talons.

Malus's heart sank. The attack on their wall had just been a feint, aimed at keeping them occupied so that they couldn't come to the gatehouse's defence. They'd outsmarted him again! 'Hauclir!' he barked. 'Form up your wolves! Now! We've got to get to the gatehouse–'

'There's no damn time,' Nuarc said, his voice tight with anger. 'Your men are spent and the enemy has a secure foothold. You'd be pulled apart before you even got close to the gatehouse.'

'I can get more of the dragon's breath–'

'And do what? Throw it at the enemy and then advance into the flames? Use some sense, boy!' Nuarc snapped. 'Remember what I said about the inner wall being easier to defend? We have to fall back now, before those bastards get the outer gate open, or we'll never make it at all. Come on!'

Without waiting for a reply, Nuarc broke away and hurried down the length of the wall, calling for the mercenaries to follow. The harbour rats, already at the limits of their endurance, were all too eager to escape. Malus took a moment to glare hatefully at the enemy champion, who wore the one thing the highborn needed to reclaim his soul and seemed capable of thwarting him at every turn.

As he glared at the armoured fiend, the champion straightened, and as though he were able to read the highborn's thoughts, the helmeted head turned and looked his way.

Malus raised his sword and levelled it at the champion. 'This isn't over yet,' he said to the baleful warrior, then he swallowed his bitter fury and turned to follow quickly in Nuarc's wake.

'First he costs us ten thousand men, and now he's cost us the fortress's outer wall!' Isilvar shouted, pointing an accusing finger at Malus. 'I tell you, he's in league with Nagaira, somehow. How else can one explain such incompetence?'

The vaulkhar and the three drachau were seated in high-backed chairs with velvet cushions, in a lesser audience chamber than the grand court chamber at the base of the Black Tower. A large, marble topped table before them was set with the remains of a sumptuous lunch, now all but forgotten in the wake of the day's disaster. Lord Myrchas studied Malus coldly, rolling a Tilean grape between his pale fingers. The Witch Lord, Balneth Bale, made a show of studying the parchment map of the inner fortress laid out on the table, but how much of it he could see amid the platters, goblets and bits of food was open to discussion. Lord Jhedir of Clar Karond chuckled at Isilvar's tirade and took another sip of wine.

Sitting in the shadows behind the four lords sat Malekith himself, fingers steepled and red light seeping from the oculars of his horned helm. The Witch King hadn't said a single word since Malus had been called to make his report. The highborn stood defiantly beyond the end of the long table, with Nuarc standing close behind him. Retainers and servants shuffled quietly about the room's perimeter; on the north end of the chamber stood a high, arched entryway that opened onto a narrow balcony which looked down over the inner wall and the city beyond. Hauclir stood by the open archway, idly cleaning his nails with a small knife and dividing his attention between events without and within.

'I wasn't aware that I'd been placed in personal command of the outer wall defences,' Malus hissed. Unlike the richly attired nobles, he'd come to the audience chamber after finding a place in the citadel for the surviving mercenaries. He was still clothed primarily in steel, blood and black ichor. 'Perhaps that explains why no one along the outer wall had the faintest idea what was happening, nor were they given any leadership or direction once the north gate fell. It would certainly explain why my section of the wall received no food, ammunition or medical orderlies in the entire two days I and my men stood guard there. Why, if only I'd known, dear brother. Perhaps I could have saved the wall and the Dark Mother only knows how many of our men!'

The retreat to the inner wall had begun well enough; the Black Tower's garrison was familiar with the plans for such a manoeuvre, as laid down by Lord Kuall, the previous vaulkhar, and they had even drilled for it regularly. But once the gate fell and the Chaos horde came swarming into the city, confusion and panic quickly took hold. With no clear chain of command there was no one to organise a rearguard to hold the attackers at bay so the rest could get to safety. Worse, the regiments from Malekith's army had to deal with their own set of conflicting orders from their individual drachau, commanding them to think of themselves first and everyone else second, if at all. The retreat quickly became a free-for-all. Regiments from the same city stuck together and left their rivals behind. Entire regiments were isolated in the city and wiped out, while there were rumours that there were at least three instances of druchii regiments fighting one another for the chance to escape the enemy.

Nuarc and Malus had done what they could, gathering up stray units and forming an ad hoc rearguard that managed to hold the central avenue outside the inner gate for some three hours before finally being forced to retreat. At this point Malus had no idea whether they'd done any good or not. Now night was drawing in, and the highborn found it hard to believe he'd been standing on the outer wall just eight hours before. He was more tired than he'd ever been in his life, and at that moment he wanted nothing in the world so much as the chance to reach over and tear out his brother's throat with his bare hands.

Isilvar met Malus's burning gaze without flinching. 'The fact remains that you were on the wall – in fact, according to your own report, you were adjacent to the main enemy attack all along. Yet you did nothing to stop it, interestingly enough.'

'I was in the middle of a *battle*,' Malus shot back. 'Where were you? In the bath? Having your teeth filed? You're the damned Vaulkhar of Hag Graef, the most powerful warlord of the most powerful city in Naggaroth. Do you even know how to use that sword you're carrying?'

Isilvar leapt to his feet, his dark eyes glittering. 'I could show you if you like.'

'You had your chance to show me in the cult chamber beneath Nagaira's tower,' Malus replied with an evil grin. 'But you ran like a frightened deer, then. Did you tell yourself you were escaping for the sake of Slaanesh and her cult, or did you save the self-serving excuses for later?' He leaned over the edge of the table. 'I should think that if anyone here is familiar with conspiring with Nagaira, it would be you.'

The vaulkar went pale – with rage or fear Malus wasn't entirely sure. 'You... you have no proof of such a thing!' he rasped, his hand rising unconsciously to his throat.

'Care to put that to the test, dear brother?' Malus said, a cruel smile playing at the corners of his mouth. He noticed Myrchas, Bale and even Jhedir casting long looks at the trembling figure of the vaulkhar.

Across the marble-floored chamber, Hauclir cleared his throat. When Malus didn't respond, he tried again, louder this time.

The highborn turned to regard Hauclir. 'Are you well?' he said icily.

'Well enough, my lord,' he said, straightening. The former guard captain gestured to the balcony with his knife. 'I think there's something out here you might want to see.'

'Do I look busy to you, Hauclir?' Malus snapped, indicating the assembled nobles with a sharp sweep of his hand.

'Of course, my lord, but–'

'Can it wait?'

Hauclir frowned. 'Well, I suppose it can,' he said.

'Then trouble me with it later!' the highborn said with a look of exasperation.

The former guardsman folded his arms, glowering at his one-time master, then shrugged. 'As you wish,' he said, turning back to the open archway.

Malus turned back to Isilvar, trying to recapture his train of thought.

Isilvar still glared at him from across the table, his hand in the hilt of his blade. His face seemed a bit calmer now, the highborn noted with a frown.

But before he could continue there was a thunderous boom that rolled through the open archway beside Hauclir. Everyone except Malekith jumped at the sound.

Malus glanced worriedly at Hauclir. 'What in the Outer Darkness is that?' he cried.

The former guardsman gave the highborn a sardonic glare. 'Evidently nothing of any import,' he said peevishly.

Snarling, Malus rushed to the archway with Nuarc in tow. Even Isilvar and the drachau rose from their chairs and made their way warily across the room.

With a passing glare at his impertinent former retainer, Malus stepped onto the balcony and looked down from a dizzying height at the top of the inner wall and the glittering ranks of the troops massed to defend it. Beyond lay the corpse-choked streets and the smouldering buildings of the outer city, teeming with looting bands of beastmen and drunken marauders.

In a wide square a few hundred yards from the inner gate however was a sight that made Malus's heart skip a beat. Long lines of straining beastmen were pulling a pair of enormous catapults down the long avenue and into firing positions alongside a third siege engine whose throwing arm was already being winched back for another shot. A pall of stone dust hung in the air above the gatehouse, indicating the catapult's intended target.

Beside Malus, Nuarc let out a low curse. 'They must have been assembling them under cover of that damned darkness,' he muttered. 'Your sister is more resourceful than I imagined.'

'She lacks martial experience, but she's well read,' Malus said grimly. 'Do you think they can knock down the gatehouse with those things?'

The warlord grunted. 'Of course they can. All they need is time and ammunition, something they seem to have in abundance.'

Malus fought down a swell of frustration. Nagaira wasn't giving him a chance to catch his breath for a single moment. He didn't have to consider the situation very long before he realised what must be done. Turning on his heel he strode back into the chamber. Isilvar and the drachau retreated as he swept inside, as though he carried some kind of plague.

The highborn turned to Lord Myrchas. 'Is there a tunnel?'

'Tunnel? What do you mean?'

'Is there a tunnel leading from the citadel into the outer city?' Malus snapped. 'Surely there must be some way to launch raids in the event the outer wall is breached.'

The drachau of the Black Tower started to speak, then paused. He frowned in bemusement.

'For the Dark Mother's sake, Myrchas! Don't you know?'

Before the drachau could embarrass himself further, Nuarc spoke up.

'There is such a tunnel. I saw it once when I was studying the plans of the citadel.'

The highborn nodded curtly. 'All right then. Lead on, my lord,' he said to Nuarc, then gestured at Hauclir. 'Let's go and get the men.'

But an armoured figure stepped into Malus's path. Isilvar stood nearly nose-to-nose with his half-brother. 'And where do you think you're going?' he said, hand on the hilt of his sword.

Furious, Malus stepped forward, catching Isilvar's sword arm and the wrist with one hand and shoving him hard with the other. The vaulkhar fell in an undignified heap, his scabbarded sword tangled beneath him.

'While the rest of you sit here peeling grapes and squabbling like children I'm going to take care of those catapults,' he snarled. 'No doubt by the time I return you'll have invented some other set of excuses to explain away your clean hands and faint hearts.'

Isilvar's face turned white with fury, but he made no reply. Malus gave his half-brother a mocking salute, then, glaring angrily at the assembled drachau, he motioned for Nuarc to take the lead and followed him from the room.

Meanwhile, in the shadows, the Witch King watched Malus go and kept his own silent counsel.

CHAPTER EIGHTEEN

THE DRAGON'S BREATH

'Oh, for the Dark Mother's sake!' Hauclir hissed in exasperation, holding open the small burlap bag so the mercenaries could see the clinking contents within. 'Which one of you halfwits thought it was a good idea to let Ten-thumbs carry the incendiaries?'

The cutthroats exchanged sheepish looks. In the light of the single witch-lamp in Malus's hand, the three mercenaries looked like mischievous shades. Pockets smirked at the former guard captain. 'Ten-thumbs only drops stuff he's trying to steal,' she said, her voice pitched just loudly enough to carry down the line of waiting troops. 'Besides, we figured if he went up in flames no one would miss him.'

Thin hisses of laughter echoed up and down the line. Even Malus found it hard not to grin. They were twenty feet underground, at the far end of a mile-long tunnel that ran from the citadel into the outer city, right in the midst of the bloodthirsty Chaos horde. The tunnel seemed well-made, its square stones slick with dark patches of moss and dripping slime, but everyone eyed the tarred black cross-beams holding up the low ceiling with evident worry. Even weak attempts at humour were welcome.

'Easy for you to say, Pockets. He doesn't owe you any coin,' Hauclir replied. Working carefully, he reached into the bag and pulled out the globes of dragon's breath one at a time. Each glass sphere was wrapped in thick wads of rough cotton to conceal the distinctive green glow and keep the volatile contents safe. He parcelled out the incendiaries among the group, handing one to Pockets, one to Cutter, one to Malus and keeping one for himself, then – with a look of pure trepidation – handing one back to Ten-thumbs. The young cutpurse accepted the deadly orb with as much aggrieved dignity as he could manage.

'I'll take the extra one,' Malus said, holding out his hand. 'And never mind what I may or may not owe you.'

'Very good, my lord,' Hauclir said, handing the orb over. The highborn set the incendiaries carefully at the bottom of a carry-bag tied to his belt, then looked over the raiding party one last time. There were only seven mercenaries, counting Hauclir; Malus felt that a smaller group had a better chance of getting close enough to the siege engines to hit them with the orbs and then slip away again in the confusion. Three of the cutthroats carried crossbows, and Malus had managed to appropriate one for himself from the citadel armoury. Hauclir had further assured him that both Cutter and Pockets were light on their feet and good with their knives.

'All right,' the highborn said, turning and raising the witchlamp to illuminate the narrow shaft at the end of the tunnel. Rusting iron staples had been hammered into the packed earth, providing a ladder to reach the surface. 'According to Nuarc, this opens into a warehouse in the armourer's district. Once we're on the surface, no lights or unnecessary talking.'

Pockets gave Malus a slow wink and a feline smile. Her alabaster skin and sharp features reminded the highborn of a maelithii. The black eyes and filed teeth didn't help. 'No worries, my lord,' she said in her rough harbour accent. 'We've a bit of experience in this sort of thing.'

'Except usually we're breaking into the warehouses instead of breaking out of them,' Ten-thumbs said. He was the youngest of the mercenaries, with a long, lean face and large, nervous eyes.

'Let's get on with this,' growled Cutter, flexing his gloved hands. The assassin was shorter than the average druchii, and slightly darker of skin, giving him an exotic appearance. His face was scarred by a pox he'd had as a child, and his right ear looked like it had been chewed by rats. As near as Malus could tell he was also unarmed; he couldn't see a knife anywhere on the druchii's body.

Malus took a deep breath and nodded. 'Cutter, Pockets, you first. See what's up there and report back.'

Cutter went right for the rungs and climbed swiftly up the shaft. Pockets moved with a bit more caution, following slowly in the assassin's wake. As the two cutthroats climbed the shaft, Malus snuffed out the witchlamp and set it carefully on the tunnel floor. He turned his head in Hauclir's direction. 'Now we just hope that there isn't a crate of iron bars sitting atop the trap door,' he muttered.

They waited in silence and utter darkness, breathing softly and listening for the slightest sound. Above them, Malus thought he heard the faint scrape of a door, and distant, muffled noises – voices, perhaps? He held his breath. Were there Chaos warriors in the warehouse?

The tiny noises faded, leaving only silence.

As the darkness and silence enfolded him like a shroud, Malus was left with only his thoughts – and the presence of the daemon.

Devoid of sensory distractions, the highborn was hyper-aware of his physical form. All at once he felt the weight of fatigue bearing down upon his shoulders and blurring his mind. He felt hunger, and pain from a half-dozen minor wounds, but as sensations they were cold and somehow distant, as though sensed from the other side of a wall of stone.

He flexed his hands, feeling them brush against the insides of his armoured gauntlets, but again, the sensation was diffused. Alarmed, he reached up and touched his face, feeling the cold steel fingertips of the gauntlet as a dull pressure against his cheek. His heart quickened fearfully, and he felt the daemon shift slightly in response. This time, however, it wasn't a sensation of snakes coiling in his chest – he felt the daemon move through his entire body, like a leviathan sliding beneath his skin.

It wasn't a barrier that separated Malus from his own body – it was Tz'arkan itself. The daemon's hold upon him was more complete than he'd dared imagine. It was as if their roles had been reversed, and now he was the dispossessed spirit lurking in a form not his own.

Immediately the daemon's presence subsided, like a predator pausing warily in mid-stride. Gritting his teeth, Malus forced himself to calm down, to slow the ragged beating of his heart. Tz'arkan was paying close attention to his reactions. Clearly the daemon did not want him to know the extent of its control. But why?

The answer suggested itself immediately. The warpsword. It had the power to counter the daemon's influence. No doubt Tz'arkan feared that if he knew how much control the daemon truly had over him, it would drive him to take up the burning blade again. So long as the warpsword remained in its scabbard on Spite's back the daemon had the upper hand – and, the highborn realised with growing horror, more freedom of action than it would have otherwise.

The nightmares, he thought. What if I wasn't stumbling about in my sleep? What if it was the daemon, moving me about like a puppet?

Suddenly there was a muffled shout from above, and the sound of running feet. Malus heard a choking cry that sounded almost directly overhead – then something metal came rattling and clanging all the way down the twenty-foot shaft, striking sparks from the iron rungs as it fell. Malus and the cutthroats spat muted curses as the object struck the floor of the tunnel next to the highborn's boot with a muted thud.

Malus bent down and groped around for the object. His armoured fingertips rang faintly on metal, then his hand found the hilt of a sword.

Faint movement sounded overhead. 'All clear,' Pockets whispered.

The highborn frowned up into the darkness. 'Is there any point whispering now?' he asked in a normal voice.

'I don't know. Maybe.' The gambler sounded defensive. 'Can't be too careful, right?'

'Evidently not,' Malus growled back. 'We're coming up. Try not to drop anything on our heads in the meantime.'

The highborn took the lead, reaching for the first of the iron rungs and then slowly working his way upwards in the cave-like darkness. His hands seemed to find the rungs effortlessly, and he wondered now if the daemon was subtly guiding his hand, using senses beyond the highborn's ken.

As he neared the top, Malus found the darkness lessened somewhat by a faint, orange glow that etched hard lines and black silhouettes out of the greater gloom. He found the top edge of the shaft and levered himself up out of the hole, finding the dark shape of Pockets waiting for him a few feet away. Large crates, many filled with what looked like metal bars or sheet stock, stood in orderly rows around the hidden trapdoor. Next to Pockets sprawled the body of a marauder, his scarred hand seemingly outstretched towards the open shaft.

'We found a group of these animals cooking meat over a small fire on the other side of these crates,' the druchii cutthroat whispered. 'Cutter and I got the lot of 'em, but this one must have been off taking a piss somewhere. It was his sword went down the shaft.'

Malus straightened and looked about. They were near the front of the building, and the orange glow he'd seen earlier came from the marauder's small fire and the shifting light of much larger fires streaming in through the building's large, open doorways. The highborn moved quietly across the cluttered space and peered warily outside. As night had fallen the Chaos horde had started fires all across the outer city, and pillars of flame and smoke billowed into the air from the warehouses scattered across the city's districts. A warm, hungry wind whispered through the eaves of the warehouse, stirred to life by the churning columns of fire, and Malus thought he could hear the faint cries of the horde borne aloft on the hot air as they celebrated their victory.

For the moment the nearby streets appeared to be empty. Malus breathed a sigh of relief. He glanced back at Pockets. 'How many marauders were there?'

'Five, counting this one,' she said.

The highborn nodded. 'Strip them of their cloaks and furs. We'll need them.'

As Pockets went to work the first of the mercenaries began appearing from the shaft. Malus kept watch in the meantime, going over his battle plan one last time and looking for possible weak points. After the debacle in the north he was determined not to tarnish his honour with yet another costly defeat.

Within minutes Hauclir was standing beside him. 'We're ready, my lord,' he said quietly.

Malus nodded and went back to join the assembled troops. He reached down and picked up the first set of stained furs atop the pile that Cutter and Pockets had gathered. 'Hauclir, you and the crossbowmen put these on,' he said, wrapping the stinking hide around his shoulders. 'Pockets, Cutter and Ten-thumbs will stay in the middle of the group.'

Hauclir's lip curled in disgust, but he obediently bent down and picked up a bloodstained cloak. 'This isn't going to fool anyone.'

'If we keep our distance it should suffice,' Malus said. 'We just have to look similar enough in the darkness that we don't raise any suspicions until we reach the square.'

Once Hauclir and the crossbowmen were wrapped in marauder attire the raiding party set off, creeping stealthily down the dark, corpse-laden streets. The exit point of the tunnel was to the south of the citadel, so they were forced to spend almost three hours in a circuitous route around the inner city until they could come within striking distance of the siege engines.

The Chaos horde had completely surrounded the inner fortress, filling the outer city like a swarm of maddened locusts. Fires burned out of control in parts of the city, and howling bands of beastmen and marauders rampaged through the once-orderly districts, looting and destroying everything in their path. Screams of terror and pain rent the night; the enemy had taken hundreds of prisoners after the outer wall had fallen, and now they sated their bestial appetites on their captives in every horrific manner possible. The small raiding party went all but unnoticed amid such pandemonium; only once did a band of marauders come close enough to get a good look at the shadowy group, and they were shot dead before they could shout an alarm. Pockets, Cutter and Ten-thumbs took their furs and the raiding party continued on.

Finally, just past midnight, the raiders found themselves north of the broad square containing the siege engines. The massive catapults had been firing without pause for hours; each siege engine was the size of a town house, resting on massive ironbound wheels and held together with iron pins as thick as shinbones. Almost a hundred slaves per engine were used to crack the massive arms into firing position, and another fifty more were put to work loading the siege engine with boulders or hunks of masonry weighing hundreds of pounds. Already the thick walls of the inner gatehouse and the tall gates themselves were showing signs of damage. Nuarc had been right; given enough time the Chaos engines would dash the fortifications to the ground.

Unfortunately for them, Malus thought with a vicious smile, their time was nearly up.

The raiding party had gone to ground in a looted barracks some two blocks north of the square, close enough to hear the crack of the taskmasters' whips and the bang of the catapults as they fired. One last time Malus considered the final stages of his plan. Everything seemed to be in place. It's all going according to plan, the highborn thought. Obviously there's something I'm missing. After a moment's thought he motioned Cutter over.

'My lord?' the cutthroat said, settling quietly into a crouch beside the highborn.

'I want you to scout around the square,' Malus said. 'We've had good fortune so far, but I'm starting to wonder how much of it we have left. Go and see if there's anything out of the ordinary.'

'Right you are, my lord,' Cutter growled, and vanished into the darkness.

In the meantime the raiders settled down in the shadows and did what they could to rest.

Another hour and a half went by. The night grew steadily colder as the night passed into early morning, and the paving stones outside glittered with a thin layer of frost. Malus was reminded of the passing of the seasons and the last few grains of sand remaining in the daemon's hourglass. Was he fighting the wrong battle, he wondered? Here he was risking his life for the defenders of the fortress when he needed to be finding a way to get the Amulet of Vaurog and escape to the north. As it was, he only had a few days left before he began cutting into the time necessary to reach Tz'arkan's distant temple.

For the moment, his plight and the fortress's plight was one and the same. So long as Nagaira and her champion were surrounded by an army they were safe. That was going to have to change.

Hauclir and several of the cutthroats were sleeping in their filthy cloaks when Cutter finally returned. He settled down beside Malus. 'It's an ambush,' the pox-marked druchii said. 'There's a hundred marauders waiting in a barracks to the west of the square, with lookouts posted on the roof.'

Startled murmurs passed among the cutthroats. Suddenly Hauclir was wide-awake. 'They expect us to hit the catapults?'

'Of course they would,' Malus said, nodding to himself. 'They know we can't afford to let them pound us at their leisure.' It's possible that they even expect me to lead the raid, Malus suddenly realised. It is, obviously, the sort of thing I would do. He rubbed his pointed chin thoughtfully. 'We still hold the advantage, though.'

'Because now we know where the ambushers are,' Hauclir said.

'Exactly,' the highborn replied. He glanced back at Cutter. 'All of the ambushers are in a single building?'

The assassin nodded. 'If it hadn't been for their lookouts I'd have never known they were there. No lights, no fires – they're a clever bunch of animals.'

Malus thought it over. A crucial decision had to be made. 'All right,' he said at length. 'Hauclir, take Cutter and the crossbowmen and circle around to the west. When you're in position, kill the lookouts and then hit the ambushers with your dragon's breath. That will be our signal to attack the siege engines.'

'*Our* signal?' Pockets said, looking to Ten-thumbs. 'What, the three of us?'

'A hundred marauders cooking alive should provide an ample distraction,' Malus replied coolly. 'Enough for us to get into the square and employ our own orbs. Then we break away in the confusion and return to the tunnel.'

The female druchii shook her head in horror. 'There's no way. It's suicide.'

But Malus smiled. 'Not at all. If there's one thing I know well, it's that you can get farther on pure audacity than anything else. Just do what I do, and we'll get through.' Without waiting for any further protests, he nodded to Hauclir. 'Get your men and get moving,' he said. 'We'll give you half an hour to get into position.'

Without a word, Hauclir rose to his feet and motioned to the crossbowmen. Within minutes Malus watched them disappear across the narrow street and down a shadowy alley to the west.

Pockets and Ten-thumbs gathered their weapons and met Malus at the doorway. 'He's as mad as you are, my lord,' she said, nodding in the direction Hauclir had gone.

Malus grinned ruefully. 'He served a highborn once who was fond of foolish risks. A complete madman. I suppose it left its mark on him.'

The female druchii frowned. 'Really? I should have guessed. What a liar!'

Malus gave her a bemused look. 'What are you talking about?'

She shrugged. 'He told us his old master was a hero, as vicious and clever as they came.'

The highborn's grin faded. 'He couldn't have been more wrong,' he said, suddenly uncomfortable. 'Come on. We've got to get closer to the square.'

Keeping to the shadows, the three druchii sidled down the long avenue towards the siege engines. Lines of slave workers came and went, dragging wagons loaded with boulders to feed the great catapults. Marauders on horseback lashed at the slaves and urged them on with savage curses. Whenever one of the riders drew close Malus led the cutthroats inside the closest building until the horseman passed.

It took nearly twenty minutes to work their way down the two blocks to the edge of the square. A small band of marauders waited there, ostensibly guarding the avenue entrance, but they were passing looted wineskins back and forth and grunting to one another in their bestial tongue. The highborn led the two mercenaries into the deep shadow of a nearby alley. 'We wait here,' he whispered. 'Get your orbs ready. When the commotion starts, I'll take the catapult to the left. Ten-thumbs, you take the one in the middle, and Pockets will go to the one on the right. Aim for the winding drums; even if they have some sorcerous means of dousing the flame, it should burn through the ropes quickly enough to knock the catapults out. We'll meet on the other side of the square and head for the tunnel.'

As it happened, they didn't have long to wait. Off to their right they heard a great *whoosh*, and a chorus of wild screams, and suddenly the marauder horsemen were racing past, heading for the square as fast as their mounts would take them. 'Now!' Malus hissed, and he dashed into the street, running along behind the horsemen. He could see a shifting green glow to the west, in the direction of the sounds, and knew that Hauclir and his men had been brutally successful.

The marauders guarding the entrance to the square were swaying on their feet and howling like the angry dead, torn between their orders and their instinct to race to the fight. They paid no attention to the horsemen or the small band of warriors trailing in their wake. The slave crews for the siege engines had been driven into three groups by their furious taskmasters and herded to the back of the square, away from the waiting siege engines. Malus turned and nodded to the cutthroats and headed straight for the catapult on his left, fishing one of his orbs of his carry-bag.

As he loped past one of the slave-gangs a whip-wielding taskmaster turned to look at him as he sped past and shouted a question in his barking tongue. Malus continued on, picking up speed. Green light shone between the fingers of his right hand.

The taskmaster yelled again, his tone sharper this time. Malus bared his teeth in a snarl. Just a dozen more yards to go.

As fast as he was, Pockets was faster. At the far end of the square bedlam erupted as the first of the catapults burst into flame. Angry cries of alarm echoed back and forth among the marauders. Throwing caution to the wind, Malus ran for his target as fast as he could.

A furious shout sounded behind the highborn, and he heard the thunder of hobnailed boots pounding after him. He reached the rear of the catapult and kept going, running for the huge winding mechanism in front. Off to the right, the second catapult was bathed in a sheet of hissing flame.

Just as he reached the far end of the catapult a chaos marauder leapt around the corner into his path, two short axes held ready. He shot the snarling man in the face with his crossbow, then half-spun on his heel and threw the green orb at the cable-wound drum looming above him.

The glass shattered and the liquid inside ignited with a roar and a dazzling green flash. Air rushed past Malus like a giant's indrawn breath, and for a terrifying moment he felt himself pulled *towards* the blaze. He staggered, then regained his footing and raced for the far end of the square as fast as his feet would carry him.

By now the entire square blazed with green light. A thrown axe whirred past his head, and he worked the reloading lever on his crossbow as quickly as he could. The shadows beckoned to him from twenty yards away. At the moment it felt like twenty miles.

Hoof beats clattered across the paving stones to the highborn's right. A horseman was spurring his wild-eyed mount right at him, a short spear held ready to throw. The crossbow's bolt racked home in the firing trough with a loud *clack*, and Malus stopped just long enough to raise his weapon and shoot the marauder high in the chest. The Chaos warrior threw his spear at the same moment, and the weapon struck Malus in the right shoulder, glancing off his enchanted armour. The blow hit hard enough to spin the highborn half-around, and he found himself stumbling backwards and facing almost a score of screaming marauders, closing fast with the burning catapults blazing at their backs.

At the sight of his face the two men in the lead drew back their axes and let fly. The first one went wide, but the second smashed into the highborn's left arm with enough force to knock the crossbow from his hand. Malus shouted a curse and tried to fumble in his bag for the second orb, but gave up in a moment and simply hurled bag and all at the oncoming enemies.

The bag sailed through the air and landed at the lead marauder's feet but swathed in cotton and the thick burlap, the orb refused to break! Malus cursed and groped for his sword – just as the lead marauder tried to knock the bag aside with a savage kick.

Whump. The marauder band disappeared in a fierce explosion, sucking away even their screams in a rushing torrent of air. Teeth bared in a feral grin, Malus turned about and all but dove into the deep shadows of an alley beyond the square.

Swallowed up by the welcoming darkness, Malus listened to the furious shouts of the enemy echo all around him. Sword and axes clashed as warriors of the horde turned on one another in confusion. The sound was sweet to the highborn's ears.

Above the sound of the enemy's disarray rose another noise, high and sharp like the whistle of a razor-edged blade. The warriors of the Black Tower were cheering.

CHAPTER NINETEEN

GHOSTS OF THE DARKNESS

Malus dreamt he was falling into darkness. Cold wind, damp and mouldy as a tomb, blew against the back of his neck and tangled his black hair as he plummeted downwards. From moment to moment his toes and fingertips would brush the packed earthen walls of the narrow shaft. Every so often he felt gnarled roots slip past his fingers, but never in enough time to snatch at them and save himself.

Slow, daemonic laughter echoed in his ears as he plunged into the Abyss.

The impact, when it came, startled him. It reverberated like thunder in the noisome blackness, and it felt as though every bone in his body shattered like glass. And yet there was no pain; just a creeping coldness, spreading through him like oil.

He could not guess how long he lay there. Malus could feel cold ichor seeping from his shattered skull and spreading across the earth beneath him. He lay there, waiting to die, but his body refused to submit to its injuries.

Then another wind brushed his face – this time from above. It reeked of blood and sickness and bodily vice, of every depravity Malus could imagine and more. And then he heard the laughter once more, and realised what was coming for him.

He rolled onto his knees, feeling bones cutting through his insides like jagged glass. His stomach spasmed, and he vomited a soup of black liquid and pulverised organs onto the unseen earth. The wind tickled at his neck like a lover, and with a groan he staggered to his feet and began to run.

Laughter echoed after him. 'I love it when you run!' the daemon's voice said behind him. 'Look over your shoulder, Malus! I'm right here behind you!'

But he didn't dare look. If he turned around, even for an instant, he knew Tz'arkan would catch him. As long as he ran, he was free.

Malus lurched and stumbled blindly down a long corridor, hands flung out before him. He crashed left and right into walls of packed earth as hard as stone and smelling of the grave. Splinters of bone pressed against the insides of his skin, burst through and then fell away in spurts of black fluid. Yet still he ran on, his body wired together by nothing more than galvanic fear and icy madness.

Then without warning he reached the end of the line, crashing headlong into an unyielding wall of earth. Malus was hurled to the ground by the impact, but the laughter of the daemon drove him back to his feet in an instant. He beat at the wall with his ragged fists; he clawed at the stone-like earth until the flesh of his fingertips was torn away. The laughter grew louder in his ears, and the air grew cold around him – and then his flailing hand closed around something hard and metallic jutting from the earthen wall.

An iron rung. He recognised it at once, and feverishly began to climb upwards, reaching frantically for the next iron staple and grabbing it with an almost hysterical wave of relief. Was he in the tunnel beneath the Black Tower? He had to be! The knowledge sped his climb even further, until it seemed that the laughter behind him was starting to fade. Tz'arkan, it seemed, didn't know how to climb. A lunatic giggle escaped his stained lips.

The trapdoor was exactly where he reckoned it would be. Malus pushed against it and it flew open, allowing a flood of warm, orange light to spill down from the space above. Now it was his turn to laugh as he struggled upwards, desperate for the glow of an honest fire.

That was when the hand closed about his ankle. 'You and I are not finished yet, Darkblade,' the daemon hissed. 'You have given yourself to the darkness, remember?'

He cried out, kicking and pulling at his leg, but the daemon was far stronger. Slowly, inexorably, he was pulled back down into the shadows.

Until he felt a strong pair of arms circle his chest and pull him upwards as though he were a child. Tz'arkan held on for a moment, struggling vainly, then the iron grip about his ankle gave way. It might have taken his foot with it, but at that moment Malus didn't care.

Strong hands hauled him upwards into the light. He hung there like a babe, laughing and weeping with relief. A shadowy figure stepped towards him, limned with fire. A cold hand caressed his cheek, tracing lines through the thick sludge coating his skin.

'There you are, beloved,' Nagaira croaked. She smiled, and rivulets of filth oozed over her ruined lips as she bent close to him. Her pale skin was marbled with pulsing, black veins, and there was only blackness where her eyes ought to be. Malus looked into their depths and realised that there were *things* living there, beings older and vaster than time. He screamed and tried to struggle, but the Chaos champion held him from behind, his armoured hands tightening around Malus's arms until black ooze ran from between his steel-clad fingers.

'We've come a very long way to find you,' Nagaira said. Her breath was cold and putrid, like air escaping from a corpse. The icy nothingness in her eyes pulled at him. 'There's so much I want to show you. So much that you need to see.'

Then her lips covered his, and he tasted icy, squirming rot against his tongue as the ancient things behind Nagaira's eyes took notice of him for the first time and the world exploded in pain.

When Malus opened his eyes he was lying on a cold, stone floor and his kidneys were aching like they'd been kicked.

'I apologise for that, my lord,' he heard Hauclir say. 'But you gave me little choice.'

He tried to move, and found himself tangled in something heavy and voluminous. With a groan he rolled onto his back and found himself wrapped in a bed sheet and blanket. Hauclir stood over him with a grim look on his face, holding his cudgel in his scarred hands. Five livid scratches ran down the right side of his face.

'Do you know who I am this time?' the former guardsman said. 'Or do I have to jog your memory again?'

'Jog my organs is more like,' Malus said with a grimace. 'Help me up, you damned rogue.'

With a grunt, Hauclir bent and pulled the highborn awkwardly to his feet. Malus looked about and realised he was standing in the hallway outside his quarters. He hissed a bitter curse. 'Again,' he muttered.

'You mean this isn't the first time you've walked in your sleep and assaulted people?' Hauclir grumbled.

'No. Not the first time,' Malus replied, entirely oblivious to Hauclir's impertinent tone. 'What in the Dark Mother's name is happening to me?'

'If I didn't know you, I'd say you were going mad,' Hauclir replied. 'Unfortunately, I *do* know you.' He glanced about quickly, ensuring that they were alone. 'Is it the daemon?' he whispered.

Malus frowned. 'I don't know. It's possible. I've lately wondered the same thing myself.' He pulled irritably at the sheets wound around his legs. 'Let's get out of this corridor before someone sees me like this. What is the hour?'

'A bit past midmorning, my lord,' Hauclir answered, setting aside his cudgel and bending to help unwind the highborn. 'Lord Nuarc told us that we were to stand down and get some rest while we could. Do you remember?'

Malus stepped out of the sweat-stained sheets and tried to focus his thoughts. 'The last thing I remember clearly is crawling across the floor of my room and climbing into bed.' He registered a familiar taste in his mouth and winced. 'There was wine involved, wasn't there?'

'Just a bit,' Hauclir agreed.

'I think I could stand some more,' Malus said, and staggered back through the open door into his apartments.

The doors to the balcony were open again, letting in a long rectangle of pale sunlight that stretched halfway across the room. His shuffling feet sent dark bottles clinking and spinning across the floor. 'Gods Below, Hauclir,' the highborn cursed, looking over the array of empty bottles. 'How much did we drink?'

'*We*, my lord?'

There wasn't a single bottle left with so much as a drop of useful liquid inside it. Growling irritably, the highborn staggered towards the balcony. A terrible disquiet lurked at the back of his mind, and he couldn't quite say why.

Or perhaps better to say I'm having a hard time being specific, the highborn thought ruefully. The Dark Mother knows I have more than enough to vex me at the moment.

Malus shaded his eyes with his left hand and squinted into the morning light. A muted clamour rose from the inner wall, and from his high vantage point he could see that the Chaos horde was assaulting the inner fortress. The sight filled him with apprehension, for reasons he couldn't explain.

'How long has the attack been going on?' Malus asked.

'Started right at dawn,' Hauclir replied, joining Malus at the balcony. 'They've been at it ever since.' He eyed the highborn. 'Good thing we're up here resting and drinking wine instead of down there fighting,' he said pointedly 'Isn't that right, my lord?'

'Wine,' the highborn said thoughtfully. 'Right. Fetch another bottle will you? And something to eat. Bread, cheese – whatever you can find. I've got to get into my armour.'

The former guardsman opened his mouth to protest, but gave it up for a lost cause. 'As you wish, my lord,' he grumbled.

Malus found Lord Nuarc giving orders by the inner gatehouse, directing three regiments of spearmen against seemingly endless waves of Chaos warriors. A battering ram still burned fitfully a few yards short of the gate, surrounded by the charred bodies of its operators, and warriors continued to repel long siege ladders cast up by swarms of enemy troops. Crossbow bolts filled the air like swarms of flies, surrounding the ladders nearest the gatehouse with dark clouds of death. A steady rain of bodies fell on either side of the high wall as marauders and beastmen were slain upon the battlements or shot through as they clung to the sixty-foot ladders.

Heads turned as the highborn reached the battlements. Spearmen from Hag Graef and the Black Ark raised their weapons in salute as he passed, and a ragged cheer followed Malus and Hauclir all the way to the gatehouse itself. The daring raid on the catapults – now just a trio of charred hulks in the square to the north – had turned Malus and the cutthroats into heroes overnight. It was a small victory, in the grand scheme of things, but it was the first of its kind for the weary defenders, and they celebrated it as only desperate soldiers can.

Even Nuarc's customary glare was tempered with a modicum of respect as the highborn joined him above the gatehouse. 'I thought I told you to get some sleep,' the warlord shouted over the din.

'I tried, but you're making too much noise down here,' the highborn shouted back. 'I don't suppose you could keep it down a bit?'

The general laughed. 'I can't help it if the bastards won't die quietly,' he replied.

Shaking his head, Malus studied the battle raging along the walls. 'How bad is it?' he asked.

'We're actually doing well so far,' Nuarc replied. 'We've got twice as much manpower here than we had at the outer wall, and it's a higher and more difficult climb. Also, the enemy attacks are fierce, but uncoordinated this time. I think you must have stirred something up when you destroyed those siege engines last night.'

'Stirred something up,' the highborn echoed thoughtfully, looking out at the wreckage in the square. 'Has there been no sign of Nagaira or her champion?'

'None,' the general said. 'I don't know why, but I've learned long ago not to question good fortune when it comes my way.'

But the more Malus thought about it, the more troubled he became.

'Something wrong, my lord?' Hauclir inquired.

'I don't know,' Malus answered. 'Wait – no. Something's not right. I just can't figure out what it is.'

Hauclir surveyed the activity on the walls and shrugged. 'Everything looks in order from up here.'

'That's part of the problem,' Malus said. 'Nuarc thinks we stirred something up last night when we attacked the catapults, but I don't think so. They were expecting a raid, and had troops waiting to ambush us.'

The former guard captain thought it over. 'They laid their trap and we blew it up in their faces. That would be enough to stir anyone up, don't you think?'

A spark of realisation struck Malus. 'The catapults were bait,' he said, a look of dread dawning on his face.

Hauclir's frown deepened. 'I suppose so,' he said. 'But we foiled the trap.'

'No!' Malus cried. 'That's not the point. They knew we would have no choice but to attack those catapults. In fact, they counted upon it!'

'To what purpose?'

'What else? Now they know we have another way out of the castle.'

Hauclir's jaw dropped. 'And if we can get out, they can get *in*. Gods Below, my lord. Could they be that clever?'

'This is Nagaira we're talking about. Of course they can be that clever,' Malus growled. Suddenly his dream took on an awful clarity that sent a chill down his spine. 'Let's go.'

'Go where?' Hauclir asked, though the tone in his voice suggested he already knew the answer.

'To gather your cutthroats and see how clever my sister truly is,' the highborn replied.

The entrance to the long tunnel lay in the bowels of the Black Tower itself, on the same level as the fortress's vast cisterns. Holding aloft a half-dozen witchlamps on long, slender poles, Malus, Hauclir and all thirty mercenaries rushed though the cavernous, arched chambers, passing broad, stone-capped basins that held the tower's water supplies. Their weapons were ready and they cast wary glances into every shadowy corner they passed. Malus led the way, fearful that they were already too late.

'Even supposing your theory is correct,' Hauclir said breathlessly, 'the beasts would still have to find the entrance to the tunnel, and I know for a fact we weren't followed.'

'They don't need to see us to be able to track us,' Malus said grimly. 'They could set hounds on our scent; they could set *beastmen* on our scent, for that matter. We're just fortunate they haven't found their way into the fortress yet.'

Pockets, jogging along behind the two druchii, piped up. 'I don't suppose either of you brought some more of those terrible little orbs with you?'

Malus shook his head. 'We've few enough left as it is, and if we tried to use one in the tunnel it would eat through the wooden supports and bring the thing down on our heads. And I don't want to cut off our only escape route unless it's absolutely necessary.'

The druchii loped along to a dark alcove at the far end of the cistern network. There, some ways off from the rest of the storage containers, lay a circular, wooden cover similar to the ones that sealed the tower's real cisterns. At Malus's direction two of the cutthroats pulled the cover aside to reveal a spiral staircase winding down into darkness.

'Crossbows up front,' Hauclir ordered, then the former guard captain turned to Ten-thumbs. 'You stay up here,' he said. 'If you hear fighting, you head upstairs as fast as you can and get reinforcements. I don't care who they are.'

'Yes, Captain,' the young thief said, his eyes wide and fearful.

Malus plucked a crossbow from a nearby cutthroat's hands and quickly loaded it. Cutter cleared his throat and spoke. 'We should douse the lights,' he said.

The mercenaries shared anxious looks. Pockets frowned. 'You want us to go down there blind?'

'Better to go in dark than lit up like daybreak,' the assassin replied. 'If those animals have found their way in, they're likely carrying torches, which gives us easy targets.'

The highborn saw the wisdom of it at once. 'Do as he says,' he commanded. When all of the lights had been extinguished, the small band of warriors were swallowed by absolute darkness. 'The two men with lamps farthest back will bring theirs along,' he said. 'The rest, leave yours aside. When I call for light, you ignite your lamps. Understood?'

Murmurs of assent rose from the back of the party. Malus nodded, feeling his heart hammering in his chest. 'All right, let's go.'

They descended the winding staircase totally blind, shuffling along one shallow step at a time. Men stumbled against one another, whispering curses, and occasionally a scabbard or sword tip would clink against the stone. The air turned chill and dank by slow degrees. Malus held his crossbow levelled, listening for the slightest sound of footsteps coming up to meet him.

At length, Malus felt his boot scrape against earth. A wisp of cold air caressed his cheek and he shuddered at the memory of the dream he'd had, little more than an hour before. Men shuffled into place on either side of him. 'Hst!' he whispered, just loud enough for keen druchii ears to hear. 'We'll walk forward slowly for a few yards and stop. Listen for my signal.' Quiet grunts to either side and behind him acknowledged the order.

They edged forward down the long tunnel, careful to make as little noise as possible. The blackness was total, infinite. The mercenaries could hear nothing but the sound of their own breath, hissing between clenched teeth. Finally, after Malus reasoned that nearly all of the troops had reached the bottom of the stairs, he whispered, 'Halt. Front rank, kneel.'

He and the two men beside him sank slowly to one knee, clutching their crossbows tightly. They peered into Abyssal blackness and listened for the slightest sound on an oncoming foe.

Minutes passed. Malus saw no hint of light in the darkness or heard any sounds of movement. There was an unmistakeable tension in the air, but his own troops could easily account for that.

Time dragged slowly on. Warriors shifted uncomfortably, drawing hissed warnings from Hauclir. Malus bared his teeth. They were out there. He was certain of it.

The warrior immediately behind Malus bent low and whispered in the highborn's ear. 'Message from Hauclir. He wants to know if we should advance down the tunnel.'

'No,' the highborn whispered. 'The enemy will have to come to us, and we're better situated here–'

He froze. Was that a faint scuff of a foot somewhere ahead? Malus listened, not daring to breathe. Another sound – perhaps the tiny rattle of a buckle or chain. Or it could be his imagination, stoked by tension and absolute blackness.

Malus thought the situation over and reached a decision. He raised his crossbow to his shoulder, aimed at waist height, and fired.

The thump of the crossbow was loud enough to startle the warriors behind Malus – but nothing like the agonised scream that rent the darkness farther down the tunnel.

'Both ranks, open fire!' Malus ordered, quickly reloading his crossbow. More bowstrings thumped, and heavy bolts thudded into shields or glanced from steel armour with glints of bright blue sparks. Some of the bolts sank into flesh, drawing more bloodcurdling screams, and then the tunnel echoed with the thunder of running feet as the Chaos troops began their charge.

The close confines of the tunnel rang with frenzied shouts and blasphemous war cries. It sounded like a thousand warriors were bearing down on Malus and his meagre force. There was no real way to tell how close they were in the bedlam of shouts and screams echoing all around him. 'Keep shooting!' he shouted into the din. 'Aim low. They can't get to us if we block the tunnel with their bodies!'

Fire. Reload. Fire. For almost a minute Malus's arms worked in deadly rhythm, working the loading lever of his repeater crossbow and firing into the darkness. Marauders screamed and stumbled with a clatter of mail and steel-rimmed shields. The sharp smell of blood and voided bowels thickened the subterranean air.

Malus fired again, and this time his victim's agonised scream sounded almost directly in front of him. 'Front rank, pass your crossbows back and draw steel!' he roared. He shoved his own weapon back to the warriors behind him and yelled back at the mercenaries as he drew his twin blades. 'Lights!' he called.

The order came just barely in time. Cold, green light flooded the narrow tunnel and revealed an axe-wielding barbarian not three feet from Malus. The human's face was twisted in a rictus of rage and pain, and a crossbow bolt was buried to the fletchings in his muscular left shoulder. The sudden glare from the witchlamps blinded the warrior for an instant, and the highborn lunged forward and thrust his right-hand blade through the muscles of the marauder's upper thigh. A fountain of arterial blood poured from the wound, and the warrior staggered, howling in pain. But before he could recover he was dashed against the side of the tunnel by the warrior behind him as his frenzied tribe-mate rushed to come to grips with his foes.

'Stay on your knees!' Malus ordered the men to either side of him. The howling barbarian came right at the highborn, his shield held low. Malus feinted with his right-hand sword and blocked a sweeping axe-stroke with his left – and then the druchii behind Malus shot the warrior point-blank in the face. The steel bolt punched clean through the warrior's skull and struck the marauder behind him in the throat.

Yet no sooner had both men collapsed than their tribe-mates were clambering over them to hack at the hard-pressed druchii line. Malus and the men in the front rank fought like rats, stabbing at exposed knees, feet, thighs and groin. They slit men's bellies where they could, and where the enemy's guard was too strong they held the barbarian off long enough for a druchii crossbow to fell him.

And yet there seemed to be no end to the bastards. Bodies began to pile so high in front of the druchii that the marauders had to drag them aside in order to reach their foes. Malus's knee was sodden with spilled blood. He soon lost count of the number of men who died trying to force their way down the tunnel, and his arms began to burn with exhaustion from near-constant battle.

The fight seemed to rage for hours, but Malus knew that it was most likely only a handful of minutes. The druchii exhausted their ammunition before long, and the second rank drew their own blades and joined in the swordplay. The marauders were able to press them more closely after that, but they still faced the difficult task of fighting two swordsmen at once.

Exhaustion began to take its toll. The druchii to Malus's right faltered for only a moment and a barbarian axe dashed out his brains. Instantly another warrior leapt forward and knelt in his place as Malus cut the barbarian's hamstring with a quick flick of his wrist. Other druchii died behind him, struck down by flung axes or the thrust of saw-edged blades. Their formation contracted slightly, falling back a few feet towards the stairs. Malus began to wonder when the reinforcements were going to arrive.

And then suddenly a horn wailed down the tunnel from out of the darkness, and the marauders fell back at once. They dragged away as many of the dead as they could, something Malus had never known the marauders to do before. A ragged cheer went up from the surviving druchii, but Malus cut them off with a sharp wave of his hand. Something wasn't right.

Then he heard it. The heavy tread of armoured feet, rolling like thunder towards the battered druchii warriors. Suddenly he realised that the enemy had used the barbarians to wear them down and soak up their ammunition, preparing them for the hammer blow.

'Mother of Night,' he cursed. 'On your feet!' he called to the men beside him. 'Get ready!'

But by then it was already too late.

The figure that loomed before them in the witchlight had once been a man. In some sense he still was, but now his body was swollen with corruption. Muscles as thick as a nauglir's threatened to burst from the warrior's taut skin, and his eyes shone like embers from behind a massive, horned helmet of dark iron. The Chaos warrior was clad in heavy armour from head to toe, adorned with jagged spikes and curling horns, heavy chains and cruel hooks festooned with shrivelled heads. His massive hands gripped a pair of hand axes that looked too large for a sane man to wield, and yet wield them the warrior did, tearing into the surprised druchii with a bloodcurdling roar.

The mercenary to Malus's left died without a sound, the front of his head shorn away by a flickering sweep of an axe. The druchii to Malus's right leapt forward with a shout, thrusting at a gap in the warrior's armour just above his thigh. But the blade missed the gap and skated harmlessly off polished iron, and the warrior punched the haft of his left-hand axe through the mercenary's skull.

Seeing an opening, the highborn lunged forward, chopping down on the warrior's left wrist and half-severing it in a spray of blood. To Malus's horror, the warrior laughed and smashed his right-hand axe into the highborn's side. It was only the enchantments woven into his armour that saved the highborn from the fearful blow; as it was, the impact knocked him from his feet and smashed him against the side of the tunnel wall.

Screaming a wild war cry, Pockets charged at the towering Chaos warrior, clutching a sword and dagger in her small hands. The warrior snarled contemptuously and swatted at her with his axe. But the nimble druchii ducked beneath the blurring sweep of the blade and then leapt onto the warrior's massive chest. Before the surprised warrior could react she howled like a mountain cat and buried her dagger to the hilt in the warrior's right eye.

With a gurgling cry the warrior fell to his knees, and Pockets sprang clear barely an instant before a heavy axe crashed into the warrior's neck and hacked away his head in a spray of hot gore. The warrior behind the headless corpse kicked the body over with a booming curse and leapt for the girl's retreating form, his axes blurring and moaning in the reeking air.

Druchii leapt at the monster from three sides, and were mown down like wheat. The charging mercenary to the warrior's right was flung back against the wall in two pieces. Dead ahead a cutthroat rushed forward, trying to cover Pockets as she retreated, and got his head struck off for his trouble. Malus ducked beneath the warrior's deadly swing and lunged in from the right. His right-hand sword crashed against the side of the warrior's armoured knee and his left-hand blade snaked upwards, catching the warrior beneath the chin and driving upwards into his fevered brain.

But the resolve of the cutthroats had collapsed before the onrushing Chosen, and a terrified flight began. Malus pulled his sword clear of the toppling warrior just as the witchlamps wobbled crazily and then abruptly dwindled as the retreating troops bore the two men back around the turn of the staircase.

More Chaos warriors howled for blood in the sudden darkness. Swearing lustily, Malus raced for the staircase after his men. The climb upwards was a frantic pursuit of crazily swinging light; the lamp men always seemed just at the verge of the turn in the stair, so the highborn could only catch wild glimpses in the shifting glow before it vanished once more. He saw terrified faces and wide, dark eyes, fearful glimpses thrown past narrow shoulders and stumbling forms practically crawling up the stairs as fast as their hands and feet could carry them. Behind Malus the darkness echoed with wild, bestial shouts as the Chosen warriors gave chase.

Then, without warning the close confines of the staircase opened up into the arched space of the cistern vaults, and the panicked retreat came to an abrupt halt. Witchlights bobbed and swung in the open space above, shedding narrow streams of pale light. All Malus could see were the backs of four or five struggling druchii trying to get off the stairs, but he clearly heard Hauclir's voice, rolling over the mercenaries like thunder. 'Any one of you takes another step forward I will split your skull myself!' he roared. 'Stand your ground! The enemy will advance no further into the citadel! We have to hold at all costs until reinforcements arrive!'

The reinforcements aren't here yet, Malus thought? Blessed Mother of Night!

He didn't know whether to thank Hauclir or kill him. On the one hand, he's stopped the rout in its tracks, but on the other hand the highborn was now trapped on the staircase at the tail end of the line with a howling Chaos horde heading his way!

Vicious oaths and bloodthirsty cries echoed crazily up the staircase. Malus turned about, levelling his swords. 'Turn and face the enemy!' he cried to the men behind him. 'They can only come at us one at a time on the stair. We can hold here for a long while if we keep our nerve!'

Thankfully the men listened. He felt them shuffling about, and blades appeared above his head. He steeled himself and crouched low, waiting for the inevitable assault.

He heard the onrushing warriors climbing the staircase, their shouts growing louder and louder. It was all but impossible to see more than a few feet down the staircase – the damned witchlamps kept swinging as though caught in a gale, creating wild patterns of light and shadow along the stairs.

Then, just as it appeared that the warriors were almost at the next turn of the staircase, the howling stopped. Silence fell like a shroud. Malus heard mercenaries gasping for breath above him. Someone moaned fearfully. He bared his teeth and tightened his grip on his blades.

There was the faint scratch of a boot heel on the stone stairs below Malus. A faint ring of harness. Then the shifting light picked out the gleaming tip of a rust-stained druchii sword. The highborn caught the scent of rot and wet earth, like a recently opened grave.

Slowly, gracefully, the Chaos champion rose into the wavering light, his helmet upturned to Malus and the Amulet of Vaurog glinting at his neck.

CHAPTER TWENTY

MIDNIGHT ALLIANCES

The Chaos champion fixed Malus with a gaze like a viper, filling his veins with dread. The armoured warrior seemed to float up the stairs towards Malus, swords outstretched like a lover's waiting arms.

'Mother of Night,' Malus cursed desperately, raising his own twin blades. 'Daemon!' he hissed. 'Attend me! Lend me your strength!'

The daemon stirred, shifting disconcertingly beneath the highborn's skin – but the customary rush of icy power did not come. Malus had barely enough time to register Tz'arkan's treachery before the champion struck.

Silver steel blades darted and slashed at the highborn's legs and abdomen, striking sparks where the keen blades slipped past Malus's guard and glanced from his enchanted armour. He parried furiously, roaring with anger at the daemon's betrayal, because he knew that, even without the terrible power of the Amulet at the champion's disposal, he was no match for the warrior's Chaos-fuelled abilities.

He took a glancing blow to the side of his knee and barely parried a swift thrust at his groin. The champion was not only skilled but well versed in the art of sariya fencing. His technique matched Malus's almost perfectly, and the realisation only enraged the highborn further. Malus channelled all his hatred and fury into his blows, allowing certain attacks through his guard in order to strike back at his foe. Powerful blows rained down on his breastplate and fauld, turned aside time and again by the potent sorceries of the armourers of Naggarond. In return he struck at the champion's arms and neck, hoping to sever a sword-hand, or better yet strike off the warrior's helmeted head. But the champion's speed was such that most often Malus's blows cut through empty air or struck a glancing blow on the champion's armour. It was as though the warrior could anticipate his every move.

There was a furious commotion among the mercenaries behind Malus, but he couldn't spare even a momentary glance over his shoulder to see what was going on. Then a dagger whirred past his head and struck the champion with such force that it penetrated his breastplate just beneath the collarbone. A normal warrior would have been staggered by the blow, but the champion scarcely noticed. It did cause the warrior to hesitate a fraction of an instant, giving Malus the chance to sweep aside the champion's left-hand sword and stab his foe through the throat. Dark blood coursed down the flat of the highborn's blade, but the warrior pulled himself off the tip of the sword as a man recoils from the prick of a thorn, and then immediately renewed his attack.

A figure brushed past Malus, charging down the staircase towards the champion. Hauclir caught the champion's right-hand sword against the side of his scarred cudgel and hacked at the warrior's wrist with his short, heavy sword, but the blade could not penetrate the champion's iron armour. Quick as a snake, the champion pivoted and lunged at Hauclir with his left-hand blade, and it was all Malus could do to knock it off-track with a blow from his own sword.

Moments later Cutter joined in the fight as well, throwing another dagger that rang off the champion's armoured leg. The Chaos warrior responded with a lightning-quick cut at the assassin's neck, but the druchii evaded the blow with astonishing speed. Seeing his opportunity, Hauclir lunged in and smashed his cudgel against the champion's right arm. The blow would have broken the bones of a lesser man, but the champion simply staggered slightly and forced the former guardsman back with a lunge at his throat.

Now, with three skilled opponents pressuring him from different angles, the Chaos champion was forced onto the defensive. Malus pressed his attack, raining blows on the warrior's left arm and shoulder. Sparks flew and fragments of iron armour were hewn away by the force of the highborn's blows, but the champion held his ground, countering each attacker in turn with swift parries and deadly feints. Malus was starting to think that they were gaining the upper hand – and then Hauclir stepped in on the champion's left, smashing his cudgel against the warrior's right knee and then reversing the blow to swing at the champion's head. The Chaos champion appeared caught off guard, thrusting his blade at Cutter's neck, but the attack was only a feint. Like a thunderbolt the champion's sword plunged down, slicing through Hauclir's right thigh. The former guard captain fell with a curse, and Cutter lunged forward with a yell, thrusting for the champion's eyes – only to have the Chaos warrior's left-hand sword bury itself deep in his right shoulder.

Seeing both druchii fall in the space of a single second filled Malus with terror and rage. Unleashing a terrible war-scream he put all of his strength and speed into a single cut that smashed into the champion's temple. Sparks flew, and the force of the blow whipped the champion's head around. Still shrieking his rage, the highborn followed up with a backhand blow that smashed into the warrior's helm right at eye level. Iron snapped with a discordant clang, and the champion's helmet burst asunder.

The warrior's head snapped back from the force of the blow. Black hair, matted with filth and old blood fell loosely to the champion's shoulders. Pallid skin, gleaming with sickness and shot through with pulsing black veins, shone greenish-white in the witchlight. A single, black eye fixed Malus with a glare of implacable hate. The other eye was sightless and glowed with grave-mould. A terrible sword wound cleft the warrior's skull above that ruined eye, its ragged edges black with corruption and squirming with parasitic life.

Malus looked into Lhunara's face and cried out in terror and anguish. 'Gods... oh Gods Below!' he cried. 'You can't be...'

Lhunara's black lips pulled back in a lunatic grin. Unlike his dreams, her teeth were still perfect and white. Her muscular body trembled, and a terrible, bubbling sound rose from her throat. It was the foulest, most vile laughter Malus had ever heard.

'With hate... all things are possible,' she croaked, drawing back her dripping blades. 'With hate... and the Dark Gods' blessing.'

She took a step towards him, and Malus looked in her ruined eyes and knew he was about to die.

He was saved by a thin, reedy voice that echoed from the top of the staircase. 'Dragon's breath!' Ten-thumbs shouted. 'Stand clear!'

Malus turned and saw the young thief standing less than ten yards away, holding a glowing green orb in his upraised hand. Hauclir shouted up at the boy through gritted teeth, 'No, you fool! You'll kill us all!'

'Throw it, boy!' Malus shouted. 'Do it now!'

But Lhunara was already gone, dashing fleet as a deer down the staircase until she was lost in darkness. Malus cursed bitterly and slumped onto the stairs, the vision of her hateful face lingering like a ghost before his eyes.

Mercenaries rushed down the stairs to grab Hauclir and Cutter and pull them clear. Hauclir glared up at Ten-thumbs. 'Who in the Dark Mother's name gave you that orb?' he snarled.

Ten-thumbs grinned. 'What? This?' he tossed the glowing ball above his head – to the horrified shouts of everyone nearby – and snatched it deftly out of the air. 'I've had this for quite a while. It's my little ace in the hole.' He tossed the orb from hand to hand.

And missed.

Ten-thumbs let out a horrified squawk and lunged for the glowing orb. The slick glass bounced through his fumbling fingers and plunged towards Malus, Hauclir and the horrified mercenaries. Dozens of hands grabbed for the orb, slapping the glowing ball this way and that, until finally it bounced free and smashed against the wall about four feet above Malus's head. Cutthroats scrambled in every direction, screaming in terror.

The small witchlamp burst with a sharp *pop* and a smell like a lightning storm. Small fragments of glass rained down on Malus's head.

'Oh, damn,' Ten-thumbs groaned. 'My mother gave me that light. I've had it since I was a child.'

Silence hung heavy in the air. The cutthroats, who moments before had been convinced they were about to burn alive, reeled like drunkards, overcome with relief. Hauclir leaned back against the outer wall of the staircase and glared up at the morose thief. 'By the Dark Mother, I don't know whether to kiss you or skin you alive.'

Nervous chuckles broke out among the cutthroats, quickly turning into gales of loud, hysterical laughter as they came to grips with their unexpected salvation. A pair of mercenaries helped Hauclir and Cutter up the staircase. Hands reached for Malus, but he pushed them away. Slowly, awkwardly, he staggered upright. His limbs felt like cold lead, and his head was cased in bitter ice.

He was the last to climb the curving stair into the cold shadows of the cistern vault. By the time he made it to the top the echoing space was full of angry warriors. Lord Isilvar stood at their head, his expression pale with fury. The cutthroats had drawn together in a tight knot around their wounded leader, glaring balefully at the sneering faces of Hag Graef's spearmen

'What is going on here?' Isilvar grated.

'A battle, dear brother. What else?' Malus shot back. He hadn't expected Ten-thumbs to be quite so successful at drumming up reinforcements. In the back of his mind he realised that they were sorely outnumbered and far from any reliable witnesses should Isilvar suddenly decide to murder the lot of them. The knowledge did nothing to blunt his impertinent tongue. 'I realise you don't see much of these, what with your duties as vaulkhar.' Before Isilvar could reply, Malus plunged onward. 'The Chaos forces have discovered the tunnel. We managed to hold them off until you arrived, but they could be massing for another assault even as we speak.' The highborn grinned mockingly. 'I yield the honour of repelling the next wave to you, as is only fitting to your rank.'

Muscles bunched furiously at the corners of Isilvar's jaws. 'We will have to fire the tunnel and collapse it,' he said. 'The Chaos horde has redoubled its assault on the walls, and every available man is needed at the parapet.'

'Then if you will excuse me, brother, I must hasten to my duty,' Malus replied. Without waiting for Isilvar's leave, he motioned to his men and made to depart. For a brief moment it looked as though the ranks of Hag Graef spearmen would refuse to let them pass, but Malus met the gaze of an older spearman who nodded curtly and stepped aside. The druchii behind the spearman followed suit, and suddenly there was a long, clear path through the spear company leading across the cistern vault. Helmeted heads, both veteran and conscript, nodded respectfully to Malus and his troops as they limped past.

Hauclir, shored up by Pockets on one side and Cutter on the other, came up alongside the highborn. 'That Chaos champion,' he began, 'she looked as though she knew you. Who is she?'

'A nightmare,' Malus said in a dead voice.

* * *

At first, all he could hear were voices. They were muffled and echoed strangely, as though heard from beneath the surface of a deep, dark lake.

'My time runs short,' Nagaira said. The sound of her voice was powerful, vibrant and utterly wrong, full of discordant tones like shattered glass. 'I have obligations to fulfil, mighty one. Obligations that will not be denied.'

'Do not speak to me of time,' Tz'arkan hissed. 'Mine runs short as well. But he knows the way, now. He knows what must be done.'

'But will he act? That is the question.' There was the faint chime of finely hammered silver, and the sound of a knife cutting through meat.

'Who can say?' the daemon growled. 'Nothing you mortals do makes any sense to me.'

The blackness began to fade. Shapes formed to either side of him. He was lying on his back, tangled in sheets. Cold air caressed his bare chest. Nagaira and the daemon spoke above his prone form like adults talking over a sleeping child.

'I fail to see why all this is necessary,' Nagaira said. 'Your scheme is overly complicated to my mind.'

'As complicated as your revenge at Hag Graef?' the daemon retorted.

'Point taken,' she said with a sigh. There was another faint ringing of metal, and this time Malus watched the blurry form of his sister lift a goblet to her lips and drink. 'Yet couldn't you simply deliver Malus to me yourself?'

Suddenly Malus was very alert. The shapes resolved further. He could see Nagaira clearly now. She was sitting in a chair, tucked close to a banquet table, turning a silver goblet in her black-veined hands. Her touch left lines of black tarnish across the gleaming curve of the metal. A knife and fork rested at the edges of the plate set before her, which was piled with steaming cuts of bloody meat. She took no notice of Malus at all, fixing the black emptiness of her gaze upon the being sitting opposite her.

'It is not so simple as that,' the daemon replied. Malus turned his head to look upon the daemon, but its shape was concealed in deep shadow. A plate of bloody meat sat untouched before it. 'You are thinking in such immediate terms, my child. Consider the implications of my plan in their full measure, and what it will mean for you once we have returned from the north.'

'Then he must be persuaded to act,' the druchii witch said. She carefully set the goblet on the table before her.

'Of course,' Tz'arkan replied. 'Do as you think best.'

Malus tried to move, but the sheets pulled tight, trapping him fast. Nagaira looked down at him, reaching to touch his cheek with a long, claw-like nail. 'How much of my brother will remain, after all is said and done?'

'Enough,' the daemon said at length. The shadowy figure reached forward and dipped a clawed hand into Malus's chest. The highborn glanced down, past his chin, to see Tz'arkan lift his still-beating heart from the gaping cavity of his chest. 'You see? It is still quite strong. So is his mind. He should satisfy your appetites for some time to come.' The daemon leaned back in his chair and gestured expansively at the highborn's ravaged body. 'Will you take any more for your plate, child?'

Nagaira leaned forward, peering thoughtfully at Malus's face. 'I should like his eyes,' she said. 'I've always loved them, you know.'

A strong hand clamped down on Malus's forehead, pressing it to the table. Another figure entered his field of vision, looming over him from above. Lhunara bent over him, her ravaged face lit with a lover's smile. Wriggling maggots fell onto his cheek from the gaping wound in her head.

She pressed a cracked thumbnail to the corner of his eye and he began to scream.

Hands were pressing him down onto the bed. Malus kicked and thrashed, screaming in rage and fear. He heard low voices cursing above him, and for a dizzying instant he wasn't sure if he was waking or still trapped in the dream. With a wild effort he tore his arms and shoulders free, shoving away the shadowy figures looming over his bed, and rolled to its edge just in time to vomit a large quantity of rancid wine onto the stone floor.

'I told you those last two bottles were mostly vinegar,' Hauclir said from across the room. 'But you wouldn't listen. Of course, you might have been too drunk to hear me at that point, but I thought it was worth a try.'

Early morning light filtered in through the bedchamber's open window. Hauclir sat in a chair near the balcony entrance, his wounded leg propped up on a low table dragged over for just that purpose. Vague figures moved quietly about in the darkened chamber, patching armour or sharpening their weapons. Pockets and Ten-thumbs were roasting meat over a brazier near the foot of the bed, whispering to one another in low voices.

Malus writhed his way out of the sodden bed sheets and staggered onto his feet. His mind swam from the aftereffects of wine and shock. The dream still hung in his mind with dreadful clarity. Was it real? Was the daemon consorting with Nagaira now? How could he know for certain? He looked to Hauclir, but what could he say that the daemon wouldn't also hear? 'What is the hour?' he asked blearily.

'Early morning,' Hauclir said. 'Too early, in fact. And thank you for asking about my wound. It's not nearly as bad as I feared.'

'We have to get to the nauglir pens,' the highborn interjected. 'Now.'

Hauclir studied Malus carefully. 'You're still drunk, my lord.'

'Since when has that ever made a difference? Help me get into my armour,' the highborn replied, tugging at his stained nightshirt.

Butchers' cleavers rose and fell outside the nauglir pens within the citadel's expansive inner compound, and vast lakes of blood glittered in the early morning sun. As Malus and Hauclir approached the low stone structure a group of young servants were pulling the bodies of beastmen and marauders from the back of a wagon and lining them up for the cutters to inspect. Several hundred nauglir consumed a great deal of meat in a given day, and the druchii saw no reason to waste anything that came their way.

The roar of battle from the inner wall, less than half a mile distant, had continued unabated since the day before. Chaos warriors were hurling themselves in endless waves against the high walls. Hauclir said that soon they wouldn't need ladders at all, but could scale the walls over the piles of their own dead.

The former guard captain was limping painfully along beside Malus, using an improvised crutch made from a pair of spear hafts. 'Why the sudden rush to visit your cold one?' he asked, a glint of suspicion showing in his dark eyes. 'If you're planning on a quick ride into the country I don't think you're going to get very far.'

'I need to get something from my saddlebags,' the highborn said curtly. His mind was still churning over the implications of his dream. In retrospect, he should have expected this, he thought angrily. Now that he'd enlisted the aid of his mother Eldire and then bound himself to the warpsword, Tz'arkan was bound to try and find ways to outmanoeuvre him and retain the upper hand. He had no idea that the daemon could speak to Nagaira through his dreams. Was it also responsible for his many nightmares about Lhunara? The thought both terrified and enraged him.

He'd been a fool to put the warpsword away, risk or no risk. That was going to change.

Malus rushed past the bloodstained butchers and down the ramp into the pens. The chamber was dark and the air dank and acrid with the scent of scores of the huge warbeasts. Each nauglir had its own pen, not unlike a horse's stall, but made of dressed stone rather than wood and secured by a stout gate of iron.

It took several minutes before the highborn found the pen where Spite was kept. The nauglir was dozing on the sandy floor, snout tucked behind its curved tail. The warbeast stirred as Malus quickly unshackled the gate and slipped inside the pen. Hauclir, his clothes still stained with fresh blood, wisely chose not to follow.

'There you are, beast of the deep earth,' Malus said. At the sound of its master's voice the cold one rose quickly to its feet. Force of habit led the highborn to check the cold one's claws, teeth and hide for signs of illness. 'It looks as though these imbeciles are treating you well,' he muttered, eyeing the bloodstained sand nearby. 'And your appetite is good.'

Malus moved his inspection to his saddle and tack, then to the saddlebags still strapped to the cold one's back. The bag containing the relics was still safely secured, and next to it lay the long, wrapped bundle of the warpsword. He fancied he could already feel the heat of the burning blade, like a brazier of banked embers waiting to be stirred to life. Taking a deep breath, the highborn reached for the sword.

Instantly a spasm of burning pain shot through Malus's body. He doubled over with an agonised groan, his hands clenching into trembling claws. Spite started at the sound, glancing back at Malus with a warning growl.

The daemon shifted and tensed beneath the highborn's skin. 'Oh, no, little druchii,' Tz'arkan purred. 'I don't think so.'

'My lord?' Hauclir cried. 'Are you all right?'

But the highborn couldn't speak; indeed, he could scarcely breathe for the pain that wracked his chest and arms. He dimly saw Spite slinking slowly away from him, and his experienced eye immediately recognised that he was in dire trouble. Beyond the roaring in his ears he heard the cold one rumble deep in its throat.

He forced every iota of his will into forcing words past his gritted teeth. 'Re... lease me,' he grated.

'Oh, I shall, little druchii,' the daemon said. 'But first, perhaps I'll let this beast of yours bite off your sword arm. I can make you stick your hand in its mouth if I wish. Would you like to see?'

A violent tremor wracked the highborn's body... and his right arm slowly, haltingly, began to rise.

'My lord!' Hauclir cried. 'What in the name of the Outer Darkness are you doing?'

Across the pen, Spite let out an angry bellow. Immediately the other nauglir in the pens took up the roar, shaking the air with their thunderous cries.

'Such weak, crude flesh you have, Darkblade,' the daemon said. 'It's no great loss if a part of it is torn away. In fact, I'm entirely happy to let your stinking beast bite both of your arms off, if that's what I must do to keep you away from that sword. I have new allies now, you see. They can finish the job you started and give me what I want.'

A thin, despairing wail rose from Malus's lips as he watched his right arm fully extend. His body moved like a children's doll, turning jerkily towards the cold one. Spite's head was lowered, its powerful tail lashing tensely across the sandy floor. The cold one was about to strike.

Suddenly a robed form lurched across the sand and knocked Malus to the floor just as the nauglir struck. Its blocky jaws clashed shut, scattering sprays of venomous drool right where Malus had been standing moments before.

'Back, you damned lump of scales!' Hauclir roared, lashing at the beast's face with his crutch in one hand and trying to drag Malus clear with the other. Spite snapped at the offending stick and ground it to splinters, but it bought Hauclir enough time to drag Malus halfway across the pen. The highborn's legs flailed at the sandy floor, trying to help push them along. The cold one let out another furious bellow, its talons digging furrows in the sand, but before it could gather itself to charge, Hauclir pulled the highborn through the gate and slammed the iron barrier closed.

'Gods Below, my lord, what was that all about?' Hauclir demanded, his breath coming in ragged gasps. Fresh blood spotted the bandage wrapping his thigh.

Before Malus could speak, the daemon whispered warningly in his ear. 'Be very careful what you say, Darkblade,' he warned. 'Or the next time you wake you'll find every one of your precious servants with their throats cut.'

The highborn gritted his teeth. 'I... was just checking on my belongings,' he said. 'The damned beast just didn't care for my scent. Too much wine, as you said.'

The former guard captain frowned. 'Are you certain that's all?' he said, his dark eyes scrutinising his former master.

'What else could it be?' Malus snapped, his voice bitter. Before Hauclir could reply he cut the druchii off with a wave of his hand. 'No more questions. I want to go to the wall and check on the state of the siege. I've got a terrible suspicion that something big is about to happen.'

CHAPTER TWENTY-ONE

BETWEEN THE LIVING AND THE DEAD

Columns of greasy, black smoke rose from behind the inner wall of the fortress, and the air was thick with the smell of roasting flesh. Every half-mile along the avenue behind the wall rose a pyre for the druchii dead, each one tended by a score of exhausted servants and a couple of hollow-eyed officers who noted down each soldier given over to the flames. The orderly removal of corpses to the funerary furnaces had been abandoned days ago. The dead were piling up far faster than the removal crews could handle, and most of the men had been pressed into service on the battlements besides.

The piles of the enemy dead were vaster still, rising in stinking heaps more than twelve feet high in places and running the entire perimeter of the wall. Malus was awed by the sheer scope of the slaughter and more than a little disturbed at the Chaos horde's near-suicidal zeal. They will bury us in their own dead if they must, he realised with a mixture of worry and admiration. All that matters to them is victory and ruin, and they will keep coming at us until their leaders are dead or the last barbarian has been cast from the walls.

He caught himself wondering what sorts of things he might accomplish with such an army at his back and ruthlessly forced such thoughts aside.

With Hauclir limping along in his wake he made his way up the long, bloodstained ramp to the battlements alongside the northern gatehouse. Bodies and bits of armour plunged past the two druchii in a grisly hailstorm as the troops on the parapet cleared away the detritus of the latest assault. The most recent attack had been seen off as the highborn had crossed the inner compound from the nauglir pens, and the sudden silence along the battlements was eerily disturbing after what seemed like hours of screams and bloodshed.

The highborn was appalled at the scene of carnage atop the wall. The dark stone parapet was mottled with a thick layer of blood, sawdust and viscera, and druchii spearmen sat or slept amid the filth, too exhausted and numbed to even notice. Broken weapons, bits of armour and pieces of flesh littered the entire length of the wall. Great ravens hopped and croaked at one another as they sought for choice morsels among the motionless bodies of the living. Even Malus, who had recently walked the blood-soaked streets of Har Ganeth, was stunned by what he saw. He glanced back at Hauclir and saw that the former guard captain's face was pale and grim.

Beyond the walls the outer city was a wasteland of burnt buildings and rude tents. Exhausted Chaos warriors sprawled like packs of wild dogs along the filth-strewn avenues, and hundreds upon hundreds of dead bodies carpeted the killing ground before the inner wall as far as Malus's eyes could see. Howls and gibbering cries rose and fell among the ruins, barking curses in a language none of the defenders could understand, but whose meaning was utterly clear. Soon, all too soon, the killing would begin once more.

There was a commotion ahead as Malus neared the door to the gatehouse. A trio of spearmen were struggling with a fourth warrior, who was shouting and struggling wildly in their grip. 'They won't stop! They won't stop coming!' he cried, his dark eyes wide in a face covered in dried blood and grime. 'We can't stay here! We can't!' The warriors struggling with the panicked druchii exchanged frightened glances. One of the soldiers drew his stabbing sword.

'What's all this?' Malus snapped, the sharp tone in his voice surprising even himself. The struggling warriors started at the barked command, and even the panicked druchii subsided in their arms.

The troops looked to one another, and the most senior man cleared his throat and replied. 'It's nothing, dread lord. We're just taking this man off the wall. He's unwell.'

'There's nothing wrong with this soldier,' Malus snarled, stepping forward and pushing his way into the knot of spearmen. He grabbed the panicked druchii by the scruff of the neck and forced him to stand. 'You've got both your eyes and all of your limbs,' he snapped. 'So what's wrong with you?'

The spearman trembled in the highborn's grip. 'We can't stay here, dread lord,' he moaned. 'It's been days, and they just keep coming–'

Malus shook the man like a rat. 'Of course they keep coming, you damned fool,' he growled. 'They're *animals*. It's all they know how to do.' He shoved the man against the battlements, forcing his body in the direction of the enemy camp. 'Listen to them! What do you hear?'

'Howls! Black curses!' the druchii shouted angrily. 'They never let up! It goes on and on for hours!'

'Of course it does!' Malus shot back. 'Every single one of those beasts are sitting out there in the muck and cursing your name loud enough that all the Dark Gods can hear it! Do you know why? Because they want nothing more than to get past these walls and slaughter every living thing they can reach, but *you won't let them*. They're the biggest damned army that's ever marched against Naggaroth, and you are standing up here on the wall with your spear and keeping them from the one thing they desire.'

The highborn dropped the man onto the filth-encrusted parapet. 'It's ridiculous! Absurd! They rise from their stinking tents each day and caper like fools before their twisted altars, working themselves into a blood-soaked frenzy that nothing on earth could stand against – and every day they slink back to their tents with their tails between their legs and lick their wounds in the shadow of these black walls. Of course they curse your name! The very thought of you burns like a coal in their guts because you've beaten them every time they've come against you. Every damned time.' He pointed out at the enemy camp. 'You should savour those sounds, soldier, because they are a lament. They're the sounds of fear and desperation. And it's all because of you.'

The spearman stared at Malus in shock. The highborn looked down at him and smiled. 'Victory is in your grasp, soldier. Are you going to let it slip away now, or will you beat these bastards once and for all?'

'You can count on us, dread lord! We'll kill every last one of the beasts!' cried a spearman just a few yards away. Malus was startled by the outcry; looking over, he realised that most of the warriors had risen to their feet while he spoke, and now they hung on his every word. Their dirty, bloodied faces beamed with fierce pride.

The panicked spearman rose shakily to his feet. He swallowed hard and looked Malus in the eye. 'Let them come, dread lord,' he said. 'I'll be waiting for them.'

A cheer went up from the assembled troops. Malus grinned, a little uncomfortably, and waved to the survivors of the regiment. 'Get some rest,' he shouted, and waved in the direction of the enemy camp. 'Enjoy the music while you can.' The warriors laughed, and Malus turned away, striding swiftly for the gatehouse.

Nuarc was waiting for him at the entrance to the fortification. The general's face was as filthy as any common soldier, its lines deepened by exhaustion and hunger. Nevertheless, he gave Malus an admiring grin. 'That was well done, boy,' he said quietly. 'I probably would have just let his file mates take care of the problem.'

The highborn shook his head. 'Then we'd just be doing the enemy's work for them,' he said. 'I'm spiteful enough to want to make those beasts work for every single one of us they kill.'

Nuarc chuckled. 'Well said.' He motioned to the highborn. 'Come inside. You look like you could stand to eat something.'

He led Malus and Hauclir into the gloomy corridors of the gatehouse, passing through deserted rooms and corridors lined with barrels of heavy bolts, until they reached a long room pierced with firing slits that looked out onto the killing ground before the gate. Perhaps a dozen weary-looking druchii soldiers, male and female alike, looked out over the corpse-strewn approach with their crossbows close to hand. A brazier in the centre of the low-ceilinged chamber provided a modicum of warmth, and upon a nearby table sat a couple of loaves of bread, some hunks of cheese and dried fish, along with a half-dozen leather jacks and several bottles of wine.

'Help yourself,' Nuarc said, waving at the contents of the table. The troops on watch cast predatory glances at the two interlopers who had been welcomed into their midst, like a pack of dogs suddenly forced to share their meat. Malus's stomach roiled at the sight of food, but Hauclir nodded his head respectfully to the warlord and helped himself to the food.

Nuarc poured some wine into one of the jacks and took a small sip. 'Word of your exploits has been spreading among the men. First the raid on the siege engines, and now the battle in the tunnel. You're fast becoming the hero of the hour.'

Malus let out a disdainful snort. 'Never mind the fact that the battle in the tunnel wouldn't have happened if I hadn't fallen for Nagaira's stratagem,' he growled. 'If those poor fools think me a hero, then things are desperate indeed.'

Hauclir chuckled around a mouthful of dried fish, but Nuarc stared into the depths of his wine jack and frowned. Malus caught the gesture and sobered at once. 'How bad is it?'

'We're barely holding on at this point,' Nuarc said gravely. 'As best we can tell, we lost just over a third of our troops in the debacle at the outer wall, and the rest are worn out. We don't lack for food or weapons, but the constant attacks have taken their toll. If we have another day of attacks like yesterday we could lose the inner wall by mid-afternoon.'

The revelation stunned Malus. 'What about the reinforcements from Har Ganeth and Karond Kar?'

Nuarc shook his head, his expression grave. 'There's been no word. At this point I doubt they will arrive in time, if at all.'

'And what of those damned lords in the Black Tower?' the highborn snarled. He began pacing the long room like a caged wolf. 'Have they any bold plans to save us from disaster?'

Nuarc reached for the wine bottle once more. 'I've heard rumours,' he said. 'Are you sure you won't take some wine?'

'Gods, no, general,' Malus said. 'I've had enough of that vinegar to last me a while.'

The warlord poured himself a healthy draught. 'There are indications that your brother the vaulkhar is contemplating a plan that will end the siege in a single stroke.'

Malus chuckled bitterly. 'He plans to lead the garrison against the Chaos horde?'

Nuarc shook his head. 'He intends to turn you over to Nagaira.'

The highborn's weak humour faded. 'You can't be serious.'

'I wish I wasn't,' Nuarc admitted. 'But you embarrassed Isilvar and the other nobles in front of the Witch King – and what's worse, your exploits are winning the admiration of the troops. That makes you very dangerous, as far as they are concerned.'

'Malekith would never allow such a thing!'

The warlord shrugged. 'I've served Malekith for more than three hundred years, boy, and I can't say what he will or won't allow. It's clear to me that he's testing Isilvar and the other lords, but to what end I can't begin to guess. The thing is, they are beginning to realise this as well, and it's making them nervous. They want the siege to end, and giving Nagaira what she wants is the quickest and easiest way to do it.'

'If Isilvar actually believes that, he's an even bigger fool than I imagined,' Malus said, torn between murderous rage and cold panic. 'If Nagaira believes that she can take the Black Tower – and humble the Witch King in the bargain – she won't hesitate to do so.'

Nuarc grimaced. 'I was afraid you were going to say something like that,' he replied. 'Then we'd best figure out another way of ending this siege before Isilvar and the other lords decide to take matters into their own hands.'

Malus bared his teeth in frustration. 'I believe I'll have a bit of that wine after all,' he said.

At that moment an earth-shaking rumble swelled up from the north, causing the oaken table to rattle and the wine bottles to wobble and clink against one another. A strange peal of thunder rent the air, like the sound of a hammer on glass. The druchii at the firing slits were suddenly alert. One of them turned to Nuarc with a frightened look on her face. 'You'd better come see this, my lord,' she said. 'Whatever it is, it can't be good.'

Nuarc and Malus rushed to the firing slits, shouldering aside wide-eyed druchii warriors. The old warlord's expression turned grim. 'Damnation,' he hissed.

Outside, beyond the far curve of the outer wall, a huge column of swirling smoke rose into the cold, clear sky. Green threads of lightning pulsed and rippled through the roiling murk, and even from almost six miles away Malus could feel the winds of sorcery tingling in waves across his skin. As they watched, the column of dark magic rose more than a thousand feet into the air and poured out its energies across the sky. Blackness spread outwards from the column in an inky, turbulent pool, casting a dreadful pall across the war-torn land beneath. More tortured thunder squealed beneath the tainted sky, and a sudden gust of cold, dank wind beat against the face of the inner wall.

'Damnation is right,' Malus said. 'I don't like the looks of this at all.'

Nuarc turned to one of the warriors. 'Sound the call to stand to,' he ordered. 'Unless I miss my guess, the enemy is about to hit us hard.' The warrior nodded, his face white with fear, and dashed from the room.

The wind picked up, skirling eerily through the narrow firing slits and filling the druchii's nostrils with the smell of damp earth. Green lightning strobed through the black sky overhead, glinting on the swords and shields of beastmen and marauders who were starting to trickle down the narrow lanes towards the killing ground before the inner fortress. Thunder keened overhead, and fat, greasy drops of rain began to spatter against the battlements. Above them, on the roof of the gatehouse, horns began to wail, their cries all but lost in the rising wind.

Within seconds the rain became a drenching downpour, tinged green by constant flashes of lightning. Cold air billowed through the firing slits; the druchii warriors recoiled with a curse, gagging on an overpowering stench of corruption. Malus cursed as well, but for a different reason entirely. A moment before he could clearly see the Chaos army massing for another assault, but now they were hidden completely by sheets of oily rain. They could be halfway across the killing ground by now.

The highborn turned to Nuarc. 'Will Morathi and her witches intercede against this awful rain? This could cost us the inner wall if we can't see the enemy until they're standing on the battlements!'

Nuarc shook his head helplessly. 'She is even harder to predict than her son. If Malekith orders her to do so, then perhaps she will.'

'Then you've got to get back to the citadel and speak to the Witch King!' The highborn turned to Hauclir, who was busy stuffing parcels of food and a bottle of wine into the sleeves of his robe. 'Hauclir! Put that down and escort Nuarc back to the Black Tower. Quickly!'

The former guard captain hurriedly folded his arms, causing the pilfered food and wine to disappear. 'As you wish, my lord,' Hauclir grumbled.

Nuarc snapped off a series of commands to the warriors, naming a half-dozen who would accompany him back to the citadel. Malus took the opportunity to join Hauclir and lead him towards the chamber doorway, out of earshot. 'When you've got Nuarc back to the citadel, round up the harbour rats and get back here as quick as you can,' he said quietly. 'We may have to do something drastic in the next few hours if we're both going to get what we want from Nagaira.'

'Drastic? Like what?' Hauclir whispered.

'Honestly? I haven't the faintest idea,' Malus replied, managing a roguish grin. 'Just like old times, eh?'

Hauclir winced. 'Old times? The ones where we nearly got drowned, or burnt up, or eaten by daemons?'

Malus glared at his former retainer. 'Now see here – what about all the good times?'

'Those *were* the good times.'

The highborn bit back a retort as Nuarc and his escorts approached. 'Just get back here as quick as you can, you damned rogue,' he said quietly.

Malus followed the small party to the rear of the gatehouse and left them at a spiral staircase that would deposit them at an iron door set beside the inner gate. Then he drew his twin blades and made his way to the outer wall.

Moments later he reached the exit leading out onto the battlements and saw the heavy oaken door rattling in its frame, buffeted by a howling wind. Shouts and screams echoed faintly from the other side. Gathering his courage, the highborn pulled open the rattling door – and found himself standing upon the brink of hell.

Druchii warriors reeled beneath the lash of reeking wind and noisome rain, many crouching and pressing the tops of their helmets against the battlements to get some relief from the hideous storm. Forks of green lightning rent the skies overhead, seemingly close enough to touch. Malus saw pale faces lit with absolute terror and heard cries of fear all up and down the struggling line of spearmen. To the highborn's horror he saw almost a dozen ladders already rising above the edge of the wall, their wooden rails quivering with the tread of hundreds of feet.

Less than twenty yards away half a dozen warriors were struggling with a thrashing figure lying on the paving stones. Malus heard shouts of anger and fury and saw a long dagger plunge again and again into the prone figure. A black rage boiled up from his heart.

'Stand and face the enemy!' he roared into the howling wind. Swords in hand, he strode out onto the parapet, heedless of the sheets of stinking water that blew into his face and into the crevices of his armour. 'The warriors of Naggaroth do not cower in the face of the storm! They fight or they die! Make your choice!'

Heads turned to Malus as he passed by. Lightning flared, lending his face a daemonic cast. Slowly but surely the spearmen of the regiment gripped their weapons and rose to the feet. Whether they did it out of honour, or shame, or fear of what he might do to them, Malus neither knew nor cared.

The brawl was still raging when Malus reached it, and with a furious shout he took to kicking the spearmen who were punching and stabbing at their victim. Fearful shouts rose in response to his angry blows. One knife-wielder even turned on Malus for a brief instant, his bloodstained knife ready, until he realised who he faced and recoiled with a frightened shout.

Now Malus could see the thrashing, snarling warrior at the bottom of the pile. Each flicker of lightning revealed ghastly wounds to the druchii's chest, belly and legs – horrible rents torn by knife, sword and axe. The warrior had his pale hands around the neck of another spearman, and was trying to pull his struggling victim within reach of his torn lips and broken, bloodstained teeth.

Malus realised how little blood there was around the snarling warrior, and then a cold knot of realisation turned his guts to ice.

The druchii was dead. He'd been dead for hours.

With a horrified shout, Malus slashed down with his blades, severing the revenant's right arm at the elbow and then shearing half its skull away. The creature recoiled and his screaming victim pulled himself free – but the revenant tried to lunge for the warrior yet again, even as his brains spilled out onto the paving stones. The highborn stepped in quickly and with a backhand swing he severed the creature's head from its shoulders. Only then did the wretched thing flop lifelessly onto the stone.

Thunder roared close to Malus's ear. Warriors cried out in terror. One of the spearmen looked up at Malus, bleeding freely from a line of deep scratches carved into his face and neck. The highborn recognised him as the panicked soldier he'd spoken to only minutes before.

'It's the rain, dread lord!' he shouted over the wind. 'It got onto Turhan's face and it brought him back to life!'

'Blessed Mother of Night,' Malus whispered, suddenly realising Nagaira's plan. He strode quickly to the inner edge of the parapet and looked down into the deep shadows at the foot of the wall.

Lightning burnt through the air overhead and Malus glimpsed the heaving mounds of rent and smashed corpses – hundreds, perhaps thousands of them – clawing their way free of the tangled piles that lined the inner avenue and staggering towards the long ramp leading to the top of the wall.

The scene was the same as far as Malus could see, all along the sections of the inner wall. His sister's infernal sorceries had trapped the defenders between two armies: one living and the other dead. And I just sent Hauclir and Nuarc down into the midst of that nightmare, he thought.

Horns began to wail all along the wall. Whether it was a cry of warning or a call to retreat, Malus could not tell. He couldn't begin to guess how such a plague of revenants could be stopped in time – all he could do was hold his part of the wall with the troops and the resources he had at his command.

Thinking quickly, Malus turned to the bleeding warrior. 'You! What's your name, spearman?'

'Anuric, dread lord,' the soldier stammered.

'You're Sergeant Anuric now,' Malus snapped. He swept his stained sword in an arc, indicating the druchii who'd struggled with the revenant. 'Take these men and get to the gatehouse as fast as you can. Grab all the dragon's breath bolts you can find and hurl them onto the ramp! Do you understand?'

The warrior nodded. 'Understood, dread lord!'

'Then why are you still sitting there? Go!' He shouted, and the warriors scrambled to obey. Shouts and screams of battle were already sounding up and down the line as the first of the Chaos attackers reached the top of the wall. As the spearmen ran back for the gatehouse Malus turned and dashed in the opposite direction, racing the shambling corpses to the top of the steep ramp.

The eight segments of the inner wall were each about three-quarters of a mile in length, but now it seemed to stretch for leagues in the flickering, chaotic darkness. Malus slipped and staggered across the oily paving stones, dodging frantic battles between screaming spearmen and howling Chaos marauders and buffeted by fierce winds that threatened to hurl him from the parapet and plunge him into the mass of shambling revenants below. Frenetic glimpses of desperate fights came and went as the highborn ran past. A spearman went down with a beastman tearing at his throat, blood bursting from the druchii's mouth even as he drove his sword again and again into his attacker's muscular chest. Another spearman crawled blindly across the paving stones, bawling like a babe from the ruined pulp that had once been his face. A pair of spearmen dragged a flailing marauder off the battlements by his braided hair and threw him face-first onto the parapet, where one of them reached down and expertly slit his throat from ear to ear. The flood of steaming blood lapped at Malus's feet as he raced past.

He was twenty yards from the end of the ramp and he could see that he was going to lose the race. The first of the revenants were almost at the top, and none of the warriors at that end of the line had any idea what was coming up behind them.

'End of the line! Look to your backs!' Malus shouted at the top of his lungs, but his words were all but lost in the roaring storm and the maelstrom of battle. Snarling in frustration, Malus started to shout again – but a figure tackled him from behind, driving him face-first into the paving stones.

Malus heard a beastman's snarl just above his head and felt its hot, foetid breath against the back of his neck. Then a sharp blow and a searing pain lanced down the length of his right jaw, and he felt hot, thick ichor splash against his cheek. Roaring like a beast himself, the highborn tried to twist beneath his attacker, driving his armoured elbow into the side of the Chaos warrior's bony snout. The beastman roared and tried to stab Malus again with his jagged knife, but the blade glanced off the highborn's backplate. Driven by pure instinct, Malus twisted back fully prone and reversed his grip on his right-hand sword with a quick flick of his wrist, then brought the sword around behind him with all the strength he could muster. The blade sank deep into the beastman's side, and Malus continued to roll, forcing the stunned and bleeding warrior off the inner edge of the parapet.

Breathing heavily, Malus clambered to one knee and saw a pair of revenants rushing towards him with grimy hands outstretched.

The undead monsters had reached the top of the wall, and already the druchii at the end of the line were being overwhelmed. Malus saw two spearmen attacked from behind and dragged down beneath a mob of tearing hands and clashing jaws. The rest were retreating with horrified screams, yielding still more of the parapet to the shambling fiends.

Malus leapt at the oncoming revenants with a fierce war-scream, his twin blades weaving a whistling pattern of dismemberment and death. Two quick swipes and the monsters' hands were chopped to jagged stumps;

then the highborn darted a step to the left and with two quick blows chopped off an arm and the leftmost revenant's head. Before the body had even hit the paving stones Malus reversed his stance and lashed out at the creature to his right, decapitating it cleanly with a single, blurring sword-stroke. 'Aim for their heads!' he shouted at the reeling warriors. 'Follow me!' And laughing like a madman, he threw himself into the press.

The undead warriors knew neither pain nor fear, but their only weapons were claws and teeth and unnatural vigour. Fuelled by rage and spiteful hate, Malus carved a fearsome swathe through the oncoming revenants. He knew that if he could reach the top of the ramp and stem the tide of creatures that reached the parapet then they could still hold the top of the wall. He sliced away fingers and parts of hands, lopped off arms and hacked away skulls. Marauders, beastmen and druchii all fell before his flickering blades.

He fought his way along twenty yards of blood-soaked parapet, felling everything that rose before him. The battle seemed to go on for hours, until the slaughter became a kind of terrible dance. Malus heard the furious shouts of the warriors behind him as they followed in his wake, and howled like a wolf loose amid the sheep. For the first time since the march on Hag Graef, many months past, he felt truly alive.

When he reached the far end of the wall it took the highborn by surprise. A pair of headless revenants slumped to the paving stones and his blades struck sparks against the wall of the far redoubt just behind them. More of the undead were trying to force their way onto the parapet, but now a solid knot of druchii spearmen at Malus's back had reached the top of the ramp and were hacking at the monsters with murderous efficiency. The highborn fetched up against the wall of the redoubt and tried to shake off the battle-madness as best he could.

Just then there was a crackling *whoosh*, and a sheet of green flame shot skyward along the back of the inner wall. Cheers went up among the druchii as the dragon's breath ignited among the shambling horde. Malus turned and saw Anuric staggering towards him, a look of weary relief plain on the young druchii's face. The spearman raised his hand in salute, then his eyes rolled back in his head and he collapsed face-first onto the parapet. A pair of marauder throwing axes jutted from the spearman's back.

Beyond the spearman's prone form the druchii line was a seething mass of fierce battles as waves of Chaos warriors poured over the battlements and leapt at the defenders. The druchii were holding on by their teeth, but there seemed to be no end to the furious assault.

Leaving the spearmen to hold the ramp, Malus advanced on the wavering line. As he passed Anuric's body he paused, then after a moment's consideration he knelt and rolled the young druchii's body off the edge of the wall, giving him over to the ravening flames as befitted a son of Naggaroth. Then he opened himself once more to the battle-madness and leapt howling into the fray.

CHAPTER TWENTY-TWO

THE BLOOD OF HEROES

There seemed no end to the killing.

As the corrupting rain fell and the wind howled its fury Malus stalked like a mountain cat along the length of the embattled druchii line, falling like a thunderbolt on the Chaos attackers and then passing on to the next desperate battle, leaving hewn limbs and twitching bodies in his wake. Always he struck the enemy from an unexpected angle, sliding a quick thrust into an unsuspecting warrior's ribs or slicing his hamstrings as he focused on the druchii in front of him. His deadly efforts had nothing to do with honour or glory; it was cold, calculated slaughter, repeated again and again all along the length of the blood-soaked wall.

The druchii fought back like the cornered animals they were. With the seething green fires raging at their backs, the spearmen knew there was nowhere to run, and so the harder they were pressed the more vicious they became. Marauders and beastmen were seized and thrown bodily into the hungry flames that raged along the ramp, or set upon from every angle like a deer beset by a pack of wolves. The druchii fought on despite grievous wounds, falling only after the last of their blood had been spilled onto the paving stones. It was as if Malus's battle-madness had infected them as well, and little by little the tide began to turn back in their favour. The knots of struggling Chaos warriors dwindled, driven further and further back towards their rain-slick ladders, then before long the defenders were standing at the ladders themselves and raining blows down on the heads of anyone who tried to scale them.

Malus could not say how long they fought. The storm raged on and on, showing no signs of slacking, and time lost all meaning, measured in lunatic flashes of green light. Again and again he caught himself searching among the struggling warriors, looking for a glimpse of Lhunara. Strangely, Nagaira's champion made no appearance during the desperate battle.

When the final wave broke against the battlements he was back at the far end of the line beside the gatehouse, standing behind a trio of roaring, blood-drenched spearmen who were crouched like snakes beneath the battlements opposite the last of the scaling ladders. For a long time they'd lurked there and ambushed each warrior that had come over the wall, stabbing upwards into the man's legs, belly and groin and then throwing the screaming victim into the fire. They had slain so many men this way that it had become a kind of routine, and so when a massive, bull-headed beastman came roaring up out of the darkness the spearmen were caught completely off-guard.

With a furious bellow the minotaur leapt over the battlements in a single bound, landing amongst the startled spearmen and laying about with a pair of enormous hand axes. One druchii was cleft in twain from shoulder to hip with a single blow; another took a splintering blow to the chest that hurled her broken body end-for-end over the inner side of the wall. The third druchii, still consumed with bloodlust, leapt at the towering beast with a fierce shout, burying his stabbing sword in the minotaur's side. But the blade penetrated barely a finger length in the monster's thick hide, and the minotaur struck the spearman a desultory blow with the back of one axe that tore the druchii's head from his body. Malus bared his teeth at the monster before him and rushed in with both swords flashing.

His first stroke slashed across the monster's enormous, muscular thigh, drawing a pained roar and the whistling stroke of a bloodstained axe. Malus tried to twist out of the way of the blow, but the weapon still caught the trailing edge of his right pauldron and the impact hurled him back against the gatehouse wall as though he'd been kicked by a nauglir. The impact knocked the breath out of him and his head struck the stones with a resounding crack that left him momentarily blind. His hearing, however, worked just fine, and he could hear the minotaur's furious bellow as it rounded on Malus and moved in to finish the highborn off.

Acting on pure instinct, Malus threw himself forward, rolling between the minotaur's legs as the beast's twin axes carved furrows in the gatehouse's stone wall. Still blinking stars from his eyes, the highborn rose to his feet and slashed his swords across the cable-like tendons behind the minotaur's knees. The crippled beast collapsed with an agonised roar, and Malus brought his swords down in a scissor-like motion that sliced open both sides of the creature's thick neck almost to the spine. Red blood sprayed in steaming arcs across the stone wall of the gatehouse, and Malus spun on his heel in search of more foes.

And that was his mistake. He'd finished with the minotaur, but the minotaur wasn't finished with him.

The highborn heard a furious bellow at his back, then a tremendous impact smashed into his left shoulder and hurled him to the paving stones. Fiery pain spread in a red wave down the left side of his back, but Malus had little time to appreciate the extent of his injury. Still roaring, the minotaur launched itself at Malus, half-leaping, half-dragging its huge bulk after him.

Cursing in pain, Malus rolled onto his back as the bull-headed monstrosity loomed over him. A heavy axe smashed into his breastplate; Malus cried out as ribs cracked beneath the ensorcelled steel, but the axe-head glanced aside from the curved plate. The minotaur drew back its weapon for another strike, but Malus lashed out like a viper, severing the creature's hand with a deft stroke of his right-hand blade. Roaring, maddened by blood loss, the monster smashed the jagged stump of its wrist into Malus's face. Splintered bone gouged the highborn's cheek and hot blood poured thickly into his eyes.

Screaming in rage, Malus lashed out blindly with his sword and connected with something as resilient as a young sapling. He struck again and sheared through – and the minotaur's head fell free, smashing the highborn in the face.

Then the heavy body, still spurting blood, collapsed on top of him.

Hot liquid flowed over the highborn's face and neck, filling his nostrils and pouring into his gasping mouth. I'm going to drown on a castle parapet in the middle of a plain of ash, he thought wildly. Coughing and sputtering, he tried to push the minotaur's heavy body aside, but the dead weight refused to budge.

After what felt like hours, the flood of gore tapered away. Dimly, Malus heard pounding foot steps and muffled shouts. The body of the minotaur shifted slightly, then suddenly rolled free. Cold rain lashed at the highborn's face – not the foetid corpse-rain of before, but honest, clean water. Malus gaped like a fish, greedily drinking it in. He rubbed thick ooze out of his eyes and blinked at the stormy sky. Green lightning still raged overhead, but the darkness had thinned somewhat, paling to an iron-grey.

Hands pulled at the highborn's arms. Silhouettes crowded at the corners of his vision. Lightning flashed, and he made out the thin, worried face of Ten-thumbs and Hauclir's cynical grin. 'I can't leave you alone for a minute without you getting into some kind of mischief, can I, my lord?' the former guard captain said.

Malus flopped about in their arms like a drunkard, wincing in pain no matter which way he turned. 'Perhaps if you'd actually been here for the battle this might not have been necessary,' the highborn snarled.

'Well, we'd have been here sooner – mind the leg, my lord! – but some fool set fire to the ramp.'

Malus found himself on his knees, using Hauclir like a ladder to haul himself upright. A black handprint stood out prominently on his bandaged thigh. Peering past Hauclir's shoulder, Malus saw the spearmen rolling the last of the enemy dead off the forward edge of the battlements. The dragon's breath had finally exhausted itself, having run out of fuel to burn. The survivors of the spear regiment staggered about in a weary daze, their bloodstained faces slack with shock and exhaustion. Malus was stunned at how few of them were left. He counted less than three score where just a short while ago there had been almost a thousand.

No one cheered. There were no celebrations of victory. The few survivors were glad enough to still be alive. That was all the glory that mattered to them.

Malus pushed himself away from his former retainer. Already the pain was subsiding, and an icy knot in the side of his chest spoke of the daemon's power knitting his broken bones back together. He looked about at the dozen cutthroats that had followed Hauclir back from the citadel. Cutter and Pockets were busy looting the enemy dead; the wounded assassin had a bloodstained bandage plastered to his shoulder and was busy pointing out places for Pockets to search. Ten-thumbs was chasing a bouncing gold earring along the parapet, his young face a mask of exasperated determination.

Malus shook his head wearily. 'Did Nuarc make it back to the citadel?'

Hauclir nodded. 'We got out just before those damned revenants started to stir and made damned good time getting back to the tower,' he said. 'Getting back here was a different story. There are packs of those revenants all over the inner compound now.'

'Did we hold the rest of the wall?'

The former guard captain nodded. 'Khaine alone knows how, but we did. For now, at least.'

Malus frowned. 'What's that mean?'

Hauclir looked back over his shoulder at the exhausted troops, then nodded his head at the gatehouse. 'Let's talk inside,' he said quietly.

A sense of foreboding crept over the highborn. Nodding wordlessly, he led the cutthroats into the gatehouse. Out of the rain, however, the stink of spilt blood and the oily residue of Nagaira's sorcerous rain rose like a cloud around the highborn, half-choking him. 'Upstairs,' he gasped. 'We'll talk on the roof.'

They found the spiral staircase leading to the top of the gatehouse and emerged once again into the howling wind and rain. Cloaked druchii huddled together around the four large bolt throwers mounted along the battlements, paying little heed to the small band of warriors at the far end of the broad, flat space.

Malus pulled off his armoured gauntlets and tried to clean them in a large puddle of rainwater. 'All right, what's going on?' he said quietly.

Hauclir knelt beside the highborn. 'Nuarc ordered me to remain once we'd reached the citadel in case he needed to relay any messages back to you. He was in talking to the Witch King for quite a while, and when he came out he wasn't alone. Your half-brother left first, looking like he'd been made to swallow a live coal, and then came a whole flock of messengers. Nuarc came out last of all, and had some interesting news.'

Malus splashed water on his face and rubbed it through his matted hair. 'Well, what did he say?'

'He said that the Witch King is getting ready to make his move,' Hauclir replied. 'Malekith is pulling the best regiments from the inner wall and bringing them inside the citadel even as we speak, as well as all the nauglir from the pens.'

Malus thought the news over. 'So we're letting the Chaos horde take the inner wall?'

Hauclir shrugged. 'At this point I'm not certain we could stop them if we wanted to. The Witch King's leaving behind enough of a rearguard to slow down the next assault, but no more.'

All at once Malus felt wearier than he'd ever felt in his life. He glanced down at the layers of blood and ichor coating the scarred surface of his armour and shook his head in frustration. 'And what does Nuarc and the Witch King ask of me?'

'Well, that's the interesting thing,' Hauclir replied. 'I'm to return you to the citadel at once.'

Malus frowned. 'And did Nuarc say why?'

'Not in so many words,' the former guard captain said. 'All Nuarc told me was that he thought Isilvar had failed the Witch King's test... and that put you in an interesting position.'

The highborn let Nuarc's words sink in for a moment. 'Are... are you telling me that Nuarc thinks the Witch King is going to name me Vaulkhar of Hag Graef over Isilvar?'

'Frankly I have no idea what I'm telling you,' Hauclir replied. 'Nothing you highborn do makes any sense to me. I'm just relating to you what Nuarc said.'

Malus nodded to himself. Would Malekith do such a thing? Why not? He'd already made Malus his champion – was it so far a leap to hand him the rank of vaulkhar? The thought of it quickened his pulse. How sweet a victory that would be: to humble Isilvar before the assembled lords and see him humiliated in the court of Hag Graef!

Only Tz'arkan stood in his way. The highborn's hands clenched into fists. Was there a way to claim his due from Malekith and still ride into the north to put an end to the daemon's infernal curse?

Perhaps, he thought. If he saw to it that the siege was broken and Nagaira destroyed.

Malus said, rising swiftly to his feet. 'I'll go straightaway to the citadel, but I want you and your warriors to get to the nauglir pens and make certain that Spite is brought into the tower.'

Hauclir chuckled. 'I'm sure the beast can take care of itself, my lord.'

'It's not Spite I'm worried about so much as the gear on its back,' the highborn said. 'There are... relics amid my saddlebags that must not fall into Nagaira's hands. Do you understand?'

The former guard captain gave Malus a searching look. 'Yes, my lord,' he said carefully. 'I understand clearly.'

'Then get moving. I don't want to keep Nuarc waiting.'

But just as the highborn and his cutthroats headed for the gatehouse stairs the air reverberated with the sullen rumble of drums.

The sound came from the broad square at the edge of the outer city. Malus hesitated, torn between a desire for haste and the need to know what the enemy was up to. Finally he turned and shouldered his way through the mercenaries, cursing under his breath as he strode swiftly to the gatehouse battlements.

His keen eyes saw a throng of bare-chested beastmen filling the square, their chests and arms painted in blood. They brandished bloody axes and bundles of severed druchii heads, still streaming trails of fresh gore. Malus could just make out the sound of a guttural chant weaving in and out of the rhythm of the great drums.

Behind the beastmen came a long line of stumbling, naked figures, spurred on by the barbed lashes of a dozen marauder overseers. Each of the druchii prisoners had suffered brutal tortures at the hands of their captors, their bodies marked with crude strokes of knife and iron.

Hauclir joined Malus's side and sneered disdainfully at the procession. 'If they think to break our will with a little torture they've come to the wrong place.'

'No,' Malus said warily. 'This is something else.'

The prisoners were herded into groups of eight and made to kneel at specific points in a rough circle at the centre of the square. Then came a band of beastmen wearing brass tokens and necklaces of skulls, each carrying a wide brass bowl and a longhaired brush. Filling the air with savage yells and barking cries, the beastmen dipped their brushes in the gleaming bowls and began to trace a complicated symbol across the stones of the square.

As they worked, Malus saw a figure clad in a dark robe and gleaming armour plate approach the edge of the square. It was no beastman or hulking marauder; Malus recognised the commanding stride of his half-sister at once.

He turned to the druchii gunners nearby. 'Can you hit those bastards from here?'

One of the warriors shook his head. 'Not a chance.'

'What if you used dragon's breath?'

The gunner let out a disgusted snort. 'We're out. Some damned officer came and took them all during that last attack.'

Nagaira walked gracefully into the centre of the expanding sigil, accompanied by a pair of hulking minotaurs who carried another druchii prisoner between them. The wretched figure had suffered the attentions of Nagaira's torturers far more than any of the other prisoners. His pale skin was covered with deep scars or fresh brands that stretched over almost every inch of his exposed skin, and his arms were bound in chains of brass. The prisoner's head rose at the sound of the drums, and even from so great a distance Malus recognised the druchii's face.

'Mother of Night!' he exclaimed. 'That's Lord Meiron!'

With a crash of drums the sigil was completed. A thousand beastmen threw back their horned heads and roared at the raging sky. Nagaira spread her arms and cried out a series of guttural words in a foul tongue that caused the assembled prisoners to writhe in fear and pain. Invisible waves of power radiated from the witch, distorting the air around her.

Something in her incantations disturbed Tz'arkan, causing the daemon to tense threateningly beneath Malus's skin. 'The little bitch has forgotten where her true allegiance lies,' the daemon hissed.

Before Malus could wonder what Tz'arkan meant, Nagaira's chant reached a crescendo. Lightning flared and a peal of thunder split the sky like the fist of an angry god. As one the beastmen raised their axes with a furious shout and turned upon the helpless prisoners, hacking them to pieces in an orgy of slaughter.

Fiery light burst from the bloody lines etched upon the stone. Lord Meiron stiffened, then screamed. The air around the druchii blurred, and his ravaged body started to swell. Malus felt his blood turn cold. 'Blessed Mother of Night,' he whispered, his voice full of dread.

Hauclir turned to Malus, his expression fearful. 'What would you have us do, my lord?' he asked.

'Run,' the highborn said. 'Run!'

Out in the square, Meiron's body continued to expand. The highborn's back was arched in agony and his muscles bulged until the skin split like an overcooked sausage, revealing the gleaming meat within. Meiron's face fell away from the dripping, shrieking skull, and a long pair of new limbs rose like blades from the highborn's back. As Malus watched, those limbs unfurled into a pair of gleaming, leathery wings.

The daemon continued to grow, wreathed in the boiling blood of the hundreds of sacrificial victims murdered in the square. Light and heat coalesced around the infernal creature's hands, taking the shape of a long, gleaming axe and a fearsome, barbed scourge.

Towering over the howling beastmen in the square, the bloodstained daemon raised its distended skull and roared a challenge at the defenders of the Black Tower.

The druchii manning the bolt throwers screamed in terror and several of the warriors ran for the stairs, hot on the heels of the fleeing mercenaries. Malus watched Hauclir and the cutthroats begin descending the spiral stair and knew that they would never reach the ground alive unless something was done to hold the daemon at bay.

He turned back to the towering fiend and met the daemon's brass eyes, raising his twin blades in challenge. Tz'arkan recoiled inside Malus's chest, sending a spasm of pain through the highborn's heart. 'What are you doing, Darkblade?' the daemon snarled.

'Do you not want Nagaira to see the error of her ways?' Malus declared.

The blood-soaked daemon spread its wings and leapt into the sky with a bloodthirsty roar. Malus threw back his head and laughed like one of the damned, and Tz'arkan's black vigour coursed through his veins.

Frantic commands echoed around Malus as the druchii still manning the bolt throwers wrestled their heavy weapons around to aim at the winged terror. The daemon seemed to fill the sky before them, its brass eyes and curved tusks gleaming in the dim light. Heavy cables banged, and four bolts streaked skyward. One missed the plunging daemon's head by less than a yard; another punched a neat hole through the creature's right wing. The last two bolts smashed full into the daemon's broad chest, their iron heads digging deep through iron-like layers of muscle and bone.

The twin impacts staggered the daemon in mid-flight. Bellowing in rage, it crashed against the edge of the gatehouse battlements, shattering the stone merlons to bits and sending a web-work of cracks along the building's thick roof. Malus was hurled backwards by the impact, throwing him beyond the sweeping arc of the daemon's fearsome axe. The blow meant for him hissed through the air and smashed a bolt thrower to splinters instead; blood and body parts of the three crew scattered in a wide arc from the impact. Snarling, the daemon lashed out at a bolt thrower to its left with its barbed scourge, wrapping it and two of its crew in a net of woven cables. Wood crackled and metal groaned as the daemon used the scourge to pull its massive bulk the rest of the way onto the battlement. The screams of the bound crewmembers turned to liquid shrieks as the barbed tendrils pulled taut and ground them into pulped flesh and bone.

Uttering a bestial roar of his own, Malus leapt back onto his feet and flew like an arrow at the axe-wielding daemon. With Tz'arkan's power burning in his limbs, the highborn was a blur of black armour and sharpened steel. He crossed the groaning roof in an eye blink, darting within the reach of the daemon's weapons and slashing fiercely at its axe arm. The keen blades rang from iron-hard muscle and bone, and then Malus felt the daemon's hot, foetid breath against his face as it snapped at him with its powerful jaws.

Malus sensed the daemon's lunge and tried to twist out of the way at the last moment, so instead of biting off his right arm the daemon's jaws closed on his armoured shoulder instead. Its fangs could not penetrate his enchanted plate but the highborn let out an agonised shriek as the metal plates compressed, twisting his arm from its socket and snapping his collarbone like a dry twig. The daemon lifted him off the ground and bit down hard once again, grinding broken bones together in Malus's chest, then it tossed him aside like a hound would a dead rat. He hit the stone roof hard, shrieking in pain once more, and skidded more than a dozen feet until he stopped near one of the last two bolt throwers at the far edge of the gatehouse roof.

Even as he ground to a halt the daemon was moving within him. Muscles spasmed and twisted of their own accord, dragging his mangled arm back into position with a crackling of sinew and bone. Malus screamed and thrashed, his eyes wild with pain, but Tz'arkan's terrible will prevented him from losing consciousness. The highborn's lunatic gaze fell upon the two bolt thrower crewmen just a few yards away, cowering in terror behind their weapon. '*Shoot... it!*' he snarled at them past ichor-flecked lips. The wide-eyed druchii took one look at Malus and leapt back into action, feverishly working at the twin cranks that drew back the weapon's steel bow.

The daemon rose to its full height, yanking its bloodied scourge loose from the mangled bolt thrower in a shower of splintered wood and steel. At the far end of the gatehouse the other surviving bolt thrower team lost their courage and ran for their lives, but their screams caught the winged fiend's attention. It lunged for the fleeing druchii, slicing one in half with a sweep of its axe and trapping the other in the barbed tails of its scourge. The daemon whirled towards Malus, swinging the scourge in an arc that sent the trapped crewman tumbling and screaming through the air. The flailing druchii missed the last bolt thrower by just a few feet before plunging into the darkness beyond the gatehouse.

With a loud *click-clack* the bolt thrower's cable locked into firing position. The crew scrambled to load another bolt in the firing channel just as the gatehouse roof trembled beneath the daemon's thundering footfalls. Malus gritted his teeth and once more surged to his feet, working the life back into his right sword hand, then rushed to meet the charging fiend.

He anticipated the lash of the daemon's scourge and ducked beneath its whistling tails, then cut to his right and drove the points of both his blades into the monster's left thigh. The weapons bit deep, drawing tendrils of black smoke from the daemon's bloodstained flesh. Roaring angrily, the winged fiend checked its pace and spun, slashing out at Malus with its axe. As fast as the highborn was, he could not move fast enough to avoid a glancing blow to the chest that broke ribs and smashed him aside like a child's toy.

As Malus tumbled once again along the gatehouse roof the last bolt thrower fired, and another iron-headed bolt punched into the daemon's abdomen. The monster staggered beneath the blow, then lashed at weapon and crew with its scourge. Both of the druchii weapon handlers were shredded in the passage of the barbed tails, and the bolt thrower itself was torn from its mount.

Baring its teeth in a feral grin, the daemon turned back to Malus, but the highborn was already on his feet again, fuelled by rage and pain as his shattered ribs were drawn back into place by Tz'arkan's will.

Malus ducked a sweeping blow of the daemon's axe, then stabbed out with his sword and raked a long, ragged gash along the length of the fiend's muscular arm. Snarling like a wolf, he nimbly dodged the fiend's backhanded swipe – and then the barbed tails of its scourge wrapped tightly around his legs.

He was pulled off his feet and dashed hard against the unyielding stone. It was Tz'arkan's power alone that allowed him to roll aside just as the daemon's axe smashed down beside him. Stone splintered, and a huge section of the gatehouse's roof collapsed in a shower of dust and debris, plunging Malus and the daemon into the space below.

Malus hit the tumbled stones hard and rolled against the side of the daemon's chest. Before the fiend could react he raised his left-hand blade and drove it with all his might into the daemon's shoulder, burying the weapon to the hilt. Roaring with rage, the daemon tried to pull Malus away with its scourge, but the highborn held on for dear life and drove his other blade into the fiend's muscular throat.

With a furious roar the daemon unfurled its wings – and suddenly more black smoke poured in a flood from its many wounds. Heat radiated from the fiend's body like a banked forge. Screaming in thwarted rage the daemon leapt skyward, and exploded in a clap of thunder and a blast of light.

Malus was hurled end-for-end through the air, striking the broken edge of the roof and bouncing along its length. The highborn fetched up hard against the line of battlements that looked over the citadel's inner compound, his skin scorched and his ears ringing from the blast. His swords were gone, lost when the daemon was banished. Gathering up his courage and trusting in Tz'arkan's power he rose to his feet and leapt over the battlements, plunging like a stooping hawk to the pavement sixty feet below. He hit the ground hard enough to crack the paving stones, but his body absorbed the blow with supernatural resilience.

It was hard not to smile. Terrible as Tz'arkan's gifts were, they could be exhilarating at times.

Guttural howls shook the air along the battlements of the inner wall. Nagaira's daemon might have lost its challenge, but it had put the druchii defenders to flight, and now the Chaos horde had seized the inner wall at last. Already, shadowy figures were racing down the long ramps into the inner courtyard itself, hard on the heels of the retreating druchii spearmen. Snarling like a wolf, Malus rose to his feet and raced off into the darkness. The siege was quickly coming to a head, and within the Black Tower the Witch King was preparing to make his move.

CHAPTER TWENTY-THREE

LORD OF RUIN

Within the walls of the inner keep the air reverberated with screams of terror and the guttural howls of the dead. The courtyards were full of panicked druchii racing for the safety of the Black Tower. Empty-handed soldiers, their spears cast aside, clambered over one another and stumbled along the cobblestones, fleeing for their lives. Craftsmen, apprentices, servants and slaves fled along with them. Like fear-maddened animals they turned upon one another in their frenzy to escape. Malus saw soldiers drawing their stabbing swords and lashing out at anyone in their path. A druchii wearing a blacksmith's apron fell with a scream, groping at the bloody wound in his back; his apprentice whirled and dashed out a spearman's brains with a heavy mallet, spattering his mates with a spray of gore. The highborn came upon a regimental officer facedown on the paving stones, a pool of dark blood spreading from his slashed throat. A sword with a jewelled pommel rested in his lifeless hand and a puddle of gold coins spilled beneath him from his torn coin-purse. It was more wealth than most low-born druchii saw in a lifetime, but no one spared it a second glance.

White faces etched with fear glimmered in the unnatural darkness, swirling like a cloud of panicked birds around Malus. Most of the panicked troops were looking back the way they'd come, listening to the exultant roars and wailing horns of the Chaos warriors swarming over the inner walls. It made them easy prey for the monsters stalking like wolves through the deep shadows of the inner compound. Nagaira's revenants dragged men down like panicked deer, tearing out their throats with claw-like fingers and feasting upon their steaming entrails. More than once Malus was forced to race past a screaming druchii buried beneath a knot of snarling, clawing monsters.

Once, a pair of pale, withered arms reached for him out the shadows of a nearby doorway. The revenant had once been a druchii spearman, his face half shorn away by the blow of a northman's axe. Cracked nails clawed at his throat; with a snarl Malus grabbed the hissing creature by the neck and tore its head from its shoulders. By the time the headless body clattered to the ground the highborn was long gone, running as fast as he could down the long avenue towards the citadel.

His body still felt cold and swollen. Muscles slid like steel cables beneath his skin, coated in thick, oily corruption. The daemon's gifts he'd summoned at the gatehouse had not ebbed, a realisation that both comforted and disturbed him at the same time.

With the daemon's unnatural speed he slipped like a ghost through the chaos of the rout. Caught between the Chaos horde and the waiting revenants, Malus feared that not one man in five among the fleeing druchii would reach the safety of the Black Tower. Malekith had been wise to pull his best troops from the walls in advance of Nagaira's attack.

He could guess the Witch King's intentions. The Chaos horde would be scattered and disorganised after the bloody pursuit, drunk with slaughter after destroying the exhausted remnants of the routing spear regiments, and Nagaira's sorceries would be depleted as well. When Malekith launched his counterattack, bolstered by the magical prowess of Morathi and the witches of the Black Tower's convent, the tables would well and truly turn. More than half of the enemy army would find itself trapped within the confines of the inner courtyard, facing fresh, disciplined infantry and the Witch King's battle-hungry knights. The slaughter would be awesome to behold, Malus reckoned, worth even the hundreds of druchii being sacrificed around him.

If Nuarc was correct about the Witch King's intentions, then it could be he who led the charge, as befit the Vaulkhar of Hag Graef. Malus smiled hungrily at the thought. After he finished massacring the troops within the inner compound he would rally the army and lead them into the outer city and beyond. They wouldn't stop until Nagaira's head dangled from one of Spite's trophy hooks.

Another of his half-sister's revenants lurched out of the shadows towards him, arms outstretched. Malus grabbed the creature's shoulder and the side of its neck and tore it down the middle like a sheet of wet parchment. He flung the dripping pieces aside and laughed lustily at the dark sky, anticipating the glories to come.

A few moments later he reached another wide courtyard that lay at the foot of the tower itself. Green fire flickered balefully from two large pyres to either side of the highborn, casting a riot of reaching shadows across the cobblestones and limning the polished helms of the two spear regiments formed up outside the doors of the great citadel. Bodies littered the broad square: revenants shot through the skull by sharp-eyed crossbowmen and a few unlucky druchii who'd been caught in the crossfire.

Malus slowed his pace somewhat as he loped into the square, showing his open hands as he approached the twin regiments. To his surprise, a ragged cheer went up from the spearmen as he strode forward. The sound quickened what little blood remained in his shrivelled veins, and he acknowledged the accolades with a raised fist and a wolfish grin.

He passed down the narrow gap between the two regiments and found a mounted officer waiting for him on the other side. The highborn raised his sword in salute. 'It is good to see you, dread lord,' the officer shouted over the thunderous din. 'The Witch King commanded me to watch for you, and bid you to attend him at his war council without delay.'

Malus's grin widened. 'I'll not keep his Dread Majesty waiting,' he shouted back. 'Has a group of infantry passed through here in the last quarter-hour with a cold one in tow? I sent my retainers to the pits to fetch my mount just before the gatehouse was attacked.'

The officer shook his head. 'We've only had a handful of troops pass through so far,' he cried. 'None of them with a nauglir.'

Malus's smile soured. He looked back the way he'd come, gauging the distance between the citadel and the nauglir pits. Where in the Dark Mother's name were they?

Something had gone wrong, he thought. They might have run afoul of a pack of revenants or been overtaken by a band of panicked troops. He fought against a tide of despair. Hauclir would get them back in time, he told himself. The insolent rogue is no end of trouble sometimes, but he's never failed me when it mattered. The highborn turned to the officer. 'Keep an eye out for them, and make certain they get inside,' he shouted. There was nothing more he could do. The officer nodded and turned his horse about, heading back to his waiting troops. Malus spared a final look at the tumult raging beyond the fires, and ran on to the tower.

Beyond the battle-line the black doors of the citadel yawned wide, ready to receive the lucky few who survived the flight from the inner wall. The green glow of witchlamps held back the darkness in the cavernous halls within, and the air rang with a different sort of clangour. Formations of spearmen stood ready, their scarred faces set in masks of concentration as they checked weapons and harness, while knights and their squires tended their wargear and the needs of their scaly mounts. The air was taut with coiled tension, like a crossbow ready to fire. Malekith had drawn back his mailed fist and now merely waited for the proper moment to strike.

Malus paused just inside the doorway, momentarily uncertain of where to proceed. Would the Witch King hold his council in the throne room, or the less formal chambers near the top of the tower? Just as he'd resolved to find a page or tower servant to ask, one appeared at his elbow.

'If you would follow me, dread lord,' the page said, bowing low. 'I am to conduct you to the council chambers.'

The highborn nodded curtly. 'Lead on, then,' he said absently, his mind awhirl. Malus fell into step behind the page, his mind immersed in drawing up hasty battle-plans for the Witch King's small army.

He followed the page upstairs, climbing the tall tower to the upper council rooms. Malus scarcely noticed the climb, buoyed by the daemon's cold strength and thoughts of the glory that awaited him. We'll have one last reunion, dear sister, the highborn thought grimly. And then I'll send you screaming into the Abyss where you belong.

Two guardsmen stood with bared blades outside the door to the council chamber. They saluted as Malus approached, and the page retreated with another deep bow. At the door, the highborn paused, suddenly realising how filthy he was. Every inch of his enamelled plate armour was coated with dust, grime and blood, and his face only slightly less so. Then he shrugged, allowing himself a grim smile. The Witch King wanted a warrior to lead his armies, he thought. A warrior he shall have. He laid his gauntleted hand on the door and pushed it wide, striding swiftly within.

The small room was dimly lit, bathed in the sullen glow of a pair of banked braziers. Maps and parchments were scattered across the broad table, just as Malus had last seen it. Retainers moved quietly among the shadows, attending upon the seated lords who watched the highborn approach. Balneth Bale glared coldly at Malus from his right, while Lord Myrchas scowled at him from the left. Lord Jhedir was conspicuously absent, Malus noted at once. Likely facedown in a puddle of wine somewhere, the highborn thought disdainfully.

As he stopped before the table the retainers retreated back to the far walls of the room, and Malus realised with a frown that none of the silver-masked Endless were present either.

His gaze fell upon the shadowy figure reclining at the far end of the table and his heart went cold.

'All hail the conquering hero,' Isilvar sneered, his ruined voice dripping with hate. He straightened in his chair and leaned towards Malus, until the red glow of the braziers painted his cheeks the dull colour of dried blood. 'You see, my lords? I told you he would reach the citadel safely. My half-brother has a talent for escaping the disasters he creates.'

'Where is Malekith?' Malus demanded, fighting a slowly rising tide of panic.

Isilvar smiled cruelly. 'Below, in the audience chamber. He is calling a council of war. Didn't you hear?'

Malus bared his teeth in a wolfish snarl, angry at having been outwitted so easily. 'I heard. He has commanded me to attend upon him.' The highborn coldly surveyed Isilvar and his allies. 'I suppose Jhedir is there as well. Interesting that the Witch King values the counsel of a drunkard over the likes of you, don't you think?'

He turned on his heel – and saw four of Isilvar's men barring his path to the door. Steel glimmered in their hands. Suddenly Malus was acutely aware of the empty scabbards at his hip.

'We have little need of councils, brother,' Isilvar replied. 'Our plan has already been set into motion. This siege begins and ends with you, Darkblade. As much as I would love to see you dragged back to the Hag in chains and taken apart one piece at a time, the needs of the moment demand that

I give you to our dear sister instead.' The vaulkar's smile widened. 'I'm certain she has something very special in mind for you.'

Malus's mind raced as he tried to think of a way out of his half-brother's trap. He looked to Lord Myrchas and Balneth Bale and wondered how strong their alliance truly was. 'You thrice-damned fool,' he said to Isilvar. 'I'm the Witch King's champion. Do you think you can just march me out through the citadel's doors and hand me to Nagaira?'

Isilvar chuckled. 'Certainly not. Thanks to you, however, we won't need to.' He beckoned to the shadows with one long-fingered hand.

A hooded figure glided silently into the crimson light, dressed in druchii robes and a worn kheitan of dwarf hide. Grave mould glowed faintly from the depths of the hood where one of the figure's eyes should have been.

Malus turned and threw himself at the druchii guarding the door. Fuelled by the daemon's power he crossed the distance between them in an instant. In a blur of motion he snatched the sword from one of the stunned warriors and smashed the druchii to the floor with an open-handed blow to his chest. The sword flickered in Malus's hand and another of the guards fell back, clutching at the gushing wound in his throat.

The highborn reached for the iron ring of the chamber door – and his entire body convulsed with a wave of icy pain. Gritting his teeth, Malus forced his hand to close about the ring, but his muscles rebelled. Tremors wracked his armoured frame as he bent every iota of will towards his escape, but it was as though flesh and bone had been transformed into solid ice.

A groan slipped past his thin lips. Inside, the daemon chuckled maliciously.

'Your sister is waiting, little druchii,' Tz'arkan said. 'We wouldn't want to disappoint her, would we?'

Slowly, achingly, his body turned away from the door. The stolen sword fell from his hand. Across the room, Isilvar watched Malus's body betray him with a mix of cruel delight and bemused wonder. He turned to Lhunara. 'I trust my sister understands the nature of the exchange?'

The hooded figure nodded. '*You will have your victory, Isilvar,*' she said, her voice bubbling up from dead lungs. '*Slay all within the inner wall, and the rest will retreat to the north. Harry the rearguard as long as you wish. We will slip away when night falls.*'

Isilvar nodded. 'Excellent.' He smiled to his fellow lords. 'By nightfall we shall all be heroes, and the Witch King will reward us well.' The vaulkhar glanced at Malus, who still trembled with thwarted rage. 'By tomorrow the Witch King will have forgotten all about my lost brother.' He gestured dismissively to Lhunara. 'Take him down the hidden stair to the cistern tunnel,' he said. 'We are late for the Witch King's war council.'

Lhunara bowed stiffly to Isilvar, then stretched out her hand to Malus. The daemon within him stirred, and to the highborn's horror his legs began to move. Slowly at first, then with gathering strength, he crossed the room like an obedient dog and fell in beside his former lieutenant.

The lords rose from their seats and filed past Malus. Balneth Bale fixed the highborn with a hateful stare and spat full in his face. 'My only regret is that I cannot slay you myself,' he growled. 'I will pray tonight that this sister of yours prolongs your suffering for a great many days.'

Lord Myrchas came next. He eyed Malus up and down, shaking his head in frightened wonder. 'You are an even greater fool than I imagined,' he said, then walked away.

Isilvar was last. He leaned close to Malus's immobile face. 'I wish you could have seen the look on your face when you walked into this room,' he said, his voice sweet poison. 'Did you honestly think I would sit meekly by and let you take my title from me? I won't see you die, brother, but I did watch your dreams turn to ash in a single instant. I will savour that moment for centuries to come.'

And then he was gone. The door swung shut, and attendants busied themselves with removing the body of the druchii Malus had killed. Lhunara turned to her former lord. Her cold breath stank of mould and corruption. She raised a gloved hand and traced a fingertip along Malus's jaw.

'*Mine at last,*' the revenant said, and her body trembled with terrible, bubbling laughter.

CHAPTER TWENTY-FOUR

THE AMULET OF VAUROG

There was a hidden stair at the far end of the council chamber that wound its way down the length of the tower and into the lower levels. Malus followed his former retainer as obediently as a hound, raging inwardly as Tz'arkan manipulated his limbs like a master puppeteer. From time to time the highborn heard voices and shouted orders emanating from the other side of spyholes and hidden doors along the stairwell. At one point he could have sworn that they passed within a scant few yards of Malekith's war council itself. Malus fought every step of the way, praying to every god and goddess he knew for someone to hear their passage or stumble onto their escape. But Lhunara's luck held out, and Tz'arkan's iron grip kept Malus helpless as a babe.

Before long a chill settled against Malus's skin, and he knew that they had descended below ground. A few minutes later Lhunara led him through a narrow door and into the cistern vaults. They walked through utter darkness, picking their way past the deep wells with unnatural ease. Malus found himself wishing with every step that the daemon would put a foot wrong and send them plunging into cold, brackish water. With all his armour he would sink like a stone. A watery death was preferable to remaining a slave in his own skin!

Isilvar had never set fire to the secret tunnel as he'd claimed. In the heat of battle it had never occurred to Malus that his half-brother would try to use it for other purposes. In retrospect, however, he was probably the one person in the tower who could treat with Nagaira effectively, owing to their ties to the Cult of Slaanesh.

They emerged into the wasteland of the outer city, now all but deserted with the bulk of the horde howling at the foot of the Black Tower. Lhunara led him down the corpse-choked lanes, past burnt-out buildings covered in obscene sigils and squares filled with victims of sacrifice and debased revelry. Ghrond had been transformed into a city of the dead; the carnage beggared anything Malus had seen in the bloody streets of Har Ganeth. The Black Tower had been transformed by the terrible siege into a city of ghosts, and there was still more hard fighting yet to come.

Beyond the outer gate waited the rude tents of the Chaos encampment. No sentries challenged Lhunara as she led Malus across the ashen plain; camp followers and wretched slaves clad in tattered rags peered warily from behind tent flaps or scattered like rats down the twisting lanes as the Chaos champion led the highborn to the pavilion of indigo-dyed tents that Malus had first spied days before. The air still roiled and seethed about the seat of Nagaira's power; the closer Malus got to her tents the more he felt a curious pressure building behind his eyes, as though something unseen was pressing insistently against the inside of his skull. Tz'arkan reacted to it as well, swelling painfully within the highborn's chest until Malus felt he was about to burst.

Huge, horned figures stood guard outside Nagaira's tent: more than a score of minotaurs, clad in crude iron armour and hefting fearsome double-bladed axes. They bellowed a challenge at Lhunara as she approached, until the Chaos champion pulled back her hood and showed them her face. At the sight of her terrible visage the monsters bent their ponderous heads as one, their nostrils twitching as Malus marched stiffly past.

The pavilion of indigo tents wasn't the elaborate, interlinked affair that Nagaira's previous abode had been. Rather, Malus counted nine smaller tents, festooned with arcane sigils and constructs of freshly cleaned druchii bones, arrayed around a larger, central enclosure. The highborn reckoned the smaller tents were given over to Nagaira's personal retainers; he wondered which one was Lhunara's. Did a creature such as she even feel the need for sleep, or to take refuge from the elements?

As they approached the central tent Malus could feel the air roiling about him, churned by otherworldly energies emanating from within. The heavy hide flaps covering the entrance billowed open at their approach, crackling like whips in an invisible wind. Faint screams and cries of terror rose and fell within.

Lhunara and the daemon led Malus inside. He could no longer tell who was leading whom, for Tz'arkan seemed to gain strength and urgency from the obscene energies seething about the tent. Beyond the entrance the large enclosure was subdivided by heavy canvas hangings, reminding the highborn of his sister's tent during the march on Hag Graef. In this case, however, the chambers were arranged in a crude spiral, leading them along a labyrinth of sorts around the circumference of the witch's tent. Along the way they passed through a succession of dimly lit spaces, each one marked with complex sigils formed of powdered gold, silver and crushed bone. The powders were the only signs of material wealth Malus could see. So much for Hauclir's visions of plunder, Malus thought bleakly.

Before long Malus could not say whether he walked in the mortal world or trod upon the threshold of another, far more terrible realm. The darkness about him stirred like ink, sliding over his skin like smoke, and strange whispers of horror and madness echoed in his ears.

Behold your future, Malus heard an unreal voice whisper to him. Whether it came from Lhunara, or Tz'arkan, or himself, he could not rightly say.

The chambers narrowed as they went. Canvas hangings pressed in about Malus, thick with oily darkness and sorcerous energies. Fear built within him, but his limbs were no longer his to command. The daemon bore him onwards through the suffocating blackness, until they rounded a final turn and the highborn found himself at the heart of Nagaira's sanctum.

There was no light. Instead, the air itself seemed leeched of shadow, creating a grey sort of gloom that hurt the eye to look upon. Malus saw no walls, or roof. A horrid, atonal chanting filled the tortured air, uttered from the twisted throats of nine beastmen shamans. They knelt in a broad circle, their horned heads thrown back and the muscles of their necks etched in taut relief in the strange half-light. Within the circle formed by the warped figures of the beastmen lay nearly a dozen shrivelled corpses, sprawled in an untidy heap before a figure that left Malus's tormented mind reeling in terror.

It was formed of inky layers of darkness and hues of smoke and shadow, swirling in the silhouette of a druchii-like figure standing with arms outstretched as though beckoning like a lover to the wailing victim floating helplessly before it. The victim was an autarii, his naked body unblemished save for dozens of ritual tattoos snaking across his muscular arms and shoulders. His body was stretched as though upon an invisible rack; each muscle tensed and twisted like ropes beneath his skin.

As Malus watched, wisps of steam began to rise from each of the autarii's tattoos, glittering like melting frost and swirling in thin tendrils about the Shade's agony-wracked form. The wisps of sorcerous power flowed towards the shadowy figure, as though drawn in by a hungry inhalation; the surface of the figure's body shifted, and Malus saw scores of horrific faces take shape along the being's limbs and torso. The obscene visages drank in the Shade's magical bindings, until the mist began to turn a pale shade of pink, then bright crimson. The autarii's body began to shrivel, his muscles softening like wax and his skin growing ashen. His screams bubbled and his eyes burst, and his tongue split apart. Within moments it was over. Another smoking, shrivelled husk clattered to the floor beside its fellows, and the beastmen's horrid chanting devolved into a chorus of joyous, barking cries.

The beckoning figure was swathed in crimson mist, swirling and mingling with the shifting currents of darkness until it smoothed into a patina of dusky skin that Malus knew all too well. The body shifted slightly, taking on beguiling curves and long, black hair. Between one heartbeat and the next the monster took the shape of his half-sister, naked and perfect.

Nagaira did not have the hollow eyes Malus saw in his dreams. They were dark orbs of jet, just like his. Her thin lips curved into a cruel smile. When she spoke, however, her voice was the same whispering chorus from his worst nightmares.

'The autarii are a bestial breed, but they understand the nature of spirits and how to bind them,' she said. 'Their souls are strong and sweet, like wine. Even that highborn fool who led them held enough power to make him savoury.' Her catlike smile widened. 'They were a fine gift, brother. I have saved them until last.' She beckoned to him with a taloned finger. 'Now you're here, and the final moves of the game are at hand.'

Within the confines of his mind, Malus snarled like a trapped wolf, but his body moved to the daemon's bidding. He and Lhunara stepped within the circle, and the beastmen bowed deeply, pressing their horned heads to the floor. Tz'arkan made no attempt to step over the piled bodies of the Black Tower's scouts. Bones snapped like twigs and grey skin turned to ash beneath Malus's boots.

The very air constricted about Malus like a fist. The air he breathed was hot and curdled, searing his lungs. When Nagaira moved towards him, the awful pressure only increased. Her vortex of power didn't emanate from her sorcerous circle, but from Nagaira herself; it seeped like acid from her skin, etching itself onto the fabric of reality around her. To the highborn's surprise, even Tz'arkan subsided as she approached, and Malus thought of the scores of unnatural voices intermingled with her own. How many pacts had she sealed with the Ruinous Powers for the strength she now possessed, and how could he hope to overcome it?

Nagaira stepped close, her eyes glittering like a serpent's. 'Have you no kiss for me, dear brother?' she said in her unearthly voice. She leaned in to him, her power rippling through his armour and sending waves of pain through his flesh. Her lips pressed lightly against the side of his neck and his heart skipped a beat at the touch. When she stepped away her lips glistened with black ichor.

Malus's jaw worked, but it was the daemon who spoke. 'Have a care, witch,' Tz'arkan said. 'This is my body now, not your brother's! I have invested too much in it for the likes of your caresses.'

Nagaira inclined her head. 'I forgot myself, oh Drinker of Worlds. It has been some time since my brother and I were together. There is much I wish to share with him.' She turned to Lhunara. 'Where are the relics?' she snapped, as though speaking to a slave.

The demand caught Lhunara unawares. She was staring intently at Malus, as though she were mapping the course of each black vein woven beneath his sickly skin. Her ruined face turned to Nagaira, blinking away her reverie. '*Relics?*' she said, a momentary frown of consternation twisting her festering brow. '*Relics? There were no relics, witch. Only him.*'

Nagaira struck the revenant with the back of her hand, swifter than a serpent. The blow echoed through the unearthly space, hard enough to break the neck of a living druchii. The witch snarled, 'Fool! Without the relics we cannot proceed! Have the maggots eaten so much of your brain that you cannot understand this?' She pointed to Malus. 'Until the great

Tz'arkan has been freed, Malus is *his*. Do you understand? We must find these relics, or you will never have the vengeance you seek.'

Lhunara rocked back on her heels from the force of the blow. Her one eye was bright with fury. '*I searched his quarters and found nothing,*' she hissed.

For a moment, Malus dared to hope. Here was an opening he might exploit. But then his lips moved, and the daemon answered them. 'He keeps the four relics on the back of his cold one,' Tz'arkan said. 'He sent his retainers to fetch it from the nauglir pits near the citadel, but they never returned.'

Lhunara's cold fists clenched at the sound of the daemon's voice. '*Then we shall find these trinkets among the dead once we've completed the destruction of the Black Tower,*' she said contemptuously.

'Prepare yourself, then,' Nagaira replied coldly. 'The Witch King is stirring in his tower, and the true battle for the city will soon begin. Do not fail again, revenant. The eyes of the Dark Gods are upon you.'

If Nagaira meant to unnerve the revenant with her threats, they came to nothing. Lhunara bowed curtly, and with a possessive glance towards Malus, she turned on her heel and strode swiftly from the chamber.

Nagaira watched her go with narrowed eyes. 'You made a grave mistake when you betrayed that one,' she said to Malus. 'She is as fierce and as implacable as a winter gale. Who knows how long she lay in the shadow of Tz'arkan's temple with that terrible wound in her head? Yet she refused to die. She lay there and prayed to the darkness with every last shred of her will, until the Gods Who Wait finally answered as she drew her last breath. They would have given her anything she asked, but she wanted one thing, and one thing only. Not wealth, nor power, nor even a whole skin. No, she wanted nothing more than pure, bloody-minded revenge.' Nagaira smiled in grudging admiration. 'By the time I found her she had already raised a sizeable army from the beastmen and the human dregs that surrounded the mountain. Once I realised how much she wanted you, it was easy enough to forge an alliance and place the Amulet of Vaurog around her neck.' She laughed coldly. 'I think the fool must have loved you, brother. Is that not rich? What else could have birthed such terrible hate?' The witch smiled at her brother. 'Sometimes, when she thinks she is alone, she whispers to herself all the terrible things she dreams of doing to you. So gloriously vicious and single-minded,' Nagaira said with a terrible sigh. 'It makes her easy to control, much like you once were. Who knows? If she serves me well in the battle to come I might even give you to her as a reward. If we triumph here I can afford to be magnanimous.'

'So you intend to betray Isilvar,' Tz'arkan said.

The witch snorted derisively. 'Betray? That implies we had an agreement in the first place,' she said. 'He came crawling to me, looking for a way out of the trap he'd fallen into. I knew from the moment the siege began that he'd try something like this. All I had to do was apply pressure and wait.'

'And the Witch King?'

Nagaira shrugged. 'Malekith grew more predictable as the siege wore on. He would never abandon the Black Tower without a fight, and once we were past the outer wall it made a counterattack inevitable. By now, Morathi's colossal arrogance has led her to believe that I have exhausted my energies during that last attack, so now is the time to strike. Do you imagine I could pass up such an opportunity?'

The daemon chuckled. 'I imagine you have little choice. You have your own masters to serve, witch. Such power does not come without fearsome promises of repayment.'

Nagaira's expression froze. 'There were... agreements... that were made,' she allowed. 'Malekith and his mother will make fine gifts for the Gods Who Wait, and they have never been as vulnerable as they are now. I should think you would be pleased,' she said haughtily. 'An ally upon the Iron Throne would make your plans much easier, I should think.'

'Plans?' the daemon said.

'You are the Scourge,' she said simply. 'The prophecy was written by you in aeons past to pave the way for your rise to power. You mean to use the druchii as the agents of your ambition in this universe.'

'And you?' the daemon asked.

The witch smiled faintly and bowed. 'I live to serve the Prince of Pleasure,' she said in her unearthly voice.

Tz'arkan smiled. 'You amuse me, witch,' it said. 'But there is little time for battle. My time grows very short. Malus will have to ride that nauglir of his to death in order to reach the temple as it is.'

'Ride? Great Tz'arkan, once I've offered the Witch King and Morathi to the Dark Gods and seized the Iron Throne, we will fly to your temple on dragon wings,' she said. 'There is time enough for the vengeance I seek.' She cocked her head, as though listening to some faint sound. 'I must take my leave of you, dread lord. Already the winds of magic are stirring. Morathi and her pitiful novices are readying themselves for the attack.' She made to leave, then paused, looking thoughtfully at Malus. The witch stared intently into his eyes, as though trying to find the highborn amid the darkness that was the daemon. 'Are you so attached to this body?' she asked, touching Malus's breastplate with a curved talon. 'Once you are freed you may take any form you like.'

'That is so,' the daemon allowed, 'but the prophecy has attached itself to his name. I must continue to be Malus for a time, once I have been set free.' Inwardly, Malus could feel the daemon's amusement. 'Of course, if you could ensure that the real Darkblade were to vanish from sight...'

Nagaira laughed. 'Be assured, dread lord. That would be no trouble whatsoever.'

'Then we will speak of this again at the temple in the north,' Tz'arkan replied. 'Go and claim your vengeance, witch. I will wait here until you return, and savour your brother's despair.'

Nagaira bowed again, and stepped from the circle. As one, the beastmen rose and followed her into the darkness.

Outside, a warhorn wailed. Malus sensed movement about the Chaos encampment, as the last reserves of the horde were called to battle. Did Nagaira truly have the power to trap and destroy the Witch King himself? After what he'd seen, the highborn thought it possible.

Still as a statue, the highborn was left to wonder as the kingdom of the druchii teetered on the edge of ruin. Despair threatened to overwhelm him.

Curled like a serpent in the darkness, Tz'arkan drank deep from the well of Malus's pain.

Malus soon lost all track of time. Few sounds penetrated the chambers of Nagaira's tent, and once she was gone there was no relief from the darkness. He might have lingered for mere minutes, or hours, or even days. Each moment was more agonising than the next, as Nagaira's stratagem inched towards completion.

He didn't notice the sounds at first. They slowly impinged on his awareness as a kind of faint scratching, like rats scampering in the walls.

Malus focused his attentions on the noise. It came and went, but always from the same general direction, off to the highborn's left.

After a time, the scratching became faint, raspy sawing. Then he heard a harsh whisper.

'How many damned compartments can one tent have?'

'Shut up and keep sawing,' hissed a familiar voice. 'We've got to be close to the centre now,' Hauclir said

'You said that the last two times,' the first voice shot back. Malus thought it sounded like Pockets.

Within Malus, the daemon stirred. He felt Tz'arkan's cold, cruel smile. 'The Dark Gods are generous,' the daemon murmured. 'We shall have pleasant diversions to occupy us while we await your sister's return.'

Tz'arkan turned Malus about and stalked across the inner chamber. His hands reached out and found the canvas wall. Moments later something sharp poked the fabric from the other side.

Malus's lips worked. 'Hauclir?' the daemon whispered, using the highborn's voice.

'My lord?' the former retainer responded. 'It's good to hear your voice! Are you bound, or injured?'

'No, I'm well,' the daemon replied. 'But Nagaira's sealed this chamber with some spell. I can't get out.'

'We'll see to that, my lord,' Hauclir answered. The object poked hard against the canvas. After a moment the needle tip of a dagger poked through.

'Gods Below,' Pockets hissed. 'This is like cutting through stone.'

'Keep at it,' Hauclir ordered. As Pockets continued to work her knife through the ensorcelled fabric, the former retainer whispered to Malus. 'We'll have you out in just a moment, my lord.'

The daemon smiled. 'What about the relics?'

'We have them as well,' Hauclir replied. 'Spite is close by.'

'That's excellent news,' Tz'arkan said. Malus could only watch in horror as his hand slid down to the dagger at his belt. Slowly, quietly, the daemon drew the weapon free.

Pockets drove her knife through the canvas wall and began sawing downward. After a few moments she'd cut a slit large enough for a man to wriggle through. The daemon raised Malus's dagger. 'Come inside,' he said. 'There are statues of gold and silver in here. It's time you got your reward.'

Malus raged helplessly within the confines of his own body, trying to regain control of his own limbs, but the daemon's grip was stronger than iron. He could see the slaughter that was about to unfold the moment Hauclir poked his head inside the chamber.

'That's the best news I've heard all day,' the former retainer answered. 'Give me your hand.'

'Of course,' the daemon replied, shifting the knife to Malus's left hand and extending the right one through the torn fragment. He reached for Hauclir blindly, groping about with Malus's armoured fingers.

Then all at once his hand found something and closed around it. Malus felt the smooth hilt of a sword – and a torrential rush of heat that poured through his hand and set his veins afire.

The daemon let out a furious shout as the Warpsword of Khaine took Malus in its burning grip. Tz'arkan tried to let go of the blade, but the highborn's fingers would no longer obey. Hungry fire seared Malus from head to foot, and he cried out in agony and triumph as the daemon's hold was broken.

After a moment Malus realised that Hauclir was hissing urgently at him. He forced himself to take a deep breath and answer. 'What is it?'

'I said, could you possibly scream a little louder? I'm pretty sure there are a few scattered tribes on the other side of the Chaos Wastes that didn't hear you.'

Malus laughed quietly, flexing his fingers around the hilt of the blade. 'Step away, you damned rogue,' he said, and sliced carefully at the tent wall. The canvas peeled back with a hiss of burnt fabric.

Hauclir, Pockets and Cutter rushed into the chamber, holding small witchlamps in their hands. The former retainer looked about the space and frowned. 'I don't see any gold or silver,' he said.

'No,' Malus replied breathlessly, holding the sword aloft. 'That was an utter lie.'

'I should have known,' Hauclir said with a sigh.

The highborn looked at the cutthroats in wonder. 'What in the Dark Mother's name are you doing here?'

Hauclir shrugged. 'Blame it on your cold one, my lord,' he said. 'It took us forever to fight our way to the nauglir pens. There were packs of those damned revenants lurking in every doorway, it seemed. Once we finally got there and let Spite loose, the damned thing sniffed at the air and just went loping off. We couldn't stop it, so we decided to follow the beast and see where it was going,' he said. 'It led us out through the south gate, then outside the city itself. We thought for sure someone would challenge us, but the camp is deserted. Nagaira's called all her troops into the city. At any rate, after a bit we worked out that the nauglir was hunting for something, and we figured it might be you.'

Malus nodded. 'But this?' he asked, showing Hauclir the sword.

'Oh. That was easy,' he replied. 'It was obvious you were trying to get it from Spite back in the nauglir pits, and the daemon managed to stop you. I figured that if you were to be found out here then the daemon must have had a hand in it, so I thought that bringing the sword along was a wise move. Was I right?'

'You have no idea,' Malus answered. 'In fact, you may have saved Naggaroth.' He quickly told the cutthroats about Nagaira's plans. 'She believes she has the power to bring down Malekith and Morathi both,' he said at last.

The cutthroats looked to one another fearfully. 'Can she?' Hauclir asked.

'After all I've seen... yes. I think she can.'

'Then I think we need to get your mount and run for our lives,' Hauclir replied.

But Malus shook his head. 'No. Malekith may be vulnerable, but so is Nagaira. She might have enough strength to master the Witch King and Morathi, but not all three of us at once,' he said. 'And she has to be destroyed.'

'For the sake of the kingdom?'

'Don't be stupid,' Malus snapped. 'For my sake. The witch knows too much.'

'Ah, of course. Your pardon, my lord,' Hauclir said dryly. 'Well, then. What would you have of us?'

Malus's hand tightened on the burning blade. He could feel its hunger now, seething like coals in his gut. 'Follow me,' he said to the cutthroats. 'And when the killing starts, stay out of my way.'

They were just emerging from the Chaos encampment when the Witch King launched his attack.

War horns screamed from the tall tower, and Malus watched as a dark form raised its serpentine neck atop the citadel and roared a challenge at the sky. With a powerful sweep of leathery wings, Malekith's dragon Seraphon launched into the dark sky. At the same moment, green lightnings smote the darkness, rending it and driving it back. In the searing flashes of light, the highborn spied an armoured figure on the dragon's back, brandishing a glowing sword at the Chaos horde.

The sword swept down and Seraphon dove with a thunderous roar, filling the inner compound with a hissing stream of dragon flame. Shouts and screams rose from the dying warriors, and the final battle was joined.

Malus, Hauclir and the cutthroats came to a halt a quarter mile from the open city gates. Spite paced alongside the small band, sniffing the air warily. The former retainer turned to the highborn. 'We're going in there?' he said, pointing to the city. Pillars of fire and smoke were already wreathing the Black Tower, and the clash of swords and armour could be heard from where they stood.

'Only so far as the square outside the inner gate,' Malus replied. 'That's where we'll find Nagaira, I expect.'

'And how do you plan on stopping her?'

'Don't worry,' Malus said. 'I have a plan.'

'Do I want to know what the plan is?' Hauclir asked.

The highborn shook his head.

'You're probably right,' Hauclir agreed. 'Lead on.'

With Malus in the lead, the small band raced through the ruins of the outer city. Forks of green lightning lashed down from the boiling skies, plunging like knives again and again onto the square outside the inner gate. Seraphon continued to swoop low over the inner compound, scouring the area with ravening bursts of fire as the outnumbered druchii army fought their way from the citadel. Somewhere ahead, in the thick of the fight, Lhunara would be wreaking bloody havoc on the Witch King's troops.

Malus expected that the Chaos horde would fall back, drawing the druchii host out past the inner gate and up to the great square. That's when Malekith would take the battle directly to Nagaira, and she would spring her trap.

They got to within less than a hundred yards of the square before their path was blocked by a herd of waiting beastmen. For the moment their attention was focused solely on the sorcerous battle being waged nearby.

Malus led the group into the shadow of a burnt-out barracks. 'Here is where we part ways,' he said. 'I must face Nagaira alone.'

'What do you want us to do?' Hauclir said.

The highborn looked his former retainer in the eye and drew a deep breath. 'I want you to circle around the square and wait,' he replied. 'When I attack Nagaira it's only a matter of time before Lhunara comes running. You will have to hold her off long enough for me to deal with my sister.'

'Blessed Murderer,' Cutter said. 'She nearly killed me the last time.'

'And me as well,' Hauclir replied.

Malus nodded. 'How is your leg?' he asked.

'Fine, oddly enough,' the former retainer said. He reached down and pulled his stained bandages aside. Only a dull, black scar showed where Lhunara's blade pierced his leg. 'I can't explain it.'

Malus noted the ichor stains darkening the bandages. It was the daemon's energies, he thought. I bled onto your bandages, and it seeped into the wound. He set his jaw. 'That's fortunate,' he said. 'Because you'll need all the luck you can get. Just hold her off long enough for me to deal with Nagaira. That's all I ask.'

The cutthroats looked to one another. Hauclir shrugged. 'We've come this far,' he said. 'We'll see this through.'

Malus nodded, clapping Hauclir on the shoulder. 'Go, then. I'll see you all shortly,' he said, hoping that it would be true.

The cutthroats moved off to the east. Malus laid a hand on Spite's snout. 'Stand,' he said, rubbing the nauglir's scales appreciatively. 'Wait until I call, beast of the deep earth. You've done enough for me already.'

Then, sword in hand, he stepped into the street and started to run.

The herd of Chaos warriors filling the street outside the square was unaware of the danger bearing down on them until it was far too late. Distracted by the pillars of lightning and deafened by the thunderous explosions, they did not notice the dark blur racing down the debris-strewn avenue until he was upon them. Half a dozen beastmen fell dead, glowing wounds smoking in their chests, before the enemy could even react.

Malus tore into the enemy with a savage howl, the warpsword carving through the tight-packed ranks like a scythe. Weapons snapped and armour melted at the blade's touch; arms and legs tumbled across the cobblestones and heads were shorn away. The highborn grew stronger with every blow, and the movements of his enemies seemed to slow, until they appeared to be standing still. He slipped past their feeble blows and slaughtered them by the score, until finally the enemy could take no more and melted away in every direction. Those who tried to run through the square itself were cut apart by the angry slashes of lightning that raged within.

Covered in steaming gore, Malus staggered drunkenly to the edge of the open space. In the centre of the square shone a hemisphere of green light more than sixty paces across. Lightning flared and rebounded from this sorcerous shield, maintained by Nagaira's shamans, who sat in their customary circle and chanted arcane phrases skyward. Within the circle, Nagaira floated a few feet off the ground. Once again she was no more that the black shadow-shape that he'd seen in the tent, surrounded by curling tendrils of black smoke that wove about her like a net of serpents.

Beyond, Malus could see fighting atop the inner wall. Malekith's counter-attack had pushed the besiegers almost to the inner gate itself. Very soon the Witch King would reach the square and fall into Nagaira's clutches. Malus was running out of time.

Brandishing the burning blade, Malus charged at the shamans' glowing sphere. Lightning seemed to drip lazily from the air, splashing against the ward and playing about the square. He struck the glowing ward with the warpsword, and a web of red cracks spread across its surface. Instantly the beastmen were aware of him, shouting magical chants and pointing fetishes of bone at the damage to the sphere. The cracks faded as he drew back his blade, but he struck the surface again and again. Slowly but surely, the damage spread.

More lightning arced down, as though Morathi sensed the change in the nature of the ward and had redoubled her efforts. The green glow began to dim as its energies were strained to the utmost. Across the square, Malus saw huge figures approaching the ward at a dead run – they were Nagaira's minotaur bodyguard. Undaunted, the highborn continued his punishing assault.

Within the hemisphere, Nagaira slowly turned to face him. Her night-haunted face was devoid of expression, but he could feel the cold pressure of her furious stare.

Another barrage of lightning bolts hammered at the ward. Malus timed his strokes with the thunderclaps, adding to Morathi's assault. Then, without warning, the shield collapsed, shattering like glass beneath a hammer blow. There was a flare of light, and several of the beastmen collapsed, blood streaming from their ears. Several more were immolated in bolts of green lightning, leaving charred husks sprawled across the paving stones. A bolt of lightning even struck Nagaira herself, momentarily staggering her.

With the shield broken, the minotaurs charged across the intervening space at Malus, axes held ready. The highborn rushed at them with a ferocious cry, and the burning blade sang through the air. One of the huge warriors swung wide and was cut in half as the highborn raced past. Another lunged at the highborn with a sweeping cut and had both hands sliced away.

An axe crashed into Malus's pauldron; the highborn spun and drove his sword through the minotaur's abdomen, boiling its guts. Another axe struck him full in the breastplate. Laughing, Malus tore his sword free and cut the legs out from under the enemy champion.

Lightning raged among the howling minotaurs, blasting warriors to the ground. A bolt struck Malus and flung him skyward, dropping him in a heap several yards away. Still smoking, he lunged back onto his feet and returned to the fray. Only three of the huge champions were left, stunned and shaken by the blast. Malus cut them down.

Then a strange buzzing filled the air, like a swarm of angry hornets, and Nagaira struck him with a bolt of pure darkness.

It passed through his armour as though it wasn't there, and he felt his organs melt at its touch. A spear of pure agony lanced through Malus's chest, and he spat sizzling ichor onto the stones. His sister loomed above him almost a dozen yards away, wreathed in tendrils of darkness. Pure rage emanated from her in palpable waves.

'You disappoint me,' Nagaira thundered. A bolt of lightning lashed at her, but his sister paid it little heed. 'I had thought you were wiser than this.' Suddenly she lunged at him, crossing the space between them in an eye blink. Her fist crashed into Malus and flung him across the square like a toy. He crashed into the wall of a warehouse fifteen yards away, striking the stone hard enough to crack it before rebounding back onto the pavement.

'A wise man would have waited in the darkness for his doom to find him,' Nagaira said. 'But you? You seek it out.'

She swept down on him again. This time Malus brought the warpsword up in a hissing arc and sliced through the witch's midsection. Nagaira staggered with a scream of countless tortured souls, but she recovered almost immediately. Her fist closed about his throat and she flung him headlong through the air.

This time he crashed against the burnt hulk of one of the Chaos catapults. Oaken timbers shattered under the impact, and he landed hard at the siege engine's base.

Nagaira stalked after him. Lightning lashed at her smoky figure again and again, slowing her flight. Still she pressed on, undeterred.

'I could swat you down like a fly, dear brother,' she seethed. 'By all the gods I should! But Tz'arkan must be freed, and so I must content myself with merely crippling you.' She swept down and slapped the highborn's chest with the flat of her hand, cracking his ribs like eggshells.

Malus screamed in agony and buried his sword in Nagaira's chest. The blade burst from the witch's back, drawing a scream of rage. Black ichor smoked from the tip of the blade. She drew back her hand to strike him again – and another bolt of sorcerous lightning struck her, blowing the two druchii apart.

Malus landed hard on his back, biting back a wave of intense pain. Nagaira landed in a heap some yards away. Her body had a grey cast now, and the tendrils of smoke that enshrouded her were all but gone. With a furious oath, she spoke an incantation that rent the air around her and her form regained a portion of its power.

Then a shadow swept over her from above. Nagaira looked up just as Seraphon bathed her in a pillar of dragon fire.

Malus could see her black form wreathed in angry fire. She screamed, spreading her arms wide within the flame, and magical power pulsed from her body. The dragon banked away, but Nagaira's ruined form turned to track it. She pointed a smoking finger at the sky, and a chorus of daemonic howls filled the air. Tendrils of smoke leapt like whipcords from her body, reaching for the armoured form riding atop the swooping dragon.

Summoning his rage, Malus staggered to his feet and charged across the square. At the last moment she saw him, and with a word sent another bolt of black fire through him. He staggered, feeling his guts turn to mush, but the blade sustained him, driving him on. Malus raised the burning blade and chopped it deep into Nagaira's chest.

She howled and writhed around the blade, her unearthly form hissing and sizzling under the weapon's touch. Still she drove the tendrils skyward, reaching for the Witch King. 'You cannot slay me!' she cried. 'The Dark Gods themselves fill me with their power!'

Malus spat a mouthful of ichor into his sister's face. 'And they do not countenance failure,' he said, twisting the blade in her body.

Nagaira screamed again – and the smoking tendrils faltered, just short of their goal. Her body turned grey, once more. Gibbering with rage, she hissed a litany of curses, calling upon the gods for more power. But she had already drawn far too much, and the patience of the fickle Chaos gods was at an end.

Like snakes, the tendrils turned, seeking easier prey. They plunged like arrows, burying themselves in Nagaira's skull.

Malus hurled himself clear of his sister, drawing the burning blade after him. As he watched, daemonic faces took shape all over her body, the mouths working hungrily as they devoured his sister from within. Still screaming, she shrank in the air before him.

The last things to go were her eyes. Nagaira glared at Malus with a look of purest hate. Then she was gone in a clap of terrible thunder.

'Enjoy the favour of the gods, dear sister,' Malus said darkly. And then, like a black wind, Lhunara was upon him.

He never heard her approach. Only the warpsword saved him; it seemed to turn in his hand, reaching skyward just as her bloodstained blades came slicing for his throat. His body moved without conscious thought, striking the twin swords aside in a shower of sparks.

There was no time for fear, or curses, or clever stratagems. She fell upon him like a storm, and it was all Malus could do just to survive.

Her glowing eye gleamed balefully from the depths of her helmet as she drove Malus across the square. The warpsword was a blur, meeting her every stroke with a ringing block that just barely kept death at bay. Already ichor was seeping from a score of shallow cuts on his face and neck.

After several long moments, Malus regained his wits in the face of Lhunara's maddened assault. She said not a word, slashing and thrusting at him with an urgency born of desperation and madness. Where Nagaira emanated rage and power, his former retainer was driven by nothing more than bitter pain and despair. Now he sensed that she knew her chance for vengeance was slipping away.

Her urgency made her sloppy. Lhunara swung for Malus's neck and he ducked beneath the blow, slicing the warpsword through her midsection. The blade parted her armour like paper, the edges turning molten from the sword's heat. Ichor poured from the wound and she groaned... but still she fought on.

The sight stunned Malus. I can't kill her, he thought. Not even the warpsword could slay her!

Lhunara leapt at the highborn and he planted his feet, blocking her twin swords and stopping her rush until she stood nearly nose-to-nose with him. He smelt her foul breath and saw burn scars etched in pale lines along her throat. Within the depths of her helmet Malus could see the deformed cheekbone that had broken beneath Nagaira's blow.

Suddenly he understood. No blade could kill the bearer of the Amulet of Vaurog.

He knew what he had to do. Gritting his teeth, he let go of the burning blade.

At once, Tz'arkan's power tore through his body, filling him with strength and wracking his body with pain. Roaring in agony, he clapped his hands against the side of Lhunara's helmet and squeezed. Face to face, he heard her scream as the steel deformed and bent inwards. She tried to pull away, but there was no room to land a blow, and the daemon's strength was irresistible. He felt Tz'arkan's power growing and wondered how long he had before the daemon regained control of him once more.

Lhunara moaned. Her body spasmed, and bone cracked. Black ichor sprayed across his face.

She drew a wracking breath. 'I... loved you,' she hissed. The words came out like a curse.

'I know,' Malus said, and crushed the helmet flat.

Lhunara's headless body collapsed to the ground. Lightning flickered on the red-gold surface of the Amulet of Vaurog as it rolled free of her body.

Stooping quickly, Malus snatched up the warpsword. For a moment he feared that the daemon would resist him; his fingers trembled, but with an effort of will he seized the hilt and felt the sword's fire hold the raging daemon at bay. Then he grasped the amulet and placed the torc around his neck.

Malus turned his face to the sky, seeking the Witch King. Seraphon was swooping low over the battlements of the inner wall, plucking beastmen from the parapet and flinging them to their deaths. More were racing down siege ladders, seeking to escape the death trap within the inner compound. Already, fleeing figures were running headlong through the darkness to either side of the square. The siege had been broken at last.

Malus wanted to roar his triumph to the heavens, but then he caught sight of a lone figure limping onto the square. The warpsword twitched in his fingers, but then he recognised who it was. Cursing under his breath, he loped across the corpse-choked space just as Hauclir collapsed onto the stones.

His short sword and trusty cudgel were gone, and his mail was soaked in blood. Lhunara had stabbed Hauclir through the chest not once, but twice. His skin was pale, and his breath was coming in shallow gasps. He blinked dully as Malus stood above him. 'I... I think we failed, my lord,' he said.

'No,' Malus replied bitterly. 'You did well, you damned rogue.'

'We held her as long as we could,' Hauclir said. 'Damn, but she was fast. She got Cutter first, then Ten-thumbs. Then she got me. I don't know what happened to Pockets. When I came to, she and that bitch were gone.'

'I'm sure she got away,' Malus said, not believing a word. 'Just rest easy. The troops will be here any minute, and we'll get you to the healers.'

Hauclir looked up at Malus. 'That's about the worst lie you've ever told,' he said. 'You're going to leave me. I can see it in your eyes.'

Malus bit back his anger. 'I have to go, Hauclir,' he said softly. 'I'm out of time.'

Suddenly Hauclir's face turned solemn. 'I know,' he said. 'So am I.' Then he turned his face away, and closed his eyes.

Malus looked down at his former retainer for a long moment, then slowly turned away. Bitterness burned like a coal in his gut. There was nothing he could do. The dire warning of the daemon still rang in his mind. *He'll have to ride that mount of his to death to make it to the temple in time.* It might already be too late to reclaim his soul, he realised.

And now I'm throwing away the last of my honour as well, he thought.

A dozen paces away he ground to a halt. Slowly he returned the warpsword to its scabbard. As its heat ebbed, he felt the daemon's strength slowly return.

'Damn me to hell,' Malus muttered, then turned and ran back to Hauclir. Gritting his teeth, he knelt by his former retainer's side and unbuckled his sword belt. Quickly he set the sword aside, and the power of the daemon surged.

Malus looked down at his ichor-stained palms and pressed them to Hauclir's wounds. 'Get up, damn you,' the highborn growled. 'Did you hear me, you damned rogue? Get up! You've vexed me for most of a year, and I'll be damned if you're going to die on me now!' Dread filled the highborn, but he focused his will and summoned Tz'arkan's power, trying to force it into Hauclir's wounds.

Hauclir gave a convulsive heave and began to cough. Malus recoiled from the druchii's body, seeing the wounds scabbing over with a dull, black crust.

Malus managed a nervous smile. 'There's your reward. You can thank me later,' he said, and lunged for the safety of the warpsword.

He fell just six inches short. In mid-leap the daemon gripped him in an invisible fist, halting his flight. He landed hard, his fingers outstretched, but salvation was just out of reach.

Agony coursed through him as Tz'arkan swelled into his brain. The pain went on and on, cutting into the depths of his heart and mind.

'Pray your precious honour gives you succour on the long ride to come,' the daemon hissed triumphantly. And the world dissolved in a haze of madness and pain.

CHAPTER TWENTY-FIVE

THE END OF TIME

The Chaos Wastes, first week of winter

The dust of ancient warlords slipped from Malus Darkblade's hands, laying out the last segments of the arcane circle that surrounded the daemon's massive crystal prison. Nearly an hour had passed since he'd begun; his skull throbbed with the daemon's blasphemous knowledge and his limbs ached with strain. He'd measured his steps with exacting care, shaping the sorcerous symbols as precisely as he could. Now the great urn was empty, and the complicated ward nearly complete.

As the powdered bone ran through his fingers he felt the final moments of his life slipping away along with it. It slid from his grasp on a tide of inevitability, driven by the daemon's implacable will. As the sorcerous circle took shape around him, Malus glimpsed the vast skein of intrigues and bloody deeds wrought by the daemon down through the millennia, all leading up to these final moments. Empires had come and gone, sorcerers and kings risen to glory and trampled into the dirt and thousands, perhaps *millions* of lives destroyed, all so that he would find himself in this chamber, at this hour, pouring the bones of conquerors upon the stone floor.

He saw what the future held. Tz'arkan had shown him hints of the world to come in the fires of Hag Graef, in the blood-soaked streets of Har Ganeth and the horrific siege of the Black Tower. An age of darkness and ruin was at hand. The daemon would walk among the druchii in the guise of the Scourge and reshape them into a weapon that would drown the world in blood.

Malus looked down at the last threads of fine powder trickling from his hand. We are all nothing but dust in the eyes of the gods, he thought, surprised to feel no sense of rage at the realisation. All the heat had gone out of him. His heart was cold and heavy as stone.

Time had run out. All of his schemes had, in the end, come to naught. Tz'arkan had millennia to lay his webs, testing their strands and pulling them taut. Now there was nothing left for him but to take the last few steps left to him.

It was time for Tz'arkan to rise from his ancient prison, and time for Malus Darkblade to die.

The last of the dust trickled through his fingers, landing in precisely the right spot to close the vast and intricate circle. The highborn felt a tremor in the air, as though the final piece of a terrible, cosmic puzzle had finally slipped into place.

'That's it,' the daemon hissed. It pressed against Malus's bones like a beast pushing at the bars of its cell. 'Now the tablet. Read the incantation inscribed upon it. Hurry!'

Stepping carefully, Malus stepped outside the circle and took his place at the foot of the mighty ward. The temple servants rose as one and moved to the five relics waiting nearby. Their ancient bodies creaking and crackling under the strain, the revenants picked up the artefacts and arranged them around the circle, then knelt beside them. The last artefact laid in place was the warpsword itself. The ancient servant placed the long blade nearly at Malus's feet.

The next thing he knew, the servant with the stone tablet was kneeling beside him, hands raised in supplication. As though in a dream, Malus reached out and plucked the tablet from the revenant's hands. He turned to the nearby pedestal and rested the tablet upon its surface. Writing older than Naggaroth, perhaps older than the very world itself, burned their angular lines into his brain. The blasphemous incantation meant nothing to the highborn, but their strange consonants came easily to his lips, thanks to the daemon's brutal tutelage.

The words burned his lips and scarred his throat, but the more he spoke, the faster they burst free. Crackling energies filled the vast treasure vault. A hot wind swirled about the gleaming crystal, pulling at Malus's hair and plucking at the servants' ancient clothes. Agony tore through Malus's chest, but the highborn had no breath to spare for tortured screams. Instead, he spoke the words before him, unravelling the ancient bindings laid upon Tz'arkan thousands of years past.

The wind grew, howling like a tormented ghost in the echoing space. He could feel the nest of snakes uncoil themselves from around his heart and begin forcing their way up his throat. Smoke seeped from Malus's mouth and nose, drawn into the cyclone like oil poured upon the surface of a turbulent sea. It spread like a black stain in the air, hovering before the crystal as the incantation reached its inevitable climax.

As the last lines of the ritual were spoken, the wind grew to a thunderous cyclone. The foul wind buffeted the undead servants, ripping at their rotten clothes and flaying their desiccated skin as it forced them to their knees. The inky smoke writhed and pulsed, lit from within by arcs of pellucid flame as it contracted into an amorphous mass before the highborn's eyes.

Then the last word burst from Malus's throat with a spray of black ichor, and it felt as though his body was being torn apart. The stone tablet shattered into razor-sharp fragments as the daemon broke its bonds at last.

With a rushing sound like an indrawn breath, the cloud of Abyssal smoke contracted further, assuming a terrible, towering form that loomed over Malus's hunched body. The daemon's body was shaped like a druchii's, only broader and far more muscular; it was beautiful, so far beyond the apex of perfection that it was maddening to look upon. Only its broad, malformed head and burning eyes betrayed its birth in the storms of Chaos. Taloned hands reached skyward, and Tz'arkan opened long, misshapen jaws and roared like a newborn god.

'FREE!' The daemon thundered. Not from the stone, but from Malus himself. The realisation did not surprise him. Indeed, a part of him had suspected it all along.

The icy touch of the daemon's power disappeared from the highborn's body in an instant, leaving behind nothing but terrible pain. Malus doubled over in agony, knocking the slim pedestal onto its side.

He knew what had to happen next, and a strange calm settled over him. 'I've done what you asked,' the highborn croaked. 'Now you must fulfil your bargain, daemon. Give me back my soul.'

Tz'arkan, Drinker of Worlds, looked down upon the highborn's pitiful form and showed triple rows of needle-like fangs. 'You shall have all you deserve,' the daemon said with a hateful laugh. 'But first, I must *feed*!'

Too fast for the eye to follow the daemon lunged forward, pressing its massive palm against Malus's breastplate. Deep inside his chest, Malus felt something give way, like a thread breaking, and he felt his heart stop at last. Pain ebbed like a swift tide, leaving only a cold emptiness in its wake.

The daemon drew back, pulling a stream of dark substance through the surface of the highborn's ensorcelled armour. Malus watched Tz'arkan pull his soul from his body and draw it to its gaping mouth. Dying, he sank slowly towards the floor.

Dying, but not yet entirely dead. The ancient sorceries of the temple wards slowed the passage of time in the great chamber. In this one place, a druchii's last breath could take a thousand years to escape.

Lost in its triumph, Tz'arkan began to feed upon the highborn's withered soul. The Drinker of Worlds failed to see Malus's hand reaching for the dark hilt of the warpsword just a few feet away.

His fingers touched the hilt of the burning blade, and felt its warmth kindle the embers of hate in Malus's dead heart. His stained lips pulled back in a bestial snarl.

With hate, all things are possible, he thought, in death as in life. The Warpsword of Khaine seemed to leap into his hands of its own accord, and he swung it in a hissing arc at Tz'arkan's towering frame.

The warpsword tore across the daemon's midsection, igniting its sorcerous shape. A howl of pain and fury tore through the treasure vault, buffeting Malus like a storm wind. It was answered by thin shrieks and wails of terror as Tz'arkan's undead servants cowered before their master's rage.

It was a gamble, perhaps the greatest wager he'd ever made. His calculations pitted the will of Khaine against the hunger of the daemon. The black blade and the sigil in the treasure vault had given him the idea; would the warpsword surrender his soul to Tz'arkan so easily? He believed it wouldn't, not if there was even the slightest hope that he could triumph against the daemon before him.

And if he was wrong, so be it, he thought, drawing back the smoking blade for another blow. He wasn't going into the Outer Darkness without putting up a fight.

The highborn's body felt light and swift as he lunged for the daemon, riding a wave of battle-hunger bequeathed by Khaine's fearsome blade. But before he could strike Malus saw the daemon's blazing eyes fix upon him, and Tz'arkan's thunderous voice spoke words of power that seared the air between them. The daemon's taloned fist clenched around Malus's night-dark soul, trapping it in a cage of crooked lightnings – then it thrust its other hand, palm out, right at the highborn's chest.

Malus felt the air between him and the daemon crackle with invisible power, and he hurled himself to the side a split-second before the bolt of power erupted from Tz'arkan's hand. The black bolt parted the air with a sound like tearing cloth and left a congealed mist of blood and bile in its wake. It licked like a dragon's tongue little more than a hair's width past the highborn's arm, and his skin recoiled from its passage, even within the confines of his enchanted armour. The bolt lashed through the wailing crowd of servants, dissolving their rotted forms with its merest touch. Gold coins melted and ran like tallow. Diamonds and rubies darkened and shattered at the energy's entropic touch. The ravening black fire burned across the length of the treasure vault and scored the thick wall with a crackle of splintering stone.

Tz'arkan still burned as well, the edges of the wound across its midsection curling and blackening like parchment as flickering yellow flames guttered and spat within its unnatural, perfect flesh. The daemon cackled insanely, its voice trembling in pitch between amusement and murderous rage as it pivoted to face Malus once more. Black vapour curled from its outstretched hand. It reached for him as though offering a benediction.

The ebon fire leapt out at Malus again. On instinct, he threw himself flat, his armoured form crashing to the polished stone floor, and once again he barely escaped the spell's all-consuming touch. It withered the pedestal where the stone tablet had rested, then scored a deep furrow along the floor as it tracked through still more of the hapless servants. Their thin screams bubbled and hissed as their bodies collapsed into steaming ash.

But the daemon wasn't finished yet. Tz'arkan continued to turn, lashing the arc of sorcerous fire at Malus like a whip. Pillars exploded at its passing touch, showering the vault with pulverised dust and whizzing fragments. Clay urns burst with sharp bangs as their contents boiled in the blink of an eye. Stands of ensorcelled armour crumpled like foil. Then the ravening fire played back across the floor, blackening the gleaming curves of the huge containment wards and then arcing against the squat, iron tripod that held the daemon's crystal prison. The dark metal sagged like hot wax, and the huge, faceted stone tipped and fell ponderously forward. Tz'arkan's entropic lash struck the gleaming crystal, and for a heart-stopping moment the facets sent tendrils of destructive power in all directions, slashing through the huge room like a storm of irresistible knives. A moment later the crystal blackened from within, a canker growing in its core with frightening speed that swelled until it reached the edges of the stone and burst it apart with an earth-shaking explosion. Malus was hurled forward by the blast, his armoured body pummelled by shards of crystal the size of a druchii's fist.

I can't keep this up, he realised. I can't get close to Tz'arkan now, and any moment my luck is going to run out. For half a moment he contemplated bargaining with the daemon – Tz'arkan needed his body to dwell in so it could return to Naggaroth, didn't it? But even as he considered it, he knew that the time for intrigues were long past. He had to think of something else, and fast.

Ears ringing, Malus cast about for somewhere to take cover from the daemon's ebon fire – and then his eyes caught a glint of brass just a few yards away, resting at the edge of the summoning circle. Of course, he thought! Gathering his legs beneath him he scrambled desperately towards the nearby relic, even as the air behind him crackled with building power.

The highborn's questing fingers closed about the brass octagon even as the daemon's sorcerous power leapt at him. Malus spun, raising the Octagon of Praan before him, and the bolt of ebon fire exploded against its surface. Jagged streaks of energy ricocheted from the amulet, deflected by its power and burying themselves like thunderbolts in the ceiling, walls and floor. Malus felt waves of heat radiate from the relic, and to his horror, he saw sizzling teardrops of molten brass running from the surface of the artefact. The daemon's full power was more fearsome than he'd imagined.

It was clear the amulet wouldn't survive another bolt. Malus tossed the damaged relic aside and sought out the next artefact along the rim of the great circle. The highborn's face turned grim. He was only going to get one more chance, and he had to make it count.

Malus lunged across the smoking floor, reaching for the relic. On the other side of the summoning circle, Tz'arkan's laughter faded. The flames licking at the tear in his chest guttered and went out.

'You insignificant little worm,' the daemon hissed. 'I've torn the life out of you, and still you wriggle. Everything you ever were, everything you ever dreamt of, I have taken all away. And yet still you refuse to accept your wretched fate! It is over, Malus Darkblade. You have been a troublesome servant indeed; at times I despaired that we would ever reach this glorious moment. But no matter how hard you fought against me, in the end you still did my bidding, whether you knew it or not.' The daemon uttered a poisonous chuckle. 'Once I have consumed your soul I will take your disgusting shape and return to Naggaroth, and the reign of the Scourge will begin,' the daemon said. Arcs of dark power crackled along its taloned fingers. 'And I could not have done it without you, Darkblade, weak as you were. And now you shall reap your reward.'

Malus closed his hand about the relic. 'Here's a token of my esteem as well,' he growled, rolling onto his back and hurling the Dagger of Torxus left-handed at the daemon.

The dagger was a dark blur, spinning end-for-end across the battered circle and burying itself in Tz'arkan's chest. There was a thunderous crackling of thwarted energies as the power the daemon was about to unleash was disrupted by the force of the relic itself. Fierce arcs of ebon fire lashed at the jutting hilt of the terrible dagger, carving gruesome wounds across the daemon's own unnatural flesh. The Dagger of Torxus began to blacken as well, its pommel and hilt vaporising under the sorcerous chain reaction. 'No!' Tz'arkan roared, clawing desperately at the dagger's hilt. Tz'arkan's body began to unravel under the onslaught, skin dissolving and flesh turning to liquid beneath. The daemon's howl of fury grew wilder by the moment. 'You cannot stop me, wretch! This world is mine, now! Hear the words of Tz'arkan and despair! The time of ruin is come! And in time you will–'

The rest was lost in a rising crescendo of concussive blasts, as the daemon's power and the energies of the Dagger of Torxus tore one another apart. With a final effort, Tz'arkan ripped the smoking weapon from its chest – and then daemon and dagger both vanished in a flare of white light and a clap of deafening thunder.

A groan brought Malus back to his senses. He had somehow risen to his knees, the burning blade still clutched in his right hand. Tendrils of smoke rose from his battered armour, and clouds of pulverised stone and metal hung heavy in the dimly lit vault.

Tz'arkan was gone. Destroyed or banished back to its goddess-forsaken realm, the highborn neither knew nor cared. Malus took a deep breath, heedless of the reek of burnt metal and scorched flesh that thickened the air. He felt light, almost weightless within his armour. He'd never realised how much of a burden the daemon's presence really was.

A soft chuckle escaped his torn lips. I won, he thought. *I won.*

His gaze fell to the gauntlet covering his right hand. Setting the warpsword across his thighs, Malus pulled the armoured glove away to reveal the ruby cabochon ring that had mocked him for so many months. With trembling fingers he gripped the ring and pulled. It slid easily from his finger, tumbling from his grasp and ringing faintly as it bounced along the floor. The highborn smiled in triumph. Another weary chuckle turned to a wild laugh of joy. 'I won!' he cried.

Something tugged at the side of his face. Absently, Malus reached up with his free hand to pluck it free. His cheek was cold to the touch.

Frowning, the highborn's fingers closed around a small, jagged shape buried in his skin. There was a dull twinge of pain as he tugged it free and held it out before him.

It was a piece of crystal the size of a gold piece, its edges sharper than any knife. He hadn't even felt it bite into his skin.

Worse, there was no blood on it. There wasn't even a dark stain of ichor. Malus's throat went dry.

He reached up once again and gingerly pressed against the side of his throat. Try as he might, he could feel no pulsing of blood in his veins. 'Oh, no,' he breathed. 'Oh, you damned, infernal bastard. You took it. You took my thrice-damned soul!'

The highborn's cry of rage was drowned out by another ominous groan. There was a crackle of breaking stone, then a thunderous crash as part of the treasure vault's ceiling collapsed. The heavy slabs of obsidian struck the already weakened floor and broke through, pouring a rain of ruined treasure and tons of debris into the level beneath.

Suddenly the air above Malus echoed with ominous groans and sharp cracks as well. 'Mother of Night,' Malus growled. The daemon might yet succeed in bringing the entire damned temple down around his ears.

The highborn eyed the open doorway. What would happen once he passed beyond the reach of the containment wards? Would death claim him at last?

There was sharp report just above Malus, and a chunk of obsidian the size of his torso crashed to the floor just a few feet to his left. That decided the highborn. If he stayed where he was he was as good as dead anyway. He gathered up his gauntlet and the warpsword and ran for his life.

He hadn't taken more than a dozen paces when the rest of the ceiling gave way in a long, grinding roar. Gusts of pulverised stone washed past him, swallowing the highborn for an instant in a smothering, black fog. Gritting his teeth, Malus ran on, aiming for the spot where he knew the doorway to lie. The floor shook beneath him as tons of rubble poured down from the temple ceiling.

Suddenly the floor seemed to fall away from him and he was stumbling headlong through empty space. He fell for a long, dizzying instant, then crashed face-first on a canted stone floor. Again the pain felt like a strange echo of true sensation; he knew he was hurt, but he wasn't certain how badly. Malus felt himself skid half a dozen feet before fetching up against a stretch of level floor. He tried to clear his head with a savage shake, belatedly realising that he'd stumbled down the long ramp leading into the living quarters on the level below the vault.

The air was still thick with dust and smoke. Malus staggered back to his feet, coughing as he struggled to breathe in the grey-brown murk. The floor continued to tremble beneath his feet, and the sounds of collapsing stone had mingled together into one long, muffled roar. Holding the warpsword out before him he ran on into the haze, navigating by memory as he sought the top of the curving stairs.

Stone fell all around him as he went; he smashed against piles of debris scattered across his path, but each time he picked himself up and drove on. The minutes stretched interminably, until he thought he'd got turned around in the murk and was hopelessly lost. Just as he began to lose heart, however, a gust of air smote his face, and he stumbled into a cleared space kept open by a furnace-like updraft of air. The spiral staircase lay before him, its curving wall lit by an ominous orange glow. 'Mother of Night,' he cursed, hesitating at the top step. Malus shook his head helplessly. 'No way out but down,' he said at last. 'If this doesn't warm my bones, nothing will.'

Taking a deep breath, he rushed down the twisting stair. The heat pressed against his flesh like a wall, but he only felt the dimmest echo of warmth. The air rippled and shimmered like a desert mirage as he descended ever lower towards the lake of fire.

He emerged upon a threshold of melting stone, at the mouth of a seething dragon's maw. Magma raged a hundred feet below; as Malus watched, chunks of rock from the cavern's ceiling plunged into the churning sea, raising plumes of molten stone dozens of feet high. The wings of the daemon at the edge of the plaza glowed white-orange along its bottom edges, dripping streams of melting rock into the lake below.

Malus sheathed the warpsword and pulled on his right-hand gauntlet, then hurried quickly down the stairs. As he stepped on the first of the floating boulders, however, the stairway shifted wildly beneath him. The multi-ton boulder wobbled – and began to sink, picking up speed.

'Blessed Mother of Night!' Malus cried, his dark eyes widening in alarm. He took a running start and leapt for the next boulder in line, and it began its death-plunge as well. Scarcely daring to stop, the highborn increased his pace, leaping from one plunging rock to the next and drawing ever closer to the lake of magma below. Behind him the massive boulders struck the lake and exploded into fragments, hurling enormous pillars of molten stone into the air.

The last section of stairs was little more than ten feet above the lake of fire. When his boots touched it the boulder plunged beneath him, striking the magma almost at once. Jets of steam burst from fissures in the stone, and the boulder burst apart beneath the highborn's feet. Screaming every oath he knew, Malus hurled himself forward and leapt the last few feet to the shimmering stones of the plaza. He landed hard on his knees and elbows, hearing the steel hiss against the burning stone.

The plaza began to tremble beneath Malus, and an ominous rumble started to build above his head. Clambering to his feet, he charged across the broad plaza, and through the chamber of the Chaos Gods that lay beyond. The faces of the Ruinous Powers leered at him from their pedestals as he passed through their midst. Had he the time he would have gladly dragged each and every one across the plaza and fed them head-first to the lake of fire.

The rumbling was increasing. Malus felt a wind growing in strength behind him as the temple's collapse accelerated. By the time he reached the temple antechamber he was howling like a madman, expecting the roof to fall in on him at any moment. The ghosts, still trapped in the chamber by the force of their ancient vows, regarded him in silent horror as he abandoned them to their fate.

Malus burst into the snowy night air with a desperate howl, just as the temple completely caved in behind him. The ground shook as though it had been struck by the hammer of a god, throwing the highborn forward onto the frozen ground. The sounds of splintering stone and settling earth went on behind him for many long minutes. When it finally stopped, the silence that stretched though the surrounding forest was deafening.

Slowly, carefully, Malus rose to his feet. He turned, and saw that the temple of Tz'arkan was no more. The huge edifice had fallen in upon itself, settling into the ravenous lake of fire. All that was left were tumbled piles of obsidian stone, wreathed by noxious vapours from the raging magma beneath. He looked upon the devastation and was surprised that he felt no relief at having escaped. Indeed, he felt nothing at all.

Small sounds of movement by the temple gate brought Malus around. Groups of beastmen were approaching, their twisted faces rapt with awe as they viewed the destruction of the great temple. Their leader, the one-eyed shaman, sank to his knees before Malus. 'What does this mean, great prince?' he croaked in his bestial tongue.

The highborn's gaze took in the swelling mob, then came to rest upon the awestruck shaman. His rage was gone. His body felt empty, his bones as cold as stone. Victory, he mused, was not supposed to feel like this.

'What does this mean?' he echoed in a dead voice. 'The end of the world, of course. For you, I mean.'

He drew Khaine's burning blade and showed it to the milling herd. Then he showed them what it could do.

Malus Darkblade squeezed the last drops of the blood from the beastman's heart into the side of Spite's fanged mouth, then tossed it onto the heap with the rest. Frowning thoughtfully, he pulled off his blood-soaked gauntlet and pressed his hand against the side of the cold one's snout. He couldn't tell if the nauglir's body heat was improving or not. 'Come on, damn you,' he whispered. 'There's enough meat here now to feed a squadron of cold ones. You just have to raise that scaly snout of yours and eat.'

The nauglir made no move to the pile of severed limbs Malus had stacked scant inches from its jaws. The war beast regarded him with one large, red eye. Shaking his head, the highborn rose to his feet. 'I've done all I can for you, you great lump of scales. If you're going to die on me now, get on with it. It's up to you. But if you're going to get me back for all the punishment I've inflicted on you in the last few weeks, you're going to need to get your strength back.'

Sighing to himself, the highborn turned away and strode to the roaring fire he'd built from molten stone and piles of severed logs. The ground surrounding the bonfire and for scores of yards in either directions had been transformed to churned, red-tinged mud. Bodies and pieces of bodies littered the earth as far as Malus could see. He'd managed to keep enough self-control to spare the last few dozen beastmen and put them to work butchering their companions and gathering logs for the fire. He'd intended to cut them down as soon as they were done, but while he busied himself feeding Spite they'd slipped away into the darkness. He doubted he would see them again.

For the next hour he busied himself by gathering the bones of his fallen retainers and feeding them one by one to the raging fire. He owed them that much, he believed, though he felt nothing as he delivered them to the flames.

I've become dead inside, he thought, watching the bones blacken in the flame. Dead within, dead without, he thought. A lord of ruin in truth.

Tz'arkan had spoken truly. The daemon had taken everything from him, just when it seemed his deepest desires lay within his grasp. I could return home, he thought. I'm still the Witch King's champion, and after the bitter victory at Ghrond he will have need of strong hands to help secure the kingdom. He could still have his reckoning with Isilvar. He could find Hauclir, if he still lived, and set about rebuilding once more.

And yet... and yet he felt nothing. No hunger. No sense of anticipation, even at the prospect of sweet revenge against his last surviving brother. No hatred for the last, treacherous blow the daemon had dealt him.

No hatred, he thought, shaking his head. This is no way for any druchii to live.

Malus stared into the flames for a long time, watching the molten stones char his retainers' bones to dust. As the night waned, more flakes of snow began to fall. By the time that dawn was paling the sky, he'd decided what must be done.

He turned back to Spite to find the nauglir on its feet, nosing hungrily through the piles of beastman flesh laid before it. The sight brought a grim smile to the highborn's face. While the war beast ate, the highborn checked Spite's feet and tail for signs of sickness or strain. Spite watched its master at work and growled ominously between bites. Malus met the nauglir's red gaze with a feigned scowl. 'I was starting to think you'd given up,' he said. 'Good to know I named you Spite with good reason.'

He let the nauglir rest until well past noon while he formulated his plan and gathered up pieces of meat for the journey ahead. He'd heard that the seer of the Black Ark of Naggor possessed a potent relic that would show the location of whatever the owner wished to find, no matter where – or in what realm – it lay. He would need such a tool if he was going to find where Tz'arkan had gone.

He was going to get his soul back. Malus had no idea how such a thing could be done, but he would do it, or die in the attempt. Wherever the daemon had fled to, even if it lay within the very storms of Chaos itself, Malus was going to find him and reclaim what was his. Naggaroth and Hag Graef could wait. What was the point of revenge, after all, if he had no means of savouring it?

By mid-afternoon, Spite was ready to travel. Malus checked his frayed bags and his fresh rations, and then swung heavily into the saddle. He led the nauglir to the square gate, past scores of snow-covered corpses, and reined in at the site of the long road dwindling into the distance.

'You're out there somewhere, daemon,' Malus whispered into the icy wind. 'And if you can hear me, you'd best prepare yourself. The Lord of Ruin is coming for you.'

Malus Darkblade rested a gloved palm against the side of Spite's scaly neck. 'On, beast of the deep earth,' he said. 'To the Black Ark, to the daemon realms, to the Abyss itself if that is where the trail leads. Our journey is over. Now the hunt begins.'

DEATHBLADE

C L Werner

Part One
NAGGAROTH

Winter 2523–2524

CHAPTER ONE

The enemy of your enemy is your friend.

The words reverberated through the drachau's brain like rolling thunder. Sharp. Persistent. Insinuating. They spoke to him with an intensity beyond that of simple speech. No sound could convey the depths of meaning and suggestion entwined within them.

The drachau stiffened in his throne of polished malachite and hydra-hide, feeling the dried scales of the seat creak beneath his weight. From the corner of his eye, he gazed longingly at the tiny whalebone table and the bottle of dark wine resting atop it. The promise of release was almost too great to resist. A few glasses and he could silence the slithering inside his skull.

Malus crushed down the urge, strangled it before the merest flicker of his desire could betray itself in his features. The wine would indeed ease the turmoil inside him, but the price for such peace was too high. More than the dark presence boiling inside him would be stifled by the brew. His own wits would be dulled, his own senses retarded by the liquor. He couldn't afford that, not now when he needed every last dreg of cunning his mind could conceive.

Look at it, Malus. Look at that simpering bag of vice and corruption. Listen to it scheme and plot. Is this petty intrigue the best you can aspire to? You who have walked in the realms of the gods themselves!

The drachau's eyes narrowed as he studied the elf who knelt before his throne. He watched the ripple that passed through the thin spider-silk cape draped across the druchii's shoulder each time the elf drew a breath. He scrutinised the subtle play of hue and texture in each scale of the elf's hauberk. He inspected the quality of the swords thrust through the elf's dragon-skin belt, the craftsmanship of the engraving on hilt and pommel. His nose drank in the smell of exotic spices and perfumes exuding from the elf's pale skin and long dark hair. His ears deciphered the practised tonalities and courtly inflections laced into each word.

Yes, everything was there. The druchii crouched before him looked, smelled and sounded the part. If there was deception here, it had been very carefully prepared. Not so long ago, Malus would have still entertained his doubts. A clever enemy would take such pains and invest such care into a plot against him. Now, however, he doubted there was anyone within Naggaroth who had the patience for such delicacy of deception. There simply wasn't the time for such games any more.

Naggaroth was a land besieged, tearing itself apart in the wake of an unprecedented invasion from the north. A tide of human barbarians, beastmen and daemons had exploded from the Wastes and smashed their way through the ring of watchtowers that guarded the borders of the druchii. There had been no warning, the sorcery of Ghrond and Morathi had failed to alert Naggaroth to its peril. The hosts of Chaos had descended, slaughtering all they confronted, despoiling and destroying everything in their path.

The time for games was over. All the craft and subtlety, the scheming and politicking, all of it was over. A new age was come upon the elves of Naggaroth, an age of crisis and cataclysm, an age that demanded actions, not words.

It was a call to action that had been brought to Malus. As drachau of Hag Graef, he was the most powerful of all the dreadlords, his armies second only to those of Naggarond itself. No, Malus corrected himself, the armies that bent their knee to his banner were mightier now than those who served the black flag of Naggarond. To the soldiery of Hag Graef had been added the warriors of vanquished Naggor and the refugees from Clar Karond, to say nothing of entire tribes of shades who had abandoned the wilds to seek sanctuary within the spires of the drachau's city. As Malus expanded his forces, those of the Witch King had lessened, bled away by constant conflict against the barbarians and monsters seeking to conquer his kingdom. How many thousands had been killed to break the horde of the daemon-thing Valkia? How many more had been lost on that long march to Ghrond to seek a reckoning with the treacherous Morathi?

Your star rises, Malus, but beware. The star that burns brightest is the first to be extinguished.

Malus gripped the arms of his throne, feeling the cold of the malachite beneath his fingers. He nodded to the messenger, the highborn emissary who had brought him the most tantalising proposition. In every line of the messenger's face he could read the smug arrogance of breeding and privilege, the surety of one who has had his every whim obeyed without question. By using such a messenger, the one who had sent him was displaying before Malus the magnitude and severity of what he was being offered.

'You may tell her ladyship that I will meet with her and her confederates,' Malus decided.

The messenger raised his eyes, just that little spark of condescension betraying itself at the corners of his gaze. 'The tzatina was certain her offer would appeal to your lordship.' He bowed his head again. 'Is there any message you wish me to convey to her?'

'I will send my own message to Khyra,' Malus said. In a single, impossibly swift motion, the drachau sprang from his throne and lunged at the messenger. The highborn was quick, fast enough to raise one hand in a warding motion while he reached with the other for a dagger cunningly sewn into the lining of his cape. Malus drove the black edge of his sword down through the messenger's hand, the enchanted metal ripping through the elf's mail as though it were butter. Fingers danced across the floor as Malus brought the Warpsword of Khaine shearing through the messenger's arm and into the druchii's breast. As blood bubbled over the dying highborn's lips, the dagger he'd been trying to free from his cape clattered against the ground.

Malus stared down at the bloodied carrion. Breeding and position counted for nothing now. The time for such frivolities was over. All that mattered was ability and ruthlessness, the vision to see and the power to take.

'Silar!' Malus called out as he wiped the edge of his sword clean with his victim's cape. From the shadows of the audience chamber a tall, powerfully built elf marched into the fitful witchlight cast by the overhanging lamps. Like the recently slain messenger, he wore an elaborate cuirass of steel scales and there was upon his face the similar qualities of breeding and nobility. There, however, the resemblance ended. Silar Thornblood was of Hag Graef and none of the sons of the Hag sneered at Malus Darkblade; even in their innermost thoughts they held their drachau in a place of fear. They were too familiar with the dreadlord's deeds and the fates of his enemies to harbour any delusions about defying him. The nobles of the Hag might hate Malus, but they would never underestimate him.

'You wish that to be removed?' Silar asked, pointing to the butchered messenger.

'Place him somewhere that the tzatina's agents will be sure to find him,' Malus said.

Silar bowed his head, not quite daring to match his lord's gaze as he spoke. 'The tzatina will know it was you who killed him.' It was true. No weapon in Naggaroth left a wound such as the warpsword dealt.

'She will,' Malus agreed. 'That is as it should be.' With a wave of his hand, he dismissed Silar, leaving the warrior to his grisly task. Soon, Silar was trudging off, the messenger's body wrapped in the silk cape and slung across his shoulder like a sack of meal.

They offer you the scraps of power. I offer you a feast. Why be content with a mortal's appetite when you can aspire to so much more?

Malus turned and made his way to the table and the bottle resting upon it. He could feel the wine calling out to him, sense the shudder of longing that coursed through his flesh. Freedom lay within that bottle, if only he was weak enough to take it.

You are weak, are you not, Darkblade?

The mockery crawled through his skull, stilling Malus's hand even as he reached for the bottle. His hand closed into a fist. With an animalistic snarl, he brought his hand smashing across the table. The bottle shattered against the floor, splashing the precious wine everywhere. Malus stared down at the spilled liquid. In his head, the voice suggested he might still drop to all fours and lap it up like a thirsty dog.

'Was that wise?' a disapproving voice called out to Malus.

Malus looked away from the wine. Advancing towards him across the audience chamber with a stately, unhurried step, was an elegant figure bedecked in flowing black robes, her carriage framed in a lacy meshwork of tiny pearls and crushed sapphires, her dark tresses bound in a coiffure of gold and jade. Her skin had an alabaster paleness beyond even that of most druchii, telling of an existence spent without the attentions of even Naggaroth's sickly sun. Across the harsh beauty of her features was stamped the fiercest determination, the sparks of her terrible will blazing in her eyes. In aspect, the elf presented a vision of both desire and dread.

'Hello, mother,' Malus greeted the elf as he stepped away from the shattered bottle. 'Your health looks as inviolate as ever.'

Lady Eldire didn't allow her son's remark to bait her. It was only through her intrigue and her assistance that Malus had survived to become drachau of Hag Graef. It was only by her sorcery that he was able to conceal the terrible affliction that gripped him and which, if exposed, would see him torn limb from limb by his own slaves. Her hold over her son was great, but so too was his over her. Lady Eldire was that rarest of creatures, a sorceress who owed no loyalty to Morathi or her convent. She had been a Naggorite, taken from the Frozen Ark by Malus's father. Only the protection of Hag Graef had kept her from being returned to Naggor or surrendered to Morathi. In placing her son upon the throne of Hag Graef, she had helped to ensure the continued protection of Naggaroth's second city.

Of late, however, Lady Eldire had been compelled to demand further indulgence from her son. She had discovered her vitality beginning to ebb, the old spells to ensure her youthfulness beginning to slip. The solution had been restorative magic that hearkened back to the forbidden pleasure cults that had corrupted the cities of Ulthuan long ago. Baths drawn from the heart's blood of elf youths and maidens, the blood of innocence to wash away the stain of age and corruption. Only through the connivance of Malus had Eldire been assured of a steady supply of sacrifices to maintain her vigour.

'I wish I could say the same for the steadfastness of your mind,' Eldire reproved him. She smiled at the flicker of disquiet that appeared on his face. 'You needn't worry. There are no spies here. I would know if there were.' She ran her fingers across the curve of her cheek, feeling the silky newness of her revivified skin. 'As you observe, my vivacity is as keen as ever it was.'

Malus scowled. 'The Hag pays a high price for your sorcery, mother. I should feel cheated if your powers were not quite as profound as you claim them to be.' He shook his head and stalked back to his throne. 'Just the same, I don't want my... affliction... mentioned in Naggarond. Not even between ourselves.'

Eldire stepped around the shattered glass and spilled wine. 'I didn't know you were so afraid of the Witch King. Certainly not after your entanglements with Lady Khyra. A usurper who fears his sovereign has lost before he begins.'

'Anyone who doesn't fear Malekith is either mad or a fool,' Malus returned. 'No, to have any chance at all, I cannot deny my fear of him.'

The sorceress circled the malachite throne, her boots clicking against the tiled floor. 'Then you will expose the tzatina's plot? Forget the chance that providence has given you?' She leaned close to the throne, her hand closing on Malus's arm. 'They are offering you his crown, the Circlet of Iron itself. You would be lord of all the druchii, master of Naggaroth!'

Malus glanced past his mother, staring regretfully at the spoiled wine. 'I will expose no one. Not yet, at least. I will hear Khyra's offer, learn how much support I can expect. The killing of her messenger was a warning to the tzatina and the other dreadlords. They must know it is I, not they, who hold the reins of power. They think to make a present to me of something only my strength and the might of the Hag can secure. When they find their highborn messenger lying in the gutter like so much garbage, they will understand that. When the Black Guard fails to arrest Khyra, they will know I haven't exposed them, that I will listen to what they would pledge to their new king.'

Eldire brought her hand up to Malus's head, running her fingers through his dark locks. 'The land is in turmoil. There is talk of treachery everywhere. The noble houses snap at one another's throats even as the daemons come crawling across their walls. It will take a strong arm to bind them once more to the service of their kingdom. It will take ruthlessness beyond that of the Witch King, savagery unmatched even by daemons, to break their pride and bind them in the shackles of terror.'

Taking hold of his mother's hand, Malus pressed it to his lips. 'I have been schooled in the cruelties of Hag Graef, I have endured the horrors of the Wastes themselves. The blood of my own father is on my hands. There is no brutality I would not indulge for the sake of power. You know that.' The drachau's grip suddenly grew tight and with a sharp pull, he brought Eldire to her knees beside him, her face level with his own. 'From the first, I think you foresaw this moment with your magic. Every torture and torment I survived, you saw before it happened. All that I have suffered was known to you, wasn't it?'

'And if it was?' Eldire demanded. 'If your entire life stood revealed to me while you were still growing inside me, how should that change this moment? Will you curse me for what you have endured or thank me for preparing the way?'

Malus shook his head. 'Neither,' he said. 'The past is done. It is the future I seek. You have brought me to this moment. Tell me what waits beyond.'

The sorceress turned her face, unable to hold the suspicious glare in Malus's gaze. 'I have seen this far, but no further. There are rules to magic, boundaries that cannot be defied. This land draws but faintly upon the lighter vibrations within the aethyr and only so much can be achieved with the lower harmonies. Your doom is obscured, but this much I can tell you – the fate of Naggaroth is bound to your own.'

Malus released his mother, sinking back against the rest of his throne. 'Mine is the doom of Naggaroth,' he mused. He kept his eyes on his mother as Eldire withdrew from the chamber. He was cautious about trusting her too far with her portents and prophecies. After all, she had benefited the most by placing him on the throne of Hag Graef. Conquest of Naggor had eliminated most of Eldire's enemies. Malus had to wonder what foes she hoped to involve in this 'doom' she now foretold.

It will be a terrible doom. An end to all things, Malus. You will lose all you possess. Nothing will be left.

The drachau pressed his fist against his forehead, trying to blot out the foul whisperings inside his skull. He'd thought himself so strong to deny the succour of the bottle, but now he wondered if he'd been clever. Hadn't he simply responded to that goading mockery? Done exactly what it wanted him to do.

A different path can be yours. A path of unending glory and horror.

'Shut up, daemon!' Malus growled at the voice creeping through his mind.

The caustic laughter of Tz'arkan was the only response to Malus's fury. The daemon could wait. What was time, after all, to something truly immortal?

'I expected more of you,' Malus said as he marched out from a concealed doorway and into the dank crypt.

The crypt was buried beneath the tower that had once been the stronghold of Oereith Kincutter. Oereith and his house had been abolished years ago, exposed as devotees of the profane god Slaanesh. The Witch King had flayed every member of the house, from Oereith himself to the lowest slave, and impaled the wet, raw bodies upon the walls of Naggarond. It had taken weeks for some of the cultists to finally die, the slobbering moans from their tongueless mouths serving as a morbid warning to all druchii that some obscenities were too much even for Naggaroth. Since the abolishment of Oereith's title, no new dreadlord had been bold enough to claim the shunned tower for his own. There were too many whispers that some of the things Oereith had called from *beyond* continued to linger in the deserted passageways and chambers. With survivors streaming into the city, with the Black Council and their entourages flocking to answer Malekith's call, the cursed tower was perhaps the only place in the city that offered the isolation the tzatina's gathering required.

Resplendent in a silver-lined gown of black, a wispy filigree adorned with bloodstones entwined with the cascade of her raven tresses, Lady Khyra looked incongruous with the macabre surroundings of the soot-blackened crypt, the smashed bones of Oereith's ancestors strewn about the floor. She looked as though she were attending a royal banquet, not orchestrating a secret plot to overthrow the Witch King. Always possessed of a flawless grace and poise, there was nevertheless something about Khyra that made the blood turn cold in Malus's veins. Looking past the beauty of her face, the enticing appeal of her body, there was a malignance ghastly even by the jaded standards of the druchii. Gazing on Khyra, for Malus, was like watching some great spider spinning its web, always wondering if the trap was being spun for him.

Malus had been fortunate to escape Khyra's web when it had been fashioned for him once before. Then he had been foolish enough to underestimate the tzatina, to think that sharing her bed gave him some immunity in her intrigues. It was a mistake he'd been fortunate to survive. Only by a shrewd piece of treachery had he been able to shield himself and leave the Witch King's wrath to fall upon Khyra.

Khyra had been fortunate, too. Malus felt his eyes drawn to the slender curve of the tzatina's right arm. It was covered in a sleeve of black adorned with sparkling diamonds and the shimmer of crushed pearl. There wasn't a real arm beneath that sleeve; it covered a surrogate carved from ivory. Khyra's real arm was adorning a spike on the battlements of the Black Tower, the price of Malekith's merciful indulgence. Being one of the Witch King's consorts, Khyra had rated such beneficent consideration.

Khyra swept past the dozen nobles and highborns who were with her in the crypt. Even the least of her companions had an air about them that betokened outrageous wealth and power. They'd made some effort to conceal their rank by adopting simple cloaks and girding themselves in the plain armour of household knights, but they couldn't efface the stamp of their breeding from their bearing. Subtle variances in costume suggested to Malus the slave markets of Karond Kar and the mines of Storag Kor, even the now-desolate shipyards of Clar Karond. He even saw a bit of scrimshaw bone adorning the dagger of one elf that was certainly in the decadent style of Har Ganeth. Khyra had cast her web far to draw in such disparate conspirators.

'I expected you to come alone,' the tzatina said, her eyes sliding past Malus to glare disapprovingly at his companions.

'You forget, Lady Khyra, I know you,' Malus reminded her. 'I will be able to concentrate on our negotiations better if I know I have someone here to watch my back.' He made a point of using his right hand as he indicated his two companions. 'Lord Silar Thornblood of my household guard. Captain Vincirix Quickdeath, commander of the Knights of the Ebon Claw.'

Malus fought down a smile when he saw the slight flush that came into Khyra's face as he introduced Vincirix. It was probable that the tzatina knew she was his current companion. Was it possible Khyra was jealous? No, not true jealousy, just the bitterness of a spoiled child who sees someone playing with one of her toys. Malus would have to remind Khyra which of them enjoyed the dominant role in this conspiracy.

'You killed my messenger because you worried if he could be trusted,' Khyra said. 'Why should we believe your *lackeys* can keep a secret any better?'

'Because they know that to betray me is to betray themselves,' Malus said. 'They each have powerful enemies. It is my strength that keeps them at bay.' Malus marched towards Khyra, pausing before he reached her to run his mailed fist across a section of fire-blackened wall. When last he'd set foot in these crypts, those fires had been raging at full force, devouring the foul creatures Oereith had bound to his service. From the corner of his eye, he watched Khyra, studying her for any trace of unease. He could find none. After what she had endured in these crypts, the hideous fate Oereith had planned for her, she must have ice water in her veins to come back.

Perhaps that was exactly why she'd chosen this place. If anyone suspected her, they'd never think to look for her here.

'The drachau places great faith in his strength, in the might of the Hag. Maybe too much.' The speaker was one of the supposed knights. Hearing his words, Malus recognised the voice as belonging to one of the elder sons of Dreadlord Ghalir of Shroktak.

Malus turned a withering look on the noble. 'The might of Hag Graef is why I'm here, and you all know it. If you didn't need my armies, you would never have invited me into your confidences. Without the strength of Hag Graef, you have nothing.'

Angry hisses and grumbles rose from the conspirators, idle threats and empty curses that Malus brushed aside like buzzing insects. Before coming here, even before he had cut down Khyra's messenger, he'd carefully considered every angle. This conspiracy had been hatched without any intention of including him. Likely, it had started as an opportunistic play to take the crown when Malekith failed to return from Ghrond. The Witch King had spoiled those plans, however. He'd survived and come back, putting Khyra and her allies in the worst possible position: a revolt all ready to unfold but without the military might to keep what it seized.

'You are sure of yourself, drachau,' Khyra said.

'Only necessity would make you welcome me back into your *arm*,' Malus answered. The look of total hate Khyra darted at him was so black that Silar took a step towards the tzatina. Malus waved him back. He'd read the situation right. Khyra did need him and would put up with anything until that was no longer the case.

'The Witch King is weak,' one of the nobles declared. 'The tyrant's grip falters. He failed to destroy the daemon-consort Valkia. He lacked the courage to relieve Clar Karond. He couldn't even bring himself to execute Morathi for her treason. He can dominate us no longer.'

Malus paced across the crypt, digesting the noble's treasonous words. There was truth in them, even divorced from the greed and hate that made them so enticing. Never in Malus's lifetime had Malekith been pressed so closely by his enemies. Driving off Valkia's horde had taxed his strength, while confronting his mother in Ghrond had tested his will. He was weakening, even as the might of Naggarond was weakening. Jackals like Khyra's allies could smell it, slinking ever closer to seize whatever they could take.

'But if the Hag were to support Malekith. If my armies were to flock to his banner, who would dare oppose him?' Malus enjoyed the looks of horror that crept onto the faces of Khyra's allies.

'You would not side with the Black Tower?' one of the highborn gasped.

Malus stopped pacing, let his fingers scrape across the scorched lid of a sarcophagus. 'Not unless it was in my best interest.' He turned towards Khyra. 'You invited me here to make a proposal. What am I promised should my armies support your cause?'

Khyra's eyes were as cold as a glacier when she answered the drachau. 'I think you have already decided what you want.'

'What I demand,' Malus corrected her. 'What I demand is the Circlet of Iron. What I demand is rule of Naggaroth. In exchange, I will support your own claims against your enemies and rivals.'

'Agreed,' Khyra said. Her answer came much too hastily for Malus's liking. 'We will acknowledge you as our king. But if you would be king, you must remove the current one.'

'Malekith's armies cannot oppose my own,' Malus said.

'Your armies cannot fight Malekith and protect the land from the hordes now despoiling it,' Khyra told him. 'It will take all the strength of Naggaroth to drive them back this time. If we spend our blood fighting among ourselves, everything will be lost.

'No, Malus Darkblade, it is not your armies alone that we need. We need you. We need the one swordsman in all Naggaroth who can do what must be done.

'You must kill Malekith, the Witch King.'

CHAPTER TWO

You know they are just using you. Once you have done what they need you to do, they will betray you as quickly as they betray their king.

'You have things backwards, daemon,' Malus growled at the presence inside his head. 'I am using them. They serve my purpose, even if their pride refuses to make them understand it. When their usefulness is at an end, even the tzatina will find that she is disposable.'

All flesh is disposable. Ponder this, when the dark reaches out for you.

Malus fought down the impulse to argue with Tz'arkan. The daemon took a perverse delight in goading him into empty arguments. The extra distraction of its poisonous advice was something he couldn't afford right now. The odds were stacked too heavily against him already.

Lady Khyra's plan had worked flawlessly thus far. Her knowledge of the Black Tower and the routine of the Black Guard who defended it had proven invaluable. Malus had been able to eliminate the sentry patrolling the desolate stretch of wall abreast of the suspended bridge that connected the tzatina's own tower to the outer ring surrounding Malekith's fortress. Silar, bedecked in the armour of the Black Guard, had assumed the sentry's place, adopting the gold sash that denoted the present rotation of warriors. The sentries wouldn't be relieved until the first light of dawn. Silar would have to make good his escape before then. Once his vassal withdrew, the empty post would be quickly discovered and real Black Guard would converge on the tzatina's bridge. Malus was certain Khyra already had some subterfuge prepared to absolve herself from any blame, but that wouldn't help him. If dawn found him still inside the Black Tower there would be no way out.

He'd be abandoned to the wrath of the Witch King.

That thought was enough to give even Malus pause. The drachau of Hag Graef, stealing through the Black Tower like a prowling shade. It wouldn't need a mind as crafty and twisted as that of the Witch King to figure out his purpose. In the long centuries of Malekith's rule there had been many assassins who had tried to depose the tyrant. Their fates had been obscene enough to horrify even the druchii.

Now, Malus was courting just such a doom. His mother's prophecy did little to cheer him. If there was one being in all the world who had the strength of will to force even fate to obey him, that being was Malekith.

Cold perspiration beaded Malus's forehead, his breath came in hot little gasps. He could feel the blood quickening in his veins. How much of it was the cocktail of herbs and elixirs he had imbibed to enhance his reflexes and heighten his senses? How much of it was his own fear, the fear that he tried to deny even to himself? He'd braved the quest for Tz'arkan's five treasures and the long quest to reclaim his soul from the devious daemon. He'd journeyed alone through the wastelands of Chaos and stood within the insane realm of the Screaming God-Child. He had dared the cursed black ark of Naggor and escaped. He'd deposed the former drachau of Hag Graef and installed himself upon the throne. All these things he had faced and survived, yet it was the spectre of his sovereign that filled him with dread.

Here, in the forgotten lower halls of the Black Tower, Malus was surrounded by the essence of the Witch King. Room after room of richly appointed chambers, their walls covered in masterworks that would have driven many a druchii noble to sell his own children into slavery simply to gaze upon them. Rugs of intricate pattern and artistry, their threads so fine that they rippled like water at the softest touch of his foot. Statues rendered from obsidian and amber, jade and crystal, their subjects rendered with such detail that they seemed to breathe as the eye passed across them. Carved tables of the rarest wood, their every curve possessing a grace and dignity that defied estimation. Jewelled goblets, platters encrusted with diamond and ruby, bowls of gold and silver and ithilmar, all of these were arranged upon the tables, awaiting the attention of some passing guest, oblivious to the faint discolouration left behind by the long-decayed viands they had once held.

Wealth beyond measure, enough to overwhelm the greed of the most avaricious druchii, yet here it stood abandoned and forgotten, caked in layers of dust that bespoke centuries of neglect. By their cast and craftsmanship, Malus knew much of the art he stalked past were relics from Nagarythe, the shattered homeland of the druchii. To any of the great houses of Naggaroth, such relics would be priceless heirlooms. To the Witch King, they were naught but idle baubles.

Nothing could impress upon Malus the absolute power of Malekith so demonstrably as this forsaken opulence. It was before the years of any living druchii that the Witch King had last employed these halls. Any living druchii save the immortal Malekith and his witch mother.

Malus ran his fingers across a goblet mired in a patina of dust and decay. Time had worn away the cup to a hollowed-out shell of corruption. It crumbled beneath his touch, collapsing to the floor in a clump of corrosion. Jewels long cheated of their lustre stared forlornly at him from the pile of decay.

The drachau felt cold fingers rush along his spine. These chambers were a lost and haunted place. Each step through the silent halls reinforced the eerie impression. It did not need the daemon's words to feed the urge to turn back, to flee to the grim horrors of Naggarond's streets, to be quit of the uncanny malignance of the Black Tower.

Hunger stayed Malus from retreat, the insatiable hunger for power that had ever driven him onwards. He stood before the ultimate power now, the promise of the Circlet of Iron and the throne of Naggaroth.

The spectre of that promise lay etched across the floor – a line of footprints pressed into the scum of dust caked upon the tiles and rugs. Malus wasn't so versed in the skills of tracking and hunting as the shades who lurked in the wilds or the beast-breakers of ravaged Clar Karond. Even he, however, could read the signs in the dust. The tracks were made by a single elf, his boots long and broad at heel and toe. The steps overlapped several times, denoting repeated circuits of this trail. All of it feeding back to what Khyra had told him about the strange turn the Witch King's habits had taken.

Since his return from Ghrond, Malekith had become prone to leaving the confines of his royal apartments at the top of the Black Tower. Many nights he spent wandering among the residue of ancient glories, pondering the relics of Nagarythe. No retinue of Black Guard protected him in these solitary forays, no complement of sorceress-consorts to follow behind him and watch over him with their magic. Whatever strange mood had gripped Malekith's mind, it was a boon for his enemies.

If that enemy was but bold enough to exploit the opportunity.

A bitter smile pulled at Malus's face. For all her intrigues and the conspiracy of powerful nobles she had gathered to her, Khyra lacked that boldness. All of them did. Only Malus had the determination to strike and slay!

Through the neglect and decay of a thousand years, Malus crept, pursuing the trail written in the dust. Every nerve in his body felt as though it were afire, and his heart beat a rapid tattoo inside his breast. His senses clawed at the stagnant air, straining it for the slightest sound, the merest odour – anything that would betray to the hunter the nearness of his quarry. His hand tightened around the warpsword's hilt. He could feel the eager pulse of the hungry blade racing up his arm, the sword's essence impatient to claim a royal soul. Soon, Malus promised, soon he would glut the warpsword's appetite.

Past a gallery of statuary that might have graced a Nagarythe garden into a broad arcade lined with wooden screens upon which some past master had painted exotic landscapes and ancient legends. Malus licked his lips, tried to moisten a mouth that felt as dry as an autarii's wit. His eyes roved along the trail he followed, watching with calculated paranoia for evidence of a trap.

The world froze around the drachau as he stepped from one gallery into another. His gaze didn't linger upon the dust-obscured portraits that filled the hall. He didn't stare at the jewelled frames and gilded settings. His attention was riveted entirely upon the lone figure who stood amid the desolation.

Tall, armoured from head to toe, an aura of imperious disdain exuded from that apparition of rune-etched metal. It was impossible to mistake the plates of black meteoric iron, the tall helm that supported the horned Circlet of Iron itself, the sheathed evil of the Destroyer hanging from the figure's hip. Malekith, the Witch King of Naggaroth.

The monarch had his back to Malus, turned to face the portraits lining the wall. Malus didn't dare breathe, felt a flush of fear at the sound of his own heartbeat. To strike now, to cut down the immortal tyrant, could he really do it? Who was he, after all, to kill an elf who had survived the Flame of Asuryan?

Now, when it is too late, do you question your pride?

The daemon's mockery poured the required measure of rage into Malus's veins. His fear was smothered beneath a surge of malice. Pride had indeed led him this far, and it would carry him still farther.

Tightening his grip on the Warpsword of Khaine, Malus leapt out from the darkness. Some slight sound, perhaps the shift of his harness as he lunged, betrayed his presence to the armoured tyrant. Malekith started to turn, fiery eyes blazing from the black depths of his helm.

Then the warpsword was chopping downwards, catching the king's shoulder, ripping through the ancient mail. The enchanted edge of Malus's blade tore through the Witch King's body, shearing through flesh and bone, cleaving ribs and breastbone before exploding from his chest.

Malus panted, gasping for breath, his entire body shivering from the magnitude of what he had done. He had killed Malekith! He had killed the Witch King! By his own hand he had made himself master of all Naggaroth!

For only a heartbeat, the grand images swam through Malus's mind. It took that long for him to accept the wrongness of what was happening before his eyes. Cut nearly in half by the warpsword, Malekith was reaching for the blade sheathed at his side. Segments of torn plate flopped obscenely about the wound, yet still the ghastly figure persisted. Malus noted that there was no blood pumping from that wound, nor was there blood upon the warpsword's hungry steel.

As the tyrant began to draw the Destroyer, Malus struck at him again. Pride had fuelled his first assault on Malekith, but the king's horrible vitality had brought all of the drachau's fear racing along his spine. Panic drove Malus back to the attack, the panic that only a condemned soul can feel. Having struck the Witch King, he knew there were only two choices now: succeed or die.

Malus struck just as the Destroyer cleared its scabbard. The warpsword came slashing down, a blur of ravenous steel that bit into the Witch King's hand, cleaving through the rune-etched gauntlet and shattering the hilt of the tyrant's weapon. The Destroyer's blade went spinning across the hall, clattering along the dusty tiles. The severed hand flopped to the floor, rolling towards Malus.

Again, Malus was stunned by the lack of blood, the absence of pain exhibited by his foe. Instead of reeling back in agony or clutching at his maimed arm, the Witch King surged forwards, reaching for his attacker with the talon-like claws of his remaining hand. Malus took a single step backwards, then, uttering a snarl of defiance, he brought the warpsword whipping back around. It licked across Malekith's shoulder, striking sparks from the armour, and tore across the tyrant's neck.

The helm and its horned crown were sent leaping into the air as Malus chopped through the Witch King's neck. He gawked in disbelief as the helm went spinning away in the darkness. The headless body remained upright, still reaching for him with its hand. Malus felt cold terror clench his heart as the beheaded tyrant lumbered towards him.

The iron talons of the outstretched hand nearly closed around Malus's throat. It was more reflex than conscious thought that made the elf dart aside at the last instant, to spin around and drive the warpsword into his attacker. This time he caught the thing in the waist. Fear infused his arms with a desperate strength and the biting edge of his weapon tore its way through the iron plate as though it were butter. When Malus ended his destructive spin, his adversary crashed to the floor in two disparate sections.

Shocked, Malus watched as the armoured legs flopped impotently against the floor. The torso, with its single hand, struggled to flip itself onto its belly. Despite the continued havoc he'd wrought against the body, still there was not a trace of blood – not even a whiff of sanguine scent in the musty air. Malus could see why, now. As the bisected body flailed on the ground, he could see inside it. He could see that the thing was empty, nothing more than a suit of armour invested with the simulacrum of vitality by some profane sorcery.

It would seem you're not going to add regicide to your accomplishments.

Malus was about to growl a response to the daemon when the sound of strident clapping brought him spinning around. His hands tightened about the warpsword as he saw shapes manifest from the darkness, illuminated by the crystal lanterns several of them bore. Like the supposed Witch King, these elves were armoured from head to toe, and in a style that was impossible to mistake. They were the Black Guard, Malekith's personal army. Leading them, his hands coming together in jeering applause, was Kouran Darkhand, the Witch King's loyal dog.

'The drachau of Hag Graef,' Kouran said, his voice laced with vicious amusement. 'How low have the mighty fallen to come slinking into their lord's tower bent upon murder. Surely you might have hired another to do it for you?'

Malus glared back at Kouran across the still-writhing bits of armour on the floor. He'd been lured into a trap, that he understood the moment he saw the armour was empty, but to have it sprung by a common-born cur like Kouran was too great an insult to bear. As he glared at Kouran, Malus's mind was already racing. The rest of the Black Guard had come armed, but Kouran had neglected to bring either sword or halberd. That was a mistake Malus was going to ensure the dog regretted for the few moments left to him.

'When you want something done right, you do it yourself,' Malus snarled at Kouran. In a blur of motion, he charged the other elf, leaping over the twitching armour to reach his foe. The warpsword came swinging downwards, gleaming in the luminance of the crystal lamps.

Malus heard the wailing shriek as the warpsword bit into its victim, wrenching the soul from the victim as it ripped through his armour. The problem was, his blow had struck the wrong victim. As he lunged for Kouran, the elf seized the arm of the Black Guard closest to him and pulled the warrior into the path of Malus's blade. Even as Malus was trying to pull free from the warrior he'd struck, Kouran was in motion, smashing the helmeted head of the dead warrior into the drachau's face.

Blood streaming from his broken nose, Malus staggered back. The weight of the dead Black Guard dragged down the warpsword and as he kicked at the body to free his weapon, Kouran came rushing at him. The captain's fist slammed into Malus's face, knocking him back in a spray of blood and curses. The momentum caused the warpsword to tear free from its victim, and as Malus stumbled back, he was able to bring his blade whipping up.

The edge of the warpsword raked across Kouran's belly, scraping along the black armour in a shriek of grinding metal. The blade failed to do more than scratch the ancient plates, but its effect was pronounced nonetheless. Malus cried out as he was struck by a piercing agony, as though a candle had been set against every nerve in his body.

'This is the Armour of Grief,' Kouran laughed, slapping his hand against the breastplate. 'The enchantment Lord Arnaethron invested into it is quite zealous about punishing those who dare strike its wearer.'

Stunned by the magical backlash of Kouran's armour, Malus's blade slipped from his weakened grasp. He staggered back, fighting to recover command of his tortured body. Kouran's cruel face split in a sadistic leer.

'Take him,' the captain ordered his warriors, waving them forwards. 'I want to bring him alive before the king.'

Kouran's smile became impossibly colder as the Black Guard swarmed around Malus and beat him down with the butts of their halberds. 'His highness could do with an amusing diversion. It might be weeks before he tires of torturing this traitor.'

Malus felt a sharp pain against his skull as one of the bludgeoning warriors brought his weapon cracking against his head. He was unconscious when his head slammed against the dusty floor.

Are you awake, Malus? I should think you'd like to see this. There might not be a chance later.

Tz'arkan's jeers echoed through Malus's throbbing head. His body felt like one big bruise. He could feel cold iron against his arms and legs, and knew he was shackled upright to some sort of frame. The chill crawling over his flesh told him his armour had been stripped away. He guessed it would prove inconvenient for his torturers. They'd prefer a clean canvas at the start of their performance.

Slowly, Malus opened his eyes, squinting through narrowed eyelids at his surroundings. He wasn't surprised that he was in a dungeon of some sort. Richly appointed with ghoulish tapestries depicting imaginative cruelties hanging on the walls, it was a room designed to enhance the terror of its occupants. Malus hoped the tapestries were decorative and not a reference guide for his tormentors. He could see them, seven pale-skinned elves wearing long smocks of serpent-hide, their arms branded with tally-marks to commemorate their many victims. Several of the torturers were so scarred that they looked like they were wearing sleeves of boiled leather.

All of the torturers were fiddling about with an assemblage of ghastly tools, arraying them along a marble table, an altar to terrible Ellinill. Tongs and probes, cruel pincers and knives, bone-scrapers and flesh-hooks, each implement the druchii removed from their ebony reliquaries was more grisly than the last. Malus tried not to imagine what sort of havoc would be inflicted upon him for his attempt at regicide. The thought of biting his own tongue and cheating his captors flashed through his mind, but the taste of a metal bit in his mouth told him the same idea had already occurred to the torturers.

Groaning in frustration, Malus tilted his head enough that he could see the black throne standing between the tapestries. In the fitful light cast by the flaming braziers scattered about the torture theatre, the throne's malachite surface glistened with an oily sheen. He had a sense of foreboding as he looked over at the throne. He knew who it was who would soon occupy that seat, and when he did, then the pain would begin.

'His highness has a great many duties, drachau.'

The words came from just behind Malus, a scratchy whisper that made his gorge rise. He tilted his head back, drawing his arms up on the chains that bound them, feeling the manacles binding his feet bite against his skin as he stretched. His reward was a view of the speaker. A spindly, almost skeletal elf adorned in robes of black and gold. Malus recognised his old adversary, one who had nearly brought him to ruin once before. It was plain that Ezresor hadn't forgotten Malus's earlier escape. It was equally plain that Malekith's spymaster was eager to make up for that lost opportunity. He reached over his captive's shoulder and rudely pulled the bit from Malus's mouth.

Malus spat the taste of metal from his mouth. 'I won't tell you anything,' he said.

Ezresor stepped around the iron framework that held Malus. He stared up at the prisoner, his gaunt face probing into the druchii's bloodied features. 'You'll tell me anything I want to hear,' he said. He pointed to the torturers. 'They will make it happen. An hour or a day, it won't make a difference. They will extract every secret buried in that brain of yours. They'll pull it out of you and pin it to a board. If you try to lie to them, they'll know and they'll make it hurt worse. Keep that in mind, Darkblade. Whatever agony they inflict on you, know they always hold a little back. When you think it can't get any worse, know that it can.'

'If I told you what you want to know, it wouldn't change anything,' Malus said.

Ezresor tapped a finger against his chin. 'No,' he admitted, 'it wouldn't. But won't you feel better knowing the ones who convinced you to betray our king will share your fate?'

Malus managed a derisive laugh. 'No, carrion-face, I won't. I'll feel better knowing they might try again and that if they succeed their first order of business will be feeding your carcass to the harpies.'

The ghoulish spymaster's hand flew towards Malus. A dagger was in Ezresor's fist, projected there by some mechanism hidden in the sleeve of his robe. He brought it against Malus's cheek.

'You'll spoil the king's show,' Malus warned Ezresor.

Ezresor scowled as he pulled back the dagger. With the sleeve of his robe he wiped away the single bead of blood he had drawn. 'I can wait, Darkblade. I've waited this long, I can wait a little longer.' A smile slithered onto his emaciated face. He cocked his head to one side, assuming an attitude of attentive listening. He turned his grin on Malus. 'I think the wait is over,' he said.

Malus followed Ezresor's gaze as the spymaster turned towards a particularly horrendous tapestry. The hanging, with its depiction of mutilation and brutality, fluttered outwards as a sudden breeze struck it. Some concealed panel had slid open, ushering in a blast of air even more frigid than that of the dungeon. No, Malus corrected himself, the intense cold was nothing felt by the body. It was a chill that scratched at the soul, even a soul shared by a daemon.

The tapestry was pushed aside and into the torture theatre there marched the same figure Malus had so recently cut to ribbons. This time it was no sorcerous puppet of iron, but the puppeteer himself. Malus could feel the awful power exuding from the Witch King like an aura of cruelty. The eyes that burned within the face of the helm were like twin embers of hate, insatiable and implacable.

'Your highness,' Ezresor greeted the tyrant as he fell to his knees. The torturers mirrored his gesture of submission and fealty. Instinctively, Malus felt his own head start to bow. It was an effort to resist the automatic obedience Malekith had compelled from every druchii since the Sundering, but resist he did. As he raised his eyes, he found himself staring into Malekith's merciless gaze. There seemed a note of sardonic humour in the tyrant's stare.

'The fleshtakers await your pleasure, highness,' Ezresor announced as he started to escort Malekith towards the marble table and the cruel implements arrayed there so that his king might inspect them. Instead, Malekith turned away and approached the frame to which Malus was shackled.

'Did you really think you could kill me?' the Witch King asked, his voice like the rumble of an angry mountain. Malus shuddered as the tyrant came towards him, reaching out with a rune-etched gauntlet to close his cold fingers about the prisoner's jaw. 'Was your daring so great? Was your arrogance so mighty? Who are you, Darkblade, to think you can kill me? You are druchii, the spawn of this miserable land! You are my creation, moulded and forged like my armour and my blade! I raised you from nothing to command my armies, to lead my warriors in battle.' With a snarl, Malekith released the captive's jaw, shoving him back on his chains.

Malus glared back at the tyrant, pride crushing down his instinctive terror of the Witch King. 'You did nothing,' he growled. 'Everything I have achieved I won for myself. I clawed my way from being the vaulkhar's bastard son to drachau of Hag Graef. I did that, not you! I crushed the black ark of Naggor's legions and vanquished their Witch Lords! It was I who...'

Ezresor came charging at Malus, the glowing length of a poker held before him. The spymaster shouted in outrage at the temerity of the traitor in daring to defy Malekith. As he ran past the tyrant, the poker was plucked from his hand and sent flying across the chamber. A backhanded swat of Malekith's gauntlet knocked Ezresor to the floor, blood trickling from his split lip.

'If my armour fails me, if my blade breaks, I discard it and forge a new one,' the Witch King declared, still glaring at the shackled elf. 'But you aren't broken, are you Malus? You still burn with enough pride to defy me even here.' Malus could feel the tyrant's tone grow colder still. 'I should take great delight in making an example of you, but there is not the time, so I must grant you a reprieve.' Malekith waved his hand at Ezresor and pointed to the iron framework.

'Highness?' the spymaster asked as he picked himself off the floor.

'Release him,' Malekith said. His eyes continued to glare into Malus's. 'Long ago, the pretender Bel Shanaar sent me into the wilds to be his ambassador among the dwarfs. Crude but clever things, the dwarf-folk. Do you know how they would check for foul vapours in their mines? They would bear with them a tiny bird and hang it from a cage where they could watch it. If the bird expired, they would know the air in the mine was becoming foul and hurry to the surface.' Malekith pressed his iron finger against Malus's chest. 'You are going to be my little bird, Darkblade. I know even you would not dare to strike against me without support from the other dreadlords. If there were time, I would rip each name from your flesh and savour every scream as I did so. But I cannot indulge in such pleasures now. Instead, I will pretend none of this ever happened. I will present the illusion that there was no attempt against my life, that you did not cut down my surrogate. I will restore you to your command of Hag Graef and none will be the wiser.'

Malus rubbed his cramped limbs as Ezresor unlocked his bindings. His mind whirled with the impossible things he was hearing, the unbelievable mercy and forgiveness Malekith was showing. Such qualities were the ultimate sign of weakness in any druchii. The society the Witch King had created was one that had long ago purged itself of such moral degeneracy.

'How do you know I won't betray you?' Malus asked.

The Witch King laughed, a sound that was far from pleasant. 'You mistake me. You are still my little bird. When I free you, when you go back among the dreadlords without any reprisal from me, what will they think? They will say that Malus has betrayed them. The cowardly ones will flee and I will have no need to worry about them. The bolder ones will stay. They'll plot against me, to be sure, but before they act they will strike against the bastard who betrayed them. You are my little bird, Malus! When the assassins come for you, that is when I will know to be on my guard.'

Malekith turned and stalked back towards the door hidden behind the tapestry. 'Ezresor will return your armour and sword to you. The Black Council meets tomorrow. I expect the drachau of Hag Graef to be in attendance.

'It would pain me to hear he has suffered an accident.'

CHAPTER THREE

There was no greater a concentration of malignance and evil in all the world than a gathering of the Black Council. From every corner of Naggaroth, the dreadlords came, hurrying to answer the Witch King's summons. Butchers who slaughtered for the simple pleasure of carnage, despots who crushed untold thousands beneath their heels, fiends who indulged in every depravity a mortal mind could conceive – all left their strongholds behind when Malekith called. Half the kingdom might be overrun by hordes of daemons and savages, the roads reduced to a nightmarish gauntlet of battle and horror, yet still the fear of their monarch was too great for anyone to defy his command.

The great throne room was situated high in the Black Tower, far above the streets and spires of Naggarond. The hall was of vast dimensions, its vaulted ceiling vanishing into shadowy heights so impenetrable that even the keen eyes of corsairs from the Underworld Sea couldn't pierce their darkness. Massive buttresses, every inch of their surfaces adorned with intricate carvings, loomed from the walls. Stone gods glowered down from the pillars: Ellinill, the Lord of Destruction, and his wrathful progeny. The eyes of each god were crafted from enormous gemstones, their lustre enhanced by an enchantment that caused them to glow with a smouldering malevolence. Between the buttresses, the walls were lost behind macabre tapestries fashioned from scalps encrusted with gore, a silent reminder of the many who had defied the Witch King's authority, and of the ultimate sanction for such defiance.

At the centre of the chamber stood the ancient throne of Aenarion, the first Phoenix King. Crafted from obsidian and iron, the massive seat was a stern reminder of Malekith's royal heritage. Of the Witch King's right to claim the Phoenix Crown.

Down the length of the hall, a blood-red carpet ran, streaming towards the great throne like a river of gore. Ornate chairs of lacquered wood flanked each side of the carpet. In each chair, some infamous leader of the dark elves reposed. Terrible names of might, equally feared and envied throughout Naggaroth. Behind each chair, standing in steely silence only a short distance away, was a warrior of the Black Guard. The halberds they bore were far from ceremonial affectations as would be normal at a meeting of the Black Council – as they had gruesomely demonstrated after Malus had himself announced by a pair of heralds. In response to the arrogant flaunting of decorum, two of the Black Guard had cut down the servants, leaving their remains strewn about the doorway.

The drachau scowled down the length of the hall to one of the chairs situated at the foot of the throne. Kouran matched Malus's glare. It had been on his order that the Hag Graef heralds had been killed, a not-so-subtle reminder to Malus of who was in command here.

Malus cast his gaze across his fellow dreadlords. He could almost smell the uncertainty and fear oozing from their pores. Ebnir Soulflayer, the general of the Witch King's armies, had died in battle – choosing death over Malekith's wrath, so the story went – and his successor tried his best to exude an air of scornful confidence and pride, but Malus could see through the warrior's pretence. The failure of Naggarond's army to utterly destroy the mongrel daemon Valkia was a responsibility that many whispered could be laid upon his shoulders rather than those of the king. He had passed blame to half a dozen lesser commanders, sealing each one alive within one of the obsidian mausoleums lining the approach to the Black Tower, but it was always possible Malekith would need one more life for his army to atone for the sin of failing him.

Hellebron's body was a shrivelled husk. The bloodthirsty Hag Queen of Har Ganeth was in her decrepit phase, but Malus had seen for himself the grisly vitality that remained in her withered bones. Entering the hall, she had paused beside the carcasses of his slain heralds to paw about in the gory wreckage. Fresh blood yet stained her fingers, and Hellebron would lick at them from time to time with her blackened tongue. Malus wasn't certain if it was magic, madness or narcotic delusions that so unhinged the Hag Queen, but whatever the cause, she was the most dangerously unpredictable of the dreadlords.

Shifting in his chair, Malus reconsidered that opinion. Hellebron might have a rival for the title of 'most dangerously insane'. Sitting across the aisle from her was Tullaris Dreadbringer, the feared executioner who had assumed the title 'Chosen of Khaine', an epithet that Malus himself had once affected when exploiting the religious mania of his half-brother Urial. With Tullaris, however, it was no mere affectation. The executioner truly believed himself marked by the Lord of Murder, to such an extent that he claimed to hear Khaine's voice inside his head. He was even bold enough to quietly decry Malekith's claims of being an avatar of the Bloody-handed God.

Lady Khyra, her false arm festooned with ornaments of pearl and silver in an audacious display of the favour Malekith had shown her – the Witch King had settled for just an arm when he might have had her executed – was several chairs to the left of Ebnir's replacement, but the way she leaned ever so slightly away from the general's direction made Malus suspicious. Was he one of her confederates, one she hadn't seen fit to let the drachau know about? The few nobles seated between the two were of such minor significance as to make their usefulness to Khyra too paltry to provoke any uneasiness. Malus was almost disappointed in the tzatina. Surely she hadn't taken it in mind to pit a fool like the general against him? A single troop of doomfire warlocks would be enough to rout any force brought against the host of Hag Graef. Malus caught Khyra's eye as he looked across at her, feeling a touch of bitter amusement at the mix of suspicion and alarm that flickered in those lustrous depths. It was natural she should worry, about how Malus was still alive and what he had told Malekith.

Ezresor, the sinister spymaster of Naggarond, was sitting further down the line from Khyra. The cadaverous elf sneered when he caught Malus looking at him. There was such a stamp of superiority in that caustic smile that the drachau at once found himself questioning his own security. Had Malekith reconsidered the usefulness of his 'little bird' and decided to make an example of him during the meeting of the Black Council? Or had Ezresor concocted some scheme of his own? Or was he simply trying to get under the drachau's skin? Malus smiled back at the spymaster and ran a finger along his cheek, mirroring the fresh scar Ezresor had suffered in the recent fighting against the barbarians. The ugly light that crept into Ezresor's eyes told Malus that the insult had struck home.

There were other lords, great and small. Venil Chillblade, Lokhir Fellheart and Drane Blackblood. Representing the Shade clans was the savage figure of Saidekh Winterclaw, his fur-trimmed armour festooned with the tongues and ears of foes slain in the recent fighting.

Seated opposite Kouran Darkhand at the foot of the throne was a newcomer to the Black Council. Never before had Ghrond been represented by anyone other than the Witch King's mother, Morathi, herself. Now, that ancient tradition had been broken. Drusala, one of the queen's handmaidens, sat in place of the exiled sorceress.

Malus had encountered Drusala only a few times over the years, typically trying to avoid any intrigues that involved Ghrond for the sake of his own sorceress-mother. Lady Eldire was the most potent enchantress in all Naggaroth who hadn't fallen under the sway of Morathi and her convent. That made her a valuable weapon in the arsenal of Hag Graef and a threat to Morathi's dominance of magic.

Malus remembered Drusala as strikingly beautiful. He found, however, that his recollection of her was far from reality. Her face was like that of a goddess rendered in flawless alabaster, milky and pale, unmarked by the stresses of time and turmoil. Her hair was a river of midnight, lustrous dark streams that swept across her shoulders and down past her waist. Charms and talismans of gold and silver and precious ithilmar were looped within her locks, tiny jewels sparkling from their polished settings. A gown of vibrant crimson hugged her shapely figure, clinging to her with all the affection of a second skin, slit at the sides to afford the greatest exposure to her slender legs. A jewelled girdle straddled her waist, tiny filigree spites clawing at one another with equal degrees of amour and violence. In her hands she held a silver chain, from which hung a pendant of Hekarti. A wispy necklace that might have been the crystallised ghost of a spider's web encircled her neck and fell across the swell of her breasts, a silver brooch in the shape of a spider holding the ethereal jewellery against the silk of her gown. Across her forehead sat a circlet of diamonds, each gemstone shaped and carved by magical rites until it looked as though it had been spun from the first frost of winter. Like icicles, two diamonds dangled from the bottom of the circlet, drawing the enraptured gaze of an observer down to the sorceress's eyes. Malus couldn't name a colour to describe Drusala's eyes. They had the same shifting, phantom quality as the aethyric aurora a bold fool might behold deep within the Wastes.

What intrigues was Morathi's handmaiden engaged in? Was she here on behalf of the king's mother, trying to pacify Malekith's ire, or was she here on some purpose of her own, without the knowledge of her patroness? And what of the Witch King? Was he privy to her schemes, a partner in them? Or was he simply keeping Drusala close as a way of monitoring a potential threat? What, Malus wondered, was her status on the Black Council? Was she Morathi's surrogate, her replacement or her scapegoat?

While he watched the sorceress from the corner of his eye, Malus saw Drusala's bosom exhibit the most momentary of shudders. A flicker of disquiet, something that senses less keen than those of an elf who had hunted a daemon lord alone across the Wastes would certainly have missed.

Malus felt resentment grow within him. He knew the cause of Drusala's disquiet. Brazenly, he looked about the hall and called out to his fellow dreadlords. 'So now we must await the pleasure of our august majesty?' He could sense the Witch King's presence, he knew Malekith was nearby. He also knew that whatever would happen had already been decided. There was nothing more to risk by making a bold show. 'I wonder how long it will be before he graces us with his presence.'

The Witch King's essence seemed to pour into the hall. The throne was suddenly filled with his cruelty, his fiery eyes burning from the depths of his iron armour. 'Not long, my good friend Malus.' The iron-encased monarch rose to his full, imposing height. He took a step down from the throne, the touch of his boot causing the carpet to smoulder. 'Not long at all,' the despot said, sweeping his gaze along the seated dreadlords.

The Witch King had kept the Black Council waiting most of the day. It was a common tactic he employed to remind his dreadlords of their status, to impress upon them who was master and who was vassal. In calmer times the king's tardiness was a necessary annoyance that the nobles knew they must suffer, but now, with cities being razed by barbarians and daemonic beasts, Malekith's eccentricity was almost unendurable. With each heartbeat, the dreadlords had wondered how far the invaders had progressed, how much of their own holdings and how many of their slaves had fallen to the enemy. To placate the tyrannical humour of their king under such circumstances was intolerable.

Malus quelled his petulant thoughts as he felt the Witch King's gaze upon him once more. He fought the urge to cower before that malignant glare. He was still somewhat in disbelief that Malekith had extended to him such left-handed leniency. He was certain that there was more to it than his king's talk of drawing out Lady Khyra and the other conspirators. Maybe if the kingdom weren't suffering such a crisis as now faced it, he would have accepted Malekith's words. But the last few weeks had shown just how nebulous the tyrant's reign had become.

Many of the dreadlords had been able to get away with acts of independence and defiance that would have been met with the most violent of reprisals only months before. The swelling of Hag Graef's armies to a point where they rivalled – if not outright exceeded – that of Naggarond was, to Malus, proof that the Witch King couldn't afford to check the autonomy of his subjects. Naggaroth had to fight the enemy without; the king didn't have the resource to also fight the enemy within.

Let him claim he had extended mercy to Malus; the truth was that the Witch King needed him, needed him to hold the great host of Hag Graef together. He couldn't afford the time that would be lost as the Dark Crag's nobles fought for Malus's title and power.

The Witch King turned away from Malus and again looked across the assembly. 'Lord Vyrath Sor shall not be joining us,' said Malekith, his voice echoing across the chamber, as cold as the iron that encased his charred body. 'He was slow to answer my summons and only arrived this morning. I reminded him of his obligations to the Circlet of Iron. The harpies should carry what's left of him back to his tower by sunset. It would pain me if the garrison of Nagrar were to think their master had fallen victim to some lesser fate.'

To emphasise his story, Malekith tossed an object out onto the carpet. The gold chain clattered as it came to rest. Though caked in blood and shreds of flesh, there was no mistaking the sigil that had represented Vyrath Sor etched onto the chain's clasp.

'Do not mourn Vyrath Sor,' the king advised with mock sympathy. 'He decreed his own doom when he placed the defence of his miserable outpost before his duty to his master. The same doom any one of you might have earned by defying me.'

'Shagrath is lost, then?' The question was uttered by Venil Chillblade, one of the admirals of the eastern corsair fleets. With much of his power and many of his holdings concentrated in Karond Kar, it was easy to understand why anxiety had overcome prudence and gained mastery of the elf's tongue. The watchtower of Shagrath was to the north of Slaver's Gate; if the fortress had fallen, Karond Kar itself would be in jeopardy. To see it suffer the fate of its rival Clar Karond was a terror that threatened Venil's every dream and ambition.

The Witch King made a deprecating wave of his hand. 'An inconsequence,' he declared. 'The garrison will fight to the last because they have no choice. They will die as druchii should, shedding their blood on behalf of their king. When the tower falls, the advance of the barbarians will falter. They will be some time plundering their conquest and slaughtering such captives as they take. It will take their warlords still more time to gather their animals back into a fighting horde.'

'But they will continue their advance, your highness?' The hesitant voice of Thar Draigoth, the great flesh-merchant, sounded more like a rodent's squeak than the words of Naggaroth's most infamous slaver. Like Venil, he had extensive holdings in Karond Kar. After seeing his interests in Clar Karond massacred by the triumphant invaders, he was doubly worried about protecting the rest of his property.

'Let them come,' Ebnir Soulflayer declared. 'With the consent of his highness, I will lead the host of Naggarond against these animals and scatter them to the winds. You may send your hunters to collect whatever strays my army leaves alive,' he told Draigoth in a tone of haughty contempt.

'Your eagerness for battle is commendable, Soulflayer,' the king said, 'but I will waste no more blood fighting these savages and daemons.'

If lightning had struck the council chamber, it wouldn't have upset the Black Council as thoroughly as Malekith's hissed words. Many of the nobles sprang to their feet, all colour draining from their faces at the madness of what they had heard. The king wasn't going to fight? He wasn't going to loose the hosts of Naggaroth, the strength of the druchii, against these marauders? Was he simply going to sit back and watch his kingdom burn?

Malus could feel the incredulity of his fellow dreadlords blackening into outright hostility. The Witch King ruled by fear, it was true, but the greater part of that fear wasn't that he could take a life, however slowly and inventively, but that he could take away everything a noble had schemed so long to possess. To lose one's life was inevitable, but to lose wealth and power before that life was through – this was a fate no druchii would accept.

With his own words, Malekith had fertilised the fields of discontent. Battle with Valkia and the treachery of his own mother must have upset the balance of his mind. It was the only explanation for why the king would incite such unrest at a time when his own reign was at its most vulnerable.

Malekith glared at his horrified vassals. 'The blood of the druchii belongs to me,' he snarled. 'I and I alone have made you what you are. Mine is the will that has stripped all weakness from your hearts. Mine is the vision that has poured strength into your bodies. All you think, all you dream, all that you are is as I have made it. The druchii are mine, formed from my hate, moulded by my spite. From the pathetic tatters of a vanquished realm I have built a great and terrible people.' The Witch King set his hand against the arm of his throne. 'To what purpose, then, have I done all this? To sulk in these black halls like a child of Drakira, supping from the poison of bitterness?'

Malekith let the question linger in the air. He waited several heartbeats, biding his time before springing whatever surprise he had in store for the Black Council. Malus was certain it could be no more shocking than the decision to keep his armies from the field of battle. In this, Malus soon found himself to be wrong.

'The *Rhana Dandra* is coming,' the Witch King proclaimed, his voice booming through the hall. 'These are the End Times. In your heart, each of you knows this to be true. Each of you has felt it in your soul.' For just an instant, Malekith stared directly at Malus. The drachau winced under that scrutiny, wondering if his king knew something more about his soul than he would like.

'Daemons and northlanders howl at the gates of our cities. They infest the land as never before. But it is not Naggaroth alone that is besieged.' Malekith paused again, letting anticipation build among his dreadlords. 'Ulthuan too is beset. Usurpers and faint-hearts strive to defend our ancient home against a foe they cannot defeat. If our people – all of our people – are to survive, they must have strong leaders. Leaders forged on the anvil of Naggaroth.'

A babble of voices rose as the dreadlords offered their full support to their king's latest campaign against Ulthuan. The nobles of Clar Karond and Karond Kar offered their warriors once the invaders were repulsed and their cities restored. The captains of the watchtowers likewise promised to dispatch elements from their garrisons once the present crisis was under control.

A grisly chuckle rose from the depths of the Witch King's armour. 'You misunderstand my intent. The End Times are coming. Chaos rises to devour the world. The northlanders will pillage everything that has not yet been warped by the storm of magic descending upon us. They will squat in our fallen towers to be preyed upon in turn by the daemons loosed by the Dark Gods they think they serve.'

Malus watched the Witch King stalk away from his throne, footprints burning into the carpet as he strode past the assembled dreadlords. Malekith stopped when he stood upon the great sigil of Aenarion set into the floor in lines of gold and malachite. An auric glow began to rise from the sigil as it reacted to the heat of Malekith's tread. Bathed in its light, the despot closed his hand about the hilt of the Destroyer hanging from his belt.

'This blasted wilderness has never been our home. It was a refuge, nothing more. Petty ambitions have allowed this place to become an anchor to the destiny of the druchii. Would you spend the blood of your warriors to protect a land that you despise, a bleak desolation that has within it nothing but scorn and mockery? I tell you, I tell all of you, this will not be! We will not bleed our armies defending this abominable wilderness. If we are to fight, then we will fight a war that is worth fighting. We will fight to take the land that belongs to us. We will fight to claim the land that is our heritage and birthright. Naggaroth? Let it burn. Let it rot. Let it fall to daemons and beasts. It is Ulthuan we desire, it is Ulthuan that is the destiny of the druchii. Ulthuan and the crown of Aenarion. Ulthuan and the birthright of Malekith!'

Ezresor was the first to raise his voice, the spymaster's tone cautious. 'The defences of Ulthuan are considerable. Even with the asur embattled by daemons, we must consider lines of supply and retreat...'

Malus could almost feel sorry for the spymaster when Malekith rounded on him and fixed him with his fiery gaze. 'There will be no retreat,' he declared. 'Naggaroth will die along with all who remain behind.' He turned, letting his gaze linger on each of the dreadlords. 'Any who try to return will die too. Do not mistake necessity for hubris. We *must* retake Ulthuan or perish in the Rhana Dandra. Victory or death, these are the only choices left to the druchii.'

The dreadlords sat in shocked silence, their outrage and resentment cowed by the mad passion of their king. Malus could guess their thoughts, for he doubted they were much different to his own. He had struggled hard to become drachau of Hag Graef. His rise had been bought with blood, far too much of it his own. Now, at the pinnacle of power, when he was the second most powerful elf in Naggaroth, it was all being cast aside, thrown away because their king believed the End Times were upon them. He was reminded of a warning Lady Eldire had given him once about prophecy: those who thought to see the future often brought it into being. Malekith believed the Rhana Dandra was upon them and now he was doing his utmost to ensure just such an apocalypse. Doom to both Naggaroth and Ulthuan.

Ulthuan. Malekith knew his people well. In his heart of hearts, every druchii coveted the lands of his forefathers. Naggaroth was a harsh, unforgiving desolation, a land of exile, not a land of glory. Nothing could change that brutal fact, not even the Circlet of Iron.

Even if he wanted to, Malus knew it would be impossible to hold Hag Graef on his own. Looking about the other dreadlords, he knew they would have reached the same conclusion. Their lands were forfeit, by royal decree. They would follow the Witch King in one final assault against Ulthuan, spending the last strength of the druchii. Either they would win new lands or they would give their lives in a final act of vengeance. Whichever doom was to be theirs, it was an ending that found harmony in the spiteful soul of every druchii.

The host of Hag Graef would follow Malekith in this final war against the asur. Malus would strip his city of every warrior, leaving only the old and the sick behind. He would muster the greatest warhost among all the druchii and, when battle was joined, the glory of victory would be his. The Witch King was selfish enough to believe this would be his war, but in any war, fortune was a fickle mistress. If Malekith showed any weakness, Malus would be there to seize upon it.

'Conquest or extinction,' the Witch King decreed. 'Naggaroth will never recover. Will the druchii stay to slowly dwindle and die, cowering behind our walls? No! We are scions of Nagarythe, the people of Aenarion. We will reclaim what is our birthright or die!' Malekith strode back to his throne as the assembled nobles cheered and shouted, each more eager to show his loyalty and support for the king than the elf beside him. Much of it was political theatre, but Malus could see that there were a few who seemed genuinely enthusiastic about the campaign ahead.

The Witch King motioned his dreadlords to silence. 'Before you depart the Black Tower, before you return to your cities to gather your warriors... a demonstration. A reminder of what must befall all who betray their king.'

Carefully Malus reached for the dagger hidden in the lining of his cloak. He froze as he saw Kouran rise to his feet. The captain wasn't interested in the drachau, however, instead marching towards the iron throne to stand beside his master. Any relief Malus might have felt vanished in the next instant. Emerging from the shadowy recesses of the chamber were the torturers who had so lately entertained him in the Black Tower's dungeons. One of the elves bore before him an ebony reliquary, which held the grisly tools of their trade.

Malus kept his hand around the dagger, every nerve on edge as he waited for some hidden foe to fall upon him. Was this why Malekith had freed him, simply to make an example of him before the whole Black Council? Watching Kouran approach the king gave him another idea. Perhaps it wasn't Malus the tyrant wanted to make an example of. Maybe it was Drusala who was the focus of the king's wrath. Making an example of her might silence some of those who thought him weak for not executing Morathi.

Kouran stood before the iron throne, the torturers flanking him at either side. The captain turned towards Drusala, then in a sudden whirl he fell upon Ezresor. The spymaster was caught utterly by surprise, the blade he'd hidden in the sleeve of his robe pinned against his wrist as Kouran restrained him. Ezresor was forced to his feet as the captain bent his other arm behind his back and pulled.

Malekith took hold of the struggling elf. His iron hand gripped Ezresor's gaunt face, forcing his mouth open. 'You were the eyes and ears of the Black Tower,' the king snarled. 'But what good are eyes and ears when the tongue will not relate what has been seen and heard?' The Witch King's iron talons reached inside Ezresor's mouth. A gargled cry escaped the spymaster as the tyrant ripped the tongue free. Malekith held the bloodied strip of flesh for all the Black Council to see. 'One of you bought Ezresor's tongue. Look well upon what you purchased.'

Dropping the gory talisman on the floor, the king withdrew from the chamber. Kouran waved the torturers forwards, supervising them as they helped him lower the mutilated Ezresor back into his chair. The elf bearing the reliquary opened the wooden box, disclosing an assortment of clawed mallets and long iron nails. While half of the torturers held Ezresor in place, the others began nailing him into his seat. When Malekith's armada sailed from Naggaroth, it would do so without the spymaster. He'd been condemned to remain behind and watch over the abandoned riches of Naggarond.

Malus shook his head. He'd suspected something untoward with Ezresor when the druchii had removed the bit from his mouth down in the dungeon. The spymaster had given Malus the chance to cheat Malekith by killing himself before any torture began. There was only one reason for extending such a mercy – Ezresor had been afraid of what Malus might say. Pride had kept Darkblade from taking such a cowardly choice. Now he rather suspected Ezresor regretted the transparency of such a mistake. He'd aroused Malekith's suspicions. Whether Ezresor was a part of Khyra's conspiracy or simply seeking to exploit it towards his own ends, the Witch King had paid him in full for his intrigues.

As he watched the torturers nailing the elf to his chair, Malus glanced across at Lady Khyra. Perhaps he'd been wrong; maybe she hadn't been leaning away from Ebnir but towards Ezresor. If so, with such a graphic display, Malekith had made the idea that the drachau had betrayed the conspiracy doubly convincing.

Malus knew Khyra wouldn't dare to act until the host of Hag Graef was embarked and on its way to Ulthuan. There was too much resting on the invasion to risk any delay in mustering the armies and setting sail. But after that, after that Malus would have good cause to worry.

His army might see the shores of Ulthuan, but would he be there to lead it?

CHAPTER FOUR

Malus watched as the towering spires of Hag Graef receded into the distance. The great black ark *Eternal Malediction* was bearing the bulk of his forces out into the Gulf of Naggarond. There they would join the rest of Malekith's armada before voyaging out into the Sea of Malice.

Hag Graef. How long and hard had he struggled to seize her crown? He'd fought against monsters and daemons, endured exile in the barbarous lands of humans and the deadly wastes of Chaos itself. He'd defeated the dread armies of Naggor on the battlefield and enslaved the Naggorites. The blood of brother and sister alike stained his hands, the life of his father had dripped down his sword. He had forfeited his soul to Tz'arkan and dared the forbidden world of the Screaming God-Child. Nothing and no one had been beyond the reach of his lust for ultimate power. Hag Graef, the second city of Naggaroth, and he had been its despotic master!

Now he watched as his kingdom faded away into the distance. Malus felt no regret at abandoning the city. The Witch King was right when he said that no druchii loved the chill wastes of Naggaroth. In their hearts burned the urge to reclaim the land to which they truly belonged, not the desolation of mocking exile. Hag Graef was a prison, a refuge, nothing more. It was in Ulthuan that true power and true glory lay, a realm worth ruling. The siren call of such a promise had fired the pride of Malus and every dreadlord in the land. Only the crazed inhabitants of Har Ganeth had refused Malekith's call, content to remain in their city, glutting their insatiable appetite for murder on the beasts and barbarians besieging their lands. Crone Hellebron and the Cult of Khaine had whipped up the people of Har Ganeth into a frenzy of blood-lust worthy of their ghastly city. It was as well for the druchii that Malekith had abandoned them to their madness.

The scenes Malus had left behind in Hag Graef were little better. Only the strong and useful had been taken aboard the *Eternal Malediction* and the other ships of the fleet. The rest of the city's population had been left to their fate, consigned to whatever horrible doom the creatures of the Wastes would bring to them once their hordes reached the Dark Crag. As his army withdrew from the city, the terror and turmoil boiling up around him had been thrilling to the drachau's black heart. He'd watched with amusement as corrupt old merchants and courtiers had tried in vain to bribe their way into the army, as though their wealth could make any warrior exchange the promise of glory in battle for the miserable end awaiting the city. He'd seen flesh traders auctioning off exotic slaves for almost nothing, seen those same slaves butchered on the spot by buyers interested only in indulging their jaded thirst for slaughter. He'd watched noble towers looted and burned, seen the mortuary vaults smashed open and the bones of ancient rivals ground into the streets under the vengeful boots of drunken wastrels. Some of the temples had been thrown open, their priests murdered by mobs of disillusioned elves, venting their feelings of divine betrayal against those who served the gods. Other temples, like that of Bloody-Handed Khaine himself, became centres of crazed worship and devotion, zealots dragging screaming sacrifices to the gore-soaked altars, as though in this last hour their religious frenzy might yet move their god to protect them.

As chaotic as the rioting and unrest in the streets was, Malus knew things were far worse in the mines below. In stripping Hag Graef of every able-bodied warrior, Malus had dispatched Kunor Kunoll's Son to gather the overseers and slavemasters in the pits below the city. He would need such experienced taskmasters to drive the captive Naggorites into battle. Leaving them behind to administer the vast numbers of human, dwarf and greenskin slaves under Hag Graef would simply be wasteful. There hadn't been time to massacre the slaves; Kunor simply withdrew the guards and locked the gates. Even as he was arranging the destruction of his own wine cellars so that no looter would profit off what he was forced to leave behind, word reached Malus that the mine slaves were in revolt. Panicked by their abandonment, the terrified throng was battering down the gates that confined them. It would only be a matter of hours before the horde won their way clear of the tunnels and spilled out into the streets.

Malus was irate he couldn't stay to watch that. It would have been amusing to behold the ragged host of starveling dogs tear their way through the decadent druchii he'd deemed unfit to fight against the asur. He was certain the carnage would be unprecedented in the history of the Hag, a final atrocity of epic scope before the foul city was blotted out.

'Do you mourn your kingdom, my lord?'

Malus turned as he felt the soft touch of Vincirix's hand against his forearm. He'd heard the knight's approach, of course. She was one of the few he trusted enough to get so near to him. It wasn't that she was beyond treachery – after all, she'd conspired with him to murder her own father – but the simple fact that she owed her position to him. Without his patronage, her own warriors would soon dispose of her. She was well aware of that. Malus wondered if that dependency added an extra note of urgency to her passion when they were alone. Certainly she'd proven to be the most delicious companion to share his bed in a long time.

The drachau rolled across the silk sheets and slid his hand down his lover's tender throat. The black arks were floating cities in their own right and the master of the *Eternal Malediction* had turned the tallest of its spires over to his fearsome passenger. The sprawling bed chamber Malus had taken for his own was very near the summit of that tower, with great windows set into three of its four walls. The resulting view was astonishing, making him feel almost as though he soared among the clouds rather than sailed upon the sea. It was easy to understand how the masters of the black arks could develop such a lordly opinion of themselves; feeling unbound by the very laws of nature, how could they respect the rules of kings and tyrants? Malus considered that it was a good thing his warriors outnumbered the black ark's corsairs by several orders of magnitude. It might remind them who exactly was in charge.

Lifting one finger, Malus stroked the knight's chin. There was just the hint of a scar there, the unhealed residue of a manticore's sting. She had far worse scars elsewhere. It had cost Vincirix much pain to impress her father, to rise through the ranks of her siblings. In some ways, her ruthless jockeying for position paralleled his own. Though, of course, his own ambitions had been much grander in scale and he, at least, had needed no help to kill his father.

He could feel Tz'arkan stirring deep inside him. Of all the things he had done, for some reason it was the vaulkhar's murder that actually seemed to disgust the daemon. Malus had never been able to figure out why. Perhaps it made the daemon question exactly how far its host would go to get what he wanted.

Vincirix tensed under his touch. She would never dare to say anything to him, but Malus knew she hated it when he ran his fingers along the lines of her scars. It reminded her that she had been weak, that she bore the marks of that weakness on her like the brand of a slave. Malus enjoyed reminding her of their respective positions. It reinforced how much she stood to lose if he tired of her.

'Do you still weep for Clar Karond?' Malus asked the knight, cupping her chin and drawing her head back so he could stare into the rich depths of her eyes. 'Do you miss the sights and smells of the slave markets, the roars from the beast-pits? Do you regret not walking the bridges between its great towers, passing between the great houses in the dead of night? How much of your heritage was lost there? How much of your blood is entombed within its tortured earth? How many companions did you leave behind, I wonder?'

The knight smiled at him, hugging him close against her in a tight embrace. 'I have no love but you, Lord Malus. What ardour could match yours? What passion could equal yours?'

Malus drew back, his hand twining Vincirix's dark locks. 'Then you are content? A pity. It is a mark of the petty that they become content. Those who aspire to greater things must never lose the flame of ambition.' Pulling her hair, he turned Vincirix back towards the diminishing image of Hag Graef. 'If I were petty, I should be content to keep the Hag. I would marshal my army and defy the Witch King's decree. I would strive to hold my realm against all foes. This I would do, if I were content to be master of a diseased dung-heap. No, Vincirix, the fire of ambition burns in me. I will have a kingdom worthy of me! Of what consequence then is the Hag or Clar Karond? Let them burn. Let them rot. They are the ghosts of the past, the symbols of our people's disgrace. The glory of the druchii doesn't lie with them. It is in Ulthuan, not Naggaroth, where our people belong!'

'You speak like Malekith,' Vincirix observed. Malus laughed and kissed her neck.

'Does that mean I sound like a king?' he asked her. He leaned back and stared again into her eyes. 'How great is your own ambition, I wonder? How far do you expect it to take you?'

Vincirix matched his stare. 'As far as it would carry my lord,' she said.

Malus laughed again and drew the knight to him.

In that moment, the great window staring out in the direction of Hag Graef burst inwards in a shower of glass and splintered wood. A lithe, nearly naked figure swept into the drachau's chamber, hip-high boots of chimera-hide and a gilded mask cast in the shape of a shrieking daemon the only raiment affected by the weird intruder. A small buckler ringed with razors was bound about the invader's right arm while in her left she gripped a hooked whip. The elf cast her masked gaze about the chamber and a hideous peal of gleeful laughter erupted from her as she spied Malus lying upon the bed.

Malus shoved Vincirix towards the masked intruder, at the same time throwing himself from bed to floor. The masked druchii swerved around Vincirix's diving form and lunged forwards at the bed. The invader's whip slashed down almost at the same moment, slicing into the bed and sending down billowing into the air. Before his attacker could fully recover, Malus kicked out with his foot, catching the elf in her shin. Instead of collapsing beneath the blow, she turned her fall into a violent spin, the razors lining her shield cutting across Malus's bare forearm. The bleeding drachau rolled away as his foe's spin brought the crooked sword sweeping towards him once again.

He knew this kind of enemy, Malus realised. He'd seen her like fight often enough in the arenas of Hag Graef. She belonged to the Sisters of Slaughter, foremost of Naggaroth's gladiator guilds – female warriors who devoted themselves to the ruthless god Eldrazor of the Blades. The gladiatrixes didn't master any technique or school of combat, instead honing their reflexes and plying their murderous trade on a savage, instinctual level. They were the most unpredictable of foes, constantly adapting and reacting to their enemy, existing only in the moment, devoid of the discipline and strategy of more refined warriors.

Whoever had sent this elf to kill him had known it was just this kind of enemy that would cause Malus the most worry. His cunning brain could outthink a normal foe, discern the pattern behind his opponent's training and plan his own strategy accordingly. Against a Sister of Slaughter, however, such ploys would be useless.

The gladiatrix was already whirling back to the attack, diving at him like a rabid wolf. Her spin brought both whip and shield slashing at him. The hooked whip gouged a furrow in the bedframe while the razored shield sent sparks flying from the stone floor. Still spinning, the elf kicked out, her boot cracking against Malus's cheek, spilling him onto his back.

More glass exploded inwards as two more of the pit fighters came crashing into the chamber, swinging into the room on ropes. Malus could afford them only the briefest glance before his first attacker was diving down on him again. His fist slammed into her chest, bruising the flesh and driving the breath out of her. As she gasped, the flash of her whip was diverted, sweeping through the drachau's hair instead of his skull. The gladiatrix's instincts recovered enough to smash the boss of her shield into Malus's face and dig the razors of its underside into his shoulder. Before she could work further harm, however, the invader was swept to the floor by Vincirix. The two she-elves rolled away, the knight's legs locked about the killer's torso, one hand trying to pry the hooked whip free while the other arm wrapped itself around the neck beneath the daemon-mask.

Malus sprang across the damaged bed, diving for the sheathed length of the Warpsword of Khaine lying upon its ebony stand. Before he could reach his sword, the other gladiatrixes were charging him, whirling at him in their eerie dance of death. The drachau recoiled before the storm of slashing whips and shields, throwing pillows and blankets at the savage she-elves in a desperate bid to hold them back. His gambit bore some slight success when one of the killers found her whip coiled around an upflung fur. Before she could disentangle herself, Malus caught her knee with a brutal kick. He heard a grisly pop as the warrior crashed to the floor.

Growling like a mother panther, the other gladiatrix lunged at him. Malus felt the murderous closeness of her whip as it snapped at his ribs. The elf's shield flashed upwards to swat away a pillow he threw at her, then her entire body described an impossible pirouette as the whip came into play once more. Malus could feel Tz'arkan's presence respond to the closeness of death to its host, the daemon's agitation threatening to intrude into his thoughts just when he needed them at their sharpest.

A shriek rose from his adversary as Malus drove his fingers into her mask. A wave of sadistic exultation swept through him as he felt the elf's eye beneath his finger. The gladiatrix tumbled away from him, pawing at her mask as she landed on the floor. With a wrench, she broke the leather straps and threw the bloodied mask at Malus. The exposed face was beauteous, or would have been but for the jellied wreckage dripping from one eye socket.

The bruising impact of the bronze mask against his bare flesh didn't stop Malus from making another dive for the warpsword. Instead, it was the brutal kick of a booted foot that drove him back. The other gladiatrix had freed herself from the blanket and was leaping to intercept the drachau. Raw pain flared through him as he was knocked back by the blow. He tried to roll as he landed back on the bed, but the pain only grew more intense. The killer's kick had fractured a rib, and blood streamed onto the sheets from the dozens of little wounds where the steel studs lining her boot had pricked his skin.

Before he could react, the mutilated gladiatrix was diving at him again. He grunted in agony as he was driven face-first into the bedding, his broken rib grinding against its fellows. The she-elf pinned him beneath her body, her legs pressing down into the small of his back. Cackling a laugh that was equal parts rage and murderous jubilation, she took hold of his hair and jerked his head back. He could see the sheen of her shield as she brought its razored edge spinning down. Desperate, Malus snatched hold of the soft flesh of the elf's thigh and gave her leg a vicious twist.

The gladiatrix was accustomed to worse pain, but the unexpectedness of Malus's assault caused her the briefest instant of surprise. Reflexively, she reared up and away from the drachau's tormenting clutch. The moment he felt her weight shift, Malus bucked up from the bedding, clenching his teeth against the surge of pain that roared through his body. His assailant was sent tumbling forwards, her uncanny knack for adaptation turning her fall into a roll. His intention had been to throw her full into the face of the other gladiatrix, but she displayed the same automatic reaction as her sister, darting aside and spinning around in a murderous counter-attack.

Malus reacted in the only way possible, doing the last thing his enemy would expect. Instead of diving back, he dived forwards. The gladiatrix adjusted the snap of her whip as he came at her; he felt the metal hook slice the skin along his shoulder. But he'd managed to slip beneath her guard, driving his head into her belly. The killer started to roll with the impact, twisting around so that she could drive her shield into Malus's neck. The drachau, however, drove a fist into her throat, crushing her windpipe. The warrior crumpled in a gasping, gagging heap.

From behind him, Malus heard a sharp cry. He turned around, putting his back to the wall and trying to keep both the choking gladiatrix and the one-eyed harridan in view. Across the room he could see Vincirix throw her enemy from her by bringing both legs up and under the killer's body. As the gladiatrix spun away, the knight kept a firm hold on her left arm. There was a sickening sound as the limb was dislocated. The crippled fighter managed to slash at Vincirix with her shield, but the knight slithered under the razored edge with an almost boneless undulation. The warrior kicked out with one of her boots, the toe cracking against Vincirix's jaw. It was a blow that would have stunned a less rugged combatant, but Vincirix had cut her teeth breaking the spirits of hydras and manticores. There was little punishment that could equal the pain of being splashed by the caustic venom of a kharibdyss. Grimly, Vincirix shrugged off the elf's kick and fell upon her foe. Wrenching the gladiatrix's knee about, she bent the killer's leg back upon itself. Even the intruder's mask couldn't muffle the resultant scream of agony.

Malus glared at the one-eyed gladiatrix, gesturing at the fighter Vincirix was dismantling piece by piece and the gagging wretch lying on the bed. 'You should have brought more help before you tried to murder me!' he snarled at her.

One-eye smiled back at him. Keeping her place near the warpsword, too cautious to risk touching the enchanted blade, the gladiatrix raised her fingers to her mouth and blew a sharp whistle.

Malus felt his insides turn sick when four more Sisters of Slaughter came rappelling down into the room through the shattered windows. He could almost hear Tz'arkan laughing at him. The daemon was right. He had asked for it.

'I'm going to peel your eyes from your skull,' One-eye promised. 'Only when you forget how to scream will I let you die.' She dived aside as Malus made a desperate lunge for his sword. The hand that reached out for the blade was smashed flat by One-eye's shield. The hook of the elf's whip cracked across his face, splitting his lip and knocking teeth from his mouth. 'Slow, Darkblade,' the murderess hissed. 'You die slow!'

The other invaders were rushing into the room now. Vincirix was crouched over the naked wreck of her own foe, trying to break the hold the killer stubbornly maintained on her whip. One of the masked gladiatrixes danced towards the unarmed knight, lash and shield describing a gleaming skein of death as she advanced.

At that moment, the door to the chamber burst inwards, blown back by a force that snapped the bolt and the heavy beam that had been set across it. A deafening roar raged through the room, like the titanic bellow of an angry volcano. Malus felt his head ring from the clamour, saw Vincirix and the gladiatrixes actually stagger before the auditory assault.

Behind that monstrous din, warriors came rushing into the chamber, falling upon the stunned gladiatrixes before they could recover their wits. Silar Thornblood led the rush, cutting down a gladiatrix with a double-handed slash of his sword. Charging past him were Kunor and a pair of elves in the battered armour of Naggorite slave-soldiers. Their assault wasn't quite as unopposed as Silar's, the gladiatrixes warding away the initial impetus with their bladed bucklers.

A howl of fury that nearly matched the deafening roar of the preceding moment struck Malus's ears. Close beside him, One-eye twisted her body, snapping her whip at his throat. The arrival of the drachau's warriors had cheated her of the opportunity to kill him slowly, but she was determined to kill him just the same.

Malus hooked his feet around One-eye's leg and threw his own body into a sidewise twist. The gladiatrix was forced to follow his motion, the whip falling lax as the two crashed against the wall. Before she could start to rise, Malus jammed the flat of his hand into her nose, crushing it into a pulpy mess. One-eye shrieked at him and raked the edge of her shield along his arm, ripping his flesh. The intense pain broke the hold Malus had gained on the killer's throat. Slamming her knee into his groin, the gladiatrix pulled back and tried to bring her whip into play once more.

Blinking through his own pain, Malus caught the butt of One-eye's whip. His tenuous clutch arrested the lash's motion, preventing the gladiatrix from drawing back for another murderous stroke. Spitting a mouthful of blood and the odd splinter of tooth into her last good eye, Malus surged upwards from the floor.

Before he could rip the whip free from the blinded gladiatrix, Malus felt his foe's entire body seized by a shivering convulsion. He could actually feel the warmth of life vanish beneath his touch. It was only the matter of a heartbeat, the pause between pulsations, and One-eye went from a living adversary to a mere carcass. He didn't need the uncanny clamminess in the air around him to recognise the taint of sorcery. He'd been around such dark arts all his life, between his mother and his treacherous sister Yasmir; he could recognise the residue of magic only too well.

Looking away from the dead gladiatrix, Malus was surprised to find Drusala standing in the doorway of his chamber. The explosive opening of the portal was now explained as well as the sudden demise of his own foe. Perhaps explained just a little too neatly.

'Silar! Kunor!' Malus shouted. 'I want one of them alive!' The drachau spared no more time for commands, but snatched up the warpsword. If Drusala didn't want any of the killers taken intact, the magic blade would make a good argument against her.

The conflict was winding down as Malus took up his sword. Two more of the gladiatrixes were dead, though they'd claimed one of Kunor's Naggorites before they went down. The last intruder was beset by the combination of Silar and Vincirix. Armed with the shield and whip of the gladiatrix she'd already killed, the knight from Clar Karond dived in upon the pit fighter as she spun away from Silar's blade. Vincirix's whip coiled around the wrist of her adversary, imprisoning both the weapon and the hand that held it. The tension of the tautened whip caused the hook at the end of the lash to tear through the gladiatrix's hand. Blood sprayed from a severed artery. Catching the masked warrior's shield with her own buckler, Vincirix pressed her assault. Closing with the gladiatrix, she drove both knees into the elf's midsection, driving the air from her body.

The crippled killer collapsed in Vincirix's arms. The knight shoved her foe away in disgust. 'Kunor,' she growled. 'Bind this thing's wound before she bleeds out.' Turning her back on the slave-driver, she smiled at Malus. 'You said alive, not whole.'

The smile Malus returned to her was as warm as a cold one's grin. 'You need to find a god and start praying that arena-meat lives long enough to tell me what I want to know.' His piece said, Malus turned away from his lover. He looked over at the gore-soaked bed. A final death rattle wheezed from the gladiatrix whose throat he'd crushed. He watched as the lithe body spasmed and fell still.

'It is fortunate that we arrived when we did, your lordship,' Drusala said, advancing into the room.

'Excuse me, I'm not really in a mood to receive visitors at the moment,' Malus told her. He directed a sharp look at Silar. The noble paused as he wiped blood off his blade.

'The sorceress saw an omen in the waves...' Silar started to explain.

'A shark in the coils of an octopus,' Drusala elaborated.

Malus didn't care for the amused twinkle in her eye as the sorceress strode towards him. Scowling, he reached for one of the sable-edged robes draped across a nearby divan. Irritated, he tried to shrug his way into the garment, his annoyance mounting when he found he'd grabbed Vincirix's robe by mistake.

'Which was I?' Malus grumbled as he threw the first robe at Vincirix and made a grab for the other. 'The shark or the octopus?'

Drusala waved her hand at the dead gladiatrixes. 'The shark ate the octopus, in the end, so you must have been the shark.'

'What does that make you?' Malus asked, not liking the superiority in Drusala's tone. 'One of the pilot fish?' He didn't give her a chance to reply. 'Silar, I want to know everything, but we can start with why you brought so few warriors to aid me.'

Silar couldn't hold his master's fierce gaze, staring instead at some imaginary fixture just over the drachau's shoulder. 'We... we weren't sure that... we'd be in time. If... if something happened...'

'You wanted only people who could keep their mouths shut,' Malus finished for him. He spun around, directing his glare at Kunor as the slavemaster finished binding the prisoner's wound. 'Can your Naggorite be trusted to hold a secret?'

Without hesitation, Kunor lunged and drove his dagger into the side of the surviving slave-soldier. The Naggorite cried out once, then wilted to the floor, his lifeblood spurting from the artery Kunor had severed.

'He can now, my lord,' Kunor said. The readiness of the slavemaster to indulge his blood-lust sometimes made Malus wonder if he wasn't the spawn of a witch elf rather than a son of Hag Graef.

'What of your captive?' Drusala asked. 'What secrets do you expect her to divulge?' The sorceress knelt beside One-eye's corpse, pulling down one of her boots and exposing a line of glyphs tattooed into her pale skin. At a glance, Malus could tell the glyphs represented various guilds, covens and noble houses. The uppermost, the most recently inked, was the glyph of Ezresor. 'Her employers are recorded here already.'

Malus smiled and shook his head. It was possible, of course, that Ezresor had made arrangements to murder Malus before his own doom claimed him in the Black Tower. It wouldn't be the first time that a schemer's designs for revenge outlived him. But such an answer would be too simple, too obvious. 'And what if she only records the mark when her job is done? No, I think it would be too reckless to trust so simple a solution.'

'Who else would want your death?' Drusala smiled. The question was much too obvious as well.

'Silar, take the prisoner to Lady Eldire,' Malus said. 'She can use her magic to wring what I want to know out of the wretch.'

Drusala snapped her fingers, calling Malus's attention back to her. 'I was handmaiden to Lady Morathi. I am a powerful sorceress in my own right. My spells can drag the truth out of that harpy-bait as easily as your mother's can.'

A twinge of amusement flashed across Malus's face as he noted the injured pride in Drusala's voice. 'Your spells are no doubt quite potent,' he told her. 'I have no doubt you could wrest the truth from this villainess. The only doubt I have is whether it would be the sort of truth I want to hear.'

Looking around the shambles of his bedchamber, Malus snapped orders to Kunor and Vincirix. 'Tell Fleetmaster Hadrith I will need a new apartment and get some of our people up here to clean this mess. Be discreet, we don't want the wrong people finding out about this.' He met Drusala's cool gaze.

'It might be dangerous if word got out before we knew who was responsible,' Malus declared. The sound of the wind whistling through the shattered windows seemed to echo his concern. An echo that rustled the bedclothes and the curtains, but somehow couldn't so much as ripple the thin silk gown that hugged Drusala's slender body.

CHAPTER FIVE

The empty wine bottle crashed against the stone floor, exploding in a nimbus of shimmering glass. Malus ignored the servant who hurried to clear away the debris and instead beckoned his mother's steward over to him. Korbus was a spindly, sour-faced druchii, with just a hint of yellow in his complexion that gave his skin a jaundiced look Malus typically associated with sickly human slaves. The expensive tunic and robe the steward wore always seemed to rest uneasily on him, like a snake not quite out of its old skin.

Korbus was an old retainer, long in his mother's service. She'd taken him on shortly after the vaulkhar's death. Malus had heard rumours that Eldire favoured him as a consort. That didn't trouble him particularly; he wasn't so insecure about his own position as to forbid his mother a toy now and then. No, what nagged at him were the stories that Korbus wasn't entirely without his own small talents in the black arts. It had been generations since Malekith, heeding some obscure prophecy about sorcerers and regicide, forbade any but she-elves to practise magic in Naggaroth. Certainly a number of sorcerers had remained, lurking in secret, but they existed under the pain of death not simply from Morathi and her convent, but from the tyranny of the Witch King himself. Why his mother, already an enemy of Morathi, should want to tempt Malekith as well by keeping a petty magician in her service was something Malus couldn't understand. One day, he felt, he would have to arrange an accident for Korbus and eliminate the potential for problems from that quarter.

For now, however, it was enough to have the dour little swine attending him like a serving wench. Korbus could do with a dose of humility and a reminder that whatever consideration Malus might accord his mother didn't extend to his mother's consort. As Malus beckoned to him, Korbus shambled over with another bottle of wine.

'Go any slower, Korbus, and I'll reconsider the wisdom of allowing you to remain on board,' Malus snapped as the steward proffered him the bottle.

'Forgive me, dread master,' Korbus said, bowing to the floor. 'I know your wounds pain you, but do you think it wise to imbibe so freely?'

Malus rolled the bottle along the side of his arm where Eldire's poultice covered the slash he'd received from one of the gladiatrixes. His mother's magic was mending his hurts well enough. It wasn't any physical pain Malus sought to deaden with the draught. It was Tz'arkan. The daemon was responding to the spells his mother had used, fattening on them like some phantom leech. The draught dulled its appetite, enticing it back into hibernation or whatever it was the daemon did when it wasn't nagging at his mind and trying to usurp his flesh.

At the moment, of course, the daemon was one of the less unsettling aspects of his life. Since sailing from Hag Graef and joining the rest of Malekith's fleet in the Gulf of Naggarond, Malus had come to appreciate the esteem with which his king regarded him. The *Eternal Malediction* had been given the dubious honour of leading the rest of the fleet out into the Sea of Malice. The vanguard position offered more than the usual hazards. The threat of an asur ship might be minimal, but they'd already fended off the mindless violence offered by dozens of barbarian dragonships. There were strange blocks of luminous ice drifting through the sea, ice that exuded fingers of lightning and which seemed to chase after the black ark with an animalistic hunger. Reefs that had never existed before menaced the vessel as she sailed across waters that should have been as familiar to the corsairs as their own boots. Eerie storms of light and sound rumbled through the sky, flashing through the clouds like primordial leviathans, sometimes reaching down to draw up part of the sea in a shrieking water spout.

Naggaroth was slipping into the abyss. The invasion besetting the realm was far more than hordes of beasts and barbarians. The corruption flowing down from the Wastes was attacking the very fabric of reality, inundating the land itself with the corrosive energies of unrestrained and unfocused magic. The Witch King's decision to abandon his kingdom was more than a last thrust at the hated asur. It was the only way for the druchii to survive as a people.

Of course, it was his own survival that was of the utmost concern to Malus. When he'd seen Drusala and her entourage from Ghrond among the passengers aboard the *Eternal Malediction,* he'd thought her presence indicated that Malekith was trying to keep a close eye on him. Despite all the talk about the Witch King falling out with his mother and leaving Morathi to rot in her tower, Malus hadn't believed it. He'd been certain that the two were yet working in concert. Drusala had been sent to watch him because Malekith expected her to faithfully attend her duty.

The turmoil of their voyage into the Sea of Malice made him reconsider that idea. He knew how precarious his own position with his king was; now he wondered if Drusala weren't in the same boat. It would be like Malekith to put all of his enemies in one cage so they might be more easily disposed of. The sorceress from Ghrond and the drachau of Hag Graef might both be living on borrowed time.

Malus stared at the bottle of wine Korbus had brought him. A cold smile played across his face. 'Steward,' he laughed, knowing how the servile title upset Korbus, 'you are forgetting that the first glass always belongs to you.'

Korbus was usually much better at hiding his emotions than he was today, Malus reflected. There was almost a suggestion of anger in his posture as he retrieved a crystal glass and poured out a small measure of the dark wine. He'd have to talk with his mother about that. A suitably brutal corrective measure might remind the petty sorcerer of exactly where he stood in the grand scheme of things.

Betraying barely a breath of hesitation, Korbus drank the measure of wine from his glass. Malus leaned back in his chair, watching with the most intense interest as the steward replaced the glass on the table and folded his arms behind his back. Seconds stretched into minutes, master studying servant while the servant stared blankly at one of the tapestries hanging from the wall. At length, Malus gave an irritated wave of his hand.

'It seems you've succeeded in keeping poisoners away from my wine,' Malus said. 'That, or maybe you have enough magic that you can keep it from affecting you.' He gripped the neck of the bottle and sketched a mocking salute to Korbus. 'I wonder what my mother will do to you if that's the case. Letting your little spells protect you while failing to save her beloved son.' Laughing, Malus took a long pull from the bottle. He could feel the welcome rush of warm numbness spread through his body. Peering down the length of the upended bottle, he saw Korbus scowling back at him. Losing patience with him, Malus gave an angry flick of his hand and dismissed his mother's consort. Considering these were the rooms Lady Eldire shared with the sorcerer, he was certain the added insult wouldn't be lost on Korbus.

As Korbus beat a graceless retreat from the room, Silar stepped away from the alcove from which he had been keeping guard. 'Is it prudent to bait him so, my lord?' he asked.

Malus shrugged his shoulders, feeling just the faintest echo of pain from the one the gladiatrix had slashed. 'No, probably not, but it is most satisfying. Someday Lady Eldire will tire of that arse-kissing conjurer and when she does, I'll get some real satisfaction out of him.'

'I shall eagerly anticipate the day, my lord,' Silar said.

A twinge of nostalgia tugged at Malus when he heard Silar speak. It was just the sort of thing Hauclir would have said, that insufferable mix of servility and sarcasm his old retainer had never been able to refrain from employing. Dear Hauclir. He'd been the closest thing to a friend Darkblade had ever had. Gone these many years, his memorial abandoned with the rest of Hag Graef...

Malus glared at the wine yet sloshing about the bottom of the bottle. It was making him maudlin, teasing out the weaker impulses and affections lying deep inside his mind. He'd almost prefer to give Tz'arkan free rein than evoke such puerile emotions. Angrily, he cast the bottle away, smiling as he heard it smack against one of the extravagant divans with which the apartment was furnished. The wine-stains would cost some corsair officer fair coin to remove once these rooms were restored to him. Allowing of course the sea-rat hadn't already been dumped over the side.

Yes, Malus reflected, there were a good many enemies who could have engaged the Sisters of Slaughter to take his life, among them the inhabitants of the black ark itself. When the drachau's enormous army had embarked, a great number of Fleetmaster Hadrith's people had been displaced, left to fend for themselves in the wilds around Hag Graef. The black ark was a floating city and, like any city, it had become bloated with the weak and wastrel. To make room for his soldiers, for their weapons and their beasts of war, Malus had ordered the removal of these worthless elves. At this stage of the game, there was no concealing from them that being left behind was a death sentence. There had been riots and rebellion, the corsairs forced to slaughter their own kin in order to maintain Hadrith's rule over the ship. The young, the old, the sick and the worthless – they had tried to resist, but it was a futile gesture against seasoned warriors. The eels and harpies had a grand feast when the black ark left Hag Graef.

Still, for all the necessity of his ruthless orders, Malus knew there would be many on the *Eternal Malediction* who bore him ill. Parents who'd seen their families cast over the side, sons and daughters who'd watched their progenitors abandoned as the black ark sailed away, any number of more torrid and unsavoury attachments that had been erased by the drachau's decree. Few druchii were so simple-minded as to let tender regards seep into their hearts, but there were even fewer who accepted their possessions being taken from them with good grace. In forcibly severing these ties of blood and intrigue, Malus had earned the hate of the corsairs.

'Someone among Hadrith's crew helped those she-daemons reach me,' Malus mused aloud. 'They must have had help getting into the rigging and knowing the right spot to rappel into my chambers.'

'Did the prisoner say as much before...' Silar shuddered, unable to finish the thought. He'd been present during most of Eldire's interrogation of the gladiatrix. The things he'd seen done were enough to shock even his sensibilities.

Malus frowned and shook his head. 'No, she didn't. But it stands to reason that they had inside help.' He tapped his chin as he considered just how obvious that connection was. Such bluntness was crude. No druchii would take any satisfaction from so direct a course of reprisal. It was the cunning behind a murder, the craft employed to conceal motive and perpetrator alike, that gave an elf pride in his sins. The very directness of the connection back to Hadrith's people made him doubt they were ultimately behind the attack. Certainly, someone had been involved at some level, but things weren't so desperate for the crew that they'd act in such a reckless fashion on their own. No, there was some other hand involved, some manipulator working from the shadows.

The question remained – who was that murderous plotter? The more Malus thought about it, the less he considered it possible Ezresor was striking at him from the beyond. The tattooed glyph on the leg of each gladiatrix was too obvious; besides there was the problem of the spymaster anticipating that Malekith would command the *Eternal Malediction* to carry the drachau and his army, a decision that the Witch King hadn't made until well after that final gathering of the Black Council. That, of course, still left entirely too many possibilities, starting with the Witch King himself. Lady Khyra and her fellow conspirators were likely candidates too, eager to obscure their own involvement in the attempt against Malekith.

Whoever was behind it, they'd had their own share of sorcery to draw upon. Despite the most heinous tortures her magic could inflict, Eldire had been unable to penetrate the barrier that had been raised inside the prisoner's mind. Some spell had partitioned the memory of whoever had engaged the troupe of gladiatrixes to kill Malus. Eldire was certain the memory was there – her own magic was powerful enough to uncover that much – but it stubbornly resisted every effort to pry it free. Before the end, after what she'd endured, Malus was certain the gladitarix would have gladly confessed if it had been in her power to do so. Instead, she'd taken her secret with her into Ereth Khial's underworld. Even Eldire's efforts to command the elf's departed spirit had been fruitless. It was rare when his mother encountered magic stronger than her own, and when she did it tended to put her into a dangerous mood.

Thinking of dangerous sorceresses made Malus turn his thoughts to Drusala. How far was he prepared to trust that her timely intervention had been caused by an omen and not arranged beforehand? What sort of game was she trying to play? If she was out of favour with Malekith, was she trying to inveigle herself into the good graces of Malus? If that were the case, anything that smacked of collusion between them would provoke the Witch King into some sort of response. Probably something involving a regiment of Black Guard. The prudent thing would be to keep the witch as far away as possible.

Malus hadn't risen to the rank of drachau by doing what was prudent.

'Where is Drusala?' Malus asked Silar as he rose from his chair.

Silar bit back whatever wise words of caution leapt to his tongue. Instead he took a moment to collect himself and tell his master what he wanted to hear. 'Lady Eldire and the witch from Ghrond have been in consultation all morning.'

That bit of information was intriguing. All his life, Malus's mother had lived in dread of Morathi's sorceresses, fearing falling into their clutches even more than she had being returned to the Witch Lords of Naggor. Why the sudden change? What had brought about such a dramatic adjustment in Eldire's sensibilities? Had the disgrace and exile of Morathi made his mother overbold? Or had her witchsight told her she would need magic beyond what her own abilities could provide on the journey ahead? Eldire had a pronounced talent for prophecy, a quality that had made her valuable to Naggor and dangerous to Ghrond. What had she foreseen that made her entertain Drusala?

Malus scowled at Silar as he realised his retainer hadn't answered his question. 'I did not ask what she's been doing,' he warned the noble. 'I asked you where she is.'

There were only a few elves Malus considered dependable and even fewer he felt comfortable allowing close to him. Silar Thornblood, with all his quaint concepts of duty and obligation, was the nearest of them all. He could be depended upon to faithfully serve the drachau because he honestly saw his own prestige as being dependent upon the drachau's power. As close as he was, however, even Silar felt a twinge of fear when his master employed that cold, flat tone of voice against him.

'Lady Eldire is meeting with Drusala in the Star Spire,' he reported. 'Several of Fleetmaster Hadrith's diviners and astrologers are with them.'

'Some great effort on mother's part to see a bit further into the future,' Malus said. He nodded as he reached a decision. 'We'll just go and see the results of her divination.'

'Shall I call your knights?' Silar asked.

Malus uttered a sneering laugh. 'Let's wait and hear what sort of prophecies these witches have conjured before I have them massacred.'

Spanning the reaches between the great spires of the black ark, vast platforms and bridges had been erected. Supported by the most powerful of old Nagarythe's ancient sorceries, the black ark was a floating city unto itself. Incapable of expanding outwards, the city had built itself upwards. Gantries and walkways coiled around the stone towers, like fungus growing on a tree. Mazes of chain and rigging spooled downwards to anchor platforms of brass, bronze, bone and timber into place. Unlike a natural ship or even the strange bastions fitted to the scaly backs of helldrakes, there was little sense of motion when standing on the platforms. The turmoil of wind and sea were largely baffled by the magics that saturated the black ark. Fierce winter storms, even the deranged tempests of shimmering light streaming down from the Wastes, were incapable of battering the seafaring citadel.

As he prowled along the bridges, making his way to the Star Spire, Malus took a sardonic pleasure from the hastily downcast eyes of the elves he passed. How many of them resented him for abandoning the Hag? They were fools, and worse, they were hypocrites. Not one of them had forsaken his place on the *Eternal Malediction*. They had all accepted the choice between sacrificing the city or remaining behind to die with it.

He could have had much better followers if he'd only cast aside the title of drachau and ridden into the north. Malus would have become master of things no earthly lord could ever aspire towards! He would have stretched forth his hand and seen eternity itself coiling about his fingers. He would know the secret names of all things and understand the fragile skein that bound the essence of worlds. His heart would have despaired from the singing of the aethyr and the great truth beyond.

Malus stopped and leaned against the iron rail lining the platform he was crossing. He could feel the darkness of Tz'arkan boiling up inside him. So far, the wine had numbed the daemon too much for it to make itself coherent and understandable. Instead he could feel it as a shadow crawling through his flesh. 'Relent,' he hissed at the abomination inside him, smashing his fist against the rail in his frustration.

'Are you ill, my lord?' The question came from a young druchii in the studded armour of a beast-keeper. Malus directed a scowl at the elf so fierce that he stumbled back towards the pack of cold ones he'd been helping to keep under control.

Silar came up beside Malus, his face imperturbable but his tone carrying a note of worry. 'Is... your trouble... becoming a problem?'

Malus grimaced. 'My guest should be impotent for hours after all I've poured into my body,' he said. 'Instead I can feel the thing's dreams slithering into my thoughts.' He uttered a bitter laugh. 'Do you remember, Silar, when I would drink for the pleasure of wine, not to quiet a monster inside my head?' The drachau looked away from his retainer, staring across the platform, at the beast-keepers and their reptilian charges.

The beast-keepers looked absolutely puny beside the twenty-foot-long reptiles. Lizard-like, with great clawed hind legs and smaller forelegs, the cold ones were the natural inhabitants of the dank caverns beneath Naggaroth. Ages ago, the huge lizards had been adopted by the druchii as beasts of war. The powerful jaws of a cold one, its rending claws and tough scaly flesh made for a much more formidable steed than a mere horse. Through special scents and perfumes, an elf knight could deceive the reptile into believing him to be a member of its pack; through the cruellest training and privation, a beast-breaker could force the cold one to adopt the knight as a superior member of its pack. When a troop of cold one knights charged across the field of battle, only the most resolute of foes had the stomach to stand against them.

The cold ones, among their other nasty qualities, exuded a poisonous slime from their skin. Over time, this poison would deaden a rider's own sense of touch. The slime also contributed to the pungent, musky smell of the reptiles. In their own caverns, the cold ones would never gather in packs so large as to smother themselves with their own toxic reek, but in the confines of the black ark, the creatures had to be removed from their pens and allowed up into the open air periodically so that their cages could be fumigated. It also allowed the beast-keepers to exercise the reptiles so that they didn't become either lethargic or too aggressive. It was often a delicate thing to remind the savage brutes of who was master and who was beast.

Malus needed the creatures to be in prime condition when his army reached Ulthuan. Despite the Witch King's assurances that the hated asur were beset by other foes, invading the island continent would not be an easy accomplishment. It would take the steel of sword and spear and the strength of claw and fang. The cold ones would need to be at their most vicious when they were unleashed against Ulthuan.

Towards that purpose, Malus had squandered precious space in the black ark's holds to embark a supply of living captives. Elves too weak to fight, as well as many human and dwarf slaves. Fresh meat was the staple of a cold one's diet. When the reptiles had to catch their dinners it helped to keep their instincts sharp and their dull wits focused. The beast-keepers were even now preparing to feed the brutes. A cluster of ragged human wretches were being herded out onto the platform. The laggards were jabbed mercilessly by the prongs of the tridents their captors stabbed into their flanks. The coppery smell of blood excited the cold ones. The lizards swung their heads around, their tongues licking the air as they sensed the injured humans marching towards them.

It had been a long time since the cold ones had been fed. Two of the brutes started to lumber forwards. The beast-keepers lashed out with their whips, driving the creatures back. It was a necessary display of discipline.

Among the clutch of reptiles there was a smaller, more sparely built creature. Great horns jutted out from the sides of its head, stabbing back over its neck. The reptile belonged to a rarer breed called 'horned ones': beasts of slighter size but much sharper intelligence. This one was actually exploiting the punishment being dispatched against the over-anxious cold ones to start its own advance upon the slaves. In its display of craft, however, the horned one missed an unengaged beast-keeper off to its left. As the beast started forwards, the beast-keeper slashed at it with his whip. The steel barbs on the end of the lash raked across the reptile's muzzle, scarring the scales and drawing blood from the flesh beneath.

In a matter of heartbeats, Malus was upon the beast-keeper, snatching the whip from the elf's hand as he made to strike the horned one again. The druchii swung around, but the expression of outrage collapsed into one of mortal terror when he saw who had taken the lash away.

'You're beating my steed, pig,' Malus growled at the beast-keeper. The elf fell to his knees, started to whine some fawning plea for forgiveness. Malus looked over at the other beast-keepers and the slave-drivers. There were many times when a necessary display of discipline was in order.

'Feed, Spite,' Malus snarled as he kicked the pleading beast-keeper. The druchii fell flat on his back. The elf didn't even have a chance to scream before the horned one pounced on him. Spite's immense weight crushed the beast-keeper's ribcage, driving a fountain of blood from his mouth.

The ravenous reptile chomped down on its former tormentor's shoulder, tearing away a ragged chunk of meat and bone.

Malus glared across at the other beast-keepers, savouring the fear he saw on their faces. 'This animal belongs to me. You will treat him accordingly,' he warned. Leaving Spite to continue its gory repast, the drachau resumed his march across the platform. Silar hurried after his master.

'After they take Spite and the others back below, I want every beast-keeper in that company stripped of rank,' Malus told Silar. 'They lose name, position and liberty. Give them over to Kunor.'

'Those are druchii of Hag Graef,' Silar cautioned. 'If they're put in with the Naggorites, they'll be killed.'

'If they are, we'll be able to feed the harpies a bit extra,' Malus said. 'They're not so particular about how lively their meals are.'

CHAPTER SIX

The Star Spire was a narrow spindle of stone and iron stabbing far above the black ark's foundations. It seemed impossible that such a delicate structure could soar to such a height, easily a hundred feet higher than Fleetmaster Hadrith's own tower. Unlike the other towers that rose from the foundation, there were few platforms and bridges connecting to the Star Spire. The mystics of the *Eternal Malediction* were fiercely protective of their privacy and the corsairs of the black ark were happy to allow them to keep their sinister secrets to themselves. Among the upper reaches of the spire, only a single bridge connected to it – a narrow ladder of steel rising from the parapets of the fleetmaster's tower. Malus eyed the high bridge with more than a little envy, but to trespass upon Hadrith's inner circle would be to expose his fears to the corsair king. He wasn't about to make a gift of his own weakness to Hadrith. It might give the fleetmaster ideas.

Instead, Malus and Silar were hurrying to one of the lower landings, the causeways that snaked up from the slave pits to the Star Spire's base. The bloody auguries and divinations of the black ark's seers required a constant stream of sacrifices. The more potent the ritual, the more blood and souls it needed to fuel its magics. Now, with the tide of slaves being herded into the tower, it seemed as though the Star Spire were trying to call up Khaine himself.

Malus was thankful for the slaves and guards trooping into the Star Spire. It would obscure his own entrance into the tower, at least from casual observers. He couldn't be too subtle; he'd need his position and authority to get inside. All he could hope was that the period of grace won by the confusion at the gate would be enough to put distance between himself and any opportunistic enemies.

The enemy is already here.

The daemon's voice was like thunder roaring inside Malus. It nearly sent him pitching from the bridge he was on, precipitating him down into the mass of slaves below. He reeled, snatching hold of a support pillar as his insides boiled from the force of Tz'arkan's intrusion. Silar started to reach for him, but quickly withdrew in alarm when he saw the distortion on his master's face. Despite the wine, despite the fierce will of Malus, the daemon was beginning to bleed through. Silar knew enough to be horrified at that prospect.

His retainer didn't know nearly enough, though. He didn't understand how Tz'arkan had mustered such strength. He didn't know the emotion in the daemon's cry. The monster was afraid. It was panic that had driven it to such a desperate exertion of power, risking the destruction of its mortal host in a bid to assert control.

'You'll kill us both,' Malus growled through teeth clenched in pain.

Death is already here.

The daemon's voice was weaker, only a whisper now. Tz'arkan had expended too much of itself in that first burst of panic. Malus could already feel it slinking back into the dark corners of himself, like a spider crawling along the threads of its web. For the first time, the drachau took no pleasure in Tz'arkan's retreat. The daemon wouldn't have panicked over nothing.

Malus was sent reeling once more, clinging to the support pillar as his legs whipped out from under him and dangled over the side of the bridge. He saw elves and cold ones hurtling past, thrown from platforms and bridges high above, their bodies smashing down into the herd of slaves below. Screams, cries of disbelief and confusion rang out from every quarter. Not simple fear, but the shrieks of beings confronted by the impossible.

The black ark, built upon the mightiest of ancient sorceries, floating inviolate upon its foundations of magic, was rolling and pitching, floundering in the sea like any mundane ship of wood and sail. The corsairs, in all the millennia since the city had ripped itself from the drowned shores of Nagarythe, had never been beset by such elemental violence.

The turmoil increased. The black ark began to list to port, throwing still more bodies from the higher ramparts and bridges. Blocks of stone, spans of iron and wood came crashing down as causeways buckled and stairways crumbled, the *Eternal Malediction*'s yaw twisting them in ways and patterns never imagined by their architects.

Screams rang out all around, rising into a deafening bedlam. But that despairing din was preferable to the ghastly silence that followed, a silence so terrible that it struck Malus like a physical blow. A silence born from blackest terror.

It was *felt* before it could be seen or smelt or heard. The druchii felt the atrocity's presence like a foulness, a spiritual contagion that spread a skein of slime across their souls. It was the phantom touch of raw evil – not the petty evil as mortal beings imagined it, but the cosmic malignance that profaned the very essence of reality. It was the hate of things impossible and unborn, the bitterness of what could not be, the profaneness of the unknown.

From the depths, it slobbered upwards, a heaving undulation of carrion-meat, flesh bloated and necrotic. It had some semblance of form about it. The things that grappled the sides of the black ark were as much like arms as they were branches; the things that oozed from the ends of those arms were not unlike titanic hands. From each hand, ropy coils that rudely simulated fingers snaked around the towers, corroding stone and iron with their touch, engulfing flesh and bone until their victims were absorbed into the necrotic essence of the tendril that gripped him.

There was a head, of sorts, and it squatted upon bony, cadaverous shoulders. It was something like a skull that had been wrapped in a veil of slime and decay, each line of bone clearly defined yet still obscured by the encrustations it had accumulated. Hagworms writhed from the thing's sunken cheeks, while anemones and polyps squirmed between its teeth. Four cavernous hollows flanked a gash-like nasal opening. In the depths of those hollows, flickering at the ends of fleshy ribbons, were hundreds of blazing red orbs. As the behemoth surged upwards and wrapped its arms about the black ark, the eye-stalks extruded themselves outwards, whipping about the skull-like face to peer and probe the world the abomination had invaded.

'By the Gates of Nethu, what is that thing?' Silar screamed. The noble had lost his footing, sprawling across the bridge like an armoured crab. A jagged piece of masonry torn from one of the towers had ripped open his arm, but he was oblivious to the injury. Like every elf on the black ark, his mind was frozen with terror, his attention focused solely upon the oceanic horror that had crawled up from the nameless depths to seize the ship.

It is doom. Tz'arkan's voice was a mere whisper, but it was enough to stir Malus from his paralysis of terrified fascination. *It is obscenity made flesh. Such a thing as this might have been your slave, Darkblade, had you but the vision to embrace me. Now we are both doomed.*

Malus stared up at the daemonic giant's face. He thought he'd seen some of those eye-stalks shift and turn when Tz'arkan whispered to him. A horrible thought came to him. 'It's looking for something, isn't it?'

I vanquished it once. Tricked and betrayed it, bound it in chains just as I was later bound until you freed me. The chains that held it were stronger, but they relied too much upon mortal substance and mortal concepts. The mortal world is dying, Darkblade. The old barriers are breaking down. The old horrors are free once more.

'It is looking for you,' Malus snarled. Even as he said it, dozens of the eye-stalks unfurled from the depths of the atrocity's face, peering down through the nest of bridges and platforms. A crawling, crippling sense of insignificance smashed down upon Malus as he felt those hideous eyes trying to find him. It was like having a mountain suddenly aware of his presence, aware with all the limitless belligerence of eternity.

It is looking for us. You are my vessel, Malus. Do you think that power will pause to make a distinction between us? Do you believe it is even capable of bothering to do so?

'You'll destroy everything,' Malus gasped. The giant was reaching around with one of its arms, stretching into the heart of the ark, trying to bring its tendrils closer. He could see now that there were chains dripping from the daemon's flesh, corroded and rusted, caked in coral and salt. From each chain, swollen and decayed like the titan itself, was shackled a body. Bodies of men and elves mostly, but there were other things too – orcs and goblins and beings even the druchii had no name for. As each of the drowned corpses fell across a bridge or platform, they jerked into a twisted semblance of life. Like horrible puppets, the things stalked and slaughtered, falling upon the shocked druchii with cutlasses and tridents.

Now you see the deceit of mortal ambition. We must both of us suffer for your short-sighted pride. We will become another of that power's toys, doomed to languish upon one of its chains until...

Again, the bloated titan reacted to Tz'arkan's whisper. Its flabby arm came crashing downwards, smashing through bridges as it reached between the towers, groping its way towards the Star Spire. Towards Malus.

'Shut up, daemon!' Malus growled. Tz'arkan couldn't have failed to notice that its persistent mutterings were drawing the thing's attention. If it was truly afraid of the titan, why would it try to draw it out? Had fear usurped the daemon's reason, or was it playing its own game? Maybe the giant wasn't here to destroy or enslave Tz'arkan, but to free it. Maybe it wasn't the daemon's ancient enemy, but rather an old friend.

Would you gamble flesh and soul on your paranoia?

Malus almost allowed Tz'arkan to distract him. Very nearly he missed the long chain dangling from the bloated wrist that was yet far overhead. The corpse at the end of the chain slapped against the surface of the bridge, then jerked into grisly animation. It still had the beard and vestments of a human barbarian and its hands gripped the crude lethality of a double-bladed axe. The drowned carcass lurched towards him as it gained its feet, two tiny eye-stalks wriggling from the sockets of its skull.

The warpsword flashed in Malus's hand, raking across the drowned man, ripping through his tattered hauberk and the blue-tinged flesh beneath. Worms and crabs spilled from the grievous wound, but the ghastly creature continued to press its attack. Malus tried to defend himself, but found his strength ebbing. Tz'arkan was draining it from him, drawing it off. He could feel the monster trying to wrest control of his body away from him. Whether the daemon fought to save them from the giant's slave or deliver them to it, Malus neither knew nor cared. He wouldn't relinquish control. He'd die before submitting to that.

Then we die.

The double-axe came chopping down, its edge crunching into Malus's pauldron. The corroded state of the blade caused it to crumble from the impact, but it didn't need to penetrate the drachau's armour to send him sprawling. As he slammed down onto his back, Malus watched the drowned barbarian raise his ancient weapon for a downward slash at his face. The warpsword felt as though it weighed as much as the entire black ark when he tried to lift it and fend off the murderous blow. Even now, however, he wasn't going to submit to Tz'arkan. He might save his life, but he'd lose everything else.

Before the chained corpse could strike, Silar was rushing the creature, bowling him over and smashing him to the ground. The barbarian struggled beneath Silar, trying to throw off the armoured elf. The noble kept his foe pinned and began stabbing him again and again with a crooked dagger. 'It won't die,' Silar snarled.

The paralysis Tz'arkan had inflicted upon Malus diminished enough that he was able to stumble over towards his retainer. He glared at the hideous barbarian and the ghoulish eye-stalks. 'It will die,' Malus swore. Driven by some instinct imparted to him by the enchanted blade, or some fragment of knowledge Tz'arkan had inadvertently left behind in his subconscious, the drachau brought his sword slashing down into the rusty chain binding the zombie to the bloated giant.

Silar rose from his abruptly lifeless foe. The severed chain flopped and flailed, flecks of rusty ichor dripping from its broken links. For all that it looked like iron, the chain was actually an extension of the behemoth, an umbilical attaching its slave to its grotesque bulk. Once that connection was broken, the power animating the drowned thrall was extinguished. Even as Silar scrambled away from the corpse, it was rapidly dissolving into a mire of putrescence.

Any jubilation at their victory over the corpse-puppet was quickly stifled. From the arm of the giant, a dozen other chains were dropping and with them a dozen more of the hideously animated carcasses. Behind the creatures came the monstrous hand of the giant itself. Malus tightened his grip on the warpsword, fearful that any moment Tz'arkan would again exert its debilitating malignance.

'Maybe Hadrith's pirates will kill it,' Silar said, pointing with his blade at the towers overhead. The giant was indeed beset by the black ark's defenders now. Repeater bolt throwers peppered the thing's ghastly flesh with yard-long spikes of steel. Bold corsairs swung out upon lines to hack at the titan with halberds and axes. Flocks of harpies darted about its skull, trying to claw eye-stalks from its face. The flash and fire of magic crackled and flamed about its body, charring small patches of the monster's skin.

An army was doing its best to fight off the giant, but Malus didn't think it would be enough. Tz'arkan might have lied to him about many things, but he was certain the daemon was right when it claimed the mortal barriers were breaking down. With the gates of reality ripped asunder, the ability of mortal weapons to visit harm against a daemonic behemoth such as this was doubtful. Such magic as was being employed against it was too little to cause any real hurt. Malus looked up towards the heights of the Star Spire. Lady Eldire and Drusala were up there, along with many of Fleetmaster Hadrith's own seers and sorceresses, yet there had been not even the slightest suggestion of attack from that quarter.

While the rest of the black ark fought for their lives, the Star Spire remained inactive. Malus would have an answer for such treachery.

'We have to get to Eldire,' Malus told Silar.

The retainer scowled as the first of the zombies reached the bridge and stirred into hideous animation. He managed to cut the chain binding one of them before it became fully active, but then was forced to retreat as the rest slashed at him with their weapons. 'I fear that won't be easy, my lord.'

Snarling, Malus sent the head of a drowned pirate hurtling from the bridge. 'Then we make it easy,' he vowed, pressing home his attack and breaking the umbilical feeding energy into the headless body.

A great shadow fell across Malus as he engaged another of the corpse-puppets. The drachau had only a second to dive aside before the gigantic paw of the giant came smashing down. The corpse he'd been fighting was obliterated by that huge hand. The whole bridge shook from the impact, chips of stone cascading down into the street below. The tendril-like fingers of the hand snaked about, squirming and oozing in every direction. Malus felt his gorge rise at the boneless, sinuous way the digits moved. Each was tipped not with a nail or claw, but a rounded leech-like mouth. He could see shreds of meat and armour caught in some of those mouths.

'You'll not feast on me!' Malus roared as one of the tendrils slithered towards him. The warpsword slashed across the finger, all but severing it. Wide as a man's body, the thing squirmed back, writhing and undulating. Other fingers came slithering around the bridge, some crawling up from beneath the span, to investigate the injury. Six gigantic tendrils turned upon Malus, their mouths uttering obscene ululations as they whipped out at him.

The warpsword severed one of the fingers, sending its wriggling hideousness into the crowd of terrified slaves below. Then the drachau was forced to retreat before the nest of abominable tentacles. It was all he could do to fend off the slobbering mouths and with each breath, the terror that Tz'arkan would immobilise him again grew.

Tremendous roars rang out from the end of the bridge. Malus was able to look past the nest of tentacles threatening him to see two enormous reptiles lumbering out onto the bridge. A company of beastmasters were goading them forwards with long spears and torches. Bigger than small whales, the reptiles stomped forwards on great clawed legs, their long bladed tails lashing angrily behind them. Bodies armoured in thick layers of scale, they ploughed through the corpse-puppets, snapping at them with their fanged maws. Each of the beasts boasted half a dozen heads, each one resting on a long, serpentine neck. There was no fear in their dull yellow eyes as they charged towards the titan's hand, only the limitless savagery of the most fearsome creatures ever bred by the beastmasters of Clar Karond: the war hydras.

Malus knew these beasts. He'd purchased them himself to augment the armies of Hag Graef, paying a small fortune to secure the biggest, most ferocious hydras ever to emerge from Clar Karond. He was still bitter over such squandered wealth. Only a few months after Griselfang and Snarclaw had been delivered to Hag Graef, the barbarian invasions and daemonic incursions had started. Clar Karond became a city under siege, desperate to sell anything and everything at any price just to bring more warriors to her defence.

Now, however, the colossal war hydras were showing their value. As they lumbered towards the titan's hand, Snarclaw reared its six heads. When it thrust them forwards once more, gouts of flame exploded from each maw, searing across the putrid meat before them. Griselfang roared, pushing past the other reptile in order to worry at the steaming flesh of the huge hand.

The tendrils that had a moment before been menacing Malus whipped back around, striking instead at Griselfang. The hydra bit back at the ropy fingers. Malus saw the hydra pull one of the wormy tentacles loose, as though uprooting a tree. The tendrils responded by wrapping around one of the reptile's necks and squeezing it mercilessly. Eventually the crushing pressure choked all life from the head. The tendrils withdrew, letting it flop lifelessly at the hydra's side. But even as life ebbed from the head, hideous new life coursed through Griselfang's frame. The dead neck and head burst, splashing gore across the bridge. Where the mangled flesh had been, two smaller heads now writhed, each snapping at the charred hand with vengeful ferocity.

Before the combined might of the two war hydras, the gigantic hand withdrew, retreating upwards. Bolts from repeater crossbows stabbed into the grotesque extremity, loosed by hundreds of Hag Graef's soldiers and the black ark's warriors. Nearer at hand, Malus saw a long spear hurled up at the hand to embed itself in the thing's palm. He locked eyes with the caster of that spear. The timely arrival of his war hydras was explained: Vincirix Quickdeath, making certain nothing dire could befall her lover and benefactor. The drachau started to walk towards her...

...Vincirix, Silar, the war hydras, the bridge itself vanished before Malus's eyes. One instant they were there, the next they were gone. Replacing them was a cold, dark room. Celestial shapes shone overhead, picked out in diamond and pearl with lines of platinum running between them to form the signs of the Cytharai and the Cadai. A great pattern glowed upon the floor beneath his feet, crushed rubies forming the lines of the Pantheonic Mandala. Upon the symbol designating each god and goddess, a disembodied heart lay in a pool of blood, the organs pulsing with impossible life. Only at the centre of the mandala, where the emblem of Khaine was depicted in bloodstone, was there no heart. Instead, a young elf boy stood, his body swaying in the grip of some hypnotic cadence.

Malus looked away from the esoteric scene, gazing instead at the people gathered around the edge of the mandala: Lady Eldire and the cabal of sorceresses she had gathered together. Somehow, he had been transported inside the Star Spire!

Eldire and the others stood in a wide circle, their hands linked. Crackling ribbons of aethyric energy played between them, provoking frost to form against their skin. Several of the sorceresses shuddered and shivered from something far more intense than the cold; two of them looked as though they had been shrivelled into mere husks, kept standing only by the hands of the druchii at either side of them.

There was only one gap in the circle. As Malus took stock of his surroundings, he saw Drusala waiting for him. Her expression was grave as she confronted the drachau. 'Your army will never reach Ulthuan if you do not protect this circle,' she warned him. 'The sea daemon will drown the *Eternal Malediction*. Our only hope for survival is to give it other prey.'

Malus looked over at his mother, but if Eldire was even aware of his presence, she gave no sign. 'How?' he demanded, returning his attention to Drusala. 'How will you save my army?'

Drusala indicated the young elf standing at the core of the mandala. 'A final offering to fuel the invocation,' she said. 'That is all you need to know. You must protect us until the ritual is finished.'

'Protect you from who? That giant?' Malus scoffed.

At a gesture from the sorceress, a door swung open at the end of the room, letting in a thin sliver of daylight. 'Stop the ones coming up the stair. If they reach this place, we are all finished.' She smiled, but it was a bitter, joyless look. 'My own precautions are not enough. Lady Eldire saw that much in her divinations.'

Drusala did not linger to explain more, but quickly returned to the circle, seizing the hands of the witches at either side of the gap. Malus wasn't sure if it was his imagination, but a shadowy knife seemed to appear beside the hypnotised youth.

Sorcery! He didn't understand how such things worked and even less did he understand the strange price demanded by magic. It was enough that such forces could be harnessed and put to use. If whatever Eldire and Drusala were conjuring could save them from the titan, he would play his part to bring such magic about.

Grimly, Malus stalked through the door. Somehow he wasn't surprised when it slid shut behind him. He was standing on a landing high upon the Star Spire. Below him, he could see the whole of the black ark. From this vantage, he could appreciate the gargantuan size of the giant and the havoc it was inflicting upon the *Eternal Malediction*. An entire tower had been ripped free, thrown into the sea by the raging behemoth. The same sorcery that supported the black ark kept the tower afloat, broken as it was. Strange sea scavengers darted about the shattered tower, picking bodies from the rubble.

Closer at hand, Malus could see the giant's head. Several clusters of eye-stalks stared back at him. There was no mistaking the abomination's hungry interest as it redoubled its efforts to batter a path through bridges now swarming with bowmen and war machines. He could feel Tz'arkan stir deep inside him, but the daemon at least had sense enough not to speak and goad the giant to greater effort.

Malus forced himself to tear his eyes from the behemoth to the stair leading down into Fleetmaster Hadrith's tower. At the edge of the stair, he saw a lone warrior standing guard. The elf had a sinister, eerie air about him, his black armour looking as though it had been hacked from a slab of malachite. His helm was tall, moulded to look like a mass of writhing serpents. He reminded Malus of a medusa, though even those terrible creatures would have had more vibrancy about them than this stony sentinel.

Beyond the guard, Malus saw a troop of corsairs rushing up the stair. At their head was Fleetmaster Hadrith, his sea-dragon cloak and cephalopod-styled armour distinct among that of his retinue. As they saw him, a cry of utter hate welled up from the corsairs. From their tone, Malus could guess that all of them had lost family to make room for Hag Graef's army.

'The fleetmaster looks upset,' Malus told the guard. He expected some kind of response, but all he got was the same stony silence. He hoped that the elf was better at fighting than he was at conversation.

The corsairs halted as they neared the top of the stair. Hadrith stepped forwards, pointing angrily at Malus. 'Stand aside, Darkblade. My business is with that scheming witch Drusala and your mother.'

'If you haven't noticed, there's a giant daemon ripping apart your black ark,' Malus said. 'I think you have bigger problems.'

Hadrith waved his sword at the drachau. 'They took my son, Darkblade. What does the black ark mean if I lose my legacy to keep it? Stand aside, and I will spare you.'

Malus shook his head. 'You seem to forget who is in command here.'

An animalistic snarl rasped through the vent in Hadrith's helm. 'Kill them!' The corsairs charged forwards at the fleetmaster's command.

What followed was a whirl of blades and bloodshed. Malus caught his first foe just as the warrior was thrusting his halberd at the drachau. The warpsword slashed through the haft of the weapon and the elbow of the arm behind it. The crippled elf shrieked as blood jetted from the stump of his arm. Malus shouted his own war-cry and kicked the mangled corsair down the stair, tripping up the pirate behind him and leaving the elf easy prey for a butchering sweep of the warpsword.

Beside him, the silent guard played his own deadly swordsmanship. Elves crippled by his blade fell screaming from the stair, hurtling to their destruction hundreds of feet below. The guard never uttered a sound, plying his gruesome art with the merciless precision of a machine. Even when a corsair's axe managed to slash his thigh, the guard didn't cry out but simply returned the hurt with a backhanded slash that opened his attacker's throat.

Fighting from the high ground, Malus and the guard held the corsairs at disadvantage. Hadrith's concern for his legacy had provoked the fleetmaster to act rashly, to ignore the development of a more cunning strategy. He'd depended too much on numbers and force of arms, perhaps upon charms and talismans to ward away sorcery. He hadn't planned on warriors of such quality defending the spire.

Suddenly, the entire ark shook, a great tremor rolling through it, the quaking sending more corsairs hurtling from the stair. A bright flash in the sky blinded Malus, causing him to stumble back. Almost at once, Hadrith was flying at him, the fleetmaster's sword upraised. Malus caught Hadrith on the warpsword's point, the enchanted blade ripping through his breastplate and the ribcage behind it.

Spitting blood, Hadrith thrust himself along the impaling blade, trying to bring his own sword slashing across Malus's neck. 'They... killed...'

Malus didn't let the fleetmaster finish. With a twist of his sword, he cut the noble in two, the severed halves rolling obscenely down the gore-slick stair. The few corsairs left standing turned and fled as they saw their leader cut down.

'I'll set Vincirix and her knights to finding them,' Malus said as he watched the corsairs flee. 'They won't be able to hide for long.' Again, his words brought no reaction from the silent guard. The sinister warrior simply turned and marched back to his place at the head of the stairs. Malus felt a chill crawl across his flesh. Even the corpse-puppets had been more lively than his late comrade-in-arms.

Thinking of the giant sea daemon, Malus cast his eyes downwards. He was shocked to find no trace of the abomination. The destruction it had wrought was all too visible, but the thing itself was gone. Vanished as completely as if the sky had swallowed it up. He could see equally shocked elves in the windows of the towers and on the bridges. He followed the pointing hands of several druchii. Far across the waves, another black ark floated upon the sea. That vessel was now listing to port, caught in the vicious embrace of the sea daemon.

Icy fingers played down Malus's spine as he considered the wrongness of what he was seeing, the uncanny magnitude of the magic his mother and the others had invoked. The shudder and the flash, that had been the mark of Lady Eldire's great spell. Hadrith had known that, recognised it as the sign that his son had been rendered up as the final sacrifice.

'The daemon has been given new prey.' Malus looked up to see Drusala standing at the head of the stairs, one arm draped teasingly across the blood-soaked shoulder of the silent guard. She smiled coyly. 'That is the *Relentless Retribution*. The ritual we cast allowed us to switch places with her in much the same way that I was able to transport you from the foot of the spire to the top. Only on a much grander scale. Six of the circle were drained completely by the spell.'

'My mother?' Malus asked.

Drusala drew back one of her raven locks, tucking it behind her ear. 'She was not one of the six. The experience has wearied her, but she will recover.' As though irritated by the question, she pointed again to the black ark. The giant was starting to pull it under, dragging it into the depths. 'I believe Lady Khyra was on that vessel. We determined that she was behind the attempt on your life. I thought you would be happy to know she won't be able to do it again.'

'Then I will be able to focus on other threats,' Malus said, just the most subtle edge of menace underlying his words.

'Just be certain who is enemy and who is ally,' Drusala advised him. Stroking the shoulder of the guard, she beckoned the warrior to follow her back inside the spire. 'Come, Absaloth. The danger is past.'

Malus watched them disappear into the Star Spire, then turned to watch as the sea daemon finished sinking the *Relentless Retribution*. The deaths of thousands didn't move him; he'd seen massacres on a such scale before. It was the thought that such a fate could so easily have been his that made Malus sombre.

Be careful of that witch.

'I intend to,' Malus growled at the daemon inside his head, annoyed by Tz'arkan's renewed intrusion. Especially to state something he already knew.

She is more dangerous than you think, Darkblade. She can see me. She knows I'm inside you.

Part Two

EAGLE GATE

Late winter 2523–Summer 2524

CHAPTER SEVEN

The ragged coastline of Ulthuan stretched away along the eastern horizon, shores so abrupt they might have been hewn by one of Addaioth's crooked swords. Here and there a crag of crumbling rock thrust itself up from the pounding waves, rotten fingers of stone that might once have been hills or mountains. At the height of the Great Sundering, when the treacherous followers of the false king Caledor sought to vanquish the faithful subjects of Malekith, the most powerful magic known to elves wrought destruction upon the realms of Nagarythe and Tiranoc.

Tidal waves a thousand feet high swept over the lands, drowning thousands, fouling the once lush countryside, obliterating the gleaming cities and soaring towers. Much of Tiranoc was sheared from the rest of Ulthuan, sent sliding into the sea. Beneath the waves, the streets of drowned cities could yet be seen, fish swimming through the weed-wrapped columns of palaces and temples.

Greatest of these sunken ruins was Tor Anroc, a place yet haunted by the ghosts of those who perished in the cataclysm. Even druchii invasion fleets gave Tor Anroc a wide berth, many of the corsairs claiming that sailing over any part of the drowned city would cause the sea god Mathlann to forsake their fleets.

As he studied the coast, Malus felt only contempt for the religious superstition of the corsairs. Mathlann had done nothing to help them against the great sea daemon that had tried to sink the *Eternal Malediction*. For the Lord of the Deeps, Mathlann had been noticeably reluctant to draw the creature back into the depths. If not for the sorcery of Eldire and Drusala, their voyage would have ended in disaster long before they came within spitting distance of Tor Anroc and the curse of its ghosts.

The real threat posed by Tor Anroc lay in that part of the city which the asur had rebuilt, a naval fortress that guarded the approaches to the western shore and whose artillery loosed pots of alchemical fire so fierce even the sea couldn't extinguish the flames. Flotillas of small, sleek galleys were anchored in the fortified harbour, ready to set sail at a moment's notice to harry any invader. The mages of Tiranoc were even known to conjure mighty merwyrms from the waters that had swallowed their old lands, and the great sea serpents were easily capable of crushing a ship in their coils, a menace to any raider not embarked on a helldrake or black ark.

And, of course, the biggest hazard offered by Tor Anroc was the simple fact that the city would spread the alarm to the rest of Ulthuan. The asur would be alerted to the return of their betrayed kin. They would muster their armies and march to repulse the druchii, to drive the invaders back into the sea. This time, with even their exile kingdom lost to them, the druchii couldn't allow their landings to be repulsed. They had to succeed, or perish in the attempt. Avoiding Tor Anroc would gain them precious hours, perhaps even a full day, to seize their beachheads. While the fleet of Drane Blackblood harried the asur naval patrols and Lokhir Fellheart led his fleet to the south and the harbours of Tor Dranil and Merokai, Malus would have a prime opportunity to wage his own war and claim his own measure of glory.

Malus crushed the scroll he held in his hand, feeling the flayed strip of skin crinkle under his grip. Dictates from the Witch King were inked in the blood of traitors on the hides of their offspring, the seals affixed to them crafted from the fat of the selfsame traitors. Such gruesome missives were a reminder that Malekith was watching, and of what the recipients' fates would be should they fail their king.

The army of Hag Graef had been given a singular honour. They would lead the attack on Ulthuan. They would be the first to land in Tiranoc, the first to confront the wrathful warriors of the shattered kingdom. The *Eternal Malediction* was to beach itself, hurl itself far out upon the shore. The ancient enchantments that kept the black ark buoyant would be dispelled, severed by the Witch King's own cabal of sorceresses. The vessel would remain as a bastion, a citadel from whence Malus would stage his attack. The ships of the fleet would be broken up, their timber used to craft siege engines and cartage for the army, their iron fastenings reforged into shields and spears, their sails cut into tents and blankets for the long march to the Annulii Mountains and the Inner Kingdoms beyond.

This was what Malekith had spared him for! A suicidal probe against the most heavily defended of Ulthuan's Outer Kingdoms! A feint to draw the attention of the asur while the rest of the invasion massed in the south. Once the asur were committed, the Witch King would order the rest of the black arks to loose their warriors on the shores of Nagarythe, reclaim the old homeland. Malus knew he was being sacrificed; he had known it the moment the black dragon had descended from the stormy sky and its rider handed him the royal command.

Yet what else was there but to obey? Naggaroth was lost; there was nowhere to sail back to. The choice of retreat had been taken away the moment he'd abandoned Hag Graef.

Still, perhaps there was a way. The army of Hag Graef was larger even than that of Naggarond, bolstered by the enslaved Naggorites and the refugees from Clar Karond. He even had the expeditionary force from Ghrond that had accompanied Drusala. If he struck swiftly, if he was ruthless enough and spared nothing to move his army at speed, there was just a chance he could outwit the Witch King. If Malus's landing was intended as a sacrificial feint, then he would turn it into a victorious conquest! Even Malekith would have a hard time arguing with victory.

Malus turned from the balcony high upon the fleetmaster's tower. After the death of Hadrith, the drachau had assumed virtual command of the black ark, installing an opportunistic corsair named Aeich as the new fleetmaster. His sycophantic minion had rendered up the royal chambers for Malus's own use. He wondered if Aeich was still so eager to please now that the order to beach the black ark had been given. He rather supposed it put a kink in Aeich's ideas about the power he thought he'd inherited.

'You have conceived a plan, my lord?' Vincirix had cast aside the brief, loose robes that she'd adopted in her role as the drachau's consort. With the shores of Tiranoc just beyond the black ark, she again wore the steel plate and chain befitting a Knight of the Ebon Claw. Malus smiled at the cold lines of her armour, the slumbering lethality of the sword and clawed mace hanging from her belt. If anything, he found her more enticing this way. Nothing soft and weak, only the merciless strength of a true daughter of Naggaroth.

He waved the ghoulish proclamation at her. 'I have an idea,' he said. 'But it will take craft to implement it properly.' Malus tapped the rolled sheet of flayed skin against his thigh. 'It is a great gamble. The wager must be everything or nothing.'

'One wins nothing without risk,' Vincirix said. 'The bigger the gamble, the greater the prize.'

Malus laid his hand against his lover's cheek, giving it an ungentle pat. 'This isn't helping a nubile wench in her patricidal fantasies,' he said, draining some of the self-assurance from her eyes. After helping save his life by leading the war hydras to the attack, she'd become a bit too certain of her place. Malus needed her insecure. The hunger to prove herself, to maintain everything she'd managed to acquire would be a valuable asset on the battlefield. If she was worried about displeasing him, she'd push her knights to the limit of endurance and beyond.

The drachau turned and paced through the opulently appointed parlour of the late Hadrith. At each step, he slapped the royal command against his leg, reminding himself of the magnitude of the responsibility resting on him now. There could be no half measures if he was going to prevail. At the same time, failure would mean complete destruction. If his name was remembered at all, it would be as that of a reckless fool.

But to dare! To trick that conniving tyrant. If he won through, his name would be heaped with glory and envy. He'd be greater than all the dreadlords. Greater, perhaps, than the Witch King himself, for he would have done what Malekith had never been able to do. The Witch King expected to spend the lives of Malus's army and eliminate the enemy within by setting him against the asur. The last thing Malekith would be ready for would be a victorious Malus.

'It is a kingdom I gamble for now,' Malus told Vincirix. 'That is why the wager must be so costly.' His hand tightened around the decree, causing the traitor-fat seal to crack. 'But maybe there is a way that I can hedge my bet.' He spun around and pointed at the knight. 'Find that buzzard Korbus. Tell him that I want my mother to disembark with the first wave. I want her ready to perform one of her auguries as soon as she is set ashore.'

Vincirix looked uneasy as she heard her lover's command. 'Your mother will listen to no one but you, my lord. If you would have her obey, you should speak to her personally.'

Malus shook his head. 'No,' he said. He removed one of the rings from his fingers and set it in the knight's hand. 'Give Korbus this and he will know the command comes from me. I will not see my mother until she is ready to relate to me what the future holds.' A scowl briefly worked itself onto his face. 'If I saw her before, she might cause me to falter in my purpose.' With a wave of his hand, Malus dismissed Vincirix to hurry away on her errand.

Left alone, the drachau stepped back to the balcony, casting his gaze once more upon the broken shore of Tiranoc. How much blood had the druchii shed here over the ages, trying to seize the land from their hated kin? How much more would it cost before they were victorious? How much was he willing to sacrifice for that triumph?

He almost expected the sneering voice of Tz'arkan to slither through his brain, mocking him for his timidity and his ruthlessness. The daemon was capricious and saw no vice in hypocrisy. A lie wrapped in a truth disguised in a falsehood, that was the parasite's favourite manner.

The daemon, however, had been curiously silent since the sea titan had taken Lady Khyra to a watery grave. Malus hadn't even felt the need to drink his draught much, just enough to keep his senses at the proper degree of wariness. What Tz'arkan was about, he couldn't begin to guess. It had claimed Drusala had seen it when they were in the Star Spire. If so, the sorceress had made no move to denounce him. Daemonic possession was the sort of affliction that no dreadlord, not even the most powerful, could survive if it was exposed to his peers. His own subjects would rise up and tear him limb from limb, even more so now that Naggaroth had been abandoned to the bestial creatures of Chaos.

The prudent thing for Malus to do would be to have Drusala murdered. That would ensure the safety of his secret. Wisdom demanded such a course. It was for that very reason he was indecisive. He still harboured suspicions that Tz'arkan had deliberately drawn the sea daemon to attack the black ark. He couldn't trust anything the parasite told him. It might share his skin, but it didn't share his life. It had its own ambitions and desires. It would do anything to break free of him. Goading him into killing someone who could help him was just the sort of ploy that would appeal to Tz'arkan's perverse humour.

No, despite the danger, Malus couldn't act until he was sure. His mother had been incapable of freeing him from the daemon, but Drusala had been handmaiden to Morathi herself. She doubtless knew things even Eldire didn't, things that might be a threat to Tz'arkan.

Such concerns were for the future, however. At the moment, the success of his invasion was the only thing that mattered. Securing a victory that even the Witch King would be unable to take away from him. Without that, even if Drusala exposed him it wouldn't matter.

He could only die once.

Columns of spearmen and swordsmen marched from the black ark's belly, trooping down iron bridges and timber platforms. As each druchii set foot upon the shore, he turned his head and spit on the sands of Tiranoc, an ancient gesture of contempt for the hated asur who had driven their ancestors from Ulthuan. Even in this, the final battle with their treacherous kin, the druchii clung to the traditions of hate.

From a small hillock, seated in Spite's saddle, Malus watched as his army disembarked from the *Eternal Malediction*. Aeich had run the black ark aground, the huge vessel gouging a deep furrow in the rock and sand as its magic failed and it entrenched itself in the shore of Tiranoc. Corsairs were already scavenging timber from their ships to erect a palisade around the beached city, a wall to hold back any asur raiders. As yet, there had been no sign of Tiranoc's people, but the druchii knew it was only a matter of time before the vengeful natives came down from their cities to repulse the invaders. By that time, the fleetmaster intended to have defences in place to protect the black ark.

Malus had encouraged Aeich in his plans. He'd sent troops of doomfire warlocks and dark riders galloping off into the countryside to ostensibly spy out the land and determine the position of a gathering enemy. On their swift horses, the squadrons of cavalry could cover a vast area in a short amount of time. He'd impressed on them the urgency of their mission; the threat of failing the drachau was enough to make even the murderous warlocks set aside their need for slaughter. They'd soon bring back the intelligence the invaders needed.

Of course, if Eldire's prophecies were auspicious, that information might not be put to the purpose Aeich expected.

Across the beach, Malus could see the baggage train of his warhost slowly taking shape. Such slaves as hadn't been butchered during the long voyage from Naggaroth were now pressed into service, toiling away under the lashes of their cruel masters. He could see Kunor mounted upon a black charger galloping up and down the beachhead, plying his whip across the backs of his Naggorites, forcing the enslaved druchii to unload the ships the corsairs had driven up onto the rocky shelf. Kunor didn't need an excuse to indulge his sadism. When purpose was linked to his penchant for brutality, the slavemaster was utterly without pity or restraint.

A tumult around the black ark marked the unloading of Griselfang and Snarclaw. The gigantic war hydras struggled against the chains with which they were bound, their jaws straining against the steel muzzles that bound their snouts closed. More chains restrained their tails, keeping the reptiles from smashing their keepers with a slap of the long, scaly columns of flesh. As the straining, vicious beasts were led down one of the bridges by a small army of beast-breakers, Vincirix Quickdeath and her Knights of the Ebon Claw waited in a solemn formation along the shore, lances at the ready and their cold ones sniffing and snarling at the air. The gigantic war hydras were a powerful weapon in the arsenal of Hag Graef. Too powerful. If they broke free and raged among Malus's forces, the toll they would take would be hideous. Better to kill the brutes than have his own warriors massacred.

A low growl rumbled from the depths of Spite's throat. Malus could feel the reptile's body become tense beneath him. He slapped the side of the horned one's snout, warning it to be still. He knew what had agitated his steed; he didn't even need to turn around to know that a rider was approaching. Spite was an excellent judge of character, but the poor brute simply didn't have the wit to understand that people of low quality and verminous morality had their uses.

A lone cold one loped towards Malus's position. When it was still a dozen yards away, the reptile's pace slackened, and it dipped its head in an attitude of submission, trying to make its huge body seem smaller than it was. Deep scars marked the creature's scales, the reminder of the claws and fangs that had likewise left their imprint on the beast's tiny brain. The cold one had made the mistake of challenging Spite once before. It wouldn't make that mistake again.

The reptile's rider dismounted and removed his helm. Unlike his steed, the knight knew better than to ever challenge Malus. He'd seen for himself what happened to those who did. Indeed, he'd helped make it happen many times.

'Dolthaic, old comrade,' Malus greeted the knight as he bowed to the drachau. Dolthaic was the deposed heir of a noble house in Naggarond. His birthright usurped, he'd taken up the mercenary trail, gathering to him a vicious cadre of warriors he'd formed into the Knights of the Burning Dark. The sell-swords had long been in the service of Hag Graef, long enough that they'd earned too many enemies elsewhere to ever leave Malus's service. Calling Dolthaic comrade was like calling a loyal dog 'brother', and the hesitation the knight exhibited as he approached told Malus that neither the irony nor the insult was lost on him.

'Dreadlord, the offerings have been rendered up to Khaine,' Dolthaic reported.

Malus sneered at the knight's piety. He seemed to believe Khaine would smile down on them because they'd spilled a few bottles of wine and opened the bellies of a dozen slaves in his name. They asked their god to deliver to them victory over the asur and offered so little for such beneficence. It would be hilarious if it wasn't so pathetic.

'Khaine respects those who do not beg his favours,' Malus said, 'those who take for themselves what they desire! The only offering worthy of Khaine is victory, Dolthaic. Remember that.'

The chastened knight bowed his head once more. 'Yes, dreadlord.'

'Lord Silar has deployed the first cohort?'

Dolthaic nodded. 'They have assembled at the edge of the plain. The bolt throwers are in position just below the shelf. The crews have been given their orders. My knights are poised to support them, should the need arise.'

Malus smiled at the report. Silar was a capable lieutenant, but sometimes insufficiently ruthless. If the asur attacked while the core of their army was disembarking, the invasion would be over before it could properly begin. Against that possibility, Malus had dispatched a small force out beyond the beach, bait the vengeful elves of Tiranoc would be certain to seize upon. The small vanguard would be routed; they'd flee back to the beaches and draw the pursuing asur straight into the waiting bolt throwers. It would, of necessity, be costly for the vanguard, but if the natives fell into the trap, it would blunt their initial assault against the landings.

'Good, Dolthaic. If we can keep the asur off the beaches until the rest of the army disembarks, this enterprise may yet prove itself.' Malus eyed the mercenary, his expression growing thoughtful. 'There should be good pickings for your knights once we penetrate into the Inner Kingdoms.'

The mercenary's face betrayed no change in expression, but Malus could read the elf's avarice in his body language. The Knights of the Burning Dark were reckoned the most dependable troops in his army not because they owed any unusual loyalty to Malus or Hag Graef, but because they didn't. Their motive was simple greed – they took the drachau's coin and he paid them better than they could expect from any other dreadlord. Among the maze of hatreds and jealousies that ruled the hearts of most druchii, greed was pure and predictable. A warrior motivated by greed could be depended upon without the undue worry about what ulterior agenda might be lurking in the shadows of his soul. That was why Malus had set Vincirix and the Knights of the Ebon Claw the task of watching his war hydras. He could afford to lose the refugees from Clar Karond far more easily than Dolthaic's mercenaries.

'When do we march?' Dolthaic asked.

'Patience, old comrade,' Malus said. 'First I must know *where* before I can know *when.*' He looked back towards the beach, chuckling as he watched an elf hurrying across the rocks towards him. From the awkwardness of his movements, it seemed that he was unaccustomed to the heavy mail he now wore. 'Unless I am mistaken, I should be getting an answer to that question very soon.' Malus dismissed Dolthaic with a wave of his hand. He didn't want the mercenary around when the messenger arrived. Saluting his master, Dolthaic hurried back to his waiting steed and rode off to where his knights were lurking.

Malus let his eyes rove across the confusion of activity along the shore, the corsairs breaking their ships with mauls and sledges, the beast-keepers herding their ghastly creatures of war through the shallows, the infantry marching stoically towards the enemy shore. Tents and pavilions had already been erected, the banners of nobles and warrior companies fluttering in the salty breeze. A plume of smoke wafted into the sky from a hastily assembled shrine to Khaine. Harpies wheeled overhead as they emerged from the cramped cages that had borne them from Naggaroth.

The thing he was looking for defied his vision. Nowhere did he see the pavilion of Lady Eldire. He knew his mother had obeyed his command and joined the first wave of invaders. Somewhere down there, her shelter had been pitched. Perhaps she'd spared some small measure of her magic to disguise the place. After the sacrifice of Hadrith's son and the deaths of so many of the black ark's seers, there were many among the fleet who bore the sorceress malice. Enemies who had their own magic to call upon. It was only prudent that she would take steps to protect herself.

The armoured messenger finally reached the rise. Malus grinned coldly at Korbus as his mother's servant bowed before him. The petty sorcerer looked absurd in the old armour he was wearing. 'You look like a rat playing wolf,' Malus scolded the servant. 'What did you do, strip a drowned Naggorite on your way here?'

Korbus kept his eyes averted and emotion from his voice when he answered. 'Lady Eldire felt I would be more inconspicuous if I looked like a warrior.'

Malus laughed at the declaration. '*If* you looked like a warrior. My mother should have disguised you as a slave, Korbus. You would wear rags better than mail.' A kick of his heels brought Spite lurching towards the servant. The horned one's forked tongue flickered out as it tasted the conjurer's smell. Korbus recoiled from the reptilian brute.

'What word do you bring me from Eldire?' Malus demanded. A rumbling hiss from Spite added still more menace to the drachau's question.

'All is in readiness, dreadlord,' Korbus said. 'She is prepared to work her auguries. She but awaits your presence.' He hesitated, licking his lips nervously. 'She says that to ensure the accuracy of her divinations, she will need some of your blood.'

'So long as mother doesn't take too much, eh, loyal Korbus?' Malus joked. He glanced back across the beachhead, still unable to find anything that resembled his mother's pavilion. 'You lead the way,' he ordered Eldire's consort. A prod of his boot against Spite's ribs brought a growl from the beast. 'Not that I doubt your loyalty, or mother's, but you should understand that if anything happens, you die first. Remember that, Korbus.'

'Of course, dreadlord,' Korbus said. The conjurer's voice was firm and properly deferential, but he couldn't quite hide the anxious tremble in his step as he led Malus down from the rise.

Malus was careful to keep a few yards between himself and Korbus as they climbed down from the rise. Just enough space so he could keep his eye on his guide, but not so much distance that Spite couldn't leap upon the elf at the first hint of treachery.

Even when it came to his own mother, Malus felt it judicious to be cautious.

CHAPTER EIGHT

The smell of death struck Malus the instant he flung aside the curtain covering the entrance to his mother's pavilion. The stench lent a still more sinister air to the place, as though its sorcerous camouflage wasn't uncanny enough. Even with Korbus guiding him, Malus had been unable to see the pavilion until he was only a few feet away from it. It wasn't invisible; the magic in play was more subtle than that. It was as if his eyes had refused to focus on the tent, sliding away from its image, straying from it to gaze elsewhere. When he came within a dozen yards of it, a clamminess wrapped itself around him, an oily sensation that repulsed him and made him want to draw away. Spite had felt it too, refusing Malus's efforts to drive the reptile onwards. He'd been forced to dismount and leave the beast behind as he followed Korbus that last leg of their journey.

Now he stood within his mother's sanctum. Malus watched as Korbus walked over and ignited a brazier of coals with a wave of his hand. The drachau shook his head at the display. Whether the conjurer had evoked some petty spell or had simply dropped some caustic powder on the smouldering coals, Malus wasn't impressed.

He glanced at the rich tapestries draped about the walls of the pavilion, arcane glyphs woven into each one in threads of silver and gold. Dried heads and hands, desiccated herbs and bundles of roots and weeds dangled from the poles that gave the grand tent its shape. On the floor, a rug cast into the patterns of the Pantheonic Mandala stretched across the floor, the symbol of Khaine at the heart of the mandala glowing with an eerie crimson light. He could feel icy fingers of magic pawing at him, blindly groping at his flesh. A phantasmal music tugged just at the edge of his hearing, indefinable melodies that both enticed and horrified. In the depths of his soul, Malus could feel Tz'arkan stir, responding to some aethyric vibration only spirits could sense.

'Lady Eldire is beyond the veil,' Korbus announced, beckoning Malus towards a dark curtain. Malus recognised that curtain. It had been woven from the tresses of Hag Graef's fallen sorceresses, shorn from their corpses before the last warmth deserted their cold flesh. The Naggorites had called such a veil a 'soul hanging', believing that the spirits of those whose hair was bound into it were enslaved and compelled to ward away inimical magics directed against those who sheltered behind them.

'Leave us,' Malus ordered Korbus. There was only the briefest flicker of hesitation on Korbus's part, then his mother's servant bowed and withdrew from the pavilion. Malus waited until the conjurer was gone, then brushed aside the soul hanging and stepped into the gloom behind the partition. The stench of death intensified and closed around him, drawing him into itself in a cadaverous embrace. His hand tightened about the warpsword's hilt.

A strange blue light slowly grew from the darkness, illuminating a space that appeared impossibly vast for it to exist within the confines of his mother's pavilion. The curtains and tapestries lining the walls were familiar to him, recalling Eldire's sanctum inside the Scion's Tower in Hag Graef. Somehow, Malus felt that if he reached out and pulled aside those hangings he would find not the canvas of the pavilion but the stone of his abandoned palace behind them. It was an impossible prospect that made his heart clench inside his chest.

Seated on the floor, her legs crossed beneath her, was Lady Eldire. She wore the black silks of a sorceress, her hair bound within the claws of a filigree basilisk, its eyes shining with a strange luminescence in the weird blue witchlight. Around her was a circle drawn in powdered bone and around it a second ring rendered from the intestines of a harpy. Between the two grisly circles were drawn the astrological symbols of each of the Cytharai.

Eldire's eyes were closed, her face drawn and pale. She held one hand against her heart, while the other was stretched before her in an arresting gesture, as though pushing against some unseen barrier. She didn't look at her son when she spoke. 'I ask you, Malus, to reconsider what you would have of me. The aethyr is in turmoil. The old magic runs wild and is slow to heed the command of even Eldire.'

Malus stepped towards his mother, careful to keep beyond the arcane circles she had crafted about herself. 'I must know,' he told her. 'You are the only one I can trust to gaze ahead and tell me what waits there. Glory or death, I must know!'

A despairing sigh shook the sorceress. For the first time, Malus noticed wrinkles marring his mother's beauty, saw hints of silver polluting her black tresses. Until this moment, he hadn't considered the toll her divinations might exact from her. There could be no going back, however. If he relented now, he would lose everything. He would be nothing more than Malekith's pawn, cast aside while the Witch King's armies fought the real battle far away. His name would be reduced to a jest – the hapless dreadlord who'd been massacred while the host of Naggaroth made war against the asur.

'The future, mother,' Malus hissed. 'I must know what it holds. I must know the path to take.'

Eldire's outstretched hand trembled, her splayed fingers twisting into patterns that threatened to dislocate every bone. 'The pattern of what is yet to come is ever in flux. Every decision we make, every choice we abandon, every action we bring into being sends ripples through that pattern. To steal secrets from the future is to catch smoke in one's hand. Only the most powerful sorceries can lend solidity to the smoke, can pour reality into what is only possibility.'

'You have such power, mother,' Malus said. 'Among all of Malekith's fleet, there is no sorceress as mighty as you.'

Eldire shook her head slowly. 'I am alone, Malus. A manticore is mighty, but it is alone. The dogs are weak, but they are many. Their numbers make a strength that can overcome the might of that which is alone.'

Malus stood and glared down at his mother. 'You delay!' he accused. 'Who would dare raise their hand against you while I am still drachau. You aren't alone. You have the might of Hag Graef to protect you. What enemy do you fear? The witches of the black ark? I'll have Aeich slaughter them for you and bring you their hearts. Drusala? What can that enchantress do to threaten someone who defied Morathi herself?'

Eldire sighed once more. 'The answers you seek are already here,' she said. 'In my auguries, I saw you would not be dissuaded from your purpose, yet I refused to abandon hope.'

Malus felt a tremor of fear pass through him. 'The omens are ill, then? You have foreseen disaster?'

'To look into the future is to give it shape,' Eldire answered. 'To give it shape is to wrap chains around the present. Prophecy binds the present to itself, compels the purpose of now to fulfil the dictates of what is yet to be.'

For the first time, she opened her eyes. Malus recoiled when he saw that Eldire's eyes had become black pits, like chips of obsidian set into her face. Little fingers of pulsating darkness wriggled from her pupils, as though beckoning to him. 'The abyss of eternity holds all that is possible. To pluck from it what might have been and transform it into what will be is a magic even the gods fear to contemplate.' Eldire's voice trailed away, losing volume and vibrancy. It seemed the most colossal effort when she pointed a finger towards something lying sprawled on the floor.

His flesh cold from the dreadful emanations of such potent magic, Malus slowly approached the prostrate form. The stink of death clung heavy to it. The mutilations visited upon it made it impossible to tell if the corpse had recently been either man or elf. What he could tell was that the victim had been alive when the worst of the atrocities were inflicted upon it. The forbidden names of Hekarti, the Mistress of Magic, entwined with the obscene glyphs of Atharti, Lady of Desires. Even an outsider like himself understood the danger of invoking both of the Cytharai sisters in the same ritual, for they were the most dire of enemies. He could only wonder at what kind of ritual demanded such power that such evocation was unavoidable.

'Reach inside the offering and remove the heart,' Eldire told her son, her voice now not much more than a whisper. 'Crush it in your hand. Squeeze the blood from the dead flesh and you will find the future you seek.'

Through one of the ghastly cuts inflicted on the corpse, Malus worked his hand between shattered ribs and torn flesh. His fingers froze when he felt the heart beneath them. The organ was moist and warm to his touch, and as his fingers lingered, he felt a hideous pulsation pass through them. The heart yet beat! By some unspeakable magic, there was life still pulsating through this abominably tortured body.

Where another elf might have quailed in horror at so obscene a spectacle, Malus firmed his grip and yanked at the beating heart. Inch by inch, he worked it free from its fleshy moorings, drawing it back through the broken chest that had once housed it. As he removed it, he saw that the thing had turned black, cancerous with the same aethyric taint he'd seen in his mother's eyes. Black worms, no more solid than a shadow, slithered and writhed from the organ as he tightened his grip and began to squeeze.

Drop by drop, the blood began to seep from the heart onto the floor – far more blood than it could possibly have held. Soon there was a puddle at Malus's feet, and within that puddle he saw things, images that flickered and changed with each drop that fell from the heart.

He saw the great army of Hag Graef marching away from the shore of Tiranoc. He saw his warriors ranging across the land, seeking battle with the asur. He saw skirmishes with the bastard kin of Nagarythe and raids mounted by the chariots of Tiranoc – far too little to threaten the mighty host he had unleashed against Ulthuan. Onwards his army pressed, the asur refusing to give them the mighty battle they sought. Then the Annulii Mountains loomed before them, towering above the landscape. Between the snow-capped peaks, there was the pass connecting the Shadowlands of old Nagarythe and Ellyrion, joining the Outer Kingdoms to the Inner Kingdoms. Blocking that pass, its battlements soaring hundreds of feet between the mountains flanking it, was the Eagle Gate.

For an instant, Malus felt his ambition turn sour. This was the fortress Malekith had commanded him to take. This was the place where the despot expected him to die. He gazed upon the massive stronghold with its megalithic gates, at the glittering spears and helms of the army garrisoning it, at the fiery wings and cold claws of the giant phoenixes that soared above it. He heard the names of great heroes whispered to him – Yvarin and Shrinastor – and he felt despair begin to bind his hopes.

Then, in the pool of blood, Malus saw a sight no druchii had ever seen. He saw the titanic doors of the Eagle Gate torn asunder. He saw the towering battlements crack and crumble. He saw the gleaming army vanquished, their dead impaled upon their own spears, a grisly forest to honour Khaine and the ancient hate of the druchii.

Malus grinned. His mother had peered into the world beyond worlds, and brought back omens of glory and victory. Victory such as would shame even the Witch King's pride!

'You may rest now, mother,' Malus said as he cast aside the shrivelled heart. He saw her hand slip away from her own heart, watched as the blackness faded from her eyes and she slumped forwards. He rushed to her side, wondering if he should have heeded her warning, if maybe he hadn't demanded too much of her sorcery.

'You have seen?' Eldire asked. With the spell broken, there was already a bit more vibrancy in her voice.

'I saw,' Malus told her. 'Your magic has told me what I must do.'

Lady Eldire looked at him, her gaze penetrating deep into his soul. 'Prophecy is a lie we tell ourselves. Be certain of what you have seen. Beware that it is not what you merely wanted to see.'

Malus laughed. 'This vision is both. It is victory.'

Eldire pulled away from him. 'Then I am pleased,' she said. 'All I have done has been for you, Malus. Always remember that. You are my legacy. Your glory is my triumph.'

With his mother's words still ringing in his ears, Malus was stunned to find himself no longer standing in the blue light. He was back among the tents, right beside the place he had hobbled Spite. Ahead of him, he could feel the clammy wrongness attached to his mother's pavilion, but he could no longer see the place.

Malus shrugged aside the disorienting wrongness of his magical ejection from Eldire's presence. She had shown him what he wanted to know. There wasn't anything else he needed of her. At least for now.

'Come along, old comrade,' Malus said to Spite as he climbed into the horned one's saddle. 'I have new orders to give my army.

'Now I can tell them where they're going.'

Lady Eldire could feel the shadows of unborn potentialities clinging to her, trying to draw existence from the magic that coursed through her body. Removing the clinging embers of possibility from her was like burning leeches from flesh. It was a revolting, painful necessity. Each dream she burned away, each parasitic hope that thought to fatten itself upon her sorcery, each reflection of what could have been but would never be, all of them took their toll upon her stamina.

She should have refused Malus's command. In more stable times, when the aethyr hadn't been transformed into a raging cataract of magic and the tides of Chaos weren't spilling into the mortal realm in a deluge of arcane malignance, she would have been able to render her divinations more easily. They wouldn't have left her feeling like a dried-out husk.

No, Eldire corrected herself, even then, even with the full resources of Hag Graef at her beck and call, what she had done for Malus would have been no easy thing. She had indeed seen his future. She had seen what would be. With her magic, she had changed what was to come. Her vision had penetrated beyond the cascade of time, into the morass of possibility, into the streams of not merely what *would* be but of what *could* be. Merely gazing upon such things was a mark of the mightiest sorcery, but to reach into that pool of impossibilities, to draw it out and graft it to the stem of eventuality, to take the unreal and compel it to become real – that was a magic only the cold-blooded toad-mages of the jungle dared to harness. One misstep, the tiniest falter of heart or mind, and such magic would do more than destroy. It would obliterate. It would erase. What it consumed wouldn't simply die, it would never have been.

She had reached into the pool of never and brought forth victory for her son. She had bound a dream of conquest to the fact of Malus's army marching from their beachhead. She had seen that impossible vision, of Malus making war upon the shores of Chrace, and she had chained it to the flow of the present.

She hoped it was enough. She begged Hekarti that it was enough. Through Malus, she could carve a legacy. Without him, she could build nothing.

Had she done enough? Had she done enough to change that awful future she'd seen, the vision she dared not even whisper? To speak the future was to give it shape – that was the true threat of prophecy. How many divinations had brought themselves into being over the long march of history? She could not risk even a single gesture, a single word, that might bring Malus to the end she had foreseen!

Eldire rose to her feet, aware that she was no longer alone in her sanctum. This refuge existed in the spaces between space, neither fixed to her pavilion on the shore of Ulthuan nor her chambers in Hag Graef. It was possible some daemon might intrude upon such a shadow place, but the presence she sensed was mortal, or at least near enough to mortality to clothe itself in flesh, to have a heart beating in its breast and a brain thinking inside its skull.

'Who is there?' Eldire called out, her hands already tightening about the protective talismans hanging about her waist.

A soft laugh answered her. 'Is your sorcery so feeble that you do not know?' a mocking voice called out from the darkness.

The note of mockery vanished as the sanctum suddenly blazed with cold blue light. The gruesome conjuring circles, the sacrificial victim, the discarded heart and the pool of blood all stood revealed in the violent illumination. So too did a slender she-elf dressed in robes of purple and scarlet, a high collar of gold circling her delicate neck.

'Drusala,' Eldire hissed. 'You dare much. What errand has Morathi set you upon? Did your mistress think to settle one of her petty jealousies through you?'

Drusala paced slowly around the sanctum, careful to avoid the pool of blood Malus had squeezed from the heart. 'I came of my own accord,' she told Eldire.

'Then you are a fool,' Eldire said. 'Your mistress did not dare to strike against me. What makes you think you can do more than she?'

'Perhaps the opportunity never presented itself before,' Drusala said. 'Or maybe you were deemed unworthy of the effort.' She stared into Eldire's face and smiled. 'Until now.'

One instant, Drusala's hand was empty, in the next she held a long staff of iron and ivory inlaid with the carved teeth of vanquished elves. A grinning skull of crystal topped the staff and from its mouth there leapt forth an icy wind, a stream of polar energy that set its elemental fury upon Eldire.

The sorceress of Hag Graef was caught in the full force of that arctic blast. Hoarfrost formed around her body, engulfing her utterly in a shroud of ice. Soon, where she had stood there was only a snowy pillar cast in the rough shape of an elf.

Drusala didn't approach the pillar. Warily, she gestured with her free hand, swinging it back and forth as little orbs of molten fire formed on the tips of her fingers. After a time, she flung her hand forwards, hurling the fiery orbs across the sanctum. They struck the icy pillar, steam and slush exploding as they burned completely through the obstacle. Consternation gripped Drusala's features when she saw no evidence of a corpse beneath the ice.

'Your arrogance must be punished,' Eldire's voice snarled through the sanctum. Drusala spun around, trying to find where her enemy had translocated herself, but as soon as she started to move, she felt the floor beneath her feet lurch and sway. She tried to leap back, but it was already too late. What had been solid stone a moment before was now a viscous, gooey sludge that pulled at her feet and tried to suck her down into the floor.

A bestial roar exploded from the trapped druchii's lips, a cry that might have been bellowed by a mammoth. The icy blue light was transformed into a hellish crimson, scarlet shadows leaping from the walls and diving into the sucking floor. Grunting with the effort, Drusala pulled her feet free as the red pulsations compelled the floor back into a state of solidity.

Even as she regained her feet, she was beset by her adversary. Spectral blades struck at Drusala from every quarter, phantom swords conjured from boiling fumes of dark magic. She whipped her iron staff around her body, using it to intercept each blade as it came slashing at her, fending them off with her parries. Faster and faster the assault came, forcing Drusala to sharpen her reactions with her own magic. The whirlwind of attack and interception became a blinding blur, the purple robes slashed to ribbons by the spectral blades, the phantom swords blunted and shattered by the flying staff.

Finally, the assault faltered. The last of the ghostly swords evaporated back into the aethyr. Victoriously, Drusala drove the end of her staff against the floor. A pulsation of raw, unfocused magic swept through the sanctum. As it passed through the chamber, Lady Eldire's figure abruptly stood revealed, the cloak of darkness that had hidden her obliterated by the force of Drusala's power.

Eldire glared at the other sorceress. 'The hag of Ghrond taught you a few tricks,' she conceded. 'What I know, I learned for myself!'

Lady Eldire now held a staff of her own, a thing of crystal and bone. At her command, the exposed crystal began to darken, to exude crawling tendrils of night. The black fingers shot across the sanctum, reaching out to seize Drusala in their clutches, to rip the soul from her flesh.

Drusala took a step back and made an arcane gesture with her hand. From her palm, a ball of nebulous energy burst forth, striking across the black fingers that reached towards her, sending little slivers of magic flying in every direction. 'You should have learned more,' Drusala spat. 'Your divinations have weakened you too much for such a conjuration. Even a mere handmaiden would know this.'

A bolt of searing darkness leapt from Eldire's staff, shearing through the shielding orb Drusala had evoked. The bolt slammed into the handmaiden, flinging her back, ripping her own staff from her hands. She crashed against the wall, almost passing through its unstable substance into the shadows beyond. By some effort of will, the stricken elf collapsed back against the semi-reality of the sanctum wall.

Eldire was already evoking another spell to strike down her foe when her concentration faltered. She'd seen something in that instant when Drusala had pierced the sanctum's illusion. Something so unexpected that it caused her concentration to slip. For an instant, for the merest fraction of time, her enemy had a different appearance. Her adversary was cloaked in a sorcerous glamour!

'Who are you?' Eldire demanded. 'How did you penetrate the wards that guard this place?'

Drusala looked up from the floor, blood trickling from her lip. 'A traitor removed the soul hanging. That is how I found this place.' She slapped her hand against the floor, sending a magical tremor through the stones. 'And to you, I am the Pale Queen,' she declared with a snarl, evoking the Cytharai goddess of the dead.

From the pool of blood, sanguinary spears erupted, striking at Eldire. She raised her staff to ward away the gruesome assault, but her enemy had prepared the attack with vicious cunning. Too much of Eldire's own magic infused the oracular liquid, too much of her own essence was yet bound within it. Aethyric sympathies, harmonies of spirit tied the sorceress to what she had conjured. The spears of solidified blood stabbed through the counter-spell Eldire raised to defend herself. In a welter of gore, they impaled her, piercing her at throat, navel and heart. The crystal staff fell from lifeless fingers to shatter upon the floor.

Drusala studied her vanquished enemy, drawing a deep sigh of contentment as she watched Eldire's life bleed away. She didn't linger to savour her triumph. Already the sanctum was beginning to lose its substance, to collapse back into the nothingness from which it had been formed. Hurriedly, she dashed through the portal that linked the place to Eldire's pavilion.

As she rushed through the doorway, Drusala found Absaloth waiting for her. The silent guard bowed his head as he saw his mistress return. She gave the warrior scarcely a glance, but instead turned to the only other druchii in the tent.

'Is it done?' Korbus asked, the soul hanging folded across his arm.

Drusala smiled at the tremor in the traitor's voice. She slid her bloodied fingers down the elf's cheek, leaving a line of gore across his skin.

'It is only beginning,' Drusala told him.

CHAPTER NINE

A cry of agony sang out from the left flank of the column, rising above the clatter of armour and the tromp of marching feet. A druchii warrior, elegant and sinister in his armour of darkened steel and cloak of deep crimson, collapsed into the dust. An arrow trembled in the pit of his eye, expertly loosed so that the shaft merely grazed the metal nasal that guarded the elf's face. The warriors around the stricken druchii didn't scatter, but came forwards, locking their shields together to form a wall of steel. Crossbows were trained upon the rocky slopes the column marched past.

Malus Darkblade swung around in his saddle, glaring at the grey desolation of the hills, the crumbling toes of the Annulii themselves. Here and there, some pattern among the rocks suggested an ancient construction, the foundation of some tower cast down ages ago. There was nothing to betray the presence of enemies, not even to eyes as keen as those of an elf or the sharp senses of the cold ones. Yet they were there just the same, lurking in the dirt and dust, stalking the druchii army, harassing it every step of the way. The toll in lives the ambushers took wasn't even worth the drachau's attention. Of what consequence was a spearman here or a knight there? Even the odd noble wasn't a serious impediment; there were plenty of druchii only too eager to assume the command of a fallen highborn.

No, the toll the ambushers were taking wasn't measured in lives but in time. The incessant attacks were taxing the discipline and morale of his warriors. Their step wasn't as firm as it had been when they left the shores of Tiranoc and abandoned the beached black ark. They were constantly looking around, watching for the next ambush, waiting for the scream that would tell of another comrade brought down by the slinking asur. Several times, entire companies of soldiers had broken, their discipline shattered by the harassing attacks. They'd stormed up onto the rocks, vengefully seeking their tormentors. Many more had been lost to deadfalls and other traps in these futile retaliations than had been felled by the black-fletched arrows. Malus had ended these breaks in discipline by employing the most ruthless measures – ordering the execution of any officer whose troops broke ranks and commanding that any soldier injured by an asur trap be left behind. Most of these injured druchii would be seen again, their butchered remains strewn across the road before the marching army by their shadowy enemy. In this, however, the vindictive asur had helped rather than hindered the determination of Malus's troops. There were no more reckless forays into the hills.

Still, it sat ill with Malus to allow the asur to assault his host with impunity. Magic would have offered the best recourse, but Lady Eldire had yet to rejoin his column. She'd remained behind at the beachhead to recover her strength after the toll her prophecy had taken on her. Until she rejoined him, the only sorceress of note in Malus's army was Drusala and he was wary of depending too much on her arcane powers. The last thing he wanted to do was to appear weak to an enchantress who might yet prove an agent of Malekith.

To that end, he'd come up with his own method of retaliation. Among the vastness of his army were his war hydras. Not only Griselfang and Snarclaw, but all the other beasts the refugees from Clar Karond had brought with them. The maws of the grotesque reptiles were fountains of corrosive, viscous bile. It was hazardous to collect that venom, to milk the ravenous hydras. The beastmasters balked at the very prospect of such labour. Fortunately, the slave-soldiers of Naggor had no choice in the matter. Under the lash of Kunor and the other slavemasters, the Naggorites had set about collecting the venom, drawing it from the glands of the multi-headed monsters. Dozens of the slave-soldiers had been lost in the process when the jaws of a hydra would slip free of the chains holding them open. In the end, however, they were able to provide gallons of the corrosive venom, storing it in clay jars and glass bottles.

As the spearmen formed their shieldwall around their dead comrade, Malus looked over to Silar and nodded. His retainer made a broad sweep of his outstretched hand. In response, a clutch of elves came marching through the ranks – more of Kunor's slave-soldiers. The Naggorites each carried a jar or bottle of hydra venom. Reaching their positions behind the shieldwall, they lobbed their burdens onto the hillside. The slaves were most energetic in this exercise, knowing that those who threw their missiles the farthest would be excused from collecting the next batch of hydra venom.

Bottles and jars shattered against the rocks, splashing the vicious liquid in every direction. Small gaps appeared in the shieldwall now, as crossbowmen took aim. Once away from the poisonous jaws of a hydra for more than a few minutes, the venom lost most of its potency, but it was still able to inflict the most hideous burns. It would take a god-like discipline to ignore such pain.

Despite their ghostly attacks, the asur proved to be mortal things of flesh and pain. As the hydra venom spattered across the rocks, grey figures rose up. Some were in such agony that they tried to rip their burning cloaks from their bodies. Others retained a bitter sense of purpose, taking swift aim with their bows and loosing arrows into their hated enemy. Several more druchii fell as the arrows stabbed into their ranks, but the retaliation of Hag Graef's crossbowmen, with their repeating weapons, ripped through any asur before they could manage a second shot.

A vengeful cheer welled up from Malus's army as he watched a score of asur ashencloaks cut down. The camouflage afforded them by their garments was almost perfect; the fault lay not in the ability of the cloak to render the elves unseen but in the weakness of the asur themselves.

Malus looked over to Silar once more, giving his loyal retainer another unspoken command. Silar barked out a string of orders and a small company of Naggorites rushed out from the column. They scrambled up the hillside, several of them vanishing as a hidden pit opened up beneath their feet. The survivors pressed on, only one of them making the mistake of turning and trying to retreat back to the column. A bolt from one of the crossbows killed the wretch before he'd gone a dozen feet. The rest picked their way among the rocks, searching out the tokens that would be their only chance to rejoin the host.

A low grumble from Spite caused Malus to look away from the Naggorites on the hill. It was a general rule in any druchii force that cold ones and horses had to be kept away from one another. The reptiles relished nothing quite so much as horseflesh, a fact that made even the strongest warhorse skittish around the scaly brutes. Now a lone rider made her way through the mass of knights, and it was the cold ones that had become skittish, recoiling from the midnight-black courser as though it were a living flame. Even Spite was uneasy, flexing its claws so that the talons scrabbled at the ground.

Malus refused to share his steed's anxiety. He had endured too much to be frightened by a mere sorceress, whatever unsettling whispers Tz'arkan tried to fill his head with. He indulged in a patronising smile as Drusala rode towards him, injecting the nuances of annoyance and condescension that would remind her of her place in his army, emphasise who was in command.

'Dreadlord,' Drusala addressed him with just the slightest measure of deference. 'You have dispatched your soldiers to recover the cloaks of our enemies. I fear that will be of no avail. The enchantment that conceals them so well is keyed to the peculiar hermetic harmonies of the asur. The air, earth and water of Naggaroth have changed the druchii too much to appeal to that magic.'

Malus shook his head. 'I haven't risked soldiers to recover those rags. That is a task fit for dogs.' From the hillside, more screams sounded. Malus turned his head to watch as an ashencloak who had been feigning death suddenly sprang into action, striking with his sword in a blur of ferocity that saw three Naggorites maimed or dead before the other slave-soldiers were able to smash him into the dirt. The crooked druchii swords slashed across the prone asur, hacking away at him without mercy.

'Nevertheless, there are better uses even for dogs,' Drusala insisted. 'If you intend to take the Eagle Gate, you will need every warrior you have.'

Malus studied the sorceress from the corner of his eye, watching her face, scrutinising her gaze. Looking for any sign that she knew, that Tz'arkan was right and that she had seen the awful secret locked away inside his soul. She could destroy him with such knowledge. If she had it, why didn't she? He should have demanded the answer to that question when he'd consulted his mother. If her auguries could reveal to him the place for a great victory, then surely she could predict the motivations of a single elf.

'I *will* take the Eagle Gate,' Malus said. 'It is my destiny.'

Drusala's face curled into an enigmatic smile. 'Destiny is what the proud call fate and the foolish call doom.'

'Are you presuming to advise me now?' Malus asked.

'Never, dreadlord,' Drusala said. 'I am well aware that you already have an advisor in matters arcane.'

Try as he might, Malus couldn't read the subtleties of tone in Drusala's choice of words. He looked the sorceress in the eye. 'Beside the Witch King himself, I am the most powerful warlord among our people. Serve me loyally, and there will always be a place for you in my court.'

'I never doubted that,' Drusala said. 'You are many things, drachau, but you aren't wasteful.' She looked back to the hillside where another of the Naggorites had fallen victim to an ashencloak playing dead. 'At least not with anyone you think is still useful to you.'

'A sorceress always has her uses,' Malus declared. He could feel a flicker of fear pass through him as he spoke. Was Tz'arkan nervous? Maybe a closer alliance with Drusala was just what he needed. Eldire had been unable to free him of the daemon; perhaps it wasn't such a bad idea to see what Drusala could do. Assuming of course he could arrange things so that if his affliction were found out the sorceress would suffer the same fate as he did.

Drusala bowed her head. There was no misunderstanding the invitation in her smile. 'I will await your pleasure, dreadlord.' She started to turn her horse, but stopped and glanced past Malus. Her body became stiff and tense, reminding Malus of a panther scenting an intruder in its territory.

He had to stifle the urge to laugh when he looked in the direction Drusala was staring and saw Vincirix riding over to join them. So, the sorceress was trying to stake out new territory. If so, she was being presumptuous. She certainly had her useful aspects, but the captain of the Knights of the Ebon Claw possessed something much more important. She was dependent on Malus for her rank and power. That gave him control over her. He didn't have a similar hold over the witch. Not yet, at least.

'You have something to report?' Malus asked Vincirix as the knight dismounted and bowed before him. He noticed that her cold one was even less willing to be around Drusala's horse than Spite was, the reptile straining at the reins she held in her hand. 'Has my mother accompanied you back from the beachhead?'

Malus had dispatched Vincirix and her knights to return to the black ark and see if Eldire was rested enough to join the march. He was anxious about leaving her behind, worrying that when Tiranoc came to assault the *Eternal Malediction,* she would be cut off from his army. His mind didn't rest any easier with the dire predictions Tz'arkan kept feeding him, allusions that his mother was gone, that her sorcery had helped him for the last time.

'There was no trace of Lady Eldire,' Vincirix reported. The knight was aware of the magical barriers that obscured the pavilion of the sorceress and had concocted a clever way of finding the place just the same, spreading her cold one knights in a wide circle and seeing at what point the reptiles began to grow agitated. It would then be a simple matter of dismounting and heading for the centre of that circle. Malus had been impressed by the simplicity of such a ploy. Now the drachau wondered if his faith in his lover's cleverness had been misplaced.

Vincirix could see the anger and doubt in Malus's eyes. 'We found her pavilion,' she hurried to explain. 'But there was no sign of your mother there.' She rose to her feet and waved her arm at a small group of knights who had followed her. 'We did find this, however.'

The knights came loping forwards on their cold ones. Between them the two elves held a large leather bag of the sort corsairs used to stash plunder when out raiding. The way the bag squirmed and shuddered, Malus could tell it held something living. The size of the bag suggested whatever was inside would be about his own size. Gruffly, the knights tossed their burden to the ground. A muffled yelp of pain sounded from whatever was inside.

Vincirix stepped over to the bag. Removing the dagger from her belt, she slashed the rope binding the mouth. With a kick, she forced the contents of the bag to wriggle out through the opening. Malus found himself glaring down at his mother's consort, Korbus. The conjurer was bound and gagged, his body bruised from the rough treatment he'd endured at the hands of Vincirix and her knights.

'I found him among the corsairs,' Vincirix explained. 'He seemed reluctant to leave their company and rejoin the host of Hag Graef.'

Spite's saddle creaked as Malus leaned forwards and fixed his cold eyes on those of Korbus, fairly willing the captive to meet his gaze. 'Did this worm tell you where my mother is?'

Vincirix grabbed Korbus by the back of his neck and jerked the servant to his feet. 'He claimed that shadow warriors infiltrated into the beachhead and attacked the pavilion. He says your mother was killed in the fighting.'

Deep inside Malus, some forgotten piece of himself turned cold. When he spoke, his words were as sharp as knives. 'Did you see any evidence of this fighting? Did the Shadowland curs leave any mark after them?'

'There was nothing,' Vincirix said. 'The corsairs had fought off a band of infiltrators several nights before, but that attack had been at the other end of their perimeter.'

Malus saw the terror in Korbus's eyes. The conjurer was desperate to speak, to make the drachau believe his story. Malus started to give the order for Vincirix to remove the gag when he noticed the frightened look the prisoner directed at Drusala. He swung around and gave the sorceress a cold smile.

'He seems to recognise you,' Malus accused.

Drusala brushed aside the accusation. 'Naturally,' she said. 'I was Morathi's closest retainer. This maggot is a sorcerer, despite the Witch King's decrees against males practising the black arts. He has probably had nightmares about our meeting for decades.'

'Perhaps,' Malus mused. He waved Vincirix to cut away the gag. 'Let's hear what he has to say.'

Korbus at once began to speak, but an expression of utter horror gripped him, as though he was frightened by his own words. Malus could understand that. The worm had, after all, just invoked Malekith's name. He closed his mouth, licked his lips. When he started to speak again, it was the Witch King he spoke of. Once more, the conjurer clamped his mouth tight, sweat pouring down his face, his eyes wide with terror.

'I grow weary of this, pig,' Malus snarled. 'Tell me what happened to my mother!'

'He is too frightened to obey,' Drusala said. 'His horror of the Witch King is greater than his fear of you. If you like, I could use my magic to draw the truth out of him, despite his fear.'

Malus glared at the trembling conjurer. He already knew something of the truth even without Drusala's magic. Whatever had befallen Eldire, it had come about because of this maggot's treachery. He waved a warning finger at the sorceress. 'This scum has betrayed me. How do I know I can trust you any better?'

'Loyalty is sometimes displayed not in what one does,' Drusala replied, 'but in what one chooses not to do.'

Malus nodded, appreciating the unstated meaning behind her words. Even if he didn't trust her, he appreciated that in such a public arena he couldn't afford to call her loyalty into question. Besides, if his mother was gone, he would need Drusala's magic. After that... after that it might be prudent to listen a little more closely to Tz'arkan's advice about her.

'So long as you do not kill him or strip away his senses,' Malus warned.

Drusala bowed in token of her understanding the restraint her powers were under. Looking back to Korbus, her eyes took on a fiery gleam, the pupils blazing until they assumed a golden hue. She reached out with her hand, the fingers splayed in a claw-like gesture. Strange words hissed across her lips. Spite and Vincirix's cold one growled, raking their claws against the ground and lashing their tails from side to side.

Korbus cried out, rearing forwards and almost slipping free of Vincirix's grip. There was absolute panic in his eyes, anguish on his face as he opened his mouth and tried to shout. The only sound that emerged was the name 'Malekith'. Hearing his own voice only increased the conjurer's despair.

'Speak, traitor!' Drusala snarled. A gibbous light began to shine from inside Korbus's mouth. Try as he might, the captive couldn't keep himself from opening his mouth. When he did, it could be seen that the light emanated from his tongue. 'Tell us what has befallen Lady Eldire,' Drusala commanded.

Korbus wept, his bound body thrashing violently in Vincirix's arms as the sordid tale of treachery and murder sprang from his tongue. He had conspired with the Witch King to kill Eldire and thereby weaken Malus. His part had been to remove and sabotage the protective spells Eldire had cast around her pavilion, opening the way for Malekith's assassins. His reward, he said, would be absolution, the Witch King's grace for Korbus's crime of practising sorcery despite the royal admonition.

Malus sat in brooding silence as the story was forced from the traitor. Drusala's magic wrenched every detail from his mother's betrayer. When the tale was told, the gibbous light faded away. All that was left in the conjurer's mouth was a burned and blackened nub of meat that had once been his tongue.

Vincirix let the traitor flop to the ground. Pulling the mace from her belt, she raised the weapon high.

'Halt! Do not touch the worm,' Malus called out before she could strike. His enraged gaze fastened itself on the shuddering figure of Korbus. 'He doesn't die so easily. This day or the next we will be at the Eagle Gate.' A cruel gleam shone in the drachau's eyes. 'I have a much better idea for how he can be paid back for the service he has rendered his king.'

The sound of rattling harnesses and marching boots echoed from the marble walls. The vibrations from two hundred warriors made the jewelled lamps sway on their golden chains, the wings of gilded eagles fluttering from where their silver talons clasped the rounded lip of each lamp. The deceptively delicate chains that held the enormous lamps high above the hall shivered in the bronze moorings that bound them to ceiling and wall. Servants in powder-blue livery hurried behind the two hundred, scrubbing and polishing the tile mosaic as they passed.

Upon a short dais, a great seat carved from the trunk of a white oak commanded the vast chamber. The back of the throne had been cunningly shaped into a lifelike semblance of a great eagle, outstretched pinions framing the sides of the throne, crooked talons making the seat itself. The brooding visage of the raptor's head loomed above the seat, the ferocity of its manner reminding all who met its gaze of the power and authority of the one who sat in the shadow of its sharp beak.

Prince Yvarin of Meletan had been commander of the Eagle Gate for only five years, a blink of the eye in the reckoning of elves. Many felt he was too raw, too untried to be given the prestigious duty of commanding the garrison, the responsibility of guarding the pass leading down from the blighted Shadowlands into the eternal summer of Ellyrion's sweeping plains. The beauty of Ellyrion, the tranquillity of that peaceful kingdom, depended upon the vigilance of the Eagle Gate. The threat of the exiled Naggarothi was perpetual, almost eternal it seemed. The pretender Malekith would never forsake his abominable claim upon the Phoenix Crown. So long as the foul Witch King of Naggaroth lived, he would never relent in his mad dream of conquest, to grind the lands of Ulthuan under his iron heel.

Amidst the turmoil besetting Ulthuan, the unprecedented numbers of strange beasts emerging from the Annulii Mountains to ravage the countryside, the burning of Chrace by mighty daemons, the horrific incidence of daemonic manifestations in the cities of Yvresse, Saphery and even Avelorn, somehow it was only to be expected that the Naggarothi would come again. Like jackals smelling a dying stag, they came from their forsaken land of chill to snap at the defences of Ulthuan. Yet another enemy at a time when the world seemed poised at the edge of the precipice. Was this, then, the final war?

Yvarin tried to banish such dire thoughts from his mind, but it was a difficult thing. It didn't need a mage to see the crimson slashes that stained the skies above the Shadowlands, a gruesome celestial corruption that grew and spread with each passing hour. The light of sun and moons had taken on a sickly quality – nothing that could be seen but something that could be felt down to an asur's very soul. The birds of summer had fled, spiralling skywards and streaming not to their winter haunts to the south but into the blighted north, the north of mutation and madness. The wind that blew through the pass bore with it little flecks of iridescence, like shards of rainbows, vibrant motes of raw magic that blighted whatever they touched.

Omens, as dire and fell as any Yvarin had ever read in the oldest legends, had become commonplace. Foremost among the evil portents had been the death of Finubar the Seafarer, last of the Phoenix Kings. His death had left Ulthuan without a leader and the turmoil besetting the land made it unlikely a new king would be chosen soon.

Then there had come the great daemon host to assault the Eagle Gate itself. That attack had been costly, both to the fortress and the garrison. Replacements were slowly arriving to reinforce the stronghold, but reconstruction of the walls the daemons had breached was advancing at a sluggish pace. The gigantic plague daemon that had struck the walls had done more than simply knock down stone and mortar. The fiend's very touch had corrupted the rock, making the rubble brittle and unusable. Fresh stone had to be brought into the pass to replace what had been ruined, an ordeal that was made all the more laborious by the turmoil afflicting the land.

The prince ran his fingers across the wand of dragon-horn he had been presented with by the last company of soldiers to arrive at the Eagle Gate. It was a splendid, marvellous piece of artistry, inlaid with rubies and fire sapphires so that whenever the light struck it, Yvarin felt like he held a sliver of frozen flame in his hand. Shrinastor, the haughty loremaster from Saphery, would no doubt be unimpressed by the token of esteem Yvarin had been given by the contingent from Caledor. The secrets of its flawless beauty would hold no surprises for the cynical mage. The prince felt it was just as well Shrinastor had slighted the soldiers sent by Prince Imrik by locking himself away in his chambers to consult his crystals and his astrological charts. He could do without the added burden of Shrinastor's presence.

Yvarin looked at the wand, turning it over in his hands, then nodded in appreciation to Jariel, the captain of the Talons of Tor Caldea. 'We thank you for your gift, but more importantly, we thank you for your service. In this hour of crisis, when the old enemy comes upon us once more, it is more important than ever to remember the honour and tradition that unites the kingdoms of the asur.'

Jariel bent to her knee, setting her ruby-encrusted helm on the tile floor. Stolid and proud, her face seemed to be chiselled from the same marble as the chamber walls until she raised her eyes and stared at the seated prince. An expression of pained humiliation swept across her heroic features. 'I bring shame to you, highness,' she said. 'Please accept my apology for this inexcusable slight upon your noble house and do not hold my error against these valiant warriors who have come to serve you.'

Yvarin stared in confusion at Jariel, then, as his fingers continued to caress the wand she had presented him, he felt a roughness beneath his touch. Lowering his eyes just the smallest fraction, he saw the ruby he was touching and the deep flaw that ran through it, a blight upon the beauteous perfection of the wand.

'There is nothing to forgive,' Yvarin said. 'At a time of crisis, the fellowship of the asur is the only jewel that is without flaw. I know that the sons and daughters of Caledor will observe their duty to Ulthuan. I know that you will fight with courage and valour. I know that you will do honour to your ancestors.'

Yvarin watched as Jariel led the Talons of Tor Caldea from the grand reception hall. They were a magnificent sight in their coats of armoured scales and their tall, dragon-winged helms. The heads of their spears were broad and sported long tassels to sop up the blood of their enemies. Their shields were thick, reinforced with the cast-off scales of the great wyrms that slept in Caledor's mountains. Such a complement of warriors was a boon to his garrison.

Even so, Yvarin couldn't help but let his eyes fall once more to the wand he held and the flawed ruby.

Another ill omen for the lords of Ulthuan.

CHAPTER TEN

There was a chill in the air as Malus stared into the pass. The shadow of the Annulii Mountains cast the foothills at their feet into darkness, little wisps of snow wafting down from their peaks whenever the wind shifted. Malus covertly glanced at the druchii warriors who surrounded him. He smiled as he noted the briskness that crept into their step, the squaring of their shoulders, the almost imperceptible eagerness in their eyes. The dark, the cold, these might be hostile and unwelcome to the soft, pampered asur. But to the druchii, reared and raised in the bleak wastes of Naggaroth, darkness and cold were their element. The kiss of snow, the shroud of shadow, these were almost welcoming to them. It was as though the land itself were calling to them, reassuring them that they were indeed coming home.

Even the most jaded and cynical of his warriors took heart from the change. The more superstitious, those who bore charms of Khaine about their necks or wore rings devoted to the various Cytharai, took these things to be an omen of victory.

Malus wasn't prepared to go so far as that. Even with his mother's last prophecy burned into his brain, he wasn't going to place too much trust in the intrigues of fate. Destiny was something that was shaped by mortal hands and mortal acts. It was in a commander's power to squander a pre-destined victory through his own mistakes and his own hubris. Having seen the future, it was in his hands to bring it to fruition.

Horsemen came galloping out from the pass, their black cloaks whipping behind them, their steeds frothing at the mouth. White-feathered arrows protruded from several of the dark riders, the shafts stabbed deep into the flesh of elf and horse alike. As they stormed towards the army, one of the horses pitched and fell, crushing its injured rider beneath it as it rolled in agony on the ground. Malus swatted the top of Spite's head, warning the reptile to keep calm despite the smell of horseblood in the air. Along the line of his knights, he could hear the sharp crack of other druchii disciplining their cold ones.

The dark riders peeled away from the cold one knights. Now that they were beyond the arrows of their enemy, the threat posed by their own comrades was impressed upon them. Two of the riders drew rein some hundred yards from the cold ones. While one rider dropped down from his saddle, the other took his horse and led it away. Malus watched the returning cavalry gallop around the flank of his infantry, headed for the rear to rest and recover from their foray into the pass.

Silar Thornblood and a small group of heavily armoured spearmen intercepted the dismounted rider. The elf was wounded, an arrow pinning his left arm to his side, but Silar was careful to remove his sword and dagger just the same before leading him through the line of cold one knights to where the drachau waited.

'Dreadlord, the scouts have returned,' Silar reported as his guards helped the rider squirm between the scaly flanks of the reptiles.

'Really?' Malus grumbled. 'I thought it was some other band of horsemen wearing the colours of Hag Graef who just happened to be riding around in the pass.' He waved his retainer away and motioned the guards to step aside. The wounded scout struggled to keep his feet. Malus could see the jewelled badge fastened to the druchii's helm that marked him as a captain. A sense of duty, this one, to bring his report despite his wound. Or perhaps he just had enough ambition in him that he didn't dare allow one of his subordinates the distinction of meeting with the drachau.

'The Eagle Gate is intact, dreadlord,' the scout said. It had been a faint hope, but there had been whispers of earthquakes and elemental upheavals when Malekith commanded his kingdom into this final assault on Ulthuan. If such turmoil had broken the defences he might have pushed his army headlong through the rubble and into the Inner Kingdoms. What a feat that would have been. A wondrous glory for Hag Graef and her drachau!

Malus scowled at the news that the asur fortress was still as formidable as it had been during the druchii invasions of ages past. Those assaults had broken upon the Eagle Gate, floundered in a futile siege until relief could arrive. The proximity of Caledor worried Malus. Prince Imrik could unleash his dragons against the host of Hag Graef. The flying wyrms were a foe that Malus didn't have the resources to vanquish. Such dragons as remained to the druchii were with Malekith and the army of Naggarond – even the beastmasters of Karond Kar had been compelled to turn over their dragons to the Witch King. Without dragons of his own to call upon and drive off any force from Caledor, there were only two choices open to Malus. He could withdraw back into the Shadowlands and try to seek shelter among the rocky hills, or he could press forward and take the fortress. If his troops were in command of the Eagle Gate, even Imrik's dragons wouldn't be able to drive them out.

Sitting atop her cold one, Vincirix listened with mounting unease as the scout related the condition of the Eagle Gate. The dark riders had suffered five dead and twice as many wounded by the archers lining the battlements.

He had marked the positions of at least half a dozen bolt throwers and suspected there might be a score more concealed on the walls. The scout had noted the banners of many asur nobles and even the colours of Caledor among the defenders.

'Caledor?' Vincirix said, running a nervous finger across the flanges of her mace.

Malus smiled at her alarm. When he spoke, it was in a voice loud enough to carry to the nearby troops. 'It is wrong to underestimate the cunning of the asur. Never let hate blind you to an enemy's ability. If the garrison is so bold as to display the colours of Caledor, it is because they want to frighten me with the idea that they've got a dragon or three hiding behind those walls.' He glared down at the scout. 'But if they did have dragons, is it not more likely they would do nothing to put that idea in my head? They'd want to lure me in and then unleash the wyrms on me.' In a single flourish, Malus drew the warpsword from its scabbard and drove the blade across the scout's neck. The stunned captain collapsed, pawing at the gushing wound in his throat. Whatever ambitions the elf had entertained were spurting into the dirt.

The drachau turned from the dying scout. 'They think to delay me here,' he mused. 'They are playing for time, trying to exploit my worries.'

'But, dreadlord, if the defences are as formidable as...' Vincirix fell silent when she saw the glare in Malus's eyes.

'I will test them,' Malus said. 'And when the asur have shown me their mettle, I will unleash my full fury against them. The Eagle Gate will fall. The glory of conquest will be mine.'

Bragath Blyte bit his lip as the lash cracked across his shoulder. The Naggorite's hands tightened about the spear he held. For the chance to drive that shaft into the belly of his tormentor... But to do so wouldn't lessen his misery or that of his people. Kunor Kunoll's Son had a vile imagination when it came to punishing rebellion. A clean death in battle might at least earn a reprieve for a slave's soul, see it carried into the Pale Queen's underworld rather than the infernal toils of Slaanesh. But broken by Kunor's tortures, his soul would be too foul to pass the Keeper of the Last Door.

No, there was nothing a war-leader of Naggor could do except swallow his pride and endure. Hope for a noble death in battle and to pass into the underworld of Mirai.

'Faster, you dogs! Close ranks!' The sharp voice of Kunor rang out above the cracking whips of his helpers. Under the bite of the lash, the slave-soldiers marched onwards.

It had been years since the Witch Lords of Naggor loosed their armies against Hag Graef. The Witch Lords had lost that battle, their sorcery and daemons unequal to the ruthlessness and cunning of Malus Darkblade. The bastard kinslayer had prevailed, seizing the crown of his own city even as he vanquished the legions of Naggor. The conquered had become slaves, chattel for the wars of the Hag. Once there had been several thousand Naggorites under Darkblade's banner. Now there were barely half that number. Privation, abuse and neglect had claimed many. Hundreds had died fighting hopeless battles when Malus rode to rescue the refugees of Clar Karond and bind what was left of their might to that of the Dark Crag.

How many more would perish today, Bragath wondered. Would his name be among those of the slain? Or would some perverse whim of providence sustain him yet again?

Staring out across the ranks of the slave-soldiers, the warrior inside Bragath cringed at the state of his comrades. Was his armour as sorry as that of his fellows, cracked and dented, crudely mended with bits of leather and scraps of cloth? Were his limbs as lean and wasted as those of the elves who marched beside him? Did his face have the same starveling thinness, the same sickly yellow colour?

Bragath turned his head and raised his eyes. Ahead, at the far side of the pass, there loomed the Eagle Gate. Hundreds of feet high, built from immense blocks of granite, the fortress blocked the pass utterly. Tier upon tier of battlements, each piled atop the last. At the centre, the gigantic sculpture of an eagle with outstretched wings. One wing merged into the side of the mountains that flanked the pass. The talons stabbed downwards, perched upon the lowest level of battlements. Between the legs, the great bronze doors rose, immense portals that were fifty feet high and nearly again as broad. The body of the eagle bulged out from the face of the fortress, each feather carved with lifelike fidelity. Bragath's keen eyes could see the little gaps between the feathers that marked the windows behind which asur archers were lurking. The enormous head of the eagle with its open mouth was more obvious in its menace, a pair of immense bolt throwers standing inside the beak.

A legion of Malekith's Black Guard couldn't take this fortress, yet Darkblade had commanded Kunor to drive the Naggorites to the attack. Bragath didn't need to turn his head to know that the rest of Malus's army was hundreds of yards behind them. They were following the advance of the slave-soldiers, but keeping well to the rear. It needed no tactical acumen to guess the purpose Darkblade had chosen for his captives. The Naggorites had been given the cheerful task of goading the asur into making the first attack.

Each step closer made the sweat drip into Bragath's eyes. It wasn't fear of death that caused his heart to pound and his back to shiver. He was resigned to death – all of the Naggorites were. It was the horror of anticipation, of knowing what must soon come but not knowing when it would strike.

At the head of the Naggorite formation, a tall standard rose into the sky. Bragath looked uneasily up at the frame of wood and iron atop the pole.

Bound to that frame was the mangled body of a druchii. Korbus, the late consort-retainer of Lady Eldire. Darkblade had been especially vicious in dealing with the traitor. The conjurer's hands had been hacked off with an axe, his lips sewn shut with wire. A metal cage bound his head in place, so that Korbus couldn't hide his face. The elf's eyes had been pinned open with needles that transfixed his eyelids. Across his stripped body, glyphs representing the most abominable curses had been carved into his flesh. Over his heart, Malus himself had cut the most profane symbol of them all, the emblem of Slaanesh the Devourer. Even for a dreadlord, such a ghastly punishment as deliberately invoking the Prince of Chaos to claim his enemy's soul was obscene.

Stoutly, the slave-soldiers maintained their march while the slavemasters barked and snapped their whips. Then a new sound entered the battle. From the walls there came a noise of whistling. The tall standard writhed and jerked as arrows slammed into the living emblem of Darkblade's hate. Blood streamed down the pole as Korbus was pin-cushioned with arrows. Then the archers on the walls turned their bows against the warriors of Naggor. Driven by the powerful longbows, the arrows arched high above the pass before streaking downwards to skewer the druchii slaves. The rude, poorly maintained armour of the Naggorites was small protection against the broad-headed missiles. By the dozen, they fell, dead or maimed.

Bragath Blyte raised his shield, feeling an asur arrow slam into it a second later. He could see the dead steel head where it had punched clean through the laminated wood. He scowled at the missile that had come so close to finishing him. Was this the warrior's death for which he'd endured years of suffering as the captive of Hag Graef?

Hate caused him to crash the shaft of his spear against his shield, breaking the arrow embedded in it. Bragath howled his fury to the uncaring sky and the asur safe behind their walls.

It was a truth the druchii had long ago learned. Where hope is lost, hate alone can drive a warrior onwards. With enough hate in his heart, a druchii could accomplish anything.

Even revenge.

Malus studied the march of Naggor with the same intensity as a gem-cutter might inspect a diamond before deciding how best to cut it. He watched every step, observed each slave-soldier as an arrow brought them down. A hundred elves lay in the dirt, killed by enemy archers or trampled by the feet of their comrades, and still the Scion of Hag Graef sat and brooded. Sometimes his hand would move to pat Spite's head as the brute's senses became excited by the smell of blood, but otherwise he was as still as a statue.

Finally, with an abruptness that caused Vincirix and Dolthaic to jump in surprise, Malus turned to the captains of his knights. 'The shooting from the right is weaker than that of the centre and the left,' he declared. 'They've tried to hide it, but there's a break in the fortifications there. A swift strike by cavalry to secure the ground followed by a rush of infantry to assault the wall.' He clenched his fist, grinding his fingers against his palm as though he were crushing the enemy in his hand. 'They try to feign strength where they are weak and weakness where they are strong, but the asur panicked at the last. They didn't want Kunor's dogs to get close to that right flank so they loosed their arrows on him too soon. Their caution has exposed their weakness instead of protecting it.'

One of my brothers has paved the way for you, Malus. This place was beset by my kind not long ago. A great plague daemon smashed his way through six of the eight walls. It is that wound your enemy hopes to protect. Do you understand now the power that could be yours?

Malus clenched his teeth against the urge to snarl down Tz'arkan's voice. Always tempting, always trying to seduce him with the promise of power. The daemon knew the desires of his heart only too well after all the years the thing had been festering inside him. The urge to quiet the daemon with wine was even greater than the fiend's wheedling, but Malus could afford neither. He had to keep his head clear if he was going to command his troops. More, with Eldire gone, he didn't know how he was going to replenish the dwindling supply of the draught he added to his wine. Drusala could make more, he was certain, but that would make him dependent on her. He still wasn't certain how much of his affliction she understood. There was great risk in adding to such knowledge as she already possessed.

She knows too much, fool! Kill her and have done before it is too late.

Malus looked down the line of knights, to where a small squadron of horsemen were galloping out, weaving a path between the main body of the army and the embattled Naggorites. His doomfire warlocks, hurrying to the attack. Even at this distance, he could see the fiery runes blazing upon their exposed hands and faces. Little coils of smoke drifted away from them as the hellish curse Malekith had inflicted upon them slowly dragged their souls into the realm of Slaanesh. The warlocks could save themselves only by sacrificing others in their stead. The murderous souls of Naggorites had done little to appease the curse – they needed pure, courageous souls to sacrifice and earn themselves a few days of respite. They needed souls such as they would find among the defenders of the Eagle Gate.

The doomfire warlocks, on their dark chargers and with their black cloaks billowing about them, weren't the focus of Malus's attention, however. Among the warlocks rode Drusala. Just as he'd tasked Kunor with drawing out the asur's physical defences, so he had charged Drusala and the warlocks with engaging the gate's magical defences. Just as the only way to defend against a dragon was with another dragon, so the only way to defend against magic was with magic of your own.

She would wait, Malus decided as he watched the sorceress ride towards the fortress. Whichever way he decided, it would wait until after the battle.

The daemon inside him would just have to be patient. For now, there was the breach in the wall to exploit.

'Wait until the riders are closer,' Malus told his captains. 'Then we use them as a screen while we rush the weak point.'

'That will be hard on the warlocks,' Vincirix observed.

Malus smiled at her. 'It's a hard life, being a warlock. They should have learned that by now.'

Drusala could feel the aethyric vibrations that pulsated around the Eagle Gate. She was surprised to find them in such a sorry condition, shocked to find the protective harmonies in such a state of discord. Extending her senses, closing her mind to the crude physical essences around her, she was able to fixate upon the ruinous energies that saturated the pass. It seemed that Malus wasn't the first enemy to try his luck against the Eagle Gate. The malefic discord of hundreds of vanquished daemons oozed all around the place. The asur had been thrown into such turmoil by the calamities besieging Ulthuan that they hadn't even been able to take the time for a proper cleansing ritual.

Such unpreparedness wasn't like the hidebound asur. This truly was the prime opportunity to attack. Malekith had been wise to abandon the wastes of Naggaroth and stake everything on this chance to seize the lands that were his birthright.

She let her witchsight canvass the walls of the fortress. She noted the great breach to the right of the gate, a gap in the defences that went beyond simply the physical. Whatever had wrought such havoc upon the Eagle Gate had done so on far more than a material level. The very atmosphere around the place was like an open wound. She could feel the dark energies bubbling and boiling there.

Turning in her saddle, Drusala wasn't surprised to find the cold one knights rushing for the breach. Both the 'household guard' of Malus Darkblade – the mercenary Knights of the Burning Dark – and the Clar Karond exiles of Vincirix Quickdeath – the Knights of the Ebon Claw – were charging down the pass. The Scion of Hag Graef was forsaking the idea of a prolonged siege and throwing his lot into a lightning assault. That he was using both the Naggorites and the doomfire warlocks to shield the initial rush of his advance was a bit of callousness that wasn't lost on her. Darkblade valued no life more than he valued his own ambition.

A flash of brilliant white light among the battlements drew Drusala's attention. Gazing upwards, she watched as a small flock of immense birds took wing. As they rose into the sky, the very plumage of the creatures burst into flame, scorching the air as they climbed. Phoenixes, great raptors whose very essence was saturated with the magical energies of the Flamespyres. Unlike most of the animals changed and twisted by the magic in the Annulii, there was a certain intelligence in the mind of a phoenix, a rationality that made the creatures respond with friendship towards the asur. The fiery birds were a powerful ally for the garrison and a terrible foe for the invaders. Attuned to aethyric harmonies, the phoenixes had been roused by the approach of the doomfire warlocks. Drusala had little doubt who the beasts had chosen for their prey.

As the birds came hurtling earthwards, Drusala urged her mount skywards. The glamour that had cloaked her steed fell away as great leathery wings unfurled from its sides. Snorting and stamping, the dark pegasus shed the illusion of being a common steed. It fanned its great wings, upsetting the ranks of the mounted warlocks. The riders cursed and raged as Drusala's steed climbed into the air. She had no need to fear reprisal. The warlocks would quickly have problems enough just surviving the assault of the phoenixes.

Soaring aloft, the pegasus gave the diving phoenixes a wide berth. Drusala could feel the heat from the creatures as they passed, could smell the acrid scent of their burning plumage. She wove her own sorcerous defences a bit more tightly around herself, hiding her presence from the hunting raptors. Soon, her flying steed had borne her high above the embattled warlocks and their bestial foes.

Drusala might have lent aid to the warlocks, but to do so would mean squandering some of her own arcane power. She needed her full strength right now, for it was her intention to go beyond the foes the warlocks had drawn out. From the aethyric harmonies of the Eagle Gate, she knew that someone, some powerful mage, had been making his own attempt at cleansing the daemonic taint. That he thought himself knowledgeable enough to attempt such a purification on his own was a testament to either his ability or his arrogance.

Drusala intended to discover which.

Warning trumpets blared from the battlements as eagle-clawed bolt throwers cast their missiles down into the pass. Drusala saw two Knights of the Burning Dark skewered by the immense shafts, their carcasses tumbling through the dust, crushed beneath the bodies of their cold ones. The rest of the knights charged onwards, however, goaded to the attack by the merciless fury of Darkblade himself.

The asur knew the objective Malus had in mind. The trumpets were calling troops down to defend the broken walls, to block the breach before the cold one knights could seize it. Archers scrambled along the battlements, but there were too few near the breach to render much help. A knight's armour wasn't so easily pierced as that of a Naggorite slave and a cold one's scaly hide was more resilient than that of a horse. The only hope the garrison had lay in the armoured spearmen who filed down into the gap.

The spearmen, and the mage whose presence Drusala now perceived. He must have worn some talisman or charm to conceal his aethyric aura, probably a ward prepared against the daemons raging across Ulthuan. Now, however, he was drawing too deeply from the stream of magic to conceal himself. Drusala could see him as a sun-like beacon of light, luminous with the power he was drawing into himself.

She could sense his purpose as well. The mage was conjuring a spell to strike down Malus, to cut the head from the force threatening the breach. There was enough power in his magic that Drusala considered the enemy had a very real chance of working harm upon Malus. There was no question that if the tyrant were incapacitated, the attack would falter.

Worse, if the mage managed to kill Malus, he might be freeing something Drusala wasn't certain she was ready to face. And that was something she wasn't willing to risk.

A bolt of rippling black energy leapt from Drusala's staff, cleaving through the crackling blaze of power the mage was loosing against Malus. The antithetical waves of magic, light and dark, collided with tempestual fury. A dull boom roared across the battlefield, a roar that had within it the violence of both spells.

The mage turned towards her. Drusala could see a lean elf in sapphire robes bedecked in gold and pearl, a tall helm rising above his thin visage. There was pride and vanity stamped across that face. In her mind she could hear the mage announcing himself. 'I am Shrinastor, Loremaster of Hoec, Hierophant of the Golden Way, Magus of the Emerald Light. This place is under my protection.'

Drusala could feel Shrinastor drawing power into himself. The loremaster intended to fight her, to pit his magic against her sorcery. Twisting the reins of her pegasus, she jerked the beast's head to one side and turned it back towards the druchii lines.

Let Shrinastor think he'd frightened her off with his magic. She'd achieved her immediate purpose. Malus had reached the breach. His knights were engaged with the asur soldiers. The loremasters were always squeamish about destroying their own troops with their magic. The drachau would be safe from Shrinastor for the moment.

More importantly, Drusala had the answer to her own question: whether her asur adversary was moved by ability or arrogance.

Their next encounter would end quite differently now that she knew who she was facing.

'Set spears! Hold your ground!' As the orders were shouted, hundreds of spears slammed into the earth, a knee set against each to help brace the weapon against the coming attack. Tall, iron-banded shields, each standing as high as the elf who carried it, were lowered across the body of each warrior. There was no expression of fright, no thought of retreat as the soldiers prepared to receive the charge of the most monstrous cavalry in the druchii horde.

Prince Yvarin, even in the midst of the battle, felt his heart pound with pride. Among his officers, he knew there had been questions about his decision to deploy these troops here, at the breach, when the position could be held by lesser troops. They had urged a sally against the druchii, to take the battle to the invader before a prolonged attack could be mounted. For such an assault, they had wanted the best warriors in the fortress. That meant these elves, the Eataine Guard.

The prince had endured the implications that he was unwise or inexperienced when he'd disagreed with the idea of an offensive attack. His officers were right – holding the Eagle Gate against a prolonged siege would be difficult with the breach in the walls. That was why he'd chosen to exploit the weakness. Turn it into a killing ground for the best their foe could send against them.

Doubt had ruled him as he saw the attack unfold, as he watched the Tyrant of Hag Graef himself leading a host of cold one knights towards the breach. Yvarin felt a sense of foreboding, the feeling that he gazed upon his own doom. It was hopeless to try and stand against such a foe. The Eagle Gate was lost, what good could come of selling their lives to no purpose? The temptation to call the retreat vexed him, nagged at him with songs of safety and peace.

The feel of the sword in his hand steadied his resolve. That blade had been handed down for fifty generations of his house. Many times, it had been borne home with the body of its owner laid upon a shield, entrusted to the living heir by a fallen hero. Never had that blade fled from battle. Ever had the elves who bore it done their duty to the Phoenix King and the people of Ulthuan. Yvarin knew what duty demanded of him this day.

He knew that to hold the gap in the outer walls was the key to maintaining the security of the Eagle Gate. Yvarin also knew that it was here the fighting would be at its hardest. The troops deployed here were effectively being given a death sentence. One and all had adopted cloaks of white before marching to the breach, a mark of purity and resolve before their final sacrifice for Ulthuan, the colour of mourning for when that sacrifice had been made. For that reason, if no other, Yvarin had decided to entrust this role to none but his personal retinue of warriors, the Eataine Guard. For that reason, he had determined to stand beside them in battle. If they prevailed, the fortress would hold. If they failed, no command he could issue would delay the catastrophe.

The stink of the Naggarothi steeds swept over the prince, bringing tears to his eyes and a cough to his throat. It was a mark of how far the druchii had degenerated since they'd followed the merciless Witch King into exile that they could abide such foul beasts.

'Ready arms,' Yvarin told his warriors. 'We fight for the Phoenix Crown! Let none of this scum past!'

The fierce cries of the druchii, the monstrous roars of their reptilian steeds rose in a deafening din. Many of the asur turned their faces behind their shields as the enemy charged their position. They could feel the ground shuddering beneath their feet as the weight of the attack came thundering towards them.

Lesser troops would have broken. The Eataine Guard held fast. Reptilian roars turned to shrieks of pain as many of the cold ones impaled themselves upon the waiting spears. Then there came the shrieks of elves as the druchii knights drove their cruel lances through the thick ironwood shields. Dozens of asur perished as the knights drove their attack home. The white cloaks of the first line were quickly stained red with the blood of friend and foe alike.

'Forward!' Yvarin cried. At his command, the second line of warriors advanced, thrusting their spears at the enemy. The druchii charge had decimated the front line, slaughtering four-fifths of the warriors, but the impetus of their assault had been blunted. Wounded cold ones flailed upon the ground, their claws slashing at anything that came near, forcing the knights behind to finish them before they could advance. Dead bodies tripped up those cold ones that tried to rush into the breach, leaving their riders exposed to the spears of the Eataine Guard. Black-armoured knights cast aside their lances, hurling them spitefully into the faces of their foes. The lance was the weapon of the charge, and the druchii charge had faltered. Now the knights drew sword and mace from their belts, the weapons best suited to close quarters.

Yvarin struck down one knight, his sword chopping through the killer's arm as he tried to negotiate his way past a thrashing cold one. The stricken knight's reptilian mount snapped at him, striving to bring him down. The axe of Yvarin's standard bearer smashed into the brute's skull, sinking almost to its jaw. The cold one collapsed in a heap, dragging the standard bearer down with it.

Before the standard bearer could regain his feet, another druchii knight was lunging at him. The reptilian mount's claws raked open his side while the knight's clawed mace dented his helm and shattered his skull. The knight snatched at the standard, catching it before it could fall to the ground. Viciously she raked her bloodied mace across it, tearing the ancient silk and fouling the emblem of the Eataine Guard.

Prince Yvarin felt fear roar through his veins. He'd watched this knight during the charge. She was one of Darkblade's war-leaders, a position she could have earned only through the most heinous atrocities. What was he beside such a fiend?

Surprisingly, Yvarin found the answer, felt it as a roar that deafened the fear inside him. Who was he? He was the commander of the Eagle Gate!

'For the Phoenix!' Yvarin screamed as he drove himself upon the war-leader. Her clawed mace crashed against his shield, but he ignored the stinging numbness the impact sent racing up his arm. Spun around by the brutal impact, he turned his rotation into a sidewise slash. It was a strategy he'd practised a thousand times in his father's palace. Now it served him well. Outstretched by the brutal blow she had struck, his enemy was exposed to the sweep of Yvarin's sword. The ancient blade rang out as it crashed against her armour, splitting the spiked pauldron and driving a sliver of the compromised mail back into the face of the knight's helm.

Blood gushed from the helm. A muffled scream rang from behind the metal mask. The clawed mace fell from a hand that now snatched at the chin-strap holding the mask in place. A moment later, it came free, or at least one side of it did. The rest simply hung in place, pinned to the war-leader's face by the sliver of steel that had impaled her eye.

Yvarin struck again, thrusting his blade at the knight. The thrust stabbed into her throat, drawing a hideous gargle from her as her body slumped sidewise in the saddle. The reptile, panicked by the dying elf slumped across it back, scrabbled away from Yvarin, snapping and barking at the other cold ones as it fled back into the pass.

The death of their war-leader appeared to embolden the knights who bore her symbol. Even as the Eataine Guard cheered Yvarin's triumph, the prince felt himself struck from behind. His shield shattered, the arm behind it cut almost to the bone. As he crashed to the ground, he saw a ghastly figure glaring down at him from the back of a horned reptile. The prince braced himself for death. He knew who this enemy was and he knew better than to expect mercy from Malus Darkblade.

The villain raised his sword, Yvarin's blood steaming on its blade; then the masked tyrant seemed to think better of it. Leaning forwards, he hissed into the earhole of his steed. 'Feed, Spite.'

Before the horned one could lunge at Yvarin, spears stabbed at Malus from almost every quarter. The tyrant lashed out, shearing through each weapon as it was thrust at him. Darkblade looked around and an animalistic cry of rage rose from behind his mask.

Painfully, Yvarin raised himself on one elbow and looked to see what had so enraged the infamous murderer. What he saw was beyond belief. The druchii attack had failed. The second group of knights, the ones following after the she-elf's company, had broken and fled. Sight of the dead captain's steed retreating through their ranks had panicked them and thrown them into headlong flight. The surviving knights of the first company, who had been holding the breach, were now falling back as well.

Seeing the fight was lost, Malus drove his spurs into his reptile's flanks. The horned beast spun around, smashing several asur with its tail, then leapt over the carcasses between itself and the breach. Archers chased Malus as he retreated back into the pass.

Attendants hurried to Yvarin's aid, but the wounded prince barely took notice of them. His wounds, his fatigue, even the terror he'd felt when he found himself facing Malus Darkblade, all of these were forgotten. His entire world now consisted of a sound. A sound that was like the roar of the ocean. A sound that rang from the walls and battlements.

The Eagle Gate had held against the druchii attack and now its defenders were cheering. A cheer that took the form of a name, a name that only days before they had still held in doubt.

'Yvarin! Yvarin! For the Phoenix and Yvarin!'

CHAPTER ELEVEN

Malus could feel the rage building up inside him. Gazing back into the pass, he could see the asur dragging the cold ones that had been killed in the assault out from behind the walls. They were building a rampart of dead flesh out ahead of their broken fortifications, an obstacle that was well within range of the archers on the battlements. There had been a chance to end the battle quickly, to establish a foothold within the fortress itself. Now that opportunity was lost.

The drachau stalked among the commanders of his knights. The Knights of the Burning Dark. His household guard. Mercenary trash that had broken at the first setback! If they'd kept their nerve, if they'd maintained the momentum of the assault... But, no, the slinking vermin had fled. They'd seen Vincirix's cold one come galloping back with her body hanging from the saddle and they'd fled.

The Warpsword of Khaine sang out as Malus removed the head from one of the disgraced commanders. Bound hand and foot, the scum awaited his rage. Silar marched behind his master, raising each gory head as Malus cut it free. Grimly, he lifted each one by its hair and cast it into the jeering mob of infantry and horsemen who'd been assembled to watch the executions. There was little sympathy for the arrogant, highborn knights. Not from the common soldiers, who were so often abused by their noble comrades.

'Have pity, dreadlord! When we saw Vincirix's body, we thought you had been slain as well.' The cries came from Dolthaic. The captain had been lashed to a skinning rack and positioned so that he could see every moment of punishment as it was meted out upon his officers.

Malus hesitated, as though considering Dolthaic's words. Then he stepped to the next bound officer. The warpsword came chopping down once again, shearing through the elf's neck. Deep inside his soul, he could feel Tz'arkan exult in the vindictive carnage. It annoyed Malus that the daemon found vengeance so satisfying when it had no vested interest in what was being avenged. For the daemon, it was all nothing more than an amusing game.

He thought again of the dwindling supply of the draught. Could he afford to indulge himself this way if it gave Tz'arkan strength? Malus dismissed the worry as unworthy. His attack had failed. If he didn't punish someone, discipline in his army would break down. His soldiers would think him weak, unfit to lead. They'd entertain ideas that someone more capable and ruthless should be their general.

The warpsword sang out again and another grovelling knight fell to the ground without his head. This last one had been a Knight of the Ebon Claw. They had their own responsibility for the failure to take the breach. If they'd fought harder, if they'd been more loyal to their captain, perhaps she wouldn't have been cut down by that damn asur prince!

When Malus struck next, it wasn't the neck of the knight he saw, but that of Prince Yvarin. The cursed asur! He'd killed Vincirix, taken away his lover and war-leader. Malus wasn't one to form deep attachments with his possessions, but he considered it an unforgivable slight when anyone took away something he owned. That the cretin had rallied the asur troops by killing Vincirix made the trespass still more insulting.

There would be retribution. Malus vowed that by Khaine he'd face Yvarin again. He'd make the prince answer for Vincirix's death. He'd make him watch as the druchii tore down his fortress stone by stone. He'd keep him alive long enough to see his family butchered like hogs. Only when the cup of vengeance had been drained to its dregs would Malus allow the scum to die.

Why stop there, Malus? It is in your power to make vengeance an eternal state of being. All you need do is stop fighting against me. Embrace the inevitable, and we can enjoy this sensation until Khorne's rage consumes all existence. You could take the soul of Yvarin and torture it until the moons crash into the sea and the sun collapses into a smouldering ember.

Quaking from the intensity of the daemon's presence, Malus hesitated as he raised the warpsword to strike down another victim. At the last instant, he kicked the wretch kneeling before him, knocking the knight into the dirt. In a loud voice, he cried out to the watching legions of druchii. 'Let this be a reminder to every captain and highborn. Let it be a lesson to every soldier and slave. The life of every one of you belongs to me. Spend it well, or by Khaine, I will claim your death for myself!' He raised the warpsword high once more, the blood of its last victim still sizzling upon the blade. The cheers and jeers of the infantry as they had watched the executions had faded now, the warriors cowed by the threat of the tyrant they served.

Malus glowered at his army, his eyes roving from elf to elf, fixing each with his merciless stare. He didn't need their loyalty, he didn't want their love. Those were the weak motivations of the contemptible asur. What he wanted was their obedience. What he needed was their fear. As he gazed upon them, Malus could see that he had claimed both. Sheathing the warpsword, the drachau dismissed his troops.

'Free the last of them,' Malus told Silar as he turned away. There were still a few officers of the Knights of the Burning Dark who had kept their heads.

Silar looked doubtful. 'Is that wise, my lord?'

An ugly chuckle rose from the drachau. He waved his hand at the officers he had spared. 'The knights will need leadership in the coming attack, and these will fight much harder than any others now that they know the fate which awaits failure.' Malus clapped his hand on Silar's shoulder. 'They are afraid of me now, too afraid to plot and scheme. By the time they gain the courage for revenge, I'll have already spent their lives taking the Eagle Gate.'

Leaving Silar to cut the bonds of the disgraced officers, Malus strode up to the skinning rack where Dolthaic's body was stretched. He stared coldly at the commander of his household guard, the mercenary renegade he'd taken into his service so long ago. 'You have wounded me, this day, old comrade.'

Dolthaic's eyes were like two pits of terror as he looked up at his master. 'Dreadlord, have I not always served you well? Have my knights not done everything you've asked of them?'

Malus scowled at Dolthaic. 'A drachau doesn't ask. A drachau commands,' he snarled. 'Your landless wastrels have accomplished the one thing that is unforgiveable. They've failed to bring me victory.'

Upon the rack, Dolthaic struggled in his bonds, his terror mounting with each word that left Malus's lips. 'Mercy! I will not fail you again!'

'Vincirix is dead,' Malus said, his hand closing about the jewelled dagger sheathed alongside the warpsword. 'You let that preening asur prince take her from me. The breach remains in the hands of the enemy. You allowed them to keep it from me. What punishment for a mere sell-sword who dares do such things to his master?'

Dolthaic cried out as Malus ripped the dagger from its sheath and slashed at him. His scream turned into a grunt of astonishment as he felt his left arm fall loose from the frame. When he dared to open his eyes, he saw Malus returning the blade to his belt. It took him a moment to fight through his own disbelief to understand that the drachau had cut him loose.

'Do not mistake a reprieve for forgiveness,' Malus cautioned. 'You've served me well over the years, Dolthaic. Because of that, I am giving you a chance to earn back your right to live. If the Knights of the Burning Dark redeem themselves, riches and glory await you. If they fail me again, it would be best for you to die on the battlefield.'

Turning his back on Dolthaic, a gesture of scornful disdain for one druchii to show another, Malus stalked off towards his tent. He could trust that Dolthaic would drive his knights mercilessly from now on. The dispossessed noble knew first-hand how vicious his master could be. There'd be no restraint any more; if Dolthaic were to fall in battle, he'd make sure his followers shared that fate.

What remained now was for Malus to decide exactly how he was going to spend their lives.

Execute them. Kill them all. Have a little fun, you miserable cretin.
'Shut up, daemon.'

The moment Malus stepped inside his tent, he could feel the icy touch of magic crawling across his skin. Deliberately he suppressed any reaction to the uncanny atmosphere. After his many audiences with his mother and the Witch Lords of Naggor, he'd become quite accomplished at denying the instinctual repugnance sorcery provoked. Calmly, he set his helmet on the ebony stand near the doorway. Without looking, he addressed the personage he knew was somewhere nearby.

'Make yourself at home,' he advised. 'Unless you already have.'

'I predicted your invitation,' Drusala's voice called to him as he started to unbuckle his sword belt.

The drachau turned his head, following the sound of her voice. To call the strip of black silk that Drusala had somehow squirmed into immodest would be like calling an orc irritable. Despite his distrust and, if he were honest, fear of the she-elf, Malus felt the blood in his veins quicken as he looked on her. She was lounging across one of the divans that had been brought all the way from Hag Graef. He'd kept it through the years, a memento of when he'd conspired with the old drachau's daughter, Malgause, to seize the Dark Crag's crown. How his ardour had burned for her and the power she had represented. He might even have kept her as his wife if she hadn't plotted to betray him with her brother.

Now, gazing upon Drusala, Malus couldn't even remember what Malgause looked like. He was sure the comparison wouldn't be favourable. It would take Atharti herself to equal that vision of seduction and desire.

Lose your head and lose your head.

Tz'arkan's voice was but the merest whisper, barely more than imagination, but it struck Malus like a peal of thunder. His nose wrinkled as he caught the subtle aroma, the soft hint of exotic perfume. He could imagine how exotic. He'd seen the degenerate slaves of Slaanesh, the barbarian marauders who devoted themselves wholly and unashamedly to the Prince of Chaos. Their shamans could obliterate the minds of those they offered up to their insidious god simply by holding a tiny flower under their nose. The scent would arouse such feelings of passion that the victim would tear out his own throat to escape the torment of longing and despair.

The key to defying any enchantment was being aware it was being cast. Malus didn't hang his sword belt on the stand with his helmet, but kept a loose grip about the sheathed length of the warpsword. Draped across the divan, Drusala's eyes exhibited just the tiniest flash of alarm. She knew Malus hadn't been caught in the web of her charms.

'Was I overbold in coming here?' Drusala asked, leaning back to better display the supple curve of her legs.

It was an effort of self-control for Malus to keep his gaze focused on her eyes. The witch didn't need perfumes or magics to enchant her prey. She was perfectly dangerous all on her own.

'I have not yet lit the pyre for Vincirix Quickdeath or entreated Nethu to allow her soul to pass the Last Door,' Malus said, trying to inject a steely firmness into his voice.

Drusala raised one eyebrow in surprise. 'Sentiment from the Scion of Hag Graef? I did not think you capable of such... indulgence. The little she-sword of Clar Karond is dead. Her usefulness to you is over.'

'And the usefulness of Drusala, lap-dog of Ghrond, is only beginning,' Malus replied venomously.

The sorceress smiled at his anger. 'Magic is always useful, drachau. Your mother should have taught you that.'

Mention of his mother only inflamed his anger. Malus stalked towards the divan. He started to reach for Drusala, but something even more primal than Tz'arkan warned him back. She was trying to goad him. He might not know why, but that didn't mean he had to walk blindly into her trap. Shaking his head, he lowered his arm and walked away.

'Your magic wasn't terribly impressive today,' Malus scolded her, 'for all your airs of arcane power and your claims of being Morathi's favourite disciple. My warlocks have been decimated by the phoenixes, but a few survived. They tell me you abandoned them when the birds came.'

Drusala matched his cold smile. 'I went to fight another, still greater enemy. He calls himself Shrinastor, one of the asur loremasters. Quite a formidable mage. Left unchecked he could have wrought great havoc on your forces.' A scolding note entered Drusala's tone as she wagged a finger at Malus. 'When you tried to kill the asur prince, did you not wonder that the warpsword failed to slay him outright? That was Shrinastor's doing. He worked a charm to dull the efficacy of your blow and allow the prince to live.'

Malus was silent a moment, thinking about Drusala's claim. It was true, the warpsword should have killed the asur prince with one blow. Instead the elf had only been wounded. If the frustration of his revenge was the doing of Shrinastor, then he owed the mage a debt of slow death.

'My warlocks have been reduced to a mere shell of their former strength,' Malus said. 'I am told they were unable to overcome the phoenixes. Lady Eldire cautioned that the birds are drawn to magic like a leech to blood. If that is true, how do you hope to prevail against both the birds and the mage?'

'Reinforcements are coming,' Drusala said. She glanced at her hand and a large ring fitted to one finger, a band of obsidian with a great sphere of crystal. 'I have seen it. By nightfall, Fleetmaster Aeich will reach your camp, bringing along a small army of corsairs and all of his surviving seers.'

'Aeich will bear me no friendship after leaving him to rot on the beach,' Malus observed.

'True, but after you left, the Tiranocii attacked. They managed enough damage to scare Aeich away from the black ark. You might have no friends among the corsairs, but they understand that their one hope for survival is to join your horde.' The sorceress tapped a finger against her chin. 'I doubt Aeich will try to have you assassinated until after the Eagle Gate is taken. A pirate knows it takes a general to capture a fortress.'

Malus clenched his fist in frustration. If it needed only a general to take the fortress, it would already be in his hands. No, after failing to seize the breach today, it would need something more. It would need luck. He had but the briefest window in which to take the gate. After that, the Eagle Gate itself would be reinforced. Worse, the dragon princes of Caledor might send a few of their wyrms to intercede. If that happened, Malus would have no chance of victory. He'd be disgraced, at best. Dead, at worst. Most likely, that had been Malekith's plan all along.

The drachau walked across the tent to the mahogany cabinet where he kept his special wine. For the first time in many months, he needed the drink not to quiet Tz'arkan but to stifle his own fears.

'You should be careful not to imbibe too freely,' Drusala called to him from the divan. 'A general must keep a clear head... and a clean spirit.'

Malus turned and scowled at her. 'Be careful how much you presume, witch. No one is indispensable.' Returning to the stand near the door, he snatched up his helmet and stormed from the tent.

Drusala watched the drachau depart. 'We shall see,' she whispered. By her estimate, a few more weeks and there would be no more of Eldire's draught left. If Malus lived that long, things would get quite interesting.

She would make a fine match for you. She wants to be lover and mother all at once. I wonder which you need more, Malus.

The most frustrating thing about the daemon was having nothing to lash out against when its taunts cut too deep. Malus growled at Tz'arkan to relent. Much more of its baiting and he'd go back to the tent and drain an entire bottle to smother the daemonic presence. That might play right into Drusala's plans for them – and he emphasised that concern. The triumph he felt when Tz'arkan receded back into the shadows of his subconscious wasn't as satisfying as he needed it to be. Something had to suffer for all the rage bottled up inside him.

Malus found that his lonely walk through the camp had brought him to the crevasse where the slave-soldiers of Naggor had been bivouacked. The grubby survivors of the day's fighting lay heaped on the ground, panting like dogs beneath ragged blankets and threadbare cloaks. A few of the vermin had been granted the privilege of starting small fires to warm themselves against the night. It was an indulgence that Kunor typically reserved for those Naggorites who informed on their fellows – or those Naggorites he wanted their fellows to believe were informants.

As he glowered at the slaves, Malus thought of the many battles he had fought against them. The war between Naggor and Hag Graef had been vicious and bloody, but in the end he had been the ultimate victor. He'd risen from being an outlaw and outcast to becoming the Dark Crag's greatest hero and drachau. In a way, he owed his position to the Naggorites. Perhaps that was why he despised them more now than even at the height of the war. That vindictiveness was why he'd brought them along, shackled in the holds of the black ark, when he'd left so many others behind.

To be strong, a druchii needed something to hate.

Malus saw the empty, beaten looks the slaves gave him – at least those brave enough to even look at their conqueror. Dogs! Vermin! To call these wretches druchii was to defile the name.

The despot turned as he heard armoured figures come rushing towards him. Silar Thornblood and a few of his guards. With them was Kunor Kunoll's Son, fresh blood smearing the leather smock the slavemaster wore. Malus knew it was Kunor's custom to personally attend the most sorely wounded of his slaves. Any Naggorite with half a brain in his head made sure to bite his own tongue rather than fall into the slavemaster's hands.

'Dreadlord!' Silar shouted, anxiety in his tone. 'You should not be alone.'

Malus waved his hand in contempt at the exhausted Naggorites. 'Your concern amuses me, old friend. What danger is there here? A whipped dog forgets how to bite.'

'And we have ways of making them forget if they remember,' Kunor grinned.

Silar stiffened at the slavemaster's mirth. He'd always pressed Malus to treat the Naggorites with some measure of consideration and restraint. They were, in his mind at least, fellow druchii. 'I was worried about asur infiltrators,' Silar said. 'The ashencloaks continue to strike down our pickets and spoil our supplies. If one of them should have the chance to strike at you...'

'Then he would end this battle with one arrow,' Malus said. The drachau's gaze became almost murderous. 'If such is my doom, the gods will answer for their jest.' He turned back around, staring across the huddled Naggorites. 'Kunor, how many troops do you still have?'

'Dreadlord, the asur struck down three score and six,' the slavemaster replied. 'Another score or so have expired from their wounds.'

Malus nodded. A grotesque strategy was occurring to him. If Drusala's prediction was right, and she would hardly have made the claim unless she was certain, he'd soon have Aeich and a host of corsairs for the next attack. Warriors accustomed to scaling the battlements of their black ark, they'd be the perfect shock troops to send against the walls of the Eagle Gate. But for him to do so, the asur would need a more immediate threat to keep them occupied.

'Your entertainment is over, Kunor,' Malus said. 'The injuries of the wounded are to be bound. You'll also pick out a hundred of the dogs in this camp. Once you've gathered them together, march them to where the beastmasters have penned the war hydras. Tell them to slather every one of the Naggorites you bring them with fellbrew.'

Silar's face went pale with shock. 'You can't mean to do such a thing?'

Malus laughed. 'Old friend, I need the war hydras at their most ferocious when we attack tomorrow. When they devour prey that has been coated in fellbrew, it will drive them berserk. Given their slow digestion, six hours should suffice to gain me the results I want.'

'But you could use horses or cold ones...' Silar protested.

'You are too timid to ever amount to anything,' Malus reproved the highborn. 'I need every horse and every cold one. I have extra Naggorites.'

Laughing at his cruel jest, the despot stalked away. Silar ordered the guards he had brought with him to follow Malus. The future of Hag Graef depended on the drachau. He wasn't going to risk that future because of their lord's hubris.

Kunor lingered long enough to give Silar a cold look of contempt before he rushed away to rouse his henchmen and carry out the drachau's command. Silar was left alone at the mouth of the crevasse. He stayed there while he heard the cries rising from the sick-tent where the injured Naggorites had been taken. It would be like Kunor to tell the wounded what was going to happen to them even as their hurts were being bandaged.

Disgusted, Silar started to walk away from the slave compound. He had only gone a short way, however, when he found his step restricted. He looked down just as the noose his foot had stepped into was jerked tight and he was sent crashing to the ground. Before he could roll onto his back, he felt the weight of a body slam on top of him, pushing his face into the dirt.

'Now, Darkblade, vengeance!' a venomous voice hissed.

Silar felt a blow against the back of his head. The thick steel of his helmet prevented the blade from striking his neck, but he knew his attacker would correct his aim for the next blow. Flailing about, Silar tried to rise, but there were other foes now, enemies who had hold of his arms. Growling in frustration, he struggled to break free before the killing blow could be struck.

'This isn't Darkblade!' a shocked voice rang out.

Silar's head was pulled back, his chinstrap snapping as his helmet was ripped free. He found himself looking into the scarred countenance of a wiry Naggorite. The slave returned his scowl with interest.

'Who is it, Lorfal?' one of the other ambushers asked.

'Silar Thornblood,' Lorfal grunted in contempt. 'One of the tyrant's lapdogs.'

The pressure on Silar's back vanished. To his surprise, the elves holding his arms released their grip. Slowly, the highborn rose to his feet. There were half a dozen slaves around him, each armed with some manner of blade. Silar was careful to keep his hands away from his own weapons. He was surprised to recognise the ambusher who'd been on top of him as Bragath Blyte, one of old General Ralkoth's captains. They'd crossed swords before, when Naggor had still been free.

Bragath saw the recognition in Silar's eyes. 'Yes, it is I. You see, I've survived all these years. When Darkblade conquered us and put all the captains of Naggor to the sword, you could have pointed me out to him.'

Silar nodded, his eyes watching the other Naggorites, wary for the first sign of treachery. 'You were a worthy foe. You deserved a death in battle, your chance to impress Khaine and Ereth Khial.'

The slave-soldier clenched his fist. 'Many years have passed and I've often wondered if I should thank you or curse you for that, Silar. I've watched you keenly when I've seen you and listened with sharp ears whenever one of our people spoke of you.' A cold smile formed on Bragath's face. 'You've always tried to deal fairly with us. You've risked Darkblade's wrath to temper the cruelties he'd heap upon us.'

'If you would kill me, give me the same chance to die with a sword in my hand I gave you,' Silar said.

'That is my intention,' Bragath said. He pointed his dagger at the scarred Lorfal. 'We thought you were Darkblade himself. That is why we attacked. It was an opportunity that could not be squandered.'

The chastened Lorfal hung his head in contrition. 'The tyrant was here. I heard him speak.'

Bragath motioned the elf to silence. 'We didn't intend to attack you, Silar, but we were looking for you. Alone among those close to Darkblade, you might give us a chance to get close to him. I know you have disagreed with his ruthless orders. A drachau must be merciless, but Darkblade goes beyond what his title demands of him.'

'You seek to draw me into a conspiracy against the dreadlord?' Silar asked, stunned by the outrageousness of such a thing.

'Indeed,' Bragath said. 'That is what we ask. What is your answer?'

Silar started to reach for his sword; then, in the distance, he heard another of the wounded Naggorites scream. Druchii fed to war hydras like so much carrion. It was a callous waste of life, an almost unthinkable atrocity.

Silar let his hand fall to his side. Looking Bragath straight in the eye, he answered the slave's question.

'Whatever you are planning, I don't think you could do it without me.'

CHAPTER TWELVE

Malus hefted the warpsword high overhead, shouting at the black legions of his horde. He evoked all the old indignities that had been heaped upon the druchii by their despised asur kin. He spoke to his warriors of the ancient hate that had divided a people. He smiled coldly as he recounted the theft of the Phoenix Crown from Malekith by a petty and ungrateful people. With his words, he conjured the vision of lost Nagarythe, now a wasteland haunted by ghosts and monsters and the deluded aesanar. He recited the promise made to the Black Council by the Witch King: that the lands of their birthright, the kingdoms of Ulthuan, would belong to them if they but had the strength to take it.

'Death and blood to the traitors!' Malus roared, his voice amplified beyond the merely mortal by the excited daemon boiling inside him. Tz'arkan was in its element now, poised upon the edge of slaughter and massacre. Briefly, Malus had considered dulling the daemon with wine, but had at last relented. He might need the accursed might of the daemon to draw upon. After all of these years sharing his flesh with the malignant fiend, he was confident that he knew how much he could tap into Tz'arkan without going too far.

Without losing control.

Without losing all that he was and all that he would ever be.

At his cry, the drachau's commanders issued the order to attack. The breach was blocked now by the piled carcasses of his own cold ones. No lightning strike by his cavalry would allow Malus to slip behind the walls and seize the Eagle Gate swiftly. No, now he would be forced into a longer fight. His army must outnumber Prince Yvarin's asur a hundredfold; there could be no question of the final outcome if he had only the garrison to worry about.

But Malus knew time was a greater enemy to him than the asur guarding the Eagle Gate. The host of Hag Graef had been bolstered during the night by Fleetmaster Aeich and those corsairs who had fled their doomed black ark. Adding thousands of battle-hardened corsairs and militia from the abandoned *Eternal Malediction* had swollen the ranks of his army, and the addition of Aeich's surviving seers and sorceresses had added a good deal more magic to his force, making Drusala not quite as essential as she so dearly wanted to be.

The problem with the arrival of the corsairs was the news they bore with them. They'd been harried by the asur along the entire line of march. Not just by the black-feathered arrows of ashencloaks, but charioteers from Tiranoc too, the advance elements of an entire Tiranocii army that had pursued them from the beachhead. Only a day or so behind Aeich, the Tiranocii force wasn't big enough to pose a threat to Malus's army. However, if they struck against the rear of his horde while they were trying to break through the Eagle Gate, the carnage they could wreak would be prodigious.

Malus didn't care so much for the loss of warriors, but he was worried about the loss of time. Every hour might bring a relief force from Ellyrion to support the Eagle Gate. Or worse, the skies might fill with dragons from Caledor. The drachau had campaigned against the asur often enough to know that whatever enmity might exist between the kingdoms, they set aside such resentments when faced by a mutual foe. If the dragons came, Malus would never take the Eagle Gate. His army would be smashed and scattered, his own disgrace absolute.

It is not too late, Malus. Set me loose and victory will yet be yours!

Spite hissed beneath its master as the horned one sensed the brief flare-up of the daemon's presence. It took an effort of will, but Malus forced Tz'arkan back into the hinterlands of his soul. Now wasn't the time to indulge the fiend's bloodthirsty ambitions. Malus had his own dreams of conquest and slaughter to achieve.

Blocks of infantry marched into the pass. Malus watched their banners snapping in the wind. He wondered how many of the asur inside recognised the bloodied flags of Hag Graef. He wondered how many hearts had filled with terror as the nature of the foe they faced became apparent. Those who didn't know the druchii would soon learn.

The warriors of Clar Karond, the enslaved Naggorites, the soldiers of the Dark Crag itself, all marched behind a screen of skirmishers drawn from the black ark's militia. Why squander his own slaves when he had those of Aeich to spend? The fleetmaster had been a good deal too vocal about blaming Malus for abandoning the beachhead. Well, now the fleetmaster would be thinking the slaughter of his slaves was his punishment. That mistake would make Aeich less appreciative of the role he and his corsairs were to play in the battle. The best illusions, after all, were those who believed in their own deceit.

Spite trotted alongside the armoured mass of spearmen, a regiment that had held the line during the final attack by Naggor against Hag Graef. For their unrivalled brutality on the field, Malus had awarded them the banner of the vanquished Witch Lords. As the spears slowly advanced on the Eagle

Gate, that banner was held high before them. A sheet of leathery skin, flayed from the bodies of enemies the Witch Lords had offered in sacrifice to dark Hekarti, the banner had been endowed with powerful enchantments by the Naggorites. As arrows came whistling down from the battlements, they veered sharply away from the dreadspears and deflected into the regiment of swordsmen marching on their flank. A few of the bleakswords fell, their armour pierced by the diverted arrows, their bodies kicked and trampled by the warriors who hastened to fill the gaps in their ranks.

Orbs of blazing arcane fire came crashing down from the Eagle Gate, incinerating dozens of druchii with each impact. In response, the sorceresses Aeich had brought unleashed their own dark magics against the walls. Lances of writhing lightning, blacker than death and lethal as the kiss of a medusa, seared along the walls. The scorched bodies of asur soldiers hurtled from the battlements, cooked inside their own armour. After an initial assault, the barrage of magic broke into isolated duels as asur mages pitted their abilities against druchii sorcery. Malus could see the white fire and the black lightning crackle and explode as the antithetical conjurations collided. Here and there, the white fire would fade, but along the front nearest the breach, it was the darker sorcery that failed. Malus scowled as he looked in that direction. The loremaster Drusala had spoken of seemed to be taking a hand in defending the gap. The asur's power must be prodigious to overcome so many sorceresses. Malus wished he could have matched Drusala against him. Whichever way such a contest went, it would make things simpler for the drachau.

Drusala, however, had other duties at the moment. Her magic was the key to this second assault on the Eagle Gate. The sorcerous deception she had worked to make her dark pegasus seem an ordinary horse had inspired Malus. He'd tasked her with working a still mightier glamour, an illusion that would conceal the true strength of the attack until it came smashing down upon the asur.

Malus laughed grimly to himself as he watched the mass of slave-soldiers being herded towards the walls. The Naggorites were again acting as a screen for better, more valuable fighters. Every arrow that pierced one of the slaves, every bolt that skewered the marching spearmen, was directed, naturally, at those nearest the wall. The asur didn't target the ranks behind, that great solid mass of druchii who stormed onwards, the whips of their masters snapping at them and forcing them on. Perhaps, if Shrinastor and the other mages weren't already occupied, they might have noticed something, detected some hint of the glamour Drusala had worked. But the mages didn't have the luxury of such wariness, not with their arcane duels unfolding all along the wall.

Piercing, bestial cries announced that other foes had noticed the deception, or at least had become aware of the great magic being worked at the rear of the Naggorites. Rising from the walls, their plumage burning like molten bronze, the phoenixes circled above the Eagle Gate, a fiery flock that was now stirring itself to action.

Malus had anticipated this as well. He'd placed his most dependable vassal, Silar Thornblood, with the contingent from Clar Karond. Silar had strict orders. When the phoenixes took wing, the beastmasters were to throw open the cages they had wheeled all the way from the *Eternal Malediction*.

Looking towards the ground the warriors of Clar Karond held, Malus watched as a great swarm rose shrieking and howling into the sky. Harpies, cruel twisted beasts cast in the roughest semblance of she-elves, with great clawed talons for feet and leathery wings sprouting from their backs. They were vile, despicable creatures, eager to torment the weak and helpless, to glut themselves upon the dead. Great flocks of them had followed the black arks – indeed, many of them had been captured in the *Eternal Malediction*'s rigging – hungry for the victims the druchii slaughtered.

Sometimes exhibiting a vicious cunning, the harpies were still little more than beasts and it was the instinct of beasts that moved them now. It didn't matter to the winged fiends that there were scores of dead druchii lying before the Eagle Gate. It didn't enter their minds to question the battle unfolding around them. Neither hunger nor curiosity governed them now. It was simple brute aggression, the fury of an animal that senses a rival in its domain. Creatures of the sky, the harpies viewed the flock of phoenixes as trespassers, intruders to be destroyed or driven away.

Even as the largest of the phoenixes, a great bird whose plumage was the colour of sapphire and diamond, started to dive towards the shaded palanquin where Drusala worked her enchantment, the harpies hurled themselves upon the phoenixes. The aerial battle was primal, primordial in its savagery. The harpies were immolated by the fires of the phoenixes, their charred bodies sent plummeting down into the massed druchii below. Sheer numbers, however, overwhelmed several of the birds. As they were slashed by the talons of their foes, burning blood spattered across the battlefield, a sizzling rain that scorched the flesh of whatever it struck. One of the phoenixes, several harpies clinging to it with their talons and mauling it with their clawed hands, went smashing down into the battlements. The fiery bird exploded as it perished, immolating its killers and the hapless asur manning that part of the wall.

The immediate threat of the phoenixes removed, Malus gave the command for the second assault to begin. Nearby, a blood-red banner was unfurled. It was the sign the waiting reaper bolt throwers had been waiting for. The fiendish engines began to pepper the face of the great gates with enormous steel arrows, each as long and thick as an elf's leg. Dark enchantments had been invested into the bolts, and as the magazines of the repeating bolt throwers churned away, the face of the Eagle Gate was pitted and scarred. Cupolas disintegrated beneath the barrage, sending archers hurtling to their deaths far below. Turrets crumbled, raining rubble onto the walls and smashing the defenders into paste.

In time with the assault by the reapers, Aeich and his corsairs launched their own attack on the left flank. Grappling irons were hurled onto the battlements while crossbows strove to hold the asur back. From behind their screen of militia and slaves, the murderous corsairs raced to the walls, their sea-dragon cloaks glistening with an oily sheen as the sun shone upon them.

The attack by the corsairs threw the asur into a panic. Here, the defenders seemed certain, was the main thrust of Malus's attack. From his vantage, he could see them diverting troops from other parts of the wall, determined to keep the corsairs from gaining a foothold on the battlements. Dozens of corsairs fell screaming as their grapples and ladders were cast down; scores more died as they tried to climb the ropes, their bodies spitted by asur arrows.

Malus waited until the corsair assault showed the first, faint hint of being driven back. Again, he motioned to the highborn bearing his signal flags. This time the banner that was unfurled was green. Even Spite seemed to understand the meaning behind that signal, the horned one hissing lowly as the command was relayed. Malus laughed at his steed's temper. He wondered what horror the asur would feel when they saw the next attack.

The great block of troops behind the Naggorites burst through their ranks, charging through the slave-soldiers as though they weren't there. The Naggorites scattered in all directions, heedless of the arrows that continued to persecute them from the walls. Some hundreds fell, smashed beneath the force that now surged through their ranks.

Drusala's glamour vanished, winking out like a snuffed candle. Where a body of slave-soldiers and their overseers had been, there now charged a dozen war hydras and their minders.

Absolute panic gripped the asur. Malus could see archers hurriedly reacting to the charging beasts, many of them leaning out from between the crenellations to loose upon the hydras. These fell victim to the bolts of druchii darkshards, plummeting from the walls. Some few sent arrows into the hydras, but the effort was far too feeble to arrest the reptilian assault.

Bolt throwers were hastily turned back to the gate, their powerful missiles smashing into the war hydras. The monsters simply snapped and gnawed at the spears embedded in their scaly flesh. Drugged by their meal of the night before, they felt no pain, the tiny brains in their many heads aware only of the burning hunger gnawing at their bellies.

More and more bowfire was unleashed against the war hydras. Now the crackle of magic struck at the beasts. Malus clenched his fist in triumph as he saw asur spearmen trying to dislodge rubble from the shattered turrets onto the heads of the monsters. Between the hydras and the corsairs, the asur were completely committed now. Two deadly foes snapped at their fortifications, enemies too dangerous to ignore.

The asur commander would doubtless be committing his reserves, any caution abandoned in the face of the double assault. Yvarin, like all of his weakling breed, valued the warriors who served under him. He'd project that same attitude onto his enemy. That was a bit of arrogance that was going to cost him. Malus didn't care how many lives he squandered. There were thousands more waiting to die so that he might have the glory of seizing the Eagle Gate!

Prince Yvarin would never guess that both of these perilous assaults were but feints. While the garrison was occupied with these distractions, Malus would be leading the real assault.

How many troops had the asur dared leave to guard the breach?

From behind the gruesome rampart of slaughtered cold ones, the Eataine Guard watched as the druchii assault intensified. Corsairs were mounting an assault on the walls, trying to secure even the smallest presence there so that they could open the way for the mass of black-armoured infantry below. The rampaging war hydras threw themselves against the silver and starwood doors of the gate itself. Two of the beasts had been felled by eagle claw bolt throwers, while three more of the monsters writhed in their death throes as magical fire was poured down on them from spouts and murder holes. Still, the surviving reptiles flung themselves at the gate, clawing it with their feet and spitting at it with their venom.

A grim silence held the Eataine Guard. They felt shame at watching their comrades fighting all across the wall while their own position was as quiet as the tomb. They longed to throw themselves at the enemy; in their minds rang the bloody song of Khaine, the call to war that stirred the heart of every elf. Unlike the foul druchii, the asur knew better than to give themselves wholly to the Bloody-handed God. Khaine had his place, he had his purpose, but the elf who harkened only to his war-song would soon become a monster. The example set by the druchii was proof of that.

A murmur swept through the white-clad warriors, astonishment as they found their commander, Prince Yvarin, returning to the breach. His arm was still swaddled in the arcane poultice Shrinastor had fashioned for him. It was crafted from feathers donated by the phoenixes and its glow shone out from beneath the prince's armour, exuding a warmth that brought beads of perspiration to the brows of those standing too near. Yvarin's shattered shield had been replaced by one gifted to him by the captain of the Silver Pelts, a mark of esteem and solidarity from the contingent from Chrace. Not to be outdone, the Talons of Tor Caldea had bestowed on him a breastplate of finely wrought ithilmar and obsidian, which, they claimed, had been forged in dragonfire by the mightiest dragon mages.

Prince Yvarin was uneasy about the heroic regard he was afforded by his troops. After the thwarting of Darkblade's first assault, Yvarin had been hailed as a champion of his people, his deeds at the wall magnified in the telling and the retelling until even the Caledorians were whispering his name in awed respect. He'd become the rallying point for his entire garrison. Elves who had gazed upon the size and evil of Darkblade's horde, who had felt the tremor of fear and doom in their hearts, now spoke of triumph and glory. Resignation to fate had been replaced with greater purpose: victory! To win the battle, not simply wear down the druchii host and break the impetus of their invasion. To finish it here and now, not lay the seeds from which would grow the triumph of another army. To be the victors themselves, not the martyred dead of future remembrance.

It was humbling to have such hope vested in him. But while Yvarin had dreamed of fame and glory, he now found it had a sour taste. Never before had he felt the weight of responsibility lie so heavily upon his shoulders. The entire garrison was united behind him; no longer disparate contingents from the ten kingdoms, they had embraced a new identity – the defenders of the Eagle Gate. He'd told them as much in the speech he'd given after Shrinastor administered to his hurts. He had been stunned by the cheers and salutes his sentiment had been met with. Not the cries of warriors resigned to their duty, but of true hope.

Darkblade's second assault was much grander than that first bold dash to the breach. Yvarin had hoped to deceive his enemy away from where the fortress was weakest. As he'd commanded his troops from the ramparts, as he'd watched the druchii attack unfold, a terrible premonition had occurred to him. He'd shown guile in trying to draw Darkblade away from the breach. Why should he expect anything less from the infamous Tyrant of Hag Graef?

The corsairs on the walls, the war hydras at the gate, these were both terrible foes, but perhaps that was exactly why they'd been set loose. Thunder to distract from the lightning. From the beak of the eagle, Yvarin had studied the deployment of Darkblade's army. As the war hydras burst out from their glamour and trampled the druchii warriors screening them, the first alarm sounded in Yvarin's brain. The survivors of the treacherous assault by the hydras were being reformed, whipped and threatened back into positions away from the gates. The haste and brutality of the slave-masters indicated that whatever purpose the regrouping had, it was both important and urgent. As they reformed at the other side of the hydras and away from the corsairs, it appeared to Yvarin that there was only one possible reason for these actions. Darkblade intended another assault on the breach.

The commanders subordinate to Yvarin didn't agree with his conclusion. Jariel had demurred at his suggestion that the Talons of Tor Caldea withdraw from the fight on the walls and strike out to the slopes of the pass to support the Eataine Guard at the breach. She'd posited that the druchii were reforming in order to rush in once the hydras were through the gate. She didn't agree with Yvarin's observation that the enemy would have put fresh warriors at the ready to act as shock troops. The druchii were as merciless to their own as they were to their enemy – she'd seen as much fighting raiders along the coasts of Caledor. She wasn't about to pull her troops out of the fight to support an attack she didn't feel was coming. The other commanders held similar views, and impressed on Yvarin that to pull any warriors from where there was already an attack would be to weaken their positions just at the time when they needed them at their strongest.

Yvarin was certain, however, that the real attack would be here. So it was back to the breach, back to the Eataine Guard, where he felt his place must be. When Darkblade made his move, it would be too late. Yvarin felt he'd anticipated the enemy. If his commanders were right, the absence of one asur on the walls wouldn't count for much. If, as he was convinced, the druchii moved again against the breach, his presence there might make all the difference. He was, after all, a hero now.

The salutes of his soldiers warmed Yvarin even more than the poultice Shrinastor had provided him. He returned their salutes with the terse nod that was expected of an elven prince, but his shining eyes told them how deeply their esteem was valued. Of all his troops, there were none he felt closer to than these warriors. To have earned their respect was a richness beyond gold.

Oerleith, the captain of the regiment, his family heraldry picked out in crimson thread against the white cloak he wore over his silver-chased armour, bowed as the prince approached him. 'Your highness, you do us a supreme honour,' he said, his eyes downcast. 'Everything has been quiet in this quarter. Except for the odd harpy dropping down from the sky, the enemy has lost interest in us.'

A tinge of hurt crept into Yvarin's eyes. Even these, his proud Eataine Guard, felt he should be elsewhere, that he should be up on the walls or at the gates inspiring his troops where the fighting was at its worst. They too didn't see the threat that Yvarin saw.

'I haven't lost interest in you,' Yvarin said. 'The breach here is the key to the Eagle Gate. Darkblade knows that as keenly as I do. Why should we believe he won't attack here?'

The captain raised his head, turning a look of confusion and astonishment on his prince. 'The druchii are already assaulting the walls and the gate. Darkblade is losing hundreds of his soldiers. He'd gain nothing by such an expensive feint.'

'He'd gain something more precious to him than the lives of his warriors,' Yvarin said. 'He'd gain time.'

Even as he spoke, warning horns sounded from the battlements. Yvarin and Oerleith rushed to the piled carcasses of the cold ones. They watched as the reformed slave-soldiers came marching towards the breach. More significantly, however, beyond them marched thousands of druchii regulars, the banners of the Dark Crag itself flying above them. Too late, Yvarin's captains on the wall saw the accuracy of their prince's premonition. An orderly redeployment was impossible now. The dribs and drabs that could make their way down from the walls would be merely a gesture. If the breach were to hold, it would be thanks to the Eataine Guard.

Yvarin hoisted himself on top of one of the cold ones, his boot resting on the reptile's head. He drew his sword, the same blade that had killed the druchii captain. He turned and faced his warriors, the finest in his garrison, the comrades-in-arms who had held this position against the cold one knights. They'd braved the best Darkblade could throw at them. It was important that they knew this as the black tide of the tyrant's army came surging towards them.

'Sons of Ellyrion! Daughters of the Summer Kingdom! Gaze upon the desperation of your foe! You, who stood here and cut down the vanguard of his horde. You who shattered the point of his spear. Now he sends a flood of dogs to drown you in blood. He thinks to strike fear into your noble hearts by this show of force. I say to you that you spit on dogs! I say to you that your hearts know no fear! You are the Eataine Guard. Let Hag Graef send a hundred slaves against us. We will slay them all and ask the scum for another thousand. We will show them what the song of Khaine means when it is sung by those with valour in their hearts and courage in their souls!'

A great cheer rose from the Eataine Guard. With spears crashing against shields, the asur answered the fiery words of their hero. Almost eagerly, they ran to the grisly pile of dead reptiles, ready to repel the first waves of Darkblade's army. Their faith in their prince had blotted out the doubt that might have ruled them otherwise. They had longed for battle, and now that battle was coming to them. With Prince Yvarin fighting beside them, how could they fail to be victorious?

Malus's retainers stacked the corpses of the knights he had executed into a pile. Digging his spurs into Spite's flanks, he sent the horned one scrambling up onto the decaying mound. The reptile snarled, digging its claws into the dead flesh until it found the purchase it wanted. Malus waited until his steed was settled before he unsheathed the warpsword and raised it high. With a downward sweep, he thrust the blade in the direction of the breach. A single word left his lips, arctic in its tone.

'Advance!'

Obediently, the warriors of Hag Graef trooped towards the rampart of dead cold ones. Already the Naggorite slave-soldiers were engaging the asur, throwing themselves at the entrenched enemy with the fatalism of all sword-fodder. They were dying by the droves, but it was of little consequence. They weren't there to win; they were there to occupy the enemy long enough for Malus's real troops to bear down on the position. Indeed, if the Naggorites did manage to hold their ground they'd be slaughtered by the soldiers coming up from behind them for being in the way. Malus considered the promise of spilling Naggorite blood before laying into the asur to be something of a reward to the soldiers of Hag Graef. The heap of dead knights beneath Spite's claws was a reminder of the punishment they'd get if they proved unworthy of that reward.

The dreadspears stabbed their way through the few Naggorites holding against the asur. A blast from the serpent-tooth horn the first regiment carried announced that they were confronting the defenders. Malus watched for the signal flag to be raised, the signal that the spearmen were through. His patience wore thinner with each passing breath. After ten minutes had elapsed, he could see that the first regiment was beginning to fall back. The second regiment advanced, thwarting the withdrawal of the first. Malus smiled coldly as he saw the warriors of the reinforcing regiment cutting down any druchii trying to retreat from the front. The orders he had issued to his captains hadn't fallen on deaf ears. Every one of them understood what was expected.

Still, even the advance of the second regiment wasn't enough to break the defenders. Worse, they themselves were beset from the flank by Caledorian archers, who'd crept out onto the face of the cliffs flanking the pass. From their precarious perches, the bowmen harassed the second regiment. Darkshards were brought up to oppose the Caledorians, but the crafty asur had positioned themselves beyond the range of the druchii's crossbows.

The third and fourth regiments swarmed forwards now, rushing to bolster the flagging strength of the second and the remnants of the first. At last, Malus thought, the breach would be taken. His anger boiled inside him as the asur continued to hold. Minute after minute, with only the Caledorian bowmen to support them, the Eataine Guard held their ground. Outnumbered a hundredfold, they refused to yield!

Elsewhere, Malus could see that his feinting attackers were faltering. The corsairs were a ravaged shell of their original strength, their robust assaults reduced to cautious probes. The harpies had been burned from the sky by the phoenixes, leaving far too many of the magical birds free to menace the druchii sorceresses.

At the gate itself, the assault of the war hydras was likewise losing its impetus. Malus saw Griselfang scorched by a shower of arcane fire poured down on it from the spouts set into the fortifications above the gate. While the huge beast writhed in pain, bones popping through its charred hide, one of the phoenixes swooped down on it. A great bird of ice and crystal, larger and older than its fiery kin, the phoenix tore into Griselfang with talons that froze the hydra's mangled hide and caused its scales to crumble into shards of frost. As the phoenix beat at the hydra with its wings, each buffet seemed to drain more of the vitality and resistance from the reptile. Its heads drooped wearily as their long necks sagged to the earth. Its lashing tail became sluggish, incapable of swatting down its avian tormentor.

Too intent on Griselfang, the cold phoenix was taken by surprise when

Snarclaw charged at it. Three of the hydra's heads sank their fangs into the bird, snowy ichor dripping from the grievous wounds it had inflicted. Even as frost began to form around the jaws that held the phoenix, Snarclaw was wrenching the creature free from the dying Griselfang. The bird slapped at the reptile with its great wings, freezing scales and sapping warmth with each touch of its icy pinions. Its other heads hissing at its prey, the hydra began to pull the phoenix apart with the jaws embedded in its body. Shrieking in agony, the phoenix was ripped to shreds, each portion of its mutilated frame freezing as it died, transforming into nothing more than slivers of ice.

Snarclaw had no time to savour its triumph. As it stood over the wreckage of the phoenix, the vengeful fire of the garrison stabbed down into it. Bolt throwers and bowmen all across the wall sought to avenge the cold phoenix. The hydra's scaly hide was pierced again and again by the missiles. In its agonies it threw itself towards the gates, there to have its flesh scorched by the same kind of molten fire that had burned Griselfang. Howling in agony, the reptile lumbered back, half of its heads lying dead and dragging behind it in the dust. Before it got more than a few yards, however, a great bolt of lightning hurtled down from the beak of the stone eagle, sent from the staff of the blue-robed elf who stood there. The arcane energies sapped the last of the hydra's monstrous vitality. With a final shudder, Snarclaw crashed to the ground and its remaining heads wilted into the dirt.

Malus cursed lividly as he saw his prize hydras cut down. The brutes had cost him a fortune. With them gone, he knew the runts Clar Karond had salvaged from their collapsing city wouldn't be able to batter their way through the gates. The asur would soon realise that, too. Then fresh forces would be diverted to the breach.

The breach! Seven regiments had now been thrown into the attack and still the Eataine Guard held their ground. What would it take to break those preening asur swine! Minutes of defiance stretched into hours. Fresh defenders could be seen scrambling down from the battlements to support the position, but the main opposition remained the Eataine Guard. Callously, Malus threw fresh troops into the assault. The ground around the breach became a mire of blood and bodies, yet he wouldn't relent. Any captain who dared think of withdrawal was butchered where he stood.

Finally, as night fell over the pass, even Malus had to accept the hideous truth. The attack had failed. He'd spent thousands of his soldiers, but the asur had held. With the darkness, the phoenixes diverted their attentions to the troops massed at the breach, swooping down on them in blazing dives that charred their victims and shattered the morale of those remaining. Assaulted from one flank by the Caledorian's arrows, the aerial attacks of the phoenixes were too much for the druchii. Their strength still in the thousands, the host of Hag Graef turned and retreated back down the pass.

Malus watched his soldiers run, cursing each and every one as a coward and worse. Threats of reprisal and revenge slashed across the fleeing warriors until the drachau's throat felt like a raw wound. Promises to torture their descendants to the fifth generation were not enough to turn his warriors back.

Turning away from the rout, Malus glared at the rampart of dead cold ones. He could see the Eataine Guard standing atop the bodies, jeering and mocking the fleeing druchii. One asur captain was even so bold as to hold out a captured banner, inviting the enemy to come back and take it.

These scenes were forgotten, however, when Malus trained his eyes on the solemn figure standing atop the rampart. There was a magical glow about the elf's shoulder and side, the place the warpsword had kissed. Malus recognised the helm and the sword in the asur's hand. Prince Yvarin, the foe who had cut down Vincirix!

Say the word, Malus. Set me loose and we can kill him. Now. We can avenge your little flesh-friend. Set me loose and we'll rip through the asur and make that princeling beg for death.

Angrily, Malus dug his heels into Spite, compelling the horned one to leap down from its perch. With a tug of the reins, he sent his steed loping back towards the druchii camp. He didn't trust himself to remain within sight of the enemy.

Not with the daemon's whispers in his ear.

… CHAPTER THIRTEEN …

There was no rest for the druchii warriors, no time for the drachau's slaves to lick their wounds. By dawn, the second assault against the Eagle Gate had been beaten back. An hour later, captains were forcing their regiments back into formation as slavemasters beat their charges back into the line. Through it all, the merciless gaze of Malus Darkblade swept across his soldiers. Every warrior could feel the hair at the back of his neck prickle and his skin crawl as he imagined the kiss of the warpsword against his flesh.

A stack of skulls rested before the drachau, heads cut from the latest victims of his ire. One soldier from every regiment, that had been the army's tithe to the dreadlord's wrath. Malus had personally cut down a hundred victims, playing the warpsword with such ferocity that his face was lost behind a patina of gore, his armour stained crimson with elven blood. Drusala and the sorceresses had been impressed into hasty service, atoning for their own failure in the battle by stripping the heads down to grinning skulls with their magic.

It was not enough. Not even the slightest gesture towards sating the fury burning inside Malus's black heart. He could feel Tz'arkan goading him on, growing stronger with each victim he claimed. He cared little. If these craven maggots lost the battle, he was dead anyway. It would be fitting punishment to turn the daemon loose upon them.

Malus crushed down that idea. That was the daemon talking, trying to make its desires sound like the drachau's own thoughts. There was still a chance for glory here, if he were bold and swift. But it had to be soon. Already, he knew his army was on borrowed time. Scouts ranging behind his army had reported the Tiranocii force drawing closer. Hours, perhaps, remained before they would reach the pass. Malus had the scouts executed before word of what they had seen could be disseminated. His warriors had only one purpose – to take the Eagle Gate. Anything else was but a distraction. If they seized the fortress, there was no need to fear the chariots of Tiranoc. If they floundered before the walls again, death beneath the wheels of the Tiranocii was a better fate than they deserved.

Despite the contempt he held them in, Malus appreciated that a reckless attack would get him nowhere. Once the regiments were reformed and the wounded dispatched, he restrained himself. Hard as it was, he sat on Spite's back and watched as the sun slowly climbed into the sky. He could see the gleam of armour on the battlements, the fiery glow as the light reflected off the phoenixes' burning plumage. The enemy was there, waiting. They too were biding their time, thinking it to be their ally.

Malus intended to teach them the error of their thinking.

When the sun reached its zenith, when its brilliant rays shone down upon the pass and straight into the eyes of the elves on the battlements, Malus drew the warpsword and again snarled out the order to attack.

Thousands of druchii advanced upon the fortress once more. Great blocks of infantry moved towards the great gates of starwood and silver, their faces pitted and scarred by the war hydras the day before. Aeich and the corsairs were doubly eager to claim the glory of seizing the gates – from their regiments Malus had demanded two victims instead of one. At their sides marched Naggorite slave-soldiers and the dreadspears of Clar Karond, both forces employing their heavy shields to fend off the archery of the asur. Harpies, those that had survived the night and been recaptured, were set loose to harry the defenders. Minds maddened by torture and magic, the harpies ran amok as they reached the asur, dragging them from behind the crenellations and tearing into them with claw and fang.

Drusala and the other sorceresses acted in concert now. They didn't ply their magic in individual duels with Shrinastor and the asur mages. Instead, they concentrated it into a great protective shell, raising it above the druchii army. While the sun thwarted the accuracy of the archers, the witches thwarted the accuracy of the spells loosed by the dragon mages and astromancers. The dark magic caught and twisted the lightning and fire called down by the asur mages, pooling the arcane energies into a dark, writhing cloud. When the cloud was powerful enough, Drusala herself sent it hurtling into the battlements. Elven warriors were slaughtered by the roiling fog of aethyric malevolence, tendrils of darkness whipping out to corrode armour and devour flesh, leaving only glistening skeletons behind.

As the attack on the gate gathered momentum, a third assault on the breach was set into motion. This time Malus didn't trust the attack to anyone but himself. He didn't leave the first charge to a lover and her knights, he didn't delegate the first wave to vassals and their warriors. He didn't linger behind and wait to see how the attack fared. This time, he led the push personally, commanding the soul-bonded warriors of his own tower, the drachau's private guard. At their back rode Dolthaic and the Knights of the Burning Dark, eager to redeem themselves in the eyes of their despotic master, only too aware that no other dreadlord would give them sanctuary should Malus fall.

Spite loped along with the soul-bonded dreadspears, the horned one snapping at those warriors too clumsy to keep their distance. The reptile disliked the nearness of allies as much as it despised the closeness of enemies, traits ingrained into its tiny brain from the moment it had hatched and found itself the runt of the nest. Malus did little to curb his steed's hostility. It reminded the soldiers of their place and warned them that death needn't come from an asur arrow or spear.

The rampart of dead cold ones drew ever closer. Malus could see the asur spearmen defending the morbid barrier. One of them turned his head and shouted to someone behind him. A moment later, a volley of arrows came arching up from the ward beyond the broken wall. Dozens of the dreadspears were struck as the barrage came raining down upon them. Those who fell were trampled by those who followed behind them. It didn't need the threats of the drachau to keep the spearmen moving. They knew they were within range of the enemy bows now. The only remedy for that was to get stuck in, engage the Eataine Guard and force the archers to hold back lest they strike friend instead of foe.

The rank smell of decaying cold ones struck Malus's senses as his assault closed upon the ghoulish obstacle. Just as he came near the barrier, he gave Spite a vicious kick in its flanks. The horned one responded with a powerful leap that brought it pouncing onto the top of the barrier. The carcass of a cold one was dislodged, sliding free to drop onto the asur below. Malus laughed as the elves caught beneath the reptilian body tried to squirm free. With deliberate viciousness, he caused Spite to drop down onto the carcass, adding his own and the horned one's weight to that already crushing the trapped asur. Screaming in pain, his white-clad enemies flailed in abject misery.

The suddenness of Malus's assault caught the other Eataine Guard by surprise. Prepared to stab their spears through gaps in the macabre wall at enemies trying to climb it, ready to repel foes who tried to circle around it, they were unprepared for an adversary who was already over the barrier. In a few heartbeats, the warpsword wrought a grim harvest from the startled warriors. Spite's jaws snapped shut upon the arm of an elf wearing the heraldry of an Ellyrian noble. A turn of the reptile's head wrenched the limb from its socket, sending the elf lurching back, feebly trying to staunch the welter of blood spurting from his mangled body.

Before the Eataine Guard could concentrate their efforts against Malus, soul-bonded druchii were scrambling up and over the reptilian wall. Spears stabbed down into the asur, spitting them like pigs. It took only a few moments for the druchii to jump down and secure the foothold they had gained, their iron-shod boots stamping out any life that clung to the elves they had impaled. Around the flanks of the dreadspears came Dolthaic and the Knights of the Burning Dark, who barrelled into the asur and hurled them back.

The orderly defence that had resisted the last assault was quickly smashed aside by Malus's troops. The drachau exulted as he butchered every asur he could reach. Spite's jaws were foul with elven blood and strips of elven flesh. Within, he could feel Tz'arkan responding to the carnage, the daemon's presence swelling and expanding.

'This is my glory!' Malus snarled at the thing inside him.

Is this glory? Even for a mortal, you are delusional, Malus. Look about you, fool.

The daemon's mockery stabbed at Malus like an icy dagger. He pulled back on Spite's reins, forcing the bloodthirsty reptile to heel. He ignored the fray unfolding around him, seized the moment to appreciate the broader situation. His face contorted into a mask of inhuman rage.

The Eataine Guard weren't trying to hold the rampart, they were falling back. They were trying to draw his warriors deeper into the breach. They were trying to pull them into a trap! He could see Prince Yvarin, the glow of magic still burning beneath his armour, leading the slow withdrawal. Nothing that would alert the druchii and make them suspicious, but now Malus could see through the methodical retreat.

He could order his troops to withdraw, to avoid the jaws of whatever deceit Yvarin planned. To do so, however, would shatter the entire assault. He'd lose another day trying to orchestrate another thrust. Another day for reinforcements to arrive. The Tiranocii would be at his rear by then, certainly. The dragons of Caledor, too, might take wing and fly to the Eagle Gate's rescue. He couldn't risk that. There could be no more delays. This attack *would* succeed. It *must* succeed!

Victory is in your power, Malus. Do you have the courage to claim it?

The druchii continued to swarm the barrier and pursue the Eataine Guard past the broken walls beyond. Malus sneered. Yvarin had overplayed his hand. He was thinking like a soft, pampered prince of the Inner Kingdoms. What matter if his trap cost Malus a hundred soldiers? Two hundred? There were more. He could afford to drown the entire garrison in blood. The host of Hag Graef alone still outnumbered the garrison a hundredfold. He would mock Yvarin for his arrogance before he ripped out the maggot's heart.

Roaring, Malus goaded his troops onwards, funnelling them into the gap, driving them at the Eataine Guard with the fury of a tempest. 'One step back!' he raged. 'One step back and you shall feel the kiss of Khaine!' He brought the warpsword flashing down into the helm of the nearest dreadspear, splitting the reinforced steel and shearing through the skull inside. The murdered warrior collapsed where he stood. Those around him redoubled their efforts to gain the walls.

'What need have I of daemons?' Malus spat at the beast inside him.

What need, Malus. Shall I tell you?

Tz'arkan's slithering words stoked the furnace of Malus's wrath. He wouldn't let the daemon's mockery poison the moment of his triumph. Savagely, he kicked Spite and sent the horned one rushing through the ranks of dreadspears. The push into the ward beyond the wall had faltered. He would know why.

Through his soul-bonded soldiers, Malus forced his reptilian steed onwards. Those elves who failed to leap out of the way were crushed underfoot. At last he reached the open ground within the ward itself. He felt his heart turn cold when he saw the battle unfolding. His dreadspears were beset on three sides by Yvarin's troops. The Eataine Guard held the ground directly before the invaders, but from the sides it was regiments adorned in the colours and lion-skins of Chrace that fought the druchii, their heavy war-axes crunching through armour and snapping bones with each strike. Archers from Ellyrion stood upon the inner walls, loosing arrows into the rear ranks of Malus's troops, felling them before they could fight their way to the front ranks.

Magnificent, are they not?

Malus could feel the daemon snicker at him. It took but a glance to understand its meaning. The archers on the walls, the Chracian axemen – these weren't the beleaguered warriors from the last two days. Their armour and raiment wasn't grimy with the foulness of war. These were fresh troops, fighters new to the battle. In the early morning, while Malus waited on the sun, the Eagle Gate had been reinforced!

The blast of a warning horn far back in the pass carried to Malus's ears, magnified and made more distinct to him by the perfidy of Tz'arkan. Tiranoc! The chariots had reached the druchii camp. The rear of his army was now beset by yet another asur host.

What glory for a fool? But, then, your king didn't expect you to win here. He expected you to die.

Snarling, Malus drove Spite forwards. The horned one swatted the druchii in its way, lashing out with fang and claw. With a lunge, it brought its master into battle. The warpsword sang out as it cleaved through the breastplate of a warrior of the Eataine Guard. Spite's jaws clamped tight about the head of a Chracian hunter.

Victory, Malus. It can still be yours. You can still have the last laugh over your king. Free me. Release me. The wild magic of these mountains rages through this land, and I have supped deeply from the storm. The pain and anguish of these mortals invigorates me. If I wanted, I could free myself, but we have been companions for so very long. It would sadden me if you weren't able to enjoy the carnage with me.

'Lies,' Malus snapped. An asur spear glanced across his knee, the warrior behind it exploiting his distraction. The drachau brought his deadly blade sweeping around, reducing the elf's face to a bloodied pulp.

What need have I for lies? You know the truth as well as I. You can feel it in your very bones. Are there not enough enemies here already, Malus? Must we fight one another as well? Think of what defeat means, Malus. Think of the Witch King laughing at you. Think of the honour and glory Prince Yvarin will enjoy, slayer of Malus Darkblade... and his lover!

Malus felt himself turning sick inside. Defeat was bitter enough to accept, but to know that in defeat he would further the ambitions of his enemies was too much to bear. How long had he resisted Tz'arkan? How many sleepless nights and hideous days? Every hour feeling the daemon's thoughts nagging at him, urging him to relent, to allow it to go free.

He knew how mighty Tz'arkan was. He knew that it never made promises it wouldn't keep. If it claimed it could still snatch victory from the jaws of defeat, it could do so.

'Very well,' Malus whispered. 'I release you, Tz'arkan. Together we will kill them all.'

We will kill them all, the daemon repeated. In that moment, Malus felt the fiend's essence boiling inside him, rising up, flowing through every nerve and every vein. Spite bucked and flailed, the horned one's terror so great that the straps of its saddle snapped and Malus was flung to the ground. Dimly he saw his loyal steed fleeing back through the press of dreadspears. Around him, druchii and asur alike drew back, gazing in horror at the fallen drachau.

It was different this time. As the pain of possession wracked him, Malus knew something was wrong. Having his body usurped by Tz'arkan was never a pleasant experience, but this time the agony was unspeakable. Screams pierced his ears, and it took the greatest effort to appreciate that the screams he heard were his own.

Now, Malus, it is your turn to be the spectator. Your chance to be the parasite. After a few centuries, you may even enjoy the experience.

Malus's skin began to flow like water, dripping away from his body, exposing the raw meat and muscle beneath. His bones began to expand, popping and cracking as they assumed new dimensions and adopted new shapes. The drachau's screams rose to a piercing wail, a cry of agony that ripped at the souls of all who heard it, tugging at them, dragging at them, trying to pull them into the private hell of the damned. The druchii and asur around the stricken tyrant backed away, retreating heedlessly into the blades of comrades and foes yet unaware of the horror unfolding so near to them.

A cackle of daemonic mirth rasped from the elongated jaws that distorted the drachau's face. Armour cracked and split, sloughing away from the transforming body in patches of twisted steel. The torn rags of Malus's rich garments fluttered in the wind as his body continued to expand, doubling in size, then redoubling once more. Long, razor-like spines erupted from his back, great horns sprouted from his forehead. Facial features withered into a skull-like semblance, eyes burned away to become embers of aethyric malevolence. The elf's long black hair thickened into a mane of worms, writhing and squirming with obscene vitality. The bubbling mass of flesh reshaped itself into thick cords of muscle; legs lengthened and broadened into pillars of bone and sinew. Thick, ape-like arms ended in blade-like talons.

The warpsword alone remained unfazed by the transformation, seeming little more than a puny knife in the clawed fist of the unleashed monster. Then it too began to change, expanding, growing into a giant blade of darkness, the weapon of some primordial titan or maniacal god.

Tz'arkan threw back its skull-like head and roared in triumph. Free! It was free! The roar that erupted from its daemonic lungs deafened the elves nearest it, shattering their eardrums. Tz'arkan the daemon king walked the mortal world once more!

One of the Eataine Guard was Tz'arkan's first victim, cut in half by a single stroke of the warpsword, his torso flung far across the battlefield. The daemon could feel the elf's soul drawn into itself, feeding the insatiable furnace of its own malefic essence. The taste brought a howl of delight from the monster. Greed, the insatiable hunger for mortal energies, flared through the daemon's mind. It had intended to keep the spirit of its bargain with Malus, to kill only the asur and spare the druchii. Now, however, it was minded to obey only the letter of their compact.

'We will kill them all,' Tz'arkan hissed, enjoying the terror that flared up from that tiny parasitic awareness lurking at the edge of its consciousness, that impotent spectator that shared its eyes. The feeble ghost that had been Malus Darkblade.

The daemon king swung around, slashing the warpsword across the druchii spearmen in its shadow. A score of elves were cut down in the blink of an eye, torn asunder by the daemon's strength and the warpsword's bite. The released spirit of each victim was channelled into Tz'arkan, further stoking the dark energies within it.

Tz'arkan howled once more. It could feel the terror of its victims and its future victims wash over it. It could feel the envy of its brother daemons, watching it from beyond the veil, straining to pierce the barrier, to emerge from the Realm of Chaos and join it in the feast. A thought, a gesture on its part, and they would be through. The daemon king laughed. The feast was rich and it had no intention of sharing. It forced down the perverse temptation to tear wide the rift. Later, perhaps, when the screams of mortals ceased to amuse it, it would let its brothers indulge themselves.

Druchii and asur alike attacked the daemon now. Dreadspears fought alongside the Eataine Guard, Knights of the Burning Dark made common cause with Chracian hunters. Spears stabbed into the monster from every side. Lances pierced its back, fangs snapped at its legs, axes hacked at its belly, swords slashed at its flanks. Tz'arkan laughed at the pathetic assault. Ichor bubbled from its wounds, closing them as soon as the violating steel was withdrawn. It plied the warpsword to left and right, spilling its enemies in every direction, each slaughtered soul serving to speed its own regeneration and invest yet more strength in its limbs.

Then, for an instant, Tz'arkan hesitated. The Eataine Guard retreated before it, but a lone warrior came striding out from their ranks. The daemon chuckled. How bold and stalwart Prince Yvarin looked, how heroically he marched to his doom. What would his vassals think, what would they say, if they could taste the desperation and fear their leader tried to hide so carefully?

Look, Malus, he is here, Tz'arkan taunted the drachau's spirit. *Pay close attention, because you surrendered more than you know just to enjoy this moment.*

The daemon reached out for Yvarin, but its arrogance, its savouring of Malus's emotions, was a distraction. The prince dived under the monster's claw and struck. The runesword, the fabulous blade that had been handed down for thousands of years, burned brighter than the sun as it slashed across the daemon's hide. Ancient enchantments blazed up from the blade, searing through the ghastly essence of Tz'arkan. The ichor that bubbled from this wound didn't knit the flesh together, didn't undo the hurt visited upon the daemon. Steaming, blackening the ground it fell upon, the ichor slopped from the cut in a continuous flow, each drop sapping some of the fiend's hideous vitality.

Yvarin started to shout in triumph, to cry out to his warriors – even to the druchii – that the beast could be hurt, the daemon could be slain. The sound died on his lips as one clawed hand closed about his runesword as he drew it from the wound. Another seized him by the neck. Tz'arkan glared at the prince with a malignity far beyond anything even Malus could have shown him.

'That hurt,' Tz'arkan growled as it crushed Yvarin's neck like a rotten stick. A flick of the daemon's claw sent the dead hero's head spinning off into the battlements.

Tz'arkan looked across the horrified ranks of the Eataine Guard as the asur began to fall back.

'Which of you wants to keep your prince company?' it called out in challenge as it stalked after them.

Drusala sensed the moment when Tz'arkan was released. The daemon's essence blazed like a pillar of fire to her witchsight, an infernal flare almost blinding in its brilliance. Amid the tumult of battle, the aethyric reverberations struck with the impact of a thunderbolt. The lesser sorceresses around her were knocked off their feet, sent tumbling through the dust, blood trickling from their ears and eyes. It would be hours before they could recover from the arcane shock and once again unleash their sorcery. Only she had the skill and power to shield herself – left shaken but otherwise unharmed.

The one consolation was that the shock wave hadn't played favourites.

The phoenixes had been sent shrieking away from the ramparts, spinning crazily up towards the mountains as they fled the daemon king's return. Drusala knew the asur mages would be suffering the same debilitation as the druchii sorceresses. They'd be out of the fight for some time.

Only one of the enemy wizards remained. Without any other mages practising their art, it was comparatively simple for Drusala to detect the workings of Shrinastor's magic. Like her own, the loremaster's willpower and knowledge had been strong enough to shield him from the aethyric blast. Now he was trying to conjure a spell that would curb the daemon's rampage.

That wouldn't play into Drusala's plans. She'd waited months for Malus to become weak enough to let loose the daemon. Now that Tz'arkan was free, she wasn't about to lose this opportunity to the loremaster's meddling. Snapping stern orders to Absaloth and the spearmen from Ghrond, Drusala dashed to her dark pegasus. A single word from her sent the winged steed soaring up into the sky. She laughed as archers loosed arrows at her, the missiles exploding into splinters as they crashed against the magical shell she'd woven about her steed.

High up in the beak of the stone eagle, Drusala could see Shrinastor siphoning magic down from the mountains into the head of his staff. It was a bold, even reckless conjuring for the mage to perform. She smiled maliciously. The loremaster was panicking, he was trying to draw too much too fast. He knew how powerful Tz'arkan was. He knew that no simple conjuration could restrain it. Pride, desperation, some foolish notion of duty – something made him unwilling to accept that reality. He was trying to hasten his spell by feeding more and more magic into it. The failing of the asur, the great weakness of their decadent breed, was that they couldn't accept when it was necessary to watch their own kind die.

The sorceress brought her pegasus soaring towards the eagle. A bolt of black lightning incinerated a clutch of archers who tried to drive her away. She stretched forth her hand and a cloud of dark, poisonous fog enveloped the bolt throwers as their crews tried to train the weapons on her. From the head of her staff, a finger of darkness struck out, ripping the souls from the armoured swordsmen who surrounded Shrinastor.

Laughing with murderous delight, Drusala leapt down from the back of her pegasus and danced over the bodies of her victims. She was alone upon the beak of the eagle. A blast of arcane fire melted the bronze door leading inside the fortress, transforming it into a wall of metal, ensuring that no rescuers would be able to rush up from below. Then she turned her attention to the loremaster.

Shrinastor had drawn a complex protective circle about himself, the asur rendition of the mandala employed by the druchii. Drusala scowled at the glowing glyphs, knowing the power they contained. It would be no easy thing, breaking such a ward.

The winds of aethyric energy Shrinastor was drawing down into the circle appeared to her magically attuned eyes as a translucent spiral of whirling colour and light. There was darkness there, too, but only the smallest traces. The mage was trying to strain the darker energies from his spell. That observation gave Drusala an idea.

Raising her staff high, Drusala whipped it through the air overhead. Faster and faster she spun the staff, and with each rotation, wisps of crawling darkness appeared in the air. The shadows coiled together, slithering into a thick morass of blackness, a patch of midnight thrust into the light of day. With a gesture, the sorceress sent the nexus of dark magic streaming into the aethyric spiral Shrinastor was calling down.

It wasn't malignant in its own right. All she had done was send more power into the energy Shrinastor was summoning. That lack of focus, that absence of immediate malevolence, allowed the dark magic to shower down into the circle. At once, it had an effect.

Shrinastor's eyes, previously unfocused and staring down towards the breach, now took on an expression of horror. His face became contorted, though his lips maintained the discipline to continue his conjuration. By degrees, the bright glyphs turned dark, their shine becoming more shadowy with each heartbeat. Threads of blackness began to ripple through the loremaster's body, squirming inside his veins.

Shrinastor's lips faltered, a syllable of his spell was lost. At once, the elf's mouth became distorted, twisting until the lower jaw tore away. Before it could strike the ground, flesh and bone had dissolved into soot. The dissolution spread as the rampant magic – far too much for the loremaster to control – ripped him apart. A hand detached itself, sprouted chitinous wings and flew away. An ear exploded into green flame, melting its way through the asur's tall helm. Lungs tore through the ribs that held them, expanding in an insane spasm of unrestrained growth.

Amidst the horrors assailing his body, Shrinastor was able to turn his gaze upon Drusala. In that last moment, a look of shocked recognition shone there. Then the eyes dissolved like wax, spilling down his face in a gelatinous tide.

Drusala sneered at the dying loremaster. Before she turned her own attention to the breach, she intensified the spells that guarded her. It might be that Tz'arkan's release had weakened some of them. It wouldn't do to take any chances.

Not until it was too late to stop her plans.

'Set spears!' Silar Thornblood shouted at the dreadspears around him. He could see the warriors hesitate. He could understand their alarm. The ground beneath their feet trembled with the fury of the Tiranoc chariots as they came rushing down the pass. Only the discipline of centuries as warriors of the Hag kept them in formation, that and the appreciation that if they tried to run now they would be slaughtered. If they held their ground, at least they had some slight chance.

Silar wasn't putting too much trust in those chances. As soon as his orders were given, he was falling back. He had other forces to command. Forces that had a real chance to blunt the asur attack.

The chariots came rushing from the distance, their silver-chased armour gleaming in the sun. Each of the chariots was drawn by two powerful horses, matched animals that had been paired for exactness of stamina, speed and strength. Two elves rode in each chariot, an armoured driver and a bowman. While the driver charged the lethal mass of the chariot towards the dreadspears, the archer loosed arrows into the massed ranks, felling warriors with each draw of the string.

Whether out of discipline or resignation, the dreadspears held their ground. Troops from the rear ranks stepped forward to replace those shot down by the archers. Horns blared, advising the soldiers how much distance yet lay between them and the enemy. When the chariots finally crashed into the ranks, a few were brought down by the wall of spears. Most, however, barrelled through, their pounding hooves and bladed wheels slashing through the packed druchii.

When the chariots won clear, however, they found Silar waiting for them. Two hundred darkshards arrayed in a double-rank opposed them now. At Silar's command, they fired their repeating crossbows into the asur. A thousand bolts punched into the chariots, slaughtering elves and horses alike. Of the Tiranocii who punched their way through the dreadspears, not a single chariot was able to retreat back into the pass and regroup with the rest of their army.

A shout, a cheer of murderous triumph, rose from Silar's troops. Even if for only a moment, the army of Hag Graef had driven off their attackers. The druchii gave small concern to the spearmen who had been sacrificed to bait the trap. Destruction of the asur was all that mattered at the moment.

With the cheers of his troops still ringing in his ears, Silar turned and gazed towards the Eagle Gate. If Malus could only seize the breach, they might yet claim the fortress.

Then his gaze rose to the skies above the Eagle Gate and Silar knew that the time for fantasies about victory was over. There was no victory for them here, only the ignominy of a useless death.

In the sky, Silar could see mighty shapes soaring towards the fortress, great winged figures of gold and crimson. What Malus had feared from the start had come to pass. The dragons of Caledor had been awakened.

The dragons were coming to save the Eagle Gate.

CHAPTER FOURTEEN

A resounding cheer rose from the battlements as the dragon princes of Caledor soared into the pass. Banners were unfurled, flags waved wildly, trumpets blared. The Eagle Gate was saved! There wasn't a chance the hated druchii could take the fortress now. In the hour of need, Caledor had come.

For the druchii in the pass, the immense reptiles flying towards the fortress were nothing less than heralds of utter doom. Many of these warriors had stood against the hordes of the Witchguard of Naggor and their doomwings. The flying demi-reptiles had seemed terrible, then. Now the memory of the doom-wings was blotted out by the enormity of the dragons. The smallest was thirty feet from horned snout to spined tail. Many were far larger, two and even three times as great. Coated in thick scales of white and gold, each of their powerful legs tipped in mighty claws, their reptilian heads adorned with sharp horns and spiny crests, the dragons were a terrifying sight. Their great leathery wings fanned the air, sending a hot, mephitic wind into the pass, the musky odour feared across the world as 'wyrmreek'.

Silar Thornblood didn't bother to redeploy his troops. If they scattered into the hills, some of them might survive, for a time, until the shadow warriors of Nagarythe tracked them down. For Silar, the verminous existence of a hunted creature didn't appeal to him. Defiantly, he held his head high and watched as the dragons began to descend. Around him, most of the druchii followed his fatalistic example. They were resigned to die and dragonfire would present them with a speedy death.

The roars of the dragons were louder than any thunder as the ancient reptiles hurtled down from the sky. The druchii cried out, final prayers to Khaine, as they saw their doom rushing down upon them. Then, abruptly, the great dragons turned, swung away from the army of Hag Graef. Silar blinked in utter shock as he saw the wyrms dive upon the Eagle Gate. The dragonfire he had expected to feel melting the flesh from his own bones was now unleashed upon the asur behind the battlements. By the hundreds, the horrified garrison were transformed into living torches, their blazing bodies raining down from the walls.

Now, Silar noticed for the first time that among the red and gold wyrms of Caledor, there were creatures of a far different and darker cast. Black-scaled dragons from Naggaroth! He could see the Caledorian nobles on the backs of the other dragons, but astride each of the black beasts there was a druchii lordling.

Silar was slow to accept the evidence of his eyes. Caledor had betrayed the asur! They had sided with Malekith! Even when he saw a flight of dragons swoop away from the walls and glide down into the pass to assault the host from Tiranoc, the highborn had difficulty accepting the unbelievable turn of events. Even as he watched the dragons of Caledor burn the asur with their fire while the dragons of Naggaroth smothered them with noxious clouds of gas, he struggled to understand. It was only when four of the dragons launched themselves at the great gates themselves and tore them asunder with their mighty claws that the truth became undeniable.

The Eagle Gate was taken! Victory was theirs!

As the druchii swarmed towards the fortress they had fought so hard to claim, the greatest of the black dragons swooped down before them. Seated upon the giant reptile's back was a figure no elf could fail to recognise. The Witch King himself, Malekith.

From the back of his monstrous steed, in a voice that was magnified by magic and boomed across the battlefield, the despot addressed the battered warriors of Hag Graef.

'The Eagle Gate is mine,' Malekith thundered. 'Caledor has acknowledged my right as true heir of Aenarion.' He raised his sword and thrust it towards the broken fortress. 'Spare all who wear the dragon,' he commanded. 'Kill the others!'

A monstrous snarl rose from the druchii. The frustration and fear of the previous days of fighting burst forth in a mad rush towards the Eagle Gate. It wasn't the organised march of an army now, but the vengeful rage of a mob. The battle was over, the dragons sweeping the walls of all organised resistance. Even the phoenixes had fled, their magical fire no match for the power of dragons.

No, the battle was over, but as Silar joined the throng charging into the fortress, he knew the killing was far from finished.

Now was the hour of slaughter and massacre. The hour of murder.

The hour of Khaine!

A veil of shadow cloaked Drusala as she hurried through the anarchy and confusion of the Eagle Gate. The betrayal of Caledor had shocked her every bit as much as the asur. Morathi had seen much in her divinations, but she hadn't foreseen the shift in alliance by the dragon princes. The entire purpose of her exodus from Ghrond seemed pointless now. Drusala had been scheming to thwart Malekith's invasion, to prevent the Witch King from gaining a hold on Ulthuan. She'd decided her best pawn in this endeavour was Malus Darkblade. If the entire army of Hag Graef were lost to him, Malekith would have been forced to reconsider his plans.

Spells to excite and enrage the daemon inside Malus had worked on the mind of the drachau. Careful strategies had been discarded in favour of bloody, ruthless slaughter. Malus had hurled his army against the Eagle Gate like a stoker shovelling coal into a furnace. A few more days of siege, and the largest army in the entire druchii armada would have been bled white by its possessed general.

The treachery of Caledor had foiled that scheme. There was no keeping Malekith from taking the Eagle Gate, no preventing his forces from securing a presence in Ulthuan. Drusala would have to adjust her plans. To do so, she'd need to return to the one she had thought almost at the end of his usefulness.

Ghost-like, Drusala stole past the stunned asur defenders. Her dark pegasus had fled when the dragons came, even its twisted heart unable to withstand the terror of so many ancient wyrms. A simple gesture had burst the beast's heart and sent it plummeting from the sky. Drusala had no pity for those who betrayed her, be they elf or brute. Without her winged steed, however, she was forced to weave an enchantment over herself, a mystic obfuscation that redirected the gaze of those who looked at her. For the asur, the only hint of her presence was a flash of movement glimpsed out of the corner of the eye.

The sounds of fighting grew louder as Drusala neared the section of wall that had been breached by the plague daemon during the last battle for the Eagle Gate. From the battlements, she could see the hulking, monstrous shape of Tz'arkan unleashed. The daemon king had left a trail of mutilation and carnage behind it as the thing glutted its appetite for death and destruction. The horrendously maimed bodies of asur and druchii alike were strewn about it.

Most of the druchii, it seemed, had the sense to understand that this was a battle they couldn't win. They were retreating from Tz'arkan, fleeing back past the rampart of dead cold ones. She could see the commander of Malus's mercenaries, the renegade noble Dolthaic, trying to regroup his knights and drive them back to the attack. Drusala smiled at that absurdity. To think his knights had any chance against the daemon was idiotic. It was a testament to his fear of Malus that a cunning opportunist like Dolthaic would consider such a plan. She wondered what he would think if she were to tell him that his master was gone. The drachau was dead.

Well, to all intents and purposes, Drusala corrected herself. Unless she took certain steps and intervened.

While the druchii retreated, the asur remained stubbornly defiant. The ragged remains of the Eataine Guard continued to attack the ghastly daemon king, refusing to submit meekly to the monster's advance. Tz'arkan took vile delight in tearing its enemies limb from limb, sometimes deliberately presenting a weakness so that some elf would rush at it. It would endure the wound the warrior delivered, then snatch him up in its claws and take its time pulling its captive apart.

As amusing as the sight of asur being butchered was, Drusala had bigger things to think about. She looked out towards the breach. Fresh druchii troops were filing past the rampart now – her own spearmen from Ghrond. She could see the cold figure of Absaloth among them. The sinister warrior had been one of Morathi's lovers once, and for that pleasure she had burned away his will and his identity. He was somewhat like a puppet now, one of the merciless Voiceless Ones. With his mind and soul chained to Morathi by links of magic and blood, his larynx had been fused into a knot of useless meat so that his words might never betray his queen. But he still had a tongue, he still had a mouth. With a minor incantation, Drusala made use of both. She had some commands to amend.

'The mistress orders that the daemon be captured, unharmed,' Drusala said. Below, she could see the Ghrondian spears turn in surprise as Absaloth repeated her command in a dry, rasping hiss. 'Keep Tz'arkan from leaving. Your mistress will join you soon.'

Drusala didn't linger to watch her spearmen charge towards the hulking daemon. Already she was hurrying down steps littered with rubble and the corpses of fallen asur. Once or twice she encountered elves wearing the heraldry of Caledor locked in mortal combat with hunters from Chrace and swordsmen from Ellyrion. Such fratricide pleased her, despite what it boded for her plans. If only all of the asur could be so obliging.

She reached the ward at the base of the walls just as the last member of the Eataine Guard was torn in half by the warpsword in Tz'arkan's fist. The daemon bellowed mockingly at the asur archers and axemen who had been supporting the noble elves.

'Are there no wolves left?' Tz'arkan raged. 'Must I drink the souls of dogs now?'

In answer to the daemon's challenge, the purple-cloaked Ghrondian spearmen rushed at Tz'arkan. The daemon swung around in amusement. It wasn't surprised. With senses far more keen than those of sight and sound, it had detected the druchii warriors stalking towards it. Now the fiend exulted in the opportunity for new atrocities.

'Your countrymen, Malus,' Tz'arkan hissed. 'Tell me, flesh-worm, are any of these walking corpses your friends? I dearly hope so!'

Laughing, Tz'arkan pounced towards the Ghrondian troops. One was crushed flat beneath the daemon's hooved feet. Another fell clutching at the string of organs the monster ripped from his bowels. A third was cleft in twain by the warpsword, his body bisected so cleanly that for a single step, the elf continued his charge before his body slopped to the ground.

The daemon's laughter became a cry of pain as one of the Ghrondian spears stabbed into its side. Tz'arkan reached a claw to the wound, surprised at the fiery ichor dribbling from the cut. Like the runesword of Prince Yvarin, the spears of Drusala's warriors could hurt the daemon. It wasn't by accident that she had dispatched these soldiers to confront the fiend. They were trained and equipped to face such foes. The sorcery within Ghrond had acted as a beacon to the twisted entities of the Wastes, drawing them down across the frontier time after time like moths to a flame. The warriors of Ghrond had been that flame.

Tz'arkan staggered back, the daemon's arrogance and audacity faltering as it now saw dozens of spears exactly like the one that had pierced its side. With grim determination, the druchii warriors formed a ring around the monster, hemming it in with a fence of steel. The daemon howled and roared and raged; threats that would have chilled the hearts of vampires slithered off its tongue. The warriors remained unmoved, determined in their purpose: to hold the beast for their mistress.

'You cannot escape,' Absaloth's rasping voice declared.

Tz'arkan fixed the Voiceless One with a murderous stare. 'I smell your magic, witch,' it snarled. 'Show yourself! Let Tz'arkan treat with the master, not the plaything.'

Drusala stepped out from the broken corner of a wall. She knew it was a reckless thing to do, foolish and stupid. She could deal with Tz'arkan without exposing herself. But the fiend's words had crawled their way into her mind, nagging at her pride. She suspected some enchantment behind that vexation, the sort of wearisome magic the daemon had used so often to manipulate Malus.

The daemon snorted derisively when it saw Drusala. 'You played your game, little one, but there is no time for games now. Tz'arkan is made flesh once more. Tz'arkan is free!' Its blazing eyes smouldered with grotesque mockery, its forked tongue licked lasciviously at its withered lips. 'Perhaps I would allow you to be my slave. If you beg. And it amuses me.'

The sorceress could feel the daemon's mind wearing at her, trying to play out her pride, trying to make her forget her schemes and plans. Trying to make her give herself over to the impulses of emotions rather than the calculations of knowledge.

'You fear me,' Tz'arkan accused.

Drusala smiled coldly at the monster. 'I think it is you who are afraid.'

Tz'arkan started to laugh at that, but it grew quiet when it saw Drusala wave her hand. Some of the spearmen raised their weapons and stepped out of formation, opening a passage for her into the cage that held the daemon. As she walked through the line, there was nothing in her step that bespoke uncertainty, not the slightest flicker of hesitancy on her face. Even when her warriors closed the ring behind her, she didn't stray.

The daemon's eyes narrowed with suspicion. There was a trap here, but try as it might, it couldn't ferret the nature of that trap from Drusala's mind. Her magic was too powerful to penetrate; all it could do was try to exploit emotions that were already there, and even this had failed it. Exploitation and manipulation end with the target's awareness.

'Who are you?' Tz'arkan hissed, offended that any mortal sorceress should have such power to resist it.

'That is the wrong question,' Drusala told it.

Tz'arkan bared its fangs, streams of venom dripping to the ground. 'What, then, is the question I should be asking?'

'You should be asking me what I want,' Drusala said.

The daemon laughed. For all the arcane power she possessed, for all her mystic knowledge, this flesh-worm was no different from any other mortal. She wanted a pact, some petty agreement between them. What would it be? Wealth? Power? Love? Revenge?

The sorceress answered her own question in a voice that was like a razor. 'I want Malus.'

Tz'arkan glowered at her. 'Darkblade is gone. There is only Tz'arkan now.'

Drusala slowly circled the hulking daemon, like a lion stalking game. Tz'arkan had made a mistake trying to manipulate her through her pride. It had forgotten that the channel worked both ways. Without the daemon appreciating it, she was playing upon its pride, provoking it with every breath. The angrier it got, the less it was aware of what else she was doing to it.

'You shouldn't lie,' the sorceress chided Tz'arkan, stepping around the gory husk of a Chracian hunter. 'I know he's still there, inside you. You wouldn't destroy him so quickly. Not when you could make him suffer.'

The daemon took a lumbering step towards her. 'Would you like to join him?' it threatened. 'All eternity as Tz'arkan's captive audience.'

Drusala continued to circle the daemon, gingerly picking her way between its victims. 'Is this how you use your freedom? Petty massacre? The great daemon king Tz'arkan, nothing more than a maniac with pretensions of grandeur.'

The daemon lashed out at her, nearly striking her with the warpsword. 'Your mind of flesh can't conceive what I am. In your blackest nightmares, you couldn't imagine the tenth part of what Tz'arkan is!'

Drusala leapt away from the enraged daemon. As Tz'arkan rushed at her, the fiend stopped short, thrust back as though it had struck an invisible wall. The beast snarled as it made a gesture with its claw. At once a scarlet circle blazed into life all around it, the circle Drusala had been furtively drawing with her foot as she taunted the daemon.

'This won't hold me,' Tz'arkan mocked. 'The merest effort and I shall be through. Then I will peel your body like a piece of fruit and feed you your own skin. I wonder how long you'll have the strength to scream.'

Drusala set one hand on her hip and actually laughed at the beast. 'You think that circle is the only magic I have worked upon you? Would you like to hear your True Name? It is neither long nor complicated as such things go. A half-brute witch doktor could learn it.'

Tz'arkan roared, the daemon's fury of such malignance that stones crumbled from the battered walls, corpses shivered on the ground. 'I will–'

'You will do nothing!' Drusala sneered. 'Or I will say that name. I will send you back.' Her voice became even more threatening as she recalled an image she'd found while she rooted about in the daemon's putrid essence. 'How do you think your brothers will greet you when you return? How will they thank you for leaving them scratching at the door when but a gesture from you could have ripped the barrier open? That should be an amusing spectacle.'

The daemon quieted, its burning eyes fading into black pits. 'What do you want?' it demanded in a sullen voice.

Drusala was wary, making no mistake of trusting Tz'arkan's seeming acceptance of defeat. 'I want Malus,' she repeated.

'You can't have him,' Tz'arkan growled. 'I am free. Do you understand me, free!'

'Soon you will be free among your brothers in the aethyr,' Drusala said.

An inarticulate cry of impotent fury shook the daemon. It knew the battle was lost. But one battle didn't lose a war. 'You can have Malus back,' the beast hissed, 'but you can't have him without Tz'arkan. Our essences are too entwined to be separated. Where he goes, I must follow, otherwise it is death for us both.'

Drusala nodded. She had expected as much. Indeed, it was vital to the revision her plans had undergone that she have both Tz'arkan and Malus Darkblade.

'Bring back the drachau,' she commanded the daemon. 'Restore your prison of flesh.'

'Shall I tell him who it was that killed his mother?' Tz'arkan asked, expecting to horrify the sorceress with a secret only a daemon could learn.

Drusala glared back at the fiend. 'If you did that, I'd be obligated to kill Malus. Then you'd lose your anchor. You'd have to go back to your waiting brothers.'

Hissing profanities to disgust the most jaded ear, Tz'arkan cast the warpsword from its hand. The weapon landed blade-first beyond the circle. For a heartbeat, Drusala's eyes glanced over at it. In that brief span, Tz'arkan rushed the sorcerous circle holding it. Wisps of colour exploded in every direction as the daemon burst through the circle. It charged at Drusala, intent on ripping her head from her shoulders before she could invoke its name.

Before Tz'arkan could reach her, however, the daemon was forced back, its body pierced by the spears of the Ghrondians. The silent Absaloth stood before his mistress, sword in hand, directing the warriors to push the daemon back.

At once, Tz'arkan sank to its knees. Its final, desperate effort had failed. Before Drusala could retaliate, could use its True Name against it, the daemon hastened to appease her. It would give her back Malus... And it would wait.

As Tz'arkan shrieked and howled like a creature damned, its monstrous frame began to collapse in upon itself. Slabs of daemonic flesh oozed away, dropping to the earth in stinking heaps. Horns crumbled into powder, spines snapped off and evaporated into smoke. Inch by inch, the daemon was melting away, each transformation bringing it a little nearer to the size and shape that had constrained it for so very long. As Tz'arkan withered away, so too did the warpsword shrink, taking back its original proportions.

Agony nearly beyond endurance had heralded Malus's transformation into Tz'arkan; now the same waves of pain coursed through him. As the daemon receded, as it restored his flesh to him, he could feel every pop and grind of his shrinking bones, experience the ghastly reshaping of muscle and tendon, the emergence of organs from the black broth of Tz'arkan's substance.

When the change was complete, Malus lay strewn upon the ground, unable to move, steam rising from his naked body. It was torture to even breathe; he had to concentrate to make his heart beat inside his chest for the first few moments, until the rhythms of his body restored themselves. He could sense Drusala's magic flowing through him, the sorceress helping guide back his mind and soul, acting to maintain his shattered body until its restoration was complete.

Around Drusala, he could see Absaloth and the Ghrondians. The spearmen stared at him in shocked disbelief, unable even now to accept that their general, the Tyrant of Hag Graef, had been the hulking daemon they'd fought. Malus grimly wondered why Drusala had bothered to restore him. With so many witnesses, there wasn't a chance of keeping the secret now. When the Witch King learned of this, he'd have Malus executed on the spot.

'Dead tongues spread no rumours,' Drusala said, reading his thoughts. Throwing both hands wide, she sent a tide of dark energies sweeping through her soldiers. The druchii stumbled and staggered as the dark magic entered them. They dropped their spears and drew the short blades on their belts. Then, in pairs, they drove their daggers into one another. The suicidal massacre was as complete as it was swift. Before a minute was out, only Drusala, Absaloth and Malus remained to bear witness to the drachau's secret.

'You needn't worry about Absaloth,' the sorceress said, motioning for her bodyguard to lift Malus from the blood-soaked ground. 'The only thoughts in his head, the only words in his mouth, are those that I put there.' She raised her hand and stroked Malus's cheek. 'We are going to be firm allies, Malus.'

Deep inside him, Malus could feel the last flicker of Tz'arkan turn cold. In as much as it was able, the daemon had abandoned him to the sorceress.

Part Three

REAVER'S MARK

Summer 2524–Autumn 2524

CHAPTER FIFTEEN

Malus moved through the carnage of the battlefield, pale and wraithlike in his nakedness. A bloodied cloak, ripped from the corpse of one of Tz'arkan's victims, was the only raiment he'd had time to adopt. Except for the Warpsword of Khaine and the icon of Hag Graef he wore about his neck, he was without accoutrements. The daemon's release had shattered his armour and destroyed his clothes. Drusala's spell to re-cage the monster had left Malus as bare as a babe. There hadn't been time to worry about propriety and modesty, however. He had to hurry if he wanted to save something more important than his dignity.

His own skin.

The Witch King himself had come to the Eagle Gate and Malus knew the dreaded tyrant would be expecting the drachau to present himself. Every moment of delay would only further provoke the despot's ire. Malus had to plead his case, make Malekith appreciate that he was still a valuable asset in the conquest of Ulthuan. Otherwise, he knew his head would be joining those of the asur lords decorating the battered walls.

Malus found his king just outside the broken fourth wall. Malekith was in conference with some of his lords and generals, poring over the maps pinned to the side of a dead cold one. As he tottered out from the shadow of a battered gatehouse, Malus was spotted by Kouran. The warrior favoured the drachau with an ugly smirk, and then hurried to draw his king's attention away from the improvised table and towards the nearly naked elf.

With an effort, Malus forced his head back and strode towards the king with such pride as his exhausted body could muster. The nobles gathered around Malekith whispered and pointed as he came shambling through the ruins, but it wasn't long before the whispers rose into open jeers and taunts. Even the harpies feasting on the corpses scattered amidst the rubble snarled and snapped at him. The columns of druchii soldiers marching into the captured fortress turned their faces towards him and laughed as they trooped past, delighted to see the high-handed Malus brought to such distress.

Each barb only served to enflame the boundless hate within the drachau. He drew upon that hate, using it to pour strength into his weary bones. He returned the taunts and jeers with a defiant arrogance that made many of his detractors choke on their laughter, suddenly appreciating just how injudicious their humour was.

Kouran stepped forwards as Malus approached the Witch King, the captain of the Black Guard closing his hand about the Crimson Blade. The drachau stopped his march when he was twenty feet away from the king, far enough away as to not provoke the uncertainty of either the despot or his hound. Malus could imagine the fearful sight he must present, his body riddled with scars and stained in blood, only the gore-soaked cloak to cover his nudity. If he were in Malekith's boots, he would be wary. It was the lone fanatic, crazed and determined, who was the greatest threat to any tyrant.

The Witch King stepped away from his maps and cast his gaze over the drachau. 'You are alive,' he said. 'Mostly.'

Malus dropped to his knee, bowing before his monarch. 'Mostly alive, your majesty,' he said. He could see the wariness on Kouran's face as he addressed Malekith. To ease some of the warrior's doubt, Malus thrust the warpsword into the ground beside him, the blade trembling ever so slightly as he withdrew his hand from its hilt. He dismissed the warrior from his mind and returned his attention to Malekith.

'Please forgive my tardiness, Lord Malekith. I was otherwise engaged during yesterday's triumph and could not share your victory.' Malus bowed his head as he made his apology, but he could hear the druchii nobles drawing closer, savouring this display of contrition and weakness, eager to see what would happen next. Jackals waiting to pick at a corpse, should the Witch King reject the drachau's apology.

It took all of Malus's willpower to fight down the fear that filled him as the Witch King walked towards him. Like a prowling lion, Malekith circled him. He could feel the despot's suspicious gaze burning against his skin as the king studied him, marking every scar and blemish on his body, trying to read on his flesh the record of his recent battle. If the Witch King guessed even a small part of the truth, Malus knew the last thing he would feel was the Destroyer stabbing into his body.

'Tell me, Malus,' the king's voice came in a low growl from behind the drachau, 'what could be so important as to delay you from my council?'

Malus tried to restrain the fear that swelled within him. He shifted his head, trying to catch some sight of the Witch King, the faintest suggestion of what the despot was doing. He strained his ears for the slightest sound that might warn him that the Destroyer was in Malekith's hand.

'Alas, majesty, I was so enthralled by the song of Khaine that I pursued the fleeing foe far down the pass. It is only this dawn that I returned.' Malus wished he could see the Witch King so he could know how favourably his lies were accepted.

'You were overcome by bloodlust?' Malekith asked, a trace of scorn in his tone.

'That is true, majesty,' Malus replied. The story had been concocted by Drusala and he'd been too exhausted by his ordeal to fabricate a better one. Now he wondered if trusting the sorceress hadn't simply guaranteed his own destruction at the hands of the Witch King.

'And you pursued the enemy so vigorously that it took you all night to return to us?'

Malus swallowed the knot that was growing in his throat. His bare back shivered, anticipating the Witch King's blade stabbing into his flesh. Malekith wasn't buying his lies. Even so, Malus knew there was nothing to be gained by abandoning the bluff.

'Which enemies did you pursue with such vigour, dear Malus?' the Witch King demanded.

Terror was racing down Malus's spine, raw despair pounding in his heart. Malekith was suspicious. A moment more and he would draw the Destroyer. Malus glanced over at the warpsword, wondering if he could reach it before either Kouran or his king could cut him down.

'I believe they were Ellyrians, your majesty.' Drusala emerged from the crowd of nobles who had gathered to watch Malus squirm under the Witch King's interrogation.

The drachau wondered if the highborn fools around her understood the power Drusala embodied. He could bear witness to the awesome might of the handmaiden. Only his mother, Lady Eldire, had ever been able to subdue Tz'arkan, and that had been with the daemon in a far less powerful state than Drusala had encountered it. How she had managed such a feat, how she had been able to not merely subdue the daemon but force it to restore his physical body, Malus couldn't begin to comprehend. He'd felt his own mind collapsing into a shrieking mire of horror and pain, but Drusala had called him back. She'd sewn his essence back together, made him once again who he had been.

Such power didn't make Malus grateful; it made him worried. He'd been forced into an alliance with Drusala. Why? What did she hope to gain from him? What was it only the Tyrant of Hag Graef could bring to her?

Malus quickly took up the thread the sorceress dangled before him, remembering more details of the story she had so hurriedly fed him before sending him to treat with his king. 'They fled towards Ellyrion, so that would make the most sense.'

'So ardent was your pursuit that you abandoned your horned one, Spite?' The Witch King's words slashed at Malus like knives. 'You abandoned your clothes? You cast aside your armour in the midst of battle?'

'Forgive me, majesty, for I made an imprudent decision when the fighting for the wall was at its fiercest.' Malus looked across the still-gloating faces of the nobles. He tried not to let his gaze linger on Drusala, but couldn't resist directing a sharp look her way. If Malekith didn't buy her story, if there was any opportunity at all Malus was going to make sure she shared his fate.

'To heighten my prowess in battle,' Malus explained, 'I drank some of the witch brew of Khaine. Just a mere mouthful to strengthen my sword-arm. I did not anticipate its effects. When an asur champion pulled me from Spite's saddle, my mind seemed to be engulfed by flames. I cut the traitorous cur in two almost as soon as I left the saddle, but that wasn't enough to satisfy the song of Khaine blazing through my veins. In my fervour, my Khaine-blessed fury to slaughter the Ellyrians, I stripped off my armour, which was weighing me down...'

Laughter rose from many of the nobles as they heard Malus explain his nudity. Before the drachau was fully aware of what he was doing, he seized the warpsword and turned on the jeering druchii lords. Belatedly he noted Kouran start towards him, but a gesture from Malekith called his hound back.

'You laugh?' Malus snarled at the nobles. 'You who allowed the king's enemies to escape? You would allow them respite? Allow the damned asur to rally and fight us again?' The drachau's eyes were nearly as fiery as those of the Witch King as he glared at the mocking crowd. Nothing so fanned the fires of his rage as the sneers of those who thought themselves his betters.

Malekith raised his hand and at once the laughter was silenced. He stared at Malus in silence for a moment. 'You cast aside your armour in order to pursue the enemy with greater speed?'

Falling to his knee once more, Malus bowed to his king. 'It is even as you say, majesty.'

The Witch King turned and pointed an iron finger at Drusala. 'You vouch for this story?'

The sorceress bowed her head. 'Even so, your majesty. Lord Malus may not remember, but he came to me last night in a battle-fever and confessed what happened.' Her voice took on the slightest note of amusement. 'He was seeking my advice, your majesty, on how to apologise for his excesses during the fight.' She produced a length of bloodied cloth and held it towards the Witch King. 'He came to me with this. He thought it to be of great importance.'

A flick of Drusala's hand and the cloth unfurled, displaying the device of silver wings upon a field of white and blue. A snarl came from Kouran as the warrior recognised the torn banner Drusala held. 'The banner of Eagle Gate,' the warrior said, reaching out to take it from the sorceress. 'The Ellyrians tried to escape with it?'

Malus looked at the banner, feigning astonishment, pressing his hand to his head as though to massage memories back into his mind. He turned to Malekith. 'Majesty, I have no reason to doubt the Lady of Ghrond's statements. My own recollections before this morning are, I fear, somewhat hazy.'

The Witch King gestured to Kouran. Malekith and his faithful dog conferred for a moment, only snatches of their conversation reaching Malus's ears. What he did hear made the drachau anxious. The king wasn't buying their lies. With that thought in mind, Malus was shocked when Malekith turned to address him.

'Your persistence in the fight is commendable, even if your tardiness to my council is less than exemplary. Your appearance is disrespectful, offensive to your king and the sensibilities of these refined highborn. It needs more than an asur shroud to be presentable at my court, whatever the custom might have been in Hag Graef.'

The king's mockery brought more jeers from the watching nobles. Malus started to raise the warpsword when Malekith again motioned for silence.

'I will overlook this discourtesy, friend Malus,' the king declared. 'The campaign ahead of us will need leaders as persistent and audacious as yourself. To you I will entrust the defeat of the Ellyrians. Your army has suffered keenly in the fighting. You will need fresh forces to bring battle to Ellyrion. To that end, I place at your disposal the warriors of Tullaris Dreadbringer. After your experience with the witch brew of Khaine, the two of you should have more in common than ever.'

Malus clenched his jaw tight as he heard the king's words. Tullaris Dreadbringer, commanding a force of executioners bigger than any left to the armies of the Witch King. With him were such warriors and soldiers as had left Har Ganeth before Hellebron declared her entire city one giant altar to Khaine. The lack of amity between Malus and the disciples of Khaine was renowned. His half-brother Urial had been a priest of the Bloody-handed God, determined to bring about an ancient prophecy surrounding the Chosen of Khaine and the Bride of Khaine. For a time, it had seemed Malus himself was the Chosen, but that had been the daemon Tz'arkan twisting fate so that his mortal slave might gain the Warpsword of Khaine and restore the daemon to corporeal form. Urial had been one of the casualties in that web of deception. So had a great many others who were involved in the cult of Khaine.

Tullaris had long been held as the Hand of Khaine, the Lord of Murder's favoured son. Now, he was universally accepted as the Chosen of Khaine by the entirety of the cult, not simply those in Har Ganeth. Violent, moved by dark dreams of carnage and slaughter, Tullaris had seized everything in his brutal life with his own hands. His accomplishments were littered with the corpses of his victims. To have the acknowledgement of his right as Chosen essentially passed over to him by Malus was a source of unending vexation to the executioner. Malus had often wondered how many of the assassins who'd tried to kill him had been dispatched on Tullaris's orders. He suspected very few – this was one enemy who would suffer no blade but his own to end the drachau's life.

One of his most dire enemies, yet Tullaris had one great mark in Malus's favour: he bore no love for Malekith. The Witch King had many times proclaimed himself as Khaine's mortal avatar. Tullaris made no secret of the divine dreams that moved and inspired him to his acts of atrocity and massacre. He presented himself as Khaine's herald, a mortal touched by the Lord of Murder. For Malekith, the executioner's claims were close to treachery. For Tullaris, the Witch King's posturing as a divine avatar was nothing less than blasphemy.

'In this war, the divine favour of Khaine is of more value than a thousand dragons,' Malus said, trying to make the statement sound sincere. 'I would deem it an unmatched distinction if I might be given command of the army brought here by Lord Tullaris. Unworthy of such command as I may be.'

'You will strike out with them across the interior of Ellyrion,' the Witch King commanded. 'It is a very simple task we set before you, Malus. We simply want you to put every settlement between here and Evershale to the sword. Do you think you can manage that?'

'If I didn't think I could achieve the task you set before me, majesty, I would be unfit for the command,' Malus said. He stood up and would have turned to walk away, but a last question from the Witch King stayed his retreat.

'What weapons will you use against the asur?' Malekith demanded.

Malus stared back at the Witch King. 'The greatest weapons of them all, majesty. The ones that have been burned into the souls of every druchii since we were cast from our homeland.

'Deceit and treachery.'

The flayed skin that formed the backing of the folding campaign chair creaked as Malus settled himself into his seat. He couldn't remember now who the skin had belonged to originally. He thought it had been one of his father's old retainers, one of the ones who had lacked the caution to treat him with proper respect while he was growing up. Emit? Razmat? He couldn't remember now. Whoever it had been, their skin surely hadn't been as comfortable to wear as it was to sit against.

Cold fury burned inside Malus every time his mind contemplated his surroundings. Despite the fawning obeisance he'd paid the Witch King, it *had* been his army that had beaten the garrison. It *had* been his leadership that broke the Eagle Gate and left it open to conquest. Malekith's contribution to the battle was little more than gutting a shark after it was already hooked and hauled into the boat. Yet the despotic monarch and his entourage were ensconced inside the fortress while Malus was left to the spare comforts of his army's camp. Instead of the prestige of sleeping in the chambers of a conquered foe, he was left to sleep in a tent like all the common sword-fodder of his army!

Despite, or rather because of, his rage, Malus was in a perversely good humour. It had been a very long time since he'd been able to indulge himself in a proper temper. Even under the influence of his mother's wine, he'd always had to be careful lest some excess of emotion allow Tz'arkan to exert too much control over him. Since Drusala's spell, however, there hadn't been a peep from the daemon. He could still feel it there, cowering in some corner of his soul, but the sorceress's magic had certainly curbed the spectral parasite.

That knowledge only further aroused Malus's temper. He hadn't risen to become drachau of Hag Graef by allowing anyone to have a hold over him. He'd refused the advances of Naggor's Belladon, refused to accept a throne on the witch's terms. It would have been easier, but to assume power at such a price would have been a shallow illusion. He would have been a slave dancing to the tune of a hidden master. He'd had enough of that sort of thing from Tz'arkan. He wouldn't simply swap the daemon for Drusala.

His eyes strayed towards the sorceress. Again, she lounged upon his divan, seemingly careless of her provocative appearance as Malus conferred with his closest advisors. She didn't fool anyone, of course, that she wasn't aware of either her beauty or the desire she provoked. But that didn't make it any easier for them to ignore her. Malus noted Dolthaic in particular attending a bit too much attention each time Drusala shifted her position and exposed a bit of her thigh. He'd have to remind the knight later about where his priorities should be. At least if he didn't want to end up as a chair.

By contrast, Tullaris Dreadbringer and his second, a noble warrior named Sarkol Narza, seemed to be sizing up a slab of meat any time their attention diverted to the sorceress. The two executioners were appropriately terrifying in their stylised armour, long-handled draichs slung over their backs, the withered heads of a few choice victims dangling from their belts. Tullaris was a tall, cheerless sort of killer, his face marked with the ghoulish imprint of the true fanatic. Sarkol Narza was more compactly built, almost stocky for an elf, but his face was no less villainous than that of his master. Matched monsters, two semi-rabid wolves in the service of Khaine. Malus had heard that Tullaris didn't even balk at offering up the hearts of those already devoted to his god when the mood struck him, once going so far as to kill a dozen witch elves during one of Khaine's holy festivals.

At present, fortunately, Tullaris gave the appearance of being far more controlled and rational. Indeed, after that exhibition of hate in the Witch King's court, the executioner had become strangely resigned to taking orders from his old enemy. What Malus couldn't decide was how much of the killer's attitude was genuine acceptance and how much was pretence. Either way, he wasn't about to let his guard down.

'If it pleases you, dreadlord,' Silar Thornblood addressed Malus, 'I think it would be best to integrate our forces gradually. Fleetmaster Aeich is dead and his corsairs almost exterminated on the walls, the Clar Karond contingent is a shell of its original strength, and the Knights of the Ebon Claw remain leaderless...'

Malus waved his hand as though swatting aside an annoying insect. 'Fold whatever is left of Vincirix's knights into Dolthaic's command. If any of them complain... the cold ones could probably use fresh meat after such a long battle. As for the rest, if they have any problems with our new allies, I suggest they get over them quickly.'

Silar turned and glowered at the imposing Tullaris, exhibiting more nerve than Malus would have given him credit for. 'I was more concerned about the discipline of our "allies", dreadlord. The denizens of Har Ganeth aren't renowned for their... professionalism... on the battlefield.'

An ophidian smile stretched across Tullaris's face. 'Is my lord Silar questioning the valour of my warriors?'

'Not their valour, only their restraint,' Silar said. It was clear he appreciated the menace in the executioner's tone. Even under the watching eyes of Malus there was no guarantee that Tullaris wouldn't kill him where he stood. It was a bold display on Silar's part. Maybe not wise, but certainly bold.

'Has it occurred to you that that is why Malekith threw this task to Tullaris?' Drusala asked. Her tone conveyed the disgust she felt, not just for the herald of Khaine but for Malus's decision to join his fate to that of the infamous marauder. 'The Witch King wants the countryside laid to waste. While we're running about butchering farms and hermitages, what do you think the Ellyrians will be doing? They'll be mustering their forces to march against us. Malekith expects us to bypass Tor Elyr and Whitefire Tor, to leave them unchallenged at our back while we strike towards Evershale and Avelorn. We will have two armies behind us and the forces of Avelorn before us.'

'Does the prospect frighten you?' Malus asked.

Drusala's eyes narrowed as she gazed over at the drachau. 'I am saying this force is nothing more than a sacrifice, Malekith's offering to Khaine so that his own victory may be assured. We draw out the hosts of Tor Elyr and Whitefire Tor, and once those armies are engaged with us, the Witch King can take the cities they've left weak and unguarded. We die while he claims all the glory.'

'Is that not the role of any dutiful subject?' Malus relished the flash of fire that came into Drusala's eyes.

'You've conveniently allowed the Witch King to put all of his worst rivals into a single force,' Drusala accused.

'And you've forgotten what I told Malekith,' Malus said. 'I warned him that my weapons would be deceit and treachery. I just didn't tell him who I'd use them against.' He rose from his chair and began to pace the floor. 'Tomorrow we march into Ellyrion, just as Malekith expects. We will begin carving a path of blood, as he has commanded. But we won't forget Tor Elyr, as he wants.' He pointed at Drusala. 'It will be your duty, witch, to observe the city. When their army sallies forth to put an end to our rampage, I need your magic to tell me.'

'And what will we do when the host of Tor Elyr comes seeking vengeance?' Dolthaic asked.

Malus grinned, his face becoming almost as bloodthirsty as those of Tullaris and Sarkol. 'We show the Witch King what a massacre really looks like.'

It was long into the night before Malus came stealing into the tent of Tullaris Dreadbringer. It was a gruesome spectacle, stitched together from the skins of sacrificial victims, the brand of Khaine still visible on each desiccated forehead. Scalps and dried fingers adorned the tent posts, fluttering in the fitful wind moaning down the pass. A mat fashioned from the facial bones of a hundred skulls grinned up at the drachau, taunting him, daring him to cross the threshold.

It would take more than that to give Malus pause, however. At his gesture, Dolthaic preceded him and drew back the curtain of witch elf hair that covered the door of the tent. A smell of blood and death wafted out from the darkened interior. Malus gave himself a moment to get accustomed to the stench. The bones in the mat cracked and creaked as his armoured boots strode across the fleshless faces and into the executioner's domain.

Tullaris was waiting for him. The Chosen of Khaine knelt on the ground, clad only in a loincloth. A pair of thin, sickly looking slaves attended him, their scarred arms rubbing at him with blood-soaked sponges. A third slave lay crumpled in a wide, trough-like basin, her blood streaming from the dozens of cuts inflicted upon her body. Sarkol Narza stood over the bleeding slave, a strange instrument gripped in his hand. It was shaped like a branding iron, but what was fitted at its end was more like a set of razors, each blade crossing and recrossing the others to form a perfect representation of the Sign of Khaine. As Malus watched, Sarkol pressed the bladed instrument into the slave's side, leaving a crimson imprint for a brief moment before the streaming blood obscured it.

'Is this how you receive your master?' Malus growled, glaring at Tullaris and his minions.

Tullaris matched the heat in the drachau's gaze. 'I serve but one master, Darkblade, and you are not Him.'

Another elf, even a dreadlord, would have been intimidated by the cold passion in Tullaris's voice, the gleam of fanaticism in his eyes. Malus had seen too much, survived too much, suffered too much, to feel impressed. 'I wonder, Tullaris. Does Khaine truly speak to you, or are you simply mad?'

From the corner of his eye, Malus noticed Sarkol reach for the dagger on his belt. He could hear Dolthaic start to draw his sword and move to intercept the executioner. He kept his own gaze upon Tullaris. The slaves were retreating from their master, cowering away from him. Even now, they were more frightened of the unarmed executioner than the armoured drachau standing a few feet away.

'I should have killed you, Darkblade,' Tullaris said, every word dripping with hate and bitterness. 'Pretender. Imposter. Blasphemer. You used the title that belongs to me towards your own purpose. For your own gain you have profaned and defiled the holy name of Khaine.'

Sarkol had turned to face Dolthaic. If it came to a fight, Malus wasn't certain he'd put his wager on the knight, even with the longer reach of his sword. At close quarters, a fanatic was more dangerous than a professional soldier.

Tullaris turned his head towards his lieutenant and nodded. Reluctantly, Sarkol relented and slammed his dagger back into its sheath. Tullaris looked back at Malus, a bitter smile appearing on his face. 'I should have killed you, Darkblade, but I *do* hear the voice of Khaine. I have seen, in my dreams, that you are the key to destiny. It has been granted that you shall atone for your blasphemies by bearing me to my apotheosis. We will walk to the Throne of Khaine together, you and I. The Witch King's pretensions of divinity shall be cast down and the true glory of Khaine will be revealed.'

With each word the executioner spoke, Malus felt his anxiety increase. Better than anyone, he knew what it was to have another voice inside one's mind. He wasn't sure which possibility was more disturbing – that Tullaris was mad or that he really did have *something* speaking to him.

'Before the Witch King offered you the choice, I knew that our doom was joined,' Tullaris continued. He rose from the ground, his body dripping with the blood his slaves had anointed him with. His brawny chest was a confusion of scars, overlapping layers of cuts, each slash representing the Mark of Khaine. 'Before you knew what you would do, I knew we would march together.'

Malus scowled at the executioner. 'Prophecy is unerringly accurate after the fact,' he sneered. 'It may interest you that my closest advisors urged me to join forces with Venil Chillblade.'

'But you didn't, Darkblade. You made the choice that Khaine demanded.' Tullaris's eyes narrowed, his tone dropping to one of warning. 'The sorceress. You must eliminate her.'

'She is... useful to me,' Malus said. He wondered if Tullaris had merely guessed or if the executioner really knew that Drusala was the 'advisor' who'd urged him against siding with the Har Ganeth exiles.

'She is a creature of the Witch King,' Tullaris said. 'She is the handmaiden of Morathi, a product of her convents. All the sorceresses of Ghrond serve Morathi, however far they fare and whatever deceits they weave.'

That idea gave Malus pause. He was certain Drusala was playing her own game, trying to fulfil some scheme that would benefit herself. Was it possible that at the same time she was acting as an agent of Morathi or the Witch King? Could it be all the seeming disfavour in which Malekith held her was simply a pretence? He already considered the witch a threat, but one that could be attended to later when the opportunity arose. If she was an agent of Malekith, however, her elimination was crucial.

'It needs magic to fight magic,' Dolthaic said. Although Sarkol had relented, the knight remained on his guard, poised to protect his master's back and flank should treachery arise.

'Only those with little ability fall outside the power of Ghrond,' Malus said. 'It will need more than a petty enchantress to oppose Drusala.'

Tullaris stepped over to the basin and the bleeding slave. He ran his hand through the dazed she-elf's hair. 'Was the Lady Eldire a petty enchantress? She opposed Morathi herself and remained independent of her control.' The executioner locked eyes with Malus. 'Perhaps that is why she was murdered.'

It took the iron resolve of a drachau not to allow any sign of emotion to show on his face. The loss of his mother was a pain Malus had yet to face. Korbus had claimed he acted for the Witch King, but what if he wasn't alone? It would need powerful magic or careful treachery to overcome someone like Eldire. Or, perhaps, a mix of both. He was reminded of what he'd witnessed while locked inside Tz'arkan's twisted form. He'd felt rather than heard Drusala's voice rising from Absaloth's tongue. Had she employed similar magic when Korbus was exposed?

Malus looked over at Dolthaic. 'The problem remains. It needs magic to fight magic. As you say, my mother was the single most powerful sorceress to defy Morathi's control.'

Almost absently, Tullaris shoved the head of his slave forwards, pushing her face under the film of blood at the bottom of the basin. 'There is no single sorceress who can equal Lady Eldire,' he said. 'But there are three whose powers combined can suit our needs.' He smiled as the slave's body thrashed about. Drowning, she had snapped from her weary stupor. Her fingers clawed at the executioner's arms, scratching at him in her agonies.

Sarkol explained his master's words. 'Three sorceresses fled Ghrond long ago. They sought shelter in Har Ganeth and the protection of Hellebron. They have become the Blood Coven, their combined sorcery enough to oppose even the great daemons of the Wastes. Perhaps only Morathi herself is the equal of their united power.'

'This Blood Coven is among your entourage?' Malus asked.

Tullaris frowned. The resistance of the drowning slave was growing weaker. 'They are not with us, but they could be. Malekith mistrusts Morathi for failing to warn him of the daemonic invasion. That suspicion runs to all who serve the convents. He knows the value of having in his keeping a body of sorceresses with no love for his mother. He has kept the Blood Coven close in case he must use them against his mother's disciples.'

'The Blood Coven appreciates how precarious their position has become,' Sarkol continued. 'They know that should Malekith reconcile with Morathi as he has so often before, they would be lost. Given the chance, they should again like the protection of Har Ganeth and the favour of Khaine.'

'Say the word, Darkblade, and when we march, the Blood Coven will march with us,' Tullaris said. He released his grip on the now unresisting slave. There was just a flicker of life left in her. If she had the strength, she might yet save herself. If she was too weak, it was a sign Khaine had accepted this offering of murder. 'Sarkol Narza knows where they are being held. He will liberate them and bring them to you. By the time their escape has been discovered, we will already be deep in Ellyrion.'

Malus pondered the offer. Not for an instant did he doubt that Tullaris had motives of his own for rescuing the Blood Coven. But it might be that such motives echoed his own. Anything that might give him an edge over Drusala was a gamble he felt he had to take. Even more now that the seed of suspicion was there.

'Very well, Tullaris,' Malus decided. 'Bring your witches.'

Tullaris smiled as he watched the last bubbles of air rise in the basin and the first touch of death steal upon the drowned slave. 'Khaine blesses this compact, Darkblade,' he said, jabbing his thumb at the unmoving corpse. 'Together, He will lead us to our destiny.'

Silar could hear the cries of agony even before he reached the compound where the Naggorites had been interred after the battle. A ring of impaled bodies greeted him, the still-living husks of those slave-soldiers wounded in battle. There were scores of them, hands bound behind them, slivers of silverwood torn from the great doors of the Eagle Gate thrust through their vitals. It was a slow, hideous death, the kind of death usually reserved for traitors and cowards, not warriors whose only failing had been to fall victim to the caprice of battle.

Such was the viciousness of Kunor Kunoll's Son, however. An inveterate sadist, the brute never squandered an opportunity for cruelty. As Silar approached, he saw the slavemaster and two of his henchmen standing over a Naggorite who'd been staked on the ground. They were busy heaping the armoured bodies of fallen slaves on the wretch, gradually pressing the elf to death. Silar noted with a start that the druchii Kunor was torturing was Bragath Blyte. One word from the tormented slave and Silar could find himself branded a traitor.

There was nothing to do, however, except keep walking. Kunor had already noted the highborn and would think it curious to see him withdraw without some manner of explanation. Silar glanced down at Bragath. For just an instant there was a silent appeal in the Naggorite's eyes.

'Has the great Silar Thornblood decided to go slumming among the commoners?' Kunor laughed. 'I thought you didn't care for this kind of diversion. Too crude for your refined palette.' He laughed again as he hefted the corpse he was holding onto the one already on Bragath's chest. The weight of two fully armoured elves now pressed down on the captive.

'I find little to enjoy in savagery without purpose,' Silar said. 'There is an art to torture that I despair of you ever appreciating, Kunor. This,' he gestured to Bragath, 'is like comparing the murmur of an idiot to the song of a diva. They are alike only in that both are sounds.'

Kunor glared at the highborn. 'I'll teach the swine to sing,' he growled, motioning for his henchmen to lug another corpse onto the pile. The slavemaster's eyes narrowed with suspicion. 'What did bring you here?'

'Orders from the drachau,' Silar said, letting the weight of that statement sink in. 'He commands that you have your Naggorites ready to march in the morning.' He glanced around the compound, at the great dark stretches between the campfires of the slave-soldiers. Over half of the Naggorites had perished over the course of the campaign. 'Such as are left,' he added with a mocking smile. 'I wonder, Kunor, how long it will be before your command vanishes completely. What use will Malus have for a slavemaster without any slaves?'

Kunor raised his hand, arresting the action of his helpers as they prepared to dump the third corpse onto Bragath's chest. 'What do you mean?' he demanded.

Silar shook his head. 'Surely you don't expect Lord Malus to give you command of a company of dreadspears or a troop of dark riders? You aren't a leader, Kunor, you are a taskmaster. You don't lead, you drive. You bully and terrorise your warriors, but you don't lead them. The host of Hag Graef may need new leaders when this war is over, but it won't need a slave-driver. Not to command troops on the battlefield.' Silar glanced down at Bragath. 'I wonder what you'll do when they're all gone. Perhaps the drachau will reward you with a post in his kitchens.'

The slavemaster shook from an apoplexy of rage. He ripped the whip from his belt, but when he played his lash, it was across the faces of his henchmen. 'Put that carrion down! Go and check that the rest of these dogs are fit to march in the morning!'

Rubbing his slashed face, one of the henchmen pointed at Bragath. 'What about him?'

'Leave him,' Kunor growled. 'If he lives until morning, cut him loose and put him in line with the rest.' The slavemaster turned back towards Silar, but the highborn was already walking away. He glared hatefully at the noble, damning him for the doubt and fear he'd set in the slavemaster's mind.

Silar walked slowly through the darkness, away from the slave compound. He'd done what little he could for Bragath. He hoped the Naggorite understood that. He hoped it would be enough to keep the elf's silence.

'Unusual friends for a noble of Hag Graef,' a soft voice whispered to Silar from the darkness.

Surprised by the abruptness of the words, Silar spun around. He discovered Drusala staring at him, an enigmatic expression on her face.

'Beasts like Kunor are an unfortunate necessity in a time of war,' Silar said.

'War makes strange bedfellows indeed.' Drusala stepped closer and slowly turned to face back at the slave compound. 'You were a hero of the war that saw Hag Graef victorious against the black ark of Naggor. It is strange to see you with such sympathy for your old enemies.'

Silar tried to hide the flash of alarm that coursed through him. How much did the sorceress know and how much did she simply guess? Or was Drusala simply fishing for a reaction, trying to tease out from him with craft what she couldn't with magic?

'That war is over. The Naggorites fight alongside Hag Graef now,' Silar said. 'I simply do not like to see Lord Malus's resources squandered needlessly.'

'A most thoughtful vassal,' Drusala said. 'It is rare to find such loyalty among the highborn. Usually it makes them too weak to accomplish anything of merit.'

As abruptly as she had appeared, so too did the sorceress depart, vanishing into the darkness of the druchii camp. Even after she was gone, however, Silar could smell the tang of her perfume and feel the uncanny chill of her presence.

CHAPTER SIXTEEN

For five days the druchii raged across the Ellyrian countryside, slaughtering and burning everything in their path. No settlement was too small to escape their hate, no victim to insignificant to be spared their wrath. The crucified bodies of tortured asur marked the march of Malus Darkblade, every victim bearing the brand of Khaine upon their brow.

Dark riders ranged far and wide, scouting the terrain, studying the lay of the land. While Drusala and the other sorceresses kept their focus upon Tor Elyr, the Griffon Gate and Whitefire Tor, the scouts fed the army a complete survey of the land. On the sixth day of their rampage, Malus had cause to put that intelligence to use.

The ravages of the druchii were known to the asur. Day by day, the outrages inflicted by the invaders continued to build until at last an army stirred from each of the great Ellyrian cities. The hosts of Tor Elyr and Whitefire Tor marched to intercept that of Naggaroth, but Malus was careful to avoid being trapped between them. His army ranged deeper into the countryside, drawing the asur after them. Eventually, the two Ellyrian armies merged, forming a united front against the despoilers of their kingdom.

It was then that Malus ordered his army to retrace their march, fading back towards the Annulii Mountains. The asur were coming for his bait, now it was time to give battle. Battle under his terms and on ground of his choosing.

From a rocky outcropping on the foothills, Malus and his generals watched the asur army closing upon them. Around a stand of forest that had been partially burned by the druchii, the Ellyrians came, their banners fluttering in the breeze, their armour gleaming in the eternal summer of Ellyrion's sun. A war-chant, as old as Aenarion's reign, rose from the marching soldiers. As it reached them, some of Malus's warriors added their own voices to the song, a reminder to the asur that it was the druchii who were the true heirs of Aenarion.

'They outnumber us, dreadlord,' Silar cautioned Malus. 'Why give battle to them at all? We can fade into the hills and force them to divide their command to pursue us.'

Malus reached down and gave Spite an affectionate pat. He appreciated the horned one's unquestioning loyalty, especially at times like these. 'After all the hard work to bring my enemies together, dividing them again is the last thing I want.'

'If you were to draw them back towards the Eagle Gate, the dragons would be able...'

An icy glare silenced Silar. 'The last thing I want is to make a present of my victory to either Imrik or Malekith. This victory will be mine! It won't be stolen from me as the Eagle Gate was.' Raising his hand, Malus brought his mailed fist flashing down. At his signal, a horn sounded, its dolorous note echoing among the rocks. Below the rise upon which Malus and Silar conferred, a great body of troops rushed out towards the enemy. Mounted slavemasters cracked their whips against the soldiers, driving them like cattle.

Silar felt his insides go cold as he watched the Naggorites herded towards the asur. He knew the slave-soldiers were greatly outnumbered, that Malus didn't expect them to stop the Ellyrian push. Well was he aware of his lord's callous deployment of the Naggorites and the fiendish plan behind it. The knowledge didn't make him like the scheme any better. Vanquished, enslaved, the Naggorites were still druchii. That meant something to Silar, much more than it had before Naggaroth was abandoned. They were the last of a breed, the last sons of the Land of Chill. To spend their lives in such a ruthless manner made him sick.

'The passes will hide the numbers of Kunor's dogs,' Malus laughed. 'For all that the asur can tell, the whole of my host is descending upon them. Our magic will prevent them from piercing that deception. When the Naggorites break, the asur will smell victory and pursue.' Malus clenched his fist, his face contorting into a visage of complete hate. 'Then they are mine. Sacrifices to *my* glory. Not that of the Witch King!'

Silar looked down into the pass. The first line of the Naggorites was just emerging out onto the plain. Immediately, a rain of arrows and spears rose from the asur lines. Scores of druchii were brought down, falling in their droves as the missiles struck their formation. Kunor and the mounted slavemasters whipped fresh troops into the gaps, driving them on, allowing them no pause for thought or fear. Yard by yard, the Naggorites clawed their way across the field towards the asur front. Beneath their feet they trampled the bodies of their own dead and wounded, deaf to the cries of the maimed and dying.

Before the Naggorites could reach the Ellyrians, a block of swordsmen in suits of mail stepped forwards. They met the initial rush of the slave-soldiers with cleaving strokes of their double-handed blades. The asur swords scythed through the druchii, cleaving through armour as though it were paper and taking scant notice of the flesh and bone within.

Kunor and the slavemasters continued to beat and threaten their troops, forcing more and more of them into the fray. At last, however, even the fatalistic determination of the Naggorites reached its limit. The surge of black-armoured elves receded, turned back upon itself. Raw, primitive cries of despair and alarm rose from the druchii as they fled back into the passes, stampeding those before them into full retreat.

The asur, the song of Khaine already sounding in their souls, the smell of enemy blood in their hearts, pursued their reeling foes. Shouting triumphantly, the Ellyrians charged after the druchii, cutting down any unfortunate enough to fall into their hands.

Upon the rise, Malus smiled, an expression of such murderous glee that it might have provoked envy in Tullaris had the executioner been there to see it. Once again, the drachau raised his hand high. Carefully he watched the Naggorites pouring back into the pass below, studying the numbers and progress of the asur pursuing them.

'Can we not wait until our warriors are clear?' Silar asked.

Malus didn't bother to look aside at his retainer. 'The Naggorites die to serve the Hag. It is all they are good for.' Extending forefinger and thumb, he gave the signal the troops positioned on the rise had been watching for.

The sorcerous glamour that had cloaked the warriors on the rise evaporated as the druchii sprang into action. Their concealment had represented something of an abuse of Drusala's magic, taxing her to the utmost. Only by remaining completely still had the warriors been able to retain the illusion of rock and brush. In motion they were revealed to the elves below. Rank upon rank of darkshards, the hideous power of their repeating crossbows magnified by the half a dozen reaper bolt throwers ranged among their ranks. Naggorite and Ellyrian alike vented a cry of despair when they saw the druchii aiming down at them.

The ensuing slaughter was horrific by any standard. The crack of bowstring, the smash of bolt through armour, the scream of ruptured flesh, all rose into a deafening tumult. In the close press of panicked warriors, the dead were pinned to the living, the wounded skewered to the walls of the pass. Ellyrian knights were shot from their saddles to impale themselves on the swords and spears of the infantry around them. The floor of the pass became a churning sea of death and terror, frantic warriors struggling to escape the massacre unfolding all around them.

Malus had schooled his soldiers well, impressing on them the penalty for restraint or hesitation. Scores of Naggorites fell alongside hundreds of Ellyrians as the gruesome harvest continued. The ground became so soaked with blood that it was reduced to a muddy mash that sucked at the feet of those trying to escape it.

The butchery was more than the asur could endure. At last they broke, fleeing back through the pass and out onto the plain. Though they left hundreds of their dead behind them, the Ellyrian force still numbered in the thousands. The trap had bloodied them, but it hadn't destroyed them.

Malus paid little notice to the surviving Naggorites as they retreated back into the hills. He was watching the asur, staring with the keen interest of a gem-cutter tending a stone. The Ellyrians were out of the pass, fleeing onto the plain. Their numbers weren't greatly diminished. But Malus hadn't expected them to be. All his trap had been designed to do was inflict disorder in the enemy host, to break up the regimental formations, to confuse the discipline that brought them unity. If he had faced a single army, the commander might have restored order as soon as the asur were clear of the pass. That was why he had waited for both armies to merge before confronting them. Instead of bringing strength, the combination had brought weakness. Two command structures, two generals, two elves to which the panicked troops were looking for leadership, for orders.

The panic of the asur continued, the commanders unable to restore order in their mixed host. The retreat brought them close to the burned forest. The forest where the real jaws of Malus's trap waited.

It had been something of a gamble, entrusting the role to Sarkol Narza and the Bloodseekers. Malus had been worried about their discipline, fearing that their lust for carnage would cause them to act too soon and betray themselves. But Tullaris had impressed upon the executioners the importance of their role, the vital turn they would play in this battle. The individual slaughter they could work on their own would pale beside the wholesale havoc they could inflict by following the drachau's plan.

It had also proved a vital test of just how powerful the Blood Coven's powers truly were. He'd taxed Drusala's magic with her illusion and demanded the Blood Coven perform a similar feat. The red-robed witches had managed their spell with a good deal more bloodshed than Drusala, offering up a dozen sacrifices to Khaine over the course of their ritual, but in the end their sorcery had proven just as effective.

The seemingly capricious burning of the forest had been exactingly deliberate: to confuse the memories of any Ellyrian who knew this ground, and to make the asur oblivious that there were more trees in the forest than there had been before. As the fleeing army retreated past those trees, the glamour cast upon Sarkol and his executioners vanished. Howling like wolves, the murderous horde fell upon the asur. This time it was the Ellyrians' turn to be cut down like wheat.

The other set of jaws in the trap Malus had prepared came galloping out from the pass. Dolthaic, leading the Knights of the Burning Dark, and Tullaris Dreadbringer, leading the Ossian Guard, the elite of his murderous army. While the cold one knights carved a path through the rear of the confused asur, Tullaris led his killers into the gaps created by the mounted warriors. Left and right, the Ossian Guard played their heavy draichs, rending the Ellyrians at every step.

'A great victory,' Malus declared as he watched the slaughter unfolding on the plain. Pinned by Sarkol at the front, Dolthaic on the flank and

Tullaris at the rear, the asur were being herded into a ring. It was still possible they might coordinate and break through, but that opportunity was quickly slipping away. The rest of Malus's army was now marching out from the pass. The survivors of Clar Karond, the veterans of Hag Graef, the Iceblades and Voiceless Ones brought by Drusala from Ghrond, the hordes of exile killers from Har Ganeth, the corsairs of the *Eternal Malediction*. The Ellyrians still outnumbered the druchii, but their numbers counted for little now. They'd lost cohesion and they'd lost the initiative. For too long, they had thought of themselves as the hunters. It wasn't an easy thing to understand that they were now the prey.

Silar listened to Malus's words. He stared down at the carnage in the pass below, at all the dead Naggorites. 'A great victory, dreadlord,' he agreed. 'But I wish it hadn't cost us so much blood.'

Malus shifted around in his saddle and favoured Silar with a withering stare. 'Be happy none of it was yours,' he told his vassal.

'I am ready to die for the Hag,' Silar answered, bowing his head.

'I will remember that, Silar,' Malus said. 'I trust you will not have cause to regret your choice of words.'

Shifting his attention back to the battle, Malus watched as the ring of asur was slowly cut to pieces. Undoubtedly some would still escape, but he actually preferred to leave some survivors. They would carry word of what had happened here back to their cities and when Malekith came to lay siege to them, the Witch King would know that it was Malus who was responsible for already decimating the asur armies.

Perhaps Drusala was already telling Malekith of what had happened here by means of her magic. Malus almost hoped she was. Anything that taxed her sorcery further was to be applauded.

'I will have need of your service this night,' Malus told Silar. 'Make yourself available. There is an urgent chore that needs attending to and I'd trust no one else to see it carried out.'

The wind carried upon it a strange warmth. By the starlight, Silar could see an eerie shimmer shining from the peaks of the Annulii. It was a fearsome thought, to understand that even someone without the uncanny gifts of a sorcerer could actually see the magic streaming down from the mountain tops. It was a manifestation of how rapidly the world was coming apart around him. Even if the druchii achieved their ancient dream of conquering Ulthuan, Silar wondered if it would be naught but a Pyrrhic victory. The might of Chaos had engulfed Naggaroth, obliterating the land that had sheltered and reshaped his exiled people for millennia. He had seen the seas tearing themselves apart on the exodus from the Land of Chill. Was it so strange, then, to question whether Ulthuan would be any more inviolable?

Silar pushed aside his doubts, focusing on the task ahead. The least distraction could prove his undoing. He regretted expressing his qualms about

Malus's ruthless strategy now. Perhaps it was that discontent that had led Malus to question his loyalty, and made him decide to employ Silar on such a perilous duty. After all they had been through, he'd half hoped the drachau considered him as something more than just another replaceable lackey. But after all these years, he knew better than that. Whatever bonds they shared, Silar knew no one was indispensable if they stood between Malus and his ambition. Hauclir, Lhunara, even his own father, the vaulkhar Lurhan Fellblade, all had been removed when they became obstacles in Malus's way.

It was one such obstacle that it had become Silar's duty to remove. Malus had been unusually frank about his reasons for having the sorceress Drusala killed. In addition to his suspicions that she was an agent and spy of Malekith, he had come to suspect she was responsible for the murder of Lady Eldire. As one of the few who was aware of the condition that afflicted the drachau, Malus told Silar that the sorceress knew of Tz'arkan and had displayed her powers over the daemon. It could be only a matter of time before she determined to use that ability to exert control over him. To protect the legacy of the Hag, Malus had to break free of such a hold. For vengeance and freedom, Drusala had to die.

The battle against the Ellyrian host had weakened the sorceress. She had drawn heavily upon her powers to conceal the druchii forces from both the spells and the eyes of the pursuing asur. Even for one of her ability, Drusala had been drained by the demands placed upon her. After the battle, she had quietly left the encampment, stealing up into the hills with only her mute bodyguard, Absaloth.

Drusala had imagined her absence to be unremarked, but in that belief her magic had failed her. The witches of the Blood Coven were using their magic to observe her. They too had been impressed to use their spells during the battle, but because they were three, they'd been able to weather the storm better than Drusala. They had enough power left over to monitor her and to warn Malus when she left the camp.

As he quietly made his way over the rocks, Silar listened for even the slightest noise from the armoured warriors he knew to be nearby. In choosing a squad of assassins to slaughter the sorceress, Malus had selected warriors not from his own army but from that of Tullaris. Disciples of Khaine, the executioners considered murder a sacred act and they harboured no love for either Malekith or the sorceresses of Ghrond. Killing Drusala, for them, would be more than vanquishing an enemy. It was an act that would bestow upon them the blessing of their god.

Twenty Bloodseekers led by the infamous Sarkol Narza. More than a match for one exhausted sorceress and her freakish bodyguard, Silar thought.

Drusala had been cautious enough to light no fires. There would be asur scouts in the area and stragglers from the vanquished Ellyrian armies. It was prudent for her to exhibit a modicum of wariness. She'd have been better served, however, to draw less heavily upon the energies streaming down from the mountains. With the aethyric emanations visible even to Silar's sight, seeing the energies converging at a single point, spiralling down to a rocky outcropping was like the blast of a trumpet or the burn of a beacon. It announced Drusala's presence for any who cared to look.

'The witch dies by my blade,' Sarkol hissed in Silar's ear. 'Do you understand that, Hag-rat? She dies in the name of Khaine, not for your master!'

Silar could see the fanatic gleam in the executioner's eyes above the face-wrapping he'd adopted. Given the slightest excuse, he knew Sarkol would leave him dead among the rocks. Cautiously, the noble nodded his understanding. 'I am here only to ensure she dies. How she dies, why she dies, is your business.'

The executioner drew back. 'See that you remember your place, then,' he warned. Sarkol pointed an armoured finger at the outcropping. 'She is there. Half of my followers are working around to the other side. We will strike from here. Between us, there will be no escape for the witch.'

Again, Silar nodded. His fingers tightened around the bronze charm the Blood Coven had bestowed upon each elf in the murder squad. In the event that Drusala wasn't as weak as they expected, the charm would offer some protection against spells. Not immunity, but a degree of resistance. Sarkol and his Bloodseekers had taken the charms with a good degree more confidence than Silar felt. Then, the killers probably thought themselves protected by Khaine and with little need for talismans and charms in the first place.

Beside him, Silar watched Sarkol's fingers rubbing a braided strangler's cord, his thumb working at the rope with careful, measured rotations. It was an old assassin's trick, a way of measuring time and synchronising an attack. At least one of the executioners circling the outcropping would be keeping time the same way. When they were in position, they would wait for the agreed upon moment to strike.

The superstitious dread of a lifetime raced down Silar's spine. It was no easy thing, killing a sorceress. If the witch was able to identify her killers before she died, her curse would haunt their bloodline to the eighth generation. It was why Sarkol and the others wore wraps across the lower half of their faces, a precaution against the death-curse. Silar swore at himself for not exhibiting similar caution, but when he'd left camp he'd been more worried about his murderous companions than Drusala's spells.

'Be ready, Hag-rat,' Sarkol whispered. 'Be vigilant and report to your blasphemous master how the children of Khaine ply their trade.'

Silar could feel more than see the Bloodseekers rise from the rocks and rush towards the outcropping. He rushed after them, determined to carry out the duty Malus had charged him with. When Sarkol struck, he intended to see every sweep of the executioner's blade.

Behind the outcropping, they found Drusala sitting on the ground, her legs folded beneath her. What seemed a column of dancing fireflies was spiralling down around her, but the glowing flickers weren't insects. They were motes of aethyric power drawn down from the mountains, seeping into Drusala as she replenished her magic. The sorceress's skin pulsed with a purple light, her clenched teeth and rolling eyes crackling with energy.

Beside her stood Absaloth, as grim and sinister as ever. The voiceless warrior had drawn his sword and turned to receive Sarkol's attack. The bodyguard appeared oblivious to the dark shapes hurrying out of the darkness behind him. As arranged, the other executioners were striking at the same moment Sarkol had chosen.

Only they weren't Sarkol's elves. Silar hissed a warning when it was obvious to him that there were too many shapes rushing out of the dark. Even as he realised the peril, crossbows were sending bolts into the charging executioners. Five of the killers, half of Sarkol's force, collapsed under the barrage. The survivors rushed onwards, determined to strike down their quarry before they too were slain.

The foe was quicker than the Bloodseekers, intercepting them before they could get close to Drusala. They were wiry, lean elves, their bodies cloaked in black, their skins pale where they hadn't been stained with tribal markings and tattoos. Autarii! The savage tribesmen of Naggaroth's wastelands, descendents of those renegades who'd been exiled from the cities and condemned to fend for themselves in the unforgiving wilds. Silar recognised the nature of the shades at once and an awful suspicion rose into his mind. The same spiral of magic that had allowed them to find Drusala had also guided these shades to her.

The sorceress had foreseen treachery and countered it with a trap of her own.

With cruel knives and crooked swords, the shades flung themselves upon the executioners. Three of the autarii were cut down by the massive blades, hacked to ribbons by the angry steel of Har Ganeth. In return, however, the cloaked savages brought down all of their foes. In the space of only a few heartbeats, only Silar and Sarkol remained.

Sarkol brought his draich crunching through the skull of one autarii and opened the belly of a second. Kicking the wretch from his path, the incensed executioner tried to reach Drusala. Absaloth fended away the butchering sweep, his sword ringing as it crashed against Sarkol's. The executioner backhanded the bodyguard, laying his cheek open to the bone. Absaloth gave no reaction to the wound, but instead slashed at Sarkol, forcing the warrior back.

The duel that ensued was as brief as it was amazing. Thrust and parry, feint and riposte, Sarkol and Absaloth circled one another. Whenever the executioner seemed about to butcher his foe, the bodyguard's sword would dance against the draich's cruel edge. When it appeared that the

Voiceless One would prevail, some killer's instinct would preserve Sarkol at the last second, causing him to weave aside or intercept the blade with the weighted hilt of his draich.

Silar was too busy trying to fend off the attentions of the autarii who came rushing at him to see the end of the fight. The shades came at him from every side, pushing him back to the edge of the outcropping. With nothing behind him except a hundred-foot fall, he had no choice but to fight. The first shade to come at him was sent rolling to the dirt, clawing at the stump of his arm. The second went hurtling to his death when Silar caught hold of his cloak as the shade lunged at him and spun the elf over the edge.

The autarii circled around him now, wary as old wolves. A snarled command from a shade with a face dominated by black tattoos caused them to back away. Falling back, they unlimbered the crossbows hidden beneath their cloaks.

'Merikaar! Leave him be!' The commanding voice boomed like a clap of thunder. The shades flinched at the sound and slipped their crossbows back beneath their cloaks. The tattooed leader scowled, but his eyes were wide with fear.

Silar looked past his attackers. He could see Sarkol staggering on his feet, a gold-hilted dagger piercing the back of his neck. While he watched, the executioner fell. Absaloth, bleeding from a deep gash in his left arm, thrust his sword into the ground and bent down to remove the dagger. Almost gingerly, he restored it to the one who had put it there.

Drusala didn't even glance at her mute bodyguard when she took the dagger from him. Her eyes were fixed entirely upon Silar. 'You will excuse Merikaar. His tribe, the Knives of Khaine, are quite devoted to me. Sometimes that devotion can be carried too far.'

The sorceress walked towards the embattled highborn, paying no notice at all to the corpses strewn about her feet. She smiled as she noted the bronze charm Silar wore. Her fingers hovered before it for an instant. She closed her eyes and sighed. 'Each spell bears a signature, and I know this one from long ago.' She opened her eyes and her smile took on a mocking quality. 'Aren't you going to attack? Aren't you going to fulfil your master's purpose?'

Silar managed to smile back at her. 'All I was supposed to do was watch and report,' he said, nodding at the dead Sarkol. 'I was warned against taking any hand in the attack.'

'You killed two of my kindred,' Merikaar accused, gesturing at Silar with the knife in his hand.

'Do be fair, Merikaar,' Drusala told the shade. 'After all, they were trying to kill him.' Her face lightened, almost wistful. 'This is Silar Thornblood, one of the highest of the highborn of Hag Graef. We mustn't be too capricious about allowing him to die.

'After all, if something were to happen to Malus Darkblade, Lord Silar would be the logical choice to succeed him as drachau.'

CHAPTER SEVENTEEN

Twenty asur captives had been the price set by the Blood Coven to work their magic and conceal the Bloodseekers of Sarkol Narza during the battle. In their time as refugees under the protection of Hellebron in Har Ganeth, the three sorceresses had many centuries to hone their craft, to merge the ritualistic powers of the cult of Khaine to their own dark sorcery. The end result had been a debased and abominable kind of magic, a magic that drew its strength from blood and suffering.

The witches gazed cruelly, hungrily, upon their prisoners. The great Tullaris himself had brought them here, bound to stakes that were driven into the ground in such a way that from the sky, from whence the gods observed the mortal realm, the stakes would form the mark of Khaine. Blood and slaughter delighted the Lord of Murder, and the witches intended to give their violent deity quite a spectacle in exchange for their own revitalisation.

Flinging aside their crimson cloaks, the witches drew long, fang-like knives from their girdles. Sacrificial blades long in the service of Har Ganeth's witch elves, the weapons exuded an aura of atrocity, the stink of blood and death soaked into the ancient bronze, perverting the very metal with the stain of murder. Gleefully, the Blood Coven kissed the hoary blades and ran their tongues along the sides. Blood welled up from the tiny scratches the knives cut into their tongues. The witches laughed in delight, rolling the blood around in their mouths until their teeth took on a crimson hue.

From the stakes, the captive asur looked on with horror and repugnance as the sorceresses worked themselves up into a frenzy, playing the knives across their nubile bodies, unheeding of the cuts and slashes they inflicted on their bare flesh. They threw themselves into a wanton dance of madness and bloodshed, cutting at one another as their bodies writhed and gyrated as though in the thrall of some phantom musician. Wilder, faster, crazier the dance became. The Blood Coven raised their voices in animalistic screeches, howls that mimicked the slavering growls of hounds and the shrieks of hawks on the hunt. The bestial chorus increased in malignance and savagery, dipping into the hisses of jungle saurians and the hellish abominations of the Wastes.

With a final wail, the Blood Coven broke away from their dance of self-mutilation. The witches rushed at the bound captives, slashing at them with their grisly knives. One after another, the asur wilted in their bonds, throats slashed and hearts stabbed as the sorceresses ran amok. Blood fountained from each of the butchered elves, the sanguine fluid taking on a lustrous black sheen as it slopped from the wounds. Ecstatic squeals leapt from the witches as they raced amongst their victims, sacrificing each in turn. The earth within the symbol of Khaine formed by the stakes soon became a bog of dark, shimmering blood.

As their last victim died, the Blood Coven returned their knives to their girdles and hurled themselves to the ground. In a spasm of obscenity, the witches squirmed and writhed through the gory mire, letting the blood soak into their pale skin. As they slithered through the muck, each of them could feel the dark magic they had trapped in the blood passing into themselves in turn. Their bodies tingled, their souls sickened, their stomachs turned as the aethyric powers were drawn into their flesh.

Abruptly, the blood-caked witches looked up, their heads snapping around to stare past the ring of stakes that surrounded them. Beyond the perimeter, they could see a lone druchii, a she-elf dressed in black, her dark hair layered in tiers upon a silver headdress. She leaned against a ghoulish-looking staff, its head aglow with the sorceries bound inside it. An expression of derisive contempt was written across her face and her eyes gleamed with the malice of an old hate long deferred.

'Wallowing in the mud like hogs,' Drusala sneered. 'Is this why you betrayed your mistress?'

One of the Blood Coven, the eldest of the trio, climbed to her feet and pointed a clawed finger at the handmaiden. 'You are a fine one to speak of betrayals. Is your place not in Ghrond, with your mistress Morathi? Do not lecture us about loyalty, Drusala!'

'And who commands your loyalty now that you have fled Hellebron?' Drusala asked. Before the witches could answer, she opened her hand, displaying the protective charm she had stripped from the body of Sarkol Narza. 'An interesting curio to find in the possession of an assassin,' she said. 'And even more curious to find each member of his entourage carrying the same.'

The Blood Coven glanced at one another uneasily. They had imagined Sarkol and his killers had simply missed Drusala in the dead of night. The foothills were, after all, quite a vast wilderness.

'You needn't worry,' Drusala told the Blood Coven. 'They are all dead... well, most of them.' She smiled at the bloody sorceresses. 'There are none left to bear witness against you.'

One of the witches uttered a dry, scoffing laugh. 'There is still you, Drusala. You are alive to bear witness against us.'

Drusala smiled coldly. 'Indeed, and what will three refugees of the convents do about that?'

Again, the witches exchanged a look, but this time there was a sly quality about it. 'We have called upon the old magic. We have drawn the blessing of Khaine into ourselves, transformed our bodies into reservoirs of dark magic. You bring your scorn and mockery at a poor time, harlot of Morathi. The Blood Coven has bathed in the favours of Khaine. Our powers are at their peak!'

'Yes,' Drusala conceded, strangely calm before the threats and boasts of the Blood Coven. 'You are indeed at the height of your ability and power. I have waited many hours to see you at your strongest. It will make beating you still more satisfying.'

A feral snarl rose from one of the witches. Throwing out her hand, the druchii sent a wave of rolling, smouldering darkness at Drusala. As the tide of darkness sped forwards, its essence pitted the wooden stakes and decayed the asur bodies bound to them.

The sorceress gestured with her staff, causing the noxious darkness to fold in upon itself. The cloud quickly disintegrated, dripping into the earth like some malefic dew. 'That was... unimpressive,' Drusala sneered.

Snarling their rage, the three witches made cabalistic symbols with their fingers, the eerie glyphs blazing for an instant in the air. As each symbol flashed into life, the blood-soaked flesh of the conjurers likewise took on a spectral glow. When the Blood Coven unleashed their fury against Drusala, the spell drew nourishment from all three witches rather than one alone. The enchantment took shape as streamers of gore flew upwards from the ground. In a few breaths, a long spear of pulsating blood hovered above the earth. Throwing their hands forwards in unison, the Blood Coven sent the gruesome lance straight at the sorceress.

Drusala drew back as the lance sped towards her. Quickly she threw the folds of her robe about her face, her staff held crosswise against her breast. The bloody spear hurtled straight at her. Like the ball of darkness, it broke against the defensive counter-spell she'd evoked. Unlike the black cloud, however, the spear didn't dissipate. Instead, it exploded into a great morass of blood, a writhing mass of gore that wrapped itself around the sorceress.

The Blood Coven laughed as the blood coiled around Drusala. Each of the witches made pulling motions with her left hand. In response the shattered spear threw more tendrils of itself about their foe. Soon, Drusala's very shape was lost beneath a blanket of pulsating liquid. Grimly, the witches stopped the pulling motions with their left hands. Now, they extended their right hands, slowly closing their fingers. In response, the shell that had formed around Drusala began to collapse in upon itself, shrinking more and more as the Blood Coven closed their hands into fists.

'Broken bones and mangled meat,' one of the witches chortled. 'A fitting end for any of Morathi's trash.' Her eyes took on a light of sadistic glee as she watched the shell contract still further, reducing itself to something on the order of a large pumpkin.

'There won't be enough of her left to fill a thimble,' a second witch observed, cackling with obscene mirth.

'Are you impressed now?' the third witch taunted the shell as it reduced itself to the size of a melon.

'Not particularly.'

The Blood Coven spun about as they heard Drusala call to them. The voice came not from within the shrinking shell, but from the centre of the sacrificial ground. The sorceress stood amongst the stakes, the unnaturally decayed husks of the asur crumbling around her. She held her staff before her, as she had at the start of the attack. Now she thrust it towards the witches, a purplish light erupting from the head of the staff.

'Let's see how you like my magic,' Drusala hissed.

The Blood Coven railed as lashes of purple light whipped around them. One of the elves was struck on the shoulder, a livid scar appearing as the arcane light seared her skin. Before another lash could strike true, however, a slobbering chant erupted from the lips of all three of the witches. The tonalities weren't entirely of elven speech, but derived from the susurrations of ancient amphibian mage-priests and the cachinnations of daemons.

The sounds themselves seemed to take on a phantasmal substance, speeding away from the witches like a storm of fireflies. Each of the knife-edged motes slashed through the whipping tendrils, sending streamers of purplish light to dissipate in the night air.

Before the lashes could be completely vanquished, Drusala magnified their power, drawing them together into a single great cord of pulsating light. Swirling her staff skywards, she caused the purple cord to shift along with it. When she brought the staff striking earthwards, the phantom luminance did likewise. The ground shook as Drusala's spell slammed against it, quivering with violent tremors that toppled many of the stakes. The purple light exploded in a burst of sound and energy, casting slivers of itself in every direction. The robes of the sorceress were slashed by the burning slivers, her pale skin cut in a dozen places. She dabbed a finger in the blood flowing from her cut cheek, for an instant her body flickering, assuming a different visage. Quickly, she reasserted her will and repaired the momentary dissipation of her protective wards.

The Blood Coven had been sent flying by the aethyric explosion. When the witches picked themselves up from the mire of blood, their bodies were scraped and bruised, the patina of sacrificial blood upon them crumbling into black ash with their every breath. The loathsome coating had preserved them against the worst of the attack, but it had drawn heavily upon their powers. They glared at Drusala as they wiped long locks of blood-matted hair from their faces.

'Enough!' Drusala shouted, slamming the butt of her staff against the earth. A sympathetic tremor rolled through the ground, causing the Blood Coven to stumble. 'You have seen that my magic is greater than yours. Must I destroy you to prove it?' She laughed, a tone of withering scorn. 'I can afford to spare you because your sorcery is no threat to me. And now you know it!'

The witches continued to glare at the sorceress. 'We know you too, Drusala. We know your devotion to Morathi. Whatever lies you've told Malekith, we know who you serve,' the eldest of the witches snarled.

Drusala nodded. 'You know much,' she said. 'But do you know enough? Do you know that Morathi is prepared to forgive your betrayal? Do you know she is prepared to welcome back her sisters? Think of it. You can slip away from the pious madness of Hellebron. You can return to the true sisterhood of sorcery.'

'What if we prefer freedom?' one of the witches demanded.

'What if we have come to favour the Lord of Murder as He favours us?' another asked.

The sorceress laughed. 'Then you are fools,' she declared. 'Think! For all of your magic, even united, you could not oppose me. And I am but Morathi's servant! How should you fare if the Queen herself were here? Do not be so foolish as to think she will be content to be exiled to Ghrond. She will stir herself when the time is right. When she does, she will know her loyal servants... and her enemies. The walls of Har Ganeth will not protect you when she does.'

A murmur swept through the Blood Coven. The three witches turned to one another, conversing without speaking, debating the things Drusala had said.

Drusala watched them with no small amount of misgiving. Their magic had been almost enough to destroy her. But for the hasty translocation spell she'd employed, their gruesome blood spear might have overwhelmed her. Certainly escaping such a fiendish evocation would have been arduous. Then there had been the ghastly survival of the witches against the malign ferocity of her own assault. Any sorceress in Naggaroth should have been obliterated, yet these renegades were merely bruised.

An offer of truce and a promise of rehabilitation hadn't been in Drusala's mind when she'd come here to confront the Blood Coven. Yet, as any druchii general knew, no plan remained intact after contact with the enemy. She felt she knew how they would decide. They had existed for too long in fear of Morathi. The chance to escape that fear was too great to let slip through their fingers now. They'd agree to Drusala's proposal.

Malus and Tullaris would find it exceedingly difficult to act against Drusala now that their pet witches were under her control. She decided not to disillusion them, however. Let them think the Blood Coven was a resource they could draw upon. Their mistake would provide her with early warning of any plan they concocted.

That was if Malus Darkblade was even around to hatch any new plots after this night. Drusala rather hoped he would be. She had a bit too much invested in Malus to see him go to waste.

Darkness had settled over the compound in which the surviving Naggorites were held. Kunor Kunoll's Son had shown unusual restraint following the vicious battle against the Ellyrian army. He'd only executed every third slave-soldier who tried to desert and escape into the hills. Barely a score of Naggorites had been impaled and set as a warning at the perimeters of the enclosure. As atrocities went, it was scarcely worth noting.

Of course, much of that restraint had to do with the attrition the Naggorites had suffered. From thousands of war-slaves, they had been bled into a force of only hundreds. Less than a twentieth of those who'd surrendered when Hag Graef defeated the black ark remained. Even Kunor recognised that the time would soon come when his slaves could no longer field a viable fighting force.

The sons of Naggor had sought noble death in battle, an end that might draw the attention of Khaine and Ereth Khial, a finish that might be worthy of the gods. To such an end they had suffered the indignities and cruelties heaped upon them by Kunor and his minions. They had forgotten their pride and sworn their service to their conqueror. At every turn, Malus had betrayed them, dispatching them not into battle, but into massacres. They weren't deployed as warriors; they were used as fodder for the arrows and blades of the enemy. Even the illusion of a glorious death in combat was stripped away from them, left to rot alongside the butchered dead.

This last callous deployment against the Ellyrians had seen the slave-soldiers decimated by their fellow druchii, shot down without remorse alongside the asur. It was the final affront for those who survived.

Through the darkened camp, three shadows moved. Silently they stole past the rows of tents in which the surviving Naggorites slept. Only a few of the survivors knew the plot that was unfolding this night. They were the only ones in the enclosure who slept the sleep of the just and whose dreams were happy ones.

The time for action had come. Now, while they yet had the strength to strike, to avenge themselves upon the tyrant who had abused them so capriciously. One last act for the glory of Naggor! One last moment when the sons of the black ark could hold their heads high and remember the pride that had once been theirs.

Bragath Blyte ran his thumb along the back of the knife he carried. The blade itself had been anointed with hydra venom during the battle for the Eagle Gate, dipped into the poison gushing from the torn remains of Griselfang. Using secrets taught to him by the Witchguard, Brek Burok's Son had preserved the envenomed blades, maintaining their potency throughout the long march across Ellyrion.

Bragath could feel the lethal power of the weapon he held. He could feel its strength flowing into him. Should he but reverse his grip, brush his finger along the edge itself, there would be an end to it all. No more doubt and fear, no more suffering. An instant of pain and it would all be over. To hold such power in his hand made his heart beat faster, made his chest swell and his stomach tighten. Death was in his hand and before the night was over, that death would sheathe itself in the breast of Malus Darkblade.

To kill the tyrant. The last act of defiance that was left to the Naggorites.

Three avengers, Brek Burok's Son, Lorfal the Sly and Bragath himself. There'd been only enough venom to anoint three blades. The other members of their conspiracy had been compelled to remain behind. It would be up to these three to bring all their plans to fruition.

The complexity of the intrigue had been complex in itself. Bribes of treasure looted from fallen asur on the battlefield had bought the service of a wine steward of Hag Graef, an elf with his own grudge against Malus having found his entire household left behind in the exodus from Naggaroth. After their victory over the Ellyrian host, the druchii had celebrated far into the night. The bribed steward had ensured drugged skins of wine reached the people Bragath needed them to reach. He was only sorry the resources weren't available to put something stronger in the wine.

Creeping through the darkness, the trio of killers soon passed the perimeter of the Naggorite compound. The sentry who should have spread a warning turned away when he saw Bragath and his companions. Suddenly he found the eerie mage-light in the sky above of far more interest than the killers slinking over the enclosure wall. It had taken a good deal of gold to buy the cooperation of guards like this, but many harboured their own resentments where the drachau was concerned and they could be depended upon to look the other way if it boded ill for Malus.

'I still think it would be wiser to wait for Lord Silar to return,' Lorfal whispered as they stole down the narrow alley between the rows of tents. Inside each bivouac, ten warriors of the Hag slumbered. There was no knowing how many of them had celebrated with a skin of drugged wine and how many would need but the slightest noise to spring from their sleep. This was the most dangerous leg of their excursion, and the murderers knew it well.

Bragath scowled at Lorfal's trepidation. 'Silar could help us,' Bragath agreed. 'But would he? It is better to strike now while he is away with Sarkol Narza. Once the deed is done, he will be unable to deny the role thrust upon him as the new drachau.'

'But would he thank us for his succession?' Brek shook his head.

'He could be no worse to our people than Malus,' Bragath answered. 'Even a quick death would be preferable to this slow hell of denigration and humiliation.'

The killers had moved through one lane and were stealing towards another when Lorfal suddenly stopped. He shook a trembling finger at one of the tents. An armoured druchii was slumped on a bench outside, her head cradled against her shoulder and a skin of wine lying at her feet. It wasn't the sight of a drugged guard that provoked Lorfal, however. Jubilantly, he wagged his finger at the banner leaning against the sleeping warrior, and at the glyph emblazoned across it. It was a symbol known and reviled by all the Naggorites.

'Kunor Kunoll's Son,' Lorfal spat. 'The swine must be inside that tent.' The murderer started towards the structure, but Bragath caught him by the shoulder.

'There isn't time,' Bragath hissed. 'We must strike down Malus before sunrise. Think of the greater goal.'

Lorfal pulled away from Bragath's grip. Scowling, he turned his head and displayed the scar on his neck, a scar left by Kunor's whip. 'I can think of no greater goal than this. Malus will wait. If there isn't time for Kunor, then we *make* the time.'

Bragath would have protested further, but Brek was already rushing past him, stealing like a hungry wolf towards the slavemaster's tent. Conceding defeat, he followed after Lorfal. While Brek stabbed his poisoned blade into the sleeping guard, Lorfal tore open the flap covering the door of the tent.

Kunor lay sprawled upon a bed of furs, moaning slightly in his drugged sleep. A skin of wine lay dangling from one hand, spilling its last dregs onto the ground.

The three Naggorites glared balefully at the sleeping slavemaster. Kunor had been their persecutor long before the invasion fleet landed in Ulthuan, but it was those recent indignities that were the most fresh in their minds. To an elf, not one of them had failed to dream of a scene like this: their enemy lain out helpless before them.

Lorfal charged at the sleeping druchii. Knife raised high, he drove it full into Kunor's chest. Dark blood was just bubbling up from the wound when Lorfal struck again. In rapid fashion, the vengeful slave-soldier stabbed his victim over and over, spattering the walls of the tent with Kunor's blood. The killer's hands became foul with gore, his face splashed crimson, yet still he stabbed and struck.

'Enough,' Bragath finally declared, pulling Lorfal away from his mutilated prey. 'He is dead.'

'I wanted a scream,' Lorfal growled, still glaring at Kunor's body. 'The drug has cheated me of my scream.'

'Then we had best find the drachau's tent,' Brek stated. 'Malus fears poisoners so he keeps his own stock of wine. He won't be drugged insensible like this dog. Stab Malus and you'll have your scream.'

Leaving the butchered Kunor behind them, the Naggorites slipped back into the night.

* * *

Silar Thornblood's heart felt as though it would burst. For hours he had been racing back to the druchii war-camp, scrambling through the underbrush and rocks as he hurried down from the foothills. His elven stamina had been taxed to the utmost by his ordeal and the haste with which it was made. Every time his boot slapped against the ground he could feel the impact throbbing in the small veins behind his eyes. The sound of his pounding blood was like a dull roar in his ears. His breath came in thin, burning gasps now, scorching his lungs and sending little slivers of suffering throughout his body.

The need for haste had never been greater. Silar was the lone survivor of the attack on Drusala. Why the sorceress had spared him and commanded the Knives of Khaine to let him go wasn't a mystery, however. Drusala had been obliging enough to explain that Silar was necessary for continuance, that the host of Hag Graef might soon demand a new leader. If Silar wasn't there to step into such a role, she was concerned that Tullaris Dreadbringer would appoint himself general. She was quite frank about her doubts that she could enjoy the same influence over the executioner that she did over the drachau. Whoever the drachau might be.

Silar clenched his teeth tight against the sensation of self-reproach that flared through him. Why had he allowed himself to be involved in the schemes of Bragath Blyte? Had it been pity for the Naggorites that kept him silent about the plot, or had he been looking for some opportunity to exploit the scheme towards his own ends? Whichever way, he knew Drusala was aware of his involvement. If anything happened to Malus, the sorceress would have a powerful piece of blackmail to wield against him. As drachau, Silar would be little more than her puppet. He knew he didn't have the strength of will to resist Drusala. It needed a resolve as mighty as that of Malus to oppose Morathi's handmaiden.

The highborn pushed himself still faster, moaning as he saw the stars of early dawn begin to creep up over the horizon behind the sheen of swirling magic crackling down from the Annulii. By the hints and suggestions Drusala had made, Bragath and his conspirators would be making their move before sunrise, while the camp was asleep. If Silar was going to warn Malus, he had to reach the camp before dawn.

The faintest hint of a rustle among the underbrush had Silar whipping around, sword in hand. The Knives of Khaine. He was certain that at least a few of the autarii were following him. Their master, Merikaar, had taken Drusala's decision to let Silar go with ill grace. He wondered if Merikaar had given the shades special orders to attend to him once he was away from the sorceress.

Silar forced his sword back into its scabbard. Even if the shades were following him, he couldn't let their presence distract him from his purpose. He had to take it on faith that Merikaar and his tribesmen understood the scope of Drusala's powers and the impossibility of concealing any treachery from her. Silar could testify to that last part from his own experiences.

After what seemed a lifetime, Silar saw the watch fires burning around the perimeter of the camp. Carefully, he forced his racing steps into a trot, smothered the panic he was feeling inside. He'd be within sight of the sentries soon. Warriors of the Hag might allow a calm, commanding highborn into the camp without too much question, but they would be certain to detain one who looked as though he'd just slipped past Nethu's gate. Adopting an imperious aloofness he didn't feel, Silar unclasped the brooch pinning his cloak in place. It was the representation of a Naggorite murder-hound, a favourite emblem of Malus's inner circle and one that would be known to any soldier of the Dark Crag.

Ahead of him, two guards materialised out of the darkness. One held a crossbow at the ready, while the other gripped the lethal length of a barbed spear. Before the soldiers could issue a challenge, Silar was holding the brooch towards them.

'Lord Silar Thornblood,' he announced in his haughtiest tone. 'Returning from an errand for the drachau.' His lip curled in a withering sneer. 'If you value your heads, let me pass.'

The spearman gave a brief inspection of the brooch and an even briefer glance at Silar. The guard turned pale as he found himself recognising both. 'Forgiveness, Lord Silar,' he said, bowing before the highborn.

Silar ignored the soldiers, marching past them with long, stately strides. The sky overhead was growing darker now, the false night before the first dawn. It was a monumental effort for Silar to maintain a measured pace until he was within the camp itself. Once out of sight of the guards, however, he broke into a frantic run. Bragath and the others had had months if not years to make their plans. Even Malus might not be able to slip through their scheme.

Hurrying towards the grand tent where the Scion of Hag Graef had ensconced himself, Silar saw the first intimations of disaster. The guards outside the tent were laying face-down in the dirt, their hauberks slashed in such a way that the mail looked as though it were partly melted. As he rushed towards the tent, Silar saw a pair of shadowy figures dart inside. A third assassin charged towards him, streams of smoke rising from the poisoned weapon in his hand.

The killer froze in mid-strike, Bragath gazing in shock at the elf he had been about to attack. 'Lord Silar?' the Naggorite gasped.

'It is I, Bragath,' Silar answered. 'Stay your hand.'

Bragath smiled at the highborn. 'With the dawn, you will be drachau. Stand with us, Lord Silar. Keep your promise to my people.'

Silar looked past Bragath, at the tent where Malus slept. There was no time for debate. He had to act now. Before the Naggorite knew what was happening, the noble's sword was flashing from its scabbard and slicing a deep furrow in his chest. 'I must do what is best for the Hag,' Silar hissed. 'I must keep the oath I made to Malus!' He blocked the vengeful sweep of

Bragath's blade and knocked the killer back with a kick of his boot. 'Alarm!' Silar shouted. 'Lord Malus, awaken! The daggers of Naggor are upon you!'

Snarling like a beast, Bragath hurled himself at Silar. A downward slash of the highborn's blade took the ear from the killer's head. The anointed knife raked across Silar's shin, the acidic hydra venom sizzling against his steel armour. The noble buffeted Bragath aside with the pommel of his sword, smashing the killer's jaw and spilling teeth into the dirt. With the Naggorite at bay, Silar hastily cut free the plate the dagger had scratched, knocking it loose before the caustic venom could burn its way down to his flesh.

Bragath glared at Silar, but instead of lunging at the highborn who had betrayed them, he spun about and charged towards the tent. Divested of his compromised armour, Silar hurried after the killer. He was just a few steps behind Bragath when the Naggorite threw open the flap.

Bragath froze in the doorway, stunned by the scene unfolding before him. That moment of surprise was all that Silar needed. Rushing up behind the Naggorite, he slammed his sword into the elf's back, driving it up under the steel backplate Bragath wore. Shuddering, the killer slid downwards, blood bubbling from his mouth as he collapsed onto the woven mats lining the floor of Malus's tent.

Silar stepped over Bragath's body. It was his turn to share the sense of shock and surprise experienced by the Naggorite. Far from finding Malus asleep and defenceless, Lorfal and Brek were engaged with a furious, armoured drachau!

'Your warning is appreciated, Lord Silar, if a bit tardy.' Malus whipped a heavy dragon-skin cloak at Lorfal, snagging the poisoned knife the Naggorite held. While Lorfal struggled to free his blade, Malus spun around, slashing the warpsword across Brek's neck. The killer's head rolled from his shoulders, bouncing across the tent. Before the decapitated body could collapse, Malus was lunging at Lorfal.

The Naggorite had just ripped his envenomed knife free of the cloak when he found the drachau charging him. Lorfal slashed at his foe, but the enraged Malus ducked beneath the sweeping blade and drove the warpsword full into the druchii's chest. Snarling at the thwarted assassin, Malus plunged his sword still deeper into Lorfal's body, impaling him upon the hungry steel. When a foot of blade stood out from the Naggorite's back, Malus gave a sidewise twist, ripping the warpsword free in a move that cut Lorfal in two.

Silar gazed in awe at the havoc his master had wrought in but a few heartbeats. Malus sneered at the dead slaves. 'When you kick a dog, sometimes it shows its teeth.' He spat into the cold eyes of Brek's head. 'When that happens you have to kick it harder.'

Silar bowed, nodding his head. 'The Naggorites sought your life, my lord.'

'And they will suffer for it,' Malus vowed. 'The cold ones will be wanting lively fare before they are fit to march and we took too few asur captive to suit that purpose.' His eyes narrowed and he studied his vassal for a moment. 'How is it that you have had the good fortune to arrive just when you did? Shouldn't you be with Sarkol Narza?'

Silar winced at the accusation, but kept all emotion from his face. Drusala had told him what to say, the explanation that would satisfy his tyrannical lord. She'd promised to fabricate whatever evidence Silar needed to back up his story. 'Sarkol Narza was a traitor, dreadlord. He plotted with Tullaris to dispose of you and me so that they could assume control of your forces. That is why he urged you to kill Drusala and abduct the Blood Coven. He knew that sorcery was the one thing that could upset his plans.'

Malus paced across his tent, blood still dripping off the warpsword's blade. 'If Sarkol wanted your life, how is it you are here to tell the tale?'

'Drusala foresaw my peril and sent her vassals, the Knives of Khaine, to intercede. They killed Sarkol and his retinue,' Silar said. 'I knew if they'd been bold enough to murder me, they wouldn't fail to send someone against you.'

The drachau paused above the body of Bragath. The Naggorite stirred feebly. Blood streaming from his mouth, the dying elf glared at Silar and reached a trembling hand towards him. 'This one seems to know you, Silar,' Malus said. He punctuated the statement by stabbing the warpsword into the druchii's back. Bragath shuddered once and fell still.

'He doubtless hoped I might display mercy towards him,' Silar suggested. 'He wouldn't be foolish enough to expect such weakness from the drachau.'

Malus nodded, satisfied with the explanation. 'You have fought beside me a long time, Silar. You would do well to remember your oath.'

'I remember my duty to the Hag,' Silar answered. He frowned, considering the implications of Drusala's lie about Sarkol and Tullaris. 'What will you do about the executioners?'

'Nothing. For the moment,' Malus said, wiping the warpsword clean on Bragath's vestment. 'They have made their play and failed. It will be a time before they work up the courage to try again. Until they do, it will be best to feign ignorance. Tullaris will fight harder if he thinks I'm unaware of this plot of his. Once his usefulness on the battlefield is at an end, so is he.'

'And... Drusala?' Silar wondered.

'A reprieve,' Malus decided, the word sour on his tongue. 'She will be needed now to counter the Blood Coven. The irony of that isn't lost on me, Silar. I don't appreciate being made a fool of.'

An ugly light shone in the drachau's eyes. 'I think a hundred Naggorites fed alive to the cold ones will remind everyone what comes of trifling with me.'

CHAPTER EIGHTEEN

There was a chill in Malus Darkblade's heart as he received the dignitaries Drusala conducted into his tent. Not so long ago, these elves would have been his most dire enemies. Now, by the edict of the Witch King himself, all who wore the World Dragon were allies to the druchii.

It wasn't the presence of the three Caledorians that discomfited the drachau. It was the knowledge that beyond the perimeter of his camp the beasts these princes had ridden awaited their return. Dragons. The strength of Caledor and by extension the might of all Ulthuan. On its own, one of the reptiles could slaughter hundreds of soldiers. In concert with its fellows and with the strategic guidance of the elven princes, the havoc these wyrms could wreak was incalculable. The threat of having such power unleashed against his troops was exceeded only by the intoxicating vision of what Malus might do with three such monsters under his command.

'Prince Iktheon of Caledor and his brothers,' Drusala announced as she presented the Caledorians. The bows they sketched might hardly have qualified as a nod. Malus wasn't certain if that was more due to arrogance or contempt for the alliance Prince Imrik had forged between their peoples.

'Well met, Iktheon,' Malus greeted the Caledorian. He glanced around at the generals and nobles who'd come to attend this audience between the dreadlord and their new allies. He noted with some pleasure the hint of uneasiness exhibited by Tullaris. First Sarkol Narza was slain in the failed plot against Drusala and now the sorceress was bringing to the army a power far in excess of the Ossian Guard and all of Tullaris's executioners. Even if Malus didn't need the dragons for the battles ahead, they would be useful to remind Tullaris who was in charge. While the wyrms were around, Malus would be able to depend on the sincerity of the Chosen of Khaine.

The more troubling issue was determining how much control Drusala had over the Caledorians that she could draw them away from the armies ransacking Tor Elyr. The sorceress was taking pains to make herself indispensable to Malus. He didn't care for that, because he knew there would be a price for her services. And when it came to a sorceress as powerful as Drusala, he was certain the price would be too dear to pay.

'It is an ill wind that brings eagles among ravens,' Iktheon replied. He cast a scornful gaze across the assembled druchii, his air as disdainful as that of a huntmaster inspecting a pack of curs in his kennel. 'My duty to Prince Imrik has never been as onerous as it is today.'

Malus leaned forwards on his wooden throne, raising one of his mailed hands and motioning for his courtiers to be silent. 'If you provoke an incident here, do not think it will shatter the alliance between your prince and my king. The dream of conquest doesn't die so easily.' The drachau smiled as he saw a little of Iktheon's haughtiness crack, the slightest sag in the proud, out-thrust chest. 'Caledor fights beside Naggaroth now. There is nothing either of us can do to change that. We are friends and as friends, we must seek out our mutual enemies.'

Drusala stepped closer to the seated drachau. In the presence of Tullaris and so many of his officers, Malus noticed that the sorceress kept close to him. He wondered if she would be quite so cosy if she knew it was he who had dispatched Sarkol to kill her.

'You have scouted the terrain between here and Avelorn,' Drusala said. 'Tell the drachau what you have seen.'

Iktheon hesitated a moment, the Caledorian choking on a revelation that only weeks before would have been the basest, most vile treachery. 'A great force marches into Ellyrion. By their deployment, it can only be that they mean to hunt the host of Hag Graef and cut it down.' The dragon prince paused again, fighting to find the strength to disclose the rest. 'The force marching from Avelorn is much smaller than your army, Lord Malus. Perhaps as little as a fifth the size.'

Malus tapped one finger against his chin. 'But there is more, is there not? Something you feel uneasy sharing with friends?'

The Caledorian glared at Malus. For a breath, it seemed he would draw his sword and leap upon the drachau. The moment passed, and instead, Iktheon spoke. 'The Phoenix Guard march in the vanguard of the army, led by Caradryan himself.'

Silar Thornblood stepped out from among the druchii nobles. 'If the Phoenix Guard is there, then they will have phoenix riders as well.' That statement brought a few uneasy mutters from Malus's generals.

The drachau clapped his armoured hands together. 'Be at ease,' he said, the commanding note in his voice brooking no dissension. 'We have friends with us now who will do their utmost to defend us from the phoenix riders.' He nodded to Iktheon. 'Surely your wyrms are the equal of any firebird?' Malus laughed at the impotent hate he saw in Iktheon's eyes. The prince's sense of duty would carry him through.

'And we have the unmatched sorcery of Lady Drusala to help us prepare for battle,' Malus declared, letting his hand fall on the sorceress's shoulder. She'd made a mistake in underestimating how fully the drachau might lean on her powers. Before the battle was through, Malus intended to drain her to the dregs. The Blood Coven could wait; Drusala was the more immediate concern. His only hesitancy came from the worry that it was Tz'arkan making that determination and not his own assessment of the threat she posed.

'If we give battle to the Phoenix Guard, it must be on ground of our choosing, not theirs,' Tullaris declared. Malus was impressed that the executioner didn't colour his words with talk about the will of Khaine and other such zealot doggerel.

Drusala opened her hand, a soft purple fire rising from her palm. In a matter of heartbeats, the fire expanded into a representation of the Ellyrian countryside. Standing stark from the rolling hills and meadows was a jagged landscape of volcanic outcroppings. 'Reaver's Mark,' Drusala explained. 'Here the aethyr hangs close to the earth and my powers will be at their strongest. It is here that I should be able to cast the glamour you wish of me. The Phoenix Guard won't see a single druchii until it is much too late for them.'

Malus nodded, appreciating the ploy. He would discuss the details with Iktheon, Tullaris and his generals later. For now, there was only the need to remind Drusala of her place. 'It isn't what I wish that concerns you, enchantress, but what I command of you. Beware you do not disappoint me.'

Reaver's Mark was a blight of ugliness marring the tranquillity of Ellyrion's eternal summer. Great heaps of volcanic rock lay strewn about the plain, breaking the landscape into eerie expanses of wind-swept cliffs and jagged gullies. Through this haunted terrain, the asur force marched, nearly a thousand strong. No scouts ranged ahead of the army, an oversight that would have bespoke perfect arrogance in any other warriors. The Phoenix Guard were different, however. To an elf, they had walked within the Shrine of Asuryan. They had formed a compact with the Creator God, binding their lives to Asuryan in exchange for the honour of serving him and the glory of his divine blessing. To them was bestowed a sense of purpose denied to other elves; in their souls each of them had been shown the place and hour of his death. In order to preserve such dire portents, to defend the sanctity of prophecy, the Phoenix Guard took an oath of silence that no foreknowledge might slip from their tongues and send ripples of discord through the skein of things yet to come.

More than any of the others, it was their leader, Caradryan of the Flame, who had been afflicted with the curse of foreknowledge. The proud lordling had violated the holiest of holies within the Shrine of Asuryan, penetrating into the sacred Chamber of Days. What secrets had been revealed to him there were known to none but himself, yet from that hour onwards, Caradryan had borne a terrible sense of destiny and upon his brow the rune of Asuryan marked his flesh in a glowing tattoo of arcane flame.

The foresight granted to Caradryan had guarded him well through the centuries. Warriors under his command knew the tide of battle before the first blow had been struck. The disposition of enemy forces, the strength of their leaders and their regiments, these were no secrets to the captain of the Phoenix Guard. To him, the outcome of any fight was already known, the lay of any battlefield already mapped in his mind. For Caradryan, even more than the warriors of his Phoenix Guard, the future was already fact, not simply a fog of possibility and potential.

Malus could have chosen no more dangerous an enemy to face. The greatest strength the druchii had lay in deceit and treachery – strengths that would count for little against a foe who already knew the future. The only counter to the divine magic of Caradryan, of course, lay in more magic. Magic of his own. Magic ruthless enough to tear apart the veil of time and space, to mock the very essence of the future. He'd heard from Lady Eldire how dangerous such magic was – only the toad-priests of the jungles could perform such violations with impunity. A lesser mage risked not simply life but soul as well attempting such a terrible ritual.

Fortunately, Malus had a sorceress on hand who would accept such risk. By playing up to her pride, Malus was able to manipulate Drusala into becoming the vital element in his battle plan. Exterminating the Phoenix Guard would be a terrible blow not simply to the defenders of Avelorn but to the asur as a whole. The key was getting around their insufferable prescience.

Much depended upon the sorceress now. Malus looked over at where Drusala stood, the blood of a dozen slaughtered Naggorites bubbling in the cauldron before her. Arrayed about the cauldron, in a twist of irony that wasn't lost on him in the slightest, were the Blood Coven. Handmaiden of Morathi and witches of Hellebron united in common purpose, determined to bring victory to the host of Hag Graef.

Spite snarled uneasily as the taint of dark magic seeped into the air around them. A spiral of darkness was growing around the cauldron, streamers of sorcery wrapping themselves about the sorceresses. Malus watched as the pale skins of Drusala and the Blood Coven blackened, becoming as dark as malachite. From their splayed fingers, sparkling flares of magic shot upwards, zipping off across the plain until they wrapped themselves about each of the assorted regiments in his army.

'Dreadlord,' Dolthaic hissed in a subdued tone. Malus turned his head slightly, trying to keep his gaze on both the knight and the witches. 'The Phoenix Guard are almost clear of Reaver's Mark. If they reach the open plain, our ambush will have no chance of stopping them, whatever magic the sorceress has promised us.'

The back of Malus's mailed fist caught Dolthaic in the side of his mouth. The knight's cold one snarled hungrily at the scent of the fresh blood dripping from its rider's face. 'I have eyes to see the same as you,' the drachau said. 'And I have a mind capable of forming my own appraisal of the situation. I suggest you hold your opinions in silence. If I want to hear anything from you, I'll tell you what to say.'

Malus left Dolthaic to nurse his wounded pride. He had bigger worries than the esteem of a chastened minion to concern him. The dire assessment Dolthaic had given echoed the thoughts running through his own mind. If Drusala's promised spell didn't exert itself quickly, the entire plan would come apart. Malus needed to cage the Phoenix Guard in Reaver's Mark, prevent them from slipping through to the plains. If a single asur survived to make his way back to Avelorn, there would be small chance of penetrating deep within its borders before Malekith's own forces were on the move again. The Witch King had already claimed victory at the Eagle Gate and would doubtless take credit for the conquest of Ellyrion. Malus was determined that the crushing of Avelorn would belong to him alone. With the Phoenix King dead, the greatest victory the druchii could have would be the capture of the Everqueen. With one blow, the battle for Ulthuan would be decided. Without their king, the asur were a shell of themselves. Without their queen, they would be nothing.

The tendrils of coruscating energy bound themselves in spectral rings around the Knights of the Burning Dark and the drachau who was their master. Malus felt the hairs on his neck prickle as the weird energies swirled faster and faster around him. He could see similar rings taking shape around the Har Ganeth regiments, Silar and the Hag Graef dreadspears, the Iceblades of Ghrond, even Drusala's sinister autarii devotees, the Knives of Khaine. Iktheon's dragons snarled as the dark magic circled them, the great wyrms voicing their distaste for this sorcery to their riders. He watched as Tullaris and his Ossian Guard closed ranks and chanted to Khaine for guidance as the spell wrapped its coils around them as well.

Malus didn't bother to hide his amusement at the sight of Tullaris's devotions. The executioners were praying to be guided into the thick of battle. Well, their prayers were going to be answered, more completely than they hoped. They would play an important role in the battle, but probably not the one Tullaris expected. He could pray to Khaine, but it wouldn't be the Bloody-handed God's doing. It would be the plan conceived by Malus and executed by Drusala.

The arcane ring circling the Knights of the Burning Dark flared, sending a pulse of energy wafting across the plain. The gyrations of the magical power grew faster, becoming more intense with each rotation. Again a pulse of power sped away from the ring. Malus could smell a copper tang in the air and felt a clammy taste in his mouth. His mind shuddered as weird sensations forced themselves into his thoughts. He could touch the colour purple, smell the sound of his heartbeat, hear the flavour of the slime oozing from Spite's scales. The drachau clamped his hands to the side of his head, trying to blot out the obscene impressions.

Then, in a blaze of light, the bizarre sensations were gone. Malus blinked in astonishment as he found himself down in one of the gullies that scratched their way across Reaver's Mark. Around him, Dolthaic and the knights muttered in confusion. They could be thankful their reptilian steeds lacked the wits to be similarly discomfited by the disorienting experience. Prepared as they were for Drusala's spell, the druchii couldn't help the awe that such mighty magic provoked in them.

What Malus and his warriors didn't expect was the sight of the Phoenix Guard just starting to march into Reaver's Mark. When he had last seen them, the asur were leaving the battleground Malus had chosen. The explanation was a simple one, though chilling for that very simplicity. Drusala's spell had moved the army not merely in place but in time as well. They'd been projected forwards to Reaver's Mark, but backwards to that moment when the sorceress had started her ritual. The realisation made Malus's stomach clench. He could hear several of the knights being sick as the same impression struck them.

Dolthaic drew his sword, ready to lead his knights to the attack. A look from Malus made him lower his sword. 'Wait,' the drachau said. 'Wait and watch. I will let you know when to sound the attack.' Dolthaic looked doubtful as he sheathed his sword. The charge of the knights was the signal that would send the rest of the Hag Graef forces into battle. Until the knights attacked, the rest of the regiments would remain where they were, in the gullies and behind the rocks Drusala's spell had sent them to.

Malus could understand Dolthaic's concern. He thought the asur would escape unless the druchii attacked right away. What the knight failed to appreciate was the bloodthirsty impetuousness of Tullaris Dreadbringer and his Ossian Guard.

As the Phoenix Guard entered Reaver's Mark, the executioners came charging out from the gully they'd been transported into. The heavily armoured druchii shrieked a murderous war cry as they flung themselves at the asur. Black draichs slashed down into shining armour and golden surcoats, rending flesh and bone with each strike. The asur were taken utterly by surprise, their shock doubled by the fact that for once Caradryan's foresight had failed to predict the ambush. Drusala's great conjuration had cheated the divine blessing of Asuryan's anointed.

Lesser warriors would have broken under the ferocity of Tullaris's attack. The Phoenix Guard, however, were the staunchest of Ulthuan's soldiers. Under the ghastly punishment of the Ossian Guard, the warriors reformed their ranks, drawing back in orderly fashion. Golden halberds crunched down into the blackened mail of the executioners. Now it was the druchii who paid a butcher's bill. The spearmen and swordsmen with Caradryan's force entered the fray from the side, assaulting the flank of the Ossian Guard. Caught between the two forces, Tullaris was swiftly outnumbered. Malus had no fear that the Chosen of Khaine would try to escape, however.

The executioners would fight so long as they had the opportunity to take some of their foes with them. Final offerings for the Lord of Murder.

'Tullaris will be overwhelmed,' Dolthaic pointed out.

Malus turned a contemptuous look on the knight. 'The Ossian Guard will keep the asur pinned down while our forces recover from Drusala's spell,' he declared. 'Tullaris will simply have to hold until we are ready to ride to his relief.'

A seething roar from the rocks to his left had Malus spinning around in Spite's saddle. He turned his eyes skywards as three immense creatures took flight. Crimson wings flashed overhead as the Caledorians guided their dragons across the battlefield. Malus slammed his fist against Spite's side in a pique of frustration. Iktheon, for all his distaste for the role, was behaving like a good ally. Despite the change in allegiance, the dragon prince was still thinking like an asur and no asur would sit back and watch comrades in arms being massacred.

As the dragons flew towards the fray, twelve fiery shapes arose from the asur ranks. Phoenix riders, and leading them, mounted upon the back of the ice-winged Ashtari, was Caradryan the Flame. The captain of the Phoenix Guard was himself taking the fight to the dragons. If the sorcerous ambush had taken Caradryan by surprise, it seemed the treachery of Caledor hadn't. Without hesitation, the phoenixes hurtled towards the dragons like arrows loosed from a bow.

'Sound the charge,' Malus growled at Dolthaic. He'd wanted to wait until the problem of Tullaris was settled, but the honour of Iktheon had made that impossible. The druchii had to attack now and in full force. If the dragons were overcome by the phoenixes, the devastating toll on the morale of Malus's troops would render them almost useless. If the wyrms made short work of the phoenixes, then the asur would break and any chance of striking Avelorn with any element of surprise would be lost.

As the cold ones charged out from the gully, hundreds of darkshards and dreadspears marched out from their own positions. The Iceblades, the grisly swordsmen from Ghrond, filed out from behind an outcropping of black volcanic rock. The Har Ganeth warriors came rushing out from one of the gullies, eager to aid their embattled Chosen of Khaine. Stealing along the periphery of the battle, the autarii, Merikaar and his shades worked their way towards the rear of the Phoenix Guard.

Cries of alarm rose from the soldiers supporting the Phoenix Guard. But for the stolid presence of the warriors of Asuryan, the rest of the asur would have broken and fled. The size of Malus's army was incomparably vast compared to their own. It was the presence of the Phoenix Guard that made them stand their ground, the reminder that they fought beside elves whose devotion to their god was stronger than fear. Unlike the Voiceless Ones from Ghrond, the Phoenix Guard held their silence not from physical mutilation but from their own oaths and determination. When one of them was cut down by an executioner, even at the moment of death he refused to let a sound pass his lips. No screams, no cries, only the silent acceptance of his doom. As the vast druchii horde came thundering down upon them, the Phoenix Guard displayed the same iron resolve, prepared to meet the foe with the same fatalism that guided all their deeds.

Malus spurred Spite onwards, reaching the asur battle line at the forefront of his knights. The warpsword flashed down, splitting the helm of a warrior of the Phoenix Guard while the flashing fangs of his horned one ripped open a second elf's pelvis. A twist of Spite's head and the asur was dragged from his regiment and tossed under the driving claws of the cold ones charging into the fight.

'Send them to sleep with their king!' Dolthaic roared, laughing as he skewered the throat of an asur spearman.

The laugh ended in a wet gurgle as the warpsword raked across Dolthaic's neck. The knight slumped in his saddle, his sword falling to the ground as he clapped his hands to his mangled throat. His eyes stared in horrified confusion at his murderous lord.

'Poor choice of words, old comrade,' Darkblade snarled as the last flicker of life left Dolthaic. The knight really had brought his execution upon himself. He should have remembered the details of his lord's parentage.

Spite shifted beneath Malus, the reptile's jaws snapping off the arm of an asur spearman as the warrior tried to attack the drachau. Malus turned away from the murdered Dolthaic and brought the warpsword shearing through the spearman's shoulder, leaving the elf's other arm lying in the dirt. The mangled body staggered back, collapsing against the warriors in the rear ranks. Spite lunged into the gap, shaking its horned head and snapping its fangs at the enemies around it. Malus played his blade about him, shattering shields and breaking spears at every turn.

Cries of dismay rose from the embattled asur. Malus saw several of the warriors in the rear ranks pointing up at the sky. Overhead, he could hear the shrieks of the phoenixes and the roars of the dragons. A hasty glance showed him Caradryan attacking Iktheon. A pivotal duel, one that might shatter the enemy's resistance if it favoured the Caledorians.

Careful to keep the asur at bay with his sword, Malus watched as Ashtari dived down upon the red-scaled dragon. Iktheon's sword crashed against Caradryan's halberd as the two elves struck at one another. Then the claws of the icy phoenix were ripping at the dragon's hide, clumps of frost forming with each buffet of the great bird's wings. The dragon gnashed its jaws, trying to snatch Ashtari from the air. The reptile's reward was the bite of Caradryan's halberd, the Phoenix Blade. Wreathed in flame, the enchanted weapon shattered several of the wyrm's fangs and drove a shard of tooth up through the top of its mouth.

Snarling in pain, the dragon started to roll in mid-air, trying to knock Ashtari loose. The roll, however, brought unintended disaster. While the wyrm seemed largely impervious to the cold generated by the phoenix, the chains holding Iktheon's saddle were far less robust. As the dragon rolled, chains already turned brittle by Ashtari's frost snapped. Iktheon managed a single wail of terror as the saddle tore loose and he plummeted to the ground far below.

Even as the dragon prince died, his monstrous steed sought to avenge him. Flipping back, turning its roll into a climb, the dragon soared upwards. Craning its head around, the brute breathed a gout of flame full into Ashtari. The cold phoenix shrieked, some of its icy feathers melting in the dragon's malignance. The pain was enough that the bird pulled its talons from the scaly hide. As it tried to glide away, the wyrm's jaws snapped at Ashtari, tearing into its left wing.

Before the dragon could work further havoc, Caradryan struck at it. Forged in the almost legendary time of Kor-Baelon, the first captain of the Phoenix Guard, the Phoenix Blade pierced the dragon's eye. Fiery ichor and molten jelly spurted from the wound, bathing Caradryan in burning slime. The stricken dragon released Ashtari, vengeance and the fallen Iktheon forgotten as it bellowed in anguish. Beating its mighty wings, the reptile soared away, driving back towards the south and the volcanic mountains of Caledor.

The asur warriors began to cheer the destruction of Iktheon and the routing of his dragon, but the celebration quickly fell silent. Ashtari, its wing maimed by the dragon's bite, came hurtling down from the sky. The bird crashed to the earth with the ferocity of a comet, scattering druchii and asur alike. Slivers of ice slashed at the elves while those closest to the impact were crushed by the phoenix.

A ragged shout did sound from the asur as the wounded phoenix stirred. Even in its fall, Ashtari had tried to protect its elven friend. Loyal to the end, the bird had shielded Caradryan from much of the impact. Now the hero emerged from the devastation, the dragon slime still steaming on his golden armour. Caradryan the Flame, bathed in smoke and wielding the fiery Phoenix Blade, stood beside the crippled Ashtari and prepared to receive his foes.

Malus sneered. It was a futile act of defiance. The asur were still vastly outnumbered. All Caradryan could do was try to sell his life as dearly as he could. The drachau was determined the elf would find no heroic end. Urging Spite away from the melee, he drove the horned one towards the regiments under Silar's command. He'd have the darkshards deploy against the arrogant lordling. There wasn't too much honour in being pierced by a hundred bolts and dying like a sick dog in the dirt.

Riding towards Silar, Malus heard a disconcerting sound ring out across the battlefield. Turning about in his saddle, he felt ice crawl down his spine. The sound was that of horns, the sharp keening blasts of war and the promise of combat. He could hear the thundering hooves of hundreds of horses, see the bright gleam of armour in the sunlight. Then Malus saw the standard of the Phoenix King, rising above a vast company of asur knights. Finubar was dead, that much Malus knew for certain. He also knew who it was who had been appointed Regent of Ulthuan.

An army was riding to rescue Caradryan and the Phoenix Guard, an army commanded by the most famed of all Ulthuan's heroes.

Prince Tyrion, the Dragon of Cothique!

CHAPTER NINETEEN

Malus could see the magic burn of Tyrion's sword, Sunfang, as the hero led his knights across the plain. Malus had imagined the Regent of Ulthuan would be far from the battlefields of Ellyrion, that he would be ensconced in some stronghold somewhere orchestrating the defence of the ten kingdoms against the elven and daemon enemies who threatened the realm. He hadn't considered that the blood of Aenarion truly coursed through Tyrion's veins, or that the regent would be as loathe to keep himself from combat as his famed ancestor.

The first victims of the asur knights were a group of Ghrondian spearmen acting as bodyguard for one of the *Eternal Malediction*'s sorceresses. As the knights thundered towards them, the dreadspears tried to brace for the assault. The sorceress drew upon her magic, hurling arcane fire into the charging Ellyrians. A clutch of knights were blasted into oblivion, their flesh melting into the backs of their panicked steeds. The malefic spell wasn't enough to break the attack. Voices raised in a cry of vengeance, demanding justice for the slaughtered elves of Tor Emyrath, the cavalry slammed into the dreadspears. The force of their impact buckled the formation, spilling druchii warriors in every direction. Tyrion himself, upon his noble stallion, Malhandhir, charged towards the sorceress.

The druchii witch hurled a blast of black lightning full into the elven prince's face. The great blood-red ruby Tyrion wore upon the brow of his winged helm pulsed and flashed with a crimson glow. The black lightning parted before him as though swept away by a spectral wind. Before the stunned sorceress could unleash another spell, Sunfang came slashing down and sent her head tumbling from her shoulders.

A flash of ghostly light, and suddenly the charge of the Ellyrian knights was blocked by a regiment of warriors from Clar Karond. The druchii soldiers locked their shields and received the brunt of the assault, resisting the driving hooves and stabbing lances of the asur.

More of the weird luminance played about the battlefield now. A company of darkshards were transplanted from where they had been menacing

Caradryan and moved to the flank of the elven knights instead. Drusala and the Blood Coven, working once again their uncanny violation of space and time. Now it was only their place in the material plane that the sorceresses adjusted, allowing the temporal positioning to remain unaffected. They didn't confine their effort to the druchii, however, and soon the spiralling rings of arcane energy were swirling about the blocks of advancing infantry moving to support Tyrion's knights. A company of Lothern archers found themselves flung to the far side of Reaver's Mark, spun around so that the arrows they loosed fell upon a cove of sun-bleached trees instead of druchii flesh. A complement of sea guard was cast full into the blades of Malus's soul-bonded dreadspears. The careful formations of the asur general were thrown into utter disarray as Drusala's sorcery scattered them about the plain.

Malus laughed. He'd thought to end Caradryan quickly, to content himself with sacrificing Tullaris and the Ossian Guard in exchange for a speedy victory. Now he found himself with a prize even greater than anything he had imagined. The Regent of Ulthuan, the mighty hero the asur had rallied to in their moment of crisis and calamity. If he could take Tyrion's head he wouldn't need to lay waste to Avelorn and capture the Everqueen. He could break the asur here and now. He could claim a victory that Malekith wouldn't be able to take from him. With the head of Tyrion hanging from his belt, the Witch King would have no choice but to make Malus his seneschal, to elevate him to a rank second only to the king himself.

Roaring commands at Silar to bring his troops, shouting threats at the Knights of the Burning Dark to follow him, Malus whipped Spite away from the Phoenix Guard and towards the new prey he had chosen for himself. The warpsword would hew the head from Tyrion's shoulders. It had been a long time since he'd faced the hero, but Malus was confident that this time their meeting would be different. He could feel the strength of Tz'arkan within him, filling his veins and muscles with power. The daemon had retreated into the hinterlands of his soul after Drusala had pacified it, but Malus found he could still call upon the fiend's strength. Even better, since the daemon wasn't trying to exert its control over him at the same time. Perhaps it understood the danger of confronting Tyrion – the Sunfang was a weapon forged to slay its kind after all. Perhaps Tz'arkan understood that if it were to endure it had to invest Malus with its strength without the usual distraction of its plots and schemes.

For Malus to endure, he had to be the one to strike down the elven prince. Yet even as he spurred Spite away from the Phoenix Guard, he could see that he wasn't alone in his ambition. Tullaris Dreadbringer had seen the Dragon of Cothique as well. A blood-curdling howl rose from the Chosen of Khaine. Driving the First Draich clean through the body of the asur he was fighting, ripping the dying elf from his blade as though he were nothing more substantial than a leaf, Tullaris turned and forced his way back through the ranks of the Ossian Guard. Those executioners too slow to part ranks for their maddened master were cut down with the same ruthlessness he had shown the asur.

There was a bitter hatred between Tullaris and Tyrion, but Malus knew on the part of Tullaris that hate was wrapped up within the divine visions and whispers the executioner believed himself to receive from Khaine. The fire that burned in Tullaris was more than simple madness: it was a religious mania that could sate itself only with the blood of the asur hero. Malus wanted the prince's head to secure his power; Tullaris wanted it merely as an offering to the Lord of Murder.

The Scion of Hag Graef was certain his claim was better, and he would make sure it was the warpsword that ended the legend of Tyrion this day. Leaning from his saddle, Malus glared back at Silar. He gestured at Tullaris and crooked two of his fingers against one another. It was an old signal between them, one that had been developed when Malus still dwelled in his father's tower and Silar was but a simple retainer. It was a sign that had brought death to a great many Malus had found inconvenient over the years. Now it would initiate still another murder.

Leaving Silar to attend the details, Malus spurred Spite onwards. Around him, the Knights of the Burning Dark urged their blood-maddened cold ones onwards, the reptiles' roars thundering across the battlefield.

The asur infantry, seeing the threat posed by the cold one knights, moved to intercept the charge, to thwart the druchii rush towards Tyrion and his cavalry. A phalanx of Sapherian spears interposed themselves in Malus's path. The spearmen were too few to overcome the knights, but they were enough to act as an obstacle to their advance. A sickening groan rattled across the field as the ponderous cold ones slammed into the hastily assembled fence of asur spears and shields. Druchii lances pierced the silverwood shields, gouging hideous wounds in the warriors behind them. A few of the cold ones were brought down, impaling themselves upon the waiting spears in their savage rush. Most of the knights on their backs were able to kick themselves free of the dying reptiles, but a couple of the elves weren't so fortunate, crushed beneath the bulk of their beasts as the brutes writhed in their death throes.

Malus brought the warpsword slashing out. Powered by the infernal strength of Tz'arkan, he sent a spearman hurtling overhead, flung like a bullet from a sling by the impact of the drachau's blade. The mangled asur crashed violently among the ranks of her comrades, breaking arms and backs as her armoured weight slammed into them. Malus urged Spite forwards, lunging into the gap he'd created; then he began to slash his enchanted blade to right and left, reaping a ghastly toll from the Sapherian soldiers. A silver-helmed champion chopped at him with a gem-encrusted axe but the elf's first blow merely glanced from the drachau's spiny sabaton. Malus answered the assault with a cleaving strike of his blade that sliced the face from the champion's head and left a screaming skull behind.

The slaughter among the Sapherians was woefully one-sided. Scores of the spearmen were cut down by the Knights of the Burning Dark or mangled by the fangs and claws of their cold ones. The stubborn defence the asur offered soon crumbled as the determination of the survivors faltered. The spearmen broke and fled, ironically causing Malus more problems in retreat than they had in battle. Bellowing threats and curses, he commanded his knights to restrain their reptilian steeds and keep them from pursuing the fleeing asur. Subduing the bestial instincts of the cold ones was a task easier said than achieved. Several of the knights broke ranks as the hungry reptiles defied their riders and loped after the Sapherians. One of the cold ones was so opposed to the idea of lingering behind that it flung its head back and caught its rider's arm, pulling the limb from its socket before any of the other druchii could come to the knight's aid.

In the confusion of restoring order among the knights, Malus looked away to the south. He could see that Tullaris had taken control of another contingent from Har Ganeth, the Bloodseekers, executioners who had once served Sarkol Narza. The Chosen of Khaine led his warriors at a loping trot across the plain, still intent on reaching Tyrion and his knights. Like Malus, however, the executioners found their path blocked, this time by a regiment of Chracian warriors. Draped in the pelts of white lions, the spearmen of Chrace met the glaives of the Bloodseekers in a display of primitive savagery that recalled to Malus the feuds of skin-clad barbarians in the Wastes. It was a forbidding reminder to him of the brute hiding beneath the veneer of civilisation, that thousands of years of culture and refinement were but a mask the elves wore to restrain the savage underneath. For the Fangs of Chrace and the Bloodseekers, such restraint had been cast into the winds.

Malus smiled when he saw Silar leading his darkshards towards the rear of the Bloodseekers. The crossbows would quickly turn the tide and settle the problem of Tullaris Dreadbringer.

Standing in his stirrups, Malus cried out to his knights. 'I want the regent's head,' he shouted. 'The knight who kills Tyrion will be given the weight of his cold one in gold! The knight who lets the regent escape will be fed to his cold one!' He brought his sword swinging down, thrusting its point to where Tyrion battled the warriors of Clar Karond. The asur were winning, but if the druchii fighters could hold out just a few minutes more, Malus could bring his cavalry smashing into the Ellyrian flank. They'd have half the asur knights lying in the dirt before the Regent could react.

Then it would just be a small matter of killing the greatest asur hero of the age. Malus was going to enjoy that. Despite his promise of reward, he would kill any druchii who tried to steal that glory from him.

* * *

Tullaris Dreadbringer hurled himself into the fray with the wanton abandon of a blood daemon. The First Draich slashed and gouged, hacked and stabbed its way through the Chracian warriors. The executioners around him gave a wide berth to the Chosen of Khaine, all too aware how easily it could be them rather than the asur who were claimed by their lord's murderous fury. Their hesitancy caused more of the asur spearmen to rush Tullaris, thinking to bring down the infamous villain before meeting the glaives of the Bloodseekers.

The song of Khaine thundered through Tullaris's veins as he met the Fangs of Chrace. Ten, then twenty of the elves lay butchered at his feet. The gore of his victims dripped from his armour and plastered his face, lending him a fiendish aspect. The slaughter thrilled Tullaris, made his heart swell inside his breast. Death! Blood! Skulls for Khaine! He would glut the Lord of Murder with the souls of his victims this day. The First Draich would reap a harvest of carnage undreamed of.

Through the blood frenzy, Tullaris could yet hear the voice of his god. Khaine's words pulsed through his very soul. The executioner snarled in rage, his entire being revelling in the havoc around him. Yet the commandments of a god couldn't be ignored.

While Tullaris wrestled to pull himself free from his own frenzy of slaughter, the commander of the Chracians fell upon him. The elf's gleaming axe came chopping down, striking for the villain's head. In a blur of motion, Tullaris spun his draich around, the ancient blade cleaving through the haft of the Chracian captain's axe. As the ancestral axe was cut in half, the draich continued its vicious sweep, slicing through the heavy lion pelt the asur wore, crumpling the steel helmet beneath and crunching through the skull inside. Before the horrified spearmen knew what was happening, their captain fell at the feet of Tullaris.

The killer's face split in an ophidian smile of diabolic satisfaction. Tullaris would heed the words of Khaine, he would march to the destiny that awaited him. But there would be blood every step of the way. Tullaris would find Tyrion even if he had to turn the whole of Reaver's Mark into a charnel house to do it.

Away from the roar of battle, Drusala watched as the asur poured more forces into the fight. With the arrival of the Ellyrian host, Caradryan had been saved. She had detected the presence of Korhil among the relieving force, Charandis-bane as the elves of Chrace had named him. An almost legendary warrior, renowned as the captain of the fearsome White Lions, Korhil would prove a formidable adversary for Malus. Perhaps too much for Darkblade to overcome.

From atop one of the volcanic spurs that rose above the field, Drusala observed the well-ordered ranks of infantry being brought into the battle. Already engaged with the Phoenix Guard and their supporting troops, the army of Hag Graef was too dispersed to react quickly enough to Korhil's advance. She could see the tall, powerful elf lord, his body draped in the hide of Charandis as he led his White Lions towards the fray. Regiments from Ellyrion and Lothern and Avelorn followed, their banners snapping in the fading light. The druchii had lost the advantage of numbers, and likewise the advantage of cohesion. There was little Drusala could do about the former, but she had tried to influence the latter, shifting regiments around the battlefield with her dark magic.

The violation of time and space had sapped her powers, however. To work the feat she now had in mind, she would need to draw upon the powers of the Blood Coven.

'Sisters, I must call upon your strength,' Drusala called to the three witches. It was a formality, really. When she'd defeated them before, she placed upon each of them a binding that laid their souls bare to her. They were as much her slaves as Absaloth and the Voiceless Ones, even if they weren't aware of it.

The Blood Coven clawed handfuls of gore from their cauldron, bathing themselves in the lifeblood of murdered druchii, drawing into themselves the terrible potentialities of the aethyr. To Drusala's attuned eyes, the three witches began to blaze with flames of dark power, each becoming a crackling pillar of arcane energy. Stretching forth her hand, she began to draw that energy into herself, to use it to shift and manipulate the fabric of reality. She ignored the cries of pain her leeching drew from the Blood Coven. It was their honour to be used by the sorceress, to fuel such a vast magical working. What matter if it would shred their souls and shatter their minds? They should be thankful for the opportunity to serve Queen Morathi.

Scattering the strands of reality, Drusala wove them into new patterns and shapes on a far greater scale that she had before. The last of the Clar Karond beastmasters in the host of Hag Graef found themselves transplanted from the flank of Caradryan's encircled forces to the fore of Korhil's White Lions. The remaining hydras in the druchii force snapped and tore at the stunned asur, decimating their front ranks as they suddenly appeared right in the path of their march.

All about the battlefield, the theme was repeated. Dreadspears manifested upon the rear of Avelorn archers, bleakswords were transferred into the path of marching Ellyrian warriors. Malignantly, Drusala stretched her will to seize the well-ordered asur regiments. One by one she scattered them about Reaver's Mark in chaotic disarray. Warriors who thought themselves protected on either side by friends now found themselves surrounded by foes. Archers ready to loose their arrows reappeared far across the field with no enemy within range. The Lothern Sea Guard were dropped in the midst of the Iceblades and the corsairs, the bewildered asur hurriedly locking their shields together in a circle of protective steel.

Drusala laughed in vicious triumph, channelling more and more power through herself. She could feel the Blood Coven being sucked dry by her magic, but it was of no concern to her. To feel this kind of power, to exert this kind of force, she would drain the lives of a dozen sorceresses! A hundred!

Lost in her hubris, Drusala failed to notice the tiny strands of magical energy that were being diverted away from her. The Blood Coven were bound to her now, and compelled to obey her, but still they had found a way to defy the sorceress. Each little coil of power that they diverted away from Drusala they sent pouring into Malus Darkblade. The process had started with the first great ritual that had sprung the drachau's ambush against Caradryan. Now, as Drusala drew more heavily upon her living fuel, so did the witches send more aethyric power into the drachau himself.

Through their arcane connection to Drusala, the Blood Coven had learned of Tz'arkan. Now they were feeding the daemon, using it to empower Malus. With enough power, the drachau would be free of Drusala's control. When he was, he would come seeking his revenge.

It was only when one of the witches was finally drained dry and her withered body wilted to the ground that Drusala noticed the energies that were being redirected. With a shriek of fury, she cut off the flow of power, leaving the two surviving witches collapsed upon the ground.

Drusala didn't spare the prostrate witches another thought, but immediately focused on what they had done. She could see the dark energies blazing within Malus. The witches had stirred up Tz'arkan's power while leaving the daemon's consciousness in retreat. Malus Darkblade with the full might of a daemon king flowing through his flesh! The prospect was one that made even her shudder.

To stop Malus now would mean horrendous risk, risk that Drusala didn't dare. Casting her awareness about the battlefield, she hesitated, wondering if there weren't perhaps another way. She saw Tullaris and the Bloodseekers cutting their way through the Fangs of Chrace. Just as they had their foe on the run, a company of darkshards under the command of Silar began to shoot down the executioners. More deceit and treachery from Malus. First the drachau had connived to have Drusala transplant Tullaris and the Ossian Guard nearest the enemy, now the drachau set his soldiers the task of outright assassination.

The Chosen of Khaine harboured a long grudge against the Scion of Hag Graef. This treachery on the battlefield would only enflame that hate. Tullaris would be her weapon against Malus.

Unable to tap into the Blood Coven's magic, Drusala exerted her own energies to once again pervert the rules of time and space. A ring of coruscating light formed around the Bloodseekers, whirring about them in a blinding spiral. When it seemed the light could spin no faster, both it and the Bloodseekers vanished. Right from under the bolts of Silar's troops, Tullaris was snatched to another part of the field, dropped down some little distance from Malus and his Knights of the Burning Dark.

Exhausted by her exertion, Drusala sank against the side of the volcanic spur. She had seen the executioners safely across the field, placed Tullaris where he could exact revenge upon Malus. What she didn't see as she tried to regain her strength was Tullaris order his troops away from the Knights of the Burning Dark. She didn't see him lead his elves towards the Ellyrian knights.

Revenge was a powerful force in the heart of Tullaris Dreadbringer, but the voice of Khaine was more powerful still.

Malus felt as though the strength of a god were in his limbs. The asur he struck down were cut asunder as if their armoured bodies were no more than pieces of bread. By his strength alone, the knights ruptured the asur regiment, decimating the warriors in an orgy of bloodshed. Cold ones ripped gory giblets from the slaughtered foe while knights stabbed their lances into the wounded elves writhing on the ground. Malus held the banner of the vanquished regiment overhead. He waved it back and forth, mocking the rest of the enemy army. Then, with no more than a snap of his fingers, he broke the stout silverwood pole and tossed the broken banner into the bloody morass of shattered warriors and feeding reptiles.

The whole of Ulthuan would tremble at his name. The asur would cower in their palaces and temples, praying to Asuryan and all the indifferent Cadai for deliverance from Malus Darkblade. He would raise a mountain of skulls such that even Malekith would beg him for mercy!

A low hiss from Spite drew Malus's attention. He followed the horned one's gaze. Red fury boiled up inside him. He'd been aware that Drusala and the Blood Coven were continuing to bend space and time to shift forces about the battlefield so that the fighting would favour the druchii. What he hadn't been aware of was the translocation of Tullaris and the Bloodseekers. The executioners had appeared a few hundred yards from the Knights of the Burning Dark. Malus could see Hag Graef crossbow bolts sticking in the armour of the Har Ganeth killers, some of them dropping to the ground from their wounds even as he watched. The sorceress had used her magic to save Tullaris just as Silar was about to destroy the Chosen of Khaine.

Drawing back on Spite's reins, Malus expected the executioners to come rushing at his knights. Instead, Tullaris goaded them forwards. It took only a second for Malus to understand his rival's intentions. Tullaris was still focused on his original purpose – determined to strike down Tyrion. Even balanced against the recent treachery of the drachau, Tullaris was intent on the asur prince. Malus felt a cold chill rush through him, wondering if the fanatic thought the voice of Khaine were guiding him to such an encounter. More disturbingly, he wondered if that voice might in fact be real.

Real or not, he was determined to reap the glory from this battle. 'The Regent!' Malus shouted at his knights, jabbing the warpsword in the direction of the Ellyrian reavers. The cavalry had won their battle, scattering the Clar Karond contingent, but it had been a costly fight. They started to turn back towards the asur positions, but thanks to the shifting magic of Drusala, there was no battle line to return to, only a hundred small skirmishes unfolding all around Reaver's Mark.

Malus saw Tyrion raise Sunfang over his head, a gesture of challenge as ancient as Aenarion. The drachau hefted the warpsword in reply, accepting the call to battle. But when the Ellyrians came galloping across the field, they wheeled to the right, away from the cold ones and their lord! Malus roared in outrage when he saw that they were charging the Bloodseekers. Tullaris, too, had raised his weapon in challenge and it was to Tullaris that the asur now drove their frothing steeds.

'I want the Regent,' Malus snarled at his knights. 'I want his blood. I want his flesh. I want his soul!' Spite growled hungrily as the drachau urged the reptile to greater effort. 'The Regent,' Malus snapped at the knights riding around him. 'Kill anyone who stands between us and the Regent!'

He knew his Knights of the Burning Dark. They wouldn't hesitate to obey his command, however murderous. The execution of Dolthaic would be a reminder to them of what it meant to offend their master.

Panic gripped Silar Thornblood when he saw the Bloodseekers vanish right from under the assault of his darkshards. From his vantage, he could see the executioners reappear across Reaver's Mark. They had rematerialised only a small distance from Malus and the Knights of the Burning Dark. At once he recognised the treachery at work here. Drusala had employed her sorcery to bring Tullaris against Malus. After the murderous fire from Silar's troops, the Chosen of Khaine would be even more enraged and maniacal than usual. He'd avenge himself on Malus, given the opportunity.

The drachau was the only one who could hold together the dwindling might of Hag Graef. Malus was the only lord with the strength and determination to rekindle the blood of the Dark Crag. Silar felt this in his heart. If his people were to have any legacy at all, Darkblade must live!

Spotting one of the mounted messengers who relayed commands between the drachau's generals, Silar broke away from the darkshards and waved the horseman towards him. As soon as the messenger was near, the noble seized him and dragged the elf from the saddle. A slash from his sword ended the messenger's protest at Silar's thievery. The smell of its former master's blood excited the black charger, the horse rearing and snorting as it tried to throw Silar from its back.

The noble jerked the reins savagely, forcing his new mount to turn. Once he had the horse pointed towards the Bloodseekers, Silar swatted its flank with the flat of his sword. The steed galloped off, its hooves pounding across the corpse-littered terrain. Dead and dying elves were smashed by the racing animal. Asur stragglers stabbed at Silar with spears and swords, druchii survivors cried to him for aid. Silar ignored them all, intent upon the desperate purpose that now ruled him. He had to save Malus. He had to honour his old oaths. The future of the Hag depended upon it.

Ahead, Silar could see the Ellyrians rushing to engage the Bloodseekers. For a moment, he debated drawing back, leaving the asur to settle with Tullaris. With Tyrion commanding them, there was every chance the Chosen of Khaine would meet his end.

Silar shook his head and urged his horse onwards. He couldn't take the chance. If Tullaris survived, it was certain that he would prosecute his vengeance against Malus. Silar was realistic about his chances against the executioner – at least in a fair fight. But he didn't intend to fight Tullaris at all. He intended to ride him down while the killer was focused on the Ellyrians.

Away to his flank, Silar could see Malus and his knights charging towards the melee. The proximity of his lord made him hurry his mount to still greater effort, lashing its flank until blood streamed down its legs. He couldn't let Darkblade fall! Not when it had been his duty to kill Tullaris in the first place. Not when so much depended on the drachau's survival.

Murderous and vicious as they were, the Bloodseekers still had a certain degree of discipline. Those at the rear of their formation parted ranks to allow Silar to pass through them, mistaking him for a mounted messenger. The noble drove his horse between the executioners. From his vantage, he soon spotted Tullaris.

Lashing the horse once more, Silar drove for the infamous fanatic. This time he didn't wait for the Bloodseekers to step aside, but used the mass of his horse to batter them aside. He saw the Ellyrians being cut down by the vicious Tullaris. He could hear the grisly Khainite chant that rose from the executioner's lips.

Raising his sword high, Silar charged his horse straight for the embattled Tullaris. Something, some uncanny sense, warned the executioner at the last instant. In a blindingly fast motion, Tullaris shifted away and brought the First Draich sweeping upwards. The murderous blade struck the horse in the neck, shearing through muscle and bone to send the animal's head flying away. The decapitated brute ploughed onwards for several yards, crashing into the Ellyrians.

Silar tried to leap clear of the saddle, but his boot caught in the stirrup. When the momentum of the beast was spent and its carcass crashed to the earth, he was pinned beneath its weight. Desperately, he tried to free himself, tried to drag his now broken leg clear of the dead animal.

A dark shadow suddenly fell across the trapped Silar. He grabbed for his sword, but even as he did, the gory blade of the First Draich came scything down, shearing through his shoulder and leaving his arm lying in the dirt.

'Loyalty to that cretin was ever your weakness, Silar,' Tullaris snarled at the maimed noble. A cruel smile twisted the executioner's face. 'Khaine warned me you would try to save your master. Fear not, he will be joining you soon enough.'

Tullaris hefted the First Draich, swinging it high above his head and bringing the murderous blade crunching into the trapped Silar's skull.

The Ellyrians crashed into the ranks of the Bloodseekers, lances piercing mail and stabbing flesh, bones crushed beneath the pounding hooves of elven steeds. Tyrion was there at the centre of the fight, his burning sword strewing the corpses of executioners all around him, his great stallion, Malhandhir, cracking skulls and shattering ribs with every kick of its powerful hooves.

Amidst the carnage, Tullaris butchered his way towards the Regent, his draich impaling foes on its blade with every thrust. Elves and horses died wherever the Chosen of Khaine stepped, their blood added to the gore already coating the butcher's armour. A low, sadistic chant rasped across Tullaris's lips as he stalked through the melee, an appeal to the Lord of Murder that the massacre should never end. A world of endless blood and slaughter, such was the only prayer Tullaris thought fit to offer up to Khaine.

When the Knights of the Burning Dark crashed into the fray they attacked with wanton abandon. Executioners were crushed beneath the claws of cold ones even as Ellyrian cavalry were lifted from their saddles by druchii lances. The warpsword sang its deathly song as Malus carved a path through enemy and ally alike. The strength of the daemon made his muscles feel as though they were corded iron; every slash reduced his victim to a mangled heap, every cut ripped through armour and pulverised bone. The drachau shouted at the magnitude of his havoc, exuberant in the glory of his might.

Ahead of him, Malus could see the banner of the Phoenix King, the standard that had been entrusted to Tyrion as Regent of Ulthuan. Redoubling his assault, the drachau cleared a way ahead. As the last Ellyrians were hacked to pieces by the warpsword, Malus drove Spite forwards in a ferocious charge that demanded every last mote of the reptile's strength.

Malhandhir smelt the horned one before it charged. Whinnying in warning, the elven steed turned towards Malus as the drachau came rushing at Tyrion. By the narrowest margin, the Regent raised Sunfang and blocked the descending strike of the warpsword. Sparks of antithetical magic flew from the crashing blades. Despite the daemonic strength flowing through the drachau's arms, Malus was unable to shatter the enchanted sword as he had the lesser blades of lesser foes. But he could see that Tyrion trembled from the strain of trying to drive back Malus's strike.

Malus reared back in his saddle, driving the warpsword again and again at Tyrion. Sunfang parried each blow, the two swords shrieking as they scraped against one another. With each strike, Malus could see Tyrion's endurance put to the test. Each assault made him drop a little lower in the saddle, each parry was just that little bit slower than the last to intercept his blade. The Regent was weakening while with every breath Malus felt his own strength growing.

Spite snapped at Malhandhir with its fangs, forcing the horse to shift and dodge the flashing jaws, further taxing the skill of its master to block Malus's attacks. Breath by breath, heartbeat by heartbeat, the drachau was winning.

Emboldened by the weakening of his foe and the daemonic might burning within his own body, Malus wasn't prepared when Tyrion changed his tactics. When the warpsword came flashing down at the Regent's head, instead of blocking the blow as he had before, Tyrion urged Malhandhir into a sidewise twist. Malus's sword cleft nothing but empty air. Without the expected impact of blade against blade, the drachau was overbalanced, falling forwards across his saddle.

Instantly, Tyrion slashed at Malus with Sunfang, but he didn't reckon upon the speed and agility of the drachau. Malus's reflexes and instincts had been honed in the horrors of Naggaroth and the perils of the Wastes. As Tyrion's blade came for him, he threw himself backwards, lying flat across Spite's back. Instead of skewering him, Sunfang merely slashed his cheek. Even so, the glancing wound brought a cry of sheer agony from Malus. The filth that bubbled up from his wound wasn't blood alone, but had within it dark purple strands of obscene ichor.

Infused with the might of a daemon, Malus's flesh had taken on some of the properties of the daemonic. Sunfang had been forged to destroy such entities in the days of Aenarion, the first Phoenix King. The agony that wracked Malus's body from even so slight a scratch was crippling. He sagged weakly against Spite's side, the warpsword dangling from his hand. His other hand clawed desperately at his scarred cheek, as though he could rip out the pain.

'Now you answer for your outrages, Tyrant of Hag Graef,' Tyrion snarled. He raised Sunfang for the killing blow. Malus saw death in the Regent's eyes.

Before the blow could land, however, Tyrion cried out in shock. Blood erupted from the hero's side, spilling across the ancient dragon armour he wore. It took Malus a few breaths to understand what had happened. When he did, a bitter laugh fell from his lips.

While drachau and Regent duelled, another foe had intruded into the fight. Tullaris drove the First Draich into Tyrion's back, the ensorcelled weapon tearing through the hero's enchanted mail, its murderous energies too great even for the armour of Aenarion to defy. Tyrion writhed in agony, his body spitted upon the unholy glaive. The executioner howled the name of Khaine as he lifted Tyrion from Malhandhir's saddle and threw the Regent to the ground.

Malus clenched his teeth as he watched Tullaris stalk towards his fallen enemy. It seemed the glory of killing the Regent would belong to Tullaris.

The satisfaction of killing Tullaris once the deed was done, however, would belong to Malus Darkblade.

CHAPTER TWENTY

Tyrion's cry echoed across Reaver's Mark as Tullaris drove his blade into the hero's back. Up on the volcanic spur, the scream stabbed into Drusala's mind, rousing her from her stupor. The sorceress turned her witchsight across the field and cursed herself for the mistake she had made.

Until that moment, she had believed Korhil was leading the asur reinforcements. She had been unaware of Tyrion's presence. The jewel the Regent wore, the Heart of Avelorn, rendered him resistant to magic. It would have taken a more direct focus for her sorcery to detect him upon the field. Even so, Drusala berated herself for allowing such an oversight. She should have considered the possibility the moment the reinforcements had arrived.

She had hoped to employ Malus Darkblade as a counter against Malekith, a pawn to send against the Witch King. Far more vital to Morathi's plans, however, was Tyrion. If the Dragon of Cothique fell, the consequences would be dire. Because of her mistake, her complacency, Drusala knew there was now a very real chance that the Regent would be killed. Alone, either Malus or Tullaris was enemy enough to test Tyrion's mettle. Against both of them, the sorceress feared Tyrion would fall. He might slay one, but then the other would pounce on the weakened hero and cut him down.

Drusala had no choice. She had to cast aside her pawn to save Tyrion. She couldn't act directly against either of the druchii warlords. The risk of her actions being made known to Malekith, the chance that the Witch King would discover her treachery, was too great. She had to act more subtly. She had to take a terrible risk, one that would allow the Regent a better chance than the odds he faced now.

Weakened by her onerous castings, Drusala turned back towards the Blood Coven. The surviving witches were only now beginning to stir. It was partly their duplicity that had brought things to such an impasse. It was only fitting that they should help set things right. Boldly, Drusala walked over to the witches. Before they could react, she clapped one of her hands against each of their foreheads.

'Your queen needs your power,' she said, a malignant glaze falling across her eyes. A sinister scarlet glow spread from Drusala's hands, slithering down into the bodies of the Blood Coven, worming through the essence of their souls for every speck of energy that yet lingered within them.

At the Eagle Gate, Drusala had re-caged the daemon Tz'arkan. A link yet existed between them. The peril was enormous and it would take more magic than she could safely harness on her own in her weakened state, but she intended to exploit that connection.

By Hekarti, she only prayed she was able to act before it was too late to salvage her carefully laid plans.

Even as Drusala began her spell, she felt the aethyric vibration sweep through her. Far away some tremendous and profane ritual had been performed, a feat of magic so colossal that its echo was roaring through the winds of magic with the fury of a tempest. The sorceress exerted her will, trying to draw down the energies blown ahead of that storm, trying to harness the magic she needed before the aethyric tidal wave struck.

Tyrion lay in the dirt, blood streaming from the wound in his back. He glared up at Tullaris as the executioner raised his bloodied draich. It was an unsettling thing, to watch as his blood dripped from the ghoulish weapon.

'Khaine told me I should find you here,' Tullaris declared. Slowly, the executioner raised the First Draich.

As Tyrion saw the murderous weapon poised to take his head, a ghastly sensation turned his insides cold. A profound sense of loss, a loneliness that gnawed at his vitals and made his heart feel as cold as iron, a numb misery that washed through him with an agony unspeakable. His daughter, Aliathra, was dead. He didn't know where or how, he only knew that she was. For an instant, he seemed to feel her soul reaching into his own. Then she was gone. Even her spirit was no more – it had been consumed by the same atrocity that had taken her life.

Fury blacker and more terrible than anything he had ever felt before filled Tyrion's mind. Long had he feared the curse of Aenarion, the murderous madness that plagued all those of the first king's bloodline. Now, he didn't care. He didn't care if this was the curse, if this was madness. All he cared about was the pain inside him. All he cared about was making it stop. All he cared about was making something suffer as he suffered.

He no longer felt the wound in his back or the weariness in his limbs. Strength poured through him – the power of rage and unbridled hate. Snarling like a rabid beast, Tyrion lunged at Tullaris as the executioner brought his draich slashing down. The Regent slid beneath the cutting blade and slammed into the druchii killer, bearing him to the ground. Roaring an inarticulate cry of unfettered savagery, Tyrion brought Sunfang stabbing into the executioner's side. Tullaris struggled against the blade as it punched its way deeper into his body, puncturing armour, crushing bone and rupturing organs. Blood gushed over Tyrion's hands as he ripped the sword free, severing the executioner's spine.

Tullaris flailed his arms on the ground for a moment and then fell still. His eyes struggled to focus on the asur prince who stood over him. 'Khaine told me I would find you here,' he repeated. 'I hear His voice even now, thundering through my brain. When this shell of flesh is finished, I will join Him.' The executioner reached his hand out, fumbling blindly at the air. 'Finish me. Set me free. Set yourself free.'

Tyrion glared down at Tullaris Dreadbringer, recounting in his mind the many atrocities, the countless sorrows this villain had inflicted upon Ulthuan. There was no mercy in him for this monster, no pity for this fiend. Let him die like a dog in the dust. It was a kinder doom than he deserved.

'You are weak,' Tullaris spat when Tyrion failed to deliver the killing blow. A cruel smile formed on the druchii's bloodied face. Attuned to the Lord of Murder, long in the service of death and slaughter, Tullaris had felt that fleeting instant when Aliathra's spirit had reached to her father. The executioner forced his paralysed body upright. His blind eyes struggled to find his enemy. A blue and gold blur was all he saw, yet towards this he turned a mocking smile.

'You are weak,' the executioner snarled again. 'That is what killed your daught–'

Tyrion drove Sunfang into the executioner's head before he could finish, cleaving it in half and spilling the fanatic's brains. 'This is what killed you,' he spat. Tyrion pressed his boot against Tullaris's chest and tried to wrench his burning blade free.

It was then that he heard Malhandhir's warning snort and he remembered that his fight wasn't with one infamous fiend but with two.

Like a jackal after the wolf is gone, Malus Darkblade came rushing in to finish the wounded Tyrion.

Tyrion's horse tried to intercept Malus as the drachau charged towards the Regent. Spite barged past Malhandhir, sending the horse stumbling back with its side torn by the reptile's claws.

Malus had eyes only for his intended prey. He had bided his time, waiting to see which of the combatants would prevail. He had to admit he was surprised to see Tyrion triumphant. He was grateful, in his murderous way, that the Regent had eliminated Tullaris for him. Now he wouldn't have to bother about that small detail. He could devote his attention fully to the asur prince. The glory of killing the Dragon of Cothique would be his and his alone.

As Tyrion struggled to free Sunfang from Tullaris's body, Malus charged. Not for an instant did he question the honour of striking his enemy from behind or taking advantage of a wounded foe. Such compunctions were for those too weak to endure, too soft to rule. He had made himself drachau by his own hand only by divesting himself of such foolish ideas as these. There was nothing, absolutely nothing, that he wouldn't do to expand and maintain his power. The head of Tyrion would help him accomplish both, and no druchii would ever question how he had claimed his trophy.

Malus raised the warpsword, ready to cut down the Regent. The strength of iron was in his arm as he hefted the blade high. Then he felt that strength expand still further, felt waves of power rushing through him. His sword fell from his hand, clattering to the ground as a spasm of searing agony coursed through him.

The drachau cried out as the familiar, hideous sensation pulsed through his body. After so long thinking the daemon subdued, he could feel Tz'arkan rising once more. The daemon brushed aside the barriers presented by Malus's mind and soul. Like wine pouring into a glass, the fiend was expanding to fill every corner of the elf's essence.

It was the change, not brought on by any act of will on the part of Malus but by Tz'arkan itself!

Spite hissed in fright and tried to unseat its master as it sensed the change that was consuming Malus. This time the transformation was too swift for the horned one. Howling in pain, the reptile collapsed beneath the expanding mass of Tz'arkan as the daemon distorted flesh and bone, twisting the form of its mortal host into a shape more to its liking. Spite flopped against the earth, its back broken by the daemon's weight. Tz'arkan grinned down at the crippled beast and brought one of its cloven hooves smashing down into Spite's skull.

'Does that make you sad, flesh-worm?' Tz'arkan taunted the retreating soul of Malus. The daemon's face twisted in a grisly leer. More of its essence came boiling up, driving the spirit of its host still further and further back into the darkness.

'The witch, I warned you about her,' Tz'arkan hissed. 'Her magic caged me, now her magic frees me.' Tz'arkan's head rotated back on its neck, staring across Reaver's Mark, glaring at the volcanic spur where Drusala stood. 'Of course, she meant only a half-measure, to leave us a quivering heap of flesh, neither Malus Darkblade or Tz'arkan. We couldn't have that, though. We're much too strong for that now.' The daemon paused, its leer turning into a snarl. 'Still, your soul acted as a bridge, a chain she used to bind me again.'

Inside it, Tz'arkan could hear Malus pleading with it, begging it for mercy.

'Shut up, mortal,' Tz'arkan growled as it sent its essence flooding into that last tiny corner where the soul of Malus Darkblade lingered. The drachau's spirit shrieked as the daemon smothered it into nothingness.

Tz'arkan's eyes glowed with vindictiveness as it stared at the spur and Drusala. 'What will you do, witch? How will you cage me now?' The daemon laughed as it plucked the sorceress's thoughts from the aethyr. 'I think I'll punish you by finishing what Malus started.'

The hulking daemon swung around. Asur and druchii alike had fled from the monster, drawing away and forgetting their own battle in the presence of this monstrous fiend. Only Tyrion remained, his blade finally torn free from the skull of Tullaris.

'An elven princeling as an appetiser and then two armies to devour,' Tz'arkan hissed at Tyrion. 'Or should I save you as a dessert and let you watch all the others die before you? Would that...' The daemon hesitated, its burning eyes shifting colours as it became aware that something wasn't right with the elf who stood before it. There was a shadow, an aura hanging over the Regent of Ulthuan, something of such ghastly power that it caused even a daemon king like Tz'arkan to feel the icy touch of fear.

Tyrion stared up at the fiend. 'What's wrong, daemon? Have you lost your appetite?'

Bellowing its fury, Tz'arkan lunged at the asur prince. Its great claws tore at the ground as Tyrion nimbly darted away. 'I shall give your soul to the furies as a plaything,' Tz'arkan vowed, venom dripping from its fangs. Again the beast charged at its foe, but this time Tyrion darted beneath the sweep of its claws. The enchantments woven into Sunfang blazed into brilliance as he raked the blade across the daemon's hide. Flesh bubbled like wax, ichor steaming from the hideous wound as writhing worms of dark magic slopped from the daemon's marrow.

The daemon shrieked, its painful screech causing hundreds of elves across the battlefield to clap their hands to their ears in a futile effort to blot out the sound. Those closest to the fray collapsed to the ground, their bodies quivering in agony as Tz'arkan's scream ripped at their souls.

Tyrion alone stood immune to the daemon's howl. Rushing in, he slashed at the injured monster, raking its flesh again and again with the burning Sunfang. Step by monstrous step, he drove the fiend back. Tz'arkan plucked elves from where they lay in the dirt, flinging both the living and the dead at its foe. The asur prince deftly avoided each flailing body. Only when he was beside the carcass of Spite did he hesitate in his pursuit of the monster. Reaching down, Tyrion retrieved something from the bloodied earth. When he stood again, he held two blades in his hands. In his right, the holy energies of Sunfang blazed. In his left, the malefic power of the warpsword.

Tz'arkan growled at its enemy, a final snarl of hate and defiance. It had felt the bite of Sunfang and it knew the power of the warpsword. Against these weapons, in the hands of a mortal who had such an ominous presence lingering around him...

The daemon turned to flee, but as it did so it found its path blocked by a force of elves who, like Tyrion, didn't cower before it. Caradryan and his Phoenix Guard had fought their way clear of the druchii and now hurried to support the Regent of Ulthuan. Their halberds stabbed at Tz'arkan, driving the beast back towards Tyrion.

Tz'arkan rounded on his pursuer. The daemon's eyes blazed with infernal fires, scorching the waxy flesh of its face. Leathery lips pulled away from monstrous fangs in a grotesque leer. 'Are you the best your people have to send against me?' Tz'arkan hissed, its voice searing across the field like some morbid echo of the ancient volcanoes beneath Reaver's Mark. The daemon cackled derisively. 'You wear the trappings of a dead maniac and you think yourself a hero? The blood of madness pulses through your veins and you think yourself virtuous? You bear the blades of both righteousness and depravity in your hands and you do not see the hypocrisy?'

The elf stalked towards Tz'arkan, Sunfang and warpsword held at his sides. 'I am Tyrion of Cothique, heir of the line of Aenarion, son of Morelion! By the faith of my people am I Regent of Ulthuan–'

A cruel laugh rumbled from the massive daemon. 'Regent? Then they would not have you as their king?' Tz'arkan's fiery eyes diminished into little slivers of malice. 'Tell me, mock-king, why do you think that is? Could it be they know you for the mad dog you are? Could it be your gods have turned their faces from you?' Tz'arkan laughed again as he saw the doubt that made Tyrion halt in his advance. The shadow of power still clung to the asur prince, but Tz'arkan thought of its own imprisonment within Malus Darkblade. However magnificent the power, the vessel was still but a mortal, and with that came mortal weakness.

'Shall I tell you of the petty scavengers you call gods?' Tz'arkan sneered. 'I have seen them, little mock-king. I have seen them cast about themselves a veil of deceit and trickery that they might drain the strength of your foolish people and fatten on them like so many leeches! You place your faith in weak parasites who will not dare stir themselves in your hour of need.'

Tz'arkan saw the doubt spread, the hissing corruption of its voice clawing into Tyrion's soul, drawing out all the doubts and fears that lurked within the hero. Still, the aura of power was there, wrapped all around the elf's essence, almost blinding the daemon in its awful potency.

'I may be benevolent,' Tz'arkan declared. 'If you like, I shall allow you to fly back to your court, mock-king. You can hide behind your fortress walls and the spears of your armies. You can find the safety of wizards and mages. Go, little mock-king! I allow you to run back to your castle. After all, if you die here, who will lead the asur in the futile fight to save their land?'

The seeds of doubt and fear provoked by the daemon's voice dropped away from Tyrion as he raised his face and stared into Tz'arkan's eyes. 'It isn't I who will die here this day, daemon.' Grimly, he hefted Sunfang and warpsword, bringing the two crashing together above his head. The clash of their antithetical enchantments was like a clap of thunder, an explosion of arcane energy that went rippling away from the Regent.

Tz'arkan felt the force of those crashing swords. It could feel the mongrel vibrations caused by their collision, vibrations magnified far beyond the magic of either sword on its own.

Brazenly, the daemon tried again to cripple its foe with doubt. 'You think to kill what is eternal, mock-king? Do you know what it is you stand before? I am Tz'arkan the Render. Tz'arkan the Woe. Tz'arkan the Blight. I was there when the star-gods fell. I was there to watch the first apes climb up from the slime and call themselves elves. I have seen the rise of continents and the collapse of empires. I have been there from before the beginning, when all was raw, primal and untainted by the unnatural harmonies of what you call order. I will be there when all of this is cast down, ravaged until it is less than dust. I will be there when Great Khorne calls the Last Slaughter and all is drowned under a tide of blood. You think to kill me, mortal? I am destiny! I am eternity! I am–'

Only two words passed Tyrion's lips as he glared at the daemon. It was the elf who now wore the mocking smile, the haughty arrogance of disdain. 'Prove it,' he challenged the daemon.

Ancient beyond even the reckoning of elves, versed in all the evils and horrors of a million nightmares, Tz'arkan was nevertheless oblivious to its own weakness. Something it had absorbed from its mortal host after so many years. Of all the things to spur the rage of Malus, the jeers of an enemy were the most certain. Now, it was the daemon who had consumed the druchii lord who felt the primitive, unthinking fury of its vanquished host boil within it. Roaring, Tz'arkan lowered its horned head and charged at Tyrion. The aura of power clinging to the elf was forgotten in the blind urge to rend and maim. The enchanted swords were dismissed as brutish blood-lust filled Tz'arkan's mind.

With the huge daemon rushing at him, Tyrion threw himself forwards in a diving roll. As he came up under the driving daemon, he stabbed his swords into Tz'arkan's body. The monster howled in pain, aethyric blood steaming from its wounds. Tyrion clenched his jaw tight, straining his muscles to their utmost, forcing the warpsword and Sunfang to shift and turn inside the daemon's body. Inch by gory inch, he forced the weapons together.

A withering blast of power exploded from Tz'arkan as the warpsword and Sunfang touched. Magnified still further by the aethyric essence of the daemon, the magical discharge ripped Tz'arkan apart. The beast's torso was flung high into the air, collapsing hundreds of yards away in a heap of bubbling corruption. The lower part of the fiend's form was blasted into dripping giblets that spattered the armour of the asur and druchii, who had forgotten their own fights to observe the Regent's duel with the daemon king.

Despite the fury of Tz'arkan's destruction, Tyrion himself was unfazed. Standing right at the centre of the arcane explosion, he was unmarred by either the violence or the gore of his enemy's annihilation. He held the warpsword before his face, watching as the fragments of Tz'arkan's essence were sucked down into the depths of the unholy blade. A fitting death for a monster that had brought such misery into the world.

* * *

As Tz'arkan's corpse corroded into puddles of stagnant filth, clouds soared into the sky, seemingly sucked into the void left by the daemon's passing. Thick, syrupy drops of black rain began to shower down upon Reaver's Mark, drawing shouts of confusion and alarm from the elves below. It seemed the very heavens were mourning the daemon king's destruction.

Only a few knew better, those who had sensed the far-distant ritual that had unleashed an unprecedented surge of magical energy across the world. The storm that swept across Reaver's Mark was much more than cloud and rain. It was the fury of the aethyr unchained.

Drusala could feel the obscene taint of Death Magic that coloured the storm. She knew that far across the sea a great evil had been revived. The clouds to the east blazed with violet fire, lightning boiling and flashing from within their smouldering depths. A deathly chill swept across Reaver's Mark, silencing the sounds of battle that yet lingered. The druchii and their asur foes drew back, gazing uneasily at the comrades around them, feeling at the very core of their beings the occult force that rippled all around them.

Then the arcane taint seeped down into the bodies lying strewn about the battlefield. The corpse of Tullaris rose to its feet, brains drooling from its split skull. The carcass of Spite slithered across the earth with its broken back. The dead of both druchii and asur rose again, granted a ghastly semblance of life by the forces surging through them. Bony hands clawed their way upwards as still more ancient dead were awakened, pulling themselves from the ground on skeletal arms and withered talons. Barbarian marauders who had been slain millennia before rose alongside skeletal elves and the rotten husks of goblins that had been slain during the rampage of Grom the Paunch.

Living warriors cowered before the graveborn, drawing away with the instinctive repugnance of all things living for all things undead. The animated corpses made no effort to close the gap between themselves and those who had been their comrades in arms. The graveborn simply stood where they were or stumbled about in directionless idiocy. It was only when the surviving witches of the Blood Coven appeared upon the volcanic spur that the undead found motivation and purpose.

The red-clad Blood Coven sent their magic wafting across the battlefield, binding those undead closest to them to their power. Following their example, the other sorceresses yet remaining to the host of Hag Graef began to exert their own power. Coldly, they stirred the desiccated hearts and tattered mentalities of the graveborn, turning them towards the asur, driving them into battle once more. Fallen asur now crossed swords with their living kinsmen while once-slain druchii were given the chance to avenge themselves against their slayers.

'Aid us,' one of the Blood Coven snarled at Drusala. 'Lend your magic to our purpose and we may yet win the day!'

Drusala knew she didn't have the power to fight the witches. Not now.

She had expended too much energy releasing Tz'arkan. What little she still possessed was sustaining the glamour that cloaked her. There was nothing she could do to defy the Blood Coven. Nothing she could do to keep the graveborn from slaughtering the asur and killing Tyrion. She had risked so much to preserve the hero that now all she could do was watch impotently as all her plans were unravelled.

As she turned her eyes towards Tyrion, Drusala saw him step boldly towards the nearest of the undead. The asur hero raised the warpsword high, brandishing it before the oncoming horde of graveborn horrors. 'This is the Warpsword of Khaine!' Tyrion shouted, his voice booming across the battlefield. 'Dead of Ulthuan, attend me! This is the blade of the Destroyer, the Murderer of Nations, he who cut the life from you and cast you into the dominion of corpses!'

The undead froze as they heard Tyrion's cry. Sightless skulls and rotting eyes turned towards him wherever the graveborn fought, staring in sepulchral fixedness at the black blade he held overhead. The Blood Coven raged and shrieked, trying to coerce the undead back into the fight, but the carcasses refused their commands. All across Reaver's Mark, the druchii sorceresses were finding themselves unable to break the uncanny fascination Tyrion exerted over the graveborn.

'I speak for the Destroyer,' Tyrion declared, slashing the warpsword through the air before him. 'You belong to Khaine. By right of conquest and death, you are the slaves of the Bloody-handed God. My enemies are the enemies of Khaine. The enemies of Khaine are your enemies.' The Regent's face became a mask of unbridled hate as he gazed across the horde of graveborn and turned towards the druchii. He thrust the warpsword towards the black-armoured warriors. 'Slay them all!' he commanded.

By the hundreds, by the thousands, the undead set themselves against the druchii, stabbing at them with splintered spears and broken swords, clawing at them with rotten fingers and bony claws. The warriors of Har Ganeth, of Clar Karond and Hag Graef met the attack with the iron resolve of their own hate, striving to push the undead back that they might again close with the living asur and sell their own lives in the killing of their ancient foes.

Upon the volcanic spur, the witches of the Blood Coven loosed their magic against the tide of skeletons climbing up towards them. Dozens of corpses were blasted into splinters by their spells, but for each corpse they vanquished three more graveborn seemed to take their place. Again, the witches called for Drusala to help them, but this time their cry was one of abject terror. Frantically they looked about them for the sorceress, but of Morathi's handmaiden there was no sign. In the confusion of shifting battle, with the Blood Coven fixated upon their undead warriors, she had vanished.

At last the undead reached the top of the spur. The first few were sent falling to earth by the sorcerous wind the Blood Coven summoned, but there were too many for the witches to resist. Their magic faltered and they were dragged beneath the oncoming swarm. Shrieking, they were torn asunder by the rotten hands of the graveborn.

Across Reaver's Mark, the sinister undead crashed against the shields and blades of the druchii. Fighting like fiends, the sons of Naggaroth tried to drive them back. Hundreds of the graveborn were cut down, but the dead cared not. Relentlessly they continued to throw themselves at their enemy. Finally, even the hate-ridden resolve of the druchii could take no more. First one regiment, then another, turned and fled, retreating back across the fields of Ellyrion they had ravaged only days before.

Tyrion raised his sword once more, but this time it was Sunfang he held and it was living warriors he addressed. 'Defenders of Ulthuan,' he shouted. 'Khaine demands blood! The blood of Naggaroth and Malekith's slaves!' A terrible cry of ancient hate and savage violence sounded from every asur on the field as they heard the song of Khaine in Tyrion's words. Viciously they followed their Regent as he led them across the field in pursuit of the broken druchii. Like wild animals, the asur fell upon their foes, hacking them to pieces when they caught them, rending their foes to ribbons even as they lay dead upon the ground. Only the Phoenix Guard, exalted and marked by Asuryan, maintained the discipline of warriors. Over them, Khaine's Bloodsong held no power.

While Tyrion led his maddened army in the massacre of their routed foe, a lone figure prowled amidst the carnage they left behind. Drusala picked her way carefully among the corpses as she emerged from the fissure at the base of the volcanic spur that had become the grave of the Blood Coven. As she drew some of the fading energies rising from the twice-slain graveborn, she found enough power to adjust the glamour she had cast about herself.

For the merest instant, the image of Drusala, handmaiden of Morathi faded. It had been a wondrous mirage, crafted from the murdered handmaiden's own soul, a semblance that had deceived even other spellcasters. Morathi was almost reluctant to cast it aside, but she knew the role of Drusala had served its purpose. The situation had changed and she had to change with it. Using the magical energies she'd gathered from the undead, she transformed herself into the likeness of a Sapherian mage.

Teasing one of her now blonde tresses behind her ear, the sorceress turned to join Tyrion in his hunt. There was a delicious flavour to the idea of hunting down the shattered druchii host. If the massacre were complete enough, it might even cause some delay in her son Malekith's schemes.

As she started towards the asur army, Morathi noted a broken corpse dragging itself along the ground. She recognised the animated remains of Spite, Malus Darkblade's steed. The thing was crawling towards the puddle of corruption that had been Tz'arkan. Even in its undead state, despite the horrific transformation of Malus's body, the reptile was trying to reach its master.

Morathi shook her head at the pathetic display and smiled. 'You were a useful pawn, for a time, Malus Darkblade. But you were, after all, only a pawn in a much greater game.'

Her eyes already envisioning the new steps she must take to ensure her plans came to fruition, the sorceress hurried to join Tyrion's triumphant asur.

BLOODWALKER

C L Werner

Ice cracked beneath the heavy, loping tread of the nauglir as it stalked through the snowdrifts. The cold one's breath turned to mist with each shuddering exhalation, its horned head undulating from side to side with almost mechanical monotony. The brute's ribs stood stark against its scaly hide, the steel barding lashed about its body sliding back and forth with each step. Oily froth trickled from the corners of its fanged mouth, freezing as it dangled from its jaws.

The armoured rider in the nauglir's saddle ran a gloved hand along the beast's neck. Leaning forwards, he spoke reassuring words to his weary stead.

'Not much farther, Spite,' he said, his voice crackling with exhaustion. 'A few more days. Only a few more days and we will be home.'

Spite gave no sign that it heard its master's voice, merely maintaining the steady league-eating trot the cold one had maintained for so many days. The lack of response troubled the nauglir's master more than any surly snarl or angry hiss could have. It was a sign that Spite was reaching the limits of its formidable endurance. The cold ones were beasts of the reptilian orders, capable of surviving the harsh cold of Naggaroth only by gorging themselves frequently, their metabolisms using the food to maintain their body heat. Without a steady supply of fresh meat, a nauglir would become steadily more lethargic until, finally, it dropped in its tracks.

It had been days since Spite had last fed. The nauglir's scaly hide felt like ice beneath its master's hand. The reptile couldn't go on for much longer. Once his steed fell, its rider's chances of survival wouldn't be worth an asur's life in Har Ganeth.

There was one thing that gave Malus Darkblade some hope. For all its seeming mindlessness, Spite was moving with purpose and direction. Once before, the nauglir had made this bold, lonely journey. Even more than its master, the reptile's brain bore the impression of the long trail that would lead it to Hag Graef. The long trail that would again put the cursed Temple of Tz'arkan behind them.

A hot rush of anger warmed the elf's cold flesh as he thought of the scheming daemon that has used him, used him to unleash itself upon the mortal world after millennia trapped within its own temple. For a year, Tz'arkan had coerced and manipulated him, lurking inside his own body, spreading its corruption through his flesh. And when it was through with him, when it had no further use for him, the daemon had betrayed him. It had sought his life, but it had taken only his soul.

The eyes of the highborn were frozen windows of hate as he thought of what Tz'arkan has stolen from him. His hand closed about the hilt of his sword, not for the first time wondering if he might not have fared better with a lesser weapon in his final confrontation with the daemon. A mortal blade wouldn't have forced Tz'arkan to abandon its attack. Only a relic of such power as the Warpsword of Khaine could have made the mighty daemon know fear. Without it, Malus would be dead.

But perhaps death was more merciful than life without a soul.

A scowl twisted the druchii's hawkish features. All his life he had struggled against the world. He would not give up now. He would not meekly submit to the cold clutch of Death. If the gods desired an end of Malus Darkblade, they would have to work for it.

Malus snapped from his thoughts as he felt Spite's body go tense beneath his caressing hand. The highborn braced himself to leap from the saddle, thinking the nauglir was about to pitch over into the snow. An instant's reflection, however, had him drawing his sword instead. Spite had long been his steed and he knew the reptile's every manner and motion better than the back of his own hand. When he saw the nauglir's neck rigid, its head pointing steadily towards a stand of snow-covered pines, he knew it was not fatigue that had changed the cold one's attitude. Spite had caught a scent upon the breeze. The scent of an enemy.

No sooner had his sword cleared its sheath than the highborn's lurking foes exploded from their hiding places. Crossbow bolts whistled through the air, glancing from Malus's armour and Spite's barding, one missile tearing through the scaly ridge of the nauglir's tail. A fluid curse rolled across the wind, bemoaning the ineffectual marksmanship. Then the ambushers came charging out onto the snow, determined to finish with sword and spear what they had failed to accomplish with crossbows.

There were five of them, lean druchii in steel dalakoi and long flowing khaitans of black silk. Tall helms with sharply angled bevors and flowing razor-edged horns obscured the visages of each elf, but there was no mistaking the crimson-scaled cold ones they rode, or the bat-winged device branded into each reptile's scaly hide. It was the device of the Black Ark of Naggor, Har Ganeth's most bitter rival and enemy.

'Dogs of Naggor!' Malus shouted at the charging elves. 'Come and embrace death!'

The highborn dug his spurs into Spite's flanks. The nauglir reared back, its foreclaws pawing at the air, then lurched forwards in a loping sprint. The smell of battle, the sight of foes, invigorated the faltering reptile, pouring fresh strength into its weakened body. Malus clung to the brute's reins, pressing his legs close to Spite's sides. He knew his steed's wind wouldn't last long. If he would survive, he had to exterminate his enemies before Spite exhausted itself and collapsed beneath him.

The warriors of Naggor thundered onwards, their cold ones hissing their fury as they bore down upon the highborn. Malus could hear the silver keikalla jangling against their armour, the little spirit bells proclaiming his foes to be knights rather than common killers. Any pretensions to honour were quashed, however, when another crossbow bolt went whistling past Darkblade's ear. One of the knights hadn't abandoned his crossbow, but was instead hanging back to allow his fellows to engage Malus while he reloaded his weapon.

Such slinking treachery brought a sharpness into Malus's eyes and murderous determination into his veins. If he was fated to die upon this blighted patch of wasteland, his killer wouldn't be the cowardly bowman.

A flash of the Warpsword and the foremost of Malus's antagonists toppled from his saddle, his helmet cleft in half by the magic blade. The dead elf's boot caught in one of the stirrups and as his cold one sprinted away it dragged the corpse after it.

Snarling like an enraged panther, the second of the knights rushed Malus, striking at him from his left side before the highborn had recovered from killing the first Naggorite. The elf's blade glanced from Malus's vambrace as he blocked the blow. Then the Warpsword was driving down at the knight. Malus's foe tried to emulate the same tactic as the highborn, to turn aside the blow with his steel vambrace. Unlike the Naggorite's sword, however, Malus's weapon bit through the thick armour, shearing through it like paper and cleaving the arm beneath. The Naggorite howled in agony, dropping his sword as he clutched at the spurting stump. Mortally wounded, he sagged low in his saddle as his nauglir dashed across the snowfield.

Another bolt came flying at Malus, this time punching into him with enough velocity that it dented the armour above his heart. Pain flared across his chest as the impacted metal drove the chain aketon biting into his skin. He glared at the circling opportunist, watching as the Naggorite wound back the string of his weapon.

Before Malus could charge the bowman, the other knights were upon him. Having learned better than to attack him singly, they tried to mount a coordinated assault. The tactic failed only because of the stubborn ferocity of their steeds, each cold one trying to sprint ahead of the other and claim the choicest morsels from the kill. It was in the truculence of the Naggorites' nauglir that Malus took advantage. When he kicked his heel against Spite's ribs, his steed didn't hesitate.

Far more intelligent than others of its kind, Spite obeyed the direction of its master immediately. Summoning a fresh burst of speed, the nauglir rushed past the first knight and lunged at the second, a tactic that caught both knights and their mounts by surprise. Before they could recover, Spite's leg delivered a savage, raking kick to the trailing cold one, slashing open its belly. The stricken nauglir's charge turned into a sprawling fall as it tripped over its own entrails. Its rider cried out in shock as the brute dragged him down with it, then crushed him under its scaly mass as it thrashed about in agony.

The other knight struggled to wheel his own nauglir back around. As he did so, Spite's powerful tail came whipping around, slapping across the other cold one's face. Instinctively, the reptile recoiled, rearing back and raking its foreclaws through the air in an effort to protect its own eyes. The knight could only hang on and curse his steed's panic, fighting to regain control over the reptile.

It took the Naggorite only a moment to assert himself, but in that moment, Malus had closed upon him. The Warpsword came slashing at the knight, crunching through his shoulder, splitting the pauldron, hewing through steel and flesh and bone. The magically keen blade didn't stop until it had cut clean through the elf's body and sheared away the top of his steed's skull. Rider and reptile sank to the earth, the centre of a spreading patch of crimson snow.

Malus turned away from his slaughtered foe, looking for the crossbowman. 'Khaine's Blood,' he cursed when he found no sign of the last Naggorite. Seeing the destruction of his comrades, the last knight had fled back into the safety of the woods. Briefly, Malus considered tracking the elf down, but he could feel Spite stumble when he tried to turn it towards the trees. The nauglir had reached its limits and beyond. Reluctantly, the highborn gave the beast its head and allowed it to stagger over to one of the dead reptiles.

As a rule, the only flesh a cold one would refuse was that of another cold one. The druchii who rode the reptiles into battle had to smear their bodies with a poisonous ointment to keep them safe from the rapacious appetites of their monstrous steeds. Spite, however, was too hungry to observe such proprieties and tore into the dead nauglir with savage abandon. It was all Malus could do to keep his steed from devouring the poisoned flesh of the dead knight as well.

'Eat up,' Malus told his steed. He again cast his eyes about, half expecting another steel bolt to come whistling at him from the trees. He had been driving Spite hard in his effort to reach Hag Graef quickly, but with warriors of Naggor on the prowl, the time for speed was past. Now he had to be more cautious. And the first rule of caution was to find a safe place where Spite and himself could rest and recover from their long journey.

'The stronghold of Yrkool should be near here,' Malus judged as he studied the range of mountains looming in the west.

The highborn smiled grimly and stroked the neck of his steed. 'Feed quickly, Spite. I fear we have a little way yet before either of us can rest.'

The last of the Naggorites dismounted from the saddle of his cold one. The armoured knight stood staring at the snow-covered pines which surrounded him, watching for any sign of movement, his ears sharp for even the slightest sound that might indicate pursuit.

The druchii felt sickness boil at the pit of his stomach as he considered the carnage Darkblade had wrought upon them. Five of the Black Ark's most lethal warriors, and their enemy had abused them like trussed slavelings on the way to Khaine's altar. Belladon could have sent twenty knights and they might not have been enough. Five against Darkblade had been nothing less than suicide.

Or perhaps that had been the hag's intention. Suspicion roared through the elf's heart as he wondered if the witch hadn't intended for the knights to succeed, if the ambush had been engineered to eliminate *them*, not the highborn.

Angrily, the druchii stripped away one of his gauntlets and flung it down into the snow. His nauglir hissed hungrily as the elf raked the edge of his knife across his palm and brought blood bubbling up from the torn flesh. The reptile grew quiet, however, as its master clenched his fist and sent bloody beads dripping onto the ground. Sibilant words rasped across the elf's tongue and the air around him began to shimmer with an icy haze. The cold one slapped its long tail against the trees, even its primitive mind unsettled by the arcane taint of sorcery.

In a matter of moments, a small puddle of blood had formed in the snow at the knight's feet. The druchii glared down at the crimson liquid. The words of his incantation fell silent as the image of a face stared back at him from the surface of the puddle. It was a cruel, hard visage, possessed of an infernal beauty at once alluring and terrifying. The knight shuddered as he felt the pitiless eyes staring back at him. Few were they who could meet the gaze of Belladon, Hag of Naggor.

'I see failure in your face,' Belladon's lips formed the words, though no sound issued from the puddle.

The knight clenched his fist, anger racing through him as Belladon reprimanded him. 'He cut through us like a raging manticore,' the elf reported. 'You should have sent more warriors.'

Belladon's expression darkened. 'Do not question me. You were given the resources to accomplish your purpose.'

'The others are dead and the enemy escaped,' the knight stated, striving to keep accusation from his tone.

'It was Malus Darkblade?' Belladon asked.

The knight nodded. 'It was Eldire's witch-spawn.'

The face in the puddle smiled. 'That is all I needed to know. You have accomplished your purpose. Another will take up the hunt now.'

Belladon's eyes hardened, her slender hands crossing before her lips, fingers splayed in a complex pattern. For an instant, the knight felt fear well up inside him, but before he could act upon the emotion it was too late. The witch's spell already had him in its coils.

Passing through the puddle of blood, invisible tendrils of magic wrapped themselves about the knight, seeping through his armour and permeating his flesh. Agonising pain roared through the druchii's body and he fell to his knees, screaming. Blood gushed from his nose, from his eyes, from his ears. A stream of gore bubbled over his lips, spilling into the snow. The hideous stream flowed into the little puddle, rapidly expanding its dimensions. By the time the knight's body was bled dry and his corpse collapsed, a pond of steaming gore stained the ground.

Now masterless, the nauglir hissed angrily at the pond, smelling the stink of sorcery rising from it. The reptile lashed its tail in fright, then turned and ran off into the fastness of the forest.

From the depths of the pool, a figure began to form. Inch by inch it grew, taking substance from the knight's blood. As its head took shape, rising from broad shoulders, two burning eyes boiled up from the pits of its skull and cast their vicious gaze upon the desiccated husk of the dead druchii. Fangs gnashed together in a hungry leer as the daemon contemplated the carrion. It lifted a half-formed arm from the edge of the pool, reaching for the corpse.

Then, reluctantly, the daemon drew back. There was a compulsion it had to fulfil before it could glut its appetite. It had to accomplish the task set before it by the one who had conjured it into the mortal world.

It had to find Malus Darkblade.

After hours following the almost invisible forest trails, it was with a supreme sense of relief that Malus saw the black walls of Yrkool suddenly appear through a break in the trees. The stronghold stood upon a small rise, a pinnacle of rock amid the sprawl of the forest. The pines had been cleared away from the fort, placing it at the centre of a half-mile-wide clearing. Banners bearing the heraldry of Hag Graef flanked the simple stone road leading up to the fort's massive darkwood doors. As Spite walked along the road, Malus noted the long stakes interspersed between the banners, each pole topped with a bleached skull. Druchast letters were cut into each forehead, proclaiming the skull that of a traitor, trespasser or outlaw. Malus's hand dropped to the hilt of his sword, as he wondered if any of these titles had been added to his name since last he'd walked the streets of his city.

The musical cry of a horn brought his eyes back to the fort. A body of armoured elves had appeared on the walls, something Malus had expected from such a lonely outpost. A closer look revealed no weapons in their hands, however, which was far more surprising. The trumpeting call of the horn wasn't sounding an alarm, but proclaiming welcome. While he watched, the huge doors of the fortress were drawn inwards and a troop of druchii soldiers filed out onto the road. They formed columns on either flank, arms crossed over their chests in the ancient gesture of respect and honour. An elf in ornate armour and wearing a flowing cloak of finest human leather stood between the two columns, his arm extended in greeting.

'My Lord Malus!' the druchii commander called out, his accent that of Hag Graef's lower nobility. 'It is an honour unparalleled for the castellan of Yrkool to welcome such a highborn into its humble halls.'

Malus cast an appraising gaze over the castellan, taking Spite's reins and stopping the cold one on the road. What was the commander's game, he wondered? Did the elf hope to weasel favours from him as a reward for Yrkool's hospitality or was he playing some deeper game? Perhaps he hoped to ingratiate himself into Malus's good graces and secure a position in the highborn's retinue, or at least a posting somewhere less forsaken than Yrkool? Lesser druchii had nurtured such ambitions, Malus reflected, thinking of Hauclir, the late captain of Hag Graef's Spear Gate.

'Forgive the spartan reception,' the castellan said, walking down the path, his hands spread to either side and well away from the swords belted about his waist. 'My scouts only noted your approach a league from the clearing. I fear this was the best I could arrange on such short notice.'

Malus favoured the castellan with the faintest hint of a nod. 'I have travelled a long way,' he said, urging Spite onwards. 'My first priority is food and rest. We can discuss any deficiencies in your courtesy later.' The highborn directed his most imperious stare at the smiling castellan. It was a look that had never failed to send servants and retainers hurrying to carry out his demands.

The castellan, however, simply continued to smile. When Malus saw the elf direct a sidewise glance at his soldiers, the highborn brought his spurs kicking into Spite's flanks. Whatever trickery the castellan was up to, he would be the first victim of it.

Before Spite had gone more than a few feet, however, the nauglir crashed onto the paving stones. In drawing closer to the fort, Malus had come abreast of the soldiers. At the castellan's motion, these had thrown open their hands, flinging what looked like dust across the road. Spite's charge carried it full into the yellow cloud.

Malus recognised the dust as soon as he noted its colour. It was the powder used by hunters to subdue cold ones in their subterranean lairs. It had a soporific effect upon nauglir, rendering them helpless for hours. Spite crumpled beneath Malus, stricken so swiftly it didn't even utter a sound. The highborn tried to throw himself from the saddle, but was too slow to leap clear. When Spite slammed against the ground, his leg was pinned beneath his steed.

'Take him alive!' the castellan shouted at his soldiers. 'He's worth nothing to me dead!'

Malus ripped his sword free from its sheath, hewing through the arm of the first soldier to close upon him. Then he felt bright stabbing pain explode through his skull as the pommel of a sword was driven against the back of his head. The shock numbed his fingers and before he could recover another soldier was wrestling the Warpsword from his weakened grip.

'Try not to damage his face,' the castellan ordered as a mass of soldiers used the pommels and flats of their swords to batter Malus into submission.

'The Drachau will want to recognise Darkblade when he is executed.'

Nehloth ran a covetous hand along the Warpsword's scabbard. It didn't take someone versed in the ancient history of Ulthuan and the elven gods to recognise a blade of quality. Even less so when he had seen with his own eyes the way the sword had sheared effortlessly through bone and steel.

The castellan leaned back in his chair, glancing apprehensively at the grim walls of his war room. There was no telling how many of his garrison were spies for the Drachau or one of the highborn families of Hag Graef. Any one of them might send word back to the Hag about his capture of Malus. That didn't worry him; the druchii was an outcast and kinslayer. No one would mourn him when he was gone. Indeed, the Drachau probably would have him executed... if Nehloth returned him to the Hag.

He wouldn't, of course. As much as the Drachau might like to see Malus disposed of, the witchlords of Naggor wanted his head even more. It was something Nehloth's own patron was counting on. Lord Severin was the Drachau's favoured son, but the highborn wasn't content with his lot. He intended to become Slavemaster of Hag Graef and wasn't willing to wait. Towards that end, Severin had been secretly negotiating with the Naggorites, seeking the support of the witchlords in securing his father's throne. Yrkool, closest of the Hag's outposts to the Black Ark, was an important rendezvous for the conspirators and Nehloth was deep in Severin's confidences.

Not so deep, however, that he was willing to let a weapon like the Warpsword slip through his fingers. The castellan would keep that for himself. When he sent word to the Naggorites about Malus's capture, they would be waiting to ambush the prisoner when Nehloth sent a few of his soldiers to take him back to the Hag. The escort would be killed, of course, and the only ones around to refute the castellan's claims that the Warpsword had been sent along with Darkblade would be the Naggorites – and even their ally Severin wouldn't believe them.

Yes, Nehloth reflected, it had been a very profitable day. All that was left was to send a messenger to Lord Severin, advising him of Malus's capture. A mere formality; the castellan already knew what was expected of him, but he knew Severin would take issue if he didn't keep him informed every step of the way.

* * *

A light snow was drifting down into Yrkool's courtyard when the messenger was ready to depart. Nehloth watched the elf exit the barracks, muffled in a heavy wolfskin cloak. The castellan knew he could trust this soldier to perform his duty. The elf was one of Severin's sworn retainers and the oaths he had made to his lord were so terrible they would make even the Dark Mother blanch.

From his position overlooking the courtyard, Nehloth nodded to the messenger as he mounted his horse. As the elf rode towards the great gates, the castellan gave the order for them to be opened. It was a foolish custom, but at night only a direct command from the castellan could open those gates. The druchii soldiers were well aware of the gruesome penalty for disobeying that custom.

As the gates swung open, however, Nehloth's elves had something far more gruesome to occupy their thoughts. Standing just beyond the portal, its eyes glowing in the darkness, was a monstrous shape. Twice the height of an elf, its blood-coloured body glistening with wet sliminess in the moonlight, the thing sprang into motion the moment the gates swung wide, its claws sweeping out for the horrified messenger.

Colour drained from Nehloth's face as he saw the monster bring its claws together, one to either side of the messenger's head. There was a gut-churning crunch as the druchii's skull disintegrated between the creature's palms. The elf's body quivered a moment after it toppled into the snow. Another sweep of the monster's claws sent the messenger's decapitated horse collapsing beside him.

To their credit, the soldiers at the gate didn't flee even after witnessing their comrade's horrible demise. With the martial discipline demanded of all Naggaroth's warriors, they rushed at the monster. The beast hovered over those it had killed, its slimy hide rippling with obscene life as it savoured its handiwork.

The spear of the first soldier to reach it stabbed clean through its waist. That of the second punched into its side. A third warrior slashed at it with his sword, hacking into its knee.

The monster rounded upon the elves who had attacked it, eyes burning malignantly from its skull-like visage. Long fangs clacked together as slimy lips pulled back in a sadistic grin. The wounds its attackers had visited upon it were already closing; in the blink of an eye its crimson skin was without the faintest trace of injury. The same could not be said for the beast's attackers. Their screams echoed across the fort as the monster literally tore them limb from limb.

Now the horn sounded the alarm, elves rushed from the barracks, crossbowmen manned the walls. Two score druchii warriors converged upon the slimy abomination, glaring with hate as they saw the carnage it had inflicted.

Nehloth retreated back inside Yrkool's keep, his body trembling in terror.

Forty warriors or four hundred, he knew the garrison had no chance against the monster. He had dealt with the Naggorites long enough to recognise one of their daemons – the hell-fiend they called the Bloodwalker. No mortal blade could harm the daemon. No spell could turn it aside. It existed only to track down the one it had been sent to find – and it would enjoy killing everything that got in its way.

The castellan rushed back into his war room, seizing the Warpsword from where it rested on the table. Mortal steel might be ineffectual against the Bloodwalker, but a magic blade might pierce its unholy essence. Nehloth turned in alarm as the door to the war room was flung open, but was relieved to find only his terrified adjutant, not the rampaging daemon.

'The monster is slaughtering the garrison!' the elf fairly shrieked. 'We must flee!'

'And have the Drachau after us for deserting the fort?' Nehloth sneered. 'No. We will fight the daemon!'

'With what?'

Nehloth stroked the Warpsword, then frowned. The magic blade might indeed work against the Bloodwalker, but was he willing to risk his own life to find out? Even as he asked himself the question, a cunning gleam entered his eye.

'Come!' Nehloth ordered. 'There is a proposition I want to make to our prisoner.'

Malus stared incredulously at Nehloth as the castellan knelt beside him in the dank squalor of the dungeon. 'You want me to do what?'

'I want you to defend Yrkool,' Nehloth repeated. 'The daemon doesn't much care who it kills. You can die down here in chains when it comes for you or die like a druchii with a blade in your hand.'

'My blade,' Malus said. He had not failed to notice that the castellan carried the Warpsword. Nehloth nodded in agreement.

'With the understanding that you will return it to me,' he said. 'I want your oath, Malus Darkblade, that you will defend Yrkool against this daemon. When it is vanquished, I shall allow you to leave – after you have returned the sword.' Nehloth craned his head to one side, listening as a thin shriek drifted down to the dungeon from the courtyard. 'I want you to swear by your mother's soul, Darkblade, that you will abide by our pact.'

The words stabbed into Malus like a dagger. Of all the oaths Nehloth could have demanded, there was none that could pain him more. Better than any living druchii, he knew what it meant to forsake one's soul.

'You have my word,' Malus snarled. 'Now undo these chains before the daemon brings this whole fort crashing down on our heads.'

Nehloth grinned as he unlocked Malus's chains, almost sneering as he handed the highborn his blade. In the back of his mind, the castellan wondered if the Bloodwalker had been sent not to destroy Yrkool, but to kill Darkblade. If so, then whatever happened, the castellan would win.

The courtyard was a scene of carnage when Malus emerged from the keep. Great blocks of stone had been ripped from the outbuildings and hurled at the battlements, smashing the crossbowmen into crimson rags. Fire raged unchecked in the barracks, devouring its timber roof. Horses screamed as the flames reached out to claim the stables. The ground was strewn with mangled bodies, mutilated in a fashion that even the highborn had never imagined possible. Streams of blood oozed through the snow, crawling with unnatural life to flow towards the Bloodwalker's feet. Whenever the streams touched the daemon, the monster's eyes blazed and its body glistened with hellish light. The daemon's skin writhed and rippled as it absorbed the blood of its victims.

Malus drew the Warpsword and pondered his next move. The Bloodwalker was busy grinding the face of a soldier into a bloody smear on the wall of the keep, but the moment the highborn stepped out into the courtyard, it lost interest in its savage amusement. The burning eyes of the daemon fixed upon Malus and its long fangs clacked together in a hungry snap.

'Not good,' the highborn cursed as the daemon lunged towards him. After the beating the soldiers had given him, Malus's body was too sore to react with its usual quickness. The daemon's claw licked out, raking across the highborn's arm. Malus felt an electric shock burn through his body as the daemon's talons tore open his skin. Blood oozed from the wound, rushing with unnatural speed towards the daemon's body.

Malus struck at the Bloodwalker with his blade, the ancient relic slashing across its forearm. The daemon recoiled, howling in pain as black steam boiled from the cut. At the same instant, the stream of blood pulsing from Malus's wound slowed to a more natural trickle.

The highborn brought his sword slashing at the daemon's claw as it came at him again. The Bloodwalker, however, had learned this blade could hurt it. Displaying inhuman agility, the daemon rolled inside the sweep of Malus's sword. Its claw smashed into his breastplate, hurling him across the courtyard as though he'd been shot from a ballista. Sparks flickered through the druchii's vision as he crashed against the flagstones.

The daemon stalked towards him, fangs exposed in a murderous grin. Malus struggled up from the ground, but he knew his battered body was moving too slowly to escape the monster.

Deliverance came from an unexpected source. Unwisely peering out from the keep to see how Malus was faring, Nehloth's adjutant made the mistake of catching the daemon's attention. The slight motion of the elf's head in the doorway brought the daemon wheeling about, pouncing on the adjutant like a raging lion. Viciously, the Bloodwalker savaged its victim, forgetting about the highborn entirely.

The grisly scene brought inspiration to Malus. Turning towards the burning stables, the highborn made a valiant dash across the courtyard. The Bloodwalker spotted him when he was passing the keep and with a ghoulish howl, it dropped the mangled adjutant and charged after its quarry.

Malus reached the stable doors an instant ahead of the daemon. He could see the portals rattling as the panicked horses kicked at them from within. Glancing back at the daemon, he brought his sword slashing down, chopping the steel bar holding the doors shut.

A dozen terrified horses leaped into the courtyard, smoke and flame billowing behind them. The daemon howled again, lashing out at the beasts as they rushed past it, bloodlust blazing in its eyes.

Malus left the thing to chase the horses. Throwing a hand before his face to shield it from the smoke, he forced his way into the burning stable. Above the crack of flames and the pop of burning timber, he could hear the furious shrieks of Spite. With as much haste as his bruised muscles could muster, Malus ran towards the source of the shrieks.

He found Spite chained by a neck-ring to a massive block of granite in a stall at the back of the stable. Burning debris showered down around the reptile, singeing its scales. The cold one snapped angrily at the flames licking down at it from the ceiling, trying to attack its tormentor.

'I have need of you, old friend,' Malus coughed. A single stroke of the Warpsword snapped the chain. For an instant Spite seemed more inclined to attack the flames than follow its master, but the nauglir quickly reverted to its training.

Climbing onto Spite's back, Malus turned the reptile towards the doors. He had seen that the Warpsword could hurt the daemon – what he couldn't overcome in his condition was its speed. But with a steed under him, the situation had changed.

With flames and smoke billowing about it, Spite charged out from the inferno like a fiend spat from hell. The Bloodwalker spun around, ignoring the horse it had caught. The daemon howled and bared its fangs.

'Let's try this again, shall we?' Malus snarled, raising the Warpsword high. Spite dropped into a crouch, its powerful legs becoming like steel coils. With a terrific display of strength, the cold one sprang at the rushing daemon. The reptile's lunge carried it clear over the Bloodwalker. As Spite passed the daemon, Malus struck, the enchanted edge of the Warpsword cleaving through its neck.

Malus was nearly thrown by the impact of Spite's landing, but he managed to retain sufficient control to not only keep his place, but even turn the nauglir around to face their stricken enemy. The highborn smiled coldly as the decapitated daemon swayed unsteadily upon its cloven feet. As he watched, the slimy body began to disintegrate, melting into a pool of blood and offal.

'You did it! You actually did it!' The castellan emerged from the keep, gawking with disbelief. Nehloth's exclamation brought the few surviving soldiers creeping out from their hiding places. Malus cast a disgusted glance at the survivors.

'You asked me to save Yrkool from the daemon,' Malus stated.

'You have honoured your oath,' Nehloth replied. 'We will make no effort to hold you now.'

Malus wasn't sure if there was treachery in the castellan's words, not that he cared. The elf was already dead and had been the moment he'd extracted that oath from him. 'You asked me to save Yrkool from the daemon.' His gaze bore into Nehloth's eyes. 'But who will save the fort from *me*?'

Malus Darkblade turned his back on the ruins of Yrkool, spurring Spite into the shelter of the forest. Between himself and the daemon, the garrison had been slaughtered to a soldier. Even Nehloth, who had been quite discomfited when the Warpsword was returned to him, blade first and through his chest.

Malus rued the petty hate that had made him kill the castellan out of hand. He should have taken his time, learned if the fool had truly been acting in the Drachau's name when he had tried to arrest him. If so, then it would inflict some adjustment to his plans about returning to Hag Graef.

Even more troubling had been the presence of the daemon. Had the fiend descended upon Yrkool by mere chance, or had there been purpose behind its rampage? Perhaps it had been following him ever since Malus left the Wastes. More troubling, perhaps it had been dispatched by Tz'arkan to hunt him down.

The very thought of such a possibility turned Malus colder than the snow falling around him. The Bloodwalker was dead, destroyed by the Warpsword. Whatever its purpose, it would trouble him no more.

Ebon wings hovered above the ruins of Yrkool, great demi-reptiles that bore armoured warriors upon their backs. In an instant, they circled the clearing, searching for any tracks. Whatever impressions there had been were lost under the fresh snow.

One of the warriors reached beneath the folds of his wyvern-hide cloak and drew forth a golden pendant, a huge bloodstone gleaming at the centre of the talisman. The cruel beauty of Belladon stared from the depths of the jewel.

'My Lady Belladon,' the Naggorite said, his voice betraying a tinge of fear. 'We have searched the fortress. There is no sign of Darkblade. Much of the fort is burned. He may have perished in the fire.'

'He lives,' Belladon's words hissed through the Naggorite's mind. 'And while he lives, he is a threat to Witchlord Bale.'

'But we do not know where he has gone,' the Naggorite protested.

From behind the bloodstone, Belladon's expression hardened. 'The Bloodwalker found Malus once; now that it has tasted his blood, it can do so again. Land your doom-wings in the courtyard. Choose the least useful of your witchguard.

'I'm afraid I will need some of his blood when I call the daemon back.'

ABOUT THE AUTHORS

Dan Abnett has written over fifty novels, including *Anarch*, the latest instalment in the acclaimed Gaunt's Ghosts series. He has also written the Ravenor, Eisenhorn and Bequin books, the most recent of which is *Penitent*. For the Horus Heresy, he is the author of the Siege of Terra novel *Saturnine*, as well as *Horus Rising*, *Legion*, *The Unremembered Empire*, *Know No Fear* and *Prospero Burns*, the last two of which were both *New York Times* bestsellers. He also scripted *Macragge's Honour*, the first Horus Heresy graphic novel, as well as numerous Black Library audio dramas. Many of his short stories have been collected into the volume *Lord of the Dark Millennium*. He lives and works in Maidstone, Kent.

Mike Lee's credits for Black Library include the Horus Heresy novel *Fallen Angels*, the Time of Legends trilogy *The Rise of Nagash*, the Warhammer 40,000 novel *Legacy of Dorn* and the Space Marine Battles novella *Traitor's Gorge*. Together with Dan Abnett, he wrote the five-volume Malus Darkblade series. An avid wargamer and devoted fan of pulp adventure, Mike lives in the United States.

C L Werner's Black Library credits include the Age of Sigmar novels *Overlords of the Iron Dragon*, *Profit's Ruin*, *The Tainted Heart* and *Beastgrave*, the novella *Scion of the Storm* in *Hammers of Sigmar*, and the Warhammer Horror novel *Castle of Blood*. For Warhammer he has written the novels *Deathblade*, *Mathias Thulmann: Witch Hunter*, *Runefang* and *Brunner the Bounty Hunter*, the Thanquol and Boneripper series and Warhammer Chronicles: The Black Plague series. For Warhammer 40,000 he has written the Space Marine Battles novel *The Siege of Castellax*. Currently living in the American south-west, he continues to write stories of mayhem and madness set in the Warhammer worlds.

YOUR NEXT READ

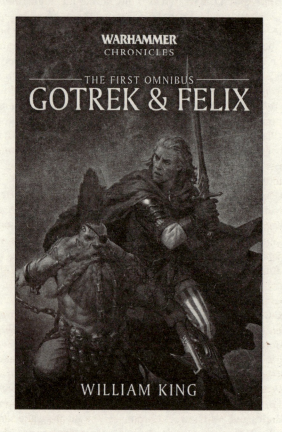

GOTREK & FELIX: THE FIRST OMNIBUS
by William King

Of all the heroes of the World-that-Was, Gotrek and Felix may be the greatest – and this collection of novels and short stories showcases their earliest adventures.

For these stories and more, go to blacklibrary.com, games-workshop.com, Games Workshop and Warhammer stores, all good book stores or visit one of the thousands of independent retailers worldwide, which can be found at games-workshop.com/storefinder

An extract from
Trollslayer
by William King
from *Gotrek & Felix: The First Omnibus*

'Damn all manling coach drivers and all manling women,' Gotrek Gurnisson muttered, adding a curse in dwarfish.

'You did have to insult the lady Isolde, didn't you?' Felix Jaeger said peevishly. 'As things are, we're lucky they didn't just shoot us. If you can call it "lucky" to be dumped in the Reikwald on Geheimnisnacht Eve.'

'We paid for our passage. We were just as entitled to sit inside as her. The drivers were unmanly cowards,' Gotrek grumbled. 'They refused to meet me hand to hand. I would not have minded being spitted on steel, but being blasted with buckshot is no death for a Trollslayer.'

Felix shook his head. He could see that one of his companion's black moods was coming on. There would be no arguing with him and Felix had plenty of other things to worry about. The sun was setting, giving the mist-covered forest a ruddy hue.

Long shadows danced eerily and brought to mind too many frightening tales of the horrors to be found under the canopy of trees.

He wiped his nose with the edge of his cloak, then pulled the Sudenland wool tight about him. He sniffed and looked at the sky where Morrslieb and Mannslieb, the lesser and greater moons, were already visible. Morrslieb seemed to be giving off a faint greenish glow. It wasn't a good sign.

'I think I have a fever coming on,' Felix said. The Trollslayer looked up at him and chuckled contemptuously. In the last rays of the dying sun, his nose-chain was a bloody arc running from nostril to earlobe.

'Yours is a weak race,' Gotrek said. 'The only fever I feel this eve is the battle-fever. It sings in my head.'

He turned and glared out into the darkness of the woods. 'Come out, little beastmen!' he bellowed. 'I have a gift for you.'

He laughed loudly and ran his thumb along the edge of the blade of his great two-handed axe. Felix saw that it drew blood. Gotrek began to suck his thumb.

'Sigmar preserve us, be quiet!' Felix hissed. 'Who knows what lurks out there on a night like this?'

Gotrek glared at him. Felix could see the glint of insane violence appear in his eyes. Instinctively Felix's hand strayed nearer to the pommel of his sword.

'Give me no orders, manling! I am of the Elder Race and am beholden only to the Kings Under the Mountain, exile though I be.'

Felix bowed formally. He was well schooled in the use of the sword. The scars on his face showed that he had fought several duels in his student days. He had once killed a man and so ended a promising academic career. But still he did not relish the thought of fighting the Trollslayer. The tip of Gotrek's crested hair came only to the level of Felix's chest, but the dwarf outweighed him and his bulk was all muscle. And Felix had seen Gotrek use that axe.

The dwarf took the bow as an apology and turned once more to the darkness. 'Come out!' he shouted. 'I care not if all the powers of evil walk the woods this night. I will face any challenger.'

The dwarf was working himself up to a pitch of fury. During the time of their acquaintance Felix had noticed that the Trollslayer's long periods of brooding were often followed by brief explosions of rage. It was one of the things about his companion that fascinated Felix. He knew that Gotrek had become a Trollslayer to atone for some crime. He was sworn to seek death in unequal combat with fearsome monsters. He seemed bitter to the point of madness – yet he kept to his oath.

Perhaps, thought Felix, I too would go mad if I had been driven into exile among strangers not even of my own race. He felt some sympathy for the crazed dwarf. Felix knew what it was like to be driven from home under a cloud. The duel with Wolfgang Krassner had caused quite a scandal.

At that moment, however, the dwarf seemed bent on getting them both killed, and he wanted no part of it. Felix continued to plod along the road, casting an occasional worried glance at the bright full moons. Behind him the ranting continued.

'Are there no warriors among you? Come feel my axe. She thirsts!'

Only a madman would so tempt fate and the dark powers on Geheimnisnacht, Night of Mystery, in the darkest reaches of the forest, Felix decided.

He could make out chanting in the flinty, guttural tongue of the Mountain Dwarfs, then once more in Reikspiel, he heard: 'Send me a champion!'

For a second there was silence. Condensation from the clammy mist ran down his brow. Then – from far, far off – the sound of galloping horses rang out in the quiet night.

What has that maniac done, Felix thought, has he offended one of the Old Powers? Have they sent their daemon riders to carry us off?

Felix stepped off the road. He shuddered as wet leaves fondled his face. They felt like dead men's fingers. The thunder of hooves came closer, moving with hellish speed along the forest road. Surely only a supernatural being could keep such breakneck pace on the winding forest road? He felt his hand shake as he unsheathed his sword.

I was foolish to follow Gotrek, he thought. Now I'll never get the poem finished. He could hear the loud neighing of horses, the cracking of a whip and mighty wheels turning.

'Good!' Gotrek roared. His voice drifted from the trail behind. 'Good!'

There was a loud bellowing and four immense jet black horses drawing an equally black coach hurtled past. Felix saw the wheels bounce as they hit a rut in the road. He could just make out a black-cloaked driver. He shrank back into the bushes.

He heard the sound of feet coming closer. The bushes were pulled aside. Before him stood Gotrek, looking madder and wilder than ever. His crest was matted, brown mud was smeared over his tattooed body and his studded leather jerkin was ripped and torn.

'The snotling-fondlers tried to run me over!' he yelled. 'Let's get after them!'

He turned and headed up the muddy road at a fast trot. Felix noted that Gotrek was singing happily in Khazalid.

Further down the Bogenhafen road the pair found the Standing Stones Inn. The windows were shuttered and no lights showed. They could hear a neighing from the stables but when they checked there was no coach, black or otherwise, only some skittish ponies and a peddler's cart.

'We've lost the coach. Might as well get a bed for the night,' Felix suggested. He looked warily at the smaller moon, Morrslieb. The sickly green glow was stronger. 'I do not like being abroad under this evil light.'

'You are feeble, manling. Cowardly too.'

'They'll have ale.'

'On the other hand, some of your suggestions are not without merit. Watery though human beer is, of course.'

'Of course,' Felix said. Gotrek failed to spot the note of irony in his voice.

The inn was not fortified but the walls were thick, and when they tried the door they found it was barred. Gotrek began to bang it with the butt of his axe-shaft. There was no response.

'I can smell humans within,' Gotrek said. Felix wondered how he could smell anything over his own stench. Gotrek never washed and his hair was matted with animal fat to keep his red-dyed crest in place.

'They'll have locked themselves in. Nobody goes abroad on Geheimnisnacht. Unless they're witches or daemon-lovers.'

'The black coach was abroad,' Gotrek said.

'Its occupants were up to no good. The windows were curtained and the coach bore no crest of arms.'

'My throat is too dry to discuss such details. Come on, open up in there or I'll take my axe to the door!'

Felix thought he heard movement within. He pressed an ear to the door. He could make out the mutter of voices and what sounded like weeping.

'Unless you want me to chop through your head, manling, I suggest you stand aside,' Gotrek said to Felix.

'Just a moment. I say: you inside! Open up! My friend has a very large axe and a very short temper. I suggest you do as he says or lose your door.'

'What was that about "short"?' Gotrek said touchily.

From behind the door came a thin, quavering cry. 'In the name of Sigmar, begone, you daemons of the pit!'

'Right, that's it,' Gotrek snapped. 'I've had enough.'

He drew his axe back in a huge arc. Felix saw the runes on its blade gleam in the Morrslieb light. He leapt aside.

'In the name of Sigmar!' Felix shouted. 'You cannot exorcise us. We are simple, weary travellers.'

The axe bit into the door with a chunking sound. Splinters of wood flew from it. Gotrek turned to Felix and grinned evilly up at him. Felix noted the missing teeth.

'Shoddily made, these manling doors,' Gotrek said.

'I suggest you open up while you still have a door,' Felix called.

'Wait,' the quavering voice said. 'That door cost me five crowns from Jurgen the carpenter.'

The door was unlatched. It opened. A tall, thin man with a sad face framed by lank, white hair stood there. He had a stout club in one hand. Behind him stood an old woman who held a saucer that contained a guttering candle.

'You will not need your weapon, sir. We require only a bed for the night,' Felix said.

'And ale,' the dwarf grunted.

'And ale,' Felix agreed.

'Lots of ale,' Gotrek said. Felix looked at the old man and shrugged helplessly.